I0784735

E. W. Hornung

BRITISH TALES OF THE BUSH: 5 Novels in One Volume
(Illustrated)

OK Publishing 2021

E. W. Hornung

BRITISH TALES OF THE BUSH: 5 Novels in One Volume

(Illustrated)

Stingaree, A Bride from the Bush, Tiny Luttrell, The Boss of Taroomba and The Unbidden Guest

Published by

MUSAICUM
Books

Advanced Digital Solutions & High-Quality book Formatting
musaicumbooks@okpublishing.info

2021 OK Publishing

ISBN 978-80-272-8026-1

Contents

"My name's Stingaree!"

Stingaree: A Voice in the Wilderness

A Voice in the Wilderness

I

"La parlate d'amor,

  O cari fior,

  Recate i miei sospiri,

  Narrate i miei matiri,

  Ditele o cari fior — —"

Miss Bouverie ceased on the high note, as abruptly as string that snaps beneath the bow, and revolved with the music-stool, to catch but her echoes in the empty room. None had entered behind her back; there was neither sound nor shadow in the deep veranda through the open door. But for the startled girl at the open piano, Mrs. Clarkson's sanctum was precisely as Mrs. Clarkson had left it an hour before; her own photograph, in as many modes, beamed from the usual number of ornamental frames; there was nothing whatever to confirm a wild suspicion of the living lady's untimely return. And yet either guilty consciences, or an ear as sensitive as it was true, had heard an unmistakable step outside.

Hilda Bouverie lived to look magnificent when she sang, her fine frame drawn up to its last inch, her throat a pillar of pale coral, her mouth the perfect round, her teeth a noble relic of barbarism; but sweeter she never was than in these days, or at this moment of them, as she sat with lips just parted and teeth just showing, in a simple summer frock of her own unaided making. Her eyes, of the one deep Tasmanian blue, were still open very wide, but no longer with the same apprehension; for a step there was, but a step that jingled; nor did they recognize the silhouette in top-boots which at length stood bowing on the threshold.

"Please finish it!" prayed a voice that Miss Bouverie liked in her turn; but it was too much at ease for one entirely strange to her, and she rose with little embarrassment and no hesitation at all.

"Indeed, no! I thought I had the station to myself."

"So you had —I have not seen a soul."

Miss Bouverie instantly perceived that honors were due from her.

"I am so sorry! You've come to see Mr. and Mrs. Clarkson?" she cried. "Mrs. Clarkson has just left for Melbourne with her maid, and Mr. Clarkson has gone mustering with all his men. But the Indian cook is about somewhere. I'll find him, and he shall make some tea."

The visitor planted himself with much gallantry in the doorway; he was a man still young, with a single eye-glass and a martial mustache, which combined to give distinction to a somewhat swarthy countenance. At the moment he had also an engaging smile.

"I didn't come to see either Mr. or Mrs. Clarkson," said he; "in fact, I never heard their name before. I was passing the station, and I simply came to see who it was who could sing like that-to believe my own ears!"

Miss Bouverie was thrilled. The stranger spoke with an authority that she divined, a sincerity which she instinctively took on trust. Her breath came quickly; she was a little nervous now.

"If you won't sing to my face," he went on, "I must go back to where I hung up my horse, and pray that you will at least send me on my way rejoicing. You will do that in any case. I didn't know there was such a voice in these parts. You sing a good deal, of course?"

"I haven't sung for months."

He was now in the room; there was no longer any necessity to bar the doorway, and the light coming through fell full on his amazement. The girl stood before him with a calm face, more wistful than ironic, yet with hints of humor in the dark blue eyes. Her companion put up the eye-glass which he had dropped at her reply.

"May I ask what you are doing in these wilds?"

"Certainly. I am Mrs. Clarkson's companion."

"And you sing, for the first time in months, the minute her back is turned: has the lady no soul for music?"

"You had better ask the lady."

And her visible humor reached the corners of Miss Bouverie's mouth.

"She sings herself, perhaps?"

"And I am here to play her accompaniments!"

The eye-glass focussed the great, smiling girl.

"*Can* she sing?"

"She has a voice."

"But have you never let her hear yours?"

"Once. I had not been here long enough to know better. And I made my usual mistake."

"What is that?"

"I thought I had the station to myself."

The questioner bowed to his rebuke. "Well?" he persisted none the less.

"I was told exactly what my voice was like, and fit for."

The gentleman turned on his heel, as though her appreciation of the humor of her position were an annoyance to him. His movement brought him face to face with a photographic galaxy of ladies in varying styles of evening dress, with an equal variety in coiffures, but a certain family likeness running through the series.

"Are any of these Mrs. Clarkson?"

"All of them."

He muttered something in his mustache. "And what's this?" he asked of a sudden.

The young man (for as such Miss Bouverie was beginning to regard him) was standing under the flaming bill of a grand concert to be given in the township of Yallarook for the benefit of local charities.

"Oh, that's Mrs. Clarkson's concert," he was informed. "She has been getting it up, and that's why she's had to go to Melbourne-about her dress, you know."

He smiled sardonically through mustache and monocle.

"Her charity begins near home!"

"It need not necessarily end there."

"Yet she sings five times herself."

"True-without the encores."

"And you don't sing at all."

"But I accompany."

"A bitter irony! But, I say, what's this? 'Under the distinguished patronage of Sir Julian Crum, Mus. Doc., D.C.L.' Who may he be?"

"Director of the Royal College of Music, in the old country," the girl answered with a sigh.

"Royal College of Music? That's something new, since my time," said the visitor, sighing also. "But what's a man like that doing out here?"

"He has a brother a squatter, the next station but one. Sir Julian's spending the English winter with him on account of his health."

"So you've seen something of him?"

"I wish we had."

"But Mrs. Clarkson has?"

"No-not yet."

"I see!" and an enlightened gleam shot through the eye-glass. "So this is her way of getting to know a poor overworked wreck who came out to patch his lungs in peace and quiet! And she's going to sing him one of his own songs; she's gone to Melbourne to dress the part; and you're not going to sing anything at all!"

Miss Bouverie refrained alike from comment and confirmation; but her silence was the less creditable in that her companion was now communing chiefly with himself. She felt, indeed, that she had already been guilty of a certain disloyalty to one to whom she owed some manner of allegiance; but that was the extent of Miss Bouverie's indiscretion in her own eyes. It caused her no qualms to entertain an anonymous gentleman whom she had never seen before. A colder course had commended itself to the young lady fresh from London; but to a Colonial girl, on a station where special provision was made for the entertaining of strange travellers, the situation was simply conventional. It might have been less onerous with host or hostess on the spot; but then the visitor would not have heard her sing, and he seemed to know what singing was.

Miss Bouverie watched him as he leant over the piano, looking through the songs which she had dared once more to bring forth from her room. She might well have taken a romantic interest in the dark and dapper man, with the military eye-glass and mustache, the spruce duck jacket and the spurred top-boots. It was her first meeting with such a type in the back-blocks of New South Wales. The gallant ease, the natural gayety, the charming manners that charmed no less for a clear trace of mannerism, were a peculiar refreshment after society racier of Riverina soil. Yet it was none of these things which attracted this woman to this man; for the susceptible girl was dead in her for the time being; but the desperate artist was alive again after many weeks, was panting for fresh life, was catching at a straw. He had heard her sing. It had brought him galloping off the track. He praised her voice; and he knew-he knew what singing was.

Who could he be? Not . . . could that be possible?

"Sing me this," he said, suddenly, and, seating himself at the piano, played the opening bars of a vocal adaptation of Handel's Largo with a just, though unpractised, touch.

Nothing could have afforded a finer hearing of the quality and the compass of her voice, and she knew of old how well it suited her; yet at the outset, from the sheer excitement of her suspicion, Hilda Bouverie was shaky to the point of a pronounced tremolo. It wore off with the lengthening cadences, and in a minute the little building was bursting with her voice, while the pianist swayed and bent upon his stool with the exuberant sympathy of a brother in art. And when the last rich note had died away he wheeled about, and so sat silent for many moments, looking curiously on her flushed face and panting bosom.

"I can't place your voice," he said, at last. "It's both voices-the most wonderful compass in the world-and the world will tell you so, when you go back to it, as go back you must and shall. May I ask the name of your master?"

"My own name-Bouverie. It was my father. He is dead."

Her eyes glistened.

"You did not go to another?"

"I had no money. Besides, he had lived for what you say; when he died with his dream still a dream, I said I would do the same, and I came up here."

She had turned away. A less tactful interlocutor had sought plainer repudiation of the rash resolve; this one rose and buried himself in more songs.

"I have heard you in Grand Opera, and in something really grand," he said. "Now I want a song, the simpler the better."

Behind his back a daring light came into the moist eyes.

"There is one of Mrs. Clarkson's," she said. "She would never forgive me for singing it, but I have heard it from her so often, I know so well how it ought to go."

And, fetching the song from a cabinet, she thrust it boldly under his nose. It was called "The Unrealized Ideal," and was a setting of some words by a real poet then living, whose name caused this reader to murmur, "London Lyrics!" The composer was Sir Julian Crum. But his name was read without a word, or a movement of the strong shoulders and the tanned neck on which Miss Bouverie's eyes were fixed.

"You had better play this yourself," said he, after peering at the music through his glass. "It is rather too many for me."

And, strangely crestfallen, Miss Bouverie took his place.

"My only love is always near, —

In country or in town

I see her twinkling feet, I hear

The whisper of her gown.

"She foots it, ever fair and young,

Her locks are tied in haste,

And one is o'er her shoulder flung

And hangs below her waist."

For that was the immortal trifle. How much of its immortality it will owe to the setting of Sir Julian Crum is a matter of opinion, but here is an anonymous view.

"I like the words, Miss Bouverie, but the setting doesn't take me. It might with repetition. It seems lacking in go and simplicity; technically, I should say, a gem. But there can be no two opinions of your singing of such a song; that's the sort of arrow to go straight to the heart of the public —a world-wide public-and if I am the first to say it to you, I hope you will one day remember it in my favor. Meanwhile it is for me to thank you-from my heart-and to say good-by!"

He was holding out a sunburnt hand.

"Must you go?" she asked, withholding her own in frank disappointment.

"Unfortunately, yes; my man is waiting for me with both horses in the scrub. But before I go I want to ask a great favor of you. It is-not to tell a soul I have been here."

For a singer and a woman of temperament, Hilda Bouverie had a wonderfully level head. She inquired his reason in no promising tone.

"You will see at Mrs. Clarkson's concert."

Hilda started.

"You are coming to that?"

"Without fail-to hear Mrs. Clarkson sing five songs-your song among them!"

"But it's hers; it has been the other way about."

The gay smile broadened on the swarthy face; a very bright eye twinkled through the monocle into those of Miss Bouverie.

"Well, will you promise to say nothing about me? I have a reason which you will be the first to appreciate in due season."

Hilda hesitated, reasoned with herself, and finally gave her word. Their hands were joined an instant, as he thanked her with gallant smile and bow. Then he was gone. And as his spurs ceased jingling on the veranda outside, Hilda Bouverie glanced again at the song on the piano and clapped her hands with unreasonable pride.

"I do believe that I was right after all!" said she.

Mr. Clarkson and his young men sat at meat that evening with a Miss Bouverie hard to recognize as the apparently austere spinster who had hitherto been something of a skeleton at their board. Coldly handsome at her worst, a single day had brought her forth a radiant beauty wreathed in human smiles. Her clear skin had a tinge which at once suggested and dismissed the thought of rouge; but beyond all doubt she had done her hair with less reserve; and it was coppery hair of a volatile sort, that sprang into natural curls at the first relaxation of an undue discipline. Mr. Clarkson wondered whether his wife's departure had aught to do with the striking change in her companion; the two young men rested mutually assured that it had.

"The old girl keeps too close an eye on her," said little Mr. Hack, who kept the books and hailed from Middlesex. "Get her to yourself, Ted, and she's as larky as they're made."

Ted Radford, the station overseer, was a personage not to be dismissed in a relative clause. He was a typical back-blocker, dry and wiry, nasally cocksure, insolently cool, a fearless hand with horse, man, or woman. He was a good friend to Hack when there was no third person of his own kidney to appreciate the overseer's conception of friendly chaff. They were by themselves now, yet the last speech drew from Radford a sufficiently sardonic grin.

"You see if she is, old man," said he, "and I'll stand by to collect your remains. Not but what she hasn't come off the ice, and looks like thoring if you take her the right way."

Ted Radford was a confirmed believer in the rightness of his own way with all mankind; his admirable confidence had not been shaken by a long succession of snubs in the quarter under discussion. As for Miss Bouverie, it was her practice to play off one young man against the other by discouraging each in his turn. But this evening she was a different being. She had a vague yet absolute conviction that her fortune was made. She could have sung all her songs to the twain, but for the reflection that Mr. Clarkson himself would hear them too, and report the matter to his wife on her return.

And the next night the male trio were strangely absorbed in some station happening which did not arouse Miss Bouverie's curiosity in the least. They were excited and yet constrained at dinner, and drew their chairs close together on the veranda afterward. The young lady caught at least one word of which she did not know the meaning. She had the tact to keep out of earshot after that. Nor was she very much more interested when she met the two young men with revolvers in their hands the following day.

"Going to fight a duel?" she inquired, smilingly, for her heart was still singing Grand Opera and Oratorio by turns.

"More or less," returned the overseer, without his usual pleasantry. "We're going to have a match at a target behind the pines."

The London bookkeeper looked an anxious clerk: the girl was glad when she saw the pair alive at dinner. There seemed to be little doing. Though the summer was already tropical, there had been plenteous rains, and Mr. Clarkson observed in Hilda's hearing that the recent day's mustering would be the last for some little time. She was thrown much in his company, and she liked Mr. Clarkson when Mrs. Clarkson was not there. In his wife's hands the good man was wax; now a mere echo, now a veritable claque in himself, he pandered indefatigably to the multitudinous vanities of a ludicrously vain woman. But it was soon Miss Bouverie's experience that he could, when he dared, be attentively considerate of lesser ladies. And in many ways these were much the happiest days that she had spent on the station.

They were, however, days of a consuming excitement for the caged and gagged nightingale that Hilda Bouverie now conceived herself to be. She sang not another note aloud. Mr. Clarkson lived in slippers on the veranda, which Hilda now associated chiefly with a stranger's spurs: for of the booted and spurred stranger she was thinking incessantly, though still without the emotions of an ordinarily romantic temperament. Would he be at the concert, or would he not? Would he turn out to be what she firmly imagined him, or was she to find out her mistake?

Might he not in any case have said or written some pregnant word for her? Was it beyond the bounds of possibility that she should be asked to sing after all?

The last question was the only one to be answered before the time, unless a point-blank inquiry of Mrs. Clarkson be included in the category. The lady had returned with a gorgeous gown, only less full of her experiences than of the crowning triumph yet to come. She had bought every song of Sir Julian's to be had in Melbourne, and his name was always on her lips. In a reckless moment Miss Bouverie had inquired his age.

"I really don't know," said Mrs. Clarkson. "What *can* it matter?"

"I only wondered whether he was a youngish man or not."

Mrs. Clarkson had already raised her eyebrows; at this answer they disappeared behind a *toupet* dating from her late descent upon the Victorian capital.

"Really, Miss Bouverie!" she said, and nothing more in words. But the tone was intolerable, and its accompanying sneer a refinement in vulgarity, which only the really refined would have resented as it deserved. Miss Bouverie got up and left the room without a word. But her flaming face left a misleading tale behind.

She was not introduced to Sir Julian; but that was not her prime disappointment when the great night came. All desire for an introduction, all interest in the concert, died a sudden death in Hilda Bouverie at her first glimpse of the gentleman who was duly presented to Mrs. Clarkson as Sir Julian Crum. He was more than middle-aged; he wore a gray beard, and the air of a somewhat supercilious martyr; his near sight was obviated by double lenses in gold rims. Hilda could have wept before the world. For nearly three weeks she had been bowing in imagination to a very different Sir Julian, bowing as though she had never beheld him in her life before; and yet in three minutes she saw how little real reason she had ever had for the illogical conclusion to which she had jumped. She searched for the sprightly figure she had worn in her mind's eye; his presence under any other name would still have been welcome enough now. But he was not there at all. In the patchy glare of the kerosene lamps, against the bunting which lined the corrugated walls of Gulland's new iron store, among flower and weed of township and of station, did Miss Bouverie seek in vain for a single eye-glass and a military mustache.

The concert began. Miss Bouverie opened it herself with the inevitably thankless pianoforte solo, in this case gratuitously meretricious into the bargain, albeit the arbitrary choice of no less a judge than Mrs. Clarkson. It was received with perfunctory applause, through which a dissipated stockman thundered thickly for a song. Miss Bouverie averted her eyes from Sir Julian (ensconced like Royalty in the centre of the first row) as she descended from the platform. She had not the hardihood to glance toward the great man until the indistinct stockman had had his wish, and Mrs. Clarkson, in her fine new raiment, had both sung and acted a coy ditty of the previous decade, wherein every line began with the word "somebody." It was an immediate success; the obstreperous stockman led the encore; but Miss Bouverie, who duly accompanied, extracted solace from the depressed attitude in which Sir Julian Crum sat looking down his nose.

The township boasted its score of dwellings, but few of them showed a light that evening; not less than ninety of the round hundred of inhabitants clapped their hands and mopped their foreheads in Gulland's new store. It might have been run up for its present purpose. There was an entrance at one end for the performers, and that on the platform level, since the ground sloped a little; at the other end was the only other entrance, by which the audience were admitted. A makeshift lobby had been arranged behind the platform, and thither Mrs. Clarkson retired to await her earlier encores; when the compliment became a recognized matter of course, she abandoned the mere form of a momentary retirement, and stood patiently smiling in the satin ball-dress brought from Melbourne for the nonce. And for the brief intervals between her efforts she descended to a throne specially reserved on the great musician's right.

The other performers did not dim her brilliance by reason of their own. There was her own dear husband, whose serious recitation was the one entertaining number. There was a Rabbit Inspector who rapped out "The Scout" in a defiant barytone, and a publican whose somewhat uneven tenor was shaken to its depths by the simple pathos of "When Sparrows Build." Mrs.

Clarkson could afford to encourage such tyros with marked applause. The only danger was that Sir Julian might think she really admired their untutored attempts.

"One must do it," she therefore took occasion to explain as she clapped. "They are so nervous. The hard thing is to put oneself in their place; it's nothing to me to sing a song, Sir Julian."

"So I can see, madam," said he.

At the extreme end of the same row Miss Bouverie passed her unemployed moments between Mr. Radford and the wall, and was not easy until she had signalled to little Mr. Hack to occupy the seat behind her. With the two together she felt comparatively comfortable. Mr. Radford's running criticism on the performers, always pungent, was often amusing, while Mr. Hack lost no opportunity of advancing his own ideals in the matter of musical entertainment.

"A song and dance," said he, again and again, with a more and more sepulchral deviltry —"a song and dance is what you want. You should have heard the Sisters Belton in their palmy days at the Pav! You don't get the best of everything out here, you know, Ted!"

"No; let's hope they've got some better men than you," returned Radford, inspired by the quorum of three to make mince-meat of his friend.

It was the interval between parts one and two. The platform was unoccupied. A cool draught blew through the iron building from open door to open door; there was no occasion to go outside. They had done so, however, at the lower end; there was a sudden stampede of returning feet. A something in the scuffling steps, a certain outcry that accompanied them, caused Miss Bouverie and her companions to turn their heads; they turned again at as sudden a jingle on the platform, and the girl caught her breath. There stood her missing hero, smiling on the people, dapper, swarthy, booted, spurred, and for one moment the man she had reason to remember, exactly as she remembered him. The next his folded arms sprang out from the shoulders, and a brace of long-barrelled revolvers covered the assembly.

"Up with your hands, every man of you!" he cried. "No, not the ladies, but every man and boy who doesn't want a bullet in his brain!"

The command was echoed in uncouth accents at the lower door, where, in fact, a bearded savage had driven in all and sundry at his pistol's point. And in a few seconds the meeting was one which had carried by overwhelming show of hands a proposition from which the ladies alone saw occasion to dissent.

"You may have heard of me before," said the man on the platform, sweeping the forest of hands with his eye-glass. "My name's Stingaree."

It was the word which Hilda Bouverie had heard on the veranda and taken for some strange expletive.

"Who is he?" she asked, in a whisper that bespoke excitement, agitation, but not alarm.

"The fancy bushranger-the dandy outlaw!" drawled Radford, in cool reply. "I've been expecting him. He was seen on our run the day Mrs. Clarkson went down to Melbourne."

That memorable day for Hilda Bouverie! And it was this manner of man who had been her hero ever since: a bushranger, an outlaw, a common robber under arms!

"And you never told me!" she cried, in an indignant whisper.

"We never told Mrs. Clarkson either. You must blame the boss."

Hilda snatched her eyes from Stingaree, and was sorry for Mrs. Clarkson for the first time in their acquaintance. The new ball-dress of bridal satin was no whiter than its wearer's face, which had aged several years in as many seconds. The squatter leant toward her with uplifted hands, loyally concerned for no one and for nothing else. Between the couple Sir Julian might have been conducting without his bâton, but with both arms. Meanwhile, the flashing eye-glass had fixed itself on Miss Bouverie's companion, without resting for an instant on Miss Bouverie.

"Silence over there!" cried Stingaree, sternly. "I'm here on a perfectly harmless errand. If you know anything about me at all, you may know that I have a weakness for music of any kind, so long as it's good of its kind."

The eye-glass dropped for a moment upon Mrs. Clarkson in the front row, and the irrepressible Radford was enabled to continue his say.

"He has, too, from a mouth-organ to a full orchestra, from all accounts, Miss Bouverie. *My revolver's in the coat-pocket next you!*"

"It is the music," continued Stingaree, looking harder than before in their direction, "which has brought me here to-night. I've come to listen, and for no other reason in the world. Unfortunately, when one has a price upon one's head, one has to take certain precautions before venturing among one's fellow-men. And, though I'm not here for gain or bloodshed, if any man of you gives me trouble I shall shoot him like a dog!"

"That's one for me," whispered the intrepid overseer, in lower key. "Never mind. He's not looking at us now. I believe Mrs. Clarkson's going to faint. *You take what I told you and slip it under your shawl, and you'll save a second by passing it up to me the instant you see her sway!*"

Hilda hesitated. A dead silence had fallen on the crowded and heated store, and in the silence Stingaree was already taking an unguarded interest in Mrs. Clarkson's appearance, which as certainly betokened imminent collapse. *"Now!"* whispered Radford, and Hilda hesitated no more. She was wearing a black lace shawl between her appearances at the piano; she had the revolver under it in a twinkling, and pressed it to her bosom with both hands, one outside the shawl and one underneath, as who should hug a beating heart.

"Mrs. Clarkson," said Stingaree, "you have been singing too much, and the quality of your song has not been equal to the quantity."

It sounded a brutal speech enough; and to do justice to a portion of the audience not hitherto remarkable for its spirit, the ungallant criticism was audibly resented in the back rows. The maudlin stockman had indeed to be restrained by his neighbors from precipitating himself upon the barrels of Stingaree. But the effect upon Mrs. Clarkson herself was still more remarkable, and revealed a subtle kindness in the desperado's cruelty. Her pale face flushed; her lack-lustre eyes blazed forth their indignation; her very clay was on fire for all the room to see.

"I don't sing for criminals and cut-throats!" the indignant lady cried out. She glanced at Sir Julian as one for whom she did sing. And Sir Julian's eyes twinkled under the bushranger's guns.

"To be sure you don't," said Stingaree, with as much sweetness as his character would permit. "You sing for charity, and spend three times as much as you are ever likely to make in arraying yourself for the occasion. Well, we must put up with some song-bird without fine feathers, for I mean to hear the programme out." His eyes ranged the front rows till they fell on Hilda Bouverie in her corner. "You young lady over there! You've been talking since I called for silence. You deserve to pay a penalty; be good enough to step this way."

Hilda's excitement may be supposed; it made her scandalously radiant in that company of humiliated men and women, but it did not rob her of her resource. Removing her shawl with apparent haste, but with calculated deliberation, she laid it in a bunch upon the seat which she had occupied, and stepped forward with a courage that won a cheer from the back rows. Stingaree stooped to hand her up to the platform; and his warm grip told a tale. This was what he had come for, to make her sing, to make her sing before Sir Julian Crum, to give her a start unique in the history of the platform and the stage. Criminal, was he? Then the dearest, kindest, most enchanting, most romantic criminal the world had ever seen! But she must be worthy of his chivalry and her chance; and, from the first, her artistic egoism insisted that she was.

Stingaree had picked up a programme, and dexterously mounted it between hammer and cartridge of the revolver which he had momentarily relinquished, much as a cornet-player mounts his music under his nose. With both weapons once more levelled, he consulted the programme now.

"The next item, ladies and gentlemen," said he, "is another pianoforte solo by this young lady. We'll let you off that, Miss Bouverie, since you've got to sing. The next song on the programme is called 'The Unrealized Ideal,' and the music is by our distinguished visitor and patron, Sir Julian Crum. In happier circumstances it would have been sung to you by Mrs. Montgomery Clarkson; as it is, I call upon Miss Bouverie to realize her ideal and ours, and on Sir Julian Crum to accompany her, if he will."

At Mrs. Clarkson's stony side the great man dropped both arms at the superb impudence of the invitation.

"Quite right, Sir Julian; let the blood run into them," said Stingaree. "It is a pure oversight that you were not exempted in the beginning. Comply with my entreaty and I guarantee that you shall suffer no further inconvenience."

Sir Julian wavered. In London he was a club-man and a diner-out; and what a tale for the Athenæum-what a short cut to every ear at a Kensington dinner-table! In the end it would get into the papers. That was the worst of it. But in the midst of Sir Julian's hesitation his pondering eyes met those of Miss Bouverie-on fire to sing him his own song-alight with the ability to do it justice. And Sir Julian was lost.

How she sang it may be guessed. Sir Julian bowed and swayed upon his stool. Stingaree stood by with a smile of personal pride and responsibility, but with both revolvers still levelled, and one of them cocked. It was a better song than he had supposed. It gained enormously from the composer's accompaniment. The last verse was softer than another would have made it, and yet the singer obeyed inaudible instructions as though she had never sung it otherwise. It was more in a tuneful whisper than in hushed notes that the last words left her lips: —

"Lightly I sped when hope was high,

And youth beguiled the chase;

I follow-follow still; but I

Shall never see her Face."

The applause, when it came, was almost overwhelming. The bushranger watched and smiled, but cocked his second pistol, and let the programme flutter to the floor. As for Sir Julian Crum, the self-contained, the cynical, he was seen for an instant, wheeled about on the music-stool, grasping the singer by both hands. But there was no hearing what he said; the girl herself heard nothing until he bellowed in her ear:

"They'll have their encore. What can you give them? It must be something they know. 'Home, Sweet Home'? 'The Last Rose'? 'Within a Mile'? The first, eh? Very well; it's a leaf out of Patti's book; but so are they all."

And he struck the opening bars in the key of his own song, but for some moments Hilda Bouverie stood bereft of her great voice. A leaf out of Patti's book, in that up-country township, before a roomful held in terror-and yet unmindful-of the loaded pistols of two bloodthirsty bushrangers! The singer prayed for power to live up to those golden words. A leaf out of Patti's book!

It was over. The last poignant note trembled into nothingness. The silence, absolutely dead for some seconds, was then only broken by a spirituous sob from the incorrigible stockman. There was never any applause at all. Ere it came, even as it was coming, the overseer Radford leapt to his feet with a raucous shout.

The bushranger had vanished from the platform. The other bushranger had disappeared through the other door. The precious pair of them had melted from the room unseen, unheard, what time every eye doted on handsome Hilda Bouverie, and every ear on the simple words and moving cadences of "Home, Sweet Home."

Ted Radford was the first to see it; for by the end of the brief song he had his revolver uncovered and cocked at last, and no quarry left for him to shoot. With a bound he was on the platform; another carried him into the canvas anteroom, a third and a fourth out into the moonlight. It was as bright as noon in a conservatory of smoked glass. And in the tinted brightness one man was already galloping away; but it was Stingaree who danced with one foot only in the stirrup of a milk-white mare.

Radford rushed up to him and fired point-blank again and again. A series of metallic clicks was all the harm he did, for Stingaree was in the saddle before the hurled revolver struck the mare on the ribs, and sent the pair flying through the moonlight with a shout of laughter, a cloud of sand, and a dull volley of thunderous hoofs. The overseer picked up his revolver and returned crestfallen to examine it in the lights of the emptying room.

"I could have sworn I loaded it," said he. "If I had, he'd have been a dead man six times over."

Miss Bouverie had been talking to Sir Julian Crum. On Radford's entry she had grown *distraite*, but at Radford's speech she turned back to Sir Julian with shining eyes.

"My wife wants a companion for the voyage," he was saying. "So that will cost you nothing, but if anything the other way, and once in London, I'll be answerable. I've adjudicated these things for years to voices not in the same class as yours. But the worst of it is you won't stay with us."

"I will."

"No; they'll want you at Covent Garden before we know where we are. And when you are ready to go to them, go you must."

"I shall do what you tell me."

"Then speak to Mrs. Clarkson at once."

Hilda Bouverie glanced over her shoulder, but her employers had left the building. Her smile was less roguish than demure.

"There is no need, Sir Julian. Mrs. Clarkson has already spoken to me, though only in a whisper. But I am to take myself off by the next coach."

The Black Hole of Glenranald

It was coming up the Murrumbidgee that Fergus Carrick first heard the name of Stingaree. With the cautious enterprise of his race, the young gentleman had booked steerage on a river steamer whose solitary passenger he proved to be; accordingly he was not only permitted to sleep on the saloon settee at nights, but graciously bidden to the captain's board by day. It was there that Fergus Carrick encouraged tales of the bushrangers as the one cleanly topic familiar in the mouth of the elderly engineer who completed the party. And it seemed that the knighthood of the up-country road had been an extinct order from the extirpation of the Kellys to the appearance of this same Stingaree, who was reported a man of birth and mystery, with an ostentatious passion for music and as romantic a method as that of any highwayman of the Old World from which he hailed. But the callow Fergus had been spared the romantic temperament, and was less impressed than entertained with what he heard.

On his arrival at Glenranald, however, he found that substantial township shaking with laughter over the outlaw's latest and least discreditable exploit, at the back-block hamlet of Yallarook; and then it was that young Carrick first conceived an ambition to open his Colonial career with the capture of Stingaree; for he was a serious immigrant, who had come out in his teens, to stay out, if necessary, for the term of his natural life.

The idea had birth under one of the many pine trees which shaded the skeleton streets of budding Glenranald. On this tree was nailed a placard offering high reward for the bushranger's person alive or dead. Fergus was making an immediate note in his pocketbook when a hand fell on his shoulder.

"Would ye like the half o' yon?" inquired a voice in his own tongue; and there at his elbow stood an elderly gentleman, whose patriarchal beard hid half the buttons of his alpaca coat, while a black skull-cap sat somewhat jauntily on his head.

"What do you mean?" said Fergus, bluntly, for the old gentleman stood chuckling gently in his venerable beard.

"To lay a hold of him," replied the other, "with the help o' some younger and abler-bodied man; and you're the very one I want."

The raw youth stared ingenuously.

"But what can you know about me?"

"I saw ye land at the wharf," said the old gentleman, nodding his approval of the question, "and says I, 'That's my man,' as soon as ever I clapped eyes on ye. So I had a crack wi' the captain o' yon steamer; he told me you hadna a billet, but were just on the lookout for the best ye could get, an' that's all he'd been able to get out o' ye in a five days' voyage. That was enough for me. I want a man who can keep his tongue behind his teeth, and I wanted you before I knew you were a brither Scot!"

"Are you a squatter, sir?" the young man asked, a little overwhelmed.

"No, sir, I'm branch manager o' the Bank o' New South Wales, the only bank within a hunder miles o' where we stand; and I can offer ye a better billet than any squatter in the Colony."

"Indeed? I'm sure you're very kind, sir, but I'm wanting to get on a station," protested Fergus with all his tact. "And as a matter of fact, I have introductions to one or two stations further back, though I saw no reason to tell our friend the skipper so."

"Quite right, quite right! I like a man who can keep his tongue in its kennel!" cried the bank manager, rubbing his hands. "But wait while I tell ye: ye'd need to work for your rations an any station I ever heard tell of, and I keep the accounts of enough to know. Now, with me, ye'd get two pound a week till your share o' the reward was wiped off; and if we had no luck for a year you'd be no worse off, but could go and try your squatters then. That's a promise, and I'll keep it as sure as my name's Andr' Macbean!"

"But how do you propose to catch this fellow, Mr. Macbean?"

The bank manager looked on all sides, likewise behind the tree, before replying under his breath: "By setting a wee trap for him! A bank's a bank, and Stingaree hasna stuck one up since he took to his trade. But I'll tell ye no more till ye give me your answer. Yes or no?"

"I'm afraid I don't even write an office hand; and as for figures ——"

Mr. Macbean laughed outright.

"Did I say I was going to take ye into the bank, mun?" cried he. "There's three of us already to do the writin' an' the cipherin,' an' three's enough. Can you ride?"

"I have ridden."

"And ye'll do any rough job I set ye to?"

"The rougher the better."

"That's all I ask. There's a buggy and a pair for ye to mind, and mebbe drive, though it's horseback errands you'll do most of. I'm an old widower, living alone with an aged housekeeper. The cashier and the clerk dig in the township, and I need to have a man of some sort about the place; in fact, I have one, but I'll soon get rid of him if you'll come instead. Understand, you live in the house with me, just like the jackeroos on the stations; and like the jackeroos, you do all the odd jobs and dirty work that no one else'll look at; but, unlike them, you get two pounds a week from the first for doing it."

Mr. Andrew Macbean had chanced upon a magic word. It was the position of "jackeroo," or utility parlor-man, on one or other of the stations to which he carried introductions, that his young countryman had set before him as his goal. True, a bank in a bush township was not a station in the bush itself. On the other hand, his would-be friend was not the first to warn Fergus against the futility of expecting more than a nominal salary as a babe and suckling in Colonial experience; and perhaps the prime elements of that experience might be gained as well in the purlieus of a sufficiently remote township as in realms unnamed on any map. It will be seen that the sober stripling was reduced to arguing with himself, and that his main argument was not to be admitted in his own heart. The mysterious eccentricity of his employer, coupled with the adventurous character of his alleged prospects, was what induced the lad to embrace both in defiance of an unimaginative hard-headedness which he aimed at rather than possessed.

With characteristic prudence he had left his baggage on board the river-steamer, and his own hands carried it piecemeal to the bank. This was a red-brick bungalow with an ample veranda, standing back from the future street that was as yet little better than a country road. The veranda commanded a long perspective of pines, but no further bricks and mortar, and but very few weather board walls. The yard behind the house was shut in by as many outbuildings as clustered about the small homesteads which Fergus had already beheld on the banks of the Murrumbidgee. The man in charge of the yard was palpably in liquor, a chronic condition from his general appearance, and Mr. Macbean discharged him on the spot with a decision which left no loophole for appeal. The woman in charge of the house adorned another plane of civilization; she was very deaf, and very outspoken on her introduction to the young gentleman, whose face she was pleased to approve, with the implied reservation that all faces were liars; but she served up the mutton of the country hot and tender; and Fergus Carrick, leaning back after an excellent repast, marvelled for the twentieth time that he was not to pay for it.

"A teetotaler, are ye?" said Macbean, mixing a third glass of whiskey, with the skull-cap on the back of his head. "And so was I at your age; but you're my very man. There are some it sets talking. Wait till the old lady turns in, and then you shall see what you shall see."

Fergus waited in increasing excitement. The day's events were worthier of a dream. To have set foot in Glenranald without knowing a soul in the place, and to find one's self comfortably housed at a good salary before night! There were moments when he questioned the complete sanity of his eccentric benefactor, who drank whiskey like water, both as to quantity and effect, and who chuckled continuously in his huge gray beard. But such doubts only added to the excitement of the evening, which reached a climax when a lighted candle was thrust in at the door and the pair advised not to make a night of it by the candid crone on her way to bed.

"We will give her twenty minutes," said the manager, winking across his glass. "I've never let her hear me, and she mustn't hear you either. She must know nothing at all about it; nobody must, except you and me."

The mystification of Fergus was now complete. Unimaginative as he was by practice and profession, he had an explanation a minute until the time was up, when the truth beat them all for wild improbability. Macbean had risen, lifting the lamp; holding it on high he led the way through baize doors into the banking premises. Here was another door, which Macbean not only unlocked, but locked again behind them both. A small inner office led them into a shuttered chamber of fair size, with a broad polished counter, glass swing-doors, and a formidable portal beyond. And one of young Carrick's theories received apparent confirmation on the spot; for the manager slipped behind his counter by another door, and at once whipped out a great revolver.

"This they provide us with," said he. "So far it is our only authorized defence, and it hangs on a hook down here behind the counter. But you march in here prepared, your pistol cocked behind your back, and which of us is likely to shoot first?"

"The bushranger," said Fergus, still rather more startled than reassured.

"The bushranger, of course. Stingaree, let us say. As for me, either my arms go up, or down I go in a heap. But supposing my arms do go up-supposing I still touch something with one foot-and supposing the floor just opens and swallows Mr. Sanguinary Stingaree! Eh? eh? What then?"

"It would be great," cried Fergus. "But could it be done?"

"It can be, it will be, and is being done," replied the manager, replacing the bank revolver and sliding over the counter like a boy. A square of plain linoleum covered the floor, overlapped by a border of the same material bearing a design. Down went Macbean upon his knees, and his beard swept this border as he began pulling it up, tacks and all.

The lamp burned brightly on the counter, its rays reflected in the burnished mahogany. All at once Fergus seized it on his own initiative, and set it on the floor before his kneeling elder, going upon his own knees on the other side. And where the plain linoleum ended, but where the overlapping border covered the floor, the planks were sawn through and through down one side of the central and self-colored square.

"A trap-door!" exclaimed Fergus in a whisper.

Macbean leant back on his slippered heels, his skull-cap wickedly awry.

"This border takes a lot o' lifting," said he. "Yet we've just got to lift it every time, and tack it down again before morning. You might try your hand over yonder on the far side."

Fergus complied with so much energy that the whole border was ripped up in a minute; and he was not mistaken. A trap-door it was, of huge dimensions, almost exactly covered by the self-colored square; but at each side a tongue of linoleum had been left loose for lifting it; and the lamp had scarcely been replaced upon the counter when the bulk of the floor leaned upright in one piece against the opposite wall. It had uncovered a pit of corresponding size, but as yet hardly deep enough to afford a hiding-place for the bucket, spade, and pickaxe which lay there on a length of sacking.

"I see!" exclaimed Carrick, as the full light flooded his brain.

"Is that a fact?" inquired the manager twinkling.

"You're going to make a deep hole of it — —?"

"No. I'm going to pay you to make it deep for me — —"

"And then — —"

"At dead o' night; you can take out your sleep by day."

"When Stingaree comes — —"

"If he waits till we're ready for him — —"

"You touch some lever — —"

"And the floor swallows him, as I said, if he waits till we are ready for him. Everything depends on that-and on your silence. We must take time. It isn't only the digging of the hole. We need to fix up some counterpoise to make it shut after a body like a mouse-trap; we must do the thing thoroughly if we do it at all; and till it's done, not a word to a soul in the same hemisphere! In the end I suppose I shall have to tell Donkin, my cashier, and Fowler the clerk. Donkin's a disbeliever who deserves the name o' Didymus more than ony mon o' my acquaintance. Fowler would take so kindly to the whole idea that he'd blurt it out within a week. He may find it out when all's in readiness, but I'll no tell him even then. See how I trust a brither Scot at sight!"

"I much appreciate it," said Fergus, humbly.

"I wouldna ha' trustit even you, gin I hadna found the delvin' ill worrk for auld shoulders," pursued Macbean, broadening his speech with intentional humor. "Noo, wull ye do't or wull ye no?"

The young man's answer was to strip off his coat and spring into the hole, and to set to work with such energy, yet so quietly, that the bucket was filled in a few almost silent seconds. Macbean carried it off, unlocking doors for the nonce, while Fergus remained in the hole to mop his forehead.

"We need to have another bucket," said the manager, on his return. "I've thought of every other thing. There's a disused well in the yard, and down goes every blessed bucket!"

To and fro, over the lip of the closing well, back into the throat of the deepening hole, went the buckets for many a night; and by day Fergus Carrick employed his best wits to make an intrinsically anomalous position appear natural to the world. It was a position which he himself could thoroughly enjoy; he was largely his own master. He had daily opportunities of picking up the ways and customs of the bush, and a nightly excitement which did not pall as the secret task approached conclusion; but he was subjected to much chaff and questioning from the other young bloods of Glenranald. He felt from the first that it was what he must expect. He was a groom with a place at his master's table; he was a jackeroo who introduced station life into a town. And the element of underlying mystery, really existing as it did, was detected soon enough by other young heads, led by that of Fowler, the keen bank clerk.

"I was looking at you both together, and you do favor the old man, and no error!" he would say; or else, "What is it you could hang the boss for, Fergy, old toucher?"

These delicate but cryptic sallies being ignored or parried, the heavy swamp of innuendo was invariably deserted for the breezy hill-top of plain speech, and Fergus had often work enough to put a guard upon hand and tongue. But his temperament was eminently self-contained, and on the whole he was an elusive target for the witticisms of his friends. There was no wit, however, and no attempt at it on the part of Donkin, the cantankerous cashier. He seldom addressed a word to Carrick, never a civil word, but more than once he treated his chief to a sarcastic remonstrance on his degrading familiarity with an underling. In such encounters the imperturbable graybeard was well able to take care of himself, albeit he expressed to Fergus a regret that he had not exercised a little more ingenuity in the beginning.

"You should have come to me with a letter of introduction," said he.

"But who would have given me one?"

"I would, yon first night, and you'd have presented it next day in office hours," replied the manager. "But it's too late to think about it now, and in a few days Donkin may know the truth."

He might have known it already, but for one difficulty. They had digged their pit to the generous depth of eight feet, so that a tall prisoner could barely touch the trap-door with extended finger-tips; and Stingaree (whose latest performance was no longer the Yallarook affair) was of medium height according to his police description. The trap-door was a double one, which parted in the centre with the deadly precision of the gallows floor. The difficulty was to make the flaps close automatically, with the mouse-trap effect of Macbean's ambition. It was managed eventually by boring separate wells for a weight behind the hinges on either side. Copper wire running on minute pulleys let into grooves suspended these weights and connected them with the flaps, and powerful door-springs supplemented the more elaborate contrivance.

The lever controlling the whole was concealed under the counter, and reached by thrusting a foot through a panel, which also opened inward on a spring.

It may be conceived that all this represented the midnight labors and the constant thought of many weeks. It was now the beginning of the cool but brilliant Riverina winter, and, despite the disparity in their years, the two Scotsmen were fast friends. They had worked together as one man, with the same patient passion for perfection, the same delight in detail for its own sake. Almost the only difference was that the old fellow refreshed his energies with the glass of whiskey which was never far from his elbow after banking hours, while the young one cultivated the local excess of continual tea. And all this time the rascally Stingaree ranged the district, with or without his taciturn accomplice, covering great distances in fabulous time, lurking none knew where, and springing on the unwary in the last places in which his presence was suspected.

"But he has not yet robbed a bank, and we have our hopes," wrote Fergus to a faithful sister at Largs. "It may be for fear of the revolvers with which all the banks are provided now. Mr. Macbean has been practising with ours, and purposely put a bullet through one of our back windows. The whole township has been chafing him about it, and the local rag has risen to a sarcastic paragraph, which is exactly what we wanted. The trap-door over the pit is now practically finished. It's too complicated to describe, but Stingaree has only to march into the bank and 'stick it up,' and the man behind the counter has only to touch a lever with his foot for the villain to disappear through the floor into a prison it'll take him all his time to break. On Saturday the cashier and the clerk are coming to dinner, and before we sit down they are to be shown everything."

This was but a fraction of one of the long letters which Fergus despatched by nearly every mail. Silent and self-contained as he was, he had one confidante at the opposite end of the earth, one escape-pipe in his pen. Not a word of the great secret had he even written to another soul. To his trusted sister he had never before been quite so communicative. His conscience pricked him as he took his letter to the post, and he had it registered on no other score.

On Saturday the bank closed at one o'clock; the staff were to return and dine at seven, the Queen's birthday falling on the same day for a sufficient pretext. As the hour approached Fergus made the distressing discovery that his friend and host had anticipated the festivities with too free a hand. Macbean was not drunk, but he was perceptibly blunted and blurred, and Fergus had never seen the pale eyes so watery or the black skull-cap so much on one side of the venerable head. The lad was genuinely grieved. A whiskey bottle stood empty on the laden board, and he had the temerity to pocket the corkscrew while Macbean was gone to his storeroom for another bottle. A solemn search ensued, and then Fergus was despatched in haste for a new corkscrew.

"An' look slippy," said Macbean, "or we'll have old Donkin here before ye get back."

"Not for another three-quarters of an hour," remarked Fergus, looking at his watch.

"Any minute!" retorted Macbean, with a ribald epithet. "I invited Donkin, in confidence, to come a good half-hour airly, and I'll tell ye for why. Donkin must ken, but I'm none so sure o' yon other impident young squirt. His tongue's too long for his mouth. Donkin or I could always be behind the counter; anyway, I mean to take his opeenion before tellin' any other body."

Entertaining his own distrust of the vivacious Fowler, Fergus commended the decision, and so took his departure by the private entrance. It was near sundown; a fresh breeze blew along the hard road, puffing cloudlets of yellow sand into the rosy dusk. Fergus hurried till he was out of sight, and then idled shamelessly under trees. He was not going on for a new corkscrew. He was going back to confess boldly where he had found the old one. And the sight of Donkin in the distance sent him back in something of a hurry; it was quite enough to have to spend an evening with the cantankerous cashier.

The bank was practically at one end of the township as then laid out; two or three buildings there were further on, but they stood altogether aloof. The bank, for a bank, was sufficiently isolated, and Fergus could not but congratulate himself on the completion of its ingenious and unsuspected defences. It only remained to keep the inventor reasonably sober for the evening, and thereafter to whistle or to pray for Stingaree. Meanwhile the present was no mean occasion, and Fergus was glad to see that Macbean had thrown open the official doors in his absence. They had often agreed that it would be worth all their labor to enlighten Donkin by letting the pit gape under his nose as he entered the bank. Fergus glanced over his shoulder, saw the other hurrying, and hurried himself in order to take up a good position for seeing the cashier's face. He was in the middle of the treacherous floor before he perceived that it was not Macbean in the half-light behind the counter, but a good-looking man whom he had never seen before.

"Didn't know I was invited, eh?" said the stranger, putting up a single eye-glass. "Don't believe it, perhaps? You'd better ask Mr. Macbean!"

And before it had occurred to him to stir from where he stood agape, the floor fell from under the feet of Fergus, his body lurched forward, and came down flat and heavy on the hard earth eight feet below. Not entirely stunned, though shaken and hurt from head to heel, he was still collecting his senses when the pit blackened as the trap-door shut in implicit obedience to its weights and springs. And in the clinging velvet darkness the young man heard a groan.

"Is that yoursel', Fergy?"

"And are you there, Mr. Macbean?"

"Mon, didn't it shut just fine!"

Curiously blended with the physical pain in the manager's voice was a sodden philosophic humor which maddened the younger man. Fergus swore where he lay writhing on his stomach. Macbean chuckled and groaned again.

"It's Stingaree," he said, drawing a breath through his teeth.

"Of course it is."

"I never breathed it to a soul."

"No more did I."

Fergus spoke with ready confidence, and yet the words left something on his mind. It was something vague but haunting, something that made him feel instinctively unworthy of the kindly, uncomplaining tone which had annoyed him but a moment before.

"No bones broken, Fergy?"

"None that I know of."

"I doubt I've not been so lucky. I'm thinkin' it's a rib, by the way it hurts to breathe."

Fergus was already fumbling in his pocket. The match-box opened with a click. The match scraped several times in vain. Then at last the scene sprang out as on the screen of a magic-lantern. And to Fergus it was a very white old man, hunched up against the muddy wall, with blood upon his naked scalp and beard, and both hands pressed to his side; to the old man, a muddy face stricken with horrified concern, and a match burning down between muddy fingers; but to both, such a new view and version of their precious hole that the corners of each mouth were twitching as the match was thrown away.

Fergus was fumbling for another when a step rang overhead; and at the sharp exchange of words which both underground expected, Fergus came on all fours to the old man's side, and together they sat gazing upward into the pall of impenetrable crape.

"You infernal villain!" they heard Donkin roar, and stamp his feet with such effect that the floor opened, and down through the square of light came the cashier feet first.

"Heaven and hell!" he squealed, but subsided unhurt on hands and knees as the flaps went up with such a snap that Macbean and Carrick nudged each other at the same moment. "Now I know who you are!" the cashier raved. "Call yourself Stingaree! You're Fowler dressed up, and this is one of Macbean's putrid practical jokes. I saw his jackal hurrying in to say I was coming. By cripes! it takes a surgical operation to see their sort, I grant you."

There was a noise of subdued laughter overhead; even in the pit a dry chuckle came through Macbean's set teeth.

"If it's practical joke o' mine, Donkin, it's recoiled on my own poor pate," said the old man. "I've a rib stove in, too, if that's any consolation to ye. It's Stingaree, my manny!"

"You're right, it is, it must be!" cried the cashier, finding his words in a torrent. "I was going to tell you. He's been at his game down south; stuck up our own mail again only yesterday, between this and Deniliquin, and got a fine haul of registered letters, so they say. But where the deuce are we? I never knew there was a cellar under here, let alone a trap-door that might have been made for these villains."

"It was made for them," replied Macbean, after a pause; and in the dead dark he went on to relate the frank and humble history of the hole, from its inception to the crooked climax of that bitter hour. A braver confession Fergus had never heard; its philosophic flow was unruffled by the more and more scornful interjections of the ungenerous cashier; and yet his younger countryman, who might have been proud of him, hardly listened to a word uttered by Macbean.

Half-a-dozen fallen from the lips of Donkin had lightened young Carrick's darkness with consuming fires of shame. "A fine haul of registered letters" —among others his own last letter to his sister! So it was he who had done it all; and he had perjured himself to his benefactor, besides, betraying him. He sat in the dark between fire and ice, chiefly wondering how he could soonest win through the trap-door and earn a bullet in his brain.

"The spree to-night," concluded Macbean, whose fall completely sobered him, "was for the express purpose of expounding the trap to you, and I asked you airly to take your advice. I was no so sure about young Fowler, whether we need tell him or no. He has an awful long tongue; but I'm thinkin' there's a longer if I knew where to look for it."

"I could tell you where," rasped Donkin. "But go on."

"I was watching old Hannah putting her feenishing touches to the table, and waiting for Fergus Carrick to come back, when I thought I heard him behind me and you with him. But it was Stingaree and his mate, and the two of us were covered with revolvers like young rifles. Hannah they told to go on with what she was doing, as they were mighty hungry, and I advised her to do as she was bid. The brute with the beard has charge of her. Stingaree himself drove me into the middle of my own trap-door, made me give up my keys, and then went behind the counter and did the trick. He'd got it all down on paper, the Lord alone knows how."

"Oh, you Scotchmen!" cried the pleasant cashier. "Talk of your land of cakes! You take every cake in the land between you!"

It seemed he had been filling his pipe while he listened and prepared this pretty speech. Now he struck a match, and with the flame to the bowl saw Fergus for the first time. The cashier held the match on high.

"You hear all the while?" he cried. "No wonder you lay low, Carrick; no wonder I didn't hear your voice."

"What do you mean by that?" growled Fergus, in fierce heat and fierce satisfaction.

"Surely, Mr. Macbean, you aren't wondering who wagged the long tongue now?"

"You mean that I wagged mine? And it's a lie!" said Fergus, hoarsely; he was sitting upon his heels, poised to spring.

"I mean that if Mr. Macbean had listened to me two months ago we should none of us be in this hole now."

"Then, my faith, you're in a worse one than you think!" cried Fergus, and fell upon his traducer as the match went out. "Take that, and that, and that!" he ground out through his teeth, as he sent the cashier over on his back and pounded the earth with his skull. Luckily the first was soft and the second hard, so that the man was more outraged than hurt when circumstances which they might have followed created a diversion.

In his turn the lively Fowler had marched whistling into the bank, had ceased whistling to swear down the barrel of a cocked revolver, and met a quicker fate than his comrades by impressing the bushranger as the most dangerous man of the quartette. Unfortunately for him, his fate was still further differentiated from theirs. Fowler's feet glanced off Carrick's back, and he plunged into the well head-first, rolling over like a stone as the wooden jaws above closed greedily upon the light of day.

Fergus at once struck matches, and in their light the cashier took the insensible head upon his knees and glared at his enemy as if from sanctuary of the Red Cross. But Fergus returned to Macbean's side.

"I never said a word to a living soul," he muttered. "It has come out some other way."

"Of course it has," said the old manager, with the same tell-tale inhalation through the teeth. Fergus felt worse than ever. He groped for the bald head and found it cold and dank. In an instant he was clamoring under the trap-door, leaping up and striking it with his fist.

"What do you want?"

"Whiskey. Some of us are hurt."

"God help you if it's any hanky-panky!"

"It's none. Something to drink, and something to drink it in, or there's blood upon your head!"

Clanking steps departed and returned.

"Stand by to catch, below there!"

And Fergus stood by, expecting to see a long barrel with the bottle and glass that broke their fall on him; but Stingaree had crept away unheard, and he pressed the lever just enough to let the glass and bottle tumble through.

Time passed: it might have been an hour. The huddled heap that was Macbean breathed forth relief. The head on Donkin's knees moved from side to side with groans. Donkin himself thanked Fergus for his ration; he who served it out alone went thirsty. "Wait till I earn some," he said bitterly to himself. "I could finish the lot if I started now." But the others never dreamt that he was waiting, and he lied about it to Macbean.

Now that they sat in silence no sound escaped them overhead. They heard Stingaree and his mate sit down to a feast which Macbean described with groaning modesty as the best that he could do.

"There's no soup," he whispered, "but there's a barr'l of oysters fetched up on purpose by the coach. I hope they havena missed the Chablis. They may as well do the thing complete." In a little the champagne popped. "Dry Monopole!" moaned the manager, near to tears. "It came up along with the oysters. O sirs, O sirs, but this is hard on us all! Now they're at the turkey-and I chopped the stuffing with my ain twa han's!"

They were at the turkey a long time. Another cork popped; but the familiar tread of deaf Hannah was heard no more, and at length they called her.

"Mother!" roared a mouth that was full.

"Old lady!" cried the gallant Stingaree.

"She's 'ard of 'earing, mate."

"She might still hear you, Howie."

And the chairs rasped backward over bare boards as one; at the same instant Fergus leapt to his feet in the earthly Tartarus his own hands had dug.

"I do believe she's done a bolt," he gasped, "and got clean away!"

Curses overhead confirmed the supposition. Clanking feet hunted the premises at a run. In a minute the curses were renewed and multiplied, yet muffled, as though there was some fresh cause for them which the prisoners need not know. Hannah had not been found. Yet some disturbing discovery had undoubtedly been made. Doors were banged and bolted. A gunshot came faint but staccato from the outer world. A real report echoed through the bank.

"A siege!" cried Fergus, striking a match to dance by. "The old heroine has fetched the police, and these beauties are in a trap."

"And what about us?" demanded the cashier.

"Shut up and listen!" retorted Fergus, without ceremony. Macbean was leaning forward, with bald head on one side and hollowed palm at the upper ear. Even the stunned man had recovered sufficiently to raise himself on one elbow and gaze overhead as Fergus struck match after match. The villains were having an altercation on the very trap-door.

"Now's the time to cut and run-now or never."

"Very well, you do so. I'm going through the safe."

"You should ha' done that first."

"Better late than not at all."

"You can't stop and do it without me."

"Oh, yes, I can. I'll call for a volunteer from below. You show them your spurs and save your skin."

"Oh, I'll stay, curse you, I'll stay!"

"And I'll have my volunteer, whether you stay or not."

The pair had scarcely parted when the trap-door opened slowly and stayed open for the first time. The banking chamber was but dimly lit, and the light in the pit less than it had been during the brief burning of single matches. No peering face was revealed to those below, but the voice of Stingaree came rich and crisp from behind the counter.

"Your old woman has got away to the police-barracks and the place is surrounded. One of you has got to come up and help, and help fair, or go to hell with a bullet in his heart. I give you one minute to choose your man."

But in one second the man had chosen himself. Without a word, or a glance at any of his companions, but with a face burning with extraordinary fires, Fergus Carrick sprang for the clean edge of the trap-door, caught it first with one hand and then with both, drew himself up like the gymnast he had been at his Scottish school, and found himself prone upon the floor and trap-door as the latter closed under him on the release of the lever which Stingaree understood so well. A yell of execration followed him into the upper air. And Stingaree was across the counter before his new ally had picked himself up.

"That's because this was expected of me," said Fergus, grimly, to explain the cashier's reiterated anathemas. "I was the writer of the registered letter that led to all this. So now I'm going the whole hog."

And the blue eyes boiled in his brick-red face.

"You mean that? No nonsense?"

"You shall see."

"I should shoot you like a native cat."

"You couldn't do me a better turn."

"Right! Swear on your knees that you won't use it against me or my mate, and I'll trust you with this revolver. You may fire as high as you please, but they must think we're three instead of two."

Fergus took the oath in fierce earnest upon his knees, was handed the weapon belonging to the bank, and posted in his own bedroom window at the rear of the building. The front was secure enough with the shutters and bolts of the official fortress. It was to the back premises that the attack confined itself, making all use of the admirable cover afforded by the stables.

Carrick saw heads and shoulders hunched to aim over stable-doors as he obeyed his orders and kept his oath. His high fire drew a deadlier upon himself; a stream of lead from a Winchester whistled into the room past his ear and over his ducked head. He tried firing from the floor without showing his face. The Winchester let him alone; in a sudden sickness he sprang up to see if anything hung sprawling over the stable-door, and was in time to see men in retreat to right and left, the white pugarees of the police fluttering ingloriously among them. Only one was left upon the ground, and he could sit up to nurse a knee.

Fergus sighed relief as he sought Stingaree, and found him with a comical face before the open safe.

"House full of paltry paper!" said he. "I suppose it's the old sportsman's custom to get rid of most of his heavy metal before closing on Saturdays?"

Fergus said it was; he had himself stowed many a strong-box aboard unsuspected barges for Echuca.

"Well, now's our time to leave you," continued Stingaree. "If I'm not mistaken, their flight is simply for the moment, and in two or three more they'll be back to batter in the bank shutters.

I wonder what they think we've done with our horses? I'll bet they've looked everywhere but in the larder next the kitchen door-not that we ever let them get so close. But my mate's in there now, mounted and waiting, and I shall have to leave you."

"But I was coming with you," cried Fergus, aghast.

Stingaree's eye-glass dangled on its cord.

"I'm afraid I must trouble you to step into that safe instead," said he, smiling.

"Man, I mean it! You think I don't. I've fought on your side of my own free will. How can I live that down? It's the only side for me for the rest of time!"

The fixed eye-glass covered the brick-red face with the molten eyes.

"I believe you do mean it."

"You shall shoot me if I don't."

"I most certainly should. But my mate Howie has his obvious limitations. I've long wanted a drop of new blood. Barmaid's thoroughbred and strong as an elephant; we're neither of us heavyweights; by the powers, I'll trust you, and you shall ride behind!"

Now, Barmaid was the milk-white mare that was only less notorious than her lawless rider. It was noised in travellers' huts and around campfires that she would do more at her master's word than had been known of horse outside a circus. It was the one touch that Stingaree had borrowed from a more Napoleonic but incomparably coarser and crueller knight of the bush. In all other respects the *fin de siècle* desperado was unique. It was a stroke of luck, however, that there happened to be an old white mare in the bank stables, which the police had impounded with solemn care while turning every other animal adrift. And so it fell out that not a shot followed the mounted bushrangers into the night, and that long before the bank shutters were battered in the flying trio were miles away.

Fergus flew like a runaway bride, his arms about the belted waist of Stingaree. Trees loomed ahead and flew past by the clump under a wonderful wide sky of scintillating stars. The broad bush track had very soon been deserted at a tangent; through ridges and billows of salt-bush and cotton-bush they sailed with the swift confidence of a well-handled clipper before the wind. Stingaree was the leader four miles out of five, but in the fifth his mate Howie would gallop ahead, and anon they would come on him dismounted at a wire fence, with the wires strapped down and his horse tethered to one of the posts till he had led Barmaid over.

It was thus they careered across the vast chessboard of the fenced back-blocks at dead of night. Stingaree and Fergus sat saddle and bareback without a break until near dawn their pioneer spurred forward yet again and was swallowed in a steely haze. It was cold as a sharp spring night in England. But for a mile or more Fergus had clung on with but one arm round the bushranger's waist; now the right arm came stealing back; felt something cold for the fraction of a second, and plucked prodigiously, and in another fraction an icy ring mouthed Stingaree's neck.

"Pull up," said Fergus, hoarsely, "or your brains go flying."

"Little traitor!" whispered the other, with an imprecation that froze the blood.

"I am no traitor. I swore I wouldn't abuse the revolver you gave me, and it's been in my pocket all the night."

"The other's unloaded."

"You wouldn't sit so quiet if it were. Now, round we go, and back on our tracks full split. It's getting light, and we shall see them plain. If you vary a yard either way, or if your mate catches us, out go your brains."

The bushranger obeyed without a word. Fergus was almost unnerved by the incredible ease of his conquest over so redoubtable a ruffian. His stolid Scottish blood stood by him; but still he made grim apology as they rode.

"I had to do it. It was through me you got to know. I had to live that down; this was the only way."

"You have spirit. If you would still be my mate — —"

"Your mate! I mean this to be the making of me as an honest man. Here's the fence. I give you two minutes to strap it down and get us over."

Stingaree slid tamely to the ground.

"Don't you dare to get through those wires! Strap it from this side with your belt, and strap it quick!"

And the bushranger obeyed with the same sensible docility, but with his back turned, so that Fergus could not see has face; and it was light enough to see faces now; yet Barmaid refused the visible wires, as she had not refused them all that night of indigo starlight.

"Coax her, man!" cried Fergus, in the saddle now, and urging the mare with his heels. So Stingaree whispered in the mare's ear; and with that the strapped wires flew under his captor's nose, as the rider took the fence, but not the horse.

At a single syllable the milk-white mare had gone on her knees, like devout lady in holy fane; and as she rose her last rider lay senseless at her master's feet; but whether from his fall, or from a blow dealt him in the act of falling, the unhappy Fergus never knew. Indeed, knowledge for him was at an end until matches burnt under his nose awakened him to a position of the last humiliation. His throat and chin topped a fence-post, the weight of his body was on chin and throat, while wrists and muscles were lashed at full stretch to the wires on either side.

"Now I'm going to shoot you like a dog," said Stingaree. He drew the revolver whose muzzle had pressed into his own neck so short a time before. Yet now it was broad daylight, and the sun coming up in the bound youth's eyes for the last time.

"Shoot away!" he croaked, raising the top of his head to speak at all. "I gave you leave before we started. Shoot away!"

"At ten paces," said Stingaree, stepping them. "That, I think, is fair."

"Perfectly," replied Fergus. "But be kind enough to make this so-called man of yours hold his foul tongue till I'm out of earshot of you all."

Huge Howie had muttered little enough for him, but to that little Stingaree put an instantaneous stop.

"He's a dog, to be shot like a dog, but too good a dog for you to blackguard!" cried he. "Any message, young fellow?"

"Any message, young fellow?"

"Not through you."
 "So long, then!"
 "Shoot away!"

The long barrel was poised as steadily as field-gun on its carriage. Fergus kept his blue eyes on the gleaming ring of the muzzle.

The hammer fell, the cartridge cracked, and from the lifted muzzle a tiny cloud flowed like a bubble from a pipe. The post quivered under Carrick's chin, and a splinter flew up and down before his eyes. But that was all.

"Aim longer," said he. "Get it over this shot."

"I'll try."

But the same thing happened again.

"Come nearer," sneered Fergus.

And Stingaree strode forward with an oath.

"I was going to give you six of them. But you're a braver man than I thought. And that's the lot."

The bound youth's livid face turned redder than the red dawn.

"Shoot me-shoot!" he shouted, like a lunatic.

"No, I shall not. I never meant to —I did mean you to sit out six-but you're the most gallant little idiot I've ever struck. Besides, you come from the old country, like myself!"

And a sigh floated into the keen morning air as he looked his last upon the lad through the celebrated monocle.

"Then I'll shoot myself when I'm free," sobbed Fergus through his teeth.

"Oh, no, you won't," were Stingaree's last words. "You'll find it's not a bit worth while."

And when the mounted police and others from Glenranald discovered the trussed youngster, not an hour later, they took the same tone. And one and all stopped and stooped to peer at the two bullet-holes in the post, and at something underneath them, before cutting poor Fergus down.

Then they propped him up to read with his own eyes the nailed legend which first helped Fergus Carrick to live down the indiscretion of his letter to Largs, and then did more for him in that Colony than letter from Queen Victoria to His Excellency of New South Wales. For it ran: —

"THIS IS THE GAMEST LITTLE COCK I HAVE EVER STRUCK. HE HAD ME CAPTIVE ONCE, COULD HAVE SHOT ME OVER AND OVER AGAIN, AND ALL BUT TOOK ME ALIVE. MORE POWER TO HIM!

"STINGAREE."

Vanheimert had been in many duststorms, but never in such a storm so far from the haunts of men. Awaking in his blanket with his mouth full of sand, he had opened his eyes to the blinding sting of a storm which already shrouded the very tree under which he lay. Other landmarks there were none; the world was swallowed in a yellow swirl that turned browner and more opaque even as Vanheimert shook himself out of his blanket and ran for the fence as for his life. He had only left it in order to camp where his tree had towered against the stars; it could not be a hundred yards away; and along the fence ran that beaten track to which the bushman turned instinctively in his panic. In a few seconds he was groping with outstretched hands to break the violence of a collision with invisible wires; in a few minutes, standing at a loss, wondering where the wires or he had got to, and whether it would not be wise to retrace his steps and try again. And while he wondered a fit of coughing drove the dust from his mouth like smoke; and even as he coughed the thickening swirl obliterated his tracks as swiftly as heavy snow.

Speckled eyeballs stood out of a sanded face as Vanheimert saw himself adrift and drowning in the dust. He was a huge young fellow, and it was a great smooth face, from which the gaping mouth cut a slice from jaw to jaw. Terror and rage, and an overpowering passion of self-pity, convulsed the coarse features in turn; then, with the grunt of a wounded beast, he rallied and plunged to his destruction, deeper and deeper into the bush, further and further from the fence.

The trees were few and mostly stunted, but Vanheimert crashed into more than one upon his headlong course. The sense was choked out of him already; he was fleeing on the wings of the storm; of direction he thought no more. He forgot that the run he had been traversing was at the best abandoned by man and beast; he forgot the "spell" that he had promised himself at the deserted homestead where he had once worked as a lad. He might have remembered that the paddock in which he was burying himself had always been the largest in the district. It was a ten-mile block without subdividing fence or drop of water from end to end. The whole station was a howling desert, little likely to be stocked a second time by enlightened man. But this was the desert's heart, and into it sped Vanheimert, coated yellow to the eyes and lips, the dust-fiend himself in visible shape. Now he staggered in his stride, now fell headlong to cough and sob in the hollow of his arm. The unfortunate young man had the courage of his desperate strait. Many times he arose and hurled himself onward with curse or prayer; many times he fell or flung himself back to earth. But at length the storm passed over and over his spent members; sand gathered by the handful in the folds of his clothes; the end was as near as end could be.

It was just then that two riders, who fancied they had heard a voice, struck an undoubted trail before it vanished, and followed it to the great sprawling body in which the dregs of life pulsed feebly. The thing groaned as it was lifted and strapped upon a horse; it gurgled gibberish at the taste of raw spirits later in the same hour. It was high noon before Vanheimert opened a seeing eye and blinked it in the unveiled sun.

He was lying on a blanket in a treeless hollow in the midst of trees. The ground had been cleared by no human hand; it was a little basin of barren clay, burnt to a brick, and drained by the tiny water-hole that sparkled through its thatch of leaves and branches in the centre of a natural circle. Vanheimert lay on the eastern circumference; it was the sun falling sheer on his upturned face that cut short his sleep of deep exhaustion. The sky was a dark and limpid blue; but every leaf within Vanheimert's vision bore its little load of sand, and the sand was clotted as though the dust-storm had ended with the usual shower. Vanheimert turned and viewed the sylvan amphitheatre; on its far side were two small tents, and a man in a folding chair reading the *Australasian*. He closed the paper on meeting Vanheimert's eyes, went to one of the tents, stood a moment looking in, and then came across the sunlit circle with his newspaper and the folded chair.

"And how do you feel now?" said he, setting up the chair beside the blanket, but still standing as he surveyed the prostrate man, with dark eyes drawn together in the shade of a great straw sombrero.

"Fine!" replied Vanheimert, huskily. "But where am I, and who are you chaps? Rabbiters?"

As he spoke, however, he searched for the inevitable strings of rabbit skins festooned about the tents, and found them not.

"If you like," replied the other, frowning a little at the immediate curiosity of the rescued man.

"I don't like," said Vanheimert, staring unabashed. "I'm a rabbiter myself, and know too much. It ain't no game for abandoned stations, and you don't go playin' it in top-boots and spurs. Where's your skins and where's your squatter to pay for 'em? Plucky rabbiters, you two!"

And he gazed across the open toward the further tent, which had just disgorged a long body and a black beard not wholly unfamiliar to Vanheimert. The dark man was a shade darker as he followed the look and read its partial recognition; but a grim light came with quick resolve, and it was with sardonic deliberation that an eye-glass was screwed into one dark eye.

"Then what should you say that we are?"

"How do I know?" cried Vanheimert, turning pale; for he had been one of the audience at Mrs. Clarkson's concert in Gulland's store, and in consecutive moments he had recognized first Howie and now Stingaree.

"You know well enough!"

And the terrible eye-glass covered him like a pistol.

"Perhaps I can guess," faltered Vanheimert, no small brain working in his prodigious skull.

"Guess, then!"

"There are tales about a new chum camping by himself-that is, just with one man ——"

"And what object?"

"To get away from the world, sir."

"And where did you hear these tales?"

"All along the road, sir."

The chastened tone, the anxious countenance, the sudden recourse to the servile monosyllable, were none of them lost on Stingaree; but he himself had once set such a tale abroad, and it might be that the present bearer still believed it. The eye-glass looked him through and through. Vanheimert bore the inspection like a man, and was soon satisfied that his recognition of the outlaw was as yet quite unsuspected. He congratulated himself on his presence of mind, and had sufficient courage to relish the excitement of a situation of which he also perceived the peril.

"I suppose you have no recollection of how you got here?" at length said Stingaree.

"Not me. I only remember the dust-storm." And Vanheimert shuddered where he lay in the sun. "But I'm very grateful to you, sir, for saving my life."

"You are, are you?"

"Haven't I cause to be, sir?"

"Well, I dare say we did bring you round between us, but it was pure luck that we ever came across you. And now I should lie quiet if I were you. In a few minutes there'll be a pannikin of tea for you, and after that you'll feel a different man."

Vanheimert lay quiet enough; there was much to occupy his mind. Instinctively he had assumed a part, and he was only less quick to embrace the necessity of a strictly consistent performance. He watched Stingaree in close conversation with Howie, who was boiling the billy on a spirit-lamp between the two tents, but he watched them with an admirable simulation of idle unconcern. They were talking about him, of course; more than once they glanced in his direction; and each time Vanheimert congratulated himself the more heartily on the ready pretence to which he was committed. Let them but dream that he knew them, and Vanheimert gave himself as short a shrift as he would have granted in their place. But they did not dream it, they were off their guard, and rather at his mercy than he at theirs. He might prove the immediate instrument of their capture-why not? The thought put Vanheimert in a glow; on the blanket where they had laid him, he dwelt on it without a qualm; and the same wide mouth watered for the tea which these villains were making, and for their blood.

It was Howie who came over with the steaming pannikin, and watched Vanheimert as he sipped and smacked his lips, while Stingaree at his distance watched them both. The pannikin was accompanied by a tin-plate full of cold mutton and a wedge of baking-powder bread, which between them prevented the ravening man from observing how closely he was himself observed as he assuaged his pangs. There was, however, something in the nature of a muttered altercation between the bushrangers when Howie was sent back for more of everything. Vanheimert put it down to his own demands, and felt that Stingaree was his friend when it was he who brought the fresh supplies.

"Eat away," said Stingaree, seating himself and producing pipe and tobacco. "It's rough fare, but there's plenty of it."

"I won't ask you for no more," replied Vanheimert, paving the way for his escape.

"Oh, yes, you will!" said Stingaree. "You're going to camp with us for the next few days, my friend!"

"Why am I?" cried Vanheimert, aghast at the quiet statement, which it never occurred to him to gainsay. Stingaree pared a pipeful of tobacco and rubbed it fine before troubling to reply.

"Because the way out of this takes some finding, and what's the use of escaping an unpleasant death one day if you go and die it the next? That's one reason," said Stingaree, "but there's another. The other reason is that, now you're here, you don't go till I choose."

Blue wreaths of smoke went up with the words, which might have phrased either a humorous hospitality or a covert threat. The dispassionate tone told nothing. But Vanheimert felt the eye-glass on him, and his hearty appetite was at an end.

"That's real kind of you," said he. "I don't feel like running no more risks till I'm obliged. My nerves are shook. And if a born back-blocker may make so bold, it's a fair old treat to see a new chum camping out for the fun of it!"

"Who told you I was a new chum?" asked Stingaree, sharply. "Ah! I remember," he added, nodding; "you heard of me lower down the road."

Vanheimert grinned from ear to ear.

"I'd have known it without that," said he. "What real bushmen would boil their billy on a spirit-lamp when there's wood and to spare for a camp-fire on all sides of 'em?"

Now, Vanheimert clearly perceived the superiority of smokeless spirit-lamp to tell-tale fire for those in hiding; so he chuckled consumedly over this thrust, which was taken in such excellent part by Stingaree as to prove him a victim to the desired illusion. It was the cleverest touch that Vanheimert had yet achieved. And he had the wit neither to blunt his point by rubbing it in nor to recall attention to it by subtle protestation of his pretended persuasion. But once or twice before sundown he permitted himself to ask natural questions concerning the old country, and to indulge in those genial gibes which the Englishman in the bush learns to expect from the indigenous buffoon.

In the night Vanheimert was less easy. He had to sleep in Howie's tent, but it was some hours before he slept at all, for Howie would remain outside, and Vanheimert longed to hear him snore. At last the rabbiter fell into a doze, and when he awoke the auspicious music filled the tent. He listened on one elbow, peering till the darkness turned less dense; and there lay Howie across the opening of the tent. Vanheimert reached for his thin elastic-sided bushman's boots, and his hands trembled as he drew them on. He could now see the form of Howie plainly enough as it lay half in the starlight and half in the darkness of the tent. He stepped over it without a mistake, and the ignoble strains droned on behind him.

The stars seemed unnaturally bright and busy as Vanheimert stole into their tremulous light. At first he could distinguish nothing earthly; then the tents came sharply into focus, and after them the ring of impenetrable trees. The trees whispered a chorus, myriads strong, in a chromatic scale that sang but faintly of the open country. There were palpable miles of wilderness, and none other lodge but this, yet the psychological necessity for escape was stronger in

Vanheimert than the bodily reluctance to leave the insecure security of the bushrangers' encampment. He was their prisoner, whatever they might say, and the sense of captivity was intolerable; besides, let them but surprise his knowledge of their secret, and they would shoot him like a dog. On the other hand, beyond the forest and along the beaten track lay fame and a fortune in direct reward.

Before departure Vanheimert wished to peep into the other tent, but its open end was completely covered in for the night, and prudence forbade him to meddle with his hands. He had an even keener desire to steal one or other of the horses which he had seen before nightfall tethered in the scrub; but here again he lacked enterprise, fancied the saddles must be in Stingaree's tent, and shrank from committing himself to an action which nothing, in the event of disaster, could explain away. On foot he need not put himself in the wrong, even with villains ready to suspect that he suspected them.

And on foot he went, indeed on tiptoe till the edge of the trees was reached without adventure, and he turned to look his last upon the two tents shimmering in the starlight. As he turned again, satisfied that the one was still shut and that Howie still lay across the opening of the other, a firm hand took Vanheimert by either shoulder; otherwise he had leapt into the air; for it was Stingaree, who had stepped from behind a bush as from another planet, so suddenly that Vanheimert nearly gasped his dreadful name.

"I couldn't sleep! I couldn't sleep!" he cried out instead, shrinking as from a lifted hand, though he was merely being shaken playfully to and fro.

"No more could I," said Stingaree.

"So I was going for a stroll. That was all, I swear, Mr. —Mr. —I don't know your name!"

"Quite sure?" said Stingaree.

"My oath! How should I?"

"You might have heard it down the road."

"Not me!"

"Yet you heard of me, you know."

"Not by name-my oath!"

Stingaree peered into the great face in which the teeth were chattering and from which all trace of color had flown.

"I shouldn't eat you for knowing who I am," said he. "Honesty is still a wise policy in certain circumstances; but you know best."

"I know nothing about you, and care less," retorted Vanheimert, sullenly, though the perspiration was welling out of him. "I come for a stroll because I couldn't sleep, and I can't see what all this barney's about."

Stingaree dropped his hands.

"Do you want to sleep?"

"My blessed oath!"

"Then come to my tent, and I'll give you a nobbler that may make you."

The nobbler was poured out of a gallon jar, under Vanheimert's nose, by the light of a candle which he held himself. Yet he smelt it furtively before trying it with his lips, and denied himself a gulp till he was reassured. But soon the empty pannikin was held out for more. And it was the starless hour before dawn when Vanheimert tripped over Howie's legs and took a contented header into the corner from which he had made his stealthy escape.

The tent was tropical when he awoke, but Stingaree was still at his breakfast outside in the shade. He pointed to a bucket and a piece of soap behind the tent, and Vanheimert engaged in obedient ablutions before sitting down to his pannikin, his slice of damper, and his portion of a tin of sardines.

"Sorry there's no meat for you," said Stingaree. "My mate's gone for fresh supplies. By the way, did you miss your boots?"

The rabbiter looked at a pair of dilapidated worsted socks and at one protruding toe; he was not sure whether he had gone to bed for the second time in these or in his boots. Certainly he had missed the latter on his second awakening, but had not deemed it expedient to make inquiries. And now he merely observed that he wondered where he could have left them.

"On your feet," said Stingaree. "My mate has made so bold as to borrow them for the day."

"He's welcome to them, I'm sure," said Vanheimert with a sickly smile.

"I was sure you would say so," rejoined Stingaree. "His own are reduced to uppers and half a heel apiece, but he hopes to get them soled in Ivanhoe while he waits."

"So he's gone to Ivanhoe, has he?"

"He's been gone three hours."

"Surely it's a long trip?"

"Yes; we shall have to make the most of each other till sundown," said Stingaree, gazing through his glass upon Vanheimert's perplexity. "If I were you I should take my revenge by shaking anything of his that I could find for the day."

And with a cavalier nod, to clinch the last word on the subject, the bushranger gave himself over to his camp-chair, his pipe, and his inexhaustible *Australasian*. As for Vanheimert, he eventually returned to the tent in which he had spent the night; and there he remained a good many minutes, though it was now the forenoon, and the heat under canvas past endurance. But when at length he emerged, as from a bath, Stingaree, seated behind his *Australasian* in the lee of the other tent, took so little notice of him that Vanheimert crept back to have one more look at the thing which he had found in the old valise which served Howie for a pillow. And the thing was a very workmanlike revolver, with a heavy cartridge in each of its six chambers.

Vanheimert handled it with trembling fingers, and packed it afresh in the pocket where it least affected his personal contour, its angles softened by a big bandanna handkerchief, only to take it out yet again with a resolution that opened a fresh sluice in every pore. The blanket that had been lent to him, and Howie's blanket, both lay at his feet; he threw one over either arm, and with the revolver thus effectually concealed, but grasped for action with finger on trigger, sallied forth at last.

Stingaree was still seated in the narrowing shade of his own tent. Vanheimert was within five paces of him before he looked up so very quickly, with such a rapid adjustment of the terrible eye-glass, that Vanheimert stood stock-still, and the butt of his hidden weapon turned colder than ever in his melting hand.

"Why, what have you got there?" cried Stingaree. "And what's the matter with you, man?" he added, as Vanheimert stood shaking in his socks.

"Only his blankets, to camp on," the fellow answered, hoarsely. "You advised me to help myself, you know."

"Quite right; so I did; but you're as white as the tent-you tremble like a leaf. What's wrong?"

"My head," replied Vanheimert, in a whine. "It's going round and round, either from what I had in the night, or lying too long in the hot tent, or one on top of the other. I thought I'd camp for a bit in the shade."

"I should," said Stingaree, and buried himself in his paper with undisguised contempt.

Vanheimert came a step nearer. Stingaree did not look up again. The revolver was levelled under one trailing blanket. But the trigger was never pulled. Vanheimert feared to miss even at arm's length, so palsied was his hand, so dim his eye; and when he would have played the man and called desperately on the other to surrender, the very tongue clove in his head.

He slunk over to the shady margin of surrounding scrub and lay aloof all the morning, now fingering the weapon in his pocket, now watching the man who never once looked his way. He was a bushranger and an outlaw; he deserved to die or to be taken; and Vanheimert's only regret was that he had neither taken nor shot him at their last interview. The bloodless alternative was to be borne in mind, yet in his heart he well knew that the bullet was his one chance with Stingaree. And even with the bullet he was horribly uncertain and afraid. But of hesitation on any higher ground, of remorse or of reluctance, or the desire to give fair play, he had none at all. The man whom he had stupidly spared so far was a notorious criminal with a high price upon his head. It weighed not a grain with Vanheimert that the criminal happened to have saved his life.

"Come and eat," shouted Stingaree at last; and Vanheimert trailed the blankets over his left arm, his right thrust idly into his pocket, which bulged with a red bandanna handkerchief. "Sorry it's sardines again," the bushranger went on, "but we shall make up with a square feed to-night if my mate gets back by dark; if he doesn't, we may have to tighten our belts till morning. Fortunately, there's plenty to drink. Have some whiskey in your tea?"

Vanheimert nodded, and with an eye on the bushranger, who was once more stooping over his beloved *Australasian*, helped himself enormously from the gallon jar.

"And now for a siesta," yawned Stingaree, rising and stretching himself after the meal.

"Hear, hear!" croaked Vanheimert, his great face flushed, his bloodshot eyes on fire.

"I shall camp on the shady side of my tent."

"And I'll do ditto at the other."

"So long, then."

"So long."

"Sweet repose to you!"

"Same to you," rasped Vanheimert, and went off cursing and chuckling in his heart by turns.

It was a sweltering afternoon of little air, and that little as hot and dry in the nostrils as the atmosphere of a laundry on ironing day. Beyond and above the trees a fiery blast blew from the north; but it was seldom a wandering puff stooped to flutter the edges of the tents in the little hollow among the trees. And into this empty basin poured a vertical sun, as if through some giant lens which had burnt a hole in the heart of the scrub. Lulled by the faint perpetual murmur of leaf and branch, without a sound from bird or beast to break its soothing monotone, the two men lay down within a few yards, though out of sight, of each other. And for a time all was very still.

Then Vanheimert rose slowly, without a sound, and came on tiptoe to the other tent, his right hand in the pocket where the bandanna handkerchief had been but was no longer. He came close up to the sunny side of the tent and listened vainly for a sound. But Stingaree lay like a log in the shade on the far side, his face to the canvas and his straw sombrero tilted over it. And so Vanheimert found him, breathing with the placid regularity of a sleeping child.

Vanheimert looked about him; only the ring of impenetrable trees and the deep blue eye of Heaven would see what really happened. But as to what exactly was to happen Vanheimert himself was not clear as he drew the revolver ready cocked; even he shrank from shooting a sleeping man; what he desired and yet feared was a sudden start, a semblance of resistance, a swift, justifiable shot. And as his mind's eye measured the dead man at his feet, the live man turned slowly over on his back.

It was too much for Vanheimert's nerves. The revolver went off in his hands. But it was only a cap that snapped, and another, and another, as he stepped back firing desperately. Stingaree sat upright, looking his treacherous enemy in the eye, through the glass in which, it seemed, he slept. And when the sixth cap snapped as harmlessly as the other five, Vanheimert caught the revolver by its barrel to throw or to strike. But the raised arm was seized from behind by Howie, who had crept from the scrub at the snapping of the first cap; at the same moment Stingaree sprang upon him; and in less than a minute Vanheimert lay powerless, grinding his teeth, foaming and bleeding at the mouth, and filling the air with nameless imprecations.

The bushrangers let him curse; not a word did they bandy with him or with each other. Their action was silent, swift, concerted, prearranged. They lashed their prisoner's wrists together, lashed his elbows to his ribs, hobbled his ankles, and tethered him to a tree by the longest and the stoutest of their many ropes. The tree was the one under which Vanheimert had found himself the day before; in the afternoon it was exposed to the full fury of the sun; and in the sun they left him, quieter already, but not so quiet as they. It was near sundown when they returned to look upon a broken man, crouching in his toils like a beaten beast, with undying malice in his swollen eyes. Stingaree sat at his prisoner's feet, offered him tobacco without a sneer, and lit up his own when the offer was declined with a curse.

"When we came upon you yesterday morning in the storm, one of us was for leaving you to die in your tracks," began Stingaree. He was immediately interrupted by his mate.

"That was me!" cried Howie, with a savage satisfaction.

"It doesn't matter which of us it was," continued Stingaree; "the other talked him over; we put you on one of our horses, and we brought you more dead than alive to the place which no other man has seen since we took a fancy to it. We saved your miserable life, I won't say at the risk of our own, but at risk enough even if you had not recognized us. We were going to see you through, whether you knew us or not; before this we should have set you on the road from which you had strayed. I thought you must know us by sight, but when you denied it I saw no reason to disbelieve you. It only dawned on me by degrees that you were lying, though Howie here was sure of it.

"I still couldn't make out your game; if it was funk I could have understood it; so I tried to get you to own up in the night. I let you see that we didn't mind whether you knew us or not, and yet you persisted in your lie. So then I smelt something deeper. But we had gone out of our way to save your life. It never struck me that you might go out of your way to take ours!"

Stingaree paused, smoking his pipe.

"But it did me!" cried Howie.

"I never meant taking your lives," muttered Vanheimert. "I meant taking you-as you deserved."

"We scarcely deserved it of you; but that is a matter of opinion. As for taking us alive, no doubt you would have preferred to do so if it had seemed equally safe and easy; you had not the pluck to run a single risk. You were given every chance. I sent Howie into the scrub, took the powder out of six cartridges, and put what anybody would have taken for a loaded revolver all but into your hands. I sat at your mercy, quite looking forward to the sensation of being stuck up for a change. If you had stuck me up like a man," said Stingaree, reflectively examining his pipe, "you might have lived to tell the tale."

There was an interval of the faint, persistent rustling of branch and leaf, varied by the screech of a distant cockatoo and the nearer cry of a crow, as the dusk deepened into night as expeditiously as on the stage. Vanheimert was not awed by the quiet voice to which he had been listening. It lacked the note of violence which he understood; it even lulled him into a belief that he would still live to tell the tale. But in the dying light he looked up, and in the fierce unrelenting face, made the more sinister by its foppish furniture, he read his doom.

"You tried to shoot me in my sleep," said Stingaree, speaking slowly, with intense articulation. "That's your gratitude! You will live just long enough to wish that you had shot yourself instead!"

Stingaree rose.

"You may as well shoot me now!" cried Vanheimert, with a husky effort.

"Shoot you? I'm not going to *shoot* you at all; shooting's too good for scum like you. But you are to die-make no mistake about that. And soon; but not to-night. That would not be fair on you, for reasons which I leave to your imagination. You will lie where you are to-night; and you will be watched and fed like your superiors in the condemned cell. The only difference is that I can't tell you when it will be. It might be to-morrow —I don't think it will-but you may number your days on the fingers of both hands."

So saying, Stingaree turned on his heel, and was lost to sight in the shades of evening before he reached his tent. But Howie remained on duty with the condemned man.

As such Vanheimert was treated from the first hour of his captivity. Not a rough word was said to him; and his own unbridled outbursts were received with as much indifference as the abject prayers and supplications which were their regular reaction. The ebbing life was ordered on that principle of high humanity which might be the last refinement of calculated cruelty. The prisoner was so tethered to such a tree that it was no longer necessary for him to spend a moment in the red eye of the sun. He could follow a sufficient shade from dawn to dusk. His boots were restored to him; a blanket was permitted him day and night; but night and day he was sedulously watched, and neither knife nor fork was provided with his meals. His fare was relatively not inferior to that of the legally condemned, whose notorious privileges and restrictions served the bushrangers for a model.

And Vanheimert clung to the hope of a reprieve with all the sanguine tenacity of his ill-starred class, though it did seem with more encouragement on the whole. For the days went on, and each of many mornings brought its own respite till the next. The welcome announcement was invariably made by Howie after a colloquy with his chief, which Vanheimert watched with breathless interest for a day or two, but thereafter with increasing coolness. They were trying to frighten him; they did not mean it, any more than Stingaree had meant to shoot the new chum who had the temerity to put a pistol to his head after the affair of the Glenranald bank. The case of lucky Fergus, justly celebrated throughout the colony, was a great comfort to Vanheimert's mind; he could see but little difference between the two; but if his treachery was the greater, so also was the ordeal to which he was being subjected. For in the light of a mere ordeal he soon regarded what he was invited to consider as his last days on earth, and in the conviction that they were not, began suddenly to bear them like a man. This change of front produced its fellow in Stingaree, who apologized to Vanheimert for the delay, which he vowed he could not help. Vanheimert was a little shaken by his manner, though he smiled behind the bushranger's back. And he could scarcely believe his ears when, the very next morning, Howie told him that his hour was come.

"Rot!" said Vanheimert, with a confident expletive.

"Oh, all right," said Howie. "But if you don't believe me, I'm sorrier for you than I was."

He slouched away, but Vanheimert had no stomach for the tea and damper which had been left behind. It was unusual for him to be suffered to take a meal unwatched; something unusual was in the air. Stingaree emerged from the scrub leading the two horses. Vanheimert began to figure the fate that might be in store for him. And the horses, saddled and bridled before his eyes, were led over to where he sat.

"Are you going to shoot me before you go," he cried, "or are you going to leave me to die alone?"

"Neither, here," said Stingaree. "We're too fond of the camp."

It was his first brutal speech, but the brutality was too subtle for Vanheimert. He was beginning to feel that something dreadful might happen to him after all. The pinions were removed from his arms and legs, the long rope detached from the tree and made fast to one of Stingaree's stirrups instead. And by it Vanheimert was led a good mile through the scrub, with Howie at his heels.

A red sun had risen on the camp, but in the scrub it ceased to shine, and the first open space was as sunless as the dense bush. Spires of sand kept whirling from earth to sky, joining other spinning spires, forming a monster balloon of yellow sand, a balloon that swelled until it burst, obscuring first the firmament and then the earth. But the mind of Vanheimert was so busy with the fate he feared that he did not realize he was in another dust-storm until Stingaree, at the end of the rope, was swallowed like a tug in a fog. And even then Vanheimert's peculiar terror of a dust-storm did not link itself to the fear of sudden death which had at last been put into him. But the moment of mental enlightenment was at hand.

The rope trailed on the ground as Stingaree loomed large and yellow through the storm. He had dropped his end. Vanheimert glanced over his shoulder, and Howie loomed large and yellow behind him.

"You will now perceive the reason for so many days' delay," said Stingaree. "I have been waiting for such a dust-storm as the one from which we saved you, to be rewarded as you endeavored to reward me. You might, perhaps, have preferred me to make shorter work of you, but on consideration you will see that this is not only just but generous. The chances are perhaps against you, and somewhat in favor of a more unpleasant death; but it is quite possible that the storm may pass before it finishes you, and that you may then hit the fence before you die of thirst, and at the worst we leave you no worse off than we found you. And that, I hold, is more than you had any right to expect. So long!"

The thickening storm had swallowed man and horse once more. Vanheimert looked round. The second man and the second horse had also vanished. And his own tracks were being obliterated as fast as footmarks in blinding snow. . . .

A Bushranger at Bay

The Hon. Guy Kentish was trotting the globe-an exercise foreign to his habit-when he went on to Australia for a reason racy of his blood. He wished to witness a certain game of cricket between the full strength of Australia and an English team which included one or two young men of his acquaintance. It was no part of his original scheme to see anything of the country; one of the Australian cricketers put that idea into his head; and it was under inward protest that Mr. Kentish found himself smoking his chronic cigar on the Glenranald and Clear Corner coach one scorching morning in the month of February. He thought he had never seen such a howling desert in his life; and it is to be feared that in his heart he applied the same epithet to his two fellow-passengers. The one outside was chatting horribly with the driver; the other had tried to chaff the Hon. Guy, and had repaired in some disorder to the company of the mail-bags inside. Kentish wondered whether these were the types he might expect to encounter upon the station to which he had reluctantly accepted an officious introduction. He wished himself out of the absurd little two-horse coach, out of an expedition whose absurdity was on a larger scale, and back again on the shady side of the two or three streets where he lived his normal life. The fare at wayside inns made the thought of his club a positive pain; and these pangs were at their sharpest when Stingaree cantered out of the scrub on his lily mare, a blessed bolt from the blue.

Mr. Kentish watched the little operation of "sticking up" without a word, but with revived interest in life. He noted the pusillanimous pallor of the driver and his friend, and felt personally indebted to the desperado who had put a stop to their unpleasant conversation. The inside passenger made a yet more obsequious surrender. Not that the trio were set any better example by their noble ally, who began by smiling at the whole affair, and was content to the last in taking an observant interest in the bushranger's methods. These were simple and in a sense humane; there was no personal robbery at all. The mail-bags were sufficient for Stingaree, who on this occasion worked alone, but led a pack-horse, to which the driver and the inside passenger were compelled to strap the long canvas bags, under his eye-glass and his long revolver. Few words were spoken from first to last; the Hon. Guy never put in his at all; but he watched the outlaw like a lynx, without betraying an undue attention, and when all was over he gave a sigh.

Mr. Kentish watched the little operation of "sticking up" without a word.

"So that's Stingaree!" he said, more to himself than to his comrades in humiliation; but the bushranger had cantered back into the scrub, and his name opened the flood-gates of a profanity which made Kentish wince, for all his knowledge of the world.

"Do you never swear at him till he has gone?" he asked when he had a chance. The driver leant across the legs of his friend.

"Not unless we want a bullet through our skulls," he answered in boorish derision; and the man between them laughed harshly.

"I thought he had never been known to shoot?"

"That's just it, mister. We don't want him to begin on us."

"Why didn't *you* give him a bit of *your* mind?" the man in the middle inquired of Kentish. "I never heard you open your gills!"

"And we expected to see some pluck from the old country," added the driver, wreaking vengeance with his lash.

Mr. Kentish produced his cigar-case with an insensitive smile, and, after a moment's deliberation, handed it for the first time to his uncouth companions. "Do you want those mail-bags back?" he asked, quite casually, when the three cigars were in blast.

"Want them? Of course I want them; but want must be my boss," said the driver, gloomily.

"I'm not so sure," said Kentish. "When does the next coach pass this way?"

"Midnight, and I drive it. I turn back when I get to Clear Corner, you see."

"Then look out for me about this spot. I'm going to ask you to put me down."

"Put you down?"

"If you don't mind pulling up. I'm not going on at present; but I'll go back with you to Glenranald instead, if you'll keep a lookout for me to-night."

Instinctively the driver put his foot upon the brake, for the request had been made with that quiet authority which this silent passenger had suddenly assumed; and yet it seemed to them such a mad demand that his companions looked at Kentish as they had not looked before. His face bore a close inspection; it was one of those which burn red, and in the redness twinkled hazel eyes that toned agreeably with a fair beard and fairer mustache. The former he had grown upon his travels; but the trail of the West-end tailor, whose shooting-jacket is as distinctive as his frock-coat, was upon Guy Kentish from head to heel. As they watched him he took an open envelope from his pocket, scribbled a few words on a card, put that in, and stuck down the flap.

"Here," said he, "is my letter of introduction to the good people at the Mazeppa Station higher up. If I don't turn up to-night, see that they get it, even if it costs you a bit of this?"

And, putting a sovereign in a startled palm, he jumped to the ground.

"But what are you going to do, sir?" cried the driver, in alarm.

"Recover your mail-bags if I can."

"What? After you've just been stuck up ——"

"Exactly. I hope to stick up Stingaree!"

"Then you were armed all the time?"

Mr. Kentish smiled as he shook his head.

"That's my affair, I imagine; but even so I am not fool enough to tackle such a fellow with his own weapons. You leave it to me, and don't be anxious. But I must be off if I'm to stalk him before he goes through the letters. No, I know what I'm doing, and I shall do better alone. Till to-night, then!"

And he was in the scrub ere they decided to take him at his madcap word, and let his blood be on the chuckle-head of the new-chummiest new chum that ever came out after the rain! Was it pluck or all pretence? It was rather plucky even to pretend in such proximity to the terrible Stingaree; on the whole, the coaching trio were disposed to concede a certain amount of unequivocal courage; and the driver, with Kentish's sovereign in his pocket, went so far as to declare that duty alone nailed him to the box.

Meantime the Hon. Guy had skirted the road until he came to double horse-tracks striking back into the bush; these he followed with the wary stealth of one who had spent his autumns, at least, in the right place. They led him through belts of scrub in which he trod like a cat, without disturbing an avoidable branch, and over treeless spaces that he crossed at a run, bent double; but always, as he followed the trail, his shadow fell at one consistent angle, showing how the bushranger rode through his natural element as the crow might have flown overhead.

At last Kentish found himself in a sandy gully bristling with pines, through which the sunlight dripped like melted gold; and in the fine warp and woof of high light and sharp shadow the bushranger's horses stood lashing at the flies with their long tails. The bushranger himself was nowhere to be seen. But at last Kentish descried a white-and-brown litter on either side of the thickest trunk in sight, from whose further side floated intermittent puffs of thin blue smoke. Kentish looked and looked again before advancing. But the tall pine threw such a shadow as should easily swallow his own. And in another minute he was peeping round the hole.

The litter on either side was, of course, the shower of miscellaneous postal matter from the mail-bags; and in its midst sat Stingaree against the tree, enjoying his pipe and a copy of *Punch*, of which the wrapper lay upon his knees. Kentish peered for torn envelopes and gaping packets; there were no more. The bushranger had evidently started with *Punch*, and was still curiously absorbed in its contents. The notorious eye-glass dangled against that kindred vanity, the spotless white jacket which he affected in summer-time; the brown, attentive face, even as Kentish saw it in less than profile, was thus purged of the sinister aspect which such an appendage can impart to the most innocent; and a somewhat passive amusement was its unmistakable note. Nevertheless, the long revolver which had once more done its nefarious work still lay ready to his hand; indeed, the Hon. Guy could have stooped and whipped it up, had he been so minded.

He was absorbed, however, in the absorption of Stingaree; and as he peered audaciously over the other's shoulder he put himself in the outlaw's place. An old friend would have lurked in every cut, a friend whom it might well be a painful pleasure to meet again. There were the oval face and the short upper lip of one imperishable type; on the next page one of *Punch's* Fancy Portraits, with lines underneath which set Stingaree incongruously humming a stave from *H.M.S. Pinafore*. Mr. Kentish smiled without surprise. The common folk in the omnibus opposite were the common folk of an inveterate master; there was matter for a homesick sigh in his hint of streaming streets-and Kentish thought he heard one as he held his breath. The page after that detained the reader some minutes. The illustrations proclaimed it an article on the new Savoy opera, and Stingaree confirmed the impression by humming more *Pinafore* when he came to the end. Kentish left him at it, and, creeping away as silently as he had come, described a circle and came noisily on the bushranger from the front. The result was that Stingaree was not startled into firing, but stopped the intruder at due distance with his revolver levelled across the open copy of *Punch*.

"I heard you singing *Pinafore*," cried Kentish, cheerily. "And I find you reading *Punch*!"

"How dare you find me?" demanded the bushranger, black with passion.

"I thought you wouldn't mind. I am perfectly innocuous-look!"

And, divesting himself of his shooting-coat, he tossed it across for the other's inspection; he wore neither waistcoat nor hip-pocket, and his innocence of arms was manifest when he had turned round slowly where he stood.

"Now may I not come a little nearer?" asked the Hon. Guy.

"No; keep your distance, and tell me why you have come so far. The truth, mind, or you'll be shot!"

"Very well," said Kentish. "They were dreadful people on the coach — —"

"Are they waiting for you?" thundered Stingaree.

"No; they've gone on; and they think me mad."

"So you are."

"We shall see; meanwhile I prefer your company to theirs, and mean to enjoy it up to the moment of my murder."

For an instant Stingaree seemed on the brink of a smile; then his dark face hardened, and he tapped the long barrel in rest between his knees.

"You may call it murder if you like," said he. "That will not prevent me from shooting you dead unless you speak the truth. You have come for something; what is it?"

"I've told you already. I was bored and disgusted. That is the truth."

"But not the whole truth," cried Stingaree. "You had some other reason."

Kentish looked down without speaking. He heard the revolver cocked.

"Come, let us have it, or I'll shoot you like the spy I believe you are!"

"You may shoot me for telling you," said Kentish, with a quiet laugh and shrug.

"No, I shall not, unless it turns out that you're ground-bait for the police."

"That I am not," said Kentish, growing serious in his turn. "But, since you insist, I have come to persuade you to give up every one of these letters which you have no earthly right to touch."

Their eyes met. Stingaree's were the wider open, and in an instant the less stern. He dropped his revolver, with a laugh, into its old place at his side.

"Mad or sane," said he, "I shall be under the unpleasant necessity of leaving you rather securely tied to one of these trees."

"I don't believe you will," returned Kentish, without losing a shade of his rich coloring. "But in any case I suppose we may have a chat first? I give you my word that you are safe from further intrusion to the level best of my knowledge and belief. May I sit down instead of standing?"

"You may."

"We are a good many yards apart."

"You may reduce them by half. There."

"I thank you," said Kentish, seating himself tailorwise within arm's length of Stingaree's spurs. "Now, if you will feel in the breast-pocket of my coat you will find a case of very fair cigars —J. S. Murias-not too strong. I shall be honored if you will help yourself and throw me one."

Stingaree took the one, and handed the case with no ungraceful acknowledgment to its owner; but before Mr. Kentish could return the courtesy by proffering his cigar-cutter, the bushranger had produced his razor from a pocket of the white jacket, and sliced off the end with that.

"So you shave every day in the wilds," remarked the other, handing his match-box instead. "And I gave it up on my voyage."

"I alter myself from time to time," said Stingaree, as he struck a light.

"It must be a wonderful life!"

But Stingaree lit up without a word, and Kentish had the wit to do the same. They smoked in silence for some minutes. A gray ash had grown on each cigar before Kentish demanded an opinion of the brand.

"To tell you the truth," said Stingaree, "I have smoked strong trash so many years that I can scarcely taste it."

And he peered rather pathetically through his glass.

"Didn't the same apply to *Punch*?"

"No; I have always read the papers when I could," said Stingaree, and suddenly he was smiling. "That's one reason why I make a specialty of sticking up the mail," he explained.

Mr. Kentish was not to be drawn into a second deliverance on the bushranging career. "Is it a good number?" he asked, nodding toward the copy of *Punch*. The bushranger picked it up.

"Good enough for me."

"What date?"

"Ninth of December."

"Nearly three months ago. I was in London then," remarked Kentish, in a reflective tone.

"Really?" cried Stingaree, under his breath. His voice was as soft as the other's, but there was suppressed interest in his manner. His dark eyes were only less alight than the red cigar he took from his teeth as he spoke. And he held it like a connoisseur, between finger and thumb, for all his ruined palate.

"I was," repeated Kentish. "I didn't sail till the middle of the month."

"To think you were in town till nearly Christmas!" and Stingaree gazed enviously. "It must be hard to realize," he added in some haste.

"Other things," replied Kentish, "are harder."

"I gather from the *Punch* cartoon that the new Law Courts are in use at last?"

"I was at the opening."

"Then you may have seen this opera that I have been reading about?"

Kentish asked what it was, although he knew.

"*Iolanthe*."

"Rather! I was there the first night."

"The deuce you were!" cried Stingaree; and for the next quarter of an hour this armed scoundrel, the terror of a district as large as England and Wales, talked of nothing else to the man whom he was about to bind to a tree. Was the new opera equal to its predecessors? Which were the best numbers? Did *Punch* do it justice, or was there some jealousy in that rival hot-bed of wit and wisdom?

Unfortunately, Guy Kentish had no ear for music, but he made a clear report of the plot, could repeat some of the Lord Chancellor's quips, and was in decided disagreement with the captious banter from which he was given more than one extract. And in default of one of the new airs Stingaree rounded off the subject by dropping once more into —

"For he might have been a Rooshian,

A French, or Turk, or Prooshian,

Or, perhaps, I-tal-i-an!

Or, perhaps, I-tal-i-an!

But in spite of all temptations

To belong to other nations

He remains an Englishman!"

"I understand that might be said of both of us," remarked Kentish, looking the outlaw boldly in the eyes. "But from all accounts I should have thought you were out here before the days of Gilbert and Sullivan."

"So I was," replied Stingaree, without frown or hesitation. "But you may also have heard that I am fond of music-any I can get. My only opportunities, as a rule," the bushranger continued, smiling mischievously at his cigar, "occur on the stations I have occasion to visit from time to time. On one a good lady played and sang *Pinafore* and *The Pirates of Penzance* to me from dewy eve to dawn. I'm bound to say I sang some of it at sight myself; and I flatter myself it helped to pass an embarrassing night rather pleasantly for all concerned. We had all hands on the place for our audience, and when I left I was formally presented with both scores; for I had simply called for horses, and horses were all I took. Only the other day I had the luck to confiscate a musical-box which plays selections from *The Pirates*. I ought to have had it with me in my swag."

So affable and even charming was the quiet voice, so evident the appreciation of the last inch of the cigar which had thawed a frozen palate, and so conceivable a further softening, that Guy Kentish made bolder than before. He knew what he meant to do; he knew how he meant to do it. And yet it seemed just possible there might be a gentler way.

"You don't always take things, I believe?" he hazarded.

"You mean after sticking up?"

"Yes."

"Generally, I fear; it's the whole meaning of the act," confessed Stingaree, still the dandy in tone and phrase. "But there have been exceptions."

"Exactly!" quoth Kentish. "And there's going to be another this afternoon!"

Stingaree hurled the stump of his cigar into the scrub, and without a word the villain was born again, with his hard eyes, his harder mouth, his sinister scowl, his crag of a chin.

"So you come back to that," he cried, harshly. "I thought you had more sense; you will make me tie you up before your time."

"You may do exactly what you like," retorted Kentish, a galling scorn in his unaltered voice. "Only, before you do it, you may as well know who I am."

"My good sir, do you suppose I care who you are?" asked Stingaree, with an angry laugh: and his anger is the rarest thing in all his annals.

"I am quite sure you don't," responded Kentish. "But you may as well know my name, even though you never heard it before." And he gave it with a touch of triumph, not for one moment to be confounded with a natural pride.

The bushranger stared him steadily in the eyes; his hand had dropped once more upon the butt of his revolver. "No; I never did hear it before," he said.

"I'm not surprised," replied the other. "I was a new member when you were turned out of the club." Stingaree's hand closed: his eyes were terrible. "And yet," continued Kentish, "the moment I saw you at close quarters in the road I recognized you as ———"

"Stingaree!" cried the bushranger, on a rich and vibrant note. "Let the other name pass your lips-even here-and it's the last word that ever will!"

"Very well," said Mr. Kentish, with his unaffected shrug. "But, you see, I know all about you."

"You're the only man who does, in all Australia!" exclaimed the outlaw, hoarsely.

"At present! I sha'n't be the only man long."

"You will," said Stingaree through teeth and mustache; and he leaned over, revolver in hand. "You'll be the only man ever, because, instead of tying you up, I'm going to shoot you."

Kentish threw up his head in sharp contempt.

"What!" said he. "Sitting?"

Stingaree sprang to his feet in a fury. "No; I have a brace!" he cried, catching the pack-horse. "You shall have the other, if it makes you happy; but you'll be a dead man all the same. I can handle these things, and I shall shoot to kill!"

"Then it's all up with you," said Kentish, rising slowly in his turn.

"All up with me? What the devil do you mean?"

"Unless I am at a certain place by a certain time, with or without these letters that are not yours, another letter will be opened."

Stingaree's stare gradually changed into a smile.

"A little vague," said he, "don't you think?"

"It shall be as plain as you please. The letter I mean was scribbled on the coach before I got down. It will only be opened if I don't return. It contains the name you can't bear to hear!"

There was a pause. The afternoon sun was sinking with southern precipitancy, and Kentish had got his back to it by cool intent. He studied the play of suppressed mortification and strenuous philosophy in the swarthy face warmed by the reddening light; and admired the arduous triumph of judgment over instinct, even as a certain admiration dawned through the monocle which insensibly focussed his attention.

"And suppose," said Stingaree —"suppose you return empty as you came?" A contemptuous kick sent a pack of letters spinning.

"I should feel under no obligation to keep your secret."

"And you think I would trust you to keep it otherwise?"

"If I gave you my word," said Kentish, "I know you would."

Stingaree made no immediate answer; but he gazed in the sun-flayed face without suspicion.

"You wouldn't give me your word," he said at last.

"Oh, yes, I would."

"That you would die without letting that name pass your lips?"

"Unless I die delirious-with all my heart. I have as much respect for it as you."

"As much!" echoed the bushranger, in a strange blend of bitterness and obligation. "But how could you explain the bags? How could you have taken them from me?"

Kentish shrugged once more.

"You left them —I found them. Or you were sleeping, but I was unarmed."

"You would lie like that-to save my name?"

"And a man whom I remember perfectly . . ."

Stingaree heard no more; he was down on his knees, collecting the letters into heaps and shovelling them into the bags. Even the copy of *Punch* and the loose wrapper went in with the rest.

"You can't carry them," said he, when none remained outside. "I'll take them for you and dump them on the track."

"I have to pass the time till midnight. I can manage them in two journeys."

But Stingaree insisted, and presently stood ready to mount his mare.

"You give me your word, Kentish?"

"My word of honor."

"It is something to have one to give! I shall not come back this way; we shall have the Clear Corner police on our tracks by moonlight, and the more they have to choose from the better. So I must go. You have given me your word; you wouldn't care to give me — —"

But his hand went out a little as he spoke, and Kentish's met it seven-eights of the way.

"Give this up, man! It's a poor game, when all's said; do give it up!" urged the man of the world with the warmth of a lad. "Come back to England and — —"

But the hand he had detained was wrenched from his, and, in the pink sunset sifted through the pines, Stingaree vaulted into his saddle with an oath.

"With a price on my skin!" he cried, and galloped from the gully with a bitter laugh.

And in the moonlight sure enough came bobbing horsemen, with fluttering pugarees and short tunics with silver buttons; but they saw nothing of the missing passenger, who had carried the bags some distance down the road, and had found them quite a comfortable couch in a certain box-clump commanding a sufficient view of the road. Nevertheless, when the little coach came swaying on its leathern springs, its scarlet enamel stained black as ink in the moonshine, he was on the spot to stop it with uplifted arms.

"Don't shoot!" he cried. "I'm the passenger you put down this afternoon." And the driver nearly tumbled from his perch.

"What about my mail-bags?" he recovered himself enough to ask: for it was perfectly plain that the pretentiously intrepid passenger had been skulking all day in the scrub, scared by the terrors of the road.

"They're in that clump," replied Mr. Kentish. "And you can get them yourself, or send someone else for them, for I have carried them far enough."

"That be blowed for a yarn!" cried the driver, forgetting his benefits in the virtuous indignation of the moment.

"I don't wonder at your thinking it one," returned the other, mildly; "for I never had such absolute luck in all my life!"

And he went on to amplify his first lie like a man.

But when the bags were really back in the coach, piled roof-high on those of the downward mail, then it was worse fun for Guy Kentish outside than even he had anticipated. Question followed question, compliment capped compliment, and a certain unsteady undercurrent of incredulity by no means lessened his embarrassment. Had he but told the truth, he felt he could have borne the praise, and indeed enjoyed it, for he had done far better than anybody was likely to suppose, and already it was irritating to have to keep that circumstance a secret. Yet one thing he was able to say from his soul before the coach drew up at the next stage.

"You should have a spell here," the driver had suggested, "and let me pick you up again on my way back. You'd soon lay hands on the bird himself, if you can put salt on his tail as you've done. And no one else can-we want a few more chums like you."

"I dare say!"
And the new chum's tone bore its own significance.
"You don't mean," cried the driver, "to go and tell me you'll hurry home after this?"
"Only by the first steamer!" said Guy Kentish.
And he kept that word as well.

The Taking of Stingaree

Stingaree had crossed the Murray, and all Victoria was agog with the news. It was not his first descent upon that Colony, nor likely to be his last, unless Sub-Inspector Kilbride and his mounted myrmidons did much better than they had done before. There is no stimulus, however, like a trembling reputation. Within four-and-twenty hours Kilbride himself was on the track of the invader, whose heels he had never seen, much less his face. And he rode alone.

It was not merely his reputation that was at stake, though nothing could restore that more effectually than the single-handed capture of so notorious a desperado as Stingaree. The dashing officer was not unnaturally actuated by the sum of three hundred pounds now set upon the outlaw's person, alive or dead. That would be a little windfall for one man, but not much to divide among five or six; on the other hand, and with all his faults, Sub-Inspector Kilbride had courage enough to furnish forth a squadron. He was a black-bearded, high-cheeked Irish-Australian, keen and over-eager to a disease, restless, irascible, but full of the fire and dash that make as dangerous an enemy as another good fighter need desire. And as a fine fighter in an infamous cause, Stingaree had his admirers even in Victoria, where the old tale of popular sympathy with a picturesque rascal was responsible for not the least of the Sub-Inspector's difficulties. But even this struck Kilbride as yet another of those obstacles which were more easily surmounted alone than at the head of a talkative squad; and with that conviction he pushed his thoroughbred on and on through a whole cool night and three parts of an Australian summer's day. Imagine, then, his disgust at the apparition of a mounted trooper galloping to meet him in the middle of the afternoon, and within a few miles of a former hiding-place of the bushranger, where the senior officer had strong hopes of finding and surprising him now.

"Where the devil do you come from?" cried Kilbride, as the other rode up.

"Jumping Creek," was the crisp reply. "Stationed there."

"Then why don't you stop there and do your duty?"

"Stingaree!" said the laconic trooper.

"What! Do you think you're after him too?"

"I am after him."

"So am I."

"Then you're going in the wrong direction."

Kilbride flushed a warm brown from beard to helmet.

"Do you know who you're speaking to?" cried he. "I'm Sub-Inspector Kilbride, and this business is my business, and no other man's in this Colony. You go back to your barracks, sir! I'm not going to have every damned fool in the force charging about the country on his own account."

The trooper was a dark, smart, dapper young fellow, of a type not easily browbeaten or subdued. And discipline is not the strong point of forces so irregular as the mounted police of a crescent colony. But nothing could have been more admirable than the manner in which this rebuke was received.

"Very well, sir, if you wish it; but I can assure you that you are off the track of Stingaree."

"How do *you* know?" asked Kilbride, rudely; but he was beginning to look less black.

"I happen to know the place. You would have some difficulty in finding it if you never were there before. I only stumbled across it by accident myself."

"Lately?"

"One day last winter when I was out looking for some horses."

"And you kept it to yourself!"

The trooper hung his head. "I knew we should have him across the river again," he said. "It was only a question of time; and-well, sir, you can understand!"

"You were keen on taking him yourself, were you?"

"As keen as you are, Mr. Kilbride!" owned the younger man, raising bold eyes, and looking his superior fairly and squarely in the face.

Kilbride returned the stare, and what he saw unsettled him. The other was wiry, trim, eminently alert; he had the masterful mouth and the dare-devil eye, and his horse seemed a part of himself. A more promising comrade at hot work was not to be desired: and the work would be hot if Stingaree had half a chance. After all, it was better for two to succeed than for one to fail. "Half the money and a whole skin!" said Kilbride to himself, and rapped out his decision with an oath.

The trooper's eyes lit with reckless mirth, and a soft cheer came from under his breath.

"By the bye, what's your name," said Kilbride, "before we start?"

"Bowen-Jack Bowen."

"Then I know all about you! Why on earth didn't you tell me before? It was you who took that black fellow who murdered the shepherd on Woolshed Creek, wasn't it?"

The admission was made with due modesty.

"Why, you're the very man for me!" Kilbride cried. "You show the way, Jack, and I'll make the going."

And off they went together at a canter, the slanting sun striking fire from their buttons and accoutrements, and lighting their sunburnt faces as it lit the red stems and the white that raced past them on either side. For a little they followed the path which Kilbride had taken on his way thither; then the trooper plunged into the thick bush on the left, and the game became follow-my-leader, in and out, out and in, through a maze of red stems and of white, where the pungent eucalyptus scent hung heavy as the sage-green, perpendicular leaves themselves: and so onward until the Sub-Inspector called a halt.

"How far is it now, Bowen?"

"Two or three miles, sir."

"Good! It'll be light for another hour and a half. We'd better give the mokes a breather while we can. And there'd be no harm in two draws."

"I was just thinking the same thing, sir."

So their reins dangled while they cut up a pipeful of apparent shoe-leather apiece: and presently the dull blue smoke was curling and circling against the dull green foliage, producing subtle half-tint harmonies and momentary arabesques as the horses ambled neck and neck.

"Native of this Colony?" puffed Kilbride.

"Well, no-old country originally-but I've been out some years."

"That's all right so long as you're not a New South Welshman," said Kilbride, with a chuckle. "I'll be shot if I wouldn't almost have turned you back if you had been!"

"Victoria is to have all the credit, is she, sir?"

"Anyhow they sha'n't have any on the other side, or I'll know the reason!" the Victorian swore. "I —I —by Jove, I'd as lief lose my man again as let them have a hand in taking him!"

"But why?"

"Why? Do you live so near the border, and can you ask? Did you never hear a Sydney-side drover blowing about his blooming Colony? Haven't you heard of Sydney Harbor till you're sick? And then their papers!" cried Kilbride, with columns in his tone. "But I'll have the last laugh yet! I swore I would, and I will! I swore I'd take Stingaree — —"

"So I heard."

"Yes, they put it in their infernal papers! But it was true-take him I will!"

"Or die in the attempt, eh?"

"Or die and be damned to me!"

All the bitterness of previous failure, indeed of notorious and much-criticized defeat, was in the Sub-Inspector's tone; that of his subordinate, though light as air, had a touch of insolence which an outsider could not have failed-but Kilbride was too excited-to detect. The outsider might possibly have foreseen a rivalry which no longer entered Kilbride's hot head.

Meanwhile the country was changing even with their now leisurely advance. The timbered flats in the region of the river had merged into a gully which was rapidly developing into a gorge, with new luxuriant growths which added greatly to the density of the forest, suggesting its very heart. The almost neutral eucalyptian tint was splashed with the gay hues of many parrots, as though the gum-trees had burst into flower. The noise of running water stole gradually through the murmur of leaves. And suddenly an object in the grass struck the sight like a lantern flashed at dead of night: it proved to be an empty sardine tin pricked by a stray lance from the slanting sun.

"We must be near," whispered Kilbride.

"We are there! You hear the creek? He has a gunyah there-that's all. Shall we rush it on horseback or creep up on foot?"

"You know the lie of the land, Bowen; which do you recommend?"

"Rushing it."

"Then here goes."

In a few seconds they had leaped their horses into a tiny clearing on the banks of a creek as relatively minute. And the gunyah —a mere funnel of boughs and leaves, in which a man could lie at full length, but only sit upright at the funnel's mouth-seemed as empty as the space on every hand. The only other sign of Stingaree was a hank of rope flung carelessly across the gunyah roof.

"He may be watching us from among the trees," muttered Kilbride, looking sharply about him. Bowen screwed up his eyes and followed suit.

"I hardly think it, Mr. Kilbride."

"But it's possible, and here we sit for him to pot us! Let's dismount, whether or no."

They slid to the ground. The trooper found himself at the mouth of the gunyah.

"What if he were in there after all!" said he.

"He isn't," said Kilbride, stepping in front and stooping quickly. "But you might creep in, Jack, and see if he's left any sign of life behind him."

The men were standing between the horses, their revolvers cocked. Bowen's answer was to hand his weapon over to Kilbride and to creep into the gunyah on his hands and knees.

"Here's something or other," his voice cried thickly from within. "It's half buried. Wait a bit."

"As sharp as you can!"

"All right; but it's a box, and jolly heavy!"

Kilbride peered nervously to right, left, and centre; then his eyes fell upon his companion wriggling back into the open, a shallow, oblong box in his arms, its polish dimmed and dusted with the mould, as though they had violated a grave.

"Kick it open!" exclaimed Kilbride, excitedly.

But there was no need for that; the box was not even locked; and the lifted lid revealed an inner one of glass, protecting a brass cylinder with steel bristles in uneven growth, and a long line of lilliputian hammers.

"A musical-box!" said the staggered Sub-Inspector.

"That's it, sir. I remember hearing that he'd collared one on one of the stations he stuck up last time he was down here. It must have lain in the ground ever since. And it only shows how hard you must have pressed him, Mr. Kilbride!"

"Yes! I headed him back across the Murray —I soon had him out o' this!" rejoined the other in grim bravado. "Anything else in the gunyah?"

"All he took that trip, I fancy, if we dig a bit. You never gave him time to roll his swag!"

"I must have a look," said Kilbride, his excitement fed by his reviving vanity.

The other questioned whether it were worth while. This settled the Sub-Inspector.

"There may be something to show where he's gone," that casuist suggested, "for I don't believe he's anywhere here."

"Shall I hold the shooters, sir?"

"Thanks; and keep your eyes open, just in case. But it's my opinion that the bird's flown somewhere else, and it's for us to find out where."

Kilbride then crept into the gunyah upon his hands and knees, and found it less dark than he had supposed, the light filtering freely through the leaves and branches. At the inner extremity he found a mildewed blanket, and the place where the musical-box had evidently lain a long time; but there, though he delved to the elbows in the loosened earth, his discoveries ended. Puzzled and annoyed, Kilbride was on the verge of cursing his subordinate, when all at once he was given fresh cause. The musical-box had burst into selections from *The Pirates of Penzance*.

"What the deuce are you at?" shouted the irate officer.

"Only seeing how it goes."

"Stop it at once, you fool! He may hear it!"

"You said the bird had flown."

"You dare to argue with me? By thunder, you shall see!"

But it was Sub-Inspector Kilbride who saw most. Backing precipitately out of the gunyah, he turned round before rising upright-and remained upon his knees after all. He was covered by two revolvers-one of them his own-and the face behind the barrels was the one with which the last hour had familiarized Kilbride. The only difference was the single eye-glass in the right eye. And the strains of the musical-box —so thin and tinkling in the open air-filled the pause.

"What in blazes are you playing at?" laughed the luckless officer, feigning to treat the affair as a joke, even while the iron truth was entering his soul by inches.

"Rise another inch without my leave and you may be in blazes to see!"

"Look here, Bowen, what do you mean?"

"Only that Stingaree happens to be at home after all, Mr. Kilbride."

The victim's grin was no longer forced; the situation made for laughter, even if the laughter were hysterical; and for an instant it was given even to Kilbride to see the cruel humor of it. Then he realized all it meant to him-certain ruin or a sudden death-and the drops stood thick upon his skin.

"What of Bowen?" he at length asked hoarsely. The idea of another victim came as some slight alleviation of his own grotesque case.

"I didn't kill him," Stingaree.

"Good!" said Kilbride. It was something that two of them should live to share the shame.

"But wing him I did," added the bushranger. "I couldn't help myself. The beggar put a bullet through my hat; he did well only to get one back in the leg."

Kilbride longed to be winged and wounded in his turn, since blood alone could lessen his disgrace. On cooler reflection, however, it was obviously wiser to feign a surrender more abject than it might finally prove to have been.

"Well," said Kilbride, "you have the whip-hand over me this time, and I give you best. How long are you going to keep me on my knees?"

"You can get up when you like," replied Stingaree, "if you promise not to play the fool. So you were really going to take me this time, were you? I have really no desire to rub it in, but if I were you I should have kept that to myself until I'd done it. And you wanted to have me all to yourself? Well, you couldn't pay me a higher compliment, but I'm going to pay you a high one in return. You really did make me run for it last time, and leave all sorts of things behind. So this time I mean to take them with me and leave you here instead. Nevertheless, you're the only Victorian trap I have any respect for, Mr. Kilbride, or I shouldn't have gone to all this trouble to get you here."

Kilbride did not blanch, but he heard his apparent doom with a glittering eye, and was deaf for a little to *The Pirates of Penzance*.

"Oh! I'm not going to harm a good man like you," continued Stingaree, "unless you make me. Your friend Bowen made me, but I don't promise to fire low every time, mark you! There's another good man on the other side-Cairns by name-you know him, do you? He'll kick up his heels when he hears of this; but they do no better in New South Wales, so don't you let that worry you. To think you held both shooters at one stage of the game! I trusted you, and so you trusted me; if only you had known, eh? Hear that tune, and know what it is? It's in your honor, Mr. Kilbride."

And Stingaree hummed the policemen's chorus *sotto voce*; but before the end, with a swift remorse, induced by the dignity of Kilbride's bearing in humiliating disaster, he swooped upon the insolent instrument and stopped its tinkle by touching the lever with one revolver-barrel while sedulously covering the Sub-Inspector with the other. The sudden cessation of the toy music, bringing back into undue prominence all the little bush noises which had filled the air before, brought home to Kilbride a position which he had subconsciously associated with those malevolent strains as something theatrical and unreal. He had known in his heart that it was real, without grasping the reality until now. He flung up his fists in sudden entreaty.

"Put a bullet through me," he cried, "if you're a man!"

Stingaree shook a decisive head.

"Not if I can help it," said he. "But I fear I shall have to tie you up."

"That's slow death!"

"It never has been yet, but you must take your chance. Get me that rope that's slung over the gunyah. It's got to be done."

Kilbride obeyed with apparent apathy; but his heart was inflamed with a sudden and infernal glow. Yes, it had never ended in death in any case that he could recall of this time-honored trick of all the bushrangers; on the contrary, sooner or later, most victims had contrived to release themselves. Well, one victim was going to complete his release by hanging himself by the same rope to the same tree! Meanwhile he confronted his captor grimly, the coil in both hands.

"There's a loop at one end," said Stingaree. "Stick your foot through it-either foot you like."

Kilbride obeyed, wondering whether his head would go through when his turn came.

"Now chuck me the other end."

It fell in coils at the bushranger's feet.

"Now stand up against that blue gum," he continued, pointing at the tree with Kilbride's revolver, his own being back at his hip. "And stand still like a sensible chap!"

Stingaree then walked round and round the tree, paying out the long rope, yet keeping it taut, until it wound round tree and man from the latter's ankles to his armpits. Instinctively Kilbride had kept his arms free to the last, but they were no use to him in his suit of hemp, and one after the other his wrists were pinned and handcuffed behind the tree. The cold steel came as a shock. The captive had counted on loosening the knots by degrees, beginning with those about his hands. But there was no loosening steel gyves like these; he knew the feel of them too well; they were Kilbride's own, that he had brought with him for Stingaree. "Found 'em in your saddle-bags while you were in my gunyah," explained the bushranger, stepping round to survey his handiwork. "Sorry to scar the kid-so to speak! But you see you were my most dangerous enemy on this side of the Murray!"

The enemy did not look very dangerous as he stood in the dusk, in the heart of that forest, lashed to that tree, with his finger-tips not quite meeting behind it, and the blood already on his wrists.

"And now?" he whispered, hoarse already, his lips cracking, and his throat parched.

"I shall give you a drink before I go."

"I won't take one from you!"

"I shall make you, if I have to be a bigger brute than ever. You must live to spin this yarn!"

"Never!"

Stingaree smiled to himself as he produced pipe and tobacco; but it was not his sinister smile; it was rather that of the victor who salutes the vanquished in his heart. Meanwhile a more striking and a more subtle change had come over the face of Kilbride. It was not joy, but it was quite a new grimness, and in his own preoccupation the bushranger did not notice it at all. He sauntered nearer with his knife and his tobacco-plug, and there was some compassion in his pensive stare.

"Cheer up, man!" said he. "There's no disgrace in coming out second best to me. You may smile. You'll find it's generally admitted in New South Wales. And after all, you needn't tell little crooked Cairns how it happened. So that stops your smile! But he's the best man left on my tracks, and I shouldn't be surprised if he's the first to find you."

"No more should I!" said a harsh voice behind the bushranger. "Hands up and empty, Stingaree, or you're the next dead man in this little Colony!"

Quick as thought Stingaree stepped in front of the tied Victorian. But his hands were up, and his eye-glass dangling on its string.

"Oh, you don't catch me kill two birds," rasped the newcomer's voice, "though I'm not sure which of you would be least loss!"

Stingaree stood aside once more, and waved his hands without lowering them, bowing from his captor to his captive as he did so.

"Superintendent Cairns, of New South Wales-Inspector Kilbride, of Victoria," said he. "You two men will be glad to know each other."

The New South Welshman drawled out a dry expression of his own satisfaction. His was a strange and striking personality. Dark as a mulatto, and round-shouldered to the extent of some distinct deformity, he carried his eyes high under the lids, and shot his piercing glance from under the penthouse of a beetling brow; a lipless mouth was pursed in such a fashion as to shorten the upper lip and exaggerate an already powerful chin; and this stooping and intent carriage was no less suggestive of the human sleuth-hound than were the veiled vigilance and dogged determination of the lowered face. Such was the man who had succeeded where Kilbride had failed-succeeded at the most humiliating moment of that most ignominious failure-and who came unwarrantably from the wrong side of the Murray. The Victorian stood in his bonds and favored his rival with such a glare as he had not levelled at Stingaree himself. But not a syllable did Kilbride vouchsafe. And the Superintendent was fully occupied with his prisoner.

"'Little crooked Cairns,' am I? There are those that look a jolly sight smaller, and'll have a worse hump than mine for the rest of their born days! Come nearer and turn your back."

And the revolver was withdrawn from its carrier on the stolen constabulary belt. The bushranger was then searched for other weapons; then marched into the bush at the pistol's point, and brought back handcuffed to the Superintendent's bridle.

"That's the way you'll come marching home, my boy; and one of us on horseback each side; don't trust *you* in a saddle on a dark night!"

Indeed, it was nearly dark already, and in the nebulous middle-distance a laughing jackass was indulging in his evening peal. Cairns jerked his head in the direction of the unearthly cackle. "Lots of 'em down here in Vic, I believe," said he, and at length turned his attention to the bound man. "You see, I wanted to land him alive and kicking without spilling blood," he continued, opening his knife. "That was why I had to let him tie you up."

"You *let* him?" thundered the Victorian, breaking his silence with a bellow. It was as though the man with the knife had cut through the rope into the bound man's body.

"Stand still," said he, "or I may hurt you. I had to let him, my good fellow, or we'd have been dropping each other like bullocks. As it is, not a scratch between us, though I found young Bowen in a pretty bad way. Our friend had stuck up Jumping Creek barracks in the small hours, put a bullet through Bowen's leg, and come away in his uniform. Pretty tall, that, eh? I shouldn't wonder if you'd swing him for it alone, down here in Vic; no doubt you've got to be more severe in a young Colony. Well, I tracked my gentleman to the barracks, and I found Bowen in his blood, sent my trooper for a doctor, and got on *your* tracks before they were half an hour old. I came up with you just as he'd stuck you up. He had one in each hand. It wasn't quite good enough at the moment."

The knife shore through the rope for the last time, and it lay in short ends all round the tree.

"Now my hands," cried Kilbride fiercely.

"I beg pardon?" said the satirical Superintendent.

"My hands, I tell you!"

"There's a little word they teach 'em to say at our State Schools. Perhaps you never heard it down in Vic?"

"Don't be a silly fool," said Kilbride, wearily. "You haven't been through what I have!"

"That's true," said Cairns. "Still, you might be decently civil to the man that gets you out of a mess."

Nevertheless, the handcuffs were immediately removed; and that instant, with the curtest thanks, Sub-Inspector Kilbride sprang forward with such vigorous intent that the other detained him forcibly by one of his stiff and aching arms.

"What are you after now, Kilbride?"

"My prisoner!"

"Your what?"

"*My* prisoner," I said.

"I like that-and you his!"

Kilbride burst into a voluble defence of his position.

"What right have you on this side of the Murray, you Sydney-sider? None at all, except as a passenger. You can't lay finger on man, woman, or child in this Colony, and, by God, you sha'n't! Nor yet upon the three hundred there's on his head; and the sons of convicts down in Sydney can put *that* in their pipe and smoke it!"

For all his cool and ready insolence, the misshapen Superintendent from the other side stood dazed and bewildered by this volcanic outpouring. Then his dark face flushed darker, and with a snarl he clinched his fists. The Victorian, however, had turned on his heel, and now his liberated hands flew skyward, as though the bushranger's revolver covered him yet again.

But there was no such weapon discernible through the shade; no New South Welshman's horse; and neither sight, sound, wraith, nor echo of Stingaree, the outlawed bushranger, the terror and the despair of the Sister Colonies!

"I thought it might be done when I saw how you fixed him," said Kilbride cheerfully. "Those beggars can ride lying down or standing up!"

"I believe you saw him clear!"

"I'll settle that with you when I've caught him."

"You catch him, you gum-sucker, when you as good as let him go!"

And a volley of further and far more trenchant abuse was discharged by Superintendent Cairns, of the New South Wales Police. But Kilbride was already in the saddle; a covert outward kick with his spurred heel, and the third horse went cantering riderless into the trees.

"He won't go far," sang the Sub-Inspector, "and he'll take you safe back to barracks if you give him his head. It's easy to get bushed in this country-for new chums from penal settlements!"

As the Victorian galloped into the darkness, and the New South Welshman dashed wildly after the third horse, the laughing jackass in the invisible middle-distance gave his last grotesque guffaw at departed day. And the laughing jackass is a Victorian bird.

The Honor of the Road

Sergeant Cameron was undressing for bed when he first heard the voices through the weather-board walls; in less than a minute there was a knock at his door.

"Here's Mr. Hardcastle from Rosanna, sir. He says he must see you at once."

"The deuce he does! What about?"

"He says he'll only tell you; but he's ridden over in three hours, and he looks like the dead."

"Give him some whiskey, Tyler, and tell him I'll be down in two ticks."

So saying, the gray-bearded sergeant of the New South Wales Mounted Police tucked his night-gown into his cord breeches, slipped into his tunic, and hastened to the parlor which served as court-room on occasion, buttoning as he went. Mr. Hardcastle had a glass to his lips as the sergeant entered. He was a very fine man of forty, and his massive frame was crowned with a countenance as handsome as it was open and bold; but at a glance it was plain that he was both shaken and exhausted, and in no mood to hide either his fatigue or his distress. Sergeant Cameron sat down on the other side of the oval table with the faded cloth; the younger constable had left the room when Hardcastle called him back.

"Don't go, Tyler," said he. "You may as well both hear what I've got to say. It's—it's Stin-garee!"

The name was echoed in incredulous undertones.

"But he's down in Vic," urged the sergeant. "He's been giving our chaps a devil of a time down there!"

"He's come back. I've seen him with my own eyes. But I'm beginning at the wrong end first," said the squatter, taking another sip and then sitting back to survey his hearers. "You know old Duncan, my overseer?"

The sergeant nodded.

"Of course you know him," the other continued, "and so does the whole back-country, and did even before he won this fortune in the Melbourne Cup sweep. I suppose you've heard how he took the news? He was fuddling himself from his own bottle on Sunday afternoon when the mail came; the first I knew of it was when I saw him sitting with his letter in one hand and throwing out the rest of his grog with the other. Then he told us he had won the first prize of thirty thousand, and that he had made up his mind to have his next drink at his own place in Scotland. He left us that afternoon to catch the coach and go down to Sydney for his money. He ought to have been back this evening before sundown."

The sergeant put in his word:

"That he ought, for I saw him come off the coach and start for the station as soon as they'd run up the horse he left behind him at the pub. I wondered what had brought him, if he was so set on getting back to the old country."

"I could tell you," said Hardcastle, after some little hesitation, "and I may as well. Poor old Duncan was the most generous of men, and nothing would serve him but that every soul on Rosanna should share more or less in his good fortune. I am ashamed to tell you how much he spoke of pressing on myself. You have probably heard that one of his peculiarities was that he would never take payment by check, like other people? I believe it was because he had knocked down too many checks in his day. In any case, we used to call him Hard Cash Duncan on Rosanna; and I am very much afraid that when you saw him he must have had the whole of his thirty thousand pounds upon him in the hardest form of cash."

"But what has happened, Mr. Hardcastle?"

"The very worst," said Hardcastle, stooping to sip. The three heads came closer together across the faded tablecloth. "There was no sign of him at seven; he ought to have been with us before six. We had done our best to make it an occasion, and it seemed that the dinner would be spoilt. So at seven young Evans, my store-keeper, went off at a gallop to meet him, and at twenty-five past he came galloping back leading a riderless horse. It was the one you saw Duncan riding this afternoon. There was blood upon the saddle. I found it. And within another hour we had found the poor old boy himself, dead and cold in the middle of the track, with a bullet through his heart."

The squatter's voice trembled with an emotion that did him honor in his hearers' eyes; and the gray-bearded sergeant waited a little before asking questions.

"What makes you think it is Stingaree?" he inquired, at length.

"I tell you I saw him on the run, with my own eyes, this morning. I passed him in one of my paddocks, as close as I am to you, and asked him if he was looking for the homestead. He answered that he was only riding through, and we neither of us stopped."

"Yet you knew all the time that it was Stingaree?"

"No; to be quite honest," replied Hardcastle, "I never dreamt of it at the time. But now I am quite positive on the point. He hadn't his eye-glass in his eye, but it was dangling on its cord all right; and there was the curled mustache, and the boots and breeches that one knows all about, if one has never seen them for oneself. Yet I own it didn't dawn on me just then. I happened to be thinking of the stations round about, and wondering if they were as burnt up as we are, and when I met this swell I simply took him for a new chum on one or other of them."

"There had been robbery, of course?"

"An absolute clearance," said Hardcastle. "The valise had been cut to ribbons with a knife, and its other contents were strewed all about; a pocketbook we found still bulging from the roll of notes which had been taken out. I waited beside him while Evans went back for the buggy, and when they started to take him in I rode on to you."

"We'll ride back with you at once," said the sergeant, "and find you a fresh horse if your own has had enough. Run up the lot, Tyler, and Mr. Hardcastle can take his choice. It seems clear enough," continued Cameron, as the trooper disappeared. "But this is a new departure for Stingaree; it's the very thing that everybody said he would never do."

"And yet it's the logical climax of his career; it might have happened long ago, but it's not his first blood as it is," argued Hardcastle, when he had drained his glass. "Didn't he wing one of you down in Victoria the other day? Your bushranger is bound to come to it sooner or later. He may much prefer not to shoot; but he has only to get up against a man of his own calibre, as resolute and as well armed as himself, to have no choice in the matter. Poor old Duncan was the very type; he would never have given way. In fact, we found him with his own revolver fast in his hand, and a finger frozen to the trigger, but not a chamber discharged."

"Yes? Then that settles it, and it must have been foul play," cried Cameron, owning a doubt in its dismissal. "And we mustn't lose a single minute in getting on this blackguard's tracks."

Yet it was midnight before the little cavalcade set out upon a ride of over thirty miles, for arrangements had to be made for a telegram to be sent to the Glenranald coroner first thing in the morning, and to insure this it was necessary to disturb the postmaster, who occupied one of the three weather-board dwellings which constituted the roadside hamlet of Clear Corner. A round moon topped the sand-hills as the trio rode away; it was near its almost dazzling zenith when they reined up at the scene of the murder. This was at a point where the sandy track ran through a belt of scrub, and the sergeant got off to examine the ground with Hardcastle, while Tyler mounted guard in the saddle. But nothing of importance was discovered by the pair on foot, and nothing seen or heard by their mounted comrade.

They found the station still astir and faintly aglow in the veiled daylight of the moon. A cluster of the men stood in a glare at the door of their hut; the travellers' hut betrayed the like symptoms of excitement; at the kitchen door were more men with pannikins, and odd glimpses of a firelit, white-capped face within. But on the broad veranda sat two young men with their backs to a closed and darkened window. And behind the window lay all that remained of an elderly man, whose brown, gnarled face was scarcely recognizable by the newcomers in its strange smooth pallor, but his grizzled beard weirdly familiar and still crisp with lingering life.

The coroner arrived in some thirty hours, which had brought forth nothing new; his jury was drawn from the men's hut and rabbiters' tents; and after a prolonged but inconclusive investigation, the inquest was adjourned for a week. But the seven days were as barren as the first, and a verdict against some person unknown a foregone result. This did not satisfy the many who were positive that they knew the person; for Stingaree had been seen a hundred miles lower down, doubtless on his way back to Victoria, and with his appearance altered in a telltale manner. But the coroner thought he knew better than anybody else, and had his way, notwithstanding the manifest feeling on the long veranda where he held his court.

So jurors and spectators drifted back to hut and tent and neighboring station, the coroner started in his buggy for Glenranald, and last of all the police departed, leading the horse which Hardcastle had ridden home from their barracks, and leaving him at peace once more with his two young men. But on the squatter the time had told; his table had been full to overflowing through it all; and he sank into a long chair, a trifle grayer at the temples, a thought looser in his dress, as the pugarees of Cameron and Tyler fluttered out of sight.

"I think we might have a drink," he said with a wry smile to Evans, who fetched the decanter from the store; the jackeroo was called from a stable which had become Augean during the week, and the three were still mildly tippling when the store-keeper came to his feet.

"Good Lord!" cried he. "I thought we'd seen the last of the plucky police!"

"You don't mean to say they're coming back?"

"I do, worse luck! Cameron, Tyler, and some new joker in plain clothes."

Hardcastle finished his drink with a resigned smile, and stood on the veranda to receive the intruders.

"After all, it will stave off the reaction I began to feel the moment they had turned their backs," said he. "Well, well, well! I thought I'd just got rid of you fellows, and back you come like base coin!"

"You mustn't blame us," said the sergeant, first to dismount. "We couldn't know that Superintendent Cairns had been sent up from Sydney, much less that we should ride right into him in your horse-paddock!"

The squatter had stepped down from the veranda with polite alacrity.

"Glad to see you, Mr. Cairns," said he. "I only wish you had come before."

The creature in the plain clothes looked about him with a dry smile, and a sharp eye upon the younger men and the empty glasses, as he and the sergeant accompanied Hardcastle to the veranda, while Tyler took charge of the three horses. The fame of Cairns had travelled before him to Rosanna, but none had been prepared for a figure so weird or for a countenance so forbidding and malign. His manners were equally uncouth. He shook his bent head to decline refreshment; he pointedly ignored a generalization of Hardcastle's about the crime; and when he spoke, it was in a gratuitously satirical style of his own.

"May I ask, Mr. Hardcastle, if you are the owner or the manager of this lodge in a howling wilderness?"

"I'm sorry to say I am both."

"I appreciate the sorrow. I failed to discern a single green blade as I came along."

"We depend on salt-bush and the like."

"In spite of which, I believe, you have had several lean years?"

"There's no denying it."

"I am sorry to be one of so many intruders in such a season, Mr. Hardcastle, but I shall not trouble you long. I hope to take the murderer to-night."

"Stingaree?"

"Not quite so loud, please. Who else, should you suppose? You may be interested to hear that he has been in hiding on your run for several days, and so have I, within fairly easy reach of him. But he is not a man to be taken single-handed without further loss of life; so I intercepted you, sergeant, and now you are both enlightened. To-night, with your assistance and that of your young colleague, I count upon a bloodless victory. But I should prefer you, Mr. Hardcastle, not to mention the matter to the very young men whom I noticed in your company on my arrival. Have I your promise to comply with my wishes on this point, and on any other which may arise in connection with the capture?"

And a steely glitter shot through the beetling eyebrows; but Hardcastle had given his word before the request was rounded to that pedantic neatness which characterized the crabbed utterances of the round-shouldered dictator.

"That is well," he went on, "for now I can admit you both into my plan of campaign. Suppose we sit down here on the veranda, at the end farthest from any door. Be good enough to draw your chairs nearer mine, gentlemen. It might be dangerous if a fourth person heard me say that I had discovered the murderer's ill-gotten hoard!"

"Not you, sir!" cried Cameron.

"Good God!" exclaimed the squatter.

"The discoverer was not divine, and indeed no human being but myself," the bent man averred, turning with mischievous humor from one to the other of his astonished hearers. "Yes, there was more gold than I would have credited a sane Scotchman with carrying through the wilds; but the bulk was in small notes and the whole has been buried in the scrub close to the scene of the murder, doubtless to avoid at once the detection and the division of such unusual spoil."

"You are thinking of his mate?"

It was Cameron who had asked the question, but Mr. Hardcastle followed immediately with another.

"Did you remove the spoil?"

"My dear Mr. Hardcastle! How you must lack the detective instinct! Of course, I left everything as nearly as possible as I found it; the man camps on the spot, or very near it; he lights no fires and is careful to leave no marks, but I am more or less convinced of it. And that is where I shall take him to-night, or, rather, early to-morrow morning."

"I wish you could make it to-night," said Hardcastle, with a yawn that put a period to a pause of some duration.

"Why?" demanded the detective, raising open eyes for once.

"Because I've had a desperate week of it," replied Hardcastle, "and am dead with sleep."

The other carried his growing geniality to the length of an almost hearty laugh.

"My dear sir, do you suppose that I thought of taking *you* with us? No, Mr. Hardcastle, the risks of this sort of enterprise are for those who are paid to run them. And there is a risk; if we timed our attack too early or too late there would be bloodshed to a certainty. But at two o'clock the average man is fast asleep; at a quarter after one, therefore, I start with Sergeant Cameron and Constable Tyler."

Hardcastle yawned again.

"I should like to have been with you, but there are compensations," said he. "I doubt if I shall even stay up to see you off."

"If you did you would sit up alone," returned the Superintendent. "I intend to turn in myself for three or four hours; and it will be in the face of all my wishes, sergeant, if you and Tyler do not do the same. No reason to tell him what a short night it's to be; it might prevent a young fellow like that from getting any sleep at all. Merely let it be arranged that we all turn in betimes in view of an early start; we three alone need know how early the start will be."

They had their simple dinner at half-past seven, when the detective took it on himself to entertain the party, and succeeded so well that the entertainment was continued on the veranda for the better part of another hour. Doubled up in his chair, abnormal, weird, he recounted in particular the exploits of Stingaree (included a garbled version of the recent fiasco across the Murray) with a zest only equalled by his confidant undertaking to avenge the death of Robert Duncan before another day was out; all listened in a rapt silence, and the younger men were duly disappointed when the party broke up prematurely between nine and ten. But they also had played their part in a fatiguing week; by the later hour all were in their rooms, and before very long Rosanna Station lay lighted only by the full white moon of New South Wales.

Cameron wondered if it could possibly be two o'clock, while Tyler sat up insensate with the full weight of his first sleep, when their chief crept into the double-bedded room in which the two policemen had been put. He owned himself before his time by an hour and more, but explained that he had an idea which had only struck him as he was about to fall asleep.

"If we hunt for the fellow in the dark," said he, "we may give him the alarm before we come on him. But if we go now there is at least a chance that we may find his fire to guide us. I am aware I said he wouldn't light one there, but everybody knows that Stingaree uses a spirit-lamp. In any case it's a chance, and with a desperate man like that we can't afford to give the ghost of a chance away."

The sergeant dressed without more ado, as did his subordinate on learning the nature of their midnight errand; meanwhile the disturber of slumbers was gone to the horse-yard to start saddling. The others followed in a few minutes. And there was the horse-yard overflowing with moonshine, but empty alike of man and beast.

"I wonder what's got him?" murmured the bewildered sergeant uneasily.

"Old Harry, for all I care!" muttered the other. "I'm no such nuts on him, if you ask me. There's a bit too much of him for my taste."

In his secret breast the sergeant entertained a similar sentiment, but he was too old an officer to breathe disaffection in the ear of his subaltern. He contented himself with a mild expression of his surprise at the conduct of the Sydney authorities in putting a "towny" over his head without so much as a word of notice.

"And such a 'towny'!" echoed Tyler. "One you never heard of in your life before, and never will again!"

"Speak for yourself!" rejoined Cameron, irritated at the exaggeration of their case. "I have heard of him ever since I joined the force."

"Well, he's a funny joke to have shoved over us, a blooming little hunchback like that."

"I always heard that he was none the worse for what he couldn't help, and now I can understand it," said the sergeant, "for he's not such a hunch — —"

The men looked at each other in the moonlight, and the ugly word was never finished. A dozen hoofs were galloping upon them, their thunder muffled by the sandy road, and into the tank of moonshine came two horses, hounded by the detective bareback on the third.

"Someone left the slip-rails down, and they were all over the horse-paddock," he panted. "But I took a bridle and managed to catch one, and it was easy enough to run up the other two."

But even Constable Tyler thought the more of their misshapen leader for the feat.

There was now no time to be lost, for it approached midnight, but the trio were soon cantering through the horse-paddock neck-and-neck, and the new day found them at the farther gate. The moon still poured unbroken brilliance upon that desert world of sandy stretches tufted with salt-bush and erratically overgrown with scrub. The shadow of the gate was as another gate lying ready to be hung; for each particular wire in the fence there was a thin black stripe upon the ground. The three passed through, and came in quick time upon the edge of that scrub in which the crime had been committed. And here the chief called a halt.

"The two to nail him must be on foot," said he. "You can creep upon him on foot as you never could with a horse; but I will remain mounted in the road and ride him down if he shows fight."

So the pair in the pugarees walked one at either stirrup of their crooked chief, leaving the two horses tethered to a tree, until of a sudden the whole party halted as one. They had rounded a bend in the road with great caution, for they all knew where they were; but only one of them was prepared for the position of the light which flashed into their eyes from the heart of the scrub.

It was a tiny light, set low upon the ground, and yet it flashed through the forest like a diamond in a bundle of hay. It burnt at no little distance from the track, for at a movement it was lost, but it was some hundreds of yards nearer the station than the scene of the murder. The chief whispered that this was where he had found the buried booty, and over half the distance he led the way, winding in and out among the trees, now throwing a leg across his horse's withers to avoid a hole, anon embracing its neck to escape contact with the branches. It was long before they could discern anything but the light itself amid the trunks and branches of the scrub.

Suddenly the horseman stopped, beckoning with his free hand to the pair afoot, pointing at the fire with the one that held the reins; and as they crept up to him he stooped in the stirrups till his mouth was close to the sergeant's ear.

"He's sitting on the far side of the light, but you can't see his face. I thought he was a log, and I still believe he's asleep. Creep on him like cats till he looks up; then rush him with your revolvers before he can draw his, and I'll support you with mine!"

Nearer and nearer stole Cameron and Tyler; the rider managed to coax a few more noiseless steps from his clever mount, but dropped the reins and squared his elbows some twenty paces from the light—a hurricane lamp now in the sharpest focus. The policemen crawled some yards ahead; all three carried revolver in hand. But still the unsuspecting figure sat motionless, his chin upon his chest, the brim of his wideawake hiding his face, a little heap of gold and notes before him on the ground. Then the Superintendent's horse flung up its head; its teeth champed upon the bit; the man sat bolt upright, and the light of the hurricane lamp fell full upon the face of Hardcastle the squatter.

"Rush him! rush him! That's the man we want!"

But the momentary stupefaction of the police had given Hardcastle his opportunity; the hurricane lamp flew between them, going out where it fell, and for a minute the revolvers spat harmlessly in the remaining patchwork of moonshine and shadow.

"Get behind trees; shoot low, don't kill him!" shouted the chief from his saddle. "Now on to him before he can load again. That's it! Pin him! Throw your revolvers away, or he'll snatch one before you know where you are! Ah, I thought he was too strong for you! Mr. Hardcastle, I'll put a bullet through you myself if you don't instantly surrender!"

And the fight ended with the bent man leaning in his stirrups over the locked and swaying group, as he brandished his revolver to suit deed to word. It was a heavy blow with the long barrel that finally turned the scale. In a few seconds Hardcastle stood a prisoner, the handcuffs fitting his large wrists like gloves, his great frame panting from the fray, and yet a marvel of monstrous manhood in its stoical and defiant carriage.

"For God's sake, Cairns, do what you say!" he cried. "Put three bullets through me, and divide what's on the ground between you!"

"I half wish we could, for your sake," was the reply. "But it's idle to speak of it, and I'm afraid you've committed a crime that places you beyond the reach of sympathy."

"That he has!" cried the sergeant, wiping blood from his gray beard. "It's plain as a pikestaff now; and to think that he was the one to come and fetch us the very night he'd done it! But what licks me more than anything is how in the world you found him out, sir!"

The hunchback looked down upon the stalwart prisoner standing up to his last inch between his two captors: there was an impersonal interest in the man's bold eyes that invited a statement more eloquently than the sergeant's tongue.

"I will tell you," said the horseman, smiling down upon the three on foot. "In the first place, I had my own reasons for knowing that Stingaree was nowhere near this place on the night of the murder, for I happen to have been on his tracks for some time. Who knew all about the dead man's stroke of luck, his insane preference for hard cash, the time of his return? Mr. Hardcastle, for one. Who swore that he had met Stingaree face to face upon the run? Mr. Hardcastle alone; there was not a soul to corroborate or contradict him. Who was in need of many thousand pounds? Mr. Hardcastle, as I suspected, and as he practically admitted to me when we discussed the bad season on my arrival. I was pretty sure of my man before I crossed the boundary fence, but I was absolutely convinced before I had spent twenty minutes on his veranda."

The prisoner smiled sardonically in the moonlight. The policemen gazed with awe upon the man who had solved a nine days' mystery in fewer hours.

"You must remember," he continued, "that I have spent some days and nights upon the run; during the days I have camped in the thickest scrub I could find, but by night I have been very busy, and last night I had a stroke of luck. I stumbled by accident on a track that led me to the place I had been looking for all along. You see, I had put myself in Hardcastle's skin, and I was quite clear that I should have buried a lapful of gold and notes somewhere in the bush until the hue and cry had blown over. Not that I expected to find it so near the scene of the crime —I should certainly have gone farther afield myself."

"But I can't make out why that wasn't enough for you, sir," ventured the sergeant, deferentially. "Why didn't you come in and arrest him on that?"

"You shall see in three minutes. Wasn't it far better to catch him red-handed as we have? You will at least admit that it was far neater. I say I have the place. I say we are all going to it at two in the morning. I say, let us sleep till a little after one. Was it not obvious what would happen? The only thing I did not expect was to find him asleep with the swag under his nose."

Then Hardcastle spoke up.

"I was not asleep," said he. "I thought I was safe for an hour or two . . . and I began to think . . . I was wondering what to do . . . whether to cut my throat at once . . ."

And his dreadful voice died away like a single chord struck in an empty room.

"But Stingaree," put in Tyler in the end. "What's happened to him?"

"He also has been here. But he was many a mile away at the time."

"What brought him here?"

The crooked Superintendent from Sydney was sitting strangely upright in his saddle; his face was not to be seen, for his back was to the moon, but he seemed to rub one of his eyes.

"He may have wished to clear his character. He may have itched to uphold the honor of that road of which he considers himself a not imperfect knight. He may have found it so jolly easy to play policeman down in Victoria, that he couldn't resist another shot in a better cause up here. At his worst he never killed a man in all his life. And you will be good enough to take his own word for it that he never will!"

He had backed his horse while he spoke; he turned a little to the light, and the eye-glass gleamed in his eye.

The young constable sprang forward.

"Stingaree!" he screamed.

But the gray sergeant flung his arms round their prisoner.

The gray sergeant flung his arms round their prisoner.

"That's right!" cried the bushranger, as he trotted off. "Your horses and even your pistols are out of reach, thanks to a discipline for which I love you dearly. You hang on to your bird in the hand, my friends, and never again misjudge the one in the bush!"

And as the trees swallowed the cantering horse and man, followed by a futile shot from the first revolver which the young constable had picked up, an embittered admiration kindled in the captive murderer's eyes.

The Purification of Mulfera

Mulfera Station, N.S.W., was not only an uttermost end of the earth, but an exceedingly loose end, and that again in more senses than one. There were no ladies on Mulfera, and this wrought inevitable deterioration in the young men who made a bachelors' barracks of the homestead. Not that they ever turned it into the perfect pandemonium you might suppose; but it was unnecessary either to wear a collar or to repress an oath at table; and this sort of disregard does not usually stop at the elementary decencies. It is true that on Mulfera the bark of the bachelor was something worse than his bite, and his tongue no fair criterion to the rest of him. Nevertheless, the place became a byword, even in the back-blocks; and when at last the good Bishop Methuen had the hardihood to include it in an episcopal itinerary, there were admirers of that dear divine who roundly condemned his folly, and enemies who no longer denied his heroism.

The Lord Bishop of the Back-Blocks had at that time been a twelvemonth or more in charge of what he himself described playfully as his "oceanic see"; but his long neglect of Mulfera was due less to its remoteness than to the notorious fact that they wanted no adjectival and alliterative bishops there. An obvious way of repulse happened to be open to the blaspheming squatter, though there is no other instance of its employment. On these up-country visitations the Bishop was dependent for his mobility upon the horseflesh of his hospitable hosts; thus it became the custom to send to fetch him from one station to another; and as a rule the owner or the manager came himself, with four horses and the big trap. The manager of Mulfera said his horses had something else to do, and his neighbors backed him up with some discreet encouragement on their own account. It was felt that a slur would be left upon the whole district if his lordship actually met with the only sort of reception which was predicted for him on Mulfera. Bishop Methuen, however, was one of the last men on earth to shirk a plague-spot; and on this one, warning was eventually received that the Bishop and his chaplain would arrive on horseback the following Sunday morning, to conduct divine service, if quite convenient, at eleven o'clock.

The language of the manager was something inconceivable upon the receipt of this cool advice. He was a man named Carmichael, and quite a different type from the neighbors who held up horny hands when the Bishop decided on his raid. Carmichael was not "a native of this colony," or of the next, but he was that distressing spectacle, the public-school man who is no credit to his public school. Worse than this, he was a man of brains; worst of all, he had promised very differently as a boy. A younger man who had been at school with him, having come out for his health, travelled some hundreds of miles to see Carmichael, whose conversation struck him absolutely dumb. "He was captain of our house," the visitor explained to Carmichael's subordinates, "and you daren't say dash in dormitory-not even dash!"

In appearance this redoubtable person was chiefly remarkable for the intellectual cast of his still occasionally clean-shaven countenance, and for his double eye-glasses, or rather the way he wore them. They were very strong and very common, without any rims, and Carmichael bought them by the box. He would not wear them with a cord, and in the heat they were continually slipping off his nose; when they did not slip right off they hung at such an angle that Carmichael had to throw his whole body and head backward in order to see anything through them except the ground. And when they fell, someone else had to find them while Carmichael cursed, for his naked eye was as blind as a bat's.

"Let's go mustering on Sunday," suggested the overseer —"every blessed man! Let him find the whole place deserted, homestead and hut!"

"Or let's get blind for the occasion," was the bookkeeper's idea —"every mother's son!"

"That would do," agreed the overseer, "if we got just blind enough. And we might get the blacks from Poonee Creek to come and join the dance."

The overseer was a dapper Victorian with a golden mustache twisted rakishly up and down at either end respectively, like an overturned letter S. He lived up to the name of Smart. The bookkeeper was a servile echo with a character and a face of putty. He had once perpetrated an opprobrious ode to the overseer, and had answered to the name of Chaucer ever since.

Carmichael leaned back to look from one of these worthies to the other, and his spectacled eyes flamed with mordant scorn.

"I suppose you think you're funny, you fellows," said he, and without the oath which was a sign of his good-will, except when he lost his temper with the sheep. "If so, I wish you'd get outside to entertain each other. Since the fellow's coming we shall have to let him come, and the thing is how to choke him off ever coming again without open insult, which I won't allow. A service of some sort we shall have to have, this once."

"I'm on to guy it," declared the indiscreet Chaucer.

"If you do I'll rehearse the men," the overseer promised.

"You idiots!" thundered Carmichael, whose temper was as short as his sight. "Can't you see I weaken on the prospect as much as the two of you stuck together? But the beggar's certain to be a public-school and 'Varsity man: and I won't have him treated as though he'd been dragged up in one of these God-forsaken Colonies!"

Now-most properly-you cannot talk like this in the bush unless you are also capable of confirming the insult with your fists. But Carmichael could; and he was much too blind to fight without his glasses. He was, in fact, the same strenuous character who had set his dogmatic face against the most harmless expletives in dormitory at school, and set it successfully, because Carmichael was a mighty man, whose influence was not to be withstood. His standard alone was changed. Or he was playing on the other side. Yet he had brought a prayer-book with him to the back-blocks. And he was seen studying it on the eve of the episcopal descent.

"He may have his say," observed Carmichael, darkly, "and then I'll have mine."

"Going to heckle him?" inquired Smart, in a nasal voice full of hope and encouragement.

"Not at the function, you fool," replied Carmichael, sweetly. "But when it's all over I should like to take him on about the Athanasian Creed and the Thirty-nine Articles." Only both substantives were qualified by the epithet of the country, for Carmichael had put himself in excellent temper for the day of battle.

That day dawned blood-red and beautiful, but in a little it was a blinding blue from pole to pole, and the thermometer in the veranda reached three figures before breakfast. It was a hot-wind day, and even Carmichael's subordinates pitied Dr. Methuen and his chaplain, who were riding from the south in the teeth of that Promethean blast. But Carmichael himself drew his own line with unswerving rigidity; and though the deep veranda was prepared as a place for worship, and covered in with canvas which was kept saturated with water, he would not permit an escort to sally even to the boundary fence to meet the uninvited prelate.

Not long after breakfast the two horsemen jogged into view, ambling over the sand-hills whose red-hot edge met a shimmering sky some little distance beyond the station pines. Both wore pith helmets and fluttering buff dust-coats, but both had hot black legs, the pair in gaiters being remarkable for their length. The homestead trio, their red necks chafed by the unaccustomed collar, gathered grimly at the open end of the veranda, where they exchanged impressions while the religious raiders bore down upon them.

"They can ride a bit, too, I'm bothered if they can't," exclaimed the overseer, in considerable astonishment.

"And do you suppose, my good fool," inquired Carmichael, with the usual unregenerate embroidery —"do you in your innocence suppose that's an accomplishment confined to these precious provinces?"

"They're as brown as my sugar," said the keeper of books and stores.

"The Bishop looks as though he'd been out here all his life."

Carmichael did not quarrel with this observation of his overseer, but colorless eyebrows were raised above the cheap glasses as he stepped into the yard to shake hands with the visitors. The bearded Bishop returned his greeting in a grave silence. The chaplain, on the other hand, seemed the victim of a nervous volubility, and unduly anxious to atone for his chief's taciturnity, which he essayed to explain to Carmichael on the first opportunity.

"His lordship feels the heat so much more than I do, who have had so many years of it; and to tell you the truth, he is still a little hurt at not being met, for the first time since he has been out here."

"Then why did he come?" demanded Carmichael, bluntly. "I never asked him, did I?"

"No, no, but-ah, well! We won't go into it," said the chaplain. "I am glad to see your preparations, Mr. Carmichael; that I consider very magnanimous in you, under all the circumstances; and so will his lordship when he has had a rest. You won't mind his retiring until it's time for the little service, Mr. Carmichael?"

"Not I," returned Carmichael, promptly. But the worst paddock on Mulfera, in its worst season, was not more dry than the manager's tone.

Shortly before eleven the bell was rung which roused the men on week-day mornings, and they began trooping over from their hut, while the trio foregathered on the veranda as before. The open end was the one looking east but the sun was too near the zenith to enter many inches, and with equal thoroughness and tact Carmichael had placed the table, the water-bag, and the tumbler, at the open end. They were all that he could do in the way of pulpit, desk, and lectern.

The men tramped in and filled the chairs, forms, tin trunks, and packing-cases which had been pressed into the service of this makeshift sanctuary. The trio sat in front. The bell ceased, the ringer entering and taking his place. There was some delay, if not some hitch. Then came the chaplain with an anxious face.

"His lordship wishes to know if all hands are here," he whispered across the desk.

Carmichael looked behind him for several seconds. "Every man Jack," he replied. "And damn his lordship's cheek!" he added for his equals' benefit, as the chaplain disappeared.

"Rum cove, that chaplain," whispered Chaucer, in the guarded manner of one whose frequent portion is the snub brutal.

"How so?" inquired Carmichael, with a duly withering glance.

Chaucer told in whispers of a word which he had overheard through the weather-board wall of the room in which the Bishop had sought repose. It was, in fact, the monosyllable of which Carmichael had just made use. He, however, was the first to heap discredit on the book-keeper's story, which he laughed to scorn with as much of his usual arrogance as could be assumed below the breath.

"If you heard it at all," said Carmichael, "which I don't for a moment believe, you heard it in the strictly Biblical sense. You can't be expected to know what that is, Chaucer, but as a matter of fact it means lost and done for, like our noble selves. And it was probably applied to us, if there's the least truth in what you say."

"Truth!" he began, but was not suffered to add another word.

"Shut up," snarled Carmichael. "Can't you hear them coming?"

And the tramp of the shooting-boots, which Dr. Methuen was still new chum enough to wear, followed by the chaplain's lighter step, drew noisily nearer upon the unseen part of the veranda that encircled the whole house.

"Stand up, you cripples!" cried Carmichael over his shoulder, in a stage whisper. And they all came to their feet as the two ecclesiastics appeared behind the table at the open end of the tabernacle.

Carmichael felt inclined to disperse the congregation on the spot.

There was the Bishop still in his gaiters and his yellow dust-coat; even the chaplain had not taken the trouble to don his surplice. So anything was good enough for Mulfera! Carmichael had lunged forward with a jutting jaw when an authoritative voice rang out across the table.

"Sit down!"

The Bishop had not opened his hairy mouth. It was the smart young chaplain who spoke. And all obeyed except Carmichael.

"I beg your lordship's pardon," he was beginning, with sarcastic emphasis, when the manager of Mulfera was cut as short as he was himself in the habit of cutting his inferiors.

"If you will kindly sit down," cried the chaplain, "like everybody else, I shall at once explain the apparent irregularity upon which you were doubtless about to comment."

Carmichael glowered through his glasses for a few seconds, and then resumed his seat with a shrug and a murmur, happily inaudible to all but his two immediate neighbors.

"On his way here this morning," the chaplain went on, "his lordship met with a misadventure from which he has not yet recovered sufficiently to address you as he fully hoped and intended to do to-day." At this all eyes sped to the Bishop, who stood certainly in a drooping attitude at the chaplain's side, his episcopal hands behind his back. "Something happened," the glib spokesman continued with stern eyes, "something that you do not often hear of in these days. His lordship was accosted, beset, and, like the poor man in the Scriptures, despitefully entreated, not many miles beyond your own boundary, by a pair of armed ruffians!"

"Stuck up!" cried one or two, and "Bushrangers!" one or two more.

"I thank you for both words," said the chaplain, bowing. "He was stuck up by the bushranger who is once more abroad in the land. Really, Mr. Carmichael——"

But the manager of Mulfera rose to his full height, and, leaning back to get the speaker into focus, stuck his arms akimbo in a way that he had in his most aggressive moments.

"And what were *you* doing?" he demanded fiercely of the chaplain.

"It was I who stuck him up," answered the *soi-disant* chaplain, whipping a single glass into his eye to meet the double ones. "My name is Stingaree!"

And in the instant's hush which followed he plucked a revolver from his breast, while the hands of the sham bishop shot out from behind his back, with one in each.

The scene of the instant after that defies ordinary description. It was made the more hideous by the frightful imprecations of Carmichael, and the short, sharp threat of Stingaree to shoot him dead unless he instantly sat down. Carmichael bade him do so with a gallant oath, at which the men immediately behind him joined with his two companions in pulling him back into his chair and there holding him by main force. Thereafter the manager appeared to realize the futility of resistance, and was unhanded on his undertaking to sit quiet, which he did with the exception of one speech to those behind.

"If any of you happen to be armed," he shouted over his shoulder, "shoot him down like a dog. But if you're all as fairly had as I am, let's hear what the beggar's got to say."

"Thank you, Mr. Carmichael," said the bushranger, still from the far side of the table, as a comparative silence fell at last. "You are a man after my own heart, sir, and I would as lief have you on my side as the simple ruffian on my right. Not a bad bishop to look at," continued Stingaree, with a jerk of the head toward his mate with the two revolvers. "But if I had let him open his mouth! Now, if I'd had you, Mr. Carmichael-but I have my doubts about your vocabulary, too!"

The point appealed to all present, and there was a laugh, in which, however, Carmichael did not join.

"I suppose you didn't come here simply to give us a funny entertainment," said he. "I happen to be the boss, or have been hitherto, and if you will condescend to tell me what you want I shall consider whether it is worth while to supply you or to be shot by you. I shall be sorry to meet my death at the hands of a thieving blackguard, but one can't pick and choose in that matter. Before it comes to choosing, however, is it any good asking what you've done with the real bishop and the real chaplain? If you've murdered them, as I ——"

Stingaree had listened thus far with more than patience, in fact with something akin to approval, to the captive who was still his master with the tongue. With all his villainy, the bushranger was man enough to appreciate another man when he met him; but Carmichael's last word flicked him on a bare nerve.

"Don't you dare to talk to me about murder," he rapped out. "I've never committed one yet, but you're going the right way to make me begin! As for Bishop Methuen, I have more respect for him than for any man in Australia; but his horse was worth two of my mate's, and that's all I troubled him for. I didn't even tie him up as I would any other man. We just relieved the two of them of their boots and clothes, which was quite as good as tying up, with your roads as red-hot as they are-though my mate here doesn't agree with me."

The man with the beard very emphatically shook a matted head, now relieved of the stolen helmet, and observed that the quicker they were the better it would be. He was as taciturn a bushranger as he had been a bishop, but Stingaree was perfectly right. Even these few words would have destroyed all chance of illusion in the case of his mate.

"The very clothes, which become us so well," continued the prince of personators, who happened to be without hair upon his face at this period, and who looked every inch his part; "their very boots, we have only borrowed! I will tell you presently where we dropped the rest of their kit. We left them a suit of pyjamas apiece, and not another stitch, and we blindfolded and drove 'em into the scrub as a last precaution. But before we go I shall also tell you where a search-party is likely to pick up their tracks. Meanwhile you will all stay exactly where you are, with the exception of the store-keeper, who will kindly accompany me to the store. I shall naturally require to see the inside of the safe, but otherwise our wants are very simple."

The outlaw ceased. There was no word in answer; a curious hush had fallen on the captive congregation.

"If there is a store-keeper," suggested Stingaree, "he'd better stand up."

But the accomplished Chaucer sat stark and staring.

"Up with you," whispered Carmichael, in terrible tones, "or we're done!"

And even as the book-keeper rose tremulously to his feet, a strange and stealthy figure, the cynosure of all eyes but the bushrangers' for a long minute, reached the open end of the veranda; and with a final spring, a tall man in silk pyjamas, his gray beard flying over either shoulder, hurled himself upon both bushrangers at once. With outspread fingers he clutched the scruff of each neck at the self-same second, crash came the two heads together, and over went the table with the three men over it.

Shots were fired in the struggle on the ground, happily without effect. Stingaree had his shooting hand mangled by one blow with a chair whirled from a height. Carmichael got his heel with a venomous stamp upon the neck of Howie; and, in fewer seconds than it would take to write their names, the rascals were defeated and disarmed. Howie had his neck half broken, and his face was darkening before Carmichael could be induced to lift his foot.

"The cockroach!" bawled the manager, drunk with battle. "I'd hoof his soul out for two pins!"

A moment later he was groping for his glasses, which had slipped and fallen from his perspiring nose, and making use of such expressions withal as to compel a panting protest from the tall man in the silken stripes.

"My name is Methuen," said he. "I know it's a special moment, but-do you mind?"

Carmichael found his glasses at that instant, adjusted them, stood up, and leant back to view the Bishop; and his next words were the apology of the gentleman he should have been.

"My dear fellow," cried the other, "I quite understand. What are they doing with the ruffians? Have you any handcuffs? Is it far to the nearest police barracks?"

But the next act of this moving melodrama was not the least characteristic of the chief performance; for when Stingaree and partner had been not only handcuffed but lashed hand and foot, and incarcerated in separate log-huts, with a guard apiece; and when a mounted messenger had been despatched to the barracks at Clare Corner, and the remnant raised a cheer for Bishop Methuen; it was then that the fine fellow showed them the still finer stuff of which he was also made. He invited all present to step back for a few minutes into the place of worship which had been so charmingly prepared, so scandalously misused, and where he hoped to see them all yet again in the evening, if it would not bore them to give him a further and more formal hearing then.

"I won't keep them five minutes now," he whispered to Carmichael, as the men went ahead to pick up the chairs and take their places, while the Bishop hobbled after, still in his pyjamas, and with terribly inflamed and swollen feet. "And then," he added, "I must ask you to send a buggy at once for my poor chaplain. He did his gallant best, poor fellow, but I had to leave him fallen by the way. I am an old miler, you know; it came easier to me; but the cinder-path and running-shoes are a different story from hot sand and naked feet! And now, if you please, I will strike one little blow while our hearts are still warm."

But how shrewdly he struck it, how straight from the shoulder, how simply, how honestly, there is perhaps no need to tell even those who have no previous knowledge of back-block Bishop Methuen and his manly ways.

What afterward happened to Stingaree is another matter, to be set forth faithfully in the sequel. This is the story of the Purification of Mulfera Station, N.S.W., in which the bushrangers played but an indirect and a most inglorious part.

The Bishop and his chaplain (a good man of no present account) stayed to see the police arrive that night, and the romantic ruffians taken thence next morning in unromantic bonds. Comparatively little attention was paid to their departure-partly on account of the truculent attitude of the police-partly because the Episcopal pair were making an equally early start in another direction. No one accompanied the armed men and the bound. But every man on the place, from homestead, men's hut, rabbiter's tent, and boundary-rider's camp-every single man who could be mustered for the nonce had a horse run up for him-escorted Dr. Methuen in close cavalcade to the Mulfera boundary, where the final cheering took place, led by Carmichael, who, of course, was font and origin of the display. And Carmichael rode by himself on the way back; he had been much with the Bishop during his lordship's stay; and he was too morose for profanity during the remainder of that day.

But it was no better when the manager's mood lifted, and the life on Mulfera slipped back into the old blinding and perspiring groove.

Then one night, a night of the very week thus sensationally begun, the ingenious Chaucer began one of the old, old stories, on the moonlit veranda, and Carmichael stopped him while that particular old story was still quite young in the telling. There was an awkward pause until Carmichael laughed.

"I don't care twopence what you fellows think of me," said he, "and never did. I saw a lot of the Bishop," he went on, less aggressively, after a pause.

"So *we* saw," assented Smart.

"You bet!" added Chaucer.

For they were two to one.

"He ran the mile for Oxford," continued Carmichael. "Two years he ran it-and won both times. You may not appreciate quite what that means."

And, with a patience foreign to his character as they knew it, Carmichael proceeded to explain.

"But," he added, "that was nothing to his performance last Sunday, in getting here from beyond the boundary in the time he did it in-barefoot! It would have been good enough in shoes. But don't you forget his feet. I can see them-and feel them-still."

"Oh, he's a grand chap," the overseer allowed.

"We never said he wasn't," his ally chimed in.

Carmichael took no notice of a tone which the youth with the putty face had never employed toward him before.

"He was also in his school eleven," continued Carmichael, still in a reflective fashion.

"Was it a public school?" inquired Smart.

"Yes."

"*The* public school?" added Chaucer.

"Not mine, if that's what you mean," returned Carmichael, with just a touch of his earlier manner. "But-he knew my old Head Master-he was quite a pal of the dear Old Man! . . . We had such lots in common," added the manager, more to himself than to the other two.

The overseer's comment is of no consequence. What the book-keeper was emboldened to add matters even less. Suffice it that between them they brought the old Carmichael to his feet, his glasses flaming in the moonshine, his body thrown pugilistically backward, his jaw jutting like a crag-the old Carmichael in deed-but not in word.

"I told you just now I didn't care twopence what either of you thought of me," he roared, "though there wasn't the least necessity to tell you, because you knew! So I needn't repeat myself; but just listen a moment, and try not to be greater fools than God made you. You saw a real man last Sunday, and so did I. I had almost forgotten what they were like-that quality. Well, we had a lot of talk, and he told me what they are doing on some of the other stations. They are holding services, something like what he held here, every Sunday night for themselves. Now, it isn't in human nature to fly from one extreme to the other: but we are going to have a try to keep up our Sunday end with the other stations; at least I am, and you two are going to back me up."

He paused. Not a syllable from the pair.

"Do you hear me?" thundered Carmichael, as he had thundered in the dormitory at school, now after twenty years in the same good cause once more. "Whether you like it or not, you fellows are going to back me up!"

And Carmichael was a mighty man, whose influence was not to be withstood.

A Duel in the Desert

It was eight o'clock and Monday morning when the romantic rascals were led away in unromantic bonds. Their arms were bound to their bodies, their feet lashed to the stirrup-irons; they sat like packs upon quiet station horses, carefully chosen for the nonce; they were tethered to a mounted policeman apiece, each with leading-rein buckled to his left wrist and Government revolver in his right hand. Behind the quartette rode the officer in command, superbly mounted, watching ever all four with a third revolver ready cocked. It seemed a small and yet an ample escort for the two bound men.

But Stingaree was by no means in that state of Napoleonic despair which his bent back and lowering countenance were intended to convey. He had not uttered a word since the arrival of the police, whom he had suffered to lift him on horseback, as he now sat, without raising his morose eyes once. Howie, on the other hand, had offered a good deal of futile opposition, cursing his captors as the fit moved him, and once struggling so insanely in his bonds as to earn a tap from the wrong end of a revolver and a bloody face for his pains. Stingaree glowered in deep delight. His mate's part was as well acted as his own; but it was he who had conceived them both, and expounded them in countless camps against some such extremity as this. The result was in ideal accordance with his calculations. The man who gave the trouble was the man to watch. And Stingaree, chin on chest, was left in peace to evolve a way of escape.

The chances were all adverse; he had never been less sanguine in his life. Not that Stingaree had much opinion of the police; he had slipped through their hands too often; but it was an unfortunate circumstance that two of the present trio were among those whom he had eluded most recently, and who therefore would be least likely to give him another chance. A lightning student of his kind, he based his only hope upon an accurate estimate of these men, and applied his whole mind to the triple task. But it was a single task almost from the first; for the policeman in charge of him was none other than his credulous old friend, Sergeant Cameron from Clear Corner; and Howie's custodian, a young trooper run from the same mould as Constable Tyler and many a hundred more, in whom a thick skull cancelled a stout heart. Both were brave men; neither was really to be feared. But the man behind upon the thoroughbred, the man in front, the man now on this side and now on that, with his braying laugh and his vindictive voice-triumphant as though he had taken the bushrangers himself, and a blatant bully in his triumph-was none other than the formidable Superintendent whose undying animosity the bushrangers had earned by the two escapades associated with his name.

Yet the outlaw never flattered him with word or look, never lifted chin from chest, never raised an eye or opened his mouth until Howie's knock on the head caused him to curse his mate for a fool who deserved all he got. The thoroughbred was caracoling on his other side in an instant.

"You ain't one, are you?" cried the taunting tongue of Superintendent Cairns. "Not much fool about Stingaree!"

The time had come for a reply.

"So I thought until yesterday," sighed the bushranger. "But now I'm not so sure."

"Not so sure, eh? You were sure enough last time we met, my beauty!"

"Yes! I had some conceit of myself then," said Stingaree, with another of his convincing sighs.

"To say nothing of when you guyed me, damn you!" added the Superintendent, below his breath and through his teeth.

"Well," replied the outlaw, "you've got your revenge. I must expect you to rub it in."

"My fine friend," rejoined Cairns, "you may expect worse than that, and still you won't be disappointed."

Stingaree made no reply; and it would have taken a very shrewd eye to have read deeper than the depth of sullen despair expressed in every inch of his bound body and every furrow of his downcast face. Even the vindictive Cairns ceased for a time to crow over so abject an adversary in so bitter an hour. Meanwhile, the five horses streamed slowly through the high lights and heavy shadows of a winding avenue of scrub. It was like a hot-house in the dense, low trees: not a wandering wind, not a waking bird; but five faces that dripped steadily in the shade, and all but caught fire in the sun. Ahead rode Howie, dazed and bleeding, with his callous young constable; the sergeant and his chief, with Stingaree between them, now brought up the rear. By degrees Stingaree raised his chin a little, but still looked neither right nor left.

"Cheer up!" cried the chief, with soothing irony.

"I feel the heat," said the bound man, uncomplainingly. "And it was just about here it happened."

"What happened?"

"We overtook the Church militant here on earth," rejoined the bushranger, with rueful irreverence.

"Well, you ran against a snag that time, Mr. Sanguinary Stingaree!"

"I couldn't resist turning Howie into the Bishop and making myself his mouthpiece. I daren't let him open his lips! It wasn't the offertory that was worth having; it was the fun of rounding up that congregation on the homestead veranda, and never letting them spot a thing till we'd showed our guns. There hadn't been a hitch, and never would have been if that old Bishop hadn't run all those miles barefoot over hot sand and taken us unawares."

Made with wry humor and a philosophic candor, alike germane to his predicament, these remarks seemed natural enough to one knowing little of Stingaree. They seemed just the sort of things that Stingaree would say. The effect, however, was rather to glorify Bishop Methuen at the expense of Superintendent Cairns, who strove to reverse it with some dexterity.

"You certainly ran against a snag," he repeated, "and now your mate's run against another." He gave the butt of his ready pistol a significant tap. "But I'm the worst snag that ever either of you struck," he went on in his vainglory. "Make no mistake about that. And the worst day's work that ever you did in your life, Mr. Sanguinary Stingaree, was when you dared to play at being little crooked Cairns."

Stingaree took a first good look at his man. After all he was not so crooked on horseback as he had seemed on foot at dusk in the Victorian bush; his hump was even less pronounced than Stingaree himself had made it on Rosanna; it looked more like a ridge of extra muscle across a pair of abnormally broad and powerful shoulders. There was the absence of neck which this deformity suggests; there was a great head lighted by flashing and indignant eyes, but mounted only on its mighty chin. The bushranger was conceited enough to find in the flesh a coarser and more common type than that created by himself for the honor of the road. But this did not make the real Superintendent a less formidable foe.

"The most poetic justice!" murmured Stingaree, and resumed in an instant his apathetic pose.

"It serves you jolly well right, if that's what you mean," the Superintendent snarled. "You've yourself and your own mighty cheek to thank for taking me out of my shell and putting me on your tracks in earnest. But it was high time they knew the cut of my jib up here; the fools won't forget me again in a hurry. And you, you devil, you sha'n't forget me till your dying day!"

On Stingaree's off-side Sergeant Cameron was also hanging an insulted head. But the bushranger laughed softly in his chest.

"Someone has got to do your dirty work," said he. "I did it that time, and the Bishop has done it now; but you shouldn't blame me for helping your fellows to bring a murderer to justice."

"You guyed me," said Cairns through his teeth. "I heard all about it. You guyed me, blight your soul!"

Stingaree felt that he was missing a strong face finely convulsed with passion—as indeed he was. But he had already committed the indiscretion of a repartee, which was scarcely consistent with an attitude of extreme despair. A downcast silence seemed the safest policy after all.

"It used to be forty miles to the Corner," he murmured, after a time. "We can't have come more than ten."

"Not so much," snapped the Superintendent.

"Going to stop for feed at Mazeppa Station?"

"That's my business."

"It's a long day for three of you, in this heat, with two of us."

"The time won't hang heavy on *our* hands."

"Not heavy enough, I should have thought. I wonder you didn't bring some of the boys from Mulfera along with you."

Superintendent Cairns brayed his high, harsh laugh.

"Yes, you wonder, and so did they," said he. "But I know a bit too much. There'll always be sympathy among scum like them for thicker scum like you!"

"You're too suspicious," said Stingaree, mildly. "But I was thinking of the Bishop and the boss."

"They've gone their own way," growled Cairns, "and it's just as well it wasn't our way. I'd have stood no interference from them!"

That had been his attitude on the station. Stingaree had heard of his rudeness to those to whom the whole credit of the capture belonged; the man revealed his character as freely as an angry child; and, indeed, a childish character it was. Arrogance was its strength and weakness: a suggestion had only to be made to call down either the insolence of office or the malice of denial for denial's sake.

"I wish you'd stop a bit at Mazeppa," whined Stingaree, drooping like a candle in the heat.

The station roofs gleamed through the trees far off the track.

"Why?"

"Because I'm feeling sick."

"Gammon! You've got some friends there; on you push!"

"But you will camp somewhere in the heat of the day?"

"I'll do as I think fit. I sha'n't consult you, my fine friend."

Stingaree drooped and nodded, lower and lower; then recovered himself with a jerk, like one battling against sleep. The party pushed on for another hour. The heat was terrible; the bound men endured torments in their bonds. But the nature of the Superintendent, deformed like his body, declared itself duly at every turn, and the more one prisoner groaned and the other blasphemed, the greater the zest and obduracy of the driving force behind them.

Noon passed; the scanty shadows lengthened; and Howie gave more trouble of an insensate sort. They reined up, and lashed him tighter; he had actually loosened his cords. But Stingaree seemed past remonstrance with friend or foe, and his bound body swayed from side to side as the little cavalcade went on at a canter to make up for lost time.

Stingaree toppled out of the saddle.

He was leading now with the kindly sergeant, and his mind had never been more alert. Behind them thundered the recalcitrant Howie with constable and Superintendent on either side. They were midway between Mazeppa and Clear Corner, or some fifteen miles from either haunt of men. Stingaree pulled himself upright in the saddle as by a superhuman effort, and shook off the helping hand that held him by one elbow.

He was about to do a thing at which even his courage quailed, and he longed for the use of his right arm. It was not absolutely bound; the hand and wrist had been badly hurt in the Sunday's fray-so badly that it had been easy to sham a fracture, and have hand and wrist in splints before the arrival of the police. They still hung before him in a sling, his good right hand and fore-arm, stiff and sore enough, yet strong and ready at a moment's notice, when the moment came. It had not come, and was not coming for a long time, when Stingaree set his teeth, lurched either way-and toppled out of the saddle in the path of the cantering hoofs. His lashed feet held him in the stirrups; the off stirrup-leather had come over with his weight; and there at his horse's hoofs, kicked and trampled and smothered with blood and dust, he dragged like an anchor, without sign of life.

And it was worse even than it looked, for the life never left him for an instant, nor ever for an instant did he fail to behave as though it had. Minutes later, when they had stopped his horse, and cut him down from the stirrups, and carried him into the shade of a hop-bush off the track, and when Stingaree dared to open his eyes, he was nearer closing them perforce, and the scene swam before him with superfluous realism.

Cairns and Cameron, dismounted (while the trooper sat aloof with Howie in the saddle), were at high words about their prostrate prisoner. Not a syllable was lost on Stingaree.

"You may put him across the horse yourself," said the sergeant. "I won't have a hand in it. But make sure you haven't killed him as it is-travelling a sick man like that."

"Killed him? He's got his eyes open!" cried Cairns in savage triumph. Stingaree lay blinking at the sky. "Do you still refuse to do your duty?"

"Cruelty to animals is no duty of mine," declared the sergeant: "let alone my fellowmen, bushrangers or no bushrangers."

"And you?" thundered Cairns at the mounted constable.

"I'm with the sergeant," said he. "He's had enough."

"Right!" cried the Superintendent, producing a note-book and scribbling venomously. "You both refuse! You will hear more of this; meanwhile, sergeant, I should like to know what your superior wisdom may be pleased to suggest."

"Send a cart back for him," said Cameron. "It's the only way he's fit to travel."

Stingaree sought to prop himself upon the elbow of the splintered wrist and hand.

"There are no more bones broken that I know of," said he, faintly. "But I felt bad before, and now I feel worse."

"He looks it, too," observed the sergeant, as Stingaree, ghastly enough beneath his blood and dust, rolled over on his back once more, and lay effectively with closed eyes. Even the Superintendent was impressed.

"Then what's to be done with him?" he exclaimed, with an oath. "What's to be done?"

"If you ask me," returned Cameron, "I should make him comfortable where he is; after all, he's a human being, and done no murder, that we should run the risk of murdering him. Leave him to me while you two push on with his mate; then one of you can get back with the spring-cart before sundown; but trust me to look after him till you do."

Stingaree held his breath where he lay. His excitement was not to be betrayed by the opening of an eye. And yet he knew that the Superintendent was looking the sergeant up and down, and he guessed what was passing through that suspicious mind.

"Trust you!" rasped the dictatorial voice at last. "That's the very thing I'm not inclined to do, Sergeant Cameron."

"Sir!"

"Keep your temper, sergeant. I don't say you'd let him go. But I've got to remember that this man has twisted you round his finger before to-day, led you by the hand like a blessed old child, and passed himself off for me! Look at the fellow; look at me; and ask yourself candidly if you're the man for the job. But don't ask me, unless you want my opinion of you a bit plainer still. No; you go on with the others. The two of you can manage Howie; if you can't, you put a bullet through him! This is my man; and I'm his, by the hokey, as he'll know if he tries any of his tricks while you're gone!"

Stingaree did not move a muscle. He might have been dead; and in his disappointment it was the easier to lie as though he were. Really bruised, really battered, really faint and stiff and sore, to say nothing of his bonds, he felt himself physically no match for so young a man-with the extra breadth of shoulder and the extra length of arm which were part and parcel of his deformity. With the elderly sergeant he might have had a chance, man to man, one arm to two; but with Superintendent Cairns his only weapons were his wits. He lay quite still and reviewed the situation, as it was, and as it had been. In the very moment of his downfall, by instinctive presence of mind he had preserved the use of his right hand, and that was a still unsuspected asset of incalculable worth. It had been the nucleus of all his plans; without a hand he must have resigned himself to the inevitable from the first. Then he had split up the party. He heard the sergeant and the constable ride off with Howie, exactly as he had intended two of the three captors to do. His fall alone introduced the element of luck. It might have killed or maimed him; but the risk had been run with open eyes. Being alive and whole, he had reduced the odds from three against two to man and man; and the difference was enormous, even though one man held all the cards. Against Howie the odds were heavier than ever, but Howie was eliminated from present calculations. And as Stingaree made them with the upturned face of seeming insensibility, he heard a nonchalant step come and go, but knew an eye was on him all the time, and never opened his own till the striking of a match was followed by the smell of bush tobacco.

The shadow of the hop-bush was spreading like spilt ink, and for the moment Stingaree thought he had it to himself. But a wreath of blue smoke hovered overhead; and when he got to his elbow, and glanced behind, there sat Cairns in his shirt-sleeves, filling the niche his body made in the actual green bush, a swollen wet water-bag at his feet, his revolver across his knees. There was an ominous click even as Stingaree screwed round where he lay.

"Give me a drink!" he cried at sight of the humid canvas bag.

"Why should I?" asked the Superintendent, smoking on.

"Because I haven't had one since we started-because I'm parched with thirst."

"Parch away!" cried the creature of suspicion. "You can't help yourself, and I can't help you with this baby to nurse."

And he fondled the cocked revolver in his hands.

"Very well! Don't give me one!" exclaimed Stingaree, and dealt the moist bag a kick that sent a jet of cold water spurting over his foot. He expected to be kicked himself for that; he was only cursed, the bag snatched out of his reach, and deeply drained before his eyes.

"I was going to give you some," said Cairns, smacking his lips. "Now your tongue may hang out before I do."

Stingaree left the last word with the foe: it was part of his preconceived policy. He still regretted his solitary retort, but not for a moment the more petulant act which he had just committed. His boots had been removed after his fall; one of his socks was now wet through, and he spent the next few minutes in taking it off with the other foot. The lengthy process seemed to afford his mind a certain pensive entertainment. It was a shapely and delicate white foot that lay stripped at last —a foot that its owner, with nothing better to do, could contemplate with legitimate satisfaction. But Superintendent Cairns, noting his prisoner's every look, and putting his own confident interpretation on them all, cursed him afresh for a conceited pig, and filled another pipe, with the revolver for an instant by his side.

Stingaree took no interest in his proceedings; the revolver he especially ignored, and lay stretched before his captor, one sock off and one sock on, one arm in splints and sling and the other bound to his ribs, a model prisoner whose last thought was of escape. His legs, indeed, were free; but a man who could not sit on a horse was not the man to run away. And then there was the relentless Superintendent sitting over him, pipe in mouth, but revolver again in hand, and a crooked finger very near the trigger.

The fiery wilderness still lay breathless in the great heat, but the lengthening shadow of the hop-bush was now a thing to be thankful for, and in it the broken captive fell into a fine semblance of natural slumber. Cairns watched with alternate envy and suspicion; for him there could not be a wink; but most likely the fellow was shamming all the time. No ruse, however, succeeded in exposing the sham, which the Superintendent copied by breathing first heavily and then stertorously, with one eye open and on his man. Stingaree never opened one of his: there was no change in the regular breathing, in the peaceful expression of the blood-stained face: asleep the man must be. The Superintendent's own experiments had gone to show him that no extremity need necessarily keep one awake in such heat. He stifled a yawn that was no part of his performance. His pipe was out; he struck a match noisily on his boot; and Stingaree just stirred, as naturally as any infant. But Stingaree's senses were incredibly acute. He smelt every whiff of the rekindled pipe, knew to ten seconds when it went out once more, and listened in an agony for another match. None was struck. Was the Superintendent himself really asleep this time? He breathed as though he were; but so did Stingaree; and yet was there hope in the fact that his own greatest struggle all this time had been against the very thing he feigned.

At last he opened one eye a little; it was met by no answering furtive glance; he opened the other, and there could be no more doubt. The terrible Superintendent was dozing in his place; but it was the lightest sort of doze, the eyes were scarcely closed, and all but watching Stingaree, as the cocked revolver in the relaxed hand all but covered him.

The prisoner felt that for the moment he was unseen, forgotten, but that the lightest movement of his body would open those terrible eyes once and for all. Be it remembered that he was lying under them lengthwise, on the bound arm, with the arm in the sling uppermost, and easily to be freed, but yet the most salient part of the recumbent figure, and that on which the hidden eyes still seemed fixed, for all their lids. To make the least movement there, to attempt the slowest withdrawal of hand and arm, was to court the last disaster of discovery in such an act. But to lie motionless down to the thighs, and to execute a flank movement with the leg uppermost, was a far less perilous exploit. It was the leg with the bare foot: every detail had been foreseen. And now at last the bare foot hovered over the revolver and the hand it held, while the upper man yet lay like a log under those drowsy, dreadful eyes.

Stingaree took a last look at the barrel drooping from the slackened hand; the back of the hand lay on the ground, the muzzle of the barrel was filled with sand, and yet the angle was such that it was by no means sure whether a bullet would bury itself in the sand or in Stingaree. He took the risk, and with his bare toe he touched the trigger sharply. There was a horrible explosion. It brought the drowsy Superintendent to his senses with such a jerk that it was as though the smoking pistol had leapt out of his hand a thing alive, and so into the hand that flashed to meet it from the sling. And almost in the same second-while the double cloud of smoke and sand still hung between them-Stingaree sprang from the ground, an armed man once more.

"Sit where you are!" he thundered. "Up with those hands before I shoot them to shreds! Your life's in less danger than mine has been all day, but I'll wing you limb by limb if you offer to budge!"

With uplifted hands above his ears, the deformed officer sat with head and shoulders depressed into the semblance of one sphere. Not a syllable did he utter; but his upturned eyes shot indomitable fires. Stingaree stood wriggling and fumbling at the coil which bound his left arm to his side; suddenly the revolver went off, as if by accident, but so much by design that there dangled two ends of rope, cut and burnt asunder by lead and powder. In less than a minute the bushranger was unbound, and before the minute was up he had leapt upon the Superintendent's thoroughbred. It had been tethered all this time to a tree, swishing tails with the station hack which Stingaree had ridden as a captive; he now rode the thoroughbred, and led the hack, to the very feet of the humiliated Cairns.

"I will thank you for that water-bag," said Stingaree. "I am much obliged. And now I'll trouble you for that nice wideawake. You really don't need it in the shade. Thank you so much!"

He received both bag and hat on the barrel of the Government revolver, hooking the one to its proper saddle-strap, and clapping on the other at an angle inimitably imitative of the outwitted officer.

"I won't carry the rehearsal any further to your face," continued Stingaree; "but I can at least promise you a more flattering portrait than the last; and this excellent coat, which you have so considerately left strapped to your saddle, should contribute greatly to the verisimilitude. Dare I hope that you begin to appreciate some of the points of my performance so far as it has gone? The pretext on which I bared my foot for its delicate job under your very eyes, eh? Not so vain as it looked, in either sense, I fancy! Should you have said that your hand would recoil from a revolver the moment it went off? You see, I staked my life on it, and I've won. And what about that fall? It was the lottery! I was prepared to have my head cracked like an egg, and it's still pretty sore. The broken wrist wasn't your fault; it had passed into the accepted situation before you turned up. And you would certainly have seen that I was shamming sleep if we hadn't both been so genuinely sleepy at the time. I give you my word, I very nearly threw up the whole thing for forty winks! Any other point on which you could wish enlightenment? Then let me thank you with all my heart for one of the worst days, and some of the greatest moments, in my whole career."

But the crooked man answered never a word, as he sat in a ball with uplifted palms, and glaring, upturned, unconquerable eyes.

"Good-by, Mr. Superintendent Cairns," said Stingaree. "I'm afraid I've been rather cruel to you-but you were never very nice to me!"

Sergeant Cameron was driving the spring-cart, toward sundown, after a variety of unforeseen delays. Of a sudden out of the pink haze came a galloping figure, slightly humped, in the inspector's coat and wideawake, with a bare foot through one stirrup and only a sock on its fellow.

"Where's Stingaree?" screamed the sergeant, pulling up. And the galloper drew rein at the driven horse's head.

"Dead!" said he, thickly. "He was worse than we thought. You fetch him while I — —"

But this time the sergeant knew that voice too well, and his right hand had flown to the back of his belt. Stingaree's shot was only first by a fraction of a second, but it put a bullet through the brain of the horse between the shafts, so that horse and shafts came down together, and the sergeant fired into the earth as he fell across the splashboard.

Stingaree pressed soft heels into the thoroughbred's ribs and thundered on and on. Soon there was a gate to open, and when he listened at that gate all was still behind him and before; but far ahead the rolling plain was faintly luminous in the dusk, and as this deepened into night a cluster of terrestrial lights sprang out with the stars. Stingaree knew the handful of gaunt, unsheltered huts the lights stood for. They were an inn, a store, and police-barracks: Clear Corner on the map. The bushranger galloped straight up to the barracks, but skirted the knot of men in the light before the veranda, and went jingling round into the yard. The young constable in charge ran through the building and met him dismounted at the back.

"What's the matter, sir?"

"He's gone!"

"Stingaree?"

"He was worse than we thought. Your man all right?"

"No trouble whatever, sir. Only sick and sorry and saying his prayers in a way you'd never credit. Come and hear him."

"I must come and see him at once. Got a fresh horse in?"

"I have so! In and saddled in the stall. I thought you might want one, sir, and ran up Barmaid, Stingaree's own mare, that was sent out here from the station when we had the news."

"That was very thoughtful of you. You'll get on, young man. Now lead the way with that lamp."

This time Stingaree had spoken in gasps, like a man who had ridden very far, and the young constable, unlike his sergeant, did not know his voice of old. Yet it struck him at the last moment as more unlike the voice of Superintendent Cairns than the hardest riding should have made it, and with the key in the door of the cell the young fellow wheeled round and held the lamp on high. That instant he was felled to the floor, the lamp went down and out with a separate yet simultaneous crash, and Stingaree turned the key.

"Howie! Not a word-out you come!"

The burly ruffian crept forth with outstretched hands apart.

"What! Not even handcuffed?"

"No; turned over a new leaf the moment we left you, and been praying like a parson for 'em all to hear!"

"This chap can do the same when he comes to himself. Lies pretty still, doesn't he? In with him!"

The door clanged. The key was turned. Stingaree popped it into his pocket.

"The later they let him out the better. Here's the best mount you ever had. And my sweetheart's waiting for me in the stable!"

Outside, in front, before the barracks veranda, an inquisitive little group heard first the clang of the door within, and presently the clatter of hoofs coming round from the yard. Stingaree and Howie —a white flash and a bay streak-swept past them as they stood confounded. And the dwindling pair still bobbed in sight, under a full complement of stars, when a fresh outcry from the cell, and a mighty hammering against its locked door, broke the truth to one and all.

The Villain-Worshipper

There was no more fervent admirer of Stingaree and all bushrangers than George Oswald Abernethy Melvin. Despite this mellifluous nomenclature young Melvin helped his mother to sell dance-music, ballads, melodeons, and a very occasional pianoforte, in one of the several self-styled capitals of Riverina; and despite both facts the mother was a lady of most gentle blood. The son could either teach or tune the piano with a certain crude and idle skill. He endured a monopoly of what little business the locality provided in this line, and sat superior on the music-stool at all the dances. He had once sung tenor in Bishop Methuen's choir, but, offended by a word of wise and kindly advice, was seen no more in surplice or in church. It will be perceived that Oswald Melvin had all the aggressive independence of Young Australia without the virility which leavens the truer type.

Yet he was neither a base nor an unkind lad. His bane was a morbid temperament, which he could no more help than his sallow face and weedy person; even his vanity was directly traceable to the early influence of an eccentric and feckless father with experimental ideas on the upbringing of a child. It was a pity that brilliantly unsuccessful man had not lived to see the result of his sedulous empiricism. His wife was left to bear the brunt —a brave exile whose romantic history was never likely to escape her continent lips. None even knew whether she saw any or one of those aggravated faults of an only child which were so apparent to all her world.

And yet the worst of Oswald Melvin was known only to his own morbid and sensitive heart. An unimpressive presence in real life, on his mind's stage he was ever in the limelight with a good line on his lips. Not that he was invariably the hero of these pieces. He could see himself as large with the noose round his neck as in coronet or halo; and though this inward and spiritual temper may be far from rare, there had been no one to kick out of him its outward and visible expression. Oswald had never learned to gulp down the little lie which insures a flattering attention; his clever father had even encouraged it in him as the nucleus of imagination. Imagination he certainly had, but it fed on strong meat for an unhealthy mind; it fattened on the sordid history of the earlier bushrangers; its favorite fare was the character and exploits of Stingaree. The sallow and neurotic face would brighten with morbid enthusiasm at the bare mention of the desperado's name. The somewhat dull, dark eyes would lighten with borrowed fires: the young fool wore an eye-glass in one of them when he dared.

"Stingaree," he would say, "is the greatest man in all Australia." He had inherited from his father a delight in uttering startling opinions; but this one he held with unusual sincerity. It had come to all ears, and was the subject of that episcopal compliment which Oswald took as an affront. The impudent little choristers supported his loss by calling "Stingaree!" after him in the street: he was wise to keep his eye-glass for the house.

There, however, with a few even younger men who admired his standpoint and revelled in his store of criminous annals, or with his patient, inscrutable mother, Oswald Melvin was another being. His language became bright and picturesque, his animation surprising. A casual customer would sometimes see this side of him, and carry away the impression of a rare young dare-devil. And it was one such who gave Oswald the first great moment of his bush life.

"Not been down from the back-blocks for three years?" he had asked, as he showed a tremulous and dilapidated bushman how to play the instrument that he had bought with the few shillings remaining out of his check. "Been on the spree and going back to drive a whim until you've enough to go on another? How I wish you'd tell that to our high and mighty Lord Bishop of all the Back-Blocks! I should like to see his face and hear him on the subject; but I suppose he's new since you were down here last? Never come across him, eh? But, of course, you heard how good old Stingaree scored off him the other day, after he thought he'd scored off Stingaree?"

The whim-driver had heard something about it. Young Melvin plunged into the congenial narrative and emerged minutes later in a dusky glow.

"That's the man for my money," he perorated. "Stingaree, sir, is the greatest chap in all these Colonies, and deserves to be Viceroy when they get Federation. Thunderbolt, Morgan, Ben Hall and Ned Kelly were not a circumstance between them to Stingaree; and the silly old Bishop's a silly old fool to him! I don't care twopence about right and wrong. That's not the point. The one's a Force, and the other isn't."

"A darned sight too much force, to my mind," observed the whim-driver with some warmth.

"You don't take my meaning," the superior youth pursued. "It's a question of personality."

"A bit more personal than you think," was the dark rejoinder.

"How do you mean?"

Melvin's tone had altered in an instant.

"I know too much about him."

"At first hand?" the youth asked, with bated breath.

"Double first!" returned the other, with a muddled glimmer of better things.

"You never knew him, did you?" whispered Oswald.

"Knew him? I've been taken prisoner by him," said the whim-driver, with the pause of a man who hesitates to humiliate himself, but is lost for the sake of that same sensation which Oswald Melvin loved to create.

Mrs. Melvin was in the back room, wistfully engrossed in an English magazine sent that evening from Bishop's Lodge. The bad blood in the son had not affected Dr. Methuen's keen but tactful interest in the mother. She looked up in tolerant consternation as her Oswald pushed an unsavory bushman before him into the room; but even through her gentle horror the mother's love shone with that steady humor which raised it above the sphere of obvious pathos.

"Here's a man who's been stuck up by Stingaree!" he cried, boyish enough in his delight. "Do keep an eye on the show, mother, and let him tell me all about it, as he's good enough to say he will. Is there any whiskey?"

"Not for me!" put in the whim-driver, with a frank shudder. "I should like a drink of tea out of a cup, if I'm to have anything."

Mrs. Melvin left them with a good-humored word besides her promise. She had given no sign of injury or disapproval; she was not one of the wincing sort; and the tremulous tramp was in her own chair before her back was turned.

"Now fire away!" cried the impatient Oswald.

"It's a long story," said the whim-driver; and his dirty brows were knit in thought.

"Let's have it," coaxed the young man. And the other's thoughtful creases vanished suddenly in the end.

"Very well," said he, "since it means a drink of tea out of a cup! It was only the other day, in a dust-storm away back near the Darling, as bad a one as ever I was out in. I was bushed and done for, gave it up and said my prayers. Then I practically died in my tracks, and came to life in a sunny clearing later in the day. The storm was over; two coves had found me and carried me to their camp; and as soon as I saw them I spotted one for Howie and the other for Stingaree!"

The narrative went no farther for a time. The thrilling youth fired question and leading question like a cross-examining counsel in a fever to conclude his case. The tea arrived, but the whim-driver had to help himself. His host neglected everything but the first chance he had ever had of hearing of Stingaree or any other bushranger at first-hand.

"And how long were you there?"

"About a week."

"What happened then?"

The whim-driver paused in doubt renewed.

"You will never guess."

"Tell me."

"They waited for the next dust-storm, and then cast me adrift in that."

Oswald stared; he would never have guessed, indeed. The unhealthy light faded from his sallow face. Even his morbid enthusiasm was a little damped.

"You must have done something to deserve it," he cried, at last.

"I did," was the reply, with hanging head. "I —I tried to take him."

"Take your benefactor-take him prisoner?"

"Yes-the man who saved my life."

Melvin sat staring: it was a stare of honestly incredulous disgust. Then he sprang to his feet, a brighter youth than ever, his depression melted like a cloud. His villainous hero was an heroic villain after all! His heart of hearts-which was not black-could still render whole homage to Stingaree! He no longer frowned on his informer as on a thing accursed. The creature had wiped out his original treachery to Stingaree by replacing the uninjured idol in its niche in this warped mind. Oswald, however, had made his repugnance only too plain; he was unable to elicit another detail; and in a very few minutes Mrs. Melvin was back in her place, though not before flicking it with her handkerchief, undetected by her son.

It was certainly a battered and hang-dog figure that stole away into the bush. Yet the creature straightened as he strode into star-light undefiled by earthly illumination; his palsy left him; presently as he went he began fingering the new melodeon in the way of a man who need not have sought elementary instruction from Oswald Melvin. And now a shining disk filled one unwashed eye.

Stingaree lay a part of that night beside the milk-white mare that he had left tethered in a box-clump quite near the town; at sunrise he knelt and shaved on the margin of a Government tank, before breaking the mirror by plunging in. And before the next stars paled he was snugly back in older haunts, none knowing of his descent upon those of men.

There or thereabouts, hidden like the needle in the hay, and yet ubiquitous in the stack, the bushranger remained for months. Then there was an encounter, not the first of this period, but the first in which shots were exchanged. One of these pierced the lungs of his melodeon-an instrument more notorious by this time than the musical-box before it —a still greater treasure to Stingaree. That was near the full of a certain summer moon; it was barely waning to the eye when the battered buyer of melodeons came for a new one to the shop in the pretty bush town.

The shop was closed for the night, but Stingaree knocked at a lighted window under the veranda, which Mrs. Melvin presently threw up. Her eyes flashed when she recognized one against whom she now harbored a bitterness on quite a different plane of feeling from her former repulsion. Even to his first glance she looked an older and a harder woman.

"I am sorry to see you," she said, with a soft vehemence plainly foreign to herself. "I almost hate the sight of you! You have been the ruin of my son!"

"His ruin?"

Stingaree forgot the speech of the unlettered stockman; but his cry was too short to do worse than warn him.

"Come round," continued Mrs. Melvin, austerely. "I will see you. You shall hear what you have done."

In another minute he was in the parlor where he had sat aforetime. He never dreamt of sitting now. But the lady took her accustomed chair as a queen her throne.

"*Is* he ruined?" asked Stingaree.

"Not irrevocably-not yet; but he may be any moment. He must be before long."

"But-but what ails him, madame?"

"Villain-worship!" cried the lady, with a tragic face stripped of all its humor, and bare without it as a winter's tree.

"I remember! Yes —I understand. He was mad about-Stingaree."

"It is madness now," said the bitter mother. "It was only a stupid, hare-brained fancy then, but now it is something worse. You're the first to whom I have admitted it," she continued, with illogical indignation, "because it's all through you!"

"All through me?"

"You told him a tale. You made that villain a greater hero in his eyes than ever. You made him real."

"He is real enough, God knows!"

"But you made him so to my son." The keen eyes softened for one divine instant before they filled. "And I —I am talking my own boy over with-with — —"

Stingaree stood in twofold embarrassment. Did she know after all who he was? And what had he said he was, the time before?

"The lowest of the low," he answered, with a twitch of his unshaven lips.

"No! That you were not, or are not, whatever you may say. You —" she hesitated sweetly — "you had been unsteady when you were here before." He twitched again, imperceptibly. "I am thankful to see that you are now more like what you must once have been. I can bear to tell you of my boy. Oh, sir, can you bear with me?"

Stingaree twitched no more. Rich as the situation was, keenly as he had savored its unsuspected irony, the humor was all over for him. Here was a woman, still young, sweet and kind, and gentle as a childish memory, with her fine eyes full of tears! That was bad enough. To make it worse, she went on to tell him of her son, him an outlaw, him a bushranger with a price upon his skin, as she might have outlined the case to a consulting physician. The boy had been born in the trouble of her early exile; he could not help his temperament. He had countless virtues; she extolled him in beaming parentheses. But he had too much imagination and too little balance. He was morbidly wrapped up in the whole subject of romantic crime, and no less than possessed with the personality of this one romantic criminal.

"I should be ashamed to tell you the childish lengths to which he has gone," she went on, "if he were quite himself on the point. But indeed he is not. He is Stingaree in his heart, Stingaree in his dreams; it is as debasing a form as mental and temperamental weakness could well take; yet I know, who watch over him half of the night. He has an eye-glass; he keeps revolvers; he has even bought a white mare! He can look extremely like the portraits one has seen of the wretched man. But come with me one moment."

She took the lamp and led the way into the little room where Oswald Melvin slept. He had slept in it from that boyhood in which the brave woman had opened this sort of shop entirely for his sake. Music was his only talent; he was obviously not to be a genius in the musical world; but it was the only one in which she could foresee the selfish, self-willed child figuring with credit, and her foresight was only equalled by her resource. The business was ripe and ready for him when he grew up. And this was what he was making of it.

But Stingaree saw only the little bed that had once been far too large, the Bible still by its side, read or unread, the parents' portraits overhead. The mother was looking in an opposite direction; he followed her eyes, and there at the foot, where the infatuated fool could see it last thing at night and first in the morning, was an enlarged photograph of the bushranger himself.

It had been taken in audacious circumstances a year or two before. A travelling photographer had been one of yet another coach-load turned out and stood in a line by the masterful masterless man.

"Now you may take my photograph. The police refuse to know me when we do meet. Give them a chance."

And he had posed on the spot with eye-glass up and pistols pointed, as he saw himself now, not less than a quarter life-size, in a great gaudy frame. But while he stared Mrs. Melvin had been rummaging in a drawer, and when he turned she was staring in her turn with glassy eyes. In her hands was an empty mahogany case with velvet moulds which ought to have been filled by a brace of missing revolvers.

"He kept it locked-he kept them in it!" she gasped. "He may have done it this very night!"

"Done what?"

"Stuck up the Deniliquin mail. That is his maddest dream. I have heard him boast of it to his friends-the brainless boys who alone look up to him —I have even heard him rave of it in his dreams!"

Stingaree was heavy for a moment with a mental calculation. His head was a time-table of Cobb's coaches on the Riverina road-system; he nodded it as he located the imperilled vehicle.

"A dream it shall remain," said he. "But there's not a moment to lose!"

"Do you propose to follow and stop him?"

"If he really means it."

"He may not. He will ride at night. He is often out as late."

"Going and coming about the same time?"

"Yes-now I think of it."

"Then his courage must have failed him hitherto, and it probably will again."

"But if not!"

"I will cure him. But I must go at once. I have a horse not far away. I will gallop and meet the coach; if it is still safe, as you may be sure it will be, I shall scour the country for your son. I can tell him a fresh thing or two about Stingaree!"

"God bless you!"

"Leave him to me."

"Oh, may God bless you always!"

His hands were in a lady's hands once more. Stingaree withdrew them gently. And he looked his last into the brave wet eyes raised gratefully to his.

The villain-worshipper was indeed duly posted in a certain belt of trees through which the coach-route ran, about half-way between the town and the first stage south. It was not his first nocturnal visit to the spot; often, as his prototype divined, had the mimic would-be desperado sat trembling on his hoary screw, revolvers ready, while the red eyes of the coach dilated down the road; and as often had the cumbrous ship pitched past unscathed. The week-kneed and weak-minded youth was too vain to feel much ashamed. He was biding his time, he could pick his night; one was too dark, another not dark enough; he had always some excuse for himself when he regained his room, still unstained by crime; and so the unhealthy excitement was deliciously maintained. To-night, as always when he sallied forth, the deed should be done; he only wished there was a shade less moon, and wondered whether he might not have done better to wait. But, as usual, the die was cast. And indeed it was quite a new complication that deterred this poor creature for the last time: he was feverishly expecting the coach when a patter of hoofs smote his ear from the opposite quarter.

This was enough to stay an older and a bolder hand. Oswald tucked in his guns with unrealized relief. It was his last instinct to wait and see whether the horseman was worth attacking for his own sake; he had room for few ideas at the same time; and his only new one was the sense of a new danger, which he prepared to meet by pocketing his pistols as a child bolts stolen fruit. There was no thinking before the act; but it was perhaps as characteristic of the naturally honest man as of the coward.

Stingaree swept through the trees at a gallop, the milk-white mare flashing in the moonlit patches. At the sight of her Oswald was convulsed with a premonition as to who was coming; his heart palpitated as even his heart had never done before; and yet he would have sat irresolute, inert, and let the man pass as he always let the coach, had the decision been left to him. The real milk-white mare affected the imitation in its turn as the coach-horses never had; and Oswald swayed and swam upon a whinnying steed. . . .

"I thought you were Stingaree!"

The anti-climax was as profound as the weakling's relief. Yet there was a strong dash of indignation in his tone.

"What if I am?"

"But you're not. You're not half smart enough. You can't tell me anything about Stingaree!"

He put his eye-glass up with an air.

Stingaree put up his.

"You young fool!" said he.

The thoroughbred mare, the eye-glass, a peeping pistol, were all superfluous evidence. There was the far more unmistakable authority of voice and eye and bearing. Yet the voice at least was somehow familiar to the ear of Oswald, who stuttered as much when he was able.

"I must have heard it before, or have I dreamt it? I've thought a good deal about you, you know!"

To do him justice, he was no longer very nervous, though still physically shaken. On the other hand, he began already to feel the elation of his dreams.

"I do know. You've thought your soul into a pulp on the subject, and you must give it up," said Stingaree, sternly.

Oswald sat aghast.

"But how on earth did you know?"

"I've come straight from your mother. You're breaking her heart."

"But how can *you* have come straight from *her*?"

"I've come down for another melodeon. I've got to have one, too."

"Another ——"

And Oswald Melvin knew his drunken whim-driver for what he had really been.

"The yarn I told you about myself was true enough," continued Stingaree. "Only the names were altered, as they say; it happened to the other fellow, not to me. I made it happen. He is hardly likely to have lived to tell the tale."

"Did he really try to betray you after what you'd done for him?"

"More or less. He looked on me as fair game."

"But you had saved his life?"

Stingaree shrugged.

"We rode across him."

"And you think he perished of dust and thirst?"

Stingaree nodded. "In torment!"

"Then he got what he jolly well earned! Anything less would have been too good for him!" cried Oswald, and with a boyish, uncompromising heat which spoke to some human nature in him still.

But Stingaree frowned up the moonlit track. There was still no sign of the coach. Yet time was short, and the morbid enthusiast was not to be disgusted; indeed, he was all enthusiasm now, and a less unattractive lad than the bushranger had hoped to find him. He looked the white screw and Oswald up and down as they sat in their saddles in the moonshine: it seemed like sunlight on that beaming fool.

"And you think of commencing bushranger, do you?"

"Rather!"

"It's a hard life while it lasts, and a nasty death to top up with."

"They don't hang you for it."

"They might hang me for the man I put back in the vile dust from whence he sprung. They'd hang you in six months. You've too many nerves. You'd pull the trigger every time."

"A short life and a merry one!" cried the reckless Oswald. "I shouldn't care."

"But your mother would," retorted Stingaree, sharply. "Don't think about yourself so much; think about her for a change."

The young man turned dusky in the moonlight; he was wounded where the Bishop had wounded him, and Stingaree was quick to see it-as quick to turn the knife round in the wound.

"What a bushranger!" he jeered. "Put your plucky little mother in a side-saddle and she'd make two of you-ten of you-twenty of a puny, namby-pamby, conceited young idiot like you! Upon my word, Melvin, if I had a mother like you I should be ashamed of myself. I never had, I may tell you, or I shouldn't have come down to a dog's life like this."

The bushranger paused to watch the effect of his insults. It was not quite what he wanted. The youth would not hang his head. And, if he did not answer back, he looked back doggedly enough; for he could be dogged, in a passive way; it was his one hard quality, the knot in a character of green deal. Stingaree glanced up the road once more, but only for an instant.

"It is a dog's life," he went on, "whether you believe it or not. But it takes a bull-dog to live it, and don't you forget it. It's no life for a young poodle like you! You can't stick up a better man than yourself, not more than once or twice. It requires something more than a six-shooter, and a good deal more than was put into you, my son! But you shall see for yourself; look over your shoulder."

Oswald did so, and started in a fashion that set the bushranger nodding his scorn. It was only a pair of lamps still close together in the distance up the road.

"The coach!" exclaimed the excited youth.

"Exactly," said Stingaree, "and I'm going to stick it up."

Excitement grew to frenzy in a flash.

"I'll help you!"

"You'll do no such thing. But you shall see how it's done, and then ask yourself candidly if it's nice work and if you're the man to do it. Ride a hundred yards further in, tether your horse quickly in the thickest scrub you can find, then run back and climb into the fork of this gum-tree. You'll have time; if you're sharp I'll give you a leg up. But I sha'n't be surprised if I don't see you again!"

There is no saying what Oswald might have done, but for these last words. Certain it is that they set him galloping with an oath, and brought him back panting in another minute. The coach-lamps were not much wider apart. Stingaree awaited him, also on foot, and quicker than the telling Oswald was ensconced on high where he could see through the meagre drooping leaves with very little danger of being seen.

"And if you come down before I'm done and gone-if it's not to glory —I'll run some lead through you! You'll be the first!"

Oswald perched reflecting on this final threat; and the scene soon enacted before his eyes was viewed as usual through the aura of his own egoism. He longed all the time to be taking part in it; he could see himself so distinctly at the work-save for about a minute in the middle, when for once in his life he held his breath and trembled for other skins.

There had been no unusual feature. The life-size coach-lamps had shown their mountain-range of outside passengers against moonlit sky or trees. A cigar paled and reddened between the teeth of one, plain wreaths of smoke floated from his lips, with but an instant's break when Stingaree rode out and stopped the coach. The three leaders reared; the two wheelers were pulled almost to their haunches. The driver was docile in deed, though profane in word; and Stingaree himself discovered a horrifying vocabulary out of keeping with his reputation. In incredibly few minutes driver and passengers were formed in a line and robbed in rotation, all but two ladies who were kept inside unmolested. A flagrant Irishman declared it was the proudest day of his life, and Oswald's heart went out to him, though it rather displeased him to find his own sentiments shared by the vulgar. The man with the cigar kept it glowing all the time. The mail-bags were not demanded on this occasion. Stingaree had no time to waste on them. He was still collecting purse and watch, when Oswald's young blood froze in the stiffening limbs he dared not move.

One of the ladies had got down from the coach on the off side, and behold! it was a man wrapped in a rug, which dropped from him as he crept round behind the horses. At their head stood the lily mare, as if doing her own nefarious part by her own kind. In a twinkling the mad adventurer was on her back, and all this time Oswald longed to jump down, or at least to shout a warning to his hero, but, as usual, his desires were unproductive of word or deed. And then Stingaree saw his man.

He did not fire; he did not shift sight or barrel for a moment from the docile file before him. "Barmaid! Barmaid, my pet!" he cried, and hardly looked to see what happened.

But Oswald watched the mare stop, prick her ears under the hammering of unspurred heels, spin round, bucking as she spun, and toss her rider like a bull. There in the moonlight he lay like lead, with leaden face upturned to the shuddering youngster in the tree.

"One of you a doctor?" asked Stingaree, checking a forward movement of the file.

"I am."

The cigar was paling between finger and thumb.

"Then come you here and have a look at him. The rest of you move at your peril!"

Stingaree led the way, stepping backward, but not as far as the injured man, who sat up ruefully as the bushranger sprang into the saddle.

"Another yard, and I'd have grabbed your ankles!" said the man on the ground.

"You're a stout fellow, but I know more about this game than you," the outlaw answered, riding to his distance and reining up. "If I didn't you might have had me-but you must think of something better for Stingaree!"

He galloped his mare into the bush and Oswald clung in lonely terror to his tree. A snatch of conversation called him to attention. The plundered party were clambering philosophically to their seats, while the driver blasphemed delightedly over the integrity of his mails.

The mare spun round, bucking as she spun.

"That wasn't Stingaree," said one.

"You bet it was!"

"How much? He hardly ever works so far south."

"And he's nuts on mails."

"But if it wasn't Stingaree, who was it?"

"It was him all right. Look at the mare."

"She isn't the only white 'orse ever foaled," remarked the driver, sorting his fistful of reins.

"But who else could it have been?"

The driver uttered an inspired imprecation.

"I can tell you. I chanst to live in this here township we're comin' to. On second thoughts, I'll keep it to myself till we get there."

And he cracked his whip.

Oswald himself rode back to the township before the moon went down. He was very heavy with his own reflections. How magnificent! It had all surpassed his most extravagant imaginings-in audacity, in expedition, in simple mastery of the mutable many by the dominant one. He forgave Stingaree his gibes and insults; he could have forgiven a horse-whipping from that king of men. Stingaree had been his imaginary god before; he was a realized ideal from this night forth, and the reality outdid the dream.

But the fly of self must always poison this young man's ointment, and to-night there was some excuse from his degenerate point of view. He must give it up. Stingaree was right; it was only one man in thousands who could do unerringly what he had done that night. Oswald Melvin was not that man. He saw it for himself at last. But it was a bitter hour for him. Life in the music-shop would fall very flat after this; he would be dishonored before his only friends, the unworthy hobbledehoys who were to have joined his gang; he could not tell them what had happened, not at least until he had invented some less inglorious part for himself, and that was a difficulty in view of newspaper reports of the sticking-up. He could scarcely tell them a true word of what had passed between himself and Stingaree. If only he might yet grow more like the master! If only he might still hope to follow so sublime a lead!

Thus aspiring, vainly as now he knew, Oswald Melvin rode slowly back into the excited town, and past the lighted police-barracks, in the innocence of that portion of his heart. But one had flown like the wind ahead of him, and two in uniform, followed by that one, dashed out on Oswald and the old white screw.

"Surrender!" sang out one.

"In the Queen's name!" added the other.

"Call yourself Stingaree!" panted the runner.

Our egoist was quick enough to grasp their meaning, but quicker still to see and to seize the chance of a crazy lifetime. Always acute where his own vanity was touched, his promptitude was for once on a par with his perceptions.

"Had your eye on me long?" he inquired, delightfully, as he dismounted.

"Long enough," said one policeman. The other was busy plucking loaded revolvers from the desperado's pockets. A crowd had formed.

"If you're looking for the loot," he went on, raising his voice for the benefit of all, "you may look. *I* sha'n't tell you, and it'll take you all your time!"

But a surprise was in store for prisoner and police alike. Every stolen watch and all the missing money were discovered no later than next morning in the bush quite close to the scene of the outrage. There had been no attempt to hide them; they lay in a heap, dumped from the saddle, with no more depreciation than a broken watch-glass. True to his new character, Oswald learned this development without flinching. His ready comment was in next day's papers.

"There was nothing worth having," he had maintained, and did not see the wisdom of the boast until a lawyer called and pointed out that it contained the nucleus of a strong defence.

"I'll defend myself, thank you," said the inflated fool.

"Then you'll make a mess of it, and deserve all you get. And it would be a pity to spoil such a good defence."

"What is the defence?"

"You did it for a joke, of course!"

Oswald smiled inscrutably, and dismissed his visitor with a lordly promise to consider the proposition and that lawyer's claims upon the case. Never was such triumph tasted in guilty immunity as was this innocent man's under cloud of guilt so apparent as to impose on every mind. He had but carried out a notorious intention; for his few friends were the first to betray their captain, albeit his bold bearing and magnanimous smiles won an admiration which they had never before vouchsafed him in their hearts. He was, indeed, a different man. He had lived to see Stingaree in action, and now he modelled himself from the life. The only doubt was as to whether at the last of that business he had actually avowed himself Stingaree or not. There might have been trouble about the horse, but fortunately for the enthusiastic prisoner the man who had been thrown was allowed to proceed on a pressing journey to the Barcoo. There was a plethora of evidence without his; besides, the hide-and-bone mare was called Barmaid, after the original, and it was known that Oswald had tried to teach the old creature tricks; above all, the prisoner had never pretended to deny his guilt. Still, this matter of the horses gave him a certain sense of insecurity in his cosey cell.

He had awakened to find himself not only deliciously notorious, but actually more of a man than in his heart of hearts he had dared to hope. The tenacity and consistency of his pose were alike remarkable. Even in the overweening cause of egoism he had never shown so much character in his life. Yet he shuddered to realize that, given the usual time for reflection before his great moment, that moment might have proved as mean as many another when the spirit had been wine and the flesh water. There was, in fine, but one feature of the affair which even Oswald Melvin, drunk with notoriety and secretly sanguine of a nominal punishment, could not contemplate with absolute satisfaction. But that feature followed the others into the papers which kept him intoxicated. And a bundle of these papers found their adventurous way to the latest fastness of Stingaree in the mallee.

The real villain dropped his eye-glass, clapped it in again, and did his best to crack it with his stare. Student of character as he was, he could not have conceived such a development in such a character. He read on, more enlightened than amused. "To think he had the pluck!" he murmured, as he dropped that *Australasian* and took up the next week's. He was filled with admiration, but soon a frown and then an oath came to put an end to it. "The little beast," he cried, "he'll kill that woman! He can't have kept it up." He sorted the papers for the latest of all —a sinful publican saved them for him-and therein read that Oswald Melvin had been committed for trial, and that his only concern was for the condition of his mother, which was still unchanged, and had seemed latterly to distress the prisoner very much.

"I'll distress him!" roared Stingaree to the mallee. "I'll distress him, if we change places for it!"

Riding all night, and as much as he dared by day, it was some hundred hours before he paid his third and last visit to the Melvins' music-shop. He rode boldly to the door, but he rode a piebald mare not to be confused in the most suspicious mind with the no more conspicuous Barmaid. It is true the brown parts smelt of Condy's Fluid, and were at once strange and seemingly a little tender to the touch. But Stingaree allowed no meddling with his mount; and only a very sinful publican, very many leagues back, was in the secret.

There were no lighted windows behind the shop to-night. The whole place was in darkness, and Stingaree knocked in vain. A neighbor appeared upon the next veranda.

"Who is it you want?" he asked.

"Mrs. Melvin."

"It's no use knocking for her."

"Is she dead?"

"Not that I know of; but she can't be long for this world."

"Where is she now?"

"Bishop's Lodge; they say Miss Methuen's with her day and night."

For it was in the days of the Bishop's daughter, who had a strong mind but no sense of humor, and a heart only fickle in its own affairs. Miss Methuen made an admirable, if a somewhat too assiduous and dictatorial, nurse. She had, however, a fund of real sympathy with the afflicted, and Mrs. Melvin's only serious complaint (which she intended to die without uttering) was that she was never left alone with her grief by day or night. It was Miss Methuen who, sitting with rather ostentatious patience in the dark, at the open window, until her patient should fall or pretend to be asleep, saw a man ride a piebald horse in at the gate, and then, half-way up the drive, suspiciously dismount and lead his horse into a tempting shrubbery.

Stingaree did not often change his mind at the last moment, but he knew the man on whose generosity he was about to throw himself, which was to know further that that generosity would be curbed by judgment, and to reflect that he was least likely to be deprived of a horse whose whereabouts was known only to himself. There was but one lighted room when he eventually stole upon the house; it had a veranda to itself; and in the bright frame of the French windows, which stood open, sat the Bishop with his Bible on his knees.

"Yes, I know you," said he, putting his marker in the place as Stingaree entered, boots in one hand and something else in the other. "I thought we should meet again. Do you mind putting that thing back in your pocket?"

Stingaree knocked in vain.

"Will you promise not to call a soul?"

"Oh, dear, yes."

"You weren't expecting me, were you?" cried Stingaree, suspiciously.

"I've been expecting you for months," returned the Bishop. "You knew my address, but I hadn't yours. We were bound to meet again."

Stingaree smiled as he took his revolver by the barrel and carried it across the room to Dr. Methuen.

"What's that for? I don't want it; put it in your own pocket. At least I can trust you not to take my life in cold blood."

The Bishop seemed nettled and annoyed. Stingaree loved him.

"I don't come to take anything, much less life," he said. "I come to save it; if it is not too late."

"To save life-here?"

"In your house."

"But whom do you know of my household?"

"Mrs. Melvin. I have had the honor of meeting her twice, though each time she was unaware of the dishonor of meeting me. The last time I promised to try to save her unhappy son from himself. I found him waiting to waylay the coach, told him who I was, and had ten minutes to try to cure him in. He wouldn't listen to reason; insult ran like water off his back. I did my best to show him what a life it was he longed to lead, and how much more there was in it than a loaded revolver. He wouldn't take my word for it, however, so I put him out of harm's way, up in a tree; and when the coach came along I gave him as brutal an exhibition of the art of bushranging as I could without spilling blood. I promise you it was for no other reason. What did I want with watches? What were a few pounds to me? I dropped the lot that the lad might know."

The Bishop started to his gaitered legs.

"And he's actually innocent all the time?"

"Of the deed, as the babe unborn."

"Then why in the wide world — —"

Dr. Methuen stood beggared of further speech. His mind was too plain and sane for immediate understanding of such a type as Oswald Melvin. But the bushranger hit off that young man's character in half-a-dozen trenchant phrases.

"He must be let out, and it may save his mother's life; but if he were mine," exclaimed the Bishop, "I would rather he had done the other deed! But what about you?" he added, suddenly, his eyes resting on his sardonic visitor, who had disguised himself far less than his horse. "It will mean giving yourself up."

"No. You know me. You can spread what I've told you."

The Bishop shifted uneasily on his hearth-rug.

"I may not see my way to that," said he. "Besides, you must have run a lot of risks to do this good action; how do you know you haven't been recognized already? I should have known you anywhere."

"But you have undertaken not to raise an alarm, my lord."

"I shall not break my promise."

There was a grim regret in the Bishop's voice. Stingaree thought he understood it.

"Thank you," he said.

"Don't thank me, pray!" Dr. Methuen could be quite testy on occasion. "I have other duties than to you, you know, and I only answer for my actions during the actual period of our interview. There are many things I should like to say to you, my brother," a gentler voice went on, "but this is hardly the time for me to say them. But there is one question I should like to ask you for the peace of both our souls, and for the maintenance of my own belief in human nature." He threw up an episcopal hand dramatically. "If you earnestly and honestly wished to save this poor lady's life, and there were no other way, would you then be man enough to give yourself up-to give your liberty for her life?"

Stingaree took time to think. His eyes were brightly fixed upon the Bishop's. Yet they saw a little bedroom just as plain, an English lady standing by the empty bed, and at its foot a portrait of himself armed to the teeth.

"For hers?" said he. "Yes, like a shot!"

"I'm thankful to hear it," replied the Bishop, with most fervent relief. "I only wish you could have the opportunity. But now you never will. My brother, if you look round, you will see why!"

Stingaree looked round without a word. In the Bishop's eyes at the last instant he had learned what to expect. A firing-party of four stocking-soled constables were drawn across the opened French windows, their levelled rifles poking through.

The bushranger looked over his shoulder with a bitter smile. "You've done me, after all!" said he, and stretched out empty hands.

"It was done before I saw you," the Bishop made answer. "I had already sent for the police."

One had entered excitedly by an inner door.

"And he didn't do you at all!" cried the voice of high hysteria. "It was I who saw you-it was I who guessed who it was! Oh, father, why have you been talking so long to such a dreadful man? I made sure he would shoot you, and you'd still be shot if they had to shoot him! Move-move-move!"

Stingaree looked at the strong-minded girl, shrill with her triumph, quite carried away by her excitement, all undaunted by the prospect of bloodshed before her eyes. And it was he who moved, with but a shrug of the shoulders, and gave himself up without another sign.

The Moth and the Star

I

Darlinghurst Jail had never immured a more interesting prisoner than the back-block bandit who was tried and convicted under the strange style and title which he had made his own. Not even in prison was his real name ever known, and the wild speculations of some imaginative officials were nothing else up to the end. There was enough color in their wildness, however, to crown the convict with a certain halo of romance, which his behavior in jail did nothing to dispel. That, of course, was exemplary, since Stingaree had never been a fool; but it was something more and rarer. Not content simply to follow the line of least resistance, he exhibited from the first a spirit and a philosophy unique indeed beneath the broad arrow. And so far from decreasing with the years of his captivity, these attractive qualities won him friend after friend among the officials, and privilege upon privilege at their hands, while amply justifying the romantic interest in his case.

At last there came to Sydney a person more capable of an acute appreciation of the heroic villain than his most ardent admirer on the spot. Lucius Brady was a long-haired Irishman of letters, bard and bookworm, rebel and reviewer; in his ample leisure he was also the most enthusiastic criminologist in London. And as President of an exceedingly esoteric Society for the Cultivation of Criminals, even from London did he come for a prearranged series of interviews with the last and the most distinguished of all the bushrangers.

It was to Lucius Brady, his biographer to be, that Stingaree confided the data of all the misdeeds recounted in these pages; but of his life during the quiet intervals, of his relations with confederates, and his more honest dealings with honest folk (of which many a pretty tale was rife), he was not to be persuaded to speak without an irritating reserve.

"Keep to my points of contact with the world, about which something is known already, and you shall have the whole truth of each matter," said the convict. "But I don't intend to give away the altogether unknown, and I doubt if it would interest you if I did. The most interesting thing to me has been the different types with whom I have had what it pleases you to term professional relations, and the very different ways in which they have taken me. You read character by flashlight along the barrel of your revolver. What you should do is to hunt up my various victims and get at their point of view; you really mustn't press me to hark back to mine. As it is you bring a whiff of the outer world which makes me bruise my wings against the bars."

The criminologist gloated over such speeches from such lips. It would have touched another to note what an irresistible fascination the bars had for the wings, despite all pain; but Lucius Brady's interest in Stingaree was exclusively intellectual. His heart never ached for a roving spirit in confinement; it did not occur to him to suppress a detail of his own days in Sydney, down to the attractions of an Italian restaurant he had discovered near the jail, the flavor of the Chianti and so forth. On the contrary, it was most interesting to note the play of features in the tortured man, who after all brought his torture on himself by asking so many questions. Soon, when his visitor left him, the bondman could follow the free in all but the flesh, through every corridor of the prison and every street outside, to the hotel where you read the English papers on the veranda, or to the little restaurant where the Chianti was corked with oil which the waiter removed with a wisp of tow.

One day, late in the afternoon, as Lucius Brady was beaming on him through his spectacles, and indulging in an incisive criticism on the champagne at Government House, Stingaree quietly garroted him. A gag was in all readiness, likewise strips of coarse sheeting torn up for the purpose in the night. Black in the face, but with breath still in his body, the criminologist was carefully gagged and tied down to the bedstead, while his living image (at a casual glance) strolled with bent head, black sombrero, spectacles and frock-coat, first through the cold corridors and presently along the streets.

The heat of the pavement striking to his soles was the first of a hundred exquisite sensations; but Stingaree did not permit himself to savor one of them. Indeed, he had his work cut out to check the pace his heart dictated; and it was by admirable exercise of the will that he wandered along, deep to all appearance in a Camelot Classic which he had found in the criminologist's pocket; in reality blinded by the glasses, but all the more vigilant out of the corners of his eyes.

A suburb was the scene of these perambulations; had he but dared to lift his face, Stingaree might have caught a glimpse of the bluest of blue water; and his prison eyes hungered for the sight, but he would not raise his eyes so long as footsteps sounded on the same pavement. By taking judicious turnings, however, he drifted into a quiet road, with gray suburban bungalows on one side and building lots on the other. No step approached. He could look up at last. And the very bungalow that he was passing was shut up, yet furnished; the people had merely gone away, servants and all; he saw it at a glance from the newspapers plastering the windows which caught the sun. In an instant he was in the garden, and in another he had forced a side gate leading by an alley to backyard and kitchen door; but for many minutes he went no further than this gate, behind which he cowered, prepared with excuses in case he had already been observed.

It was in this interval that Stingaree recalled the season with a thrill; for it was Christmas week, and without a doubt the house would be empty till the New Year. Here was one port for the storm that must follow his escape. And a very pleasant port he found it on entering, after due precautionary delay.

Clearly the abode of young married people, the bungalow was fitted and furnished with a taste which appealed almost painfully to Stingaree; the drawing-room was draped in sheets, but the walls carried a few good engravings, some of which he remembered with a stab. It was the dressing-room, however, that he wanted, and the dressing-room made him rub his hands. The dainty establishment had no more luxurious corner, what with the fitted bath, circular shaving-glass, packed trouser-press, a row of boots on trees, and a fine old wardrobe full of hanging coats. Stingaree began by selecting his suit; and it may have been his vanity, or a strange longing to look for once what he once had been, but he could not resist the young man's excellent evening clothes.

"This fellow comes from Home," said he. "And they are spending their Christmas pretty far back, or he would have taken these with him."

He had wallowed in the highly enamelled bath, and was looking for a towel when he saw his head in the shaving-glass; he was dry enough before he could think of anything else. There was a dilemma, obvious yet unforeseen. That shaven head! Purple and fine linen could not disguise the convict's crop; a wig was the only hope; but to wear a wig one must first try it on-and let the perruquier call the police. The knot was Gordian. And yet, desperately as Stingaree sought unravelment, he was at the same time subconsciously as deep in a study of a face so unfamiliar that at first he had scarcely known it for his own. It was far leaner than of old; it was no longer richly tanned; and the mouth called louder than ever for a mustache. The hair, what there was of it, seemed iron-gray. It had certainly receded at the temples. What a pity, while it was about it — —

Stingaree clapped his hands; his hunt for the razor was feverish, tremulous. Such a young man must have many razors; he had, he had-here they were. Oh, young man blessed among young men!

It was quite dark when a gentleman in evening clothes, light overcoat, and opera hat, sallied forth into the quiet road. Quiet as it was, however, a whistle blew as he trod the pavement, and his hour or two of liberty seemed at an end. His long term in prison had mixed Stingaree's ideas of the old country and the new; he had forgotten that it is the postmen who blow the whistles in Australia. Yet this postman stopped him on the spot.

"Beg your pardon, sir, but if it's quite convenient may I ask you for the Christmas-box you was kind enough to promise me?"

"I think you are mistaking me for someone else," said Stingaree.

"Why, so I am, sir! I thought you came out of Mr. Brinton's house."

"Sorry to disappoint you," said the convict. "If I only had change you should have some of it, in spite of your mistake; but, unfortunately, I have none."

He had, however, a handsome pair of opera-glasses, which he converted into change (on the gratuitous plea that he had forgotten his purse) at the first pawnbroker's on the confines of the city. The pawnbroker talked Greek to him at once.

"It's a pity you won't be able to see 'er, sir, as well as 'ear 'er," said he.

"Perhaps they have them on hire in the theatre," replied Stingaree at a venture. The pawnbroker's face instantly advised him that his observation was wide of the obscure mark.

"The theatre! You won't 'ear 'er at any theatre in Sydney, nor yet in the Southern 'Emisphere. Town 'Alls is the only lay for 'Ilda Bouverie out 'ere!"

At first the name conveyed nothing to Stingaree. Yet it was not wholly unfamiliar.

"Of course," said he. "The Town Hall I meant."

The pawnbroker leered as he put down a sovereign and a shilling.

"What a season she's 'aving, sir!"

"Ah! What a season!"

And Stingaree wagged his opera-hatted head.

"'Undreds of pounds' worth of flowers flung on to every platform, and not a dry eye in the place!"

"I know," said the feeling Stingaree.

"It's wonderful to think of this 'ere Colony prodoocin' the world's best primer donner!"

"It is, indeed."

"When you think of 'er start."

"That's true."

The pawnbroker leant across his counter and leered more than ever in his customer's face.

"They say she ain't no better than she ought to be!"

"Really?"

"It's right, too; but what can you expect of a primer donner whose fortune was made by a blood-thirsty bushranger like that there Stingaree?"

"You little scurrilous wretch!" cried the bushranger, and flung out of the shop that second.

It was a miracle. He remembered everything now. Then he had done the world a service as well as the woman! He gave thanks for the guinea in his pocket, and asked his way to the Town Hall. And as he marched down the middle of the lighted streets the first flock of newsboys came flying in his face.

"Escape of Stingaree! Escape of Stingaree! Cowardly Outrage on Famous Author! Escape of Stingaree!!"

The damp pink papers were in the hands of the overflow crowd outside the hall; his own name was already in every mouth, continually coupled with that of the world-renowned Hilda Bouverie. It did not deter the convict from elbowing his way through the mass that gloated over his deed exactly as they would have gloated over his destruction on the gallows. "I have my ticket; I have been detained," he told the police; and at the last line of defence he whispered, "A guinea for standing-room!" And the guinea got it.

It was the interval between parts one and two. He thought of that other interval, when he had made such a different entry at the same juncture; the other concert-room would have gone some fifty times into this. All at once fell a hush, and then a rising thunder of applause, and some one requested Stingaree to remove his hat; he did so, and a cold creeping of the shaven flesh reminded him of his general position and of this particular peril. But no one took any notice of him or of his head. And it was not Hilda Bouverie this time; it was a pianiste in violent magenta and elaborate lace, whose performance also was loud and embroidered. Followed a beautiful young barytone whom Miss Bouverie had brought from London in her pocket for the tour. He sang three little songs very charmingly indeed; but there was no encore. The gods were burning for their own; perfunctory plaudits died to a dramatic pause.

And then, and then, amid deafening salvos a dazzling vision appeared upon the platform, came forward with the carriage of a conscious queen, stood bowing and beaming in the gloss and glitter of fabric and of gem that were yet less radiant than herself. Stingaree stood inanimate between stamping feet and clapping hands. No; he would never have connected this magnificent woman with the simple bush girl in the unpretentious frocks that he recalled as clearly as her former self. He had looked for less finery, less physical development, less, indeed, of the grand operatic *tout-ensemble*. But acting ended with her smile, and much of the old innocent simplicity came back as the lips parted in song. And her song had not been spoilt by riches and adulation; her song had not sacrificed sweetness to artifice; there was even more than the old magic in her song.

”Is this a dream?

Then waking would be pain!

Oh! do not wake me;

Let me dream again.”

It was no new number even then; even Stingaree had often heard it, and heard great singers go the least degree flat upon the first “dream.” He listened critically. Hilda Bouverie was not one of the delinquents. Her intonation was as perfect as that of the great violinists, her high notes had the rarefied quality of the E string finely touched. It was a flawless, if a purely popular, performance; and the musical heart of one listener in that crowded room was too full for mere applause. But he waited with patient curiosity for the encore, waited while courtesy after courtesy was given in vain. She had to yield; she yielded with a winning grace. And the first bars of the new song set one full heart beating, so that the earlier words were lost upon his brain.

”She ran before me in the meads;

And down this world-worn track

She leads me on; but while she leads

She never gazes back.

”And yet her voice is in my dreams,

To witch me more and more;

That wooing voice! Ah me, it seems

Less near me than of yore.

”Lightly I sped when hope was high,

And youth beguiled the chase;

I follow-follow still; but I

Shall never see her Face.”

So the song ended; and in the ultimate quiet the need of speech came over Stingaree.

“‘The Unrealized Ideal,’” he informed a neighbor.

"Rather!" rejoined the man, treating the stale news as a mere remark. "We never let her off without that."

"I suppose not," said Stingaree.

"It's the song the bushranger forced her to sing at the back-block concert, and it made her fortune! Good old Stingaree! By the way, I heard somebody behind me say he had escaped. That can't be true?"

"The newsboys were yelling it as I came along late."

"Well," said Stingaree's neighbor, "if he has escaped, and I for one don't hope he hasn't, this is where he ought to be. Just the sort of thing he'd do, too. Good old sportsman, Stingaree!"

It was an embarrassing compliment, eye to eye and foot to foot, wedged in a crowd. The bushranger did not fish for any more; neither did he wait to hear Hilda Bouverie sing again, though this cost him much. But he had one more word with his neighbor before he went.

"You don't happen to know where she's staying, I suppose? I've met her once or twice, and I might call."

The other smiled as on some suicidal moth.

"There's only one place good enough for a star like her in Sydney."

"And that is?"

"Government House."

His Excellency of the moment was a young nobleman of sporting proclivities and your true sportsman's breadth of mind. He was immensely popular with all sects and sections but the aggressively puritanical and the narrowly austere. He graced the theatre with his constant presence, the Turf with his own horses. His entertainment was lavish, and in quality far above the gubernatorial average. Late life and soul of exalted circle, he was hide-bound by few of the conventional trammels that distinguished the older type of peer to which the Colonies had been accustomed. It was the obvious course for such a Governor and his kindred lady to insist upon making the great Miss Bouverie their guest for the period of her professional sojourn in the capital; and a semi-Bohemian supper at the Government House was but a characteristic *finale* to her first great concert.

The *prima donna* sat on the Governor's right, and at the proper point his Excellency sang her praises in a charmingly informal speech, which delighted and amused the press men, actors and actresses whom he had collected for the occasion. Only the guest of honor looked a little weary and condescending; she had a sufficient experience of such entertainments in London, where the actors were all London actors, the authors and journalists men whose names one knew. Mere peers were no great treat either; in a word, Hilda Bouverie was not a little spoilt. She had lost the girl's glad outlook on the world, which some women keep until old age. There were stories about her which would have accounted for a deeper deterioration. Yet she was the Governor's guest, and her behavior not unworthy of the honor. On him at least she smiled, and her real smile, less expansive than the platform counterfeit, had still its genuine sweetness, its winning flashes; and, at its worst, it was more sad than bitter.

To-night the woman was an exhausted artist-unnerved, unstrung, unfitted for the world, yet only showing it in a languid appreciation which her host and hostess were the first to understand. Indeed, it was the great lady who carried her off, bowing with her platform bow, and smiling that smile, before the banquet was at an end.

A charming suite of rooms had been placed at the disposal of the *prima donna*; the boudoir was like a hot-house with the floral offerings of the evening, already tastefully arranged by madame's own Swiss maid. But the weary lady walked straight through to her bedroom, and sank with a sigh into the arm-chair before the glass.

"Who brought this?" she asked, peevishly picking a twisted note from amid the golden furniture of her toilet-table.

"I never saw it until this minute, madame!" the Swiss maid answered, in dismay. "It was not there ten minutes ago, I am sure, madame!"

"Where have you been since?"

"Down to the servants' hall, for one minute, madame."

Miss Bouverie read the note, and was an animated being in three seconds. She looked in the glass, the flush became her, and even as she looked all horror died in her dark-blue eyes. Instead there came a glitter that warned the maid.

"I am tired of you, Lea," cried madame. "You let people bring notes into my room, and you say you were only out of it a minute. Be good enough to leave me for the night. I can look after myself, for once!"

The maid protested, wept, but was expelled, and a key turned between them; then Hilda Bouverie read her note again: —

> "Escaped this afternoon. Came to your concert. Hiding in boudoir. Give me five minutes, or raise alarm, which you please. —STINGAREE."

So ran his words in pencil on her own paper, and they were true; she had heard at supper of the escape. Once more she looked in the glass. And to her own eyes in these minutes she looked years younger-there was a new sensation left in life!

A touch to her hair, a glance in the pier-glass, and all for a notorious convict broken prison! So into the boudoir with her grandest air; but again she locked the door behind her, and, sweeping round, beheld a bald man bowing to her in immaculate evening clothes.

"Are you the writer of a note found on my dressing-table?" she demanded, every syllable off the ice.

"I am."

"Then who are you, besides being an impudent forger?"

"You name the one crime I never committed," said he. "I am Stingaree."

And they gazed into each other's eyes; but not yet were hers to be believed.

"He only escaped this afternoon!"

"I am he."

"With a bald head?"

"Thanks to a razor."

"And in those clothes?"

"I found them where I found the razor. Look; they don't fit me as well as they might."

And he drew nearer, flinging out an abbreviated sleeve; but she looked all the harder in his face.

"Yes. I begin to remember your face; but it has changed."

"It has gazed on prison walls for many years."

"I heard . . . I was grieved . . . but it was bound to come."

"It may come again. I care very little, after this!"

And his dark eyes shone, his deep voice vibrated; then he glanced over a shrugged shoulder toward the outer door, and Hilda darted as if to turn that key too, but there was none to turn.

"It ought to happen at once," she said, "and through me."

"But it will not."

His assurance annoyed her; she preferred his homage.

"I know what you mean," she cried. "You did me a service years ago. I am not to forget it!"

"It is not I who have kept it before your mind."

"Perhaps not; but that's why you come to me to-night."

Stingaree looked upon the spirited, spoilt beauty in her satin and diamonds and pearls; villain as he was, he held himself at her mercy, but he was not going to kneel to her for that. He saw a woman who had heard the truth from very few men, a nature grown in mastery as his own had inevitably shrunk: it was worth being at large to pit the old Adam still remaining to him against the old Eve in this petted darling of the world. But false protestations were no counters in his game.

"Miss Bouverie," said Stingaree, "you may well suppose that I have borne you in mind all these years. As a matter of honest fact, when I first heard your name this evening, I was slow to connect it with any human being. You look angry. I intend no insult. If you have not forgotten the life I was leading before, you would very readily understand that I have never heard your name from those days to this. That is my misfortune, if also my own fault. It should suffice that, when I did remember, I came at my peril to hear you sing, and that before I dreamt of coming an inch further. But I heard them say, both in the hall and outside, that you owed your start to me; now one thinks of it, it must have been a rather striking advertisement; and I reflected that not another soul in Sydney can possibly owe me anything at all. So I came straight to you, without thinking twice about it. Criminal as I have been, and am, my one thought was and is that I deserve some little consideration at your hands."

"You mean money?"

"I have not a penny. It would make all the difference to me. And I give you my word, if that is any satisfaction to you, I would be an honest man from this time forth!"

"You actually ask me to assist a criminal and escaped convict-me, Hilda Bouverie, at my own absolute risk!"

"I took a risk for you nine years ago, Miss Bouverie; it was all I did take," said Stingaree, "at the concert that made your name."

"And you rub it in," she told him. "You rub it in!"

"I am running for my life!" he exclaimed, in answer. "It wouldn't have been necessary-that would have been enough for the Miss Bouverie I knew then. But you are different; you are another being, you are a woman of the world; your heart, your heart is dead and gone!"

He cut her to it, none the less; he could not have inflicted a deeper wound. The blood leapt to her face and neck; she cried out at the insult, the indignity, the outrage of it all; and crying she darted to the door.

It was locked.

She turned on Stingaree.

"You dared to lock the door-you dared! Give me the key this instant."

"I refuse."

"Very well! You have heard my voice; you shall hear it again!"

Her pale lips made the perfect round, her grand teeth gleamed in the electric light.

He arrested her, not with violence, but a shrug.

"I shall jump out of the window and break my neck. They don't take me twice-alive."

She glared at him in anger and contempt. He meant it. Then let him do it. Her eyes told him all that; but as they flashed, stabbing him, their expression altered, and in a trice her ear was to the keyhole.

"Something has happened," she whispered, turning a scared face up to him. "I hear your name. They have traced you here. They are coming! Oh! what are we to do?"

He strode over to the door.

"If you fear a scandal I can give myself up this moment and explain all."

He spoke eagerly. The thought was sudden. She rose up, looking in his eyes.

"No, you shall not," she said. Her hand flew out behind her, and in two seconds the brilliant room had click-clicked into a velvet darkness.

"Stand like a mouse," she whispered, and he heard her reach the inner door, where she stood like another.

Steps and voices came along the landing at a quick crescendo.

"Miss Bouverie! Miss Bouverie! Miss Bouverie!"

It was his Excellency's own gay voice. And it continued until with much noise Miss Bouverie flung her bedroom door wide open, put on the light within, ran across the boudoir, put on the boudoir light, and stooped to parley through the keyhole.

"The bushranger Stingaree has been traced to Government House."

"Good heavens!"

"One of your windows was seen open."

"He had not come in through it."

"Then you were heard raising your voice."

"That was to my maid. This is all through her. I don't know how to tell you, but she leaves me in the morning. Yes, yes, there was a man, but it was not Stingaree. I saw him myself through coming up early, but I let him go as he had come, to save a fuss."

"Through the window?"

"I am so ashamed!"

"Not a bit, Miss Bouverie. I am ashamed of bothering you. Confound the police!"

When the voices and steps had died away, Hilda Bouverie turned to Stingaree, her whole face shining, her deep blue eyes alight.

"There!" said she. "Could you have done that better yourself?"

"Not half so well."

"And you thought I could forget!"

"I thought nothing. I only came to you in my scrape."

After years of imprisonment he could speak of this life-and-death hazard as a scrape! She looked at him with admiring eyes; her personal triumph had put an end to her indignation.

"My poor Lea! I wonder how much she has heard? I shall have to tell her nearly all; she can wait for me at Melbourne or Adelaide, and I can pick her up on my voyage home. It will be no joke without her until then. I give her up for your sake!"

Stingaree hung his head. He was a changed man.

"And I," he said grimly-not pathetically —"and I am a convict who escaped by violence this afternoon."

Hilda smiled.

"I met Mr. Brady the other day," she said, "and I heard of him to-night. He is not going to die!"

He stared at her unscrupulous radiance.

"Do you wonder at me?" she said. "Did you never hear that musical people had no morals?"

And her smile bewitched him more and more.

"It explains us both!" declared Miss Bouverie. "But do you know what I have kept all these years?" she went on. "Do you know what has been my mascot, what I have had about me whenever I have sung in public, since and including that time at Yallarook? Can't you guess?"

He could not. She turned her back, he heard some gussets give, and the next moment she was holding a strange trophy in both hands.

It was a tiny silken bandolier, containing six revolver cartridges, with bullet and cap intact.

"Can't you guess now?" she gloried.

"No. I never missed them; they are not like any I ever had."

"Don't you remember the man who chased you out and misfired at you six times? He was the overseer on the station; his name may come back to me, but his face I shall never forget. He had a revolver in his pocket, but he dared not lower a hand. I took it out of his pocket and was to hand it up to him when I got the chance. Until then I was to keep it under my shawl. That was when I managed to unload every chamber. These are the cartridges I took out, and they have been my mascot ever since."

She looked years younger than she had seemed even singing in the Town Hall; but the lines deepened on the bushranger's face, and he stepped back from her a pace.

"So you saved my life," he said. "You had saved my life all the time. And yet I came to ask you to do as much for me as I had done for you!"

He turned away; his hands were clenched behind his back.

"I will do more," she cried, "if more could be done by one person for another. Here are jewels." She stripped her neck of its rope of pearls. "And here are notes." She dived into a bureau and thrust a handful upon him. "With these alone you should be able to get to England or America; and if you want more when you get there, write to Hilda Bouverie! As long as she has any, there will be some for you!"

Tears filled her eyes. The simplicity of her girlhood had come back to the seasoned woman of the world, at once spoiled and satiated with success. This was the other side of the artistic temperament which had enslaved her soul. She would swing from one extreme of wounded and vindictive vanity to this length of lawless nobility; now she could think of none but self, and now not of herself at all. Stingaree glanced toward the window.

"I can't go yet, I'm afraid."

"You sha'n't! Why should you?"

"But I still fear they may not be satisfied downstairs. I am ashamed to ask it-but will you do one little thing more for me?"

"Name it!"

"It is only to make assurance doubly sure. Go downstairs and let them see you; tell them more details, if you like. Go down as you are, and say that without your maid you could not find anything else to put on. I promise not to vanish with everything in your absence."

"You do promise?"

"On my-liberty!"

She looked in his face with a very wistful sweetness.

"If they were to find me out," she said, "I wonder how many years they would give *me*? I neither know nor care; it would be worth a few. I thought I had lived since I saw you last . . . but this is the best fun I have ever had . . . since Yallarook!"

She stood for a moment before opening the door that he unlocked for her, stood before him in all her flushed and brilliant radiance, and blew a kiss to him before she went.

The Governor was easily found. He was grieved at her troubling to descend at such an hour, and did not detain her five minutes in all. He thought she was in a fever, but that the fever became her beyond belief. Reassured on every point, Miss Bouverie was back in her room but a very few minutes after she had left it.

It was empty. She searched all over, first behind the curtains, then between the pedestals of the bureau, but Stingaree was nowhere in the room, and the bedroom door was still locked. It was a second look behind the curtains that revealed an open window and the scratch of a boot upon the white enamel. It was no breakneck drop into the shrubs.

So he had gone without a word, but also without breaking his word; for, with wet eyes and a white face, between anger and admiration, Hilda Bouverie had already discovered her bundle of notes and her rope of pearls.

There are no more tales of Stingaree; tongue never answered to the name again, nor was face ever recognized as his. He may have died that night; it is not very likely, since the young married man in the well-appointed bungalow, which had been broken into earlier in the day, missed a suit of clothes indeed, but not his evening clothes, which were found hung up neatly where he had left them; and it is regrettable to add that his opera-glasses were not the only article of a marketable character which could never be found on his return. There is none the less reason to believe that this was the last professional incident in one of the most incredible criminal careers of which there is any record in Australia. Whether he be dead or alive, back in the old country or still in the new, or, what is less likely, in prison under some other name, the gratifying fact remains that neither in Australia nor elsewhere has there been a second series of crimes bearing the stamp of Stingaree.

A Bride from the Bush

'She looked very fresh and buoyant in the summer morning.'

Chapter I
A Letter from Alfred

There was consternation in the domestic camp of Mr Justice Bligh on the banks of the Thames. It was a Sunday morning in early summer. Three-fourths of the family sat in ominous silence before the mockery of a well-spread breakfast-table: Sir James and Lady Bligh and their second son, Granville. The eldest son-the missing complement of this family of four-was abroad. For many months back, and, in fact, down to this very minute, it had been pretty confidently believed that the young man was somewhere in the wilds of Australia; no one had quite known where, for the young man, like most vagabond young men, was a terribly meagre corespondent; nor had it ever been clear why any one with leisure and money, and of no very romantic turn, should have left the beaten track of globe-trotters, penetrated to the wilderness, and stayed there-as Alfred Bligh had done. Now, however, all was plain. A letter from Brindisi, just received, explained everything; Alfred's movements, so long obscure, were at last revealed, and in a lurid light-that, as it were, of the bombshell that had fallen and burst upon the Judge's breakfast-table. For Alfred was on his way to England with an Australian wife; and this letter from Brindisi, was the first that his people had heard of it, or of her.

'Of course,' said Lady Bligh, in her calm and thoughtful manner, 'it was bound to happen sooner or later. It might have happened very much sooner; and, indeed, I often wished that it would; for Alfred must be-what? Thirty?'

'Quite,' said Granville; 'I am nearly that myself.'

'Well, then,' said Lady Bligh gently, looking tenderly at the Judge (whose grave eyes rested upon the sunlit lawn outside), 'from one point of view —a selfish one-we ought to consider ourselves the most fortunate of parents. And this news should be a matter for rejoicing, as it would be, if-if it were only less sudden, and wild, and-and ——'

Her voice trembled; she could not go on.

'And alarming,' added Granville briskly, pulling himself together and taking an egg.

Then the Judge spoke.

'I should like,' he said, 'to hear the letter read slowly from beginning to end. Between us, we have not yet given it a fair chance; we have got only the drift of it; we may have overlooked something. Granville, perhaps you will read the letter aloud to your mother and me?'

Granville, who had just laid open his egg with great skill, experienced a moment's natural annoyance at the interruption. To stop to read a long letter now was, he felt, treating a good appetite shabbily, to say nothing of the egg. But this was not a powerful feeling; he concealed it. He had a far stronger appetite than the mere relish for food; the intellectual one. Granville had one of the nicest intellects at the Junior Bar. His intellectual appetite was so hearty, and even voracious, that it could be gratified at all times and places, and not only by the loaves and fishes of full-bodied wit, but by the crumbs and fishbones of legal humour-such as the reading aloud of indifferent English and ridiculous sentiments in tones suitable to the most chaste and classic prose. This he had done in court with infinite gusto, and he did it now as he would have done it in court.

' "My dear Mother" ' (he began reading, through a single eyeglass that became him rather well), —' "Before you open this letter you'll see that I'm on my way home! I am sorry I haven't written you for so long, and *very* sorry I didn't before I sailed. I should think when I last wrote was from Bindarra. But I must come at once to my great news-which Heaven knows how I'm to tell you, and how you'll take it when I do. Well, I will, in two words-the fact is, *I'm married*! My wife is the daughter of 'the boss of Bindarra' —in other words, a 'squatter' with a 'run' (or territory) as big as a good many English counties.' "

The crisp forensic tones were dropped for an explanatory aside. 'He evidently *means* —father' (Granville nearly said 'my lord,' through force of habit), 'that his father-in-law is the squatter; not his wife, which is what he *says*. He writes in such a slipshod style. I should also think he means that the territory in question is equal in size to certain English counties, individually (though this I venture to doubt), and not-what you would infer-to several counties put together. His literary manner was always detestable, poor old chap; and, of course, Australia was hardly likely to improve it.'

The interpolation was not exactly ill-natured; but it was received in silence; and Granville's tones, as he resumed the reading, were even more studiously unsympathetic than before.

' "Of my Bride I will say very little; for you will see her in a week at most. As for myself, I can only tell you, dear Mother, that I am the very luckiest and happiest man on earth!" ' ('A brave statement,' Granville murmured in parenthesis; 'but they all make it.') '"She is typically Australian, having indeed been born and bred in the Bush, and is the first to admit it, being properly proud of her native land; but, if you knew the Australians as I do, this would not frighten you. Far from it, for the typical Australian is one of the very highest if not *the* highest development of our species."' (Granville read that sentence with impressive gravity, and with such deference to the next as to suggest no kind of punctuation, since the writer had neglected it.) '"But as you, my dear Mother, are the very last person in the world to be prejudiced by mere mannerisms, I won't deny that she has one or two —*though, mind you, I like them!* And, at least, you may look forward to seeing the most beautiful woman you ever saw in your life-though I say it.

'"Feeling sure that you will, as usual, be 'summering' at Twickenham, I make equally sure that you will be able and willing to find room for us; at the same time, we will at once commence looking out for a little place of our own in the country, with regard to which we have plans which will keep till we see you. But, while we are with you, I thought I would be able to show my dear girl the principal sights of the Old Country, which, of course, are mostly in or near town, and which she is dying to see.

'"Dear Mother, I know I *ought* to have consulted you, or at least told you, beforehand. The whole thing was impulsive, I admit. But if you and my Father will forgive me for this-take my word for it, you will soon find out that it is all you have to forgive! Of course, I am writing to my Father as much as to you in this letter-as he will be the first to understand. With dearest love to you both (not forgetting Gran), in which Gladys joins me (though she doesn't know I am saying so).

'"Believe me as ever,
'"Your affectionate Son,

'"Alfred."'

'Thank you,' said the Judge, shortly.

The soft dark eyes of Lady Bligh were wet with tears.

'I think,' she said, gently, 'it is a very tender letter. I know of no man but Alfred that could write such a boyish, simple letter-not that I don't enjoy your clever ones, Gran. But then Alfred never yet wrote to me without writing himself down the dear, true-hearted, affectionate fellow he is; only here, of course, it comes out doubly. But does he not mention her maiden name?'

'No, he doesn't,' said Granville. 'You remarked the Christian name, though? Gladys! I must say it sounds unpromising. Mary, Eliza, Maria — —one would have rather liked a plain, homely, farm-yard sort of name for a squatter's daughter. But Ermyntrude, or Elaine, or Gladys! These are names of ill-omen; you expect de Vere coming after them, or even worse.'

'What *is* a squatter, Gran?' asked Lady Bligh abruptly.

'A squatter? I don't know,' said Gran, paring the ham daintily as he answered. 'I don't know, I'm sure; something to do with bushranging, I should imagine-but I really can't tell you.'

But there was a set of common subjects of which Gran was profoundly and intentionally ignorant; and it happened that Greater Britain was one of them. If he had known for certain whether Sydney (for instance) was a town or a colony or an island, he would have kept the knowledge carefully to himself, and been thoroughly ashamed of it. And it was the same with other subjects understood of the Board-scholars. This queer temper of mind is not indeed worth analysing; nevertheless, it is peculiar to a certain sort of clever young fellows, and Granville Bligh was a very fair specimen of the clever young fellow. He was getting on excellently at the Bar, for so young a man. He also wrote a little, with plenty of impudence and epigram, if nothing else. But this was not his real line. Still, what he did at all, he did more or less cleverly. There was cleverness in every line of his smooth dark face; there was uncommon shrewdness in his clear gray eyes. His father had the same face and the same eyes-with this difference added to the differences naturally due to age: there were wisdom, and dignity, and humanity in the face and glance of the Judge; but the nobility of expression thus given was not inherited by the Judge's younger son.

The Judge spoke again, breaking a silence of some minutes: —

'As you say, Mildred, it seems to have been all very wild and sudden; but when we have said this, we have probably said the worst there is to say. At least, let us hope so. Of my own knowledge many men have gone to Australia, as Alfred went, and come back with the best of wives. I seem to have heard, Granville, that that is what Merivale did; and I have met few more admirable women than Mrs Merivale.'

'It certainly is the case, sir,' said Granville, who had been patronised to some extent by Merivale, Q.C. 'But Mrs Merivale was scarcely "born and bred in the Bush"; and if she had what poor Alfred, perhaps euphemistically, calls "mannerisms" —I have detected no traces of any myself-when Merivale married her, at least she had money.'

'Your sister-in-law may have "money," too,' said Sir James, with somewhat scornful emphasis. 'That is of no consequence at all. Your brother has enough for both, and more than enough for a bachelor.'

There was no need to remind the young man of that; it had been a sore point, and even a raw one, with Granville since his boyhood; for it was when the brothers were at school together-the younger in the Sixth Form, the elder in the Lower Fifth-and it was already plain which one would benefit the most by 'private means,' that a relative of Sir James had died, leaving all her money to Alfred.

Granville coloured slightly-very slightly-but observed: —

'It is a good thing he has.'

'What do you mean?' the Judge asked, with some asperity.

'That he needs it,' said Granville, significantly.

Sir James let the matter drop, and presently, getting up, went out by the open French window, and on to the lawn. It was not his habit to snub his son; he left that to the other judges, in court. But Lady Bligh remonstrated in her own quiet way —a way that had some effect even upon Granville.

'To sneer at your brother's inferior wits, my son, is not in quite nice taste,' she said; 'and I may tell you, now, that I did not at all care for your comments upon his letter.'

Granville leant back in his chair and laughed pleasantly.

'How seriously you take one this morning! But it is small wonder that you should, for the occasion is a sufficiently serious one, in all conscience; and indeed, dear mother, I am as much put out as you are. Nay,' Granville added, smiling blandly, 'don't say that you're *not* put out, for I can see that you *are*. And we have reason to be put out' —he became righteously indignant —'all of us. I wouldn't have thought it of Alfred, I wouldn't indeed! No matter whom he wanted to marry, he ought at least to have written first, instead of being in such a violent hurry to bring her over. It is treating *you*, dear mother, to say the best of it, badly; and as for the Judge, it is plain that he is quite upset by the unfortunate affair.'

'We have no right to assume that it is unfortunate, Gran.'

'Well, I hope it is not, that's *all*,' said Gran, with great emphasis. 'I hope it is not, for poor Alfred's sake. Yet, as you know, mother, he's the very kind of old chap to get taken in and imposed upon; and —I tell you frankly —I tremble for him. If he is the victim of a designing woman, I am sorry for him, from my soul I am! If he has married in haste-and he has-to repent at leisure-as he may-though this is trite and detestable language, I pity him, from my soul I do! You have already rebuked me —I don't say unjustly-for making what, I admit, had the appearance of an odious and egotistical comparison; I will guard against conveying a second impression of that kind; yet I think I may safely say, without bragging, that I know the world rather better than old Alfred does. Well, I have, I will not say my fears, but my dreads; and I cannot help having them. If they are realised, no one will sympathise with poor dear Alfred more deeply than I shall.'

Lady Bligh looked keenly at her eloquent son; a half-smile played about her lips: she understood him, to some extent.

'But what if your fears are *not* realised?' she said, quietly.

'Why, then,' said Gran, less fluently, 'then I —oh, of course, I shall be delighted beyond words; no one will be more delighted than I.'

'Then you shall see,' said Lady Bligh, rising, with a sweet and hopeful smile, 'that is how it is going to turn out; I have a presentiment that it will all turn out for the best. So there is only one thing to be done-we must prepare to welcome her to our hearts!'

Granville shrugged his shoulders, but his mother did not see him; she had gone quietly from the room and was already climbing (slowly, for she was stout) the stairs that led up to her own snuggery on the first floor. This little room was less of a boudoir than a study, and more like an office than either, for it was really a rather bare little room. Its most substantial piece of furniture was a large unlovely office-table, and its one picture was framed in the window-sashes —a changeful picture of sky and trees, and lawn and river, painted this morning in the most radiant tints of early summer. At the office-table, which was littered with letters and pamphlets, Lady Bligh spent diligent hours every day. She was a person of both mental and manual activity, with public sympathies and interests that entailed an immense correspondence. She was, indeed, one of the most charitable and benevolent of women, and was to some extent a public woman. But we have nothing to do with her public life, and, on this Sunday morning, no more had she.

There were no pictures on the walls, but there were photographs upon the chimney-piece. Lady Bligh stood looking at them for an unusually long time-in fact, until the sound of the old church bells, coming in through the open window, called her away.

One of the photographs was of the Judge-an excellent one, in which the dear old gentleman looked his very best, dignified but kindly. Another was a far too flattering portrait of Granville. A third portrait was that of an honest, well-meaning, and rather handsome face, with calm dark eyes, exactly like Lady Bligh's; and this was the erratic Alfred. But the photograph that Lady Bligh looked at longest, and most fondly, was a faded one of Alfred and Granville as mere schoolboys. She loved her two sons so dearly! One of them was much changed, and becoming somewhat spoilt, to phrase it mildly; yet that son was rather clever, and his mother saw his talents through a strong binocular, and his faults with her eyes at the wrong end of it; and she loved him in spite of the change in him, and listened-at least with tolerance-to the airings of a wit that was always less good natured, and generally less keen, than she imagined it. But the other son had never changed at all; even his present fatal letter showed that. He was still a boy at heart —a wild, stupid, affectionate schoolboy. There was no denying it: in his mother's heart the elder son was the best beloved of the two.

And it was this one who had married with so much haste and mystery-the favourite son, the son with money, the son who might have married any one he pleased. It was hard to choke down prejudice when this son was bringing home a wife from the Bush, of all places!

What would she be like? What *could* she be like?

Chapter II
Home in Style

'He must be mad!' said Granville, flourishing a telegram in his hand.

'He must be very fond of her,' Lady Bligh replied, simply.

Granville held the telegram at arm's length, and slowly focussed it with his eyeglass. He had already declaimed it twice, once with horror in his voice, once with a running accompaniment of agreeable raillery. His third reading was purely compassionate, in accordance with his latest theory regarding the mental condition of the sender.

'"Arrived both well. Chartered launch take us Gravesend Twickenham; show her river. Join us if possible Westminster Bridge 3 o'clock. —Alfred."'

Granville sighed.

'Do you comprehend it, dear mother? I think I do, at last, though the prepositions *are* left to the imagination. He has saved at least twopence over those prepositions-which, of course, is an item, even in a ten-pound job.'

'You don't mean to say it will cost him ten pounds?'

'Every penny of it: it would cost you or me, or any ordinary person, at least a fiver. I am allowing for Alfred's being let in rather further than any one else would be.'

'At all events,' said Lady Bligh, 'you will do what he asks you; you will be at Westminster at the time he mentions?'

Granville shrugged his shoulders. 'Certainly, if you wish it.'

'I think it would be kind.'

'Then I will go, by all means.'

'Thank you-and Granville! I do wish you would give up sneering at your brother's peculiarities. He *does* do odd and impulsive things, we know; and there is no denying the extravagance of steaming up the river all the way from Gravesend. But, after all, he has money, and no doubt he wants to show his wife the Thames, and to bring her home in a pleasant fashion, full of pleasant impressions; and upon my word,' said Lady Bligh, 'I never heard of a prettier plan in my life! So go, my dear boy, and meet them, and make them happier still. If that is possible, no one could do it more gracefully than you, Gran!'

Granville acknowledged the compliment, and promised; and punctually at three he was at Westminster Bridge, watching with considerable interest the rapid approach of a large launch — a ridiculously large one for the small number of people on board. She had, in fact, only two passengers, though there was room for fifty. One of the two was Alfred, whose lanky figure was unmistakable at any distance; and the dark, straight, strapping young woman at his side was, of course, Alfred's wife.

The meeting between the brothers was hearty enough, but it might have been more entirely cordial had there been a little less effusiveness on one side-not Granville's. But Alfred-who was dressed in rough tweed clothes of indeterminate cut, and had disfigured himself with a beard-was so demonstrative in his greeting that the younger brother could not help glancing anxiously round to assure himself that there was no one about who knew him. It was a relief to him to be released and introduced to the Bride.

'Gladys, this is Gran come to meet us-as I knew he would-like the brick he is, and always was!'

Gran was conscious of being scrutinised keenly by the finest dark eyes he had ever encountered in his life; but the next moment he was shaking his sister-in-law's hand, and felt that it was a large hand —a trifling discovery that filled Granville with a subtle sense of satisfaction. But the Bride was yet to open her lips.

'How do you do?' she said, the olive tint of her cheek deepening slightly. 'It was awfully nice of you to come; I *am* glad to see you —I have heard such lots about you, you know!'

It was said so glibly that the little speech was not, perhaps, exactly extempore: and it was spoken-every word of it-with a twang that, to sensitive ears like Granville's, was simply lacerating.

Granville winced, and involuntarily dropped his eyeglass; but otherwise he kept a courteous countenance, and made a sufficiently civil reply.

As for Alfred, he, of course, noticed nothing unusual in his wife's accents; he was used to them; and, indeed, it seemed to Granville that Alfred spoke with a regrettable drawl himself.

'You've got to play showman, Gran,' said he, when some natural questions had been hurriedly put and tersely answered (by which time they were opposite Lambeth Palace). 'I've been trying, but I'm a poor hand at it; indeed, I'm a poor Londoner, and always was: below Blackfriars I was quite at sea, and from here to Richmond I'm as ignorant as a brush.'

'No; he's no good at all,' chimed in the Bride, pleasantly.

'Well, I'm not well up in it, either,' said Gran, warily.

This was untrue, however. Granville knew his Thames better than most men-it was one of the things he *did* know. But he had a scholar's reverence for classic ground; and in a young man who revered so very little, this was remarkable, if it was not affectation. Granville would have suffered tortures rather than gravely point out historic spots to a person whose ideas of history probably went no farther back than the old Colonial digging days; he would have poured sovereigns into the sea as readily as the coin of sacred associations into Gothic ears. At least, so he afterwards said, when defending his objection to interpreting the Thames for his sister-in-law's benefit.

'What nonsense!' cried Alfred, good-humouredly. 'You know all about it-at all events, you used to. There-we've gone and let her miss Lambeth Palace! Look, dear, quick, while it's still in sight-that's where the Archbishop of Canterbury hangs out.'

'Oh,' said Gladys, 'I've heard of *him.*'

'And isn't that Cheyne Walk, or some such place, that we're coming to on the right there?' said Alfred.

'Yes,' said Granville, briefly; 'that's Cheyne Walk.'

Luckily the Bride asked no questions-indeed, she was inclined to be silent-for of all localities impossible to discuss with an uneducated person, Granville felt that Chelsea and Cheyne Walk were the most completely out of the question. And that the Bride was a sadly uneducated person was sufficiently clear, if only from her manner of speaking. Granville accepted the fact with creditable equanimity-he had prophesied as much-and sat down to smoke a cigarette and to diagnose, if he could, this new and wonderful dialect of his sister-in-law. It was neither Cockney nor Yankee, but a nasal blend of both: it was a lingo that declined to let the vowels run alone, but trotted them out in ill-matched couples, with discordant and awful consequences; in a word, it was Australasiatic of the worst description. Nor was the speech of Alfred free from the taint-Alfred, whose pronunciation at least had been correct before he went out; while the common colloquialisms of the pair made Granville shudder.

'If I did not hope for such surprisingly good looks,' said he to himself, 'yet even *I* was not prepared for *quite* so much vulgarity! Poor dear Alfred!'

And Granville sighed, complacently.

Yet, as she leant upon the rail in the summer sunlight, silent and pensive, there was certainly no suggestion of vulgarity in her attitude; it was rather one of unstudied grace and ease. Nor was there anything at all vulgar in the quiet travelling dress that fitted her tall full form so closely and so well. Nor was her black hair cut down to within an inch of her eyebrows-as, of course, it should have been-or worn in a fringe at all. Nor was there anything the least objectionable in the poise of the small graceful head, or in the glance of the bold dark eyes, or in the set of the full, firm, crimson lips; and thus three more excellent openings-for the display of vulgarity-were completely thrown away. In fact, if she had never spoken, Granville would have been at a loss to find a single fault in her. Alas! about her speech there could be no two opinions-it bewrayed her.

Presently Alfred sat down beside his brother, and began to tell him everything, and did all the talking; while the Bride still stood watching the shifting panorama of the banks, and the golden sunlight upon the water, and the marvellous green of all green things. It was practically her first experience of this colour. And still she asked no questions, her interest being perhaps too intense; and so the showman-business was forgotten, to the great relief of Granville; and the time slipped quickly by. At last-and quite suddenly-the Bride clapped her hands, and turned with sparkling eyes to her husband: they had entered that splendid reach below Richmond, and the bridges were in sight, with the hill beyond.

'I give this best!' she cried. 'It *does* knock spots out of the Yarra and the Murray after all!'

Alfred glanced uneasily at his brother, but found an impassive face.

'Come, old fellow,' said Alfred, 'do your duty; jump up and tell her about these places.'

So at last Granville made an effort to do so; he got up and went to the side of the Bride; and presently he was exercising a discreet if not a delicate vein of irony, that was peculiarly his own.

'That was Kew we passed just now-you must see the gardens there,' he said; 'and this is Richmond.'

'Kew and Richmond!' exclaimed the Bride, innocently. 'How rum! We have a Kew and a Richmond in Melbourne.'

'Ah!' said Gran. 'I don't fancy the theft was on our side. But look at this gray old bridge-picturesque, isn't it? —and I dare say you have nothing like it out there. And there, you see-up on the left yonder-is Richmond Hill. Rather celebrated, Richmond Hill: you may have heard of it; there was a lass that lived there once.'

'Yes-what of her?'

'Oh, she was neat and had sweet eyes-or sweet, with neat eyes —I really forget which. And there was a somebody or other who said he'd resign any amount of crowns-the number wasn't specified-to call her his. He was pretty safe in saying that-unless, indeed, he meant crown-*pieces* —which, now I think of it, would be rather an original reading.'

'Alfred,' said the Bride abruptly, 'are we nearly there?'

'Not far off,' said Alfred.

Granville bit his lip. 'We are very nearly there,' he said; 'this is the beginning of Twickenham.'

'Then where's the Ferry?' said the Bride. 'I know all about "Twickenham Ferry"; we once had a storekeeper —a new chum-who used to sing about it like mad. Show it me.'

'There, then: it crosses by the foot of the island: it's about to cross now. Now, in a minute, I'll show you Pope's old place; we don't go quite so far-in fact, here we are — but you'll be able just to see it, I think.'

'The Pope!' said Gladys. 'I never knew *he* lived in England!'

'No more he does. Not *the* Pope —*Pope*; a man of the name of Pope: a scribbler: a writing-man: in fact, a poet.'

The three were leaning over the rail, shoulder to shoulder, and watching eagerly for the first glimpse of the Judge's retreat through the intervening trees. Granville was in the middle. The Bride glanced at him sharply, and opened her lips to say something which-judging by the sudden gleam of her dark eyes-might possibly have been rather too plain-spoken. But she never said it; she merely left Granville's side, and went round to the far side of her husband, and slipped her hand through his arm. Granville walked away.

'Are we there?' whispered Gladys.

'Just, my darling. Look, that's the house-the one with the tall trees and the narrow lawn.'

'*Hoo-jolly-ray!*'

'Hush, Gladdie! For Heaven's sake don't say anything like that before my mother! There she is on the lawn, waving her handkerchief. We'll wave ours back to her. The dear mother! Whatever you do, darling girl, don't say anything of that sort to *her*. It would be Greek to my mother and the Judge, and they mightn't like it.'

Chapter III
Pins and Needles

Slanting mellow sunbeams fell pleasantly upon the animated face of the Bride, as she stepped lightly across the gangway from the steam-launch to the lawn; and, for one moment, her tall supple figure stood out strikingly against the silver river and the pale eastern sky. In that moment a sudden dimness came over Lady Bligh's soft eyes, and with outstretched arms she hurried forward to press her daughter to her heart. It was a natural motherly impulse, but, even if Lady Bligh had stopped to think, she would have made sure of being met half-way. She was not, however, and the mortification of the moment was none the less intense because it was invisible. The Bride refused to be embraced. She was so tall that it would have been impossible for Lady Bligh to kiss her against her will, but it never came to that; the unbending carriage and man-like outstretched hand spoke plainly and at once-and were understood. But Lady Bligh coloured somewhat, and it was an unfortunate beginning, for every one noticed it; and the Judge, who was hurrying towards them across the lawn at the time, there and then added a hundred per cent of ceremony to his own greeting, and received his daughter-in-law as he would have received any other stranger.

'I am very happy to see you,' he said, when Alfred had introduced them-the Judge waited for that. 'Welcome, indeed; and I hope you have received agreeable impressions of our River Thames.'

'Oh, rather!' said Gladys, smiling unabashed upon the old gentleman. 'We've no rivers like it in Australia. I've just been saying so.'

Granville, who had been watching for a change in his mother's expression when she should first hear the Bride speak, was not disappointed. Lady Bligh winced perceptibly. Judges, however, may be relied upon to keep their countenances, if anybody may; it is their business; Sir James was noted for it, and he merely said dryly, 'I suppose not,' and that was all.

And then they all walked up the lawn together to where tea awaited them in the veranda. The Bride's dark eyes grew round at sight of the gleaming silver teapot and dainty Dresden china; she took her seat in silence in a low wicker chair, while the others talked around her; but presently she was heard exclaiming: —

'No, thanks, no milk, and I'll sweeten it myself, please.'

'But it's cream,' said Lady Bligh, good-naturedly, pausing with the cream-jug in the air.

'The same thing,' returned Gladys. 'We never took any on the station, so I like it better without; and it can't be too strong, if you please. We didn't take milk,' she turned to explain to Sir James, 'because, in a general way, our only cow was a tin one, and we preferred no milk at all. We ran sheep, you see, not cattle.'

'A tin cow!' said Sir James.

'She means they only had condensed milk,' said Alfred, roaring with laughter.

'But our cow is *not* tin,' said Lady Bligh, smiling, as she still poised the cream-jug; 'will you not change your mind?'

'No, thanks,' said the Bride stoutly.

It was another rather awkward moment, for it did seem as though Gladys was disagreeably independent. And Alfred, of all people, made the moment more awkward still, and, indeed, more uncomfortable than any that had preceded it.

'Gladdie,' he exclaimed in his airiest manner, 'you're a savage! A regular savage, as I've told you over and over again!'

No one said anything. Gladys smiled, and Alfred chuckled over his pleasantry. But it was a pleasantry that contained a most unpleasant truth. The others felt this, and it made them silent. It was a relief to all-with the possible exception of the happy pair, neither of whom appeared to be over-burdened with self-consciousness —when Lady Bligh carried off Gladys, and delivered her in her own room into the safe keeping of Miss Bunn, her appointed maid.

This girl, Bunn, presently appeared in the servants' hall, sat down in an interesting way, and began to twirl her thumbs with great ostentation. Being questioned, in fulfilment of her artless design, she said that she was not wanted upstairs. Being further questioned, she rattled off a string of the funny things Mrs '*H*alfred' had said to her along with a feeble imitation of Mrs '*H*alfred's' very funny way of saying them. This is not a matter of importance; but it was the making of Bunn below stairs; so long as Mrs Alfred remained in the house, her maid's popularity as a kitchen entertainer was assured.

The Bride wished to be alone; at all events she desired no personal attendance. What should she want with a maid? A lady's-maid was a 'fixing' she did not understand, and did not wish to understand; she had said so plainly, and that she didn't see where Miss Bunn 'came in'; and then Miss Bunn had gone out, in convulsions. And now the Bride was alone at last, and stood pensively gazing out of her open window at the wonderful green trees and the glittering river, at the deep cool shadows and the pale evening sky; and delight was in her bold black eyes; yet a certain sense of something not quite as it ought to be —a sensation at present vague and undefined-made her graver than common. And so she stood until the door was burst suddenly open, and a long arm curled swiftly round her waist, and Alfred kissed her.

'My darling! tell me quickly — —'

'Stop!' said Gladys. 'I'll bet I guess what it is you want me to tell you! Shall I?'

'Yes, if you can, for I certainly do want you to tell me something.'

'Then it's what I think of your people!'

'How you like them,' Alfred amended. 'Yes, that was it. Well, then?'

'Well, then —I like your mother. She has eyes like yours, Alfred, large and still and kind, and she is big and motherly.'

'Then, oh, my darling, why on earth didn't you kiss her?'

'Kiss her? Not *me*! Why should I?'

'She meant to kiss you; I saw she did.'

'Don't you believe it! Even if she had, it would have been only for your sake. You wait a little bit; wait till she knows me, and if she wants to kiss me then-let her!'

Alfred was pained by his young wife's tone; he had never before heard her speak so strangely, and her eyes were wistful. He did not quite understand her, but he did not try to, then; he varied the subject.

'How about Gran?'

'Oh, that Gran!' cried Gladys. 'I can't suffer him at all.'

'Can't suffer Gran! What on earth do you mean, Gladys?'

'I mean that he was just a little beast in the boat! You think he was as glad to see you as you were him, because you judge by yourself; but not a bit of it; I know better. It was all put on with him, and a small "all" too. Then you asked him to tell me about the places we passed, and he only laughed at me. Ah, you may laugh at people without moving a muscle, but people may see it all the same; and I did, all along; and just before we got here I very near told him so. If I had, I'd have given him one, you stake your life!'

'I'm glad you didn't,' said Alfred devoutly, but in great trouble. '*I* never heard him say anything to rankle like that; I thought he was very jolly, if you ask me. And really, Gladdie, old Gran's as good a fellow as ever lived; besides which, he has all the brains of the family.'

'Perhaps,' said Gladys, softening, 'my old man has got a double share of something better than brains!'

'Nonsense, darling! But at least the Judge was pleasant; what did you think of the Judge?'

'I funked him.'

'Good gracious! Why?'

'He's so dreadfully dignified; and he looks you through and through-not nastily, like Gran does, but as if you were something funny in a glass case.'

'What stuff and nonsense, Gladdie! You're making me miserable. Look here: talk to the Judge: draw him out a bit. That's all he wants, and he likes it.'

'What am I to call him —"Judge"?'

'No: not that: never that. For the present, "Sir James," I think.'

'And what am I to talk about?'

'Oh, anything-Australia. Interest him about the Bush. Try, dearest, at dinner-to please me.'

'Very well,' said Gladys; 'I'll have a shot.'

And she had one, though it was not quite the kind of shot Alfred would have recommended-at any rate, not for a first shot. For, on thinking it over, it seemed to Gladys that, with relation to the Bush, nothing could interest a Judge so much as the manner of administering the law there, which she knew something about. Nor was the subject unpromising or unsafe: it was only her way of leading up to it that was open to criticism.

'I suppose, Sir James,' she began, 'you have lots of trying to do?'

'Trying?' said the Judge, looking up from his soup; for the Bride had determined not to be behindhand in keeping her promise, and had opened the attack thus early.

'As if he were a tailor!' thought Granville. 'Trials, sir,' he suggested suavely. He was sitting next Gladys, who was on the Judge's right.

'Ah, trials!' said the Judge with a faint —a very faint-smile. 'Oh, yes —a great number.'

A sudden thought struck Gladys. She became the interested instead of the interesting party. She forgot the Bush, and stared at her father-in-law in sudden awe.

'Are there many murder trials among them, Sir James?'

By the deliberate manner with which he went on with his soup, the Judge apparently did not hear the question. But Lady Bligh and Alfred heard it, and were horrified; while Granville looked grave, and listened for more with all his ears. He had not to wait long. Gladys feared she had expressed herself badly, and quickly tried again.

'What I mean is-Sir James-do you often have to go and put on the black cap, and sentence poor unfortunate people to be hung? Because that can't be very nice, Sir James-is it?'

A faint flush mounted into the Judge's pale cheeks. 'It is not of frequent occurrence,' he said stiffly.

Granville, sitting next her, might easily have stopped his sister-in-law by a word or a sign before this; but Alfred was practically hidden from her by the lamp, and though he tried very hard to kick her under the table, he only succeeded in kicking footstools and table-legs; and Lady Bligh was speechless.

The Bride, however, merely thought that Alfred had exaggerated the ease with which his father was to be drawn out. But she had not given in yet. That would have been contrary to her nature.

'What a good thing!' she said. 'It would be so-so horrid, if it happened *very* often, to wake up and say to yourself, "That poor fellow's got to swing in a minute or two; and it's me that's done it!" It would be a terror if that was to happen every week or so; and I'm glad for your sake, Sir James — —'

She broke off suddenly; why, it is difficult to say, for no one had spoken; but perhaps that was the very reason. At all events, she remembered her experience of Bush law, and got to her point, now, quickly enough.

'I was once at a trial myself, Sir James, in the Bush,' she said (and there was certainly a general sense of relief). 'My own father was boss-or Judge, if you like-that trip. There were only four people there; the sergeant, who was jailer and witness as well, father, the prisoner, and me; I looked on.'

'Is your father a member of the Colonial Bar?' inquired Sir James, mildly.

'Lord, no, Sir James! He's only a magistrate. Why, he'd only got to remand the poor chap down to Cootamundra; yet he had to consult gracious knows how many law-books (the sergeant had them ready) to do it properly!'

They all laughed; but there was a good deal that ought not to have been laughed at. A moment before, when her subject was about as unfortunate as it could have been, she had chosen her mere words with a certain amount of care and good taste; but now that she was on her native heath, and blameless in matter, her manner had become dreadful-her expressions were shocking-her twang worse than ever. The one subject that she was at home in excited her to an unseemly degree. No sooner, then, had the laugh subsided than Lady Bligh seized upon the conversation, hurled it well over the head of the Bride, and kept it there, high and dry, until the end of dessert; then she sailed away to the drawing-room with the unconscious offender.

It was time to end this unconsciousness.

'My dear,' said Lady Bligh, 'will you let me give you a little lecture?'

'Certainly,' said Gladys, opening her eyes rather wide, but won at once by the old lady's manner.

'Then, my dear, you should never interrogate people about their professional duties, least of all a judge. Sir James does not like it; and even I never dream of doing it.'

'Goodness gracious!' cried the Bride. 'Have I been and put my foot in it, then?'

'You have said nothing that really matters,' Lady Bligh replied hastily; and she determined to keep till another time some observations that were upon her mind on the heads of 'slang' and 'twang;' for the poor girl was blushing deeply, and seemed, at last, thoroughly uncomfortable; which was not what Lady Bligh wanted at all.

'Only, I must tell you,' Lady Bligh continued, 'it *was* an unfortunate choice to hit upon the death-sentence for a subject of conversation. All judges are sensitive about it; Sir James is particularly so. But there! there is nothing for you to look grieved about, my dear. No one will think anything more of such a trifle; and, of course, out in Australia everything must be quite different.'

Gladys bridled up at once; she would have no allowances made for herself at the expense of her country. It is a point on which Australians are uncommonly sensitive, small blame to them.

'Don't you believe it!' she cried vigorously. 'You mustn't go blaming Australia, Lady Bligh; it's no fault of Australia's. It's *my* fault —*my* ignorance —*me* that's to blame! Oh, please to remember: whenever I do or say anything wrong, you've not to excuse me because I'm an Australian! Australia's got nothing to do with it; it's me that doesn't know what's what, and has got to learn!'

Her splendid eyes were full of trouble, but not of tears. With a quick, unconscious, supplicating gesture she turned and fled from the room.

A few minutes later, when Lady Bligh followed her, she said, very briefly and independently, that she was fatigued, and would come down no more. And so her first evening in England passed over.

Chapter IV
A Taste of Her Quality

Mr Justice Bligh was an inveterate and even an irreclaimable early riser. In the pleasant months at Twickenham he became worse in this respect than ever, and it was no unusual thing for the slow summer dawns to find this eminent judge, in an old tweed suit, and with a silver frost upon his cheeks and chin, pottering about the stables, or the garden, or the river's brim.

The morning following the arrival of the happy pair, however, is scarcely a case in point, for it was fully six when Sir James sat down in his dressing-room to be shaved by his valet, the sober and vigilant Mr Dix. This operation, for obvious reasons, was commonly conducted in dead silence; nor was the Judge ever very communicative with his servants; so that the interlude which occurred this morning was remarkable in itself, quite apart from what happened afterwards.

A series of loud reports of the nature of fog-signals had come suddenly through the open window, apparently from some part of the premises. The Judge held up his finger to stop the shaving.

'What is that noise, Dix?'

'Please, Sir James, it sounds like some person a-cracking of a whip, Sir James.'

'A whip! I don't think so at all. It is more like pistol-shooting. Go to the window and see if you can see anything.'

'No, Sir James, I can't see nothing at all,' said Dix from the window; 'but it do seem to come from the stable-yard, please, Sir James.'

'I never heard a whip cracked like that,' said the Judge. 'Dear me, how it continues! Well, never mind; lather me afresh, Dix.'

So the shaving went on; but in the stable-yard a fantastic scene was in full play. Its origin was in the idle behaviour of the stable-boy, who had interrupted his proper business of swilling the yard to crack a carriage-whip, by way of cheap and indolent variety. Now you cannot crack any kind of whip well without past practice and present pains; but this lad, who was of a mean moral calibre, had neither the character to practise nor the energy to take pains in anything. He cracked his whip as he did all things-execrably; and, when his wrist was suddenly and firmly seized from behind, the shock served the young ruffian right. His jaw dropped. 'The devil!' he gasped; but, turning round, it appeared that he had made a mistake-unless, indeed, the devil had taken the form of a dark and beautiful young lady, with bright contemptuous eyes that made the lad shrivel and hang his head.

'Anyway, *you* can't crack a whip!' said the Bride, scornfully-for of course it was no one else.

The lad kept a sulky silence. The young lady picked up the whip that had fallen from his unnerved fingers. She looked very fresh and buoyant in the fresh summer morning, and very lovely. She could not have felt real fatigue the night before, for there was not a lingering trace of it in her appearance now; and if she had been really tired, why be up and out so very early this morning? The stable-boy began to glance at her furtively and to ask himself this last question, while Gladys handled and examined the whip in a manner indicating that she had handled a whip before.

'Show you how?' she asked suddenly; but the lad only dropped his eyes and shuffled his feet, and became a degree more sulky than before. Gladys stared at him in astonishment. She was new to England, and had yet to discover that there is a certain type of lout —a peculiarly English type-that infinitely prefers to be ground under heel by its betters to being treated with the least approach to freedom or geniality on their part. This order of being would resent the familiarity of an Archbishop much more bitterly than his Grace would resent the vilest abuse of the lout. It combines the touchiness of the sensitive-plant with the soul of the weed; and it was the Bride's first introduction to the variety-which, indeed, does not exist in Australia. She cracked the whip prettily, and with a light heart, and the boy glowered upon her. The exercise pleased her, and brought a dull red glow into her dusky cheeks, and heightened and set off her beauty, so that even the lout gaped at her with a sullen sense of satisfaction. Then, suddenly, she threw down the whip at his feet.

'*Take* the beastly thing!' she cried. 'It isn't half a whip! But you just hold on, and I'll show you what a real whip is!'

She was out of the yard in a twinkling. The lout rubbed his eyes, scratched his head, and whistled. Then a brilliant idea struck him: he fetched the coachman. They were just in time. The Bride was back in a moment.

'Ha! two of you, eh?' she exclaimed. 'Well, stand aside and I'll show you how we crack stock-whips in the Bush!'

A short, stout handle, tapering towards the lash, and no longer than fifteen inches, was in her hand. They could not see the lash at first, because she held it in front of her in her left hand, and it was of the same colour as her dark tailor-made dress; but the Bride jerked her right wrist gently, and then a thing like an attenuated brown snake, twelve feet long, lay stretched upon the wet cement of the yard as if by magic. Swiftly then she raised her arm, and the two spectators felt a fine line of water strike their faces as the lash came up from the wet cement; looking up, they saw a long black streak undulating for an instant above the young lady's head, and then they heard a whiz, followed by an almost deafening report. The lash lay on the ground again, quivering. Coachman and stable-boy instinctively flattened their backs against the coach-house door.

'That,' said the Bride, 'is the plain thing. Smell this!'

Again the long lash trembled over her head; again it cracked like a gun-shot somewhere in front of her, but this time, by the help of the recoil and by the sheer strength of her wrist, the lash darted out again behind her-as it seemed, under her very arm-and let out the report of a second barrel in the rear. And this fore-and-aft recoil cracking went on without intermission for at least a minute-that minute during which the Judge's shaving was interrupted. Then it stopped, and there was a fine wild light in the Bride's eyes, and her breath came quickly, and her lips and cheeks were glowing crimson.

The phlegmatic lad was quite speechless, and, in fact, with his gaping mouth and lolling tongue he presented a rather cruel spectacle. But the coachman found an awestruck word or two: 'My soul and body!' he gasped.

'Ah!' said the Bride, 'that *is* something flash, ain't it though? I wonder I hadn't forgotten it. And now *you* have a try, old man!'

Honest Garrod, the coachman, opened his eyes wide. He knew that this was Mrs Alfred; he had heard that Mrs Alfred was an Australian; but he could scarcely believe his ears.

'No, miss-no, mum-thank you,' he faltered. The 'miss' came much more naturally than the 'mum.'

'Come on!' cried the Bride.

'I'd rather not, miss —*mum*,' said the coachman.

'What rot!' said Gladys. 'Here-that's it-bravo! *Now* blaze away!'

The old man had given in, simply because this extraordinary young lady was irresistible. The first result of his weakness was a yell of pain from the stable-boy; the poor lad's face was bleeding where the lash had struck it. Rough apologies followed. Then the old coachman-who was not without mettle, and was on it, for the moment-took off his coat and tried again. After many futile efforts, however, he only succeeded in coiling the lash tightly round his own legs; and that made an end of it; the old man gave it up.

'Show us some more, mum,' said he. 'I've got too old and stiff for them games,' —as if in his youth he had been quite at home with the stock-whip, and only of late years had got rusty in the art of cracking it.

'Right you are,' said Gladys, gaily, when her laughter was over-she had a hearty, but a rather musical laugh. 'Give me the whip. Now, have you got a coin —a sixpence? No? No odds, here's half a sov. in my purse that'll do as well; and you shall have it, either of you that do this side o' Christmas what I'm going to do now. I'm going to show you a trick and a half!'

Her eyes sparkled with excitement: she was rather over-excited, perhaps. She placed the coin upon the ground, retreated several paces, measured the distance with her eye, and smartly raised the handle of the stock-whip. The crack that followed was the plain, straightforward crack, only executed with greater precision than before. Then she had resembled nothing so much as an angler idly flogging a stream; the difference was that now, as it were, she was throwing at a rise. And she threw with wonderful skill; for, at the first crack, the half-sovereign spun high into the air and fell with a ring upon the cement; she had picked it up on the point of the lash!

It was a surprising feat. That she managed to accomplish it at the first attempt surprised no one so much as the Bride herself. This also added in a dangerous degree to her excitement. She was now in little less than a frenzy. She seemed to forget where she was, and to think that she was back on the station in New South Wales, where she could do what she liked.

'Now that you've seen I can do that,' she cried to the lad, 'stand you with your back to the wall there, and I'll take your hat off for you!'

The answer of the dull youth was astonishingly wise; he said nothing at all, but beat a hasty retreat into the safety of the saddle-room.

She turned to the trembling Garrod. 'Then you!'

Even as he demurred, he saw her hand go up. Next moment the whipcord hissed past his face and there was a deafening report in his right ear, and the next a fearful explosion just under his left ear, and many more at every turn and corner of his face, while the poor man stood with closed eyes and unuttered prayers. It was an elaborate substitute for the simpler fun of whipping his cap off, the unhappy creature being bareheaded already. At last, feeling himself still untouched, Garrod opened his eyes, watched his opportunity, and, while the lash still quivered in mid-air, turned and made a valiant bolt for shelter. His shirt was cut between the shoulder-blades as cleanly as though a knife had done it, but he reached the saddle-room with a whole skin.

'Ye cowardly devils!' roared the Bride, now beside herself-her dark eyes ablaze with diabolical merriment. 'I'll keep you there all day, so help me, if you don't come out of it!' And, in the execution of her threat, the long lash cracked in the doorway with terrifying echoes.

At that moment, wildly excited as she was, she became conscious of a new presence in the yard. She turned her head, to see a somewhat mean-looking figure in ancient tweed, with his back to the light, but apparently regarding her closely from under the shadow of his broad felt wideawake.

'Another of 'em, I do declare!' cried the Bride. And with that the lash cracked in the ears of the unfortunate new-comer, who stood as though turned to stone.

The blue sky, from this luckless person's point of view, became alive with the writhings of serpents, hell-black and numberless. His ears were filled and stunned with the fiendish musketry. He stood like a statue; his hands were never lifted from the pockets of his Norfolk jacket; he never once removed his piercing gaze from the wild face of his tormentor.

'Why don't you take off your hat to a lady?' that lunatic now shouted, laughing hoarsely, but never pausing in her vile work. 'Faith, but I'll do it for you!'

The wideawake then and there spun up into the air, even as the half-sovereign had spun before it. And the very next instant the stock-whip slipped from the fingers of the Bride. She had uncovered the gray hairs of her father-in-law, Sir James Bligh! At the same moment there was a loud shout behind her, and she staggered backward almost into the arms of her horror-stricken husband. Even then the Bride knew that Granville was there too, watching her misery with grinning eyes. And the Judge did not move a muscle, but stood as he had stood under her fire, piercing her through and through with his stern eyes; and there was an expression upon his face which the worst malefactors he had ever dealt with had perhaps not seen there; and a terrible silence held the air after the mad uproar of the last few minutes.

That awful stillness was broken by the patter of unsteady footsteps. With a crimson face the Bride tottered rather than ran across the yard, and fell upon her knees on the wet cement, at the Judge's feet.

'Forgive me,' she said; 'I never saw it was you!'

Chapter V
Granville on the Situation

It was in the forenoon of the same day that Granville entered abruptly his mother's sanctum. Lady Bligh was busily writing at the great office-table, but she looked up at once and laid down her pen. Granville threw himself into her easiest chair with an air of emancipation.

'They have gone!' he ejaculated. If he had referred to the British workman or to the bailiffs he could not have employed more emphatic tones of relief; so Lady Bligh naturally asked to whom he did refer.

'To the happy pair!' said Granville.

'They have gone to town, then?'

'To town for the day.'

Lady Bligh took up her pen again, but only to wipe it, deliberately. 'Now, Granville,' she said, leaning back in her chair, 'I want you to tell me the truth about-about whatever happened before breakfast. I don't know yet quite what did happen. I want to get at the truth; but so far I have been able to gather only shreds and patches of the truth.'

Granville rose briskly to his feet and took his stand upon the hearthrug. Then he leant an elbow on the chimney-piece, adjusted his eyeglass, and smiled down upon Lady Bligh. One easily might have imagined that the task imposed upon him was congenial in the extreme. Without further pressing he told the story, and told it succinctly and well, with a zest that was vaguely felt rather than detected, and with an entire and artistic suppression of his usual commentaries. The mere story was so effective in itself that the most humorous parenthesis could not have improved it, and Granville had the wit to tell it simply. But when he reached the point where the Judge appeared on the scene Lady Bligh stopped him; Granville was disappointed.

'I think perhaps I have been told what happened then,' said Lady Bligh; 'at all events I seem to know, and I don't care to hear it again. Oh! it was too scandalous! But tell me, Gran, how did your father bear it? —at the time, I mean.'

'Like a man!' said Granville, with righteous warmth. 'Like a man! With that vile whip cracking under his very nose, he did not flinch-he did not stir. Then she whipped his hat from his head; and then she saw what she had done, and went down on her knees to him-as if *that* would undo it!'

'And your father?'

'My father behaved splendidly; as no other man in England in his position and-in *that* position-would have behaved. He told her at once, when she said she had not seen it was he, that he quite understood that; that, in fact, he had seen it for himself from the first. Then he told her to get up that instant; then he smiled-actually smiled; and then-you will hardly believe this, but it is a fact-he gave his arm to Mistress Gladys and took her in to breakfast!'

Lady Bligh sighed, but made no remark.

'It was more than she deserved; even Alfred admitted that.'

Lady Bligh did not answer.

'Even Alfred was knocked out of time. I never saw a fellow look more put out than he did at breakfast. He had warned us to prepare for "mannerisms," but —— '

Granville made a tempting pause. Lady Bligh, however, refused to fill it in. She was engrossed in thought. Her line of thought suddenly flashed across Granville, and he caught it up dexterously.

'As for the Judge,' said he, 'what the Judge feels no one can say. As I said, he behaved as only he could have behaved in the infamous circumstances. But I did see him steal a quiet glance at Alfred; and that glance said plainer than words: "*You've* done it, my boy; this is irrevocable!"'

Lady Bligh was drawn at last.

'This is very painful,' she murmured; 'this is too painful, Granville!'

'Painful?' cried Granville. 'I grant you it's painful; but it's the fact; it's got to be faced.'

'That may be,' said Lady Bligh, sadly; 'that may be. But we ought not to be hasty; and we certainly ought not to make too much of this one escapade.'

Granville shook his head wisely, and smiled.

'I don't think there is much fear of *that*. On the contrary, I doubt if our eyes are even yet fully open to the enormity of this morning's work. I don't think we any of us realise the hideous indignity to which my father has been subjected. But we should. We should think of it-and of him. Here we have one of the oldest and ablest of Her Majesty's judges—a man of the widest experience and of the fairest fame, whose name is a synonym for honour and humanity, not only in the Profession, but throughout every section of the community—a man, my dear mother, with whom the very smartest of us—I tell you frankly-would fight shy of a tilt in court, yet whom we all respect and honour; in very truth, "a wise and upright judge," though I say it who am his son. And what has happened to him? How has he been treated?' cried Granville. 'Well, we know. No need to go into that again. Only *try* to realise it, dear mother; try to realise it. To me there is, I confess, something almost epic in this business!'

'I don't wish to realise it; and I don't know, I am sure, why you should wish to make me.'

'For no reason,' said Granville, shrugging his shoulders, and also looking hurt; 'for no kind of reason, except that it *did* strike me that my father's character had never-never, that is, in his home life-come out more strongly or more generously. Why, I should like to lay ruinous odds that he never refers to the matter again, even to you; while, you shall see, his manner to her will not suffer the slightest change in consequence of what has happened.'

'It would be a terrible thing if it did,' said Lady Bligh; and she added after a pause: 'She *is* so beautiful!'

Granville drummed with his fingers upon the chimney-piece. His mother wanted a reply. She wanted sympathy upon this point; it was a very insignificant point, the Bride's personal beauty; but as yet it seemed to be the only redeeming feature in Alfred's unfortunate marriage.

'You can't deny *that*, Gran?' she persisted.

'Deny what? The young woman's prepossessing appearance? Certainly not; nobody with eyes to see could deny that.'

'And after all,' said Lady Bligh, 'brought up as she evidently has been, it would be astonishing indeed if her ways were *not* wild and strange. Consequently, Gran, there is every hope that she will fall into our ways very soon; is there not?'

'Oh, of course there is *hope*,' said Gran, with an emphasis that was the reverse of hopeful; 'and there is hope, too, that she will ultimately fall into our way of speaking: her own "mannerisms," in that respect, are just a little too marked. Oh, yes, there is hope; there is hope.'

Lady Bligh said no more; she seemed to have no more to say. Observing this, Granville consulted his watch, said something about an engagement in town, and went to the door.

'Going to London?' said Lady Bligh. 'You might have gone with them, I think.'

'I think not,' said Granville. 'I should have been out of place. They were going to Madame Tussaud's, or the Tower of London, or the Zoological Gardens—I don't know which-perhaps to all three. But the Bride will tell us all about it this evening and how the sights of London compare with the sights of Melbourne; we may look forward to that; and, till then-good-bye.'

So Lady Bligh was once more alone. She did not at once resume her correspondence, however. Leaning back in her chair, she gazed thoughtfully through the open window at her side, and across the narrow lawn to where the sunlit river was a silver band behind the trunks and nether foliage of the trees. Lady Bligh was sad, and no wonder; but in her heart was little of the wounded pride, and none of the personal bitterness, that many mothers would feel-and do feel every day-under similar circumstances. What were the circumstances? Simply these: her eldest son had married a wife who was beautiful, it was true, and good-tempered, it appeared; but one who was, on the other hand, both vulgar and ignorant, and, as a daughter, in every way impossible. These hard words Lady Bligh pronounced deliberately in her mind. She was facing the fact, as Granville had said that it should be faced. Yet Granville had used no such words as these; if he had, he would have been given reason to regret them.

For, as has been said already, Lady Bligh had a tolerably just estimate of her son Granville; she thought him only rather more clever, and a good deal more good-natured, than he really was. She knew that a man of any cleverness at all is fond of airing his cleverness-and, indeed, must air it-particularly if he is a young man. For this reason, she made it a rule to listen generously to all Granville had to say to her. But there was another reason: Lady Bligh was a woman who valued highly the confidence and companionship of her sons. Sometimes, it is true, she thought Granville's cynicism both cheap and worthless; and sometimes (though more rarely) she told him so. Often she thought him absurd: she was amused, for instance, when he solemnly assured her of the Judge's high standing and fair fame in 'the Profession' —as if she needed *his* assurance on that point! But it very seldom seemed to her that the things he said were really ill-natured. There, in the main, she was right. There was no downright malice (as a rule) in Granville; he was merely egotistical and vain; he merely loved more than most things the sound of his own voice. He did not designedly make unkind remarks-at least, not often; but he never took any pains to make kind ones. He passed among men for a fellow of good nature, and unquestionably he was good company. Certainly Lady Bligh overestimated his good nature; but to a great extent she understood Granville; and in any case-of course-she loved him. But she loved Alfred more; and it was Alfred who had made this marriage.

Yet it was only with grief that she could think of the marriage, at present; she found it impossible to harbour bitter feeling against the young handsome face and honest brave eyes that had taken poor Alfred by storm, though they had blinded him to a hundred blemishes. The fact is, her daughter-in-law's face was haunting Lady Bligh. As the day wore on she found herself longing wistfully to see it again. When she did see it again, the face was changed; its expression was thoughtful, subdued, and even sad. Nor were there any *gaucheries* at dinner that night, for both Alfred and Gladys were silent and constrained in manner.

Then Lady Bligh took heart afresh.

'It *is* only her bringing up,' she said. 'She will fall into our ways in time; indeed, she is falling into them already-though not in the way I wish her to; for it must not make her sad, and it must not make her feel ashamed. It shall not; for I mean to help her. I mean to be to her what, indeed, I already am without choice-her mother-if she will only let me!'

Chapter VI
Comparing Notes

But, during those first few days, Lady Bligh did not get many opportunities of carrying out her good intentions towards her daughter-in-law. For several mornings in succession Alfred carried off his wife to London, and they never returned until late in the afternoon, while twice during the first week the pair went to the theatre. They were seeing the sights of the town; and the Bride did appear to be impressed with what she saw; but the prospect of an unreserved and racy commentary upon everything, which the first hour of her installation in her husband's family had seemed to hold out-and which Granville, for one, had counted upon-was not properly realised. And at this Alfred perhaps, was scarcely less disappointed than Granville.

'Why don't you tell them more what you think of things?' said Alfred. 'They won't fancy you half appreciate the Old Country.'

'I can't help it,' replied his young wife. 'You know that I *do* like what I see, dear: you know that I am just delighted with everything: but how can I tell them so, unless I tell them in my own way? Well, then, I see they don't like it when I drag in the Colonies; yet you must compare what you see with something you've seen before; and the Colonies is the only other country ever I did see.'

But the fact is, it was not so much their daughter-in-law's comparisons, which were inoffensive in themselves, as the terms in which these comparisons were expressed, that Lady Bligh and Sir James felt bound to discourage. For it soon became plain that Gladys could not talk for two minutes about her native country without unseemly excitement; and this excitement was invariably accompanied by a small broadside of undesirable phrases, and by an aggravation of the dreadful Australian twang, even if some quite indecorous Bush idiom did not necessitate a hasty change of subject. When Australia was rigorously tabooed the Bride was safe, and stupid; when it was not, she might be bright and animated and amusing-but you could never tell what she would say next-the conversation was full of perils and pitfalls.

The particular conversations that revealed the thinness of the ice in this quarter were trivial in the extreme. In them it was mere touch-and-go with the dangerous subject, nothing more: nothing more because Gladys was quick to perceive that the subject was unpopular. So she became rather silent in the long evenings at the dinner-table and in the drawing-room; for it was her only subject, this one that they did not seem to like. To strangers, however, who were glad to get up a conversation with one of the prettiest women they had ever met in their lives, this seemed the likeliest topic in the world; *they* could not know that Australia was dangerous ground. The first of them who ventured upon it did not soon forget the experience; it was probably always a more amusing reminiscence to him than to Gladys's new relatives, who heard all that passed, and grinned and bore it.

The stranger in question was by way of being illustrious. He was a Midland magnate, and his name, Travers, was a good one; but, what was for the moment much more to the point, he was a very newly elected Member of the House of Commons; in fact, 'the new boy' there. He came down to dinner at Twickenham flushed with the agreeable heat of successful battle. Only the week before he had snatched his native borough from the spreading fire of Democracy, and won one of the very closest and most keenly contested by-elections of that year. Naturally enough, being a friend of some standing, he talked freely of his electioneering experiences, and with a victor's rightful relish. His manner, it must be owned, was a trifle ponderous; according to Granville, he was an inflated bore. But Mr Travers, M.P., was sufficiently well listened to (Lady Bligh was such a wonderful listener); and he fought his good fight over and over again with such untiring energy, and depicted it from so many commanding points of view, that, even when it came to tea in the drawing-room, the subject was still unfinished. At all events, it then for the first time became lively; for it was then that Mr Travers turned to young Mrs Bligh (also for the first time), and honoured her with an observation: —

'No doubt you order these things better in Australia; eh?'

'What things?' asked the Bride, with some eagerness; for of Australia she had been thinking, but not of Mr Travers or his election.

'Why,' said the Member, with dignity, 'your elections. I was speaking of the difficulty of getting some of the lower orders to the poll; you have almost to drive them there. What I say is, that very probably, in Australia, you manage these things on a superior system.'

'We do,' said the Bride laconically.

The new Member looked astonished; he had expected a more modest answer.

'Indeed!' he said stiffly, and addressed himself to his tea-cup.

'For,' explained the Bride, exhibiting dangerous symptoms, 'we *do* drive 'em to the poll out there, and make no bones about it either!'

'Indeed?' said Mr Travers again; but this time there was some curiosity in his tone. 'This is interesting. I always thought Australia was such a superlatively *free* country!'

The Bride scented a sarcasm.

'So it is,' she cried warmly, beginning to speak at a perilous pace, and with her worst twang; '*my* word it is! But you don't understand me. It's like this: we *do* drive 'em to the poll, up the Bush; I've driven 'em lots o' times myself. They're camped out-the voters, like-all over the runs, for all the hands have a vote; and to get 'em to the police-barracks (the poll, d'ye see?) on election day, each squatter's got to muster his own men and drive 'em in. I used to take one trap with four horses, and father another. Gracious, what a bit of fun it was! But the difficulty was —— '

She hesitated, for Lady Bligh was staring at her; and, though her ladyship's face was in shadow, the Bride was disturbed, for a moment, by the rigid pose of the old lady's head. A queer expression was come over the face of the new Member, moreover; but this Gladys could not see, for he was a tall man, standing, while she was seated.

'What *was* the difficulty?' asked Granville from a corner, in an encouraging tone.

Gladys instantly forgot Lady Bligh. 'To keep 'em from going to the shanty *first*,' she answered, with a merry laugh.

'The shanty?' repeated Mr Travers, with a vague idea of sailors' songs.

'The pub., then. Of course they all went afterwards, and-but we were obliged to keep them sober till they'd voted; and that's where the difficulty came in.'

The assembly shuddered; but, before new ground could be broken, Mr Travers, for the first time interested in somebody else's electioneering experiences, said inquiringly: —

'These squatters I presume, represent the landed interest; *my* party, in fact?'

'Oh, I don't know nothing about that,' replied the Bride.

At this juncture Alfred announced, in an uncommonly loud and aggressive tone, that-what do you think? —the glass was going down!

'Is it?' cried Sir James, with a lively concern quite foreign to his habit. 'Dear, dear! And Mr Travers just now assured me that the weather was quite settled. I fear that this will disappoint-er-Mr Travers!'

But it failed even to attract that gentleman's attention; and Granville, in the background, chuckled satanically over the ingenuousness of the device. Mr Travers, in fact, was sufficiently interested elsewhere. 'Yet, of course,' he was saying, 'there *are* two parties?'

'*My* word, there are!' returned the Bride.

'And do you call them Whig and Tory?'

'I don't think it' —doubtfully.

'Conservative and Liberal, perhaps?'

'Not that I know of.'

'Yet you say you have two parties —— '

'Of course we have, same as you,' broke in the Bride, who would brook anything rather than the implied inferiority of Australia in the most trivial respect. 'But all ever *I* heard 'em called was the squatters' candidate and the selectors' *man*!'

'And your men, I suppose, voted for the squatters' candidate?'

'I should rather hope so!' said Mrs Alfred, with severe emphasis. 'Even Daft Larry-who's both deaf and mad-had sense enough to give us his vote!'

Mr Travers, though astonished at her tone, said nothing at the moment; but Granville asked from his corner: —

'What if they didn't, Gladys?'

The Bride was seized with a sudden fit of uncontrollable mirth. Some reminiscence evidently tickled her.

'There *was* one man that we knew of that voted wrong,' she said, 'and he got it pretty hot, I can tell you!'

'Advanced Australia!' murmured Granville.

'I am sorry to hear that, Mrs Bligh,' said Mr Travers (who had ceased to deal with those local tradesmen, at his place in the Midlands, who were suspected of having 'voted wrong' the previous week). 'I am sorry indeed to hear that. May I ask who punished him?'

'Certainly —*I* did.'

It was a startling reply. The Judge quietly quitted the room. Alfred, with his back to every one, surveyed his red face in the mantel-mirror, and ground his teeth; only Lady Bligh sat stoically still.

'He came back to the trap very drunk-blind, speechless, paralytic,' the Bride explained rapidly, 'and owned up what he'd done as bold as brass. So I let him have it with the whip, pretty sudden, I can tell you. It was chiefly for his drunken insolence-but not altogether,' said Gladys, candidly.

Mr Travers had been glad to pick up a thing or two concerning Australian politics, but he seemed now to consider himself sufficiently enlightened.

'Do you sing, Mrs Bligh?' he asked somewhat abruptly.

'Not a note,' said the Bride, perceiving with regret that the subject was changed.

'You play, perhaps? If so ——'

'No, I can't play neither,' said the Bride, smiling broadly-and bewitchingly. 'I'm no good at all, you see!'

It seemed too true. She had not the saving grace of a single accomplishment-nothing, nothing, nothing but her looks!

Chapter VII
In Richmond Park

The day after Mr Travers dined at Twickenham was almost the first day that passed without the happy pair running up to London together.

'It's far too hot to think of town, or of wearing anything but flannels all day,' said Alfred in the morning. 'But there's plenty to see hereabouts, Gladdie. There's Bushey Park and Hampton Court, and Kew Gardens, and Richmond Park. What do you say to a stroll in Richmond Park? It's as near as anything, and we shall certainly get most air there.'

Gladys answered promptly that she was 'on' (they were alone); and they set out while the early haze of a sweltering day was hanging closely over all the land, but closest of all about the river.

There was something almost touching in the air of serious responsibility with which these two went about their daily sight-seeing; though Granville derived the liveliest entertainment from the spectacle. The worst of guides himself, and in many respects the least well-informed of men, Alfred nevertheless had no notion of calling in the aid of a better qualified cicerone, and of falling into the rear himself to listen and learn with his wife. At the same time, the fierce importance, to his wife, of this kind of education exaggerated itself in his mind; so he secretly armed himself with 'Baedeker,' and managed to keep a lesson ahead of his pupil, on principles well known to all who have ever dabbled in the noble art of 'tutoring.' But, indeed, Alfred's whole conduct towards his wife was touching-touching in its perpetual tenderness, touching in its unflagging consideration, and ten times touching in the fact that his devotion was no longer blind. His eyes had been slowly and painfully opened during this first week at home. Peculiar manners, which, out there in the Bush, had not been peculiar, seemed worse than that here in England. They had to bear continual comparison with the soft speech and gentle ways of Lady Bligh, and the contrast was sharp and cruel. But the more Alfred realised his wife's defects the more he loved her. That was the nature of his simple heart and its simple love. At least *she* should not know that he saw her in a different light, and at first he would have cut his tongue out rather than tell her plainly of her peculiarities. Presently she would see them for herself, and then, in her own good time, she would rub down of her own accord the sharper angles; and then she would take Lady Bligh for her model, instinctively, without being told to do so: and so all would be well. Arguing thus, Alfred had not allowed her to say a word to him about that escapade with the stock-whip on the first morning, for her penitence was grievous to him-and was it a thing in the least likely to happen twice? Nevertheless, he was thoroughly miserable in a week-that electioneering conversation was the finisher-and at last he had determined to speak. Thus the walk to Richmond was strangely silent, for all the time he was casting about for some way of expressing what was in his mind, without either wounding her feelings or letting her see that his own were sore.

Now they walked to Richmond by the river, and then over the bridge, but, before they climbed the hill to the park gates, a solemn ceremony, insisted upon by Alfred, was duly observed: the Bride ate a 'Maid-of-Honour' in the Original Shop; and when the famous delicacy had been despatched and criticised, and Alfred had given a wild and stumbling account of its historic origin, his wife led the way back into the sunshine in such high spirits that his own dejection deepened sensibly as the burden of his unuttered remonstrances increased. At last, in despair, he resolved to hold his tongue, for that morning at least. Then, indeed, they chatted cheerfully together for the first time during the walk, and he was partly with her in her abuse of the narrow streets and pavements of Richmond, but still stuck up for them on the plea that they were quaint and thoroughly English; whereat she laughed him to scorn; and so they reached the park.

But no sooner was the soft cool grass under their dusty feet, and the upland swelling before them as far as the eye could travel, than the Bride became suddenly and unaccountably silent. Alfred stole curious glances as he walked at her side, and it seemed to him that the dark eyes roving so eagerly over the landscape were grown wistful and sad.

'How like it is to the old place!' she exclaimed at last.

'You don't mean your father's run, Gladdie?'

'Yes, I do; this reminds me of it more than anything I've seen yet.'

'What nonsense, my darling!' said Alfred, laughing. 'Why, there is no such green spot as this in all Australia!'

'Ah! you were there in the drought, you see; you never saw the run after decent rains. If you had, you'd soon see the likeness between those big paddocks in what we call the "C Block" and this. But the road spoils this place; it wants a Bush road; let's get off it for a bit.'

So they bore inward, to the left, and Gladys was too thoroughly charmed, and too thoughtful, to say much. And now the cool bracken was higher than their knees, and the sun beat upon their backs very fiercely; and now they walked upon turf like velvet, in the shadow of the trees.

'You don't get many trees like these out there,' said Alfred.

'Well-not in Riverina, I know we don't,' Gladys reluctantly admitted; and soon she added: 'Nor any water-holes like this.'

For they found themselves on the margin of the largest of the Pen Ponds. There was no wind, not a ripple could be seen upon the whole expanse of the water. The fierce sun was still mellowed by a thin, gauzy haze, and the rays were diffused over the pond in a solid gleam. The trees on the far side showed fairly distinct outlines, filled in with a bluish smoky gray, and entirely without detail. The day was sufficiently sultry, even for the Thames Valley.

'And yet,' continued Gladys, speaking slowly and thoughtfully, 'it *does* remind one of the Bush, somehow. I have sometimes brought a mob of sheep through the scrub to the water, in the middle of the day, and the water has looked just like this-like a great big lump of quicksilver pressed into the ground and shaved off level. That'd be on the hot still days, something like to-day. We now and then did have a day like this, you know-only, of course, a jolly sight hotter. But we had more days with the hot wind, hot and strong; what terrors they were when you were driving sheep!'

'You were a tremendous stock-rider, Gladdie!' remarked her husband.

'Wasn't I just! Ever since I was *that* high! And I was fond, like, of that old run-knew every inch of it better than any man on the place-except the old man, and perhaps Daft Larry. Knew it, bless you! from sunrise-you remember the sunrise out there, dull, and red, and sudden-to sundown, when you spotted the station pines black as ink against the bit of pink sky, as you came back from mustering. Let's see —I forget how it goes-no, it's like this: —

> ''Twas merry 'mid the black-woods when we spied the station roofs,
> To wheel the wild scrub cattle at the yard,
> With a running fire of stock-whips and a fiery run of hoofs,
> Oh, the hardest day was never then too hard!

That's how it goes, I think. We used sometimes to remember it as we rode home, dog-tired. But it was sheep with us, not cattle, more's the pity. Why, what's wrong, Alfred? Have you seen a ghost?'

'No. But you fairly amaze me, darling. I'd no idea you knew any poetry. What is it?'

'Gordon-mean to say you've never heard of him? Adam Lindsay Gordon! You *must* have heard of him, out there. *Everybody* knows him in the Bush. Why, I've heard shearers, and hawkers, and swagmen spouting him by the yard! He was our Australian poet, and *you* never had one to beat him. Father says so. Father says he is as good as Shakespeare.'

Alfred made no contradiction, for a simple reason: he had not listened to her last sentences; he was thinking how well she hit off the Bush, and how nicely she quoted poetry. He was silent for some minutes. Then he said earnestly: —

'I wish, my darling, that you would sometimes talk to my mother like that!'

Gladys returned from the antipodes in a flash. 'I shall never talk to any of your people any more about Australia!' And, by her tone, she meant it.

'Why not?'

'Because they don't like it, Alfred; I see they don't, though I never see it so clearly as when it's all over and too late. Yet why should they hate it so? Why should it annoy them? I've nothing else to talk about, and I should have thought they'd like to hear of another country. I know *I* liked to hear all about England from *you*, Alfred!'

Faint though it was, the reproach in her voice cut him to the heart. Yet his moment had come. He had decided, it is true, to say nothing at all; but then there had been no opening, and here was one such as might never come again.

'Gladdie,' he began, with great tenderness, 'don't be hurt, but I'm going to tell you what *may* have something to do with it. You know, you are apt to get —I won't say excited-but perhaps a little *too* enthusiastic, when you talk of the Bush. Quite right-and no wonder, *I* say-but then, here in England, somehow, they very seldom seem to get enthusiastic. Then, again —I think-perhaps-you say things that are all right out there, but sound odd in our ridiculous ears. For we are an abominable, insular nation of humbugs — —' began poor Alfred with a tremendous burst of indignation, fearing that he had said too much, and making a floundering effort to get out of what he *had* said. But his wife cut him short.

The colour had mounted to her olive cheeks. Denseness, at all events, was not among her failings-when she kept calm.

She was sufficiently calm now. 'I see what you mean, and I shall certainly say no more about Australia. "I like a man that is well-bred!" Do you remember how Daft Larry used to wag his head and say that whenever he saw you? "You're not one of the low sort," he used to go on; and how we did laugh! But I've been thinking, Alfred, that he couldn't have said the same about me, if I'd been a man. And-and that's at the bottom of it all!' She smiled, but her smile was sad.

'You are offended, Gladys?'

'Not a bit. Only I seem to understand.'

'You *don't* understand! And that *isn't* at the bottom of it!'

'Very well, then, it isn't. So stop frowning like that this instant. I'd no idea you looked so well when you were fierce. I shall make you fierce often now. Come, you stupid boy! I shall learn in time. How do you know I'm not learning already? Come away; we've had enough of the water-hole, I think.'

She took his arm, and together they struck across to Ham Gate. But Alfred was silent and moody; and the Bride knew why.

'*Dear* old Alfred,' she said at last, pressing his arm with her hand; 'I *know* I shall get on well with all your people, in time.'

'All of them, Gladdie?'

'At any rate, all but Granville.'

'Still not Gran! I was afraid of it.'

'No; I shall never care much about Gran. I can't help it, really I can't. He is everlastingly sneering, and he thinks himself so much smarter than he is. Then he enjoys it when I make a fool of myself; I see he does; and-oh, I can't bear him!'

A pugnacious expression came into Alfred's face, but passed over, and left it only stern.

'Yes,' he said, 'I know his infernal manner; but, when he sneers, it's only to show what a superior sort of fellow he is; he doesn't mean anything by it. The truth is, I fear he's becoming a bit of a snob; but at least he's a far better fellow than you think; there really isn't a better fellow going. Take my word for it, and for Heaven's sake avoid words with *him*; will you promise me this much, Gladdie?'

'Very well-though I *have* once or twice thought there'd be a row between us, and though I *do* think what he'd hear from me would do him all the good in the world. But I promise. And I promise, too, not to gas about Australia, to any of them for a whole week. So there.'

They walked on, almost in silence, until Ham Common was crossed and they had reached the middle of the delightful green. And here-with the old-fashioned houses on three sides of them, and the avenue of elms behind them and the most orthodox of village duck-ponds at their feet-Gladys stopped short, and fairly burst into raptures.

'But,' said Alfred, as soon as he could get a word in, which was not immediately, 'you go on as though this was the first real, genuine English village you'd seen; whereas nothing could be more entirely and typically English than Twickenham itself.'

'Ah, but this seems miles and miles away from Twickenham, and all the other villages round about that I've seen. I think I would rather live here, where it is so quiet and still, like a Bush township. I like Twickenham; but on one side there's nothing but people going up and down in boats, and on the other side the same thing, only coaches instead of boats. And I hate the sound of those coaches, with their jingle and rattle and horn-blowing; though I shouldn't hate it if I were on one.'

'Would you so very much like to fizz around on a coach, then?'

'Would I *not*!' said Gladys.

The first person they saw, on getting home, was Granville, who was lounging in the little veranda where they had taken tea on the afternoon of their arrival, smoking cigarettes over a book. It was the first volume of a novel, which he was scanning for review. He seemed disposed to be agreeable.

'Gladys,' he said, 'this book's about Australia; what's a "new chum," please? I may as well know, as, so far, the hero's one.'

'A "new chum," ' his sister-in-law answered him readily, 'is some fellow newly out from home, who goes up the Bush; and he's generally a fool.'

'Thank you,' said Granville; 'the hero of this story answers in every particular to your definition.'

Granville went on with his skimming. On a slip of paper lying handy were the skeletons of some of the smart epigrammatic sentences with which the book would presently be pulverised. Husband and wife had gone through into the house, leaving him to his congenial task; when the Tempter, in humorous mood, put it into the head of his good friend Granville to call back the Bride for a moment's sport.

'I say' —the young man assumed the air of the innocent interlocutor —'is it true that every one out there wears a big black beard, and a red shirt, and jack-boots and revolvers?'

'No, it is not; who says so?'

'Well, this fellow gives me that impression. In point of fact, it always *was* my impression. Isn't it a fact, however, that most of your legislators (I meant to ask you this last night, but our friend the senator gave me no chance) —that most of your legislators are convicts?'

'Does your book give you that impression too?' the Bride inquired coolly.

'No; that's original, more or less.'

'Then it's wrong, altogether. But, see here, Gran: you ought to go out there.'

'Why, pray?'

'You remember what I said a "new chum" was?'

'Yes; among other things a fool.'

'Very good. You ought to go out there, because there are the makings of such a splendid "new chum" in *you*. You're thrown away in England.'

Granville dropped his book and put up his eyeglass. But the Bride was gone. She had already overtaken her husband, and seized him by the arm.

'Oh, Alfred,' she cried, 'I have done it! I have broken my promise! I have had words with Gran! Oh, my poor boy —I'm beginning to make you wish to goodness you'd never seen me —I feel I am!'

Chapter VIII
Gran's Revenge

All men may be vain, but the vanity of Granville Bligh was, so to speak, of a special brand. In the bandying of words (which, after all, was his profession) his vanity was not too easily satisfied by his own performances. This made him strong in attack, through setting up a high standard, of the kind; but it left his defence somewhat weak for want of practice. His war was always within the enemy's lines. He paid too much attention to his attack. Thus, though seldom touched by an adversary, when touched he was wounded; and, what was likely to militate against his professional chances, when wounded he was generally winged. His own skin was too thin; he had not yet learned to take without a twinge what he gave without a qualm: for a smart and aggressive young man he was simply absurdly sensitive.

But, though weaker in defence than might have been expected, Granville was no mean hand at retaliation. He neither forgot nor forgave; and he paid on old scores and new ones with the heavy interest demanded by his exorbitant vanity. Here again his vanity was very fastidious. First or last, by fair means or foul, Granville was to finish a winner. Until he did, his vanity and he were not on speaking terms.

There were occasions, of course, when he was not in a position either to *riposte* at once or to whet his blade and pray for the next merry meeting. Such cases occurred sometimes in court, when the bench would stand no nonsense, and brusquely said as much, if not rather more. Incredible as it may seem, however, Granville felt his impotency hardly less in the public streets, when he happened to be unusually well dressed and gutter-chaff rose to the occasion. In fact, probably the worst half-hour he ever spent in his life was one fine morning when unaccountable energy actuated him to walk to Richmond, and take the train there, instead of getting in at Twickenham; for, encountering a motley and interminable string of vehicles *en route* to Kempton Park, he ran a gauntlet of plebeian satire during that half-hour, such as he never entirely could forget.

To these abominable experiences, the Bride's piece of rudeness unrefined (which she had the bad taste to perpetrate at the very moment when he was being rude to her, but in a gentleman-like way) was indeed a mere trifle; but Granville, it will now be seen, thought more of trifles than the ordinary rational animal; and this one completely altered his attitude towards Gladys.

If, hitherto, he had ridiculed her, delicately, to her face, and disparaged her-with less delicacy-behind her back, he had been merely pursuing a species of intellectual sport, without much malicious intent. He was not aware that he had ever made the poor thing uncomfortable. He had not inquired into that. He was only aware that he had more than once had his joke out of her, and enjoyed it, and felt pleased with himself. But his sentiment towards her was no longer so devoid of animosity. She had scored off him; he had felt it sufficiently at the moment; but he felt it much more when it had rankled a little. And he despised and detested himself for having been scored off, even without witnesses, by a creature so coarse and contemptible. He was too vain to satisfy himself with the comfortable, elastic, and deservedly popular principle that certain unpleasantnesses and certain unpleasant people are 'beneath notice.' Nobody was beneath Granville's notice; he would have punished with his own boot the young blackguards of the gutter, could he have been sure of catching them, and equally sure of not being seen; and he punished Gladys in a fashion that precluded detection-even Gladys herself never knew that she was under the lash.

On the contrary, she ceased to dislike her brother-in-law. He was become more polite to her than he had ever been before; more affable and friendly in every way. Quite suddenly, they were brother and sister together.

'How well those two get on!' Lady Bligh would whisper to her husband, during the solemn game of *bezique* which was an institution of their quieter evenings; and, indeed, the Bride and her brother-in-law had taken to talking and laughing a good deal in the twilight by the open window. But, sooner or later, Granville was sure to come over to the card-table with Gladys's latest story or saying, with which he would appear to be hugely amused: and the same he delighted to repeat in its original vernacular, and with its original slips of grammar, but with his own faultless accent-which emphasised those peculiarities, making Lady Bligh sigh sadly and Sir James look as though he did not hear. And Alfred was too well pleased that his wife had come to like Granville at last, to listen to what they were talking about; and the poor girl herself never once suspected the unkindness; far from it, indeed, for she liked Granville now.

'I thought he would never forgive me for giving him that bit of my mind the other day; but you see, Alfred, it did him good; and now I like him better than I ever thought possible in this world. He's awfully good to me. And we take an interest in the same sort of things. Didn't you hear how interested he was in Bella's sweetheart at lunch to-day?'

Alfred turned away from the fresh bright face that was raised to his. He could not repress a frown.

'I *do* wish you wouldn't call the girl Bella,' he said, with some irritation. 'Her name's Bunn. Why don't you *call* her Bunn, dear? And nobody dreams of making talk about their maids' affairs, let alone their maids' young men, at the table. It's not the custom-not in England.'

A week ago he would not have remonstrated with her upon so small a matter; but the ice had been broken that morning in Richmond Park. And a week ago she would very likely have told him, laughingly, to hang his English customs; but now she looked both pained and puzzled, as she begged him to explain to her the harm in what she had said.

'Harm?' said Alfred, more tenderly. 'Well, there was no real *harm* in it-that's the wrong word altogether-especially as we were by ourselves, without guests. Still, you know, the mother doesn't want to hear all about her servants' family affairs, and what her servants' sweethearts are doing in Australia, or anywhere else. All that-particularly when you talk of the woman by her Christian name-sounds very much-why, it sounds almost as though you made a personal friend of the girl, Gladdie!'

Gladys opened wide her lovely eyes. 'Why, so I do!'

Alfred looked uncomfortable.

'So I do!' said the Bride again. 'And why not, pray? There, you see, you know of no reason why I shouldn't be friends with her, you goose! But I won't speak of her any more as Bella, if you don't like-except to her face. I shall call her what I please to her face, sir! But, indeed, I wouldn't have spoken about her at all to-day, only I *was* interested to know her young man was out there; and Gran seemed as interested as me, for he went on asking questions ——'

Alfred was quite himself again.

'Any way, darling,' he said, interrupting her with a kiss, 'I am glad you have got over your prejudice against Gran!' —and he went out, looking it; but leaving behind him less of gladness than he carried away.

The conversation had taken place in the little morning-room in the front of the house, which faced the west; and the strong afternoon sunshine, striking down through the trembling tree-tops, dappled the Bride's face with lights and shadows. It was not, at the moment, a very happy face. All the reckless, radiant, aggressive independence of two or three weeks ago was gone out of it. The bold, direct glance was somewhat less bold. The dark, lustrous, lovely eyes were become strangely wistful. Gladys was in trouble.

It had crept upon her by slow degrees. Shade by shade the fatal truth had dawned even upon her-the fatal disparity between herself and her new relatives. This was plainer to no one now than to the Bride herself; and to her the disparity meant despair-it was so wide-and it grew wider day by day, as her realisation of it became complete. Well, she had made friends with Granville: but that was all. The Judge had been distant and ceremonious from the first: he was distant and ceremonious still. He had never again unbent so much as at that tragic moment when he bade her rise from her knees in the wet stable-yard. As for Lady Bligh, she had begun by being kind enough; but her kindness had run to silent sadness. She seemed full of regrets. Gladys was as far from her as ever. And Gladys knew the reasons for all this-some of them. She saw, now, the most conspicuous among her own shortcomings; and against those that she did see (Heaven knows) she struggled strenuously. But there were many she could not see, yet; she felt this, vaguely; and it was this that filled her with despair.

It was green grass that she gazed out upon from the morning-room window, as the trouble deepened in her eyes; and in Australia she had seldom seen grass that was green. But just then she would have given all the meadows of England for one strip of dry saltbush plain, with the sun dropping down behind the far-away line of sombre, low-sized scrub, and the sand-hills flushing in the blood-red light, and the cool evening wind coming up from the south. The picture was very real to her-as real, for the moment, as this shaven grass-plot, and the line of tall trees that shadowed it, with their trunks indistinguishable, in this light, against the old brick wall. Then she sighed, and the vision vanished-and she thought of Alfred.

'He can't go on loving me always, unless I improve,' she said dismally. 'I *must* get more like his own people, and get on better with them, and all that. I *must*! Yet he doesn't tell me how to set to work; and it's hard to find out for oneself. I am trying; but it's very hard. If only somebody would show me how! For, unless I find out, he can't care about me much longer —I see it-he can't!'

Yet it seemed that he did.

If attending to the most extravagant wish most lightly spoken counts for anything, Alfred could certainly care for his wife still, and did care for her very dearly indeed. And that wish that Gladys had expressed while walking through the village of Ham-the desire to drive about in a coach-and-four —had been at least lightly uttered, and had never since crossed her mind, very possibly. Nevertheless, one day in the second week of June the coach-and-four turned up-spick and span, and startling and fairylike as Cinderella's famous vehicle. It was Alfred's surprise; he had got the coach for the rest of the season; and when he saw that his wife could find no words to thank him-but could only gaze at him in silence, with her lovely eyes grown soft and melting, and his hand pressed in hers-then, most likely, the honest fellow experienced a purer joy than he had ever known in all his life before. Nor did the surprise end there. By collusion with Lady Bligh and Granville, a strong party had been secretly convened for Ascot the very next day; and a charming dress, which Gladys had never ordered, came down from her dressmaker in Conduit Street that evening-when Alfred confessed, and was hugged. And thus, just as she was getting low and miserable and self-conscious, Gladys was carried off her feet and whirled without warning into a state of immense excitement.

Perhaps she could not have expressed her gratitude more eloquently than she did but a minute before they all drove off in the glorious June morning; when, getting her husband to herself for one moment, she flung her arms about his neck and whispered tenderly: —

'I'm going to be as good as gold all day-it's the least I can do, darling!'

And she was no worse than her word. The racing interested her vastly-she won a couple of sweepstakes too, by the way-yet all day she curbed her wild excitement with complete success. Only her dark eyes sparkled so that people declared they had never seen a woman so handsome, and in appearance so animated, who proved to have so little-so appallingly little-to say for herself. And it was Gladys herself who drove them all home again, handling the ribbons as no other woman handled them that season, and cracking her whip as very few men could crack one, so that it was heard for half a mile through the clear evening air, while for half that distance people twisted their necks and strained their eyes to see the last of the dark, bewitching, dashing driver who threaded her way with such nerve and skill through the moving maze of wheels and horseflesh that choked the country roads.

And, with it all, she kept her promise to the letter. And her husband was no less delighted than proud. And only her brother-in-law felt aggrieved.

'But it's too good to last,' was that young man's constant consolation. 'It's a record, so far; but she'll break out before the day is over; she'll entertain us yet-or I'll know the reason why!' he may have added in his most secret soul. At all events, as he sat next her at dinner, when the Lady Lettice Dunlop-his right-hand neighbour-remarked in a whisper the Bride's silence, Granville was particularly prompt to whisper back: —

'Try her about Australia. Sound her on the comparative merits of their races out there and Ascot. Talk in front of me, if you like; I don't mind; and she'll like it.'

So Lady Lettice Dunlop leant over gracefully, and said she had heard of a race called the Melbourne Cup; and how did it compare with the Gold Cup at Ascot?

The Bride shook her head conclusively, and a quick light came into her eyes. 'There is *no* comparison.'

'You mean, of course, that your race does not compare with ours? Well, it hardly would, you know!' Lady Lettice smiled compassionately.

'Not a bit of it!' was the brusque and astonishing retort. 'I mean that the Melbourne Cup knocks spots —I mean to say, is ten thousand times better than what we saw to-day!'

The Lady Lettice sat upright again and manipulated her fan. And it was Granville's opening.

'I can quite believe it,' chimed in Gran. 'I always *did* hear that that race of yours was the race of the world. Englishmen say so who have been out there, Lady Lettice. But you should tell us wherein the superiority lies, Gladys.'

The Bride complied with alacrity.

'Why, the course is ever so much nicer; there are ever so many more people, but ever so much less crowding; the management of everything is ever so much better; and the dresses are gayer —*ever* so much!'

'Ever so much' was a recent reform suggested by Alfred. It was an undoubted improvement upon 'a jolly sight,' which it replaced; but, like most reforms, it was apt to be too much *en evidence* just at first.

She rattled off the points at a reckless rate, and paused fairly breathless. Her speaking looks and silent tongue no longer presented their curious contradiction; she not only looked excited, but spoke excitedly now. Lady Lettice smiled faintly, with elevated eyes and eyebrows, as she listened-till the comparison between Colonial and English dress, at which home-touch Lady Lettice was momentarily overcome behind her fan. But the Bride had other hearers besides Lady Lettice; and those who heard listened for more; and those who listened for more heard Granville remark pleasantly: —

'You used to come down from the Bush for the Melbourne Cup, then?'

'Did once,' Gladys was heard to reply.

'Have a good time?'

'Did *so*.'

'Old gentleman in luck, then?'

'Pretty well. No; not altogether, I think.'

'Didn't care about going again, eh?'

'No; but that was because he knocked up when we got back.'

The conversation had become entirely confidential between the two. Lady Lettice was out of it, and looked as though she were glad of that, though in reality she was listening with quite a fierce interest. Others were listening too, and not a few were watching the Bride with a thorough fascination: the good humour and high spirits with which she was now brimming over enhanced her beauty to a remarkable degree.

'What was it that knocked him up?' inquired Granville softly, but in distinct tones.

She smiled at him. 'Never you mind!'

'But I am interested.' He looked it.

She smiled at him again, not dreaming that any other eye was upon her; then she raised her champagne glass two inches from the table and set it down again; and her smile broadened, as though it were the best joke in the world.

The refined tale was told. The action was understood by all who had listened to what went before.

The Judge was one of those who both saw and heard; and he spoke to Granville on the subject afterwards, and with some severity. But Gran's defence was convincing enough.

'Upon my honour, sir,' he protested, 'I had no kind of idea what was coming.'

'Well,' said the Judge, grimly, 'I hope *everybody* did not take it in. Her own father, too! Apart from the offensiveness of the revelation, there was a filial disrespect in it which, to me, was the worst part of it all.'

Granville looked at his father humorously through his eyeglass.

'I fear, sir, she is like *our* noble Profession-no Respecter of Persons!'

But the Judge saw nothing to smile at. 'It is nothing to joke about, my boy,' he observed. 'It has provoked me more than I can say. It is enough to frighten one out of asking people to the house. It forces me to do what I am very unwilling to do: I shall speak seriously to Alfred before we go to bed.'

Chapter IX
E Tenebris Lux

Wild weather set in after Ascot. The break-up was sudden; in England it generally is. In a single night the wind flew into the east, and clouds swept into the sky, and thermometers and barometers went down with a run together. One went to bed on a warm, still, oppressive night in June; one got up four months later, in the rough October weather. The Bride came down shivering and aggrieved; the whims and frailties of the English climate were new to her, and sufficiently disagreeable. She happened to be down before any one else, moreover; and there were no fires in the rooms, which were filled with a cheerless, pallid light; while outside the prospect was dismal indeed.

The rain beat violently upon the windows facing the river, and the blurred panes distorted a picture that was already melancholy enough. The sodden leaves, darkened and discoloured by the rain, swung heavily and nervelessly in the wind; the strip of river behind the trees was leaden, like the sky, and separable from it only by the narrow, formless smear that marked the Surrey shore. In the garden, the paths were flanked with yellow, turbid runnels; the lawn alone looked happy and healthy; the life seemed drowned out of everything else-in this single night after Ascot. Gladys shivered afresh, and turned her back on the windows in miserable spirits. And, indeed, in downright depressing spectacles, a hopeless summer's day in the Thames Valley is exceptionally rich.

The Bride, however, had no monopoly of bad spirits that morning. This became plain at breakfast, but it was not so plain that the dejection of the others arose from the same simple cause as her own. Vaguely, she felt that it did not. At once she asked herself if aught that she had done or said unwittingly could be connected in any way with the general silence and queer looks; and then she questioned herself closely on every incident of the previous day and her own conduct therein —a style of self-examination to which Gladys was becoming sadly used. But no, she could remember nothing that she had done or said amiss yesterday. With respect to that day, at least, her conscience was clear. She could say the same of no other day, perhaps; but yesterday morning she had promised her husband golden behaviour; and she honestly believed, this morning, that she had kept her promise well. Yet *his* manner was strangest of all this morning, and particularly strange towards her, his wife. It was as though he had heard something against her. He barely looked at her. He only spoke to her to tell her that he must go up to town on business, and therefore alone; and he left without any tenderness in bidding her good-bye, though it was the first time he had gone up without her.

Gladys was distressed and apprehensive. What had she done? She did not know; nor could she guess. But she did know that the longer she stood in the empty rooms, and drummed with her fingers upon the cold, bleared panes, gazing out at the wretched day, the more she yearned for one little glimpse of the sunlit bush. The barest sand-hill on her father's run would have satisfied her so long as its contour came with a sharp edge against the glorious dark-blue sky; the worst bit of mallee scrub in all Riverina-with the fierce sun gilding the leaves-would have presented a more cheery prospect than this one on the banks of the renowned (but overrated) Thames. So thought Gladys; and her morning passed without aim or occupation, but with many sad reflections and bewildering conjectures, and in complete solitude; for Lady Bligh was upstairs in her little room, and everybody else was in town. Nor did luncheon enliven matters in the least. It was virtually a silent, as it was certainly a disagreeable, *tête-à-tête*.

And yet, though Lady Bligh went up again to her little room without so much as inquiring into her daughter-in-law's plans for the afternoon, neither was she without a slight twinge of shame herself.

'But I could not help it!' Lady Bligh exclaimed to herself more than once-so often, in fact, as to prove conclusively that she *could* have helped it. 'I could not help it-indeed I could not. Once or twice I did try to say something-but there, I could not do it! After all, what have I to talk to her about? What is there in common between us? On the other hand, is not talking to her hanging oneself on tenter-hooks, for dread of what she will say next? And this is Alfred's wife! No pretensions-none of the instincts-no, not one!'

A comfortable fire was burning in the sanctum, lighting up the burnished brass of fender and guard and the brown tiles of the fireplace with a cheerful effect; and this made the chill gray light that hung over the writing-table under the window less inviting, if possible, than it had been before luncheon. Lady Bligh immediately felt that, for this afternoon, writing letters over there in the cold was out of the question. She stood for a moment before the pleasant fire, gazing regretfully at Alfred's photograph on the chimney-piece. Then a thought smote her-heavily. She rang the bell. A maid answered it.

'Light a fire for Mrs Alfred downstairs-in the morning-room, I think-and this minute. How dreadful of me not to think of it before!' said Lady Bligh, when the servant was gone. 'Poor girl! Now I think of it, she *did* look cold at the table. I feel the cold myself to-day, but she must feel it ten times more, coming from that hot country. And I have had a fire all the morning, and she has not! She looked sad, too, as well as cold, now I think of it. I wonder why? She seems so unconscious of everything, so independent, so indifferent. And, certainly, I blame myself for seeing so little of her. But does the smallest advance ever come from *her* side? Does *she* ever try to meet *me* half-way? If only she had done so-if only she were to do so now ——'

Lady Bligh stopped before following further a futile and mortifying train of speculation. No; it were better, after all, that no advances should be made now. It was a little too late for them. If, in the beginning, her daughter-in-law had come to her and sought her sympathy and her advice, it would have been possible then to influence and to help her; it might have been not difficult, even, to break to her-gently and with tact-many of her painful peculiarities as they appeared. But she had not come, and now it was too late. The account might have been settled item by item; but the sum was too heavy to deal with in the lump.

'Yet her face troubles me,' said Lady Bligh. 'It is so handsome, so striking, so full of character and of splendid possibilities; and I cannot understand why it should sometimes look so wistful and longing; for at all events this must be a very different-and surely a preferable-existence to her old rough life out there, with her terrible father' (Lady Bligh shuddered), 'and no mother.'

She could not write, so she drew the easy-chair close to the fire, and wrapped a shawl about her shoulders, and placed a footstool for her feet, and sat down in luxury with a Review. But neither could Lady Bligh read, and ultimately her brooding would probably have ended in a nap, had not some one tapped at the door.

Lady Bligh —a hater of indolence, who commonly practised her principle-being taken un-awares, was weak enough to push back her chair somewhat, and to kick aside the footstool, before saying, 'Come in.' Then she looked round-and it was the Bride herself.

'Am I disturbing you very much?' asked Gladys, calmly; indeed, she shut the door behind her without waiting for the answer.

Lady Bligh was taken aback rather; but she did not show it. 'Not at all. Pray come in. Is it something you want to ask me about?'

'There's lots of things I want to ask you about; if it isn't really bothering you too much altogether, Lady Bligh.'

'Of course it is not, child; I should say so if it were,' Lady Bligh answered, with some asperity. But her manner was not altogether discouraging.

'Thank you. Then I think I will sit down on that footstool by the fender-it is so cold. May I? Thanks. There, that won't keep the fire from you at all. Now, first of all, may I do *all* the questioning, Lady Bligh, please?'

Lady Bligh stared.

'What I mean is, may I ask you questions without you asking me any? You needn't answer if you don't like, you know. You may even get in a —in a rage with me, and order me out of the room, if you like. But please let me do the questioning.'

'I am not likely to get in a rage with you,' said Lady Bligh, dryly, 'though I have no idea what is coming; so you had better begin, perhaps.'

'Very well; then what I want to know is this-and I do want to know it very badly indeed. When you married, Lady Bligh, were you *beneath* Sir James?'

Lady Bligh sat bolt upright in her chair, and stared severely at her daughter-in-law. Gladys was sitting on the low stool with her hands clasped about her knees, and leaning backward with half her weight thus thrown upon her long straight arms. And she was gazing, not at the fire nor at Lady Bligh, but straight ahead at the wall in front of her. Her fine profile was stamped out sharply against the fire, yet touched at the edge with the glowing light, which produced a kind of Rembrandt effect. There was no movement of the long eyelashes projecting from the profile; the well-cut lips were firm. So far as could be seen from this silhouette, the Bride was in earnest. Lady Bligh checked the exclamation that had risen to her lips, and answered slowly: —

'I do not understand you, Gladys.'

'No?' Gladys slowly turned her face to that of her companion; her eyes now seemed like still black pools in a place of shadows; and round her head the red firelight struggled through the loopholes and outworks of her hair. 'Well, I mean-was it considered a very great match for *you*?'

'No; it certainly was not.'

'Then he was not much above you-in riches or rank or anything else?'

'No; we were both very poor; our early days were a struggle.'

'But you were equals from the very beginning-not only in money?'

'Yes; socially we were equals too.'

Gladys turned her face to the fire, and kept it so turned. 'I am rather sorry,' she said at length, and sighed.

'You are sorry? Indeed!'

'Yes, Lady Bligh, and disappointed too; for I'd been hoping to find you'd been ever so much beneath Sir James. Don't you see, if you *had* been ever so much beneath him, you aren't a bit now; and it would have proved that the wife can become what the husband is, if she isn't that to begin with-and if she tries hard. No-you mustn't interrupt unless it's to send me away. I want you to suppose a case. Look back, and imagine that your own case was the opposite to what it really was. That Sir James was of a very good family. That you were not only not that, but were stupid and ignorant, and a worse thing-vulgar. That you had lived your rough life in another country; so that when he brought you to England as his wife, your head was full of nothing but that other country, which nobody wanted to know anything about. That you couldn't even talk like other people, but gave offence, not only without meaning to, but without knowing how. That — —'

Lady Bligh could hear no more. 'Oh, Gladys!' she exclaimed in a voice of pain, 'you are not thinking of yourself?'

'That's a question! Still, as it's your first, I don't mind telling you you've hit it, Lady Bligh. I *am* thinking of myself. But you must let me finish. Suppose-to make short work of it-that you had been me, what would you have done to get different, like?'

'My poor child! I cannot bear to hear you talk like this!'

'Nonsense, Lady Bligh. I want you to tell me how you'd have gone about it-you know what I mean.'

'I can't tell you, Gladys; I can't indeed!'

'What! Can't tell me what you would have done-what I ought to do?'

'I cannot!' Lady Bligh commanded her voice with difficulty. 'I cannot!'

'Oh! then it's no good saying anything more about that.' There was a touch of bitterness in the girl's tone. 'But, at any rate, you might give me a hint or two how to be more like what you *are*. Can't you do that, even?'

'No, my dear-how can I? I am no model, Heaven knows!'

'Aren't you? Then I will get up. I am going, Lady Bligh. It's no good staying and bothering you any longer. I have asked my questions.'

She rose sadly from the stool, and her eyes met Lady Bligh's again. For some minutes she had kept her face turned steadily to the fire. The rich warm glow of the fire still flushed her face and lingered in her luminous eyes. In the half-lit room, with the rain rattling ceaselessly against the panes, the presence of the Bride was especially attractive and comforting; but perhaps it was chiefly the rarity of her companionship to Lady Bligh that made the latter clutch Gladys's hand so eagerly.

'Don't go, my dear. Stop, and let us talk. This is practically our first talk together, Gladys, dear; you needn't be in such a hurry to end it. Sit down again. And-and I do wish you would not always call me "Lady Bligh"!'

'Then what am I to call you, pray?' Gladys smiled up into the old lady's face; she could not help facing her now, for Lady Bligh would hold her hand; she was even forced to draw the footstool closer to the easy-chair; and thus she was now sitting at Lady Bligh's feet, touching her, and holding her hand.

'Could you not-sometimes-call me —"mother"?'

Gladys laughed. 'It wouldn't be easy.'

'But why not?'

'Because you could never be a mother to *me*. You might to another daughter-in-law, but not to me. You, who are so gentle and graceful and-and *everything*, could never seem like a mother to a —well, to me. People would say so, too, if they heard me call you "mother." It would make everybody laugh.'

'Gladys! Gladys! How cruel you are to yourself! You are not what you say you are. Here-just now — —'

'Ah,' said the Bride, sadly. 'Here! Just now! Yes, it is easy enough here and now. Here in the quiet, by the fireside, alone with you, it is easy enough to be well-behaved. I am on my good behaviour, and no one knows it better than I do. And I know it, too, when I behave badly; but not till afterwards. I go forgetting myself, you see. I believe it's principally when they talk to me about Australia. I suppose I lose my head, and talk wildly, and less like a lady than usual even. Alfred has told me, you see; though I don't know where it was I went wrong yesterday. I thought I was so very good all day. I hardly opened my mouth to anybody. But somehow I can't help it when the Bush crops up. You see, I'm a Bush girl. *All* the girls out there aren't like me; don't you believe it. They would think me as bad as you do. I'm not a sample, you see. I should be riled if I was taken for one; nothing riles me so much as people speaking or thinking meanly of Australia! But here, alone with you, with everything so quiet, it would be difficult not to be quiet too. What's more, I like it, Lady Bligh —I do indeed. I can't come lady-like all at once, perhaps; but if I was oftener beside you, like just now, I might by degrees get more like you, Lady Bligh.'

'Then you shall be oftener with me-you shall, my dear!'

'Thank you-thank you so much! And I shan't mind if you send me away; yet I won't speak if you're busy. If you'll only let me come in sometimes, for a little bit, that's all I ask.'

'You shall come in as often as ever you like, my darling!'

The old lady had drawn her daughter-in-law's head backward upon her lap, and was caressing the lovely hair, more and more nervously, and bending over the upturned face. Gladys leant back with half-closed eyes. Suddenly a scalding drop fell upon her cheek. Next moment the girl was upon her feet. The moment after that she had fallen upon her knees and caught Lady Bligh's hands in her own.

'You are crying!' said Gladys, hoarsely. 'You are crying, and because of me! Oh, Lady Bligh, forgive me! How could I know I should bring you such trouble as this? I never knew —I never dreamt it would be like this. Alfred told me that I should get on well with you all. He was blind, poor boy, but *I* might have known; only we loved each other so! Oh, forgive me-forgive me for marrying him! Say that you forgive me! Before God, I never thought it would be like this!'

'My daughter! I have nothing to forgive! Kiss me, Gladys-kiss me!'

'Yes, I will kiss you; but I have brought misery upon you all; and I will never forgive myself.'

'Gladys-you have *not*! Do not think it-and don't go, Gladys.'

'I must go. You have been good and kind to me; but this is hard for me too, though I am not crying. I never cry, though sometimes I feel inclined to, when I think of everything.'

'But now you will often come beside me, Gladys?'

'Yes, I will come. And I will try to change; you have helped me already. It will not come all at once; but perhaps I can prevent myself giving you any fresh cause to be downright ashamed of me. Nay, I must. That's the least I can do. If I fail ———'

She stopped, as though to think well of what she was saying. Her face became pale and stern-Lady Bligh never forgot it.

'If I fail,' she repeated slowly, 'after this, you will know that I am hopeless!'

She went to the door, but turned on the threshold, as though wishful to carry away a distinct impression of the scene-the half-lit room, the failing fire still reflected in the burnished brasses, the darkening panes still beaten by the wild rain, and the figure of Lady Bligh, dimly outlined and quivering with gentle weeping. Then she was gone.

Chapter X
Plain Sailing

Among unexpected pleasures there are few greater than the sudden discovery that one has become the living illustration of a common proverb. Of course the proverb must be of the encouraging order; but then most proverbs are. Equally of course, the conditions of this personal illustration should be exceptionally delightful; yet will there still remain an intrinsic charm in your relations with the proverb. You will feel benignantly disposed towards it for evermore. You will receive it henceforth with courtesy, even in the tritest application. Nor need the burden of obligation be all on your side: you can give that proverb a good character among your friends —a thing that few people will do for any proverb. You can tell it frankly: 'Sir, I always thought you were a humbug, like the rest of them. Now I know better. I admit that I was hasty. I apologise. I shall speak up for *you*, sir, till my dying day!'

That good-hearted fellow, Alfred Bligh, awaking gradually to a sensation of this sort, became very rapidly the happiest of men. The proverb in his case was the one about the dawn and the darkest hour. Alfred's darkest hour had been the day after Ascot, when, after a perfectly amicable conversation with the Judge, he had rushed up to town with ice at his heart and schemes of instant removal in his head. His dawn was the same evening, at dinner, when an indefinable *je ne sais quoi* in the mutual manner of Gladys and his mother attracted his attention and held him in suspense. And after dinner his sun rose quickly up.

The happiness of the succeeding days-to Alfred, to Gladys, and to Lady Bligh-was complete and pure. Nothing much happened in those last perfect days of June, when the rain had all fallen, and the wind changed, and summer was come back. There was some rowing on the sunlit river, and a good deal of coaching, in small parties; but on the whole they were quiet days. Yet these were the days that stood out most plainly through the dim distance of after years.

To be closely intimate with Lady Bligh meant an intimacy with a nature that was generous and sweet and womanly; and it included a liberal education-for those who would help themselves to it-in gentle, unaffected manners. Gladys came under this very desirable influence at a favourable moment, and in precisely the right frame of mind to profit most by it. And profit she did. As she herself had predicted, no miracle was wrought; she did not become everything that she ought to have been in a day; but several small alterations of manner, all of them for the better, did very quickly take place.

The Bride felt her feet at last. Then, becoming thoroughly in touch with Lady Bligh, she waxed bold in a less approachable direction, and with the best results. Not only did she start lively little conversations with Sir James, but she got him to carry them on in the same light strain, and sustained her part in them very creditably indeed, all things considered. But the subject of his judicial functions was now avoided far more sedulously by Gladys than by the old gentleman himself. She even joined the Judge more than once in his early morning prowls; but the stock-whip was always left behind in her room. On these occasions she showed herself to be an admirable assistant-potterer; while she delighted her old companion still further by many pretty and even delicate attentions, to which he was not used, having no daughters of his own. Thus there were mornings when the Judge would come in to breakfast with quite a startling posy in his button-hole, and with a certain scarcely perceptible twitching of the lips and lowering of the eyelids, such as had been observed in him sometimes on the bench when the rest of the court were 'convulsed with laughter.' It invariably transpired that the decoration was the work and gift of the Judge's daughter-in-law; and, as the old gentleman had never before been seen by his family to sport any such ornament, the departure was extremely gratifying to most of them.

Granville, it is true, found fault with the taste displayed in the composition of the button-holes, and one morning flatly refused one that had been made for him expressly; but the fact is, Granville was of rather small account in the house just now. He was busy, certainly, and was seen very little down at Twickenham; but he might have been seen more-his temporary occupation of a back-seat was in a great measure voluntary. Nor was he really malicious at this time. It is true that he spoke of the leopard's spots, and used other phrases equally ominous but less hackneyed; for the most part, however, he made these observations to himself. He could have found nowhere a more appreciative and sympathetic audience. But, though he looked on sardonically enough at the Bride's conquests, Granville did not lay himself out to hinder them. This should be clearly understood. The fellow was not a full-blown Mephistopheles.

And the happy pair were indeed happy. But for an occasional wistful, far-away look-such as will come sometimes to every exile, for all the 'pleasures and palaces' of new worlds-Gladys seemed to everybody to be gay and contented as the midsummer days were long. As for Alfred, he considered the sum of his earthly happiness complete. Even the ideal farm (which his solicitors were doing their best to find for him) in the ideal sleepy hollow (which *he* meant to do *his* best to wake up, by the introduction of vigorous Bush methods) —when purchased, stocked, furnished, inhabited, and in full swing-could not, he felt, add much to his present happiness. Poor Alfred! He was laying out the future on idyllic lines. But, meanwhile, the present was full of happy days; and that was well.

There was one evening that Alfred did not soon forget.

It was the last Sunday in June. There had been a thunderstorm early in the afternoon and a smart shower. The evening air was a long, cool, delicious draught, flavoured with the exquisite fragrance of dripping leaves and petals; and this, and the sound of the church bells, and the sunlight glittering upon the wet lanes, came back to Alfred afterwards as often as he remembered the conversation which made the walk to the old church all too short. Alfred walked with his mother; Gladys, some little distance ahead, with the Judge.

'I think Gladys likes England a little better now,' observed Lady Bligh.

'And can't England say the same thing of Gladys?' cried Alfred. 'Don't answer the question-it's idiotic. But oh, mother, I'm a fool with very joy!'

'Because Gladys has won all our hearts, dear?'

'Yes; and I really think she has. You have all been so good, so patient and forgiving. Don't stop me, mother. If you had been different, I know I never should have allowed that you had anything to forgive; but now that you are like this, I own that there was much. Look at her now with the Judge; he has given her his arm. Now think of the beginning between these two!'

'Why think of that? We have all forgotten it. You must forget it too.'

'I think of it,' said Alfred, 'because it is all over; because you have civilised my wild darling; and because I like to realise this. But, upon my soul, if you had seen her life out there; if you knew her father (she doesn't remember her mother); if you had any idea of the work she did on that run; you would simply be amazed-as I am, now that I look back upon it-at what your tenderness has done. But do you know, mother, what the dear girl says? I had nearly forgotten to tell you.'

One would have counted upon a joke, and possibly a good one; for Alfred stopped to chuckle before coming out with it; though, certainly Alfred was not the best judge of jokes.

'She says that if ever she makes you feel regularly ashamed of her again, she may be considered hopeless; and though you forgive her, she'll never forgive herself! That's rather rich, eh?'

Lady Bligh failed to see it in that light. On the contrary, for one moment she seemed both surprised and pained.

'Perhaps, Alfred,' she said, thoughtfully, 'she still feels the restraint, and hates our conventionalities. I often think she must; I sometimes think she does.'

'Not she! Not a bit of it! She's as safe as the Bank, and as happy as they make 'em, *I* know her!'

Poor Alfred!

'Perhaps,' said Lady Bligh again; 'but there may be a constant effort which we cannot see; and I have once or twice caught a look in her eyes-but let that pass. I may be wrong; only I think it has been rather slow for her lately. She must have more amusement. There are one or two amusing things coming on presently. But just now I should like to think of something quite fresh to interest her. My dear boy! you are whistling! —in the churchyard!'

In fact, Alfred was foolish with joy, as he himself had said. He could not control his spirits long when speaking of Gladys, and hearing her well spoken of by the others, and marvelling at the change that a few days had brought about. It was a case of either laughing or crying with him then; and the tears never got a chance.

But, in the solemn twilight of the church; standing, kneeling, sitting by his wife's side; sharing her book; listening with her to the consummate language of the Common Prayer; watching with her the round stained window fail and fade against the eastern sky-then, indeed, the boisterous, boyish spirits of this singularly simple-minded man of thirty melted into thankfulness ineffable and perfect peace.

It so happened that they sang an anthem in the old church that evening. This neither attracted nor distracted Alfred at first. He was a man without very much more music in his soul than what he was able to whistle when in high spirits. It did not strike him that this anthem was lovelier than most 'tunes.' The sweet sensations that stole over his spirit as the singing of it proceeded certainly were not credited to the music. To the words he never would have attempted to listen but for an accident.

To Alfred the anthem presented but one of the many opportunities presented by the Church Service for private reverie on the part of worshippers. Of course his reverie was all about the future and Gladys. And while he mused his arm touched hers, that was the delightful part of it. But on glancing down to see her face again (he had actually not looked upon it for five whole minutes) his musing swiftly ended. Her singular expression arrested his whole attention. And this was the accident that made him listen to the words of the anthem, to see if *they* could have affected her so strangely.

The Bride's expression was one of powerful yearning. The first sentence Alfred managed to pick out from the words of the anthem was: 'Oh, for the wings, for the wings of a dove!' piped in a boy's high treble.

The melting wistfulness in the Bride's liquid eyes seemed to penetrate through that darkening east window into far-away worlds; and the choir-boy sang: 'Far away, far away would I rove!'

The solo went on:

> In the wilderness build me a nest:
> And remain there for ever at rest.

Then, with some repetition which seemed vain to Alfred, the chorus swallowed the solo. And to Alfred's mind the longing in his wife's face had grown definite, acute, and almost terrible.

As they knelt down after the anthem, his eyes met those of his mother. She, too, had seen Gladys's expression. Was it the expression she had referred to on the way to church? Was such an expression a common one with his darling, and concealed only from him? Was it possible that she was secretly longing and pining for the Bush-now-when they were all so happy?

Much later in the evening-long after church-Lady Bligh made an opportunity of speaking again alone with Alfred. 'I have been maturing my little plans,' she said, smiling.

'As regards Gladys?' he asked.

'Yes; and I have been thinking that really, after all, she need not be so dull during the next few days ——'

Alfred interrupted her hastily.

'I also have been thinking; and, do you know, after all, I half fancy that she *is* a bit dull. I shall be very glad indeed if you have thought of something to 'liven her up a little.'

Lady Bligh regarded him shrewdly; but she was not entirely astonished at this complete change of opinion. She, too, had seen Gladys's longing, far-away expression in church. She, too, remembered it.

'Well, she will be less dull during the next few days than just lately,' said Lady Bligh, after a slight pause. 'On Tuesday, to begin with, there is this garden-party of ours; a dull thing enough in itself, but the people may amuse Gladys. On Wednesday, there is to be the Opera for her, at last. Thursday and Friday you must boat and drive. But for Saturday-when the Lord Chief is coming-you are all invited to lawn-tennis somewhere; are you not? After this week it is simply *embarras*; the two matches at Lord's, and Henley too, one on top of the other; then Wimbledon. Gladys must miss none of these. But can you guess what my happy thought is?'

'You seem to have so many happy thoughts!'

'No; but my little plan for to-morrow?'

'I have no idea. But I think Gladys would be content to do nothing much to-morrow, perhaps.'

'Alfred,' said Lady Bligh, severely, 'Gladys tells me you have never once had her in the Park! How is that?'

'I —well, the fact is, I'm such a duffer in the *very* swagger part of the town,' said poor Alfred; 'and I never did know the run of the parks properly.'

'Then you shall drive with Gladys and me, and learn. It is getting near the end of the season, when every day makes a difference. So, not to lose another day, we'll drive in to-morrow. This is my happy thought! I think Gladys will like it-though Garrod won't.'

'You mean he'll say it's too much for *his* horses? I should think he'll give warning,' said Alfred, encouragingly.

'He may,' said Lady Bligh, with a fine fearlessness which can be properly appraised only by ladies who keep, or once kept, their coachman. 'He may. I defy him!'

Chapter XI
A Thunder-Clap

Fully ten days were wanting before the Eton and Harrow cricket-match, which appears to be pretty generally recognised as the last 'turn' in the great variety entertainment of the season; there was plenty of life, and of high life, too, in the town yet; and, what was even more essential to a thorough enjoyment of the Park, the afternoon, as regarded the weather, was for once beyond all praise. Moreover, Royalty was there for at least half an hour; so that the circumstances attendant upon young Mrs Bligh's first appearance in the ring of fashion were in every way all that could be desired.

It was an 'appearance'; for Lady Bligh, though in no sense a woman of fashion, was sufficiently well known to attract attention, which was heightened by the increasing rarity of her appearances in the fashionable world. Even had it been otherwise, the robust, striking beauty of the dark young woman at her side must have awakened interest on its own account. It did, among those who did not know the Blighs by sight. But with most people the questions were: Where had Lady Bligh discovered such a fresh and taking type of prettiness? Was the girl a relative? Was that Alfred Bligh sitting opposite to the ladies, come back from Australia disfigured by a beard? Was she his fiancée-or were they already married? It is intended by no means to imply that the modest and even homely equipage of Lady Bligh became the cynosure of Hyde Park; but it was certainly seen; and few saw it with unawakened curiosity.

One or two persons were able to satisfy to some extent this curiosity, and took a delight in doing so; Lady Lettice Dunlop, for one. The curiosity that Lady Lettice relieved was of a languid and peculiarly well-bred kind. A coronet adorned the barouche in which she rode. She said rather more than she knew, yet not quite all that she did know, and said it with a gentle disdain. But Lady Lettice was stopped by a deprecatory gesture of her mother the Countess before she came to the end-which made her regret having over-elaborated the beginning. The Countess considered the story most coarse, and regretted the almost friendly nature of the bow with which she had just favoured poor Lady Bligh. Yet, as the Lady Lettice was generous enough to fancy, the Colonial creature did seem on her very best behaviour this afternoon. And in her fancy Lady Lettice was nearer the mark than in her facts.

Another person, in an even better position to answer questions concerning the Bride, was Mr Travers, M.P. —now the newest M.P. but one. He was walking under the trees with his daughter, whom he was boring somewhat with his political 'shop'; for he was enough of a new boy still to be full of his nice new lessons. This Miss Travers, however, was no young girl, but a woman of thirty, with a kind, sweet, sympathetic face, and a nature intensely independent. She was best known for her splendid work in Whitechapel, though how splendid that work really was no one knew outside the slums, where her face was her only protection-but a greater one than a cordon of police. But she had also a reputation as a singer, which need not have been confined to a few drawing-rooms in the West, and numberless squalid halls in the East, had she been ambitiously inclined. And this Miss Travers was attracted and charmed by the bold, conspicuous beauty of young Mrs Bligh; pressed for an introduction; pressed all the harder on hearing some plain truths about the Bride and her Bush manners; and presently had her way.

It was now six o'clock. The crowning period of the afternoon had commenced with the arrival of Royalty a few minutes before the hour. Carriages were drawn up by the rails on either side in long, regular ranks. The trough between presented visions of glossy horseflesh and flashing accoutrements and flawless japan, to say nothing of fine looks and finer dress; visions changeful as those of the shaken kaleidoscope; marvellous, magical visions-no matter how much or how little they owed to the golden glamour of the sinking sun, visions of intrinsic wonder.

The Blighs' serviceable vehicle had found an anchorage by the inner rails in the thick of all this, but not in the thickest. They were, in fact, no farther than a furlong from the Corner, and thus in comparatively open water. At this point the shrubs planted between the two converging courses come to an end, and the two roads are separated by little more than twenty yards. A little way farther on you can see only the bobbing heads of the riders over in Rotten Row; but at this point you have indeed 'the whole show' before you. The position had been taken up on the Bride's express petition. It was the riding that interested Gladys. She had no eyes for the smart people in the carriages when once she could watch with as little trouble the hacks and their riders in Rotten Row. The little interest she took in the passing and re-passing of Royalty was somewhat disappointing. But it was plain that she was enjoying herself in her own way; and that was everything. When the Traverses came up, the interruption of this innocent enjoyment was a distinct annoyance to Gladys.

Alfred-to whom it was not an afternoon of wild delight-got out of the carriage with some alacrity; and Miss Travers, with a very engaging freedom of manner, got in. She button-holed the Bride (if that is not an exclusively masculine act-as between man and man), and at first the Bride did not like it. Very soon, however, Gladys was pleased to withdraw her attention, partially, from Rotten Row and transfer it to Miss Travers. Like everybody else, the Bride was immensely attracted; Miss Travers's manner was so sympathetic, yet unaffected, and so amazingly free (Gladys thought) from English stiffness; and her face was infinitely kind and sweet, and her voice musical and soft.

So Mr Travers, with one foot upon the carriage-step, brought Lady Bligh up to date in her politics generally, and in his own political experiences in particular; and Alfred made aimless patterns on the ground with his feet; and Miss Travers questioned Gladys on the subject upon which all strangers who were told where she came from invariably and instantly did question her. But Miss Travers did this in a way of her own, and a charming way. You would have thought it had been the dream of her life to go to Australia; you would have inferred that it was her misfortune and not her fault that her lines were cast in England instead of out there; and yet you would not, you could not, have suspected her of hypocrisy. She was one of those singular people who seem actually to prefer, in common conversation, the *tuum* to the *meum*. Gladys was charmed. But still she stole furtive glances across the space dividing them from the tan; and her answers, which would have been eager and impetuous enough in any other circumstances, came often slowly; she was obviously *distraite*.

Miss Travers saw this, and followed the direction of the dark, eager eyes, and thought she understood. But suddenly there came a quick gleam into the Bride's eyes which Miss Travers did not understand. A horsewoman was crossing their span of vision in the Row at a brisk canter. The Bride became strangely agitated. Her face was transfigured with surprise and delight and incredulity. Her lips came apart, but no breath escaped them. Her flashing eyes followed the cantering horsewoman, who, in figure and in colouring, if not in feature, was just such another as Gladys herself, and who sat her horse to perfection. But she was cantering past; she would not turn her head, she would not look; a moment more and the shrubs would hide her from Gladys-perhaps for ever.

Before that moment passed, Gladys stood up in the carriage, trembling with excitement. Careless of the place-forgetful of Lady Bligh, of all that had passed, of the good understanding so hardly gained-attracting the attention of Royalty by conspicuously turning her back upon them as they passed for the fourth time-the Bride encircled her lips with her two gloved palms, and uttered a cry that few of the few hundreds who heard it ever forgot: —

'*Coo-ee!*'

That was the startling cry as nearly as it can be written. But no letters can convey the sustained shrillness of the long, penetrating note represented by the first syllable, nor the weird, die-away wail of the second. It is the well-known Bush call, the 'jodel' of the black-fellow; but it has seldom been heard from a white throat as Gladys Bligh let it out that afternoon in Hyde Park, in the presence of Royalty.

To say that there was a sensation in the vicinity of the Blighs' carriage-to say that its occupants were for the moment practically paralysed-is to understate matters, rather. But, before they could recover themselves, the Bride had jumped from the carriage, pressed through the posts, rushed across to the opposite railings, and seized in both hands the hand of the other dark and strapping young woman, who had reined in her horse at once upon the utterance of the '*Coo-ee!*'

And there was a nice little observation, audible to many, which Gladys had let fall in flying: —
'Good Lord deliver us-it's *her!*'

Chapter XII
Past Pardon

Patience and sweetness of disposition may not only be driven beyond endurance; they may be knocked outside in, knocked into their own antitheses. And one need not go to crime or even to sin to find offences which no amount of abstract angelicalness could readily forgive or ever forget. It is a sufficiently bad offence, if not an actual iniquity, to bring well-to-do people into public derision through an act of flagrant thoughtlessness and unparalleled social barbarity. But if the people are not only well-to-do, but well and honourably known, and relatives by your marriage, who have been more than kind to you, you could scarcely expect a facile pardon. Sincerity apart, they would be more than mortal if they so much as pretended to forgive you out of hand, and little less than divine if they did not tell you at once what they thought of you, and thereafter ignore you until time healed their wounds.

Woman of infinite sweetness though she was, Lady Bligh was mortal, not divine; and she showed her clay by speaking very plainly indeed, as the carriage swept out of the Park, and by speaking no more (to Gladys) that day. A good deal of cant is current about people whose anger is violent ('while it lasts'), but short-lived ('he gets over it in a moment'); but it is difficult to believe in those people. If there be just cause for wrath, with or without violence, it is not in reason that you can be in a rollicking good humour the next minute. That is theatrical anger, the anger of the heavy father. Lady Bligh, with all her virtues, could nurse the genuine passion-an infant that thrives at the breast. Indeed, it is probable that before the end of the silent drive to Twickenham (Alfred never opened his clenched teeth all the way) this thoroughly good woman positively detested the daughter whom she had just learnt to love. For it is a fallacy to suppose that the pepper-and-salt emotion of love and hatred in equal parts is the prerogative of lovers; you will find it oftener in the family.

What penitence Gladys had expressed had been lame-crippled by an excuse. Moreover, her tone had lacked complete contrition. Indeed, if not actually defiant, her manner was at least repellent. She had been spoken to hotly; some of the heat was reflected; it was a hot moment.

As for her excuse, it, of course, was ridiculous —*qua* excuse.

She had seen her oldest-indeed, her only-girl friend, Ada Barrington. Ada (Gladys pronounced it 'Ida') was another squatter's daughter; their fathers had been neighbours, more or less, for many years; but Ada's father owned more stations than one, was a wealthy man-in fact, a 'woollen king.' Gladys had known they were in Europe, but that was all. And she had seen Ada cantering past, but Ada had not seen her. So she had '*coo-ee'd*.' What else was there to be done? Gladys did not exactly ask this question, but she implied it plainly. As it happened, if she had not '*coo-ee'd*,' she never would have seen Ada again, to a certainty; for the Barringtons had taken a place in Suffolk, and were going down there the very next day. That was all. Perhaps it was too much.

Silence ensued, and outlasted the long drive. What afterwards passed between the young husband and wife did not, of course, transpire. There was no further expression of regret than the very equivocal and diluted apology comprehended in the Bride's excuses; indeed, Lady Bligh and her daughter-in-law never spoke that night; nor did Alfred attempt to mediate between them. As a matter of fact, his wife had told him-with a recklessness that cut him to the heart-that, this time, she neither expected nor deserved, nor so much as desired, any one's forgiveness; that now she knew what she had feared before, that she was hopeless; that-but the rest was wild talk.

Next morning, however, Alfred went to Lady Bligh with a letter, one that Gladys had received by the early post. It was an invitation from the Barringtons, the wording of which was sufficiently impulsive and ill-considered. Ada besought her darling Gladys to go stay with them in Suffolk immediately, on the following Saturday, and for as many days as she could and would; and the invitation included the darling's husband in a postscript.

'An extraordinary kind of invitation!' observed Lady Bligh, handing back the letter.

'Ignorance,' said Alfred laconically.

'Did you meet the people out there?'

'Only this girl's brother; the others had been in Europe some time. I thought him a very pleasant fellow, I remember, though his contempt for me and for all "home" birds was magnificent.'

'Well,' said Lady Bligh, 'it is hardly the kind of invitation that Gladys can accept. Is it?'

'She refuses to think of it,' Alfred answered, with a frown that rather puzzled Lady Bligh. 'But I hope she will change her mind. I wish her to go.'

His mother was silent for more than a minute. 'Does the letter say Saturday?' she then inquired.

'Yes.' Alfred gazed steadily in his mother's face as though he would search her inmost thoughts. 'Yes, it says Saturday. And it is on Saturday that the Lord Chief is coming down to stay over Sunday, is it not? I thought so. I very much wish I could induce her to go.'

'Not on that account, my boy, I hope?' Lady Bligh seemed slightly embarrassed.

'Partly,' said Alfred, speaking firmly and distinctly, but not without an effort; 'partly on that account, but by no means altogether.'

'She could not go without you,' remarked Lady Bligh; 'and they do not ask you civilly, to say the least of it.'

'She *could* go without me,' returned Alfred emphatically. 'What's more, I want her to. It's she that won't hear of it. These are quite old and intimate friends of Gladys and her father. She might easily spend a week with them alone, without me. Mother —I think she would like it so, if only she would go! They are probably free-and-easy, roughish folks, and it would do her good, a week with them. There would be no restraints-nay, she has observed none here, God knows! —but there there might be none to observe. She could do and say what she liked. She would hurt no one's feelings. She would scandalise no one. And-do you know what, mother? —I have got it into my head that when she came back she would see the difference, and appreciate your ways here more than she ever might otherwise. I have got it into my head that one week of that kind, just now, would open her eyes for good and all. And I think-there might be no more relapses! Yes, I thought that before; but I was wrong, you see-after yesterday! Besides, this week would bring us within a few weeks of Scotland; and, after Scotland, we shall have our own little place to go to —I have almost settled upon one. But if I went with her, restraint would go with her too.'

His voice had broken more than once with emotion. He commanded it with difficulty, and it became hard and unnatural. In this tone he added: —

'Besides-it would be more comfortable for every one if she were not here with the Lord Chief Justice.'

'Do not say that-do not think that!' said Lady Bligh; but faintly, because her heart echoed his sentiment.

'Oh, there's no disguising it-my wife's dynamite!' said Alfred, with a short, harsh laugh. 'Only an explosion is worse at one time than at another.' He went hastily from the room, neither of them having referred more directly to the scandalous scene in the Park.

He went straight to his wife, to try once more to coax her into accepting the Barringtons' invitation. But it was of no use. She would not listen to him. She would go nowhere without her husband; she should write that to Ada plainly.

Later in the morning, Lady Bligh, of her own deliberate design, came in contact with her daughter-in-law. Gladys attempted escape. Lady Bligh caught her by the hand.

'You are angry, Gladys!'

Gladys said nothing.

'I don't think *you* are the one to be angry,' Lady Bligh said, nettled by the other's sullen manner.

Gladys raised her eyes swiftly from the ground; they were filled with bitterness. 'Haven't I a right to be what I like with myself?' she cried. 'I am angry with no one else. But I shall never forgive myself-no, nor I won't be forgiven either; I am hopeless! I feared it before; now I know it. Let me go, Lady Bligh!'

She broke away, and found a quiet spot, by-and-by, among the trees by the river.

'If only I were in *there*!' cried Gladys, out of the tumult of shame and rebellion within her. 'In there-or else back in the Bush! And one is possible and easy; and the other is neither!'

By a single grotesque act she had brought her happiness, and not hers alone, to wreck and ruin!

Chapter XIII
A Social Infliction

Happily for all concerned, there was something else to be thought about that day: it was the day of Lady Bligh's garden-party.

The British garden-party is possibly unique among the social gatherings of the world. It might be a revelation to most intelligent foreigners. It is held, of course, in the fresh air; the weather, very likely, is all that can be desired. The lawn is soft and smooth and perfectly shaven; sweeping shadows fall athwart it from the fine old trees. The flower-beds are splendidly equipped; their blended odours hover in the air. The leaves whisper and the birds sing. The scene is agreeably English. But let in the actors. They are English too. The hostess on the lawn receiving the people, and slipping them through her busy fingers into solitude and desolation-anywhere, anywhere, out of her way; the stout people in the flimsy chairs, in horrid jeopardy which they alone do not realise; the burly, miserable male supers, in frock-coats and silk hats, standing at ease (but only in a technical sense) around the path, ashamed to eat the ices that the footman proffers them, ashamed of having nobody to talk to but their sisters or wives-who are worse than no one: it is so feeble to be seen speaking only to *them*. This is the British garden-party in the small garden, in the suburbs. In the large garden, in the country, you may lose yourself among the fruit-trees without being either missed or observed; but this is not a point in favour of the institution. Even in suburban districts there are bold spirits that aspire to make their garden-parties different from everybody else's, and not dull; who write 'Lawn Tennis' in the corner of their invitation-cards before ascertaining the respective measurements of a regulation court and of their own back gardens. But beware of these ambitious souls; they add yet another terror to the British garden-party. To go in flannels and find everybody else in broadcloth; to be received as a champion player in consequence, and asked whether you have 'entered at Wimbledon'; to be made to play in every set (because you are the only man in flannels), with terrible partners, against adversaries more terrible still-with the toes of the onlookers on the side lines of the court, and the dining-room windows in peril should you but swing back your racket for your usual smashing service, once in a way, to show them how it is done: all this amounts to spending your afternoon in purgatory, in the section reserved for impious lawn-tennis players. Yet nothing is more common. The lawn must be utilised, either for lawn-tennis or for bowls (played with curates), or by the erection of a tent for refreshments. By Granville's intervention, the Blighs had the refreshment-tent.

Lady Bligh would not have given garden-parties at all, could she have been 'at home' in any other way; but as her set was largely composed of people living actually in town, who would not readily come ten miles out for a dinner-party, still less for an after-dinner party, she had really no choice in the matter. Still, Lady Bligh's garden-parties were not such very dull affairs after all. They were immensely above the suburban average. To the young and the curious they held out attractions infinitely greater than garden-party lawn-tennis, though these could not be advertised on the cards of invitation. For instance, you were sure of seeing a celebrity or two, if not even the highest dignitaries, with some of the dignity in their pockets. And it is inexpressible how delightful it was to come across a group of Her Majesty's Judges gorging strawberry ices unblushingly in a quiet corner of the marquee. On the present occasion, when the stoutest and most pompous Q.C. at the Bar-Mr Merivale-sat down on the slenderest chair in the garden, and thence, suddenly, upon the grass, the situation was full of charm for Granville and some of his friends, who vied with one another in a right and proper eagerness to help the great man to his feet. Even Gladys (who was so very far from being in a laughing mood) laughed at this; though she was not aware that the stout gentleman was a Q.C., nor of the significance of those initials, had any one told her so.

But this was all the entertainment that Gladys extracted from the long afternoon. She was amused, at the moment, in spite of herself; she was not amused a second time. She kept ingeniously in the background. Alfred was attentive to her, of course, but not foolishly attentive, this afternoon. And Granville introduced to her one of his clean-shaven friends, whom Gladys conversed with for perhaps a minute. She was also presented by the Judge-in his recent genial, fatherly manner-to one or two of his colleagues. Plainly, the disgraceful scene in Hyde Park had not yet reached Sir James's ears. But that scandal was being discreetly discussed by not a few of the guests. Gladys suspected as much, though she did not know it. She imagined herself to be a not unlikely subject of conversation in any case, but quite a tempting one in the light of her last escapade. But this idea did not worry her. In some moods it is possible to be acutely self-conscious without being the least sensitive; Gladys's present mood was one. More often than at the people, she gazed at the window of her own room, and longed to be up there, alone. She neither took any interest in what was going on around her, nor cared what the people were whispering concerning her. No doubt they *were* whispering, but what did it matter? Misery is impervious to scorn and ridicule and contempt. These things wound the vanity; misery deadens it. Gladys was miserable.

Among the later arrivals was Miss Travers. Her father could not come: he was doing the fair thing by the Party and his constituents: it was his first term. Miss Travers came alone, and intended to go back alone, the later the better. Whitechapel had made her fearless and independent. She rather hoped to be asked to stop to dinner: some people were certain to stay, for the Blighs were uncommonly hospitable, and in many things quite unconventional; and Miss Travers intended to be one of those people, if she got the opportunity. She also intended to cultivate the most original specimen of her sex that she had ever yet met with; and for this she tried to make the opportunity.

But the most original of her sex was also one of the most slippery, when she liked; she dodged Miss Travers most cleverly, until the pursuer was herself pursued, and captured. Her captor was a rising solicitor, a desirable gentleman and an open admirer; but he did not improve his chances by that interview. Miss Travers was disappointed, almost annoyed. The unlucky lawyer sought to make her smile with a story: the story of the '*coo-ee!*' as he had heard it. He knew Miss Travers intimately; her appreciation of humour was vast, for a woman; he felt sure she would be tickled. But, unfortunately, the version he had heard was already fearfully exaggerated, and, as Miss Travers drew him on gently, yet without smiling as he wished her to, the good fellow improvised circumstances still more aggravating and scandalous; and then-sweet Miss Travers annihilated him in a breath.

'I was in their carriage at the time, myself; but-you will excuse my saying so —I shouldn't have recognised the incident from your description!'

It was a staggerer; but Miss Travers did not follow up the blow. She reproved him, it is true, but so kindly, and with such evident solicitude for his moral state, that the wretch was in ecstasies in two minutes.

'At all events,' he said, with enthusiasm, 'she has you for her champion! I won't hear another word about her; *I'll* champion her too!'

'If you spoke to her for one moment,' Miss Travers replied, 'you would own yourself that she is charming. You never saw such eyes!'

This the lawyer seemed to question, by the rapt manner in which he gazed into Miss Travers's own eyes; but the speech was the prettier for being left unspoken; and here the lawyer showed some self-restraint and more wisdom. But immediately the lady left him: she had descried her quarry.

Gladys dodged again, and, passing quickly through the tent, heard two words that sent the blood to her cheeks. The words were in close conjunction —'*coo-ee!*' and 'disgrace.' Without turning to see who had uttered them-the voice was unfamiliar-she hurried through into the house, and finding the little morning-room quite empty, went in there to sit down and think.

She was not wounded by the chance words; her lifeless pride had not quickened and become vulnerable all in a moment-it was not that. But it was this: what she had done, she realised now, for the first time, fully. Disgrace! She had disgraced Lady Bligh, Sir James, Alfred, Granville, all of them; in a public place, she, the interloper in the family, had brought down disgrace upon them all. Disgrace!—that was what people were saying. Disgrace to the Blighs-that was why she minded what the people said. And she minded this so much, now, that she rocked herself to and fro where she sat, and wrung her large strong hands, and groaned aloud.

And it was not only once; she had disgraced them many times. And all had been forgiven. But this could never be forgiven.

If only she had never married poor Alfred; if only she had never come among his family, to behave worse than their very servants! The servants? Would Bella Bunn have behaved so in her place? It was not likely, for even Bella had been able to give her hints, and she had consulted Bella upon points on which she would have been ashamed to confess her ignorance, even to Alfred. But, in spite of all their goodness and patience, she had brought only unhappiness to them all; there could be no more happiness for them or for her while she remained in the family.

'I ought to be dead-or back in the Bush!' she cried again, in her heart. 'Oh, if only one was as easy as the other!'

These were her sole longings. Of the two, one was strong and not new (being intensified, not produced, by the circumstances), but sufficiently impracticable. The other was easy to compass, easy to the point of temptation, but as yet not nearly so strong, being entirely the impulse of events. But neither longing was at present anything more than a longing; no purpose showed through either yet. The reality of Alfred's love, the feeling that it would kill him to lose her, was accountable for this. Gladys's resolution was, so far, a blank tablet, not because purpose was absent, but because it was not yet become visible.

A rough analogy may be borrowed from the sensitive film used for the production of a photographic negative. The impression is taken, yet the film remains blank as it was before, until the proper acid is applied, when the impression becomes visible.

Now, a moral acid, acting upon that blank tablet of the mind, would produce a precisely similar effect. Suppose Gladys became convinced that Alfred would be a happier man without her, that it would be even a relief to him to lose her: this would supply the moral acid.

The effect of this moral acid would coincide with that of the photographer's acid. In either case something that had been imperceptible hitherto would now start out in sharp outline. The blank film would yield the negative picture; the vague longings of Gladys would take the shape of two distinct alternatives, one of them inevitable.

Suppose this happened, one of these alternatives was so simple as to be already, in its embryo state, something of a temptation; while the other would remain a moral impossibility.

It must be remembered that the Bride confronted no such alternatives yet, but merely experienced vague, passionate longings. In this state of mind, however, but one drop of acid was needed to produce 'development.'

Miss Travers did not, after all, succeed in cornering Gladys at the garden-party, but she did contrive to get herself asked to stay later, and without much difficulty (she would probably have found it far more difficult to go with the rest-hostesses were tenacious of Miss Travers); and after dinner, when the ladies went off to the drawing-room, her stubborn waiting was at last rewarded.

Some other people had stayed to dinner also, in the same informal way, and among them one or two of Granville's friends. These young men had come to the garden-party by no advice of Gran's — in fact, those who chanced to have mentioned to him Lady Bligh's invitation he had frankly told to stay away and not to be fools. But, having come, he insisted on their staying. 'For,' he said, 'you deserve compensation, you fellows; and the Judge's wine, though I say it, hasn't a fault-unless it's spoiling a man for his club's.'

And while the young men put the truth of this statement to a more earnest test than could be applied before the ladies left the table, Miss Travers, in the drawing-room, at last had Gladys to herself. And Miss Travers was sadly disappointed-as, perhaps, she deserved to be. Gladys had very little to say to her. As a matter of fact, it was no less irksome to the Bride to listen than to talk herself. But they happened to be sitting close to the piano, and it was not long before a very happy thought struck Gladys, which she instantly expressed in the abrupt question: —

'You sing, Miss Travers, don't you?'

'In a way.'

'In a way! I've heard all about the way!' Gladys smiled; Miss Travers thought the smile sadly changed since yesterday. 'Sing now.'

'You really want me to?'

'Yes, really. And you must.' Gladys opened the piano.

Miss Travers sang a little song that Gladys had never heard before, accompanying herself from memory. She sang very sweetly, very simply-in a word, uncommonly well. The voice, to begin with, was an exceptionally sound soprano, but the secret and charm of it all was, of course, in the way she used her voice. Gladys had asked for a song to escape from a chat, but she had forgotten her motive in asking-she had forgotten that she *had* asked for it-she had forgotten much that it had seemed impossible to forget, even thus, for one moment-before the song was half finished. Very possibly, with Gladys, who knew nothing of music, this was an appeal to the senses only; but it gave her some peaceful, painless moments when such were rare; and it left her, with everything coming back to her, it is true, but with a grateful heart. So grateful, indeed, was Gladys that she forgot to express her thanks until Miss Travers smilingly asked her how she liked that song; and then, instead of answering, she went over to where Lady Bligh was sitting, bent down, and asked a question, which was answered in a whisper.

Then Gladys came back to the piano. 'Yes, I *do* like that song, very, very much; and I beg your pardon for not answering you, Miss Travers, but I was thinking of something else; and I want you, please, to sing Mendelssohn's "Hear my Prayer!"' These words came quickly-they were newly learnt from Lady Bligh.

Miss Travers could not repress a smile. 'Do you know what you are asking me for?'

'Yes; for what we heard in church last Sunday evening. That's the name, because I've just asked Lady Bligh. I would rather you sang that than anything else in the world!'

'But — —' Miss Travers was puzzled by the Bride's expression; she would have given anything not to refuse, yet what could she do? 'But-it isn't the sort of thing one can sit down and sing —*really* it isn't. It wants a chorus, and it is very long and elaborate.'

'Yes?' Gladys seemed strangely disappointed. 'But there was one part-the part I liked-where the chorus didn't come in, I am sure. It was sung by a boy. You could do it so much better! It was about the wings of a dove, and the wilderness. You know, I come from the wilderness my-self' —the Bride smiled faintly —'and I thought I'd never heard anything half so lovely before; though of course I've heard very little.'

'No matter how little you have heard, you will never hear anything much more beautiful than that,' said Miss Travers, with sympathetic enthusiasm.

'Since I cannot hear it now, however, there is an end of it.'

Gladys sighed, but her eyes pleaded still; it was impossible to look in them long and still resist. Miss Travers looked but for a moment, then, turning round to the keys, she softly touched a chord. 'I will try the little bit you liked,' she whispered, kindly, 'whatever I make of it!'

What she did make of it is unimportant, except in its effect upon Gladys. This effect was very different from that produced a few minutes before by the song; this, at least, was no mere titillation of the senses by agreeable sounds. And it differed quite as much from the effect produced by the same thing in church on Sunday, when Gladys, after being surprised into listening, had listened only to the words. Then, indeed, the music had seemed sweet and sad, but to-night each note palpitated with a shivering, tremulous yearning, dropping into her soul a relief as deep as that of sorrow unbosomed, a comfort as soothing as the comfort of tears. And there was now an added infinity of meaning in the words; though it was the words that had thrilled her then-then, before she had brought all the present misery to pass.

> O for the wings, for the wings of a dove!
> Far away, far away would I rove:
> In the wilderness build me a nest,
> And remain there for ever at rest.

It is only a few bars, the solo here; and at the point where the chorus catches up the refrain Miss Travers softly ceased. She turned round slowly on the stool, then rose up quickly in surprise. Her ardent listener was gone. And as Miss Travers stood by the piano, peering with raised eyebrows into every corner of the room, and out into the night through the open French window, the men entered the room in a body-she was surrounded.

But Gladys had stepped softly through the window on to the lawn, re-entered the house by another way, and stolen swiftly up to her room. The last strains came to her through the open window of the drawing-room, and in at her own window, at which Gladys now knelt: and this short passage through the outer air brought them upward on the breath of the night, rarefied and softened as though from the lips of far-off angels: and so they reached her trembling ears.

The scent of roses was in the air. The moon was rising, and its rays spanned the river with a broad bridge of silver, against which some of the foliage at the garden-end stood out in fine filigree. It was a heavenly night; it was a sweet and tranquil place; but yet —

> O for the wings of a dove!

Gladys had been home-sick before; she had been miserable and desperate for many, many hours; but at this moment it seemed as though hitherto she had never known what it was to pant and pray in real earnest for her old life and her own country. She was almost as a weak woman in the transports of spiritual fervour, her vision riveted upon some material mental picture, the soul for one ecstatic instant separated from the flesh-only Gladys missed the ecstasy.

There was no light in the room; and the girl remained so entirely motionless, as she knelt, that her glossy head, just raised above the level of the sill, would have seemed in the moonlight a mere inanimate accessory, if it had been seen at all. But only the bats could have seen Gladys, and they did not; at all events, it was the touch of a bat's wing upon the forehead that recalled her to herself, making her aware of voices within earshot, immediately below her window. Her room was over the dining-room. The voices were men's voices, and the scent of cigars reached her as well. She could hear distinctly, but she never would have listened had she not heard her own name spoken; and then-the weakness of the moment prevented her from rising.

'No,' said one of the voices, 'not a bit of it; oh dear, no! Gladys has her good points; and, frankly, I am getting rather to like her. But she is impossible in her position. The whole thing was a fearful mistake, which poor old Alfred will live to repent.'

The voice was unmistakable; it was Granville's.

'But' —and the other voice was that of Granville's most intimate friend, whom he had introduced to Gladys during the course of the afternoon —'doesn't he repent it already, think you?'

'Upon my word, I'm not sure that he doesn't,' said Granville.

'If you ask me,' said his friend, 'I should say there isn't a doubt of it. I've been watching him pretty closely. Mark my words, he's a miserable man!'

'Well, I'm half inclined to agree with you,' said Granville. 'I didn't think so two or three days since, but now I do. You see, there are camels' backs and there are last straws (though I wish there were no proverbs); and there never was a heavier straw than yesterday's —'gad! 'twas as heavy as the rest of the load! I mean the perfectly awful scene in the Park, which you know about, and the whole town knows about, and the low papers will publish, confound them! Yes, I believe you're right; he *can't* get over this.'

'Poor chap!' said Granville's friend.

'You may well say that. Alfred is no genius' —Granville was, apparently —'but he has position; he has money-luckily for him; he means to settle down in the country somewhere, and, no doubt, he'd like to be somebody in the county. But how could he? Look at his wife!'

'There ought to be a separation,' said the friend, feelingly.

'Well, I don't think it's quite as bad as that,' said Granville, wearing ship. 'Anyway, there never will be one; you may trust her for that. And, I must own, I don't think it's all the main chance with her, either; they're sufficiently spooney. Why, she will not even leave him for a week on a visit, though, as I understand, he's doing his best to persuade her to.'

Gladys's hands tightened upon the woodwork of the window-frame.

'Can't persuade her to?' cried the friend. 'What did I tell you? Why, Lord love you, he wants to get rid of her already!'

This was rather strong, even for an intimate friend, and even though the intimate friend had drunk a good deal of wine. Granville's tone cooled suddenly.

'We'll drop the subject, I think. My cigar's done, and you've smoked as much as is good for you. You can do as you like, but I'm going inside.'

Their footsteps sounded down the gravel-path; then the sound ceased; they had gone in by the drawing-room window.

Gladys had never once altered her position; she did not alter it now. The moon rose high in the purple sky, and touched her head with threads of silver. It was as though gray hairs had come upon her while she knelt. The sudden turning of the door-handle, and a quick step upon the threshold, aroused her. It was Alfred come for an easier coat. The people were gone.

'What —*Gladys!*' he cried. She rose stiffly to her feet, and confronted him with her back to the moonlight. 'Up here-alone?'

'You didn't miss me, then?' Her tone was low and hoarse-the words ran into one another in their hurried, eager utterance.

'Why, no,' cried Alfred; 'to tell you the truth, I didn't.'

He seemed to her in better spirits than he had been all day; his voice was full and cheery, and his manner brisk. Why? Evidently the evening had gone off very agreeably. Why? Was it because he had got rid of her for an hour? Was it, then, true that he was doing his best to get rid of her for a week-that he would be only too glad to get rid of her for ever? It was as though a poniard were being held to her breast. She paused, and nerved herself to speak calmly, before, as it were, baring her bosom to the steel.

'Alfred,' she said at length, with slow distinctness, but not with the manner of one who is consciously asking a question of life or death, 'I have been thinking it over, about the Barringtons; and I think I *should* like to go to them on Saturday after all. May I go?'

'May you?' Alfred fairly shouted. 'I am only too delighted, Gladdie! Of course you may.'

The poniard went in-to the hilt.

So delighted was Alfred that he caught her in his arms and kissed her. Her cheek was quite cold, her frame all limp. Though she reeled on her feet, she seemed to shrink instinctively from his support.

'What's the matter, Gladdie?' he cried, in sudden alarm. 'What's wrong-are you ill? Stop, I'll fetch ——'

She interrupted him in a whisper.

'Fetch no one.' She dropped one hand upon the dressing-table, leant her weight upon it, and motioned him back with the other. 'I am not ill; I only was faint, just for a moment. I am all right now. There, that's a long breath; I can speak quite properly again. You see, it was only a passing faintness. I must have fallen asleep by the window. I was enjoying the lovely night, and that must have done it. There, I am only tired now, and want-sleep!'

That acid had been applied, and not in drops. Its work was complete.

Chapter XV
The First Parting

It was Saturday forenoon, and everything was ready for the departure of Gladys. Moreover, the moment had come. Garrod was at the door with the carriage; the phlegmatic stable-boy, having performed feats of unsuspected strength with the luggage, had retired into his own peculiar shell, and lurked in sullen humility at the far side of the horse; while Mr Dix figured imposingly in the hall. Alfred was here too, waiting for Gladys to come down. But Gladys was upstairs saying good-bye to Lady Bligh, and lingering over the parting somewhat strangely, for one who was going away for a week only.

'If I hear any more such absurd talk,' Lady Bligh said at last, and with some impatience, 'about forgiveness and the like, I shall punish you by not allowing you to leave me at all.'

'It is too late to do that,' Gladys hastily put in. 'But oh, Lady Bligh! if only you knew how happy you have made me-how happily I go away, having your forgiveness for everything, for everything — —'

'Except for what you are saying now. How wildly you do talk, child! One would think you were going for ever.'

'Who knows, Lady Bligh? There are accidents every day. That's why I'm thankful to be leaving like this.'

Lady Bligh hated sentimentality. Only the intense earnestness of the girl's voice and manner restrained her from laughing; sentimentality was only fit to be laughed at; but this was sentimentality of a puzzling kind.

A minute later, with passionate kisses and incoherent expressions, out of all proportion to the occasion, and fairly bewildering to poor Lady Bligh, Gladys was gone.

Alfred scanned her narrowly as they drove to the station. By the way she kept turning round to gaze backward, you would have thought her anxious to 'see the last of' things, as small boys are when the holidays are over, and bigger boys when they go finally out into the world. Alfred was going with her to Liverpool Street. She had refused to go at all if he took her (as he wanted to) all the way into Suffolk, to return himself by the next train.

'Gladdie,' he said, after watching her closely, 'you look cut up; is it from saying good-bye to the *mater*?'

'I suppose it must be-if I really look like that.'

'There is still, perhaps, some soreness — —'

'No, there is none now,' said Gladys, quickly.

'Then what is it?'

'Only that it is so dreadful, saying good-bye!'

'My darling! —by the way you talk you might be going for good and all. And it is only for a week.'

She did not answer, but pressed the hand that closed over her own.

During the half-hour's run to Waterloo he continued to glance furtively, and not without apprehension, at her face. It was unusually pale; dark rings encircled the eyes, and the eyes were unusually brilliant.

They had a compartment to themselves. He held her hand all the way, and she his, like a pair of moonstruck young lovers; and, for the most part, they were as silent.

'You have not been yourself these last few days,' he said at length; 'I am glad you are going.'

'And I am glad of that,' she answered.

Her tone was odd.

'But I shall be wretched while you are gone,' he quickly added.

She made no reply to this; it seemed to her an afterthought. But, if it was, it grew upon him with swift and miserable effect as the minutes remaining to them gradually diminished. When they drove up to Liverpool Street he was in the depths of dejection.

It was their first parting.

She insisted on sending the necessary telegram to the Barringtons herself. His depression made him absent, and even remiss. He stood listlessly by while she filled in the form; at any other time he would have done this for her, or at least looked over her shoulder-humorously to check the spelling; but this afternoon he was less attentive in little things than she had ever known him, because she had never known him so depressed.

It was their first parting.

He had got her a compartment to herself, but only at her earnest insistence; *he* had spoken for a carriage full of people, or the one reserved for ladies-anything but solitary confinement. It was the Cambridge train; there were few stoppages and no changes.

Gladys was ensconced in her corner. For the moment, her husband sat facing her. Four minutes were left them.

'You have a Don in the next carriage to you; an ancient and wonderfully amiable one, I should say,' observed Alfred, with a sickly attempt at levity. 'I wish you were under his wing, my dear!'

Gladys made a respondent effort, an infinitely harder one. 'No, thanks,' she said; 'not *me!*'

'Come, I say! Is it nervousness or vanity?'

'It is neither.'

'Yet you look nervous, Gladdie, joking apart-and, honestly, I never felt less like joking in my life. And you are pale, my darling; and your hand is so cold!'

She withdrew the hand.

But one more minute was left. 'Better get out, sir,' said the guard, 'and I'll lock the lady in.'

Gladys felt a shiver pass through her entire frame. With a supreme effort she controlled herself. They kissed and clasped hands. Then Alfred stepped down heavily on to the platform.

The minute was a long one; these minutes always are. It was an age in passing, a flash to look back upon. These minutes are among the strangest accomplishments of the sorcerer Time.

'It is dreadful to let you go alone, darling, like this,' he said, standing on the foot-board and leaning in. 'At least you ought to have had Bunn with you. You might have given way in that, Gladdie.'

'No,' she whispered tremulously; 'I—I like going alone.'

'You must write at once, Gladdie.'

'To-morrow; but you could only get it latish on Monday.'

The bell was ringing. You know the clangour of a station bell; of all sounds the last that it resembles is that of the funeral knell; yet this was its echo in the heart of Gladys.

'Well, it's only for a week, after all, isn't it, Gladdie? It will be the weariest week of my life, I know. But I shan't mind-after all, it's my own doing-if only you come back with a better colour. You have been so pale, Gladdie, these last few days-pale and excitable. But it's only a week, my darling, eh?'

She could not answer.

The guard blew his whistle. There was an end of the minute at last.

'Stand back,' she whispered: her voice was stifled with tears.

'Back?'—Alfred peered up into her face, and a sudden pallor spread upon his own—'with your dear eyes full of tears, where I never yet saw tears before? Back?—God forgive me for thinking of it, I'll come with you yet!'

He made as though to dive headlong through the window; but, looking him full in the eyes through her tears, his girl-wife laid a strong hand on each of his shoulders and forced him back. He staggered as the platform came under his feet. The train was already moving. He stood and gazed.

Gladys was waving to him, and smiling through her tears. So she continued until she could see him no more. Then she fell back upon the cushions, and, for a time, consciousness left her.

It was their first parting.

Chapter XVI
Traces

Alfred did not become unconscious, nor even feel faint: he was a man. But he did feel profoundly wretched. He tried to shake off this feeling, but failed. Later, on his way back through the City, he stopped somewhere to try and lunch it off, and with rather better success. He was a man: he proceeded to throw the blame upon the woman. It was Gladys who had supplied all the sentiment (and there had been an absurd amount of it) at their parting; it was the woman who had exaggerated this paltry week's separation, until it had assumed, perhaps for them both-at the moment-abnormal dimensions; he, the man, was blameless. If *his* way had obtained, she should have gone away in highest spirits, instead of in tears-and all for one insignificant week! He should write her a serious, if not a severe, letter on the subject. So Alfred went down to Twickenham in quite a valiant mood to face his week of single-blessedness, and to affect a droll appreciation of it in the popular, sprightly manner of the long-married man.

But the miserable feeling returned-if, indeed, it had ever been chased fairly away; and it returned with such force that Alfred was obliged to own at last that it, too, was exaggerated and out of all proportion to the exciting cause. He, in his turn, was sentimentalising as though Gladys had gone for a term of years. He was conscious of this; but he could not help it. His thoughts seemed bound to the parting of this Saturday, powerless to fly forward to the reunion of the next. A vague, dim sense of finality was the restraining bond; but this sense was not long to remain dim or vague. Meanwhile, so far as Alfred was concerned, the Sunday that followed was wrapped in a gloom that not even the genial presence of the distinguished (but jocular) guest could in any way pierce or dissipate. Nevertheless, it contained the last tranquil moments that Alfred was to know at that period of his life; for it led him to the verge of an ordeal such as few men are called upon to undergo.

He was not a little surprised on the Monday morning to find among the letters by the first post one addressed to his wife. She had received scarcely any letters since her arrival in England-two or three from tradesmen, an invitation or so, nothing from Australia; but this letter was directed in a large, bold hand, with which Alfred fancied he was not wholly unfamiliar; and he suddenly remembered that he had seen it before in Miss Barrington's note of invitation. Now, the post-mark bore the name of the town to which Gladys had booked from Liverpool Street, and the date of the day before; and how could Miss Barrington write to Gladys at Twickenham, when Gladys was staying with Miss Barrington in Suffolk?

He tore open the envelope, and his hand shook as he did so. When he had read to the end of the letter, which was very short, his face was gray and ghastly; his eyes were wild and staring; he sank helplessly into a chair. The note ran thus: —

> 'Dearest Glad, —We are *so* disappointed, you can't think. As for me, I've been in the sulks ever since your telegram came this afternoon. What *ever can* have prevented your coming, at the *very last minute* —for your wire from *Liverpool Street*? Do write at once, for I'm *horribly* anxious, to your loving
>
> 'Ada.
>
> 'PS. —And do *come* at once, if it's nothing serious.
> 'Saturday.'

Alfred read the letter a second time, and an extraordinary composure came over him.

He folded the letter, restored it to its envelope, and put the envelope in his pocket. Then he looked at the clock. It wanted a quarter to eight. The Judge was no doubt up and about somewhere; but none of the others were down. Alfred rang the bell, and left word that he had received a letter begging an early interview on important business, and that he would breakfast in town.

Alfred was stunned; but he had formed a plan. This plan he proceeded to put into effect; or rather, once formed, the plan evolved itself into mechanical action without further thought. For some hours following he did not perfectly realise either what he was doing or why he was doing it. He never thoroughly pulled himself together, until a country conveyance, rattling him through country lanes, whisked into a wooded drive, and presently past a lawn where people were playing lawn-tennis, and so to the steps of a square, solid, country house. But he had all his wits about him, and those sharpened to the finest possible point, when he looked to see whether Gladys was, or was not, among the girls on the lawn. She was not. That was settled. He got out and rang the bell. He inquired for Mr Barrington; Mr Barrington was playing at lawn-tennis. In answer to a question from the butler, Bligh said that he would rather see Mr Barrington in the house than go to him on the tennis-court. He could wait until the set was finished. He had come from London expressly to speak for a few minutes with Mr Barrington. His name would keep until Mr Barrington came; but he was from Australia.

The last piece of information was calculated to fetch Mr Barrington at once; and it did. He came as he was, in his flannels, his thick hairy arms bare to the elbow: a bronzed, leonine man of fifty, with the hearty, hospitable manner of the Colonial 'squatocracy.' Alfred explained in a few words who he was, and why he had come. He had but one or two questions to ask, and he asked them with perfect self-possession. They elicited the assurance that nothing had been heard of Gladys in that quarter, beyond the brief message received on the Saturday. Mr Barrington found the telegram, and handed it to his visitor. It read: 'Prevented coming at last moment. Am writing-Gladys.' By the time of despatch, Bligh knew that it was the message she had written out in his presence.

'Of course she never wrote?' he said coolly to the squatter.

'We have received nothing,' was the grave answer.

'Yet she started,' said Alfred. 'I put her in the train myself, and saw her off.'

His composure was incredible. The Australian was more shaken than he.

'Did you make any inquiries on the line?' asked Barrington, after a pause.

'Inquiries about what?'

'There might have been-an accident.'

Bligh tapped the telegram with his finger. 'This points to no accident,' he said, grimly. 'But,' he added, more thoughtfully, 'one might make inquiries down the line, as you say. It might do good to make inquiries all along the line.'

'Do you mean to say you have made *none?*'

'None,' said Alfred, fetching a deep sigh. 'I came here straight. I could think of nothing else but getting here-and-perhaps-finding her! I thought —I thought there might be some-mistake!' His voice suddenly broke. The futility of the hope that had sustained him for hours had dawned upon him slowly, but now the cruel light hid nothing any longer. She was not here; she had not been heard of here; and precious hours had been lost. He grasped his hat and held out his trembling hand.

'Thank you! Thank you, Mr Barrington! Now I must be off.'

'Where to?'

'To Scotland Yard. I should have gone there first. But —I was mad, I think; I thought there had been some mistake. Only some mistake!'

The squatter was touched to the soul. 'I have known her, off and on, since she was a baby,' he said. 'Bligh-if you would only let me, I should like to come with you.'

Alfred wrung the other's hand, but refused his offer.

'No. Though I am grateful indeed, I would rather go alone. It would do no good, your coming; I should prefer to be alone. So only one word more. Your daughter was a great friend of Gladys; better not tell her anything of this. For it may still be only some wild freak, Mr Barrington-God knows what it is!'

It was evening when he reached London. A whole day had been wasted. He stated his case to the police; and then there was no more to be done that night. With an eagerness that all at once became feverish he hastened back to Twickenham. It was late when he arrived at the house; only Granville was up; and, for an instant, Granville thought his brother had been drinking. The delusion lasted no longer than that instant. It was not drink with Alfred: his excitement was suppressed: he stood staring at Granville with a questioning, eager expression, as though he expected news. What could it mean? What could be the explanation of such fierce excitement in stolid Alfred, of all people in the world?

Granville thought of the one thing, or rather of the one person, likely, and threw out a feeler: —

'Have you heard from Gladys?'

'No,' said Alfred, in a hollow voice. *'Have you seen her?'*

This was the last idea that had possessed him: that Gladys might have come home, that he might find her there on his return. It was the second time that day that he had cheated himself with vain, unreasoning hopes.

'Seen her?' Granville screwed in his eyeglass tighter. 'Of course I haven't seen her! How should we see her here, my good fellow, when she's down in Suffolk?'

Alfred turned pale, and for an instant stood glaring; then he burst into a harsh laugh.

'You know how odd she is, Gran! I thought she might have tired of her friends and come back. She's capable of it, and I feared it-that's all!'

He left the room abruptly.

'Poor chap!' said Granville, with a sentient shake of the head; 'he *is* far gone, if you like.'

Next morning Alfred walked into Scotland Yard as the clocks were striking eleven. His appointment was for that hour, and he had striven successfully to keep it to the second; though commonly he was a far from punctual man. In point of fact, he had been sitting and loitering about the Embankment for a whole hour, waiting until the moment of his appointment should come, as unwilling to go to it a minute before the time as a minute late. So he entered the Yard while Big Ben was striking. And this was a young man with a reputation for unpunctuality, and all-round unbusinesslike, dilatory habits.

Moreover, for a man who, as a rule, was not fastidious enough about such matters, his appearance this morning was wellnigh immaculate. Yet, perhaps, he had only sought, by a long and elaborate toilet, to while away the long, light hours of the early morning: for, on looking at him closely, it was impossible to believe that he had slept a wink. The fact is, abnormal circumstances had conduced to bring about in Alfred an entirely abnormal state of mind. In a word, and a trite one, he was no longer himself. A crust of insensibility had hardened upon him. Had there been no news for him at all at the Yard this morning, possibly this crust might have been broken through: for he was better prepared for one crushing blow than for the bruises of repeated disappointment. Thus, the very worst news might have affected him less, at the moment, than no news, which is supposed, popularly, to be of the best. But there was some news.

Official investigation had thus far discovered what a person of average intelligence, with a little more presence of mind than Alfred had shown, might have ascertained, perhaps for himself. Yet the information was important. Gladys had left the train, with her luggage, two stations before her destination. This was testified by the guard of the train. But there was a later fact still. It was certain that Gladys had returned to town by the next up-train: for she had personally deposited her luggage in the cloak-room at Liverpool Street between the hours of six and seven on the Saturday evening. There all trace of her was lost, for the present; but it was extremely likely that fresh traces would be forthcoming during the course of the day.

The simple nature of the inquiries that had elicited the above information will be at once apparent; but Alfred went away with an exalted opinion of the blood-hound sagacity of the police. In his present condition of mind, his opinion, good or bad, was not worth much. He went to a club which he had not been in for years, and of which he had long ceased to look upon himself as a member; but his bankers, doubtless, still paid his subscription; and in any case it was not likely that he would be turned out. He would find some quiet corner and sit down and wait until the messenger came from Scotland Yard; for, of course, something more would be discovered during the course of the day-had they not promised as much? The quiet corner that he chose was an upstairs window, from which there was a fair glimpse of the river. The river fascinated him most strangely to-day. During the hour he had loitered on the Embankment, between ten and eleven, he had raised his eyes but seldom from the river.

He sat long at the window-so long that minutes ran into hours and the summer afternoon melted into the summer evening. The room was a reading-room; the windows were in snug recesses. Alfred had his recess to himself for hours and hours. He was conscious of no other presence; certainly no one spoke to him: very possibly, with his beard, no one recognised him.

The sun was sinking. He could not see it from this window; but he could see the heightened contrast of light and shadow among the ripples of the river, and the shadows deepening far away under Westminster Bridge. This was where his gaze rested. It was a stony gaze; his lips were compressed and bloodless, his features pointed and pale. A hideous vision filled his mind; but it was a vision only; it had no meaning. He did not realise it. He realised nothing....Some one came and asked if he was Mr Bligh. It was a club servant. A man awaited him below. Alfred went down; the messenger from Scotland Yard was come at last.

The messenger was the bearer of these few words: —

'A lady's hat and jacket have been found in the river below Blackwall. If you wish to see them, they are here.'

Five minutes later Alfred walked into the office in which he had heard the result of the investigations that morning, and identified instantly the jacket and hat awaiting his inspection.

Gladys had gone away in them on Saturday.

Chapter XVII
Waiting for the Worst

For the second time, it was Granville whom Alfred first encountered on his return from town. They met in the twilight. Dinner was over, and Granville sauntered alone in the bit of garden between the house and the road, smoking a cigarette. Suddenly the gate was opened, and the one brother, looking up, saw the other coming quickly towards him through the dusk.

It was too dark for the ready reading of faces; but it struck Granville that the approaching footsteps were hasty and unusual. He recalled Alfred's unaccountable manner of the night before. Indeed, all his movements, during the past two days, were mysterious: up to London first thing in the morning, back late, and not a word to any one; whereas the whole household, as a general rule, were in possession of most of Alfred's private plans and hopes and fears. But Granville had no time to speculate now. Alfred came straight up to him.

'I want to speak to you, Gran,' he said. 'I'm glad I found you here.'

The step had been suspicious; the voice was worse. It was calm enough, but it was not Alfred's voice at all. Something had happened. Granville put up his eyeglass; but in that light it did not avail him much.

'Let us sit down, then,' said Granville, leading the way to a seat under the trees.

'What is it about?'

Then Alfred began, in set tones and orderly phrases. The affectation of his manner was almost grotesque.

'I want a kind of professional opinion from you, Gran, about-let us say, about a case that interests me, rather. That will be near enough to the mark, I think.'

'Delighted to help you, if I can.' Granville lounged back carelessly on the garden-seat, but his keen glance lost not a line of the other's profile, as Alfred bent forward with his eyes upon the ground; and those lines seemed strangely hardened.

'Thank you. The case is, briefly, this,' Alfred continued: 'somebody-no matter who-has been missing for some days. The number of days is of no consequence either. The police were not informed immediately. They only heard of it last night. But, this afternoon, they found — —'

Alfred checked himself, sat upright, shifted his position, and met Granville's gaze.

'What should you consider incontestable evidence of drowning, Gran?'

'The body.'

'Of course. But you have to look for bodies. What should you find, to make you search with the absolute certainty of discovering the body at last?'

'Nothing else could make it an absolute certainty. But lots of things would set you search-ing —a hat, for instance.'

'They have found her hat!' said Alfred, through his clenched teeth.

'*Her* hat! Whose?'

Alfred stretched over, caught Granville's arm in a nervous grip, and whispered rapidly in his ear. In a moment Granville knew all. But he did not speak immediately. When he did speak, it was to ask questions. And there was another unnatural voice now, besides Alfred's —Granville's was quite soft.

'Was she unhappy at all?' he asked.

'Just the reverse, I thought, until last week. You know what happened in the Park yesterday week. She said some very wild things after that, and spoke as though she had never been quite happy here; she vowed she would never forgive herself for what she had done; and she said she wished she was dead. Well, I did not think much about her words; I thought more of what she had done; I put down what she said to the shame and temper of the moment, not to real unhappiness. But, when I said good-bye to her, then she *was* unhappy-more so than I ever knew her before.'

From his tone, no one could have guessed that he was speaking of his wife.

'And you think she-she — —'

Granville could not bring his lips to utter the words.

Alfred could. 'I think she has drowned herself,' he said calmly.

Granville shuddered. Callous as he was himself by nature, callousness such as this he could not have imagined possible; it was horrible to see and to hear.

Neither spoke for some little time.

'Did it never occur to you,' said Granville, at last, 'that she might have drowned herself without all this trouble, simply by walking to the bottom of the garden here?'

'What?' cried Alfred, sharply. His fingers tightened upon Granville's arm. His voice fell, oddly enough, into a natural tone.

Granville repeated his question.

'No,' said Alfred, hoarsely, 'that never crossed my mind. But there's something in it. God bless you, Gran, for putting it into my head! It's almost like a ray of hope-the first. If I hadn't seen the things and identified them as hers ——'

'The things! You did not say there was anything else besides the hat. What else was there?'

'The jacket she went away in.'

'You are sure it was hers?'

'Yes.'

'You could swear to both hat and jacket?'

'Yes.'

Granville leapt to his feet.

'Who throw their things into the water' —he asked, in strange excitement, for him —'the people who mean to sink or the people who mean to swim-or the people who mean to stay on the bank?'

Alfred stared at him blankly. Gradually the light dawned upon him that had entered Granville's quicker intelligence in a flash.

'What do you mean?' whispered Alfred; and, in a moment, his voice and his limbs were trembling.

'Nothing very obscure,' replied Granville, with a touch of contempt, which, even then, he could not manage to conceal (Alfred's slow perception always had irritated him); 'simply this: Gladys has *not* drowned herself. She was never the girl to do it. She had too much sense and vitality and courage. But she may mean us to think there's an end of her-God knows with what intention. She may have gone off somewhere-God knows where. We must find out ——'

He stopped abruptly, and nearly swore: for Alfred was wringing his hand, and weeping like a child.

Granville hated this, but bore it stoically. It was now plain to him that Alfred had been driven very nearly out of his senses: and no wonder-Granville himself could as yet scarcely realise or believe what he had heard. And this outburst was the natural reaction following upon an unnatural mental condition. But *was* there any ground for hope? Granville was less confident than he appeared when he amended his last words and said: —

'I *will* find out.'

Alfred wrung his hand again. He was calmer now, but terribly shaken and shattered. The weakness that he had been storing up during the past two days had come over him, as it were, in the lump. Granville led him to his room. Alfred had never in his life before known Granville half so good-natured and sympathetic; he blessed him fervently.

'You were her friend,' he said, huskily. 'She thought no end of you, Gran! You got on so splendidly together, after the first few days; and she was always talking about you. Find her-find her for me, Gran; and God bless you-and forgive her for this trick she has played us!'

Granville did not often feel contrition, or remorse, or shame: but he felt all three just then. He knew rather too well the measure of his own kindness to Gladys. For the first time in his life-and not, perhaps, before it was time-he disliked himself heartily. He felt vaguely that, whatever had happened, he had had something to do with it. He had had more to do with it than he guessed. 'I'll do my best —I'll do my best,' he promised; and he meant his 'best' to be better than that of the smartest detective at Scotland Yard.

He left Alfred, shut himself up alone, and reviewed the situation. An hour's hard thinking led to a rather ingenious interview-one with the girl Bunn. It took place on the stairs, of all places. Granville saw her set foot upon the bottom stair; he immediately sat down upon the top one, produced a newspaper, and blocked the gangway.

'Bunn, you have a sweetheart in Australia. Don't pout and toss your head; it's nothing to be ashamed of-quite the contrary; and it's the fact, I think-eh?'

'Lor', Mr Granville, what if I have?'

'Well, nothing; only there is something about it in this newspaper-about Australia, I mean; not about you-that's to come. You shall have the newspaper, Bunn; here it is. I thought you'd like it, that's all.'

Bunn took the paper, all smiles and blushes.

'Oh, thank you, Mr Granville. And-and I beg your pardon, sir.'

'Don't name it, my good girl. But, look here, Bunn; stay one moment, if you don't mind.' (She could scarcely help staying, he gave her no chance of passing; besides, he had put her under an obligation.) 'Tell me now, Bunn-didn't Mrs Alfred know something about him? And didn't Mrs Alfred talk to you a good deal about Australia?'

'That she did, sir. But she didn't know my young man, Mr Granville. She only got his address from me just as she was going away, sir.'

'Ah! she wanted his address before she went away, did she?'

'Yes, sir. She said she would name him in writing to her father, or in speaking to Mr Barrington, or that, any way, it'd be nice to have it, against ever she went out there again, sir.'

'Oh, she gave three reasons all in one, eh? And did she say she'd like to go out again, Bunn?'

'She always said that, sir, between ourselves —"between you and I, Bella," it used to be. But, time I gave her the address, she went on as if she would like to go, and meant a-going, the very next day.'

'Yet she didn't like leaving this, even for a week-eh, Bunn?'

'Lor', no, sir! She spoke as if she was never coming back no more. And she kissed me, Mr Granville-she did, indeed, sir; though I never named that in the servants' hall. She said there might be a accident, or somethink, and me never see her no more; but that, if ever she went back to Australia, she'd remember my young man, and get him a good billet. Them were her very words. But, oh, Mr Granville! —oh, sir! ——'

'There, there. Don't turn on the waterworks, Bunn. I thought Mrs Alfred had been cut up about something; but I wasn't sure-that's why I asked *you*, Bunn; though I think, perhaps, you needn't name this conversation either in the servants' hall, or tell any one else what you have told me. Yes, you may go past now. But-stop a minute, Bunn-here's something else that you needn't name in the servants' hall.'

The something else was a half-sovereign.

'It was worth it, too,' said Granville, when the girl was gone; 'she has given me something to go upon. These half-educated and impulsive people always do let out more to their maids than to any one else.'

He went back to Alfred.

'There was something I forgot to ask you. How much money do you suppose Gladys had about her when she went away?'

'I have no idea,' said Alfred.

'Do you know how much money you have given her since you have been over-roughly?'

'No; I don't know at all.'

'Think, man. Fifty pounds?'

'I should say so. I gave her a note or so whenever it struck me she might want it. She never would ask.'

'Do you think she spent much?'

'I really can't tell you, Gran; perhaps not a great deal, considering everything; for, when I was with her, I never would let her shell out. I never knew of her spending much; but she had it by her, in case she wanted it; and that was all I cared about.'

And that was all Granville cared about. He ceased his questioning; but he was less ready to leave Alfred alone than he had been before. He had found him sitting in the dark by the open window, and staring blankly into the night. Granville had insisted on lighting the gas: only to see how the room was filled with Gladys's things. In every corner of it some woman's trifle breathed of her. Granville felt instinctively that much of this room, in the present suspense, might turn a better brain than Alfred's, in Alfred's position.

'Look here,' said Granville, at last: 'I have been thinking. Listen, Alfred.'

'Well?' said Alfred absently, still gazing out of window.

'I have got a theory,' went on Granville —'no matter what; only it has nothing to say to death or drowning. It is a hopeful theory. I intend to practise it at once: in a day or two it ought to lead me to absolute certainty of one thing, one way or the other. No matter what that one thing is; I have told you what it is not. Now, I shall have to follow out my idea in town; and if I find the truth at all, I shall most likely come across it suddenly, round a corner as it were. So I have been thinking that you may as well be in town too, to be near at hand in case I am successful. If you still have a club, you might hang about there, and talk to men, and read the papers; if not — — Why do you shake your head?'

'I am not going to town any more,' said Alfred, in low, decided tones. 'If you are right, and she is not dead, she may come back-she may come back! Then I shall be here to meet her-and-and — — But you understand me, Gran?'

'Not very well,' said Granville, dryly, and with a shrug of his shoulders that was meant to shift from them all responsibility for Alfred's possible insanity. 'In your case I should prefer to be in town rather than here. However, a man judges for himself. There is one thing, however; if you stay here all day — —'

'What's that?'

'The question whether you should tell the Judge and the *mater*.'

'No,' said Alfred, resolutely; 'I shall not tell them-not, that is, until the worst is known for certain. They think she is at the Barringtons'. I shall say I have heard from her. I would tell a million lies to save them the tortures of uncertainty that I am suffering, and shall suffer, till-till we know the worst. Oh, Granville! —for God's sake, find it out quickly!'

'I'll do my best —I've already told you I would,' said Granville almost savagely; and he left the room.

Granville's best, in matters that required a clear head and some little imagination, was always excellent. In the present instance his normal energies were pushed to abnormal lengths by the uncomfortable feeling that he himself had been not unconcerned in bringing about that state of unhappiness which alone could have driven his sister-in-law to her last rash, mysterious step; by a feverish desire to atone, if the smallest atonement were possible; and by other considerations, which, for once, were unconnected with the first person singular. Nevertheless, on the Wednesday-the day following the foregoing conversation-he found out nothing at all; and nothing at all on the Thursday. Then Alfred made up his mind that nothing but the very worst could now come to light, and that that was only a question of time; and he fell into an apathy, by day, that Granville's most vigorous encouragement, in the evening, could do nothing to correct. Thus, when the news did come, when the terrible suspense was suddenly snapped, Alfred was, perhaps, as ill-prepared for a shock (though he had expected one for days) as it was possible for a man to be.

It was on the Friday night. Lady Bligh and Sir James were deep in their game of *bezique*. Alfred sat apart from them, without a hope left in his heart, and marvellously altered in the face. His pallor was terrible, but perhaps natural; but already his cheekbones, which were high, seemed strangely prominent; and the misery in his large still eyes cried out as it sometimes does from the eyes of dumb animals in pain. He was conscious of his altered looks, perhaps;

for he sedulously avoided looking his parents in the face. They did not know yet. It added to his own anguish to think of the anguish that must come to them too, sooner or later-sooner now-very soon indeed.

The door opened. Granville entered, with a brisk, startling step, and a face lit up-though it was Granville's face-with news.

Alfred saw him-saw his face-and rose unsteadily to his feet.

'Speak! Say you have found her! No —I see it in your face-she is there. Let me come to her!'

As Alfred stepped forward, Granville recoiled, and the light left his face.

Alfred turned to his parents. The Judge had risen, and glanced in mute amazement from one son to the other: both were pale, but their looks told nothing. Lady Bligh sat back in her chair, her smooth face wrinkled with bewilderment and vague terror.

'It is Gladys come back,' said Alfred, in tremulous explanation; 'it is only that Gladys has come back, mother!'

Even then he chuckled in his sleeve to think that they had never known, and never need know, anything of this, the worst of his wife's many and wild escapades.

But Granville recoiled still farther, and his face became gray.

'I have not seen her,' he said, solemnly. 'She is *not* here.'

'Not seen her? Not here?' Alfred was quickly sobered. 'But you know where she is? I see it in your face. She is within reach-eh? Come, take me to her!'

'She is not even within reach,' Granville answered, squeezing out the words by a strenuous effort. 'I cannot take you to her. Gladys sailed for Australia last Monday morning!'

Alfred sunk heavily into a chair. No one spoke. No one was capable of speech. Before any one had time to think, Alfred was on his feet again, tottering towards the door.

'I must follow!' he whispered, in hoarse, broken tones. 'I will follow her to-night! Stand aside, Gran; thanks; and God bless you! Good-bye! I shall know where to find her out there. I have no time to stop!'

Granville stood aside in obedience; but for one instant only: the next-he sprang forward to catch in his arms the falling form of Alfred.

Chapter XVIII
The Boundary-Rider of the Yelkin Paddock

Picture the Great Sahara. The popular impression will do: it has the merit of simplicity: glaring desert, dark-blue sky, vertical sun, and there you are. Omit the mirage and the thirsty man; but, instead, mix sombre colours and work up the African desert into a fairly desirable piece of Australian sheep-country.

This, too, is a simple matter. You have only to cover the desert with pale-green saliferous bushes, no higher than a man's knee; quite a scanty covering will do, so that in the thickest places plenty of sand may still be seen; and there should be barren patches to represent the low sand-hills and the smooth clay-pans. Then have a line of low-sized dark-green scrub at the horizon; but bite in one gleaming, steely speck upon this sombre rim.

Conceive this modification of the desert, and you have a fair notion of the tract of country-six miles by five-which was known on Bindarra Station as the 'Yelkin Paddock,' the largest paddock in the 'C Block.'

Multiply this area by six; divide and subdivide the product by wire fences, such as those that enclose the Yelkin Paddock; water by means of excavations and wells and whims; stock with the pure merino and devastate with the accursed rabbit; and (without troubling about the homestead, which is some miles north of the Yelkin) you will have as good an idea of the Bindarra 'run,' as a whole, as of its sixth part, the paddock under notice.

The conspicuous mark upon the distant belt of dingy low-sized forest-the object that glitters in the strong sunlight, so that it can be seen across miles and miles of plain-is merely the galvanised-iron roof of a log-hut, the hut that has been the lodging of the boundary-rider of the Yelkin Paddock ever since the Yelkin Paddock was fenced.

A boundary-rider is not a 'boss' in the Bush, but he is an important personage, in his way. He sees that the sheep in his paddock 'draw' to the water, that there is water for them to draw to, and that the fences and gates are in order. He is paid fairly, and has a fine, free, solitary life. But no boundary-rider had ever stopped long at the Yelkin hut. The solitude was too intense. After a trial of a few weeks-sometimes days-the man invariably rolled up his blankets, walked in to the homestead, said that there was moderation in all things, even in solitude, and demanded his cheque. The longest recorded term of office in the Yelkin Paddock was six months; but that boundary-rider had his reasons: he was wanted by the police. When, after being captured in the hut, this man was tried and hanged for a peculiarly cold-blooded murder, the Yelkin post became even harder to fill than it had been before.

During the Australian summer following that other summer which witnessed the events of the previous chapters, this post was not only filled for many months by the same boundary-rider, but it was better filled than it had ever been before. Moreover, the boundary-rider was thoroughly satisfied, and even anxious to remain. The complete solitude had been far less appreciated by the gentleman with the rope round his neck; for him it had terrors. The present boundary-rider knew no terrors. The solitude was more than acceptable; the Crusoe-like existence was entirely congenial; the level breezy plains, the monotonous procession of brilliant, blazing days, and the life of the saddle and the hut, were little less than delightful, to the new boundary-rider in the Yelkin. They were the few pleasures left in a spoilt life.

There could have been no better cabin for 'a life awry' (not even in the Bush, the living sepulchre of so many such) than the Yelkin hut. But it was not the place to forget in. There are, however, strong natures that can never forget, and still live on. There are still stronger natures that do not seek to forget, yet retain some of the joy of living side by side with the full sorrow of remembrance. The boundary-rider's was one of these.

The boundary-rider saw but few faces from the home-station; none from anywhere else. But, one glowing, hot-wind day, early in January, a mounted traveller entered the Yelkin Paddock by the gate in the south fence. He was following the main track to the homestead, and this track crossed a corner of the Yelkin Paddock, the corner most remote from the hut. He did not seem a stranger, for he glanced but carelessly at the diverging yet conterminous wheel-marks which are the puzzling feature of all Bush roads. He was a pallid, gaunt, black-bearded man: so gaunt and so pallid, indeed, that no one would have taken him at the first glance, or at the second either, for Alfred Bligh.

Yet it was Alfred-straight, virtually, from his sick-bed. As soon as he could stand (which was not for weeks) he had been taken on board the steamer. The voyage, it was hoped, would do him good, and he was bent on going-to find his wife. It did not do him much good; the eyes that swept at last the territory of his father-in-law were the sunken, wistful eyes of a shattered man.

Nothing had been heard of Gladys. Granville, indeed, had written to Bindarra, but there had been no reply. Of this Alfred had not been informed. From the first moments of returning consciousness he had expressed himself strongly against writing at all.

So, as he crossed the corner of the Yelkin Paddock, all he knew was that Gladys had sailed for Australia six months before.

'If she is here, she is here,' he muttered a hundred times; 'and there will have been no warning of my coming to frighten her away. If she is not here-if she were dead — —'

His eyes dropped upon the bony hand holding the reins.

'Well, it would be an easier matter to follow her there than here. It would take less time!'

But, as often as this contingency presented itself, his thin hand involuntarily tightened the reins. Indeed, the nearer he got to the homestead the slower he rode. Many a thousand times he had ridden in fancy this last stage of his long, long journey, and always at a hand-gallop; but, now that he was riding it in fact, he had not the courage to press on. He let his tired horse make the speed, and even that snail's pace was, at moments, too quick for him.

At the hour wherein he needed his utmost nerve to meet his fate-his nerve, and the stout heart that had brought him, weak as he was, from the opposite end of the earth, were failing him.

The gate in the west fence was in sight, when Alfred, awaking from a fit of absence, became aware that a man with a cylinder of rolled blankets upon his back (his 'swag') was tramping along the track to meet him. For a moment Alfred's heart thumped; he would know his fate now; this man, who was evidently from the home-station, would tell him. Then he recognised the man. It was Daft Larry, the witless stockman, who, being also stone deaf, was incapable of answering questions.

Larry was a short man, strongly built though elderly, and probably less old than he looked. He had a fresh complexion, a short gray beard, and eyes as blue (and as expressionless) as the flawless southern sky. He recognised Alfred, stood in his path, threw down his swag, put his hands in his pockets, and smiled delightedly; not in surprise; in mere idiotic delight. On beholding Alfred, this had been his invariable behaviour. They had beheld one another last a year ago; but last year and yesterday were much the same date to Larry.

'I like a man that is well-bred!' exclaimed Larry, with a seraphic smile, his head critically on one side. On beholding Alfred, this had been his invariable formula.

Alfred stopped his horse.

Daft Larry cocked his head on the other side. 'You're not one of the low sort!' he went on.

Alfred smiled.

'*You're* well-bred,' continued Larry, in the tone of a connoisseur. Then, wagging his head gravely: 'I like a man that's not one of the low sort; I like a man that is well-bred!'

That was the end, as it always had been. Larry picked up his swag with the air of a man who has proved his case.

Alfred had ridden on some yards, when a call from the idiot made him stop.

'Look there!' shouted Larry, with an ungainly sweep of the arm. 'Dust-storm coming up-bad dust-storm. Don't get catched, mister-you aren't one of the low sort-not you!'

Daft Larry had been known to give gratuitous information before, though he could not answer questions. Alfred, instead of riding on, now looked about him. There was sense enough in the warning; though Larry, apparently, did not mind being 'catched' himself, since he was plodding steadily on, leaving the station, probably for good, as he periodically did leave it. There was every indication of a dust-storm, though the sun still shone brilliantly. The hot-wind had become wild and rampant. It was whipping up the sandy coating of the plain in every direction. High in the air were seen whirling spires and cones of sand —a curious effect against the deep-blue sky. Below, puffs of sand were breaking out of the plain in every direction, as though the plain were alive with invisible horsemen. These sandy cloudlets were instantly dissipated by the wind; it was the larger clouds that were lifted whole into the air, and the larger clouds of sand were becoming more and more the rule.

Alfred's eye, quickly scanning the horizon, descried the roof of the boundary-rider's hut still gleaming in the sunlight. He remembered the hut well. It could not be farther than four miles, if as much as that, from this point of the track; but it was twelve miles at least from this to the homestead. He also knew these dust-storms of old; Bindarra was notorious for them. Without thinking twice, Alfred put spurs to his horse and headed for the hut. Before he had ridden half the distance, the detached clouds of sand banded together in one dense whirlwind; and it was only owing to his horse's instinct that he did not ride wide of the hut altogether; for, during the last half mile, he never saw the hut until its outline loomed suddenly over his horse's ears; and by then the sun was invisible.

'I never saw one come on quicker!' gasped Alfred, as he jumped off and tethered his quivering horse in the lee of the hut.

The excitement, and the gallop, had made Alfred's blood tingle in his veins. It was a novel sensation. He stepped briskly into the hut.

Almost his first sight on entering was the reflection of his own face in a little mirror, which was neatly nailed to the wall, close to the door. Alfred had never been vain, but he did pause to gaze at himself then; for his face was covered with a thin veneer of sand, as a wall becomes coated with driven snow. He dashed off the sand, and smiled; and for the moment, with some colour in his cheeks and a healthy light in his eyes, Alfred scarcely knew himself. Then he turned his back upon the glass, merely noting that it was a queer thing to find in a boundary-rider's hut, and that it had not been there a year ago.

The door had been ajar, and the window was blocked up. The sand, however, had found free entry through the crevices between the ill-fitting pine-logs of the walls, and already the yellow coating lay an eighth of an inch thick all over the boarded floor and upon the rude bench and table.

Alfred sat down and watched the whirling sand outside slowly deepen in tint. He had left the door open, because otherwise the interior of the hut would have been in complete darkness. As it was, it was difficult to distinguish objects; but Alfred, glancing round, was struck with the scrupulous tidiness of everything.

'Ration-bags all hung up; nothing left about; fireplace cleaned out-daily, I should say; pannikins bright as silver; bunk made up. All this is most irregular!' exclaimed Alfred. 'This boundary-rider must be a curiosity. I never saw anything half so neat during all the months I was in the Bush before. One might almost suspect a woman's hand in it-especially in that mirror. Which reminds me, Gladys told me she was once out here for a week, alone, riding the boundaries, when they were short-handed. My darling! What nerve! Would to Heaven you had had less nerve!'

The thick sand rattled in continuous assault upon the iron roof. It was becoming a difficult matter to see across the hut. But the storm, and the gallop, had had a curiously exhilarating effect upon Alfred. His spirits had risen.

'I wish that boundary-rider would come in; but the storm's bound to fetch him. I want a pannikin of tea badly, to lay the dust inside; there's as much there as there was outside, I'll be bound. Besides, he will have news for me. Poor Larry! —the same old drivel! And to think that I was something like that in my delirium-that I might have been left like Larry!'

His attention was here attracted by the illustrated prints pasted upon a strip of sackcloth nailed to the pine-logs over the bunk: a feature, this, of every bushman's hut. He went over to look at them, and, the better to do so, leant with one knee upon the bed-the rudely-framed bed that was so wonderfully well 'made.'

'Ah!' remarked Alfred, 'some of them are the old lot; I remember them. But some are new, and-why, that's a cabinet photograph down there by the pillow; and' —bending down to examine it —'good Heavens! it's of *me!*'

It was a fact. The photograph, fixed so close to the pillow, was an extremely life-like one of Alfred Bligh. But how had it got there? Of what interest or value could it be to the boundary-rider of the Yelkin Paddock? It had been taken last summer, at Richmond; and-oh, yes, he remembered now-Gladys had sent one out to her father. That was it, of course. The boundary-man had found it lying about the veranda or the yard at the homestead (Alfred knew his father-in-law), and had rescued it for the wall of his hut. No matter (to the boundary-man) who it was, it was a picture, and one that would rather set off the strip of sackcloth. That was it, of course; a simple explanation.

Yet Alfred trembled. The photograph was in a far from conspicuous position; nor did it look as if it had been left lying about. What if it belonged to Gladys? What if Gladys had fastened it there with her own hands? What if she came sometimes to the hut-this hut in which he stood? What if she had spent another week here riding the boundaries, when her father was short of men?

All at once he felt very near to her; and the feeling made him dizzy. His eyes roved once again round the place, noting the abnormal neatness and order that had struck him at first; a look of wild inquiry came into his haggard face; and even then, as the agony of surmise tightened every nerve —a sound broke plainly upon his ears. It was heard above the tinkle of the sand upon the roof: a horse's canter, muffled in the heavy sand outside.

Alfred sprang to the door. At the same instant a rider drew rein in front of him. They were not five paces apart, but such was the density of the flying sand and dust that he could see no more than the faint outline of the horse and its rider. Then the rider leapt lightly to the ground. It was the boundary-rider of the Yelkin Paddock; but the boundary-rider was a woman.

Alfred reeled forward, and clasped her to his heart.

'Gladdie! Darling!'

He had found her.

Chapter XIX
Another Letter from Alfred

'Bindarra Station, N.S.W., *April 13*.

'Dearest Mother,—Your dear letter, in answer to my first, written in January, has just reached me. Though I wrote so fully last mail, I can't let a mail go without some sort of an answer. But, as a matter of fact, I am in a regular old hurry. The mail-boy is waiting impatiently in the veranda, with his horse "hung up" to one of the posts; and the store keeper is waiting in the store to drop my letter in the bag and seal it up. So I must be short. Even with lots of time, however, you know I never could write stylish, graphic letters like Gran can. So you must make double allowances for me.

'And now, dear mother, about our coming back to England; and what you propose; and what you say about my darling. To take the best first-God bless you for your loving words! I can say nothing else. Yes, I knew you were getting to love her in spite of all her waywardness; and I know —I *know* —that you would love her still. And you would love her none the less for all that has happened; you would remember what I explained in my first letter, that it was *for my sake*; you would think no longer of what she did, but why she did it.

'But, about coming back, we have, as you already know, made up our minds to live out our lives here in Australia. After all, it's a far better country —a bigger and a better Britain. There is no poverty here, or very little; you never get stuck up for coppers in the streets of the towns; or, if you do, it's generally by a newly-landed immigrant who hasn't had time to get out of bad old habits. There's more room for everybody than at home, and fairer rations of cakes and ale all round. Then there's very little ill-health, because the climate is simply perfect-which reminds me that *I* am *quite* well now-have put on nearly two stone since I landed! But all this about Australia's beside the mark: the real point is that it suits Gladdie and me better than any other country in the world.

'Now for some news. We have decided upon our station at last. It is the one in Victoria, in the north-eastern district — — I think I mentioned it among the "probables" in my last. It is not large as stations go; but "down in Vic" you can carry as many sheep to the acre as acres to the sheep up here in the "back-blocks." You see, it is a grass country. But the scenery is splendid: great rugged ranges covered with the typical gum-trees, of which there are none up here, and a fine creek clean through the middle of the "run." Then there are parrots and 'possums and native bears all over the place, none of which you get up here, though I fear there will be more snakes too. The only drawback is the "cockatoos." I don't mean the *bird*, dear mother, but the "cockatoo selectors." Personally, I don't think these gentry are the vermin my father-in-law makes them out to be; *he* brackets them with the rabbits; but *I* mean to make friends with them-if I can. The homestead is delightful: good rooms, and broad veranda round three sides. We are going to be absurdly happy there.

'We shall not take possession though till after shearing —*i.e.* in your autumn, though the agreement is signed and everything arranged. Meanwhile, we shall stay on here, and I am to get a little more Colonial experience. I need it badly, but not perhaps so badly as my father-in-law makes out. He ridiculed the idea of my turning squatter on my own account, unless Gladys was "boss." But, now that we have fixed on the Victorian station, he is a bit more encouraging. He says any fool could make *that* country pay, referring of course to the rainfall, which just there, in the ranges, is one of the best in Australia. Still, he is right: experience *is* everything in the Colonies.

'So I am not quite idle. All day I am riding or driving about the "run," seeing after things, and keeping my eyes open. In the evenings Gladdie and I have taken to reading together. This was her doing, not mine, mind; though I won't yield to her in my liking of it. The worst of it is, it's so difficult to know where to begin; *I* am so painfully ignorant. Can *you* not help us, dear mother, with some hints? Do! —and when we come home some day (just for a trip) you will find us both such reformed and enlightened members of society!

'But, long before that, *you* must come out and see *us*. Don't shake your head. *You simply must.* England and Australia are getting nearer and nearer every year. The world's wearing small, like one of those round balls of soap, between the hands of Time —(a gem in the rough this, for Gran to polish and set!) Why, there's a Queensland squatter who for years has gone "home" for the hunting season; while, on the other hand, Australia is becoming *the* crack place to winter in.

'Now, as you, dear mother, always *do* winter abroad, why not here as well as anywhere else? You must! You shall! If not next winter, then the following one; and if the Judge cannot bring you, then Gran must. That reminds me: how are they both? And has Gran been writing anything specially trenchant lately? I'm afraid I don't appreciate very 'cutely —"miss half the 'touches,'" he used to tell me (though I think I have made him a present of a "touch" to-day). But you know how glad we would both be to read some of his things; so *you* might send one sometimes, dear mother, without him knowing. For we owe him so much! And, besides what he did for me afterwards, he was always so nice and brotherly with Gladys. I know she thought so at the time, though she doesn't speak about him much now —I can't think why. *You're* the one she thinks of most, dearest mother; you're her model and her pattern for life!

'The mail-boy has begun to remonstrate. He'll have to gallop the whole way to the "jolly" township, he says, if I am not quick. So I must break off; but I will answer your dear letter more fully next mail, or, better still, Gladdie shall write herself. Till then, good-bye, and dearest love from us both.

'Ever your affectionate son,

'Alfred.

'PS. —Gladys has read the above: so one last word on the sly.

'Oh, mother, if you only saw her at this moment! She is sitting in the veranda —I can just see her through the door. She's in one of those long deck-chairs, with a book, though she seems to have tired of reading. I can't see much of her face, but only the sweep of her cheek, and the lashes of one lid, and her little ear. But I can see she isn't reading-she's threading her way through the pines into space somewhere-perhaps back to Twickenham, who knows? And she's wearing a white dress; you would like it-it's plain. And her cheek is quite brown; you'll remember how it was the day she landed from the launch. But there! I can't describe like Gran, so it's no good trying. Only I do know this: I simply love her more and more and more, and a million times more for all that has happened. And you, and all of you, and all your friends, would fairly worship her now. You couldn't help it!'

Tiny Luttrell

TO

C. A. M. D.
FROM
E. W. H.

Chapter I
The Coming of Tiny.

Swift of Wallandoon was visibly distraught. He had driven over to the township in the heat of the afternoon to meet the coach. The coach was just in sight, which meant that it could not arrive for at least half an hour. Yet nothing would induce Swift to wait quietly in the hotel veranda; he paid no sort of attention to the publican who pressed him to do so. The iron roofs of the little township crackled in the sun with a sound as of distant musketry; their sharp-edged shadows lay on the sand like sheets of zinc that might be lifted up in one piece; and a hot wind in full blast played steadily upon Swift's neck and ears. He had pulled up in the shade, and was leaning forward, with his wide-awake tilted over his nose, and his eyes on a cloud of dust between the bellying sand-hills and the dark blue sky. The cloud advanced, revealing from time to time a growing speck. That speck was the coach which Swift had come to meet.

He was a young man with broad shoulders and good arms, and a general air of smartness and alacrity about which there could be no mistake. He had dark hair and a fair mustache; his eye was brown and alert; and much wind and sun had reddened a face that commonly gave the impression of complete capability with a sufficiency of force. This afternoon, however, Swift lacked the confident look of the thoroughly capable young man. And he was even younger than he looked; he was young enough to fancy that the owner of Wallandoon, who was a passenger by the approaching coach, had traveled five hundred miles expressly to deprive John Swift of the fine position to which recent good luck had promoted him.

He could think of nothing else to bring Mr. Luttrell all the way from Melbourne at the time of year when a sheep station causes least anxiety. The month was April, there had been a fair rainfall since Christmas, and only in his last letter Mr. Luttrell had told Swift that all he need do for the present was to take care of the fences and let the sheep take care of themselves. The next news was a telegram to the effect that Mr. Luttrell was coming up country to see for himself how things were going at Wallandoon. Having stepped into the managership by an accident, and even so merely as a trial man, young Swift at once made sure that his trial was at an end. It did not strike him that in spite of his youth he was the ideal person for the post. Yet this was obvious. He had five years' experience of the station he was to manage. The like merit is not often in the market. Swift seemed to forget that. Neither did he take comfort from the fact that Mr. Luttrell was an old friend of his family in Victoria, and hitherto his own highly satisfied employer. Hitherto, or until the last three months, he had not tried to manage Mr. Luttrell's station. If he had failed in that time to satisfy its owner, then he would at once go elsewhere; but for many things he wished most keenly to stay at Wallandoon; and he was thinking of these things now, while the coach grew before his eyes.

Of his five years on Wallandoon the last two had been infinitely less enjoyable than the three that had gone before. There was a simple reason for the difference. Until two years ago Mr. Luttrell had himself managed the station, and had lived there with his wife and family. That had answered fairly well while the family were young, thanks to a competent governess for the girls. But when the girls grew up it became time to make a change. The squatter was a wealthy man, and he could perfectly well afford the substantial house which he had already built for himself in a Melbourne suburb. The social splashing of his wife and daughters after their long seclusion in the wilderness was also easily within his means, if not entirely to his liking; but he was a mild man married to a weak woman; and he happened to be bent on a little splash on his own account in politics. Choosing out of many applicants the best possible manager for Wallandoon, the squatter presently entered the Victorian legislature, and embraced the new interests so heartily that he was nearly two years in discovering his best possible manager to be both a failure and a fraud.

It was this discovery that had given Swift an opening whose very splendor accounted for his present doubts and fears. Had his chance been spoilt by Herbert Luttrell, who had lately been on Wallandoon as Swift's overseer, for some ten days only, when the two young fellows had failed to pull together? This was not likely, for Herbert at his worst was an honest ruffian, who had taken the whole blame (indeed it was no more than his share) of that fiasco. Swift, however, could think of nothing else; nor was there time; for now the coach was so close that the crack of the driver's whip was plainly heard, and above the cluster of heads on the box a white handkerchief fluttered against the sky.

The publican whom Swift had snubbed addressed another remark to him from the veranda:

"There's a petticoat on board."

"So I see."

The coach came nearer.

"She's your boss's daughter," affirmed the publican —"the best of 'em."

"So you're cracking!"

"Well, wait a minute. What now?"

Swift prolonged the minute. "You're right," he said, hastily tying his reins to the brake.

"I am so."

"Heaven help me!" muttered Swift as he jumped to the ground. "There's nothing ready for her. They might have told one!"

A moment later five heaving horses stood sweating in the sun, and Swift, reaching up his hand, received from a gray-bearded gentleman on the box seat a grip from which his doubts and fears should have died on the spot. If they did, however, it was only to make way for a new and unlooked-for anxiety, for little Miss Luttrell was smiling down at him through a brown gauze veil, as she poked away the handkerchief she had waved, leaving a corner showing against her dark brown jacket; and how she was to be made comfortable at the homestead, all in a minute, Swift did not know.

"She insisted on coming," said Mr. Luttrell, with a smile. "Is it any good her getting down?"

"Can you take me in?" asked the girl.

"We'll do our best," said Swift, holding the ladder for her descent.

Her shoes made a daintier imprint in the sand than it had known for two whole years. She smiled as she gave her hand to Swift; it was small, too, and Swift had not touched a lady's hand for many months. There was very little of her altogether, but the little was entirely pleasing. Embarrassed though he was, Swift was more than pleased to see the young girl again, and her smiles that struggled through the brown gauze like sunshine through a mist. She had not worn gauze veils two years ago; and two years ago she had been content with fare that would scarcely please her to-day, while naturally the living at the station was rougher now than in the days of the ladies. It was all very well for her to smile. She ought never to have come without a word of warning. Swift felt responsible and aggrieved.

He helped Mr. Luttrell to carry their baggage from the coach to the buggy drawn up in the shade. Miss Luttrell went to the horses' heads and stroked their noses; they were Bushman and Brownlock, the old safe pair she had many a time driven herself. In a moment she was bidden to jump up. There had been very little luggage to transfer. The most cumbrous piece was a hamper, of which Swift formed expectations that were speedily confirmed. For Miss Luttrell remarked, pointing to the hamper as she took her seat:

"At least we have brought our own rations; but I am afraid they will make you horribly uncomfortable behind there?"

Swift was on the back seat. "Not a bit," he answered; "I was much more uncomfortable until I saw the hamper."

"Don't you worry about us, Jack," said Mr. Luttrell as they drove off. "Whatever you do, don't worry about Tiny. Give her travelers' rations and send her to the travelers' hut. That's all she deserves, when she wasn't on the way-bill. She insisted on coming at the last moment; I told her it wasn't fair."

"But it's very jolly," said Swift gallantly.

"It was just like her," Mr. Luttrell chuckled; "she's as unreliable as ever."

The girl had been looking radiantly about her as they drove along the single broad, straggling street of the township. She now turned her head to Swift, and her eyes shot through her veil in a smile. That abominable veil went right over her broad-brimmed hat, and was gathered in and made fast at the neck. Swift could have torn it from her head; he had not seen a lady smile for months. Also, he was beginning to make the astonishing discovery that somehow she was altered, and he was curious to see how much, which was impossible through the gauze.

"Is that true?" he asked her. He had known her for five years.

"I suppose so," she returned carelessly; and immediately her sparkling eyes wandered. "There's old Mackenzie in the post office veranda. He was a detestable old man, but I must wave to him; it's so good to be back!"

"But you own to being unreliable?" persisted Swift.

"I don't know," Miss Luttrell said, tossing the words to him over her shoulder, because her attention was not for the manager. "Is it so very dreadful if I am? What's the good of being reliable? It's much more amusing to take people by surprise. Your face was worth the journey when you saw me on the coach! But you see I haven't surprised Mackenzie; he doesn't look the least impressed; I dare say he thinks it was last week we all went away. I hate him!"

"Here are the police barracks," said Swift, seeing that all her interest was in the old landmarks; "we have a new sergeant since you left."

"If *he's* in *his* veranda I shall shout out to him who I am, and how long I have been away, and how good it is to get back."

"She's quite capable of doing it," Mr. Luttrell chimed in, chuckling afresh; "there's never any knowing what she'll do next."

But the barracks veranda was empty, and it was the last of the township buildings. There was now nothing ahead but the rim of scrub, beyond which, among the sand-hills, sweltered the homestead of Wallandoon.

"I've come back with a nice character, have I not?" the girl now remarked, turning to Swift with another smile.

"You must have earned it; I can quite believe that you have," laughed Swift. He had known her in short dresses.

"Ha! ha! You see he remembers all about you, my dear."

"Do you, Jack?" the girl said.

"Do I not!" said Jack.

And he said no more. He was grateful to her for addressing him, though only once, by his Christian name. He had been intimate with the whole family, and it seemed both sensible and pleasant to resume a friendly footing from the first. He would have called the girl by her Christian name too, only this was so seldom heard among her own people. Tiny she was by nature, and Tiny she had been by name also, from her cradle. Certainly she had been Tiny to Swift two years ago, and already she had called him Jack; but he saw in neither circumstance any reason why she should be Tiny to him still. It was different from a proper name. Her proper name was Christina, but unreliable though she confessedly was, she might perhaps be relied upon to jeer if he came out with that. And he would not call her "Miss Luttrell." He thought about it and grew silent; but this was because his thoughts had glided from the girl's name to the girl herself.

She had surprised him in more ways than one-in so many ways that already he stood almost in awe of the little person whom formerly he had known so well. Christina had changed, as it was only natural that she should have changed; but because we are prone to picture our friends as last we saw them, no matter how long ago, not less natural was Swift's surprise. It was unreasoning, however, and not the kind of surprise to last. In a few minutes his wonder was that Christina had changed so little. To look at her she had scarcely changed at all. A certain finality of line was perceptible in the figure, but if anything she was thinner than of old. As for her face, what he could see of it through the maddening gauze was the face of Swift's memory. Her voice was a little different; in it was a ring of curiously deliberate irony, charming at first as a mere affectation. A more noteworthy alteration had taken place in her manner: she had acquired the manner of a finished young woman of the world and of society. Already she had shown that she could become considerably excited without forfeiting any of the grace and graciousness and self-possession that were now conspicuously hers; and before the homestead was reached she exhibited such a saintly sweetness in repose as only enhanced the lambent deviltry playing about most of her looks and tones. If Swift was touched with awe in her presence, that can hardly be wondered at in one who went for months together without setting eyes upon a lady.

The drive was a long one-so long that when they sighted the homestead it came between them and the setting sun. The main building with its long, regular roof lay against the red sky like some monstrous ingot. The hot wind had fallen, and the station pines stood motion-less, drawn in ink. As they drove through the last gate they could hear the dogs barking; and Christina distinguished the voice of her own old short-haired collie, which she had bequeathed to Swift, who was repaid for the sound with a final smile. He hardly knew why, but this look made the girl's old self live to him as neither look nor word had done yet, though her face was turned away from the light, and the stupid veil still fell before it.

But the less fascinating side of her arrival was presently engaging his attention. He hastily interviewed Mrs. Duncan, an elderly godsend new to the place since the Luttrells had left it, and never so invaluable as now. Into Mrs. Duncan's hands Christina willingly submitted herself, for she was really tired out. Swift did not see her again until supper, which afforded further proofs of Mrs. Duncan's merits in a time of need. Meanwhile, Mr. Luttrell had finally disabused him of the foolish fears he had entertained while waiting for the coach. Swift's youth, which has shown itself in these fears, comes out also in the ease with which he now forgot them. They had made him unhappy for three whole days; yet he dared to feel indignant because his owner, who had confirmed his command instead of dismissing him from it, chose to talk sheep at the supper table. Swift seemed burning to hear of the eldest Miss Luttrell, who was Miss Luttrell no longer, having married a globe-trotting Londoner during her first season and gone home. He asked Christina several questions about Ruth (whose other name he kept forgetting) and her husband. But Mr. Luttrell lost no chance of rounding up the conversation and yarding it in the sheep pens; and Swift had the ingratitude to resent this. Still more did he resent the hour he was forced to spend in the store after supper, examining the books and discussing recent results and future plans with Mr. Luttrell, while his subordinate, the storekeeper, enjoyed the society of Christina. The business in the store was not only absurdly premature and irksome in itself, but it made it perfectly impossible for Swift to hear any more that night of the late Ruth Luttrell, whose present name was not to be remembered. He found it hard to possess his soul in patience and to answer questions satisfactorily under such circumstances. For an hour, indeed, he did both; but the station store faced the main building, and when Tiny Luttrell appeared in the veranda of the latter with a lighted candle in her hand, he could do neither any longer. Saying candidly that he must bid her good-night, he hurried out of the store and across the yard, and was in time to catch Christina at one end of the broad veranda which entirely surrounded the house.

At supper Mr. Luttrell had made him take the head of the table, by virtue of his office, declaring that he himself was merely a visitor. And on the strength of that Swift was perhaps justified now in adding a host's apology to his good-night. "I'm afraid you'll have to rough it most awfully," was what he said.

"Far from it. You have given me my old room, the one we papered with *Australasians*, if you remember; they are only a little more fly-blown than they used to be."

This was Christina's reply, which naturally led to more.

"But it won't be as comfortable as it used to be," said Swift unhappily; "and it won't be what you are accustomed to nowadays."

"Never mind, it's the dearest little den in the colonies!"

"That sounds as if you were glad to get back to Riverina?"

"Glad? No one knows how glad I am."

One person knew now. The measure of her gladness was expressed in her face not less than in her tones, and it was no ordinary measure. Over the candle she held in her hand Swift was enabled for the first time to peer unobstructedly into her face. He found it more winsome than ever, but he noticed some ancient blemishes under the memorable eyes. She had, in fact, some freckles, which he recognized with the keenest joy. She might stoop to a veil-she had not sunk to doctoring her complexion; she had come back to the bush an incomplete worldling after all. Yet there was that in her face which made him feel a stranger to her still.

"Do you know," he said, smiling, "that I'm in a great funk of you? I can't say quite what it is, but somehow you're so grand. I suppose it's Melbourne."

Miss Luttrell thanked him, bowing so low that her candle shed grease upon the boards. "You've altered too," she added in his own manner; "I suppose it's being boss. But I haven't seen enough of you to be sure. You evidently told off your new storekeeper to entertain me for the evening. He is a trying young man; he *will* talk. But of course he is a new chum fresh from home."

"Still he's a very good little chap; but it wasn't my fault that he and I didn't change places. Mr. Luttrell wanted to speak to me about several things, besides glancing through the books; I thought we might have put it off, and I wondered how you were getting on. By the way, it struck me once or twice that your father was coming up to give me the sack; and it's just the reverse, for now I'm permanent manager."

He told her this with a natural exultation, but she did not seem impressed by it. "Do you know why he did come up?" she asked him.

"Yes; for his Easter holidays, chiefly."

"And why I would come with him?"

"No; I'm afraid we never mentioned you. I suppose you came for a holiday too?"

"Shall I tell you why I did come?"

"I wish you would."

"Well, I came to say good-by to Wallandoon," said Christina solemnly.

"You're going to be married!" exclaimed Swift, with conviction, but with perfect nonchalance.

"Not if I know it," cried Christina. "Are you?"

"Not I."

"But there's Miss Trevor of Meringul!"

"I see them once in six months."

"That may be in the bond."

"Well, never mind Miss Trevor of Meringul. You haven't told me how it is you've come to say good-by to the station, Miss Luttrell of Wallandoon."

"Then I'll tell you, seriously: it's because I sail for England on the 4th of May."

"For England!"

"Yes, and I'm not at all keen about it, I can tell you. But I'm not going to see England, I'm going to see Ruth; Australia's worth fifty Englands any day."

Swift had recovered from his astonishment. "I don't know," he said doubtfully; "most of us would like a trip home, you know, just to see what the old country's like; though I dare say it isn't all it's cracked up to be."

"Of course it isn't. I hate it!"

"But if you've never been there?"

"I judge from the people-from the samples they send out. Your new storekeeper is one; you meet worse down in Melbourne. Herbert's going with me; he's going to Cambridge, if they'll have him. Didn't you know that? But he could go alone, and if it wasn't for Ruth I wouldn't cross Hobson's Bay to see their old England!"

The serious bitterness of her tone struck him afterward as nothing less than grotesque; but at the moment he was gazing into her face, thoughtfully yet without thoughts.

"It's good for Herbert," he said presently. "I couldn't do anything with him here; he offered to fight me when I tried to make him work. I suppose he will be three or four years at Cambridge; but how long are you going to stay with Mrs. —Mrs. Ruth?"

"How stupid you are at remembering a simple name! Do try to remember that her name is Holland. I beg your pardon, Jack, but you have been really very forgetful this evening. I think it must be Miss Trevor of Meringul."

"It isn't. I'm very sorry. But you haven't told me how long you think of staying at home."

"How long?" said the young girl lightly. "It may be for years and years, and it may be forever and ever!"

He looked at her strangely, and she darted out her hand.

"Good-night again, Jack."

"Good-night again."

What with the pauses, each of them an excellent opportunity for Christina to depart, it had taken them some ten minutes to say that which ought not to have lasted one. But you must know that this was nothing to their last good-night, on the self-same spot two years before, when she had rested in his arms.

Chapter II
Swift of Wallandoon.

Christina was awakened in the morning by the holland blind flapping against her open window. It was a soft, insinuating sound, that awoke one gradually, and to Christina both the cause and the awakening itself seemed incredibly familiar. So had she lain and listened in the past, as each day broke in her brain. When she opened her eyes the shadow of the sash wriggled on the blind as it flapped, a blade of sunshine lay under the door that opened upon the veranda, and neither sight was new to her. The same sheets of the *Australasian* with which her own hands had once lined the room, for want of a conventional wallpaper, lined it still; the same area of printed matter was in focus from the pillow, and she actually remembered an advertisement that caught her eye. It used to catch her eye two years before. Thus it became difficult to believe in those two years; and it was very pleasant to disbelieve in them. More than pleasant Christina found it to lie where she was, hearing the old noises (the horses were run up before she rose), seeing the old things, and dreaming that the last two years were themselves a dream. Her life as it stood was a much less charming composition than several possible arrangements of the same material, impossible now. This is not strange, but it was a little strange that neither sweet impossibilities nor bitter actualities fascinated her much; for so many good girls are morbidly introspective. As for Christina, let it be clearly and early understood that she was neither an introspective girl by nature nor a particularly good one from any point of view. She was not in the habit of looking back; but to look back on the old days here at the station without thinking of later days was like reading an uneven book for the second time, leaving out the poor part.

In making, but still more in closing that gap in her life (as you close a table after taking out a leaf) she was immensely helped by the associations of the present moment. They breathed of the remote past only; their breath was sweet and invigorating. Her affection for Wallandoon was no affectation; she loved it as she loved no other place. And if, as she dressed, her thoughts dwelt more on the young manager of the station than on the station itself, that only illustrates the difference between an association and an associate. There is human interest in the one, but it does not follow that Tiny Luttrell was immoderately interested in Jack Swift. Even to herself she denied that she had ever done more than like him very much. To some "nonsense" in the past she was ready to own. But in the vocabulary of a Tiny Luttrell a little "nonsense" may cover a calendar of mild crimes. It is only the Jack Swifts who treat the nonsense seriously and deny that the crimes are anything of the sort, because for their part they "mean it." Women are not deceived. Besides, it is less shame for them to say they never meant it.

"He must marry Flo Trevor of Meringul," Christina said aloud. "It's what we all expect of him. It's his duty. But she isn't pretty, poor thing!"

The remarks happened to be made to Christina's own reflection in the glass. She, as we know, was very pretty indeed. Her small head was finely turned, and carried with her own natural grace. Her hair was of so dark a brown as to be nearly black, but there was not enough of it to hide the charming contour of her head. If she could have had the altering of one feature, she would probably have shortened her lips; but their red freshness justified their length; and the crux of a woman's beauty, her nose, happened to be Christina's best point. Her eyes were a sweeter one. Their depth of blue is seen only under dark blue skies, and they seemed the darker for her hair. But with all her good features, because she was not an English girl, but an Australian born and bred, she had no complexion to speak of, being pale and slightly freckled. Yet no one held that those blemishes prevented her from being pretty; while some maintained that they did not even detract from her good looks, and a few that they saved her from perfection and were a part of her charm. The chances are that the authorities quoted were themselves her admirers one and all. She had many such. To most of them her character had the same charm as her face; it, too, was freckled with faults for which they loved her the more.

One of the many she met presently, but one of them now, though in his day the first of all. Swift was hastening along the veranda as she issued forth, a consciously captivating figure in her clean white frock. He had on his wide-awake, a newly filled water-bag dripped as he carried it, the drops drying under their eyes in the sun, and Christina foresaw at once his absence for the day. She was disappointed, perhaps because he was one of the many; certainly it was for this reason she did not let him see her disappointment. He told her that he was going with her father to the out-station. That was fourteen miles away. It meant a lonely day for Christina at the homestead. So she said that a lonely day there was just what she wanted, to overhaul the dear old place all by herself, and to revel in it like a child without feeling that she was being watched. But she told a franker story some hours later, when Swift found her still on the veranda where he had left her, but this was now the shady side, seated in a wicker chair and frowning at a book. For she promptly flung away that crutch of her solitude, and seemed really glad to see him. Her look made him tingle. He sat down on the edge of the veranda and leaned his back against a post. Then he inquired, rather diffidently, how the day had gone with Miss Luttrell.

"I am ashamed to tell you," said Christina graciously, for though his diffidence irritated her, she was quite as glad to see him as she looked, "that I have been bored very nearly to death!"

"I knew you would be," Swift said quite bitterly; but his bitterness was against an absent man, who had gone indoors to rest.

"I don't see how you could know anything," remarked Christina. "I certainly didn't know it myself; and I'm very much ashamed of it, that's another thing! I love every stick about the place. But I never knew a hotter morning; the sand in the yard was like powdered cinders, and you can't go poking about very long when everything you touch is red hot. Then one felt tired. Mrs. Duncan took pity on me and came and talked to me; she must be an acquisition to you, I am sure; but her cooking's better than her conversation. I think she must have sent the new chum to me to take her place; anyway I've had a dose of him, too, I can tell you!"

"Oh, he's been cutting his work, has he?"

"He has been doing the civil; I think he considered that his work."

"And quite right too! Tell me, what do you think of him?"

Christina made a grotesque grimace. "He's such a little Englishman," she simply said.

"Well, he can't help that, you know," said Swift, laughing; "and he's not half a bad little chap, as I told you last night."

"Oh, not a bit bad; only typical. He has told me his history. It seems he missed the army at home, front door and back, in spite of his crammer —I mean his cwammer. He was no use, so they sent him out to us."

"And he is gradually becoming of some use to us, or rather to me; he really is," protested Swift in the interests of fair play, which a man loves. "You laugh, but I like the fellow. He's much more use-forgive my saying so-than Herbert ever would have been-here. At all events he doesn't want to fight! He's willing, I will say that for him. And I think it was rather nice of him to tell you about himself."

"It's nicer of you to think so," said Christina to herself. And her glance softened so that he noticed the difference, for he was becoming sensitive to a slight but constant hardness of eye and tongue distressing to find in one's divinity.

"He went so far as to hint at an affair of the heart," she said aloud, and he saw her eyes turn hard again, so that his own glanced off them and fell. But he forced a chuckle as he looked down.

"Well, you gave him your sympathy there, I hope?"

"Not I, indeed. I urged him to forget all about her; she has forgotten all about him long before now, you may be sure. He only thinks about her still because it's pleasant to have somebody to think about at a lonely place like this; and if she's thinking about him it's because he's away in the wilderness and there's a glamour about that. It wouldn't prevent her marrying another man to-morrow, and it won't prevent him making up to some other girl when he gets the chance."

"So that's your experience, is it?"

"Never mind whose experience it is. I advised the young man to give up thinking about the young woman, that's all, and it's my advice to every young man situated as he is."

Swift was not amused. Yet he refused to believe that her advice was intended for himself: firstly, because it was so coolly given, which was his ignorance, and secondly, because, literally speaking, he was not himself situated as the young Englishman was, which was merely unimaginative. In his determination, however, not to meet her in generalizations, but to get back to the storekeeper, he was wise enough.

"I know something about his affairs, too," he said quietly; "he's the frankest little fellow in the world; and I have given him very different advice, I must say."

Tiny Luttrell bent down on him a gaze of fiendish innocence.

"And what sort of advice does he give you, pray?"

"You had better ask him," said Swift feebly, but with effect, for he was honestly annoyed, and man enough to show it. As he spoke, indeed, he rose.

"What, are you going?"

"Yes; you go in for being too hard altogether."

"I don't go in for it. I am hard. I'm as hard as nails," said Christina rapidly.

"So I see," he said, and another weak return was strengthened by his firmness; for he was going away as he spoke, and he never looked round.

"I wouldn't lose my temper," she called after him.

Her face was white. He disappeared. She colored angrily.

"Now I hate you," she whispered to herself; but she probably respected him more, and that was as it only should have been long ago.

But Swift was in an awkward position, which indeed he deserved for the unsuspected passages that had once taken place between Tiny Luttrell and himself. It is true that those passages had occurred at the very end of the Luttrells' residence at Wallandoon; they had not been going on for a period preceding the end; but there is no denying that they were reprehensible in themselves, and pardonable only on the plea of exceeding earnestness. Swift would not have made that excuse for himself, for he felt it to be a poor one, though of his own sincerity he was and had been unwaveringly sure. Beyond all doubt he was properly in love, and, being so, it was not until the girl stopped writing to him that he honestly repented the lengths to which he had been encouraged to go. It is easy to be blameless through the post, but they had kept up their perfectly blameless correspondence for a very few weeks when Christina ceased firing; she was to have gone on forever. He was just persistent enough to make it evident that her silence was intentional; then the silence became complete, and it was never again broken. For if Swift's self-control was limited, his self-respect was considerable, and this made him duly regret the limitations of his self-control. His boy's soul bled with a boy's generous regrets. He had kissed her, of course, and I wonder whose fault you think that was? I know which of them regretted and which forgot it. The man would have given one of his fingers to have undone those kisses, that made him think less of himself and less of his darling. Nothing could make him love her less. He heard no more of her, but that made no difference. And now they were together again, and she was hard, and it made this difference: that he wanted her worse than ever, and for her own gain now as much as for his.

But two years had altered him also. In a manner he too was hardened; but he was simply a stronger, not a colder man. The muscles of his mind were set; his soul was now as sinewy as his body. He knew what he wanted, and what would not do for him instead. He wanted a great deal, but he meant having it or nothing. This time she should give him her heart before he took her hand; he swore it through his teeth; and you will realize how he must have known her of old even to have thought it. The curious thing is that, having shown him what she was, she should have made him love her as he did. But that was Tiny Luttrell.

She was half witch, half coquette, and her superficial cynicism was but a new form of her coquetry. He liked it less than the unsophisticated methods of the old days. Indeed, he liked the girl less, while loving her more. She had given him the jar direct in one conversation, but even on indifferent subjects she spoke with a bitterness which he thoroughly disliked; while some of her prejudices he could not help thinking irredeemably absurd. As a shrill decrier of

England, for instance, she may have amused him, but he hardly admired her in that character. In a word, he thought her, and rightly, a good deal spoilt by her town life; but he hated towns, and it was a proof of her worth in his eyes that she was not hopelessly spoilt. He saw hope for her still-if she would marry him. He was a modest man in general, but he did feel this most strongly. She was going to England without caring whether she went or not; she would do much better by marrying him and coming back to her old home in the bush. That home she loved, whether she loved him or not; in it she had grown up simple and credulous and sweet, with a wicked side that only picked out her sweetness; in it he believed that her life and his might yet be beautiful. The feeling made him sometimes rejoice that she had fallen a little out of love with her life, so that he might show her with all the effect of contrast what life and love really were; it thrilled his heart with generous throbs, it brought the moisture to his honest eyes, and it came to him oftener and with growing force as the days went on, by reason of certain signs they brought forth in Christiana. Her voice lost its bitterness in his ears, not because he had grown used to notes that had jarred him in the beginning, but because the discordant strings came gradually into tune. Her freshness came back to her with the charm and influence of the wilderness she loved; her old self lived again to Jack Swift. On the other hand, she came to realize her own delight in the old good life as she had never realized it before; she felt that henceforward she should miss it as she had not missed it yet. Now she could have defined her sensations and given reasons for them. She spent many hours in the saddle, on a former mount of hers that Swift had run up for her; often he rode with her, and the scent of the pines, the swelling of the sand-hills against the sky, the sense of Nothing between the horses' ears and the sunset, spoke to her spirit as they had never done of old. And even so on their rides would she speak to Swift, who listened grimly, hardly daring to answer her for the fear of saying at the wrong moment what he had resolved to say once and for all before she went.

And he chose the wrong moment after all. It was the eve of her going, and they were riding together for the last time; he felt that it was also his last opportunity. So in six miles he made as many remarks, then turned in his saddle and spoke out with overpowering fervor. This may be expected of the self-contained suitor, with whom it is only a question of time, and the longer the time the stronger the outburst. But Christina was not carried away, for she did not quite love him, and the opportunity was a bad one, and Swift's honest method had not improved it. She listened kindly, with her eyes on the distant timbers of the eight-mile whim; but her kindness was fatally calm; and when he waited she refused him firmly. She confessed to a fondness for him. She ascribed this to the years they had known each other. Once and for all she did not love him.

"Not now!" exclaimed the young fellow eagerly. "But you did once! You will again!"

"I never loved you," said the girl gravely. "If you're thinking of two years ago, that was mere nonsense. I don't believe its love with you either, if you only knew it."

"But I do know what it is with me, Tiny! I loved you before you went away, and all the time you were gone. Since you have been back, during these few days, I have got to love you more than ever. And so I shall go on, whatever happens. I can't help it, darling."

Neither could he help saying this; for the hour found him unable to accept his fate quite as he had meant to accept it. Her kindness had something to do with that. And now she spoke more kindly than before.

"Are you sure?" she said.

"Am I sure!" he echoed bitterly.

"It is so easy to deceive oneself."

"I am not deceived."

"It is so easy to imagine yourself——"

"I am not imagining!" cried Swift impatiently. "I am the man who has loved you always, and never any girl but you. If you can't believe that, you must have had a very poor experience of men, Tiny!"

For a moment she looked away from the whim which they were slowly nearing, and her eyes met his.

"I have," she admitted frankly; "I have had a particularly poor experience of them. Yet I am sorry to find you so different from the rest; I can't tell you how sorry I am to find you true to me."

"Sorry?" he said tenderly; for her voice was full of pain, and he could not bear that. "Why should you be sorry, dear?"

"Why-because I never dreamt of being true to you."

For some reason her face flamed as he watched it. There was a pause. Then he said:

"You are not engaged; are you in love?"

"Very far from it."

"Then why mind? If there is no one else you care for you shall care for me yet. I'll make you. I'll wait for you. You don't know me! I won't give you up until you are some other fellow's wife."

His stern eyes, the way his mouth shut on the words, and the manly determination of the words themselves gave the girl a thrill of pleasure and of pride; but also a pang; for at that moment she felt the wish to love him alongside the inability, and all at once she was as sorry for herself as for him.

"What should you mind?" repeated Swift.

"I can't tell you, but you can guess what I have been."

"A flirt?" He laughed aloud. "Darling, I don't care two figs for your flirtations! I wanted you to enjoy yourself. What does it matter how you've enjoyed yourself, so long as you haven't absolutely been getting engaged or falling in love?"

Her chin drooped into her loose white blouse. "I did fall in love," she said slowly —"at any rate I thought so; and I very nearly got engaged."

Swift had never seen so much color in her face.

Presently he said, "What happened?" but immediately added, "I beg your pardon; of course I have no business to ask." His tone was more stiff than strained.

"You *have* business," she answered eagerly, fearful of making him less than friend. "I wouldn't mind telling you the whole thing, except the man's name. And yet," she added rather wistfully, "I suppose you're the only friend I have that doesn't know! It's hard lines to have to tell you."

"Then I don't want to know anything at all about it," exclaimed Swift impulsively. "I would rather you didn't tell me a word, if you don't mind. I am only too thankful to think you got out of it, whatever it was."

"I didn't get out of it."

"You don't —mean-that the man did?"

Swift was aghast.

"I do."

He did not speak, but she heard him breathing. Stealing a look at him, her eyes fell first upon the clenched fist lying on his knee.

She made haste to defend the man.

"It wasn't all his fault; of that I feel sure. If you knew who he was you wouldn't blame him anymore than I do. He was quite a boy, too; I don't suppose he was a free agent. In any case it is all quite, quite over."

"Is it? He was from England-that's why you hate the home people so!"

"Yes, he was from home. He went back very suddenly. It wasn't his fault. He was sent for. But he might have said good-by!"

She spoke reflectively, gazing once more at the whim. They were near it now. The framework cut the sky like some uncouth hieroglyph. To Swift henceforward, on all his lonely journeys hither, it was the emblem of humiliation. But it was not his own humiliation that moistened his clenched hand now.

"I wish I had him here," he muttered.

"Ah! you know nothing about him, you see; I know enough to forgive him. And I have got over it, quite; but the worst of it is that I can't believe any more in any of you —I simply can't."

"Not in me?" asked Swift warmly, for her belief in him, at least, he knew he deserved. "I have always been the same. I have never thought of any other girl but you, and I never will. I love you, darling!"

"After this, Jack?"

He seemed to disappoint her.

"After the same thing if it happens all over again in England! There is no merit in it; I simply can't help myself. While you are away I will wait for you and work for you; only come back free, and I will win you, too, in the end. You are happier here than anywhere else, but you don't know what it is to be really happy as I should make you. Remember that-and this: that I will never give you up until someone else has got you! Now call me conceited or anything you like. I have done bothering you."

"I can only call you foolish," said the girl, though gently. "You are far too good for me. As for conceit, you haven't enough of it, or you would never give me another thought. I still hope you will quite give up thinking about me, and-and try to get over it. But nothing is going to happen in England, I can promise you that much. And I only wish I could get out of going."

He had already shown her how she might get out of it; he was not going to show her afresh or more explicitly, in spite of the temptation to do so. Even to a proud spirit it is difficult to take No when the voice that says it is kind and sorrowful and all but loving. Swift found it easier to bide by his own statement that he had done bothering her; such was his pride.

But he had chosen the wrong moment, and though he had shown less pride than he had meant to show, he was still too proud to improve the right one when it came. He was too proud, indeed, to stand much chance of immediate success in love. Otherwise he might have reminded her with more force and particularity of their former relations; and playing like that he might have won, but he would rather have lost. Perhaps he did not recognize the right moment as such when it fell; but at least he must have seen that it was better than the one he had chosen. It fell in the evening, when Christina's mood became conspicuously sentimental; but Swift happened to be one of the last young men in the world to take advantage of any mere mood.

As on the first evening, Mr. Luttrell was busy in the store, but this time with the storekeeper, who was making out a list of things to be sent up in the drays from Melbourne. Tiny and the manager were thrown together for the last time. She offered to sing a song, and he thanked her gratefully enough. But he listened to her plaintive songs from a far corner of the room, though the room was lighted only by the moonbeams; and when she rose he declared that she was tired and begged her not to sing any more. She could have beaten him for that.

But in leaving the room they lingered on the threshold, being struck by the beauty of the night. The full moon ribbed the station yard with the shadows of the pines, a soft light was burning in the store, and all was so still that the champing of the night-horse in the yard came plainly to their ears, with the chirping of the everlasting crickets. Christina raised her face to Swift; her eyes were wet in the moonlight; there was even a slight tremor of the red lips; and one hand hung down invitingly at her side. She did not love him, but she was beginning to wish that she could love him; and she did love the place. Had he taken that one hand then the chances are he might have kept it. But even Swift never dreamt that this was so. And after that moment it was not so any more. She turned cold, and was cold to the end. Her last words from the top of the coach fell as harshly on a loving ear as any that had preceded them by a week.

"Why need you remind me I am going to England? Enjoy myself! I shall detest the whole thing."

Her last look matched the words.

Chapter III
The Tail of the Season.

"What do you say to sitting it out? The rooms are most awfully crowded, and you dance too well for one; besides, one's anxious to hear your impressions of a London ball."

"One must wait till the ball is over. So far I can't deny that I'm enjoying myself in spite of the crush. But I should rather like to sit out for once, though you needn't be sarcastic about my dancing."

"Well, then, where's a good place?"

"There's a famous corner in the conservatory; it should be empty now that a dance is just beginning."

It was. So it became occupied next moment by Tiny Luttrell and her partner, who allowed that the dimly illumined recess among the tree-ferns deserved its fame. Tiny's partner, however, was only her brother-in-law, Mr. Erskine Holland.

The Luttrells had been exactly a fortnight in England. It was in the earliest hour of the month of July that Christina sat out with her brother-in-law at her first London party; and if she had spent that fortnight chiefly in visiting dressmakers and waiting for results, she had at least found time to get to know Erskine Holland very much better than she had ever done in Melbourne. There she had seen very little of him, partly through being away from home when he first called with an introduction to the family, but more by reason of the short hurdle race he had made of his courtship, marriage, and return to England with his bride. He had taken the matrimonial fences as only an old bachelor can who has been given up as such by his friends. Mr. Holland, though still nearer thirty than forty, had been regarded as a confirmed bachelor when starting on a long sea voyage for the restoration of his health after an autumnal typhoid. His friends were soon to know what weakened health and Australian women can do between them. They beheld their bachelor return within four months, a comfortably married man, with a pleasant little wife who was very fond of him, and in no way jealous of his old friends. That was Mrs. Erskine's great merit, and the secret of the signal success with which she presided over his table in West Kensington, when Erskine had settled down there and returned with steadiness to the good, safe business to which he had been virtually born a partner. For his part, without being enslaved to a degree embarrassing to their friends, Holland made an obviously satisfactory husband. He was good-natured and never exacting; he was well off and generous. One of a wealthy, many-membered firm driving a versatile trade in the East, he was as free personally from business anxieties as was the hall porter at the firm's offices in Lombard Street. There Erskine was the most popular and least useful fraction of the firm, being just a big, fair, genial fellow, fond of laughter and chaff and lawn tennis, and fonder of books than of the newspapers-an eccentric preference in a business man. But as a business man the older partners shook their heads about him. Once as a youngster he had spent a year or two in Lisbon, learning the language and the ropes there, the firm having certain minor interests planted in Portuguese soil on both sides of the Indian Ocean; and those interests just suited Erskine Holland, who had the handling of them, though the older partners nursed their own distrust of a man who boasted of taking his work out of his head each evening when he hung up his office coat. At home Erskine was a man who read more than one guessed, and had his own ideas on a good many subjects. He found his sister-in-law lamentably ignorant, but quite eager to improve her mind at his direction; and this is ever delightful to the man who reads. Also he found her amusing, and that experience was mutual.

A Londoner himself, with many reputable relatives in the town, who rejoiced in the bachelor's marriage and were able to like his wife, he was in a position to gratify to a considerable extent Mrs. Erskine's social desires. That he did so somewhat against his own inclination (much as in Melbourne his father-in-law had done before him) was due to an acutely fair mind allied with a thoroughly kind and sympathetic nature. His own attitude toward society was not free from that slight intellectual superiority which some of the best fellows in the world cannot help; but at least it was perfectly genuine. He treated society as he treated champagne, which he seldom touched, but about which he was curiously fastidious on those chance occasions. He cared as little for the one as for the other, but found the drier brands inoffensive in both cases. The ball to-night was at Lady Almeric's.

"Not a bad corner," Erskine said as he made himself comfortable; "but I'm afraid it's rather thrown away upon me, you know."

"Far from it. I wish I had been dancing with you the whole evening, Erskine," said Christina seriously.

"That's rather obsequious of you. May I ask why?"

"Because I don't think much of my partners so far, to talk to."

"Ha! I knew there was something you wouldn't think much of," cried Erskine Holland. "Have they nothing to say for themselves, then?"

"Oh, plenty. They discover where I come from; then they show their ignorance. They want to know if there is any chance for a fellow on the gold fields now; they have heard of a place called Ballarat, but they aren't certain whether it's a part of Melbourne or nearer Sydney. One man knows some people at Hobart Town, in New Zealand, he fancies. I never knew anything like their ignorance of the colonies!"

Mr. Holland tugged a smile out of his mustache. "Can you tell me how to address a letter to Montreal-is it Quebec or Ontario?" he asked her, as if interested and anxious to learn.

"Goodness knows," replied Christina innocently.

"Then that's rather like their ignorance of the colonies, isn't it? There's not much difference between a group of colonies and a dominion, you see. I'm afraid your partners are not the only people whose geography has been sadly neglected."

Christina laughed.

"My education's been neglected altogether, if it comes to that. As you're taking me in hand, perhaps you'll lend me a geography, as well as Ruskin and Thackeray. Nevertheless, Australia's more important than Canada, you may say what you like, Erskine; and your being smart won't improve my partners."

"Oh! but I thought it was only their conversation?"

"You force me to tell you that their idea of dancing seems limited to pushing you up one side of the room, and dragging you after them down the other. Sometimes they turn you round. Then they're proud of themselves. They never do it twice running."

"That's because there are so many here."

"There are far too many here-that's what's the matter! And I'm a nice person to tell you so," added Tiny penitently, "when it's you and Ruth who have brought me here. But you know I don't mean that I'm not enjoying it, Erskine; I'm enjoying it immensely, and I'm very proud of myself for being here at all. I can't quite explain myself—I don't much like trying to-but there's a something about everything that makes it seem better than anything of the kind that we can do in Melbourne. The music is so splendid, and the floor, and the flowers. I never saw such a few diamonds-or such beauties! Even the ices are the best I ever tasted, and they aren't too sweet. There's something subdued and superior about the whole concern; but it's too subdued; it needs go and swing nearly as badly as it needs elbow-room —of more kinds than one! I'm thinking less of the crowd of people than of their etiquette and ceremony, which hamper you far more. But it's your old England in a nutshell, this ball is: it fits too tight."

"Upon my word," said Erskine, laughing, "I don't think it's at all bad for you to find the old country a tight fit! I'm obliged to you for the expression, Tiny. I only hope it isn't suggested by personal suffering. I have been thinking that you must have a good word to say for our dressmakers, if not for our dancing men."

Christina slid her eyes over the snow and ice of the shimmering attire that had been made for her in haste since her arrival.

"I'm glad you like me," she said, smiling honestly. "I must own I rather like myself in this lot. I didn't want to disgrace you among your fine friends, you see."

"They're more fine than friends, my dear girl. Lady Almeric's the only friend. She has been very nice to Ruth. Most of the people here are rather classy, I can assure you."

He named the flower of the company in a lowered voice. Christina knew one of the names.

"Lady Mary Dromard, did you say?" said she, playing idly with her fan.

"Yes; do you know her?"

"No, but her brother was in Melbourne once as aid-de-camp to the governor. I knew him."

"Ah, that was Lord Manister; he wasn't out there when I was."

"No, he must have come just after you had gone. He only remained a few months, you know. He was a quiet young man with a mania for cricket; we liked him because he set our young men their fashions and yet never gave himself airs. I wonder if he's here as well?"

"I don't think so. I know him by sight, but I haven't seen him. I'm glad to hear he didn't give himself airs; you couldn't say the same for the sister who is here, though I only know her by sight, too."

"He was quite a nice young man," said Christina, shutting up her fan; and as she spoke the music, whose strains had reached them all the time, came to its natural end.

The conservatory suffered instant invasion, Christina and Mr. Holland being afforded the entertainment of disappointing couple after couple who came straight to their corner.

"We're in a coveted spot," whispered Erskine; and his sister-in-law reminded him who had shown the way to it. It was less secluded than remote, so the present occupiers found further entertainment as mere spectators. The same little things amused them both; this was one reason why they got on so well together. They were amused by such trifles as a distant prospect of Ruth, who was innocently enjoying herself at the other end of the conservatory, unaware of their eyes. Erskine might have felt proud, and no doubt he did, for many people considered Ruth even prettier than Christina, with whom, however, they were apt to confuse her, though Holland himself could never see the likeness. He now sat watching his wife in the distance while talking to her sister at his side until a new partner pounced upon Ruth, and bore her away as the music began afresh.

"There goes my chaperon," remarked Christina resignedly.

"Who's your partner now? I'm sorry to say I see mine within ten yards of me," whispered Erskine in some anxiety.

Tiny consulted her card. "It's Herbert," she said.

"Herbert!" said Mr. Holland dubiously. "I'm afraid Herbert's going it; he's deeply employed with a girl in red —I think an American. Shall I take you to Lady Almeric?" His eyes shifted uneasily toward his expectant partner.

"No, I'll wait here for Herbert. Mayn't I? Then I'm going to. You're sure to see him, and you can send him at once. Don't blame Ruth. What does it matter? It will matter if you don't go this instant to your partner; I see it in her eye!"

He left her reluctantly, with the undertaking that Herbert should be at her side in two minutes. But that was rash. Christina soon had the conservatory entirely to herself, whereupon she came out of her corner, so that her brother might find her the more readily. Still he kept her waiting, and she might as well have been lonely in the corner. It was too bad of Herbert to leave her standing there, where she had no business to be by herself, and the music and the throbbing of the floor within a few yards of her. These awkward minutes naturally began to disturb her. They checked and cooled her in the full blast of healthy excitement, and that was bad; they threw her back upon herself straight from her lightest mood, and this was worse. She became abnormally aware of her own presence as she stood looking down and impatiently tapping with her little white slipper upon the marble flags. Even about these there was the grand air which Christina relished; she might have seen her face far below, as though she had been standing in still water; but her thoughts had been given a rough jerk inward, her outward vision fell no deeper than the polished surface, while her mind's eye saw all at once the dusty veranda boards of Wallandoon. She stood very still, and in her ears the music died away, and through three months of travel and great changes she heard again the night-horse champing in the yard, and the crickets chirping further afield. And as she stood, her head bowed by this sudden memory, footsteps approached, and she looked up, expecting to see Herbert. But it was not Herbert; it was a young man of more visible distinction than Herbert Luttrell. It is difficult to look better dressed than another in our evening mode; but this young man overcame the difficulty. He stood erect; he was well built; his clothes fitted beautifully; he was himself nice looking, and fair-haired, and boyish; and, even more than his clothes, one admired his smile, which was frank and delightful. But the smile he gave Christina was followed by a blush, for she had held out her hand to him, and asked him how he was.

"I'm all right, thanks. But-this is the most extraordinary thing! Been over long?"

He had dropped her hand.

"About a fortnight," said Christina.

"But what a pity to come over so late in the season! It's about done, you know."

"Yes. I thought there was a good deal going on still."

"There's Henley, to be sure."

"I think I'm going to Henley."

"Going to the Eton and Harrow?"

"I am not quite sure. That was your match, wasn't it?"

The young man blushed afresh.

"Fancy your remembering! Unfortunately it wasn't my match, though; my day out was against Winchester."

"Oh, yes," said Tiny, less knowingly.

"And how are you, Miss Luttrell?"

This had been forgotten, Tiny reported well of herself. Her friend hesitated; there was some nervousness in his manner, but his good eyes never fell from her face, and presently he exclaimed, as though the idea had just struck him:

"I say, mayn't I have this dance, Miss Luttrell-what's left of it?"

"Thanks, I'm afraid I'm engaged for it."

"Then mayn't I find your partner for you?"

Now this second request, or his anxious way of making it, was an elaborate revelation to Christina, and wrote itself in her brain. "Do you remember Herbert?" she, however, simply replied. "He is the culprit."

"Your brother? Certainly I remember him. I saw him a few minutes ago, and made sure I had seen him somewhere before; but he looks older. I don't fancy he's dancing. He's somewhere or other with somebody in red."

"So I hear."

"Then mayn't I have a turn with you before it stops?"

She hesitated as long as he had hesitated before first asking her; there was not time to hesitate longer. Then she took his arm, and they passed through a narrow avenue of ferns and flowers, round a corner, up some steps, and so into the ball room.

The waltz was indeed half over, but the second half of it Christina and her fortuitous partner danced together, without a rest, and also without a word. He led her a more enterprising measure than those previous partners who had questioned her concerning Australia. The name of Australia had not crossed this one's lips. As Tiny whirled and glided on his arm she saw a good many eyes upon her: they made her dance her best; and her best was the best in the room, though her partner was uncommonly good, and they had danced together before. Among the eyes were Ruth's, and they were beaming; the others were mostly inquisitive, and as strange to Christina as she evidently was to them; but once a turn brought her face to face with Herbert, on his way from the conservatory, and alone. He was a lanky, brown-faced, hook-nosed boy, with wiry limbs and an aggressive eye, and he followed his sister round the room with a stare of which she was uncomfortably conscious. He had looked for her too late, when forced to relinquish the girl in red to her proper partner, who still seemed put out. Christina was put out also, by her brother's look, but she did not show it.

"You are staying in town?" her partner said after the dance as they sat together in the conservatory, but not in the old corner.

"Yes, with my sister, Mrs. Holland; you never met her, I think. We are in town till August."

"Where do you go then?"

"To the country for a month. My sister and her husband have taken a country rectory for the whole of August. They had it last year, and liked the place so much that they have taken it again; it is a little village called Essingham."

"Essingham!" cried Christina's partner.

"Yes; do you know it?"

"I know of it," answered the young man. "I suppose you will go on the Continent after that?" he added quickly.

"Well, hardly; my brother-in-law has so little time; but he expects to have to go to Lisbon on business at the end of October, and he has promised to take us with him."

"To Lisbon at the end of October," repeated Tiny's friend reflectively. "Get him to take you to Cintra. They say it's well worth seeing."

Yet another dance was beginning. Christina was interested in the movements of a young man in spectacles, who was plainly in search of somebody. "He's hunting for me," she whispered to her companion, who was saying:

"Portugal's rather the knuckle end of Europe, don't you think? But I've heard Cintra well spoken of. I should go there if I were you."

"We intend to. Do you mind pulling that young man's coat tails? He has forgotten my face."

"Yes, I do mind," said Tiny's partner with unexpected earnestness. "I may meet you again, but I should like to take this opportunity of explaining — —"

Tiny Luttrell was smiling in his face.

"I hate explanations!" she cried. "They are an insult to one's imagination, and I much prefer to accept things without them." There was a gleam in her smile, but as she spoke she flashed it upon the spectacles of her blind pursuer, who was squaring his arm to her in an instant.

And that was the last she saw of the only partner for whom she had a good word afterward, and he had come to her by accident. But it was by no means the last she heard of him. The next was from Herbert, as they drove home together in one hansom, while Ruth and her husband followed in another. The morning air blew fresh upon their faces; the rising sun struck sparks from the harness; the leaves in the park were greener than any in Australia, and the dew on the grass through the railings was as a silver shower new-fallen. But the most delicious taste of London that had yet been given her was poisoned for Christina by her brother Herbert.

"To have my claim jumped by that joker!" said he through his nose.

"But you had left it empty," said Tiny mildly. "I was all alone."

"It isn't so much that," her brother said, shifting the ground he had taken in preliminary charges; "it's your dancing with that brute Manister!"

"My dear old Herbs," said Miss Luttrell with provoking coolness, "Lord Manister asked me to dance with him, and I didn't see why I should refuse. I certainly didn't see why I should consult you, Herbs."

"By ghost," cried Herbert, "if it comes to that, he once asked you to marry him!"

"Now you are a treat," said the girl, before the blood came.

"And then bolted! I should be ashamed of myself for dancing with him if I were you. He said I was a larrikin, too. I'd like to fill his eye for him!"

"He'll never say a truer thing!" Christina cried out; but her voice broke over the words, and the early sun cut diamonds on her lashes.

Now this was Herbert: he was rough, but not cowardly. His nose had become hooked in his teens from a stand-up fight with a full-grown man. There is not the least doubt that in such a combat with Lord Manister that nobleman, though otherwise a finer athlete, would have suffered extremely. But it was not in Herbert to hit any woman in cold blood with his tongue. Having done this in his heat to Christina, his mate, he was man enough to be sorry and ashamed, and to slip her hands into his.

"I'm an awful beast," he stammered out. "I didn't mean anything at all-except that I'd like to fill up Manister's eye! I can't go back on that when-when he called me a larrikin!"

Chapter IV
Ruth and Christina.

Here is the difference between Ruth and Christina, who were considered so much alike.

Of the two, Ruth was the one to fall in love with at sight-of which Erskine Holland supplies the proof. She was less diminutive than her sister; she had a finer figure, a warmer color, and indeed, despite the destructive Australian sun, a very beautiful complexion. In the early days at Wallandoon she had given herself a better chance in this respect than Christina had done, not from vanity at all, but rather owing to certain differences in their ideas of pleasure, into which it is needless to enter. The result was her complexion; and this was not her only beauty, for she had good brown eyes that suited her coloring as autumn leaves befit an autumn sunset. These eyes are never unkind, but Ruth's were sweet-tempered to a fault. So the glance of one scanning both girls for the first time rested naturally upon Ruth, but on all subsequent occasions it flew straight to Christina, because there was an end to Ruth; but there was no coming to an end of Tiny, about whom there was ever some fresh thing to charm or disappoint one.

Thus, but for the businesslike dispatch of Erskine Holland, it might have been Ruth's fate to break in Christina's admirers until Christina fancied one of them enough to marry him. For Ruth's was perhaps the more unselfish character of the two, as it was certainly the simpler one, in spite of a peculiar secretive strain in her from which Tiny was free. Tiny, on the other hand, was much more sensitive; but to perceive this was to understand her better than she understood herself. For she did not know her own weaknesses as the self-examining know theirs, and hardly anybody suspected her of this one until her arrival in England-when Erskine Holland came to treat her as a sister, and to understand her more or less.

In Australia he had seen very little of her, though enough to regard her at the time as an arrant little heartless flirt, for whom sighed silly swains innumerable. That she was, indeed, a flirt there was still no denying; but as his knowledge of her ripened, Holland was glad to unharness the opprobrious epithets with which Ruth's sister had first driven herself into his mind. He discovered good points in Christina, and among them a humor which he had never detected out in Australia. Probably his own sense of it had lost its edge out there, for love-making blunts nothing sooner; while Ruth, for her part, was naturally wanting in humor. Holland had never been blind to this defect in his wife, but he seemed resigned to it; one can conceive it to be a merit in the wife of an amusing man.

Some people called Erskine amusing-it is not hard to win this label from some people-but at any rate he was never likely to find it difficult to amuse Ruth. Now no companion in this world is more charming for all time than the person who is content to do the laughing. As a novelty, however, Christina had her own distinctive attraction for Erskine Holland. And they got on so well together that presently he saw more in Tiny than her humor, which others had seen before him; he saw that her heart was softer than she thought; but he divined that something had happened to harden it.

"She has been falling in love," he said to Ruth —"and something has happened."

"What makes you think so? She has told me nothing about it," Ruth said.

"Ah, she is sensitive. I can see that, too. It's her bitterness, however, that makes me think something has turned out badly."

"She is sadly cynical," remarked Ruth.

"Cynically sad, I rather think," her husband said. "I don't fancy she's languishing now; I should say she has got over the thing, whatever it has been-and is rather disappointed with herself for getting over it so easily. She has hinted at nothing, but she has a trick of generalizing; and she affects to think that one person doesn't fret for another longer than a week in real life. I don't say her cynicism is so much affectation; something or other has left a bad taste in her mouth; but I should like to bet that it wasn't an affair of the most serious sort."

"Her affairs never were very serious, Erskine."

"So I gathered from what I saw of her before we were married. It's a pity," said Erskine musingly. "I'd like to see her married, but I'd love to see her wooed! That's where the sport would come in. There would be no knowing where the fellow had her. He might hook her by luck, but he'd have to play her like fun before he landed her! There'd be a strong sporting interest in the whole thing, and that's what one likes."

"It's a pity I didn't know what you liked," Ruth said, with a smile; "and a wonder that you liked me, and not Tiny!"

"My darling," laughed her husband, "that sort of sport's for the young fellows. I'm past it. I merely meant that I should like to see the sport. No, Tiny's charming in her way, but God forbid that it should be your way too!"

Now Ruth was such a fond little wife that at this speech she became too much gratified on her own account to care to discuss her sister any further. But in dismissing the subject of Tiny she took occasion to impress one fact upon Erskine:

"You may be right, dear, and something may have happened since I left home; but I can only tell you that Tiny hasn't breathed a single word about it to me."

And this is an early sample of the disingenuous streak that was in the very grain of Ruth. Christina, indeed, had told her nothing, but Ruth knew nearly all that there was to know of the affair whose traces were plain to her husband's insight. Beyond the fact that the name of Tiny Luttrell had been coupled in Melbourne with that of Lord Manister, and the *on dit* that Lord Manister had treated her rather badly, there was, indeed, very little to be known. But Ruth knew at least as much as her mother, who had written to her on the subject the more freely and frequently because her younger daughter flatly refused the poor lady her confidence. There was no harm in Ruth's not showing those letters to her husband. There was no harm in her keeping her sister's private affairs from her husband's knowledge. There was the reverse of harm in both reservations, as Erskine would have been the first to allow. Ruth had her reasons for making them; and if her reasons embodied a deep design, there was no harm in that either, for surely it is permissible to plot and scheme for the happiness of another. I can see no harm in her conduct from any point of view. But it was certainly disingenuous, and it entailed an insincere attitude toward two people, which in itself was not admirable. And those two were her nearest. However amiable her plans might be, they made it impossible for Ruth to be perfectly sincere with her husband on one subject, which was bad enough. But with Christina it was still more impossible to be at all candid; and this happened to be worse, for reasons which will be recognized later. In the first place, Tiny immediately discovered Ruth's insincerity, and even her plans. Tiny was a difficult person to deceive. She detected the insincerity in a single conversation with Ruth on the afternoon following Lady Almeric's ball, and before she went to bed she was as much in possession of the plans as if Ruth had told her them.

The conversation took place in Erskine's study, where the sisters had foregathered for a lazy afternoon.

"Oh, by the way," said Ruth, apropos of the ball, "it was a coincidence your dancing with Lord Manister."

"Why a coincidence?" asked Christina. She glanced rather sharply at Ruth as she put the question.

"Well, it is just possible that we shall see something of him in the country. That's all," said Ruth, as she bent over the novel of which she was cutting the pages.

Christina also had a book in her lap, but she had not opened it; she was trying to read Ruth's averted face.

"I thought perhaps you meant because we saw something of him in Melbourne," she said presently. "I suppose you know that we did see something of him? He even honored us once or twice."

"So you told me in your letters."

The paper knife was still at work.

"What makes it likely that we shall see him in the country?"

"Well, Mundham Hall is quite close to Essingham, you know."

"Mundham Hall! Whose place is that?"

"Lord Dromard's," replied Ruth, still intent upon her work.

"Surely not!" exclaimed Christina. "Lord Manister once told me the name of their place, and I am convinced it wasn't that."

"They have several places. But until quite lately they have lived mostly at the other side of the county, at Wreford Abbey."

"That was the name."

"But they have sold that place," said Ruth, "and last autumn Lord Dromard bought Mundham; it was empty when we were at Essingham last year."

For some moments there was silence, broken only by the leisurely swish of Ruth's paper knife. Then Christina said, "That accounts for it," thinking aloud.

"For what?" asked Ruth rather nervously.

"Lord Manister told me he knew of Essingham. He never mentioned Mundham. Is it so very close to your rectory?"

"The grounds are; they are very big; the hall itself is miles from the gates-almost as far as our home station was from the boundary fence."

"Surely not," Tiny said quietly.

"Well, that's a little exaggeration, of course."

"Then I wish it wasn't!" Tiny cried out. "I don't relish the idea of living under the lee of such very fine people," she said next moment, as quietly as before.

"No more do I —no more does Erskine," Ruth made haste to declare. "But we enjoyed ourselves so much there last August that we said at the time that we would take the rectory again this August. We made the people promise us the refusal. And it seemed absurd to refuse just because Lord Dromard had bought Mundham; shouldn't you have said so yourself, dear?"

"Certainly I should," answered Tiny; and for half an hour no more was said.

The afternoon was wet; there was no inducement to go out, even with the necessary energy, and the two young women, on whose pillows the sun had lain before their faces, felt anything but energetic. The afternoon was also cold to Australian blood, and a fire had been lighted in Erskine's den. His favorite armchair contained several cushions and Christina-who might as well have worn his boots-while Ruth, having cut all the leaves of her volume, curled herself up on the sofa with an obvious intention. She was good at cutting the leaves of a new book, but still better at going to sleep over them when cut. She had read even less than Christina, and it troubled her less; but this afternoon she read more. Ruth could not sleep. No more could Tiny. But Tiny had not opened her book. It was one of the good books that Erskine had lent her. She was extremely interested in it; but just at present her own affairs interested her more. Lying back in the big chair, with the wet gray light behind her, and that of the fire playing fitfully over her face, Christina committed what was as yet an unusual weakness for her, by giving way voluntarily to her thoughts. She was in the habit of thinking as little as possible, because so many of her thoughts were depressing company, and beyond all things she disliked being depressed. This afternoon she was less depressed than indignant. The firelight showed her forehead strung with furrows. From time to time she turned her eyes to the sofa, as if to make sure that Ruth was still awake, and as often as they rested there they gleamed. At last she spoke Ruth's name.

"Well?" said Ruth. "I thought you were asleep; you have never stirred."

"I'm not sleepy, thanks; and, if you don't mind, I should like to speak to you before you drop off yourself."

Ruth closed her novel.

"What is it, dear? I'm listening."

"When you wrote and invited me over you mentioned Essingham as one of the attractions. Now why couldn't you tell me the Dromards would be our neighbors there?"

Ruth raised her eyes from the younger girl's face to the rain-spattered window. Tiny's tone was cold, but not so cold as Tiny's searching glance. This made Ruth uncomfortable. It did not incapacitate her, however.

"The Dromards!" she exclaimed rather well. "Had they taken the place then?"

"You say they bought it before Christmas; it was after Christmas that you first wrote and expressly invited me."

"Was it? Well, my dear, I suppose I never thought of them; that's all. They aren't the only nice people thereabouts."

"I'm afraid you are not quite frank with me," the young girl said; and her own frankness was a little painful.

"Tiny, dear, what a thing to say! What does it mean?"

Ruth employed for these words the injured tone.

"It means that you know as well as I do, Ruth, that it isn't pleasant for me to meet Lord Manister."

"Was there something between you in Melbourne?" asked Ruth. "I must say that nobody would have thought so from seeing you together last night. And-and how was I to think so, when you have never told me anything about it?"

Christina laughed bitterly.

"When you have made a fool of yourself you don't go out of your way to talk about it, even to your own people. It is kind of you to pretend to know nothing about it —I am sure you mean it kindly; but I'm still surer that you have been told all there was to tell concerning Lord Manister and me. I don't mean by Herbert. He's close. But the mother must have written and told you something; it was only natural that she should do so."

"She did tell me a little. Herbert has told me nothing. I tried to pump him, —I think you can't wonder at that, —but he refused to speak a word on the subject. He says he hates it."

"He hates Lord Manister," said Christina, smiling. "It came round to him once that Lord Manister had called him a larrikin, and he has never forgiven him. But he has been less of a larrikin ever since. And, of course, that wasn't why he was so angry with me for dancing with Lord Manister last night; he was dreadfully angry with me as we drove home; but he is a very good boy to me, and there was something in what he said."

"What made you dance with him?" Ruth said curiously.

"I was alone. I hadn't a partner. He asked me rather prettily-he always had pretty manners. You wouldn't have had me show him I cared, by snubbing him, would you?"

"No," said Ruth thoughtfully; and suddenly she slipped from the sofa, and was kneeling on the hearthrug, with her brown eyes softly searching Christina's face and her lips whispering, "Do you care, Tiny? *Do* you care, Tiny, dear?"

Tiny snapped her fingers as she pushed back her chair.

"Not that much for anybody-much less for Lord Manister, and least of all for myself! Now don't you be too good to me, Ruth; if you are you'll only make me feel ungrateful, and I shall run away, because I'm not going to tell you another word about what's over and done with. I can't! I have got over the whole thing, but it has been a sickener. It makes me sick to think about it. I don't want ever to speak of it again."

"I understand," said Ruth; but there was disappointment in her look and tone, and she added, "I should like to have heard the truth, though; and no one can tell it me but you."

"I thank Heaven for that!" cried Christina piously. "The version out there was that he proposed to me and I accepted him, and then he bolted without even saying good-by. It's true that he didn't say good-by; the rest is not true. But you must just make it do."

Her face was scarlet with the shame of it all; but there was no sign of weakness in the curling lips. She spoke bitterly, but not at all sadly, and her next words were still more suggestive of a wound to the vanity rather than to the heart.

"Does Erskine know?"

"Not a word."

"Honestly?"

"Quite honestly; at least I have never mentioned it to him, and I don't think anybody else has, or he would have mentioned it to me."

"Oh, Herbert wouldn't say anything. Herbert's very close. But-don't you two tell each other everything, Ruth?"

The young girl looked incredulous; the married woman smiled.

"Hardly everything, you know! Erskine has lots of relations himself, for instance, and I'm sure he wouldn't care to tell me the ins and outs of their private affairs, even if I cared to know them. It's just the same about you and your affairs, don't you see."

"Except that he knows me so well," Christina reflected aloud, with her eyes upon the fire. "If I had a husband," she added impulsively, "I should like to tell him every mortal thing, whether I wanted to or not! And I should like not to want to, but to be made. But that's because I should like above all things to be bossed!"

"You would take some bossing," suggested Ruth.

"That's the worst of it," said Christina, with a little sigh, and then a laugh, as she snatched her eyes from the fire. "But I can't tell you how glad I am you haven't told Erskine. Never tell him, Ruth, for you don't know how I covet his good opinion. I like him, you know, dear, and I rather think he likes me-so far."

"Indeed he does," cried Ruth warmly; and a good point in her character stood out through the genuine words. "Nothing ever made me happier than to see you become such friends."

"He laughs at me a good deal," Tiny remarked doubtfully.

"That's because you amuse him a good deal. I can't get him to laugh at me, my dear."

"He would laugh," said Christina, with her eyes on the fire again, "if you told him I had aspired to Lord Manister!"

"But I'm not going to tell him anything at all about it." Ruth paused. "And after all, the Dromards won't take any notice of us in the country." She paused again. "And we won't speak of this any more, Tiny, if you don't like."

The shame had come back to Christina's face as she bent it toward the fire. Twice she had made no answer to what was kindly meant and even kindlier said. But now she turned and kissed Ruth, saying, "Thank you, dear. I am afraid I don't like. But you have been awfully good and sweet about it-as I shan't forget." And the fire lit their faces as they met, but the tear that had got upon Tiny's cheek was not her own.

Ruth, you see, could be tender and sympathetic and genuine enough. But she could not be sensible and let well alone.

She did that night a very foolish thing: she brought up the subject again. Tempted she certainly was. Never since her arrival in England had Tiny seemed so near to her or she to Tiny as in the hours immediately following the chat between them in Erskine's study. But Christina stood further from Ruth than Ruth imagined; she had not advanced, but retreated, before the glow of Ruth's sympathy. This was after the event, when some hours separated Christina from those emotional moments to which she had not contributed her share of the emotion, leaving the scene upon her mind in just perspective. She still could value Ruth's sweetness at the end of their talk, but her own suspicions, aroused at the outset, to be immediately killed by a little kindness, had come to life again, and were calling for an equal appreciation. The extent of Tiny's suspicions was very full, and the suspicions themselves were uncommonly shrewd and convincing. They made it a little hard to return Ruth's smiles during the evening, and to kiss her when saying good-night, though Tiny did these things duly. She went upstairs before her time, however, and not at all in the mood to be bothered any further about Lord Manister. Yet she behaved very patiently when Ruth came presently to her room and thus bothered her, being suddenly tempted beyond her strength. For Christina was discovered standing fully dressed under the gas-bracket, and frowning at a certain photograph on an orange-colored mount, which she turned face downward as Ruth entered. Whereupon Ruth, discerning the sign manual of a Melbourne photographer, could not help saying slyly, "Who is it, Tiny?"

"A friend of mine," Tiny said, also slyly, but keeping the photograph itself turned provokingly to the floor.

"In Australia?"

"Er-it was taken out there."

"It's Lord Manister!"

"Perhaps it is-perhaps it isn't."

"Tiny," said Ruth with pathos, "you might show me!"

But Tiny drummed vexatiously on the wrong side of the mount; and here Ruth surely should have let the matter drop, instead of which:

"You are very horrid," she said, "but I must just tell you something. I have heard things from Lady Almeric, who is very intimate with Lady Dromard, and I don't believe *he* is so much to blame as you think him. I have heard it spoken about in society. But don't look frightened. Your name has never been mentioned. I don't think it has ever come out. Indeed, I know it hasn't, for *I*, actually, have been asked the name of the girl Lord Manister was fond of in Melbourne-by Lady Almeric!"

"And what did you say?"

"What do you suppose? I glory in that fib —I am honestly proud of it. But, dear, the point is, not that Lord Manister has never mentioned your name, but that he can bear neither name nor sight of the girl he is expected to marry! Lady Almeric told me when —I couldn't help her."

"He is a nice young man, I must say!" remarked Christina grimly. "My fellow-victim has a title, no doubt?"

"Well, it's Miss Garth, and her father's Lord Acklam, so she's the honorable," said Ruth gravely. (Tiny smiled at her gravity.) "But I've seen her, and-he can't like her! And oh! Tiny dear, they all say he left his heart in Australia, but his mother sent for him because she heard something-but not your name, dear-and he came. They say he is devoted to his mother; but this has come between them, and she's sorry she interfered, because after all he won't marry poor Miss Garth. I had it direct from Lady Almeric when she tried to get that out of me. But I lied like a trooper!" exclaimed poor Ruth.

"I'm grateful to you for that," Christina said, not ungraciously —"but I must really be going to bed."

With a last wistful glance at the orange-colored cardboard, Ruth took the hint. Christina turned away in time to avoid an embrace without showing her repugnance, because she had still some regard for Ruth's good heart. But she had never experienced a more grateful riddance, and the look that followed Ruth to the threshold would have kept her company for some time had she turned there and caught one glimpse of it.

"Now I understand!" said Christina to the closed door. "I suppose I ought to love you for it, Ruth; but I don't —no, I don't!"

She turned the photograph face upward, and stared thoughtfully at it for some minutes longer; then she put it away.

Chapter V
Essingham Rectory.

Essingham Rectory, which the Erskine Hollands had taken for the month of August, was a little old building with some picturesque points to console one for the tameness of the view from its windows. The surrounding country was perfectly flat but for Gallow Hill, and not at all green but for the glebe and the riverside meadows, while the only trees of any account were the rectory elms and those in the Mundham grounds. It is true that on Gallow Hill three wind-crippled beeches brandished their deformities against the sky, as they may do still; but the country around Essingham is no country for trees. It is the country for warrens and rabbits and roads without hedges. So it struck Christina as more like the back-blocks than anything she had hoped to see in England, and pleased her more than anything she had seen. She showed her pleasure before they arrived at Essingham. She forgot to disparage the old country during the long drive from the county town; and that was notable. She had actually no stone to cast at the elaborate and impressive gates of Mundham Hall; apparently she was herself impressed. But opposite the gates they turned to the left, into a narrow road with hedges, from which you can see the rectory, and as Herbert put it afterward:

"That's what knocked our Tiny!"

For the girl's first glimpse of the old house was over the hedge and far away above a brilliant sash of meadow green. The cream-colored walls were aglow in the low late sunshine, what was to be seen of them, for they were half hidden by a creeper almost as old as themselves. The red-tiled, weather-beaten roof was dark with age. Even at a distance one smelt rats in the wainscot within the stuccoed walls. Around the house, and towering above the tiles, the elms stood as still against the evening sky as the square church tower but a little way to the right. To the right of that, but farther away, rose Gallow Hill. Thereabouts the sun was sinking, but the clock on the near side of the church tower had gilt hands, which marked the hour when Christina stood up in the fly and astonished her friends with her frank delight. It was a point against this young lady, on subsequent occasions when she did not forget to decry the old country, that at ten minutes past seven on the evening of the 1st of August she had given way to enthusiasm over a scene that was purely English and very ordinary in itself.

Not that her immediate appreciation of the place became modified on a closer acquaintance with it. At the end of the first clear day at Essingham she informed the others that thus far she had not enjoyed herself so much since leaving Australia. Of course she had enjoyed herself in London. That did not count. London only compared itself with Melbourne, Christina did not care how favorably; but Essingham was for comparison with the place that was dearer to her than any other in the world. You will understand why all her appreciations were directly comparative. This is natural in the very young, and fortunately Tiny Luttrell was still very young in some respects. Blessed with observant eyes, and having at this time an irritable memory to keep her prejudices at attention, her mind soon became the scene of many curious and specific contests between England and Australia. In the match between Wallandoon and Essingham the latter made a better fight than you would think against so strong an opponent. The rectory was homely and convenient in its old age, and Christina was greatly charmed with her own room, because it was small; and if the wall-paper was modern and conventional, and not to be read from the pillow in the early morning, it was almost as pleasant to lie and watch the elm tops trembling against the sky. And if the sky was not really blue in England, the leaves in Australia were not really green, as Christina now knew. So there they were quits. But England and Essingham scored palpably in some things; the kitchen garden was one. Christina had never seen such a kitchen garden; she found it possible to spend half an hour there at any time, to her further contentment; and there were other attractions on the premises, which were just as good in their way, while their way was often better for one.

For instance, there was a lawn tennis court which satisfied the soul of Erskine, who played daily for its express refreshment. That was what brought him to Essingham. The neighboring clergy were always ready for a game. But they laughed at Erskine for being so keen; he would get up before breakfast to roll the court, which passed their understanding. Christina played also, by no means ill, and Herbert uncommonly well; but this player neither won nor lost very prettily. He was more amiable over the photography which he had taken up in partnership with Tiny; but his photographs were uncommonly bad. Yet this was another amusement in the country, where, however, Christina was most amused by the neighbors who called. These were friendly people, and they had all called on the Hollands the previous year. Half of them were clergymen, though the stranger who met them found this difficult to believe in some cases; the other half were the clergymen's wives. Very grand families apart, there is no other society round about Essingham. And what could man wish better? Even Christina found it impossible to disapprove of the well-bred, easy-going, tennis-playing, unprofessional country clergy, as acquaintances and friends. But she did find fault with the rector of Essingham as a rector, though she had never seen him, and though Ruth assured her that he was a dear old man.

"He may be a dear old man," Miss Luttrell would allow, "but he's a bad old rector! His flock don't find him such a dear old man, either. They only see him once a week, in the pulpit; and then they can't hear him!"

"Who has been telling you that, Tiny?" asked Ruth.

"You've been talking sedition in the village!" said Erskine Holland.

"Well, I've been making friends with two or three of the people, if that's what you call talking sedition," Tiny replied; "and I think your dear old rector neglects them shamefully. He does worse than that. There's some fund or other for buying coals and blankets for the poor of the parish; and there's old Mrs. Clapperton. Mrs. Clapperton's a Roman Catholic; so, if you please, she never gets her coals or blankets, and she's too proud to ask for them. That's a fact-and I tell you what, I'd like to expose your dear old man, Ruth! As for the village, if it's a specimen of your English villages, let me tell you, Erskine, that it's leagues behind the average bush township. Why, they haven't even got a state school, but only a one-horse affair run by the rector! And the schoolmaster's the most ignorant man in the village. I wonder you don't copy us, and go in for state schools!"

"'Copy us, and go in for state schools,'" echoed Ruth with gentle mirth, as she sometimes would echo Tiny's remarks, and with a smile that traveled from Tiny to Erskine. But Erskine did not return the smile. His eyes rested shrewdly upon Christina, and Ruth feared from their expression that he thought the girl an utter fool; but she was wrong.

Christina was not, if you like, an intellectual girl, but she was by no means a fool. Neither was her brother-in-law, who perceived this. Her comments on the books he lent her were sufficiently intelligent, and she pleased him in other ways too. He was glad, for instance, to see her interesting herself in the local peasants; she was particularly glad that she did not give this interest its head, though as a matter of fact it never pulled. Christina was not the girl for interests that gallop and have not legs. Not the least of her attractions, in the eyes of a male relative of middle age, was a certain solid sanity that showed through every crevice of her wayward nature. It was sanity of the cynical sort, which men appreciate most. And it was least apparent in her own actions, which is the weak point of the cynically sane.

"At all events, Tiny, you can't find the country a tight fit, like London," said Erskine once, during the first few days. "Come, now!"

"No," replied Tiny thoughtfully, "I must own it doesn't fit so tight. But it tickles! You mayn't go here and you mayn't go there; in Australia you may go anywhere you darn please. Excuse me, Erskine, but I feel this a good deal. Only this morning Ruth and I were blocked by a notice board just outside the wicket at the far end of the churchyard; we were thinking of going up Gallow Hill, but we had to turn back, as trespassers would be prosecuted. There's no trespassing where I come from. And Ruth says the board wasn't there last year."

"Ah, the Dromards weren't there last year! They've stuck it up. You should pitch into your friend Lord Manister. It's rather vexatious of them, I grant you; they can't want to have tea on Gallow Hill; and it's a pity, because there's a fine view of the Hall from the top."

"Indeed? Ruth never told me that," remarked Christina curiously. "Have they arrived yet?" she added in apparent idleness.

"Last night, I hear-if you mean the Dromards. And a rumor has arrived with them."

Now Christina was careful not to inquire what the rumor was; but Erskine told her; and, oddly enough, what he had heard and now repeated was to come true immediately.

The great family at Mundham were about to entertain the county. That was the whisper, which was presently to be spoken aloud as a pure fact. It ran over the land with "At last!" hissing at its heels, and a still more sinister whisper chased the pair of them; for the Dromards might have entertained the county months before; a house-warming had been expected of them in the winter, but they had chosen to warm Mundham with their own friends from a distance; and since then the general election had become a moral certainty for the following spring, and-the point was-Viscount Manister had declared his willingness to stand for the division. The corollary was irresistible, but so, it appears, was Countess Dromard's invitation, which few are believed to have declined-for those that did so made it known. Some disgust, however, was expressed at the kind of entertainment, which, after all, was to be nothing more than a garden party. But nearly all who were bidden accepted. The notice, too, was shorter than other people would have presumed to give; but other people were not the Dromards. The countess' invitation conveyed to a hundred country homes a joy that was none the less keen for a certain shame or shyness in showing any sort of satisfaction in so small a matter. Nevertheless, though not adorned by a coronet, as it might have been, nor in any way a striking trophy, the card obtained a telling position over many a rectory chimney-piece, where in some instances it remained, accidentally, for months. In justice to the residents, however, it must be owned that not one of them read it with a more poignant delight, nor adjusted it in the mirror with a nicer care and a finer show of carelessness, nor gazed at it oftener while ostensibly looking at the clock, than did Mrs. Erskine Holland during the next ten days.

But when it came she acted cleverly. There was occasion for all her cleverness, because in her case the invitation was a complete surprise; she had not dared to expect one; and you may imagine her peculiar satisfaction at receiving an invitation that embraced her "party." Yet she was able to toss the card across the breakfast table to Erskine, merely remarking, "Should we go?" And when Tiny at once stated that for her part she was not keen, Ruth gave her a sympathetic look, as much as to say, "No more am I, my dear," which might have deceived a less discerning person. But Tiny saw that her sister was holding her breath until Erskine spoke his mind.

"Have we any other engagement?" said he directly. "If not, it would hardly do to stick here playing tennis within sight of their lodge. I'm no more keen than you are, Tiny, but that would look uncommon poor. It was very kind of them to think of asking us; I'm afraid we must go; but I am sure you will find it amusing."

"Thanks," replied Christina, to whom this assurance was addressed, "but you needn't send me there to be amused; you see, I have plenty to amuse me here," she added, with a smile that had been slow to come. "I'll go, of course, and with pleasure; but there would be more pleasure in some hard sets with you, Erskine, or in taking your photograph."

"Ah, you don't know what you'd miss, Tiny! I can promise you some sport, if you keep your eyes and ears open. Then you knew Lord Manister in Melbourne. In any case, you oughtn't to go back there without a glimpse of some of our fine folks at home, when you can get it."

"Oh, I'll go; but not for the sport of seeing your clergy and gentry on their knees to your fine folks, nor yet to be amused. As for Lord Manister, he was well enough in Melbourne; he didn't give himself airs, and there he was wise. But on his native heath! One would be sorry to set foot on the same soil. It must be sacred."

"Come, I say, I don't think you'll find the parsons on their knees. We think a lot of a lord, if you like; but we try to forget that when we're talking to him. We do our best to treat him as though he were merely a gentleman, you know," said Erskine, smiling, but giving, as he felt, an informing hint.

"Ah, you try!" said Christina. "You do your best!"

"Our best may be very bad," laughed Erskine; "if so, you must show us how to better it, Tiny."

"I should get Tiny to teach you how to treat a lord, dear," said Ruth, who saw nothing to laugh at, and seemed likely to lend her husband a severer support than the occasion needed.

"Say Lord Manister!" suggested Erskine. "Will you show me on him?"

"I may if you're good-you wait and see," said Tiny lightly. And lightly the matter was allowed to drop. For Herbert, as usual, was late for breakfast, which was for once a very good thing; and as for Ruth, it was merely her misfortune to have a near sight for the line dividing chaff from earnest, but now she saw it, and on which side of it the others were, for she had joined them and was laughing herself.

But Herbert would not have laughed at all; indeed, he had not a smile for the subject when he did come down and Ruth gave him his breakfast alone. It seemed well that Christina was not in the room. Her brother took the opportunity of saying what he thought of Manister, and what Manister had once called him behind his back, and what he would have done to Manister's eye had half as much been said to his face. His personal decision about the garden party was merely contemptuous. He was not going. Nor did he go when the time came. Meanwhile, however, something happened to modify for the moment his opinion of the young viscount whom it was Herbert's meager satisfaction to abuse roundly whenever his noble name was spoken.

Having been provided with two rooms at the rectory, in one of which he was expected to read diligently every morning, Herbert entered that room only when his pipe needed filling. He kept his tobacco there, and also, to be sure, his books; but these he never opened. He read nothing, save chance items in an occasional sporting paper; he simply smoked and pottered, leaving the smell of his pipe in the least desirable places. When he took photographs with Tiny, that was pottering too, for neither of them knew much about it, and Herbert was too indolent to take either pains or care in a pursuit which essentially demands both. He had rather a good eye for a subject; he could arrange a picture with some judgment. That interested him, but the subsequent processes did not, and these invariably spoilt the plate. All his actions, however, suggested an underlying theory that what is worth doing is not necessarily worth doing well. This applied even to his games, about which Herbert was really keen; he played lawn tennis carelessly, though with a verve and energy somewhat surprising in the loafing, smoking idler of the morning. He had been fond of cricket, too, in Australia; it was a disappointment to him that no cricket was to be had at Essingham. He looked forward to Cambridge for the athletic advantages. He had no intention of reading there; so what, he wanted to know, was the good of his reading here? Certainly Herbert had entered at an accommodating college, which would receive young men quite free from previous knowledge; but he might have been reading for his little-go all this time; and he never read a word.

But one morning he loitered afield, and came back enthusiastic about a place for a photograph; the next, Tiny and the implements were dragged to the spot; and really it was not bad. It was a scene on the little river just below Mundham bridge. The thick white rails of the bridge standing out against a clump of trees in the park beyond, the single arch with the dark water underneath and some sunlit ripples twinkling at the further side, seemed to call aloud for a camera; and Herbert might have used his to some purpose, for a change, had he not forgotten to fill his slides with plates before leaving home. This discovery was not made until the bridge was in focus, and it put young Luttrell in the plight of a rifleman who has sighted the bull's-eye with an empty barrel. It was a question of returning to the rectory to load the slides or of giving up the photograph altogether. On another occasion, having forgotten the lens, Herbert had packed up the camera and gone back in disgust. But that happened nearer home. To-day he had carried the camera a good mile. Two journeys with something to show for them were preferable to one with a tired arm for the only result. Within a minute after the slides were found empty Christina was alone in the meadow below the bridge; Herbert had found it impossible to give up the photograph altogether.

The girl had not lost patience, for she was herself partly to blame. There were, however, still better reasons for her resignation. She happened to have the second volume of "The Newcomes" in her jacket pocket, and the little river seemed to ripple her an invitation from the bridge to make herself comfortable with her book in its shade. There was no great need for shade, but the idea seemed sensible. With her hand on the book in her pocket, and her eyes hovering about the bridge for the coolest corner, she felt perhaps a little ashamed as she thought of Herbert making a cool day hot by running back alone for what they had both forgotten. It was hardly this feeling, however, that kept her standing where she was.

She had known no finer day in England. The light was strong and limpid, the shadows abrupt and deep. The sky was not cloudless, but the clouds were thin and clean. There was a refreshing amount of wind; the tree tops beyond the bridge swayed a little against the sky; the focusing cloth flapped between the tripod legs, and for some minutes the girl stood absently imbibing all this, without a thought in her head.

Presently she found herself wondering whether there was enough movement in the trees to mar a photograph; later she tucked her head under the cloth to see. As she examined the inverted picture on the ground glass, she held the cloth loosely over her head and round her neck. But suddenly she twitched it tighter. For first the sound of wheels had come to her ears. Then a dogcart had been pulled up on the bridge. And now on the focusing screen a figure was advancing upside down, like a fly on the ceiling, and doubling its size with each stride, until there occurred a momentary eclipse of the inverted landscape by Lord Manister, who had stalked in broad daylight to our Tiny's side.

Chapter VI
A Matter of Ancient History.

The focusing cloth clung to her head like a cowl as she raised it and bowed. There must have been nervousness on both sides, for the moment, but it did not prevent Lord Manister from taking off his hat with a sweep and swiftness that amounted almost to a flourish, nor Christina from noticing this and his clothes. He was so admirably attired in summer gray that she took pleasure in reflecting that she was herself unusually shabby, her idea being that contact with the incorrect was rather good for him. Correctness of any kind, it is to be feared, was ridiculously wrong in her eyes. Otherwise she might have been different herself.

"I knew it was you!" Lord Manister declared, having shaken her hand.

"How could you know?" said Christina, smiling. "You must be very clever."

"I wish I was. No; I met your brother running like anything with some wooden things under his arm. He wouldn't see me, but I saw him. I was going to pull up, but he wouldn't see me."

Miss Luttrell explained that her brother had gone back for plates, which they had both very stupidly forgotten; she added that she was sure he could not have recognized Lord Manister.

"Plates!" said this nobleman. "Ah, they're important, I know."

"Well, they're your cartridges; you can't shoot anything without them."

Lord Manister gave a louder laugh than the remark merited; then he studied his boots among the daisies. Christina smiled as she watched him, until he looked up briskly, and nearly caught her.

"I say, Miss Luttrell, I should like immensely to be on in this scene, if you would let me! I mean to say I should like to see the thing taken. Perhaps you could do with the trap and my mare on the bridge; she's something special, I assure you. And I have been thinking-if you think so too-that my man might go back for your brother and give him a lift. It must be monstrous hot walking. It's a monstrous hot day, you know."

This was not only an exaggeration, but a puff of smoke revealing hidden fires within the young man's head. Christina fanned the fire until it tinged his cheek by willfully hesitating before giving him a gracious answer. For when she spoke it was to say, with a smile at his anxiety, "Really, you are very considerate, Lord Manister, and I am sure Herbert will be grateful." They walked to the bridge, and stood upon it the next minute, watching the dogcart swing out of sight where the road bent.

"Your brother is very likely halfway back by this time," remarked Lord Manister, who would have been very sorry to believe what he was saying. "I dare say my man will pick him up directly; if so, they'll be back in a minute."

"I hope they will," said Christina —"the light is so excellent just now," she was in a hurry to add.

"Ah, the light in Australia was better for this sort of thing."

"As a rule, yes; but it would surely be difficult to beat this morning anywhere; the great thing is, over here, that you are so free from glare."

"Then you like England?"

"Well, I must say I like this corner of England; I haven't seen much else, you know."

"Good! I am glad you like this corner; you know it's ours," said the young fellow simply. Then he paused. "How strange to meet you here, though!" he added, as if he could not help it, nor the slight stress that laid itself upon the personal pronoun.

"It should rather strike me as strange to meet you," Miss Luttrell replied pointedly; "for I am sure I told you that my sister and her husband had taken Essingham Rectory for August. You may have forgotten the occasion. It was in London."

"Dear me, no, I'm not likely to forget it. To be sure you told me-at Lady Almeric's."

"Then perhaps you remember saying that you knew *of* Essingham?"

It was not, perhaps, because this was very dryly said that Lord Manister smiled. Nor was the smile one of his best, which were charming; it was visibly the expression of his nervousness, not his mirth.

"Yes, I am sorry to say I do remember that," he confessed with an awkwardness and humility which made Christina tingle in a sudden appreciation of his position in the world. "It was very foolish of me, Miss Luttrell."

"I wonder what made you?" remarked Christina reflectively, but in a friendlier tone.

"Ah! don't wonder," he said impatiently. His eyes fell upon her for one moment, then wandered down the road, as he added strangely: "You do and say so many foolish things without a decent why or wherefore. They're the things for which you never forgive yourself! They're the things for which you never hope to be forgiven!"

The girl did not look at him, but her glance chased his down the road to the bend where the dogcart had vanished and would reappear. She, however, was the next to speak, for something had occurred to her that she very much desired to explain.

"You see, I didn't know you lived here. I had never heard of Mundham when we met in town; if I had I shouldn't have known it was yours. I never dreamt that I should meet you here. You understand, Lord Manister?"

"My dear Miss Luttrell," cried Manister earnestly, "anybody could see that!"

So Christina lost nothing by her little exhibition of anxiety to impress this point upon him; for his reply was a triumphant flourish of the opinion she desired him to hold, to show her that he had it already; and his anxiety in the matter was even more apparent than her own.

"Thank you, Lord Manister," said Christina, looking him full in the face. Then her glance dropped to his hand; and his fingers were entangled in his watch-chain; and in the knowledge that the greater awkwardness was on his side she raised her eyes confidently, and met the dogged stare of a young Briton about to make a clean breast of his misdeeds.

"Do you want to know why I didn't mention our having taken this place-that time in town?"

"That depends on whether you want to tell me."

"I must tell you. It was because I feared —I mean to say, it crossed my mind-that perhaps you mightn't care to come here if you knew."

He paused and watched her. She was looking down, with her chin half buried in the focusing cloth, which had slipped from her head and fallen round her shoulders. The coolness of her face against the black velvet exasperated him, and the more so because he felt himself flushing as he added, "I see I was a fool to fear that."

"It was certainly unnecessary, Lord Manister," said the girl calmly, and not without a note of amusement in her voice.

"So you don't mind meeting one!"

"Lord Manister, I am delighted. Why should I mind?"

"You know I behaved like a brute."

"You did, I'm afraid." He winced. "You went away without saying good-by to your friends."

"I went away without saying good-by to you."

"Among others."

"No!" he cried sharply. "You and I were more than friends."

Christina drummed the ground with one foot. Her glance passed over Lord Manister's shoulder. He knew that it waited for the dogcart at the bend of the road.

"We were more than friends," he repeated desperately.

"I don't think we ever were."

"But you thought so once!"

The girl's lip curled, but her eyes still waited in the road.

"I wonder what you yourself thought once, Lord Manister?" she said quietly. "Whatever it was, it didn't last long; but I forgive that freely. Do you know why? Why, because it was exactly the same with me."

"Do you forgive me for getting you talked about?" exclaimed Lord Manister.

"Yes-because it is the only thing I have to forgive," returned Christina after a moment's hesitation. "The rest was nonsense; and I wish you wouldn't rake it up in this dreadfully serious way."

We know what Christina might mean by nonsense. Lord Manister was not the first of her friends whom she had offended by her abuse of the word. "It was not nonsense!" he cried. "It was something either better or worse. I give you my word that I honestly meant it to be something better. But my people sent for me. What could I do?"

His voice and eyes were pitiable; but Christina showed him no pity.

"What, indeed!" she said ironically. "I myself never blamed you for going. I was quite sure that you were the passive party, though others said differently. All I have to forgive is what you made other people say; but the whole affair is a matter of ancient history-and do you think we need talk about it any more, Lord Manister?"

"It is not all I have to forgive myself," he answered bitterly, disregarding her question. "If only you would hate me, I could hate myself less; but I deserve your contempt. Yet, if you knew what has been in my heart all this time, you would pity one. You have haunted me! I have been good for nothing ever since I came back to England. My people will tell you so, when you get to know them. My mother would tell you in a minute. She has never heard your name ... but she knows there was someone ... she knows there is someone still!"

Christina had colored at last; but, as she colored, the trot of a horse came gratefully to her attentive ears.

"You must think no more about it," she whispered; and her flush deepened.

"You wipe it all out?" he cried eagerly.

"Of course I do."

Her eyes met the dogcart at the bend. Herbert was in it.

"And we start afresh?"

He thought he was to get no answer. She was gazing anxiously at Herbert as the trap approached; as it drew up on the bridge she murmured, "I think we had better let well alone," without looking at Lord Manister. "Herbert, you remember Lord Manister?" she cried aloud in the same breath.

Herbert's look was not reassuring. He was, in fact, disgusted with all present but the groom, and most of all with himself, for being where he was. Nor was he the young man to trouble to hide his feelings, and he showed them now in so black a look that Christina, who knew him, was filled with apprehension. Thanks to Lord Manister's tact, that look did not last. Manister, who had his own impression of young Luttrell's character, and had not to be shrewd to guess the other's attitude toward himself, brought his most graceful manner to bear on the situation. With Tiny Luttrell, during the bad quarter of an hour which he had deserved and now endured, his best manner had not been at his command; but it returned to him with the return of the dogcart, and in time to do him a service. He had hardly shaken hands with Herbert when he asked him as an Australian, and therefore a judge, his opinion of the mare.

The touch would have been too heavy for an older man; but Herbert was barely twenty, and it flattered him to the marrow. Christina was relieved to hear his knowing but laudatory comments on the mare's points. She knew that, despite her brother's aggressive independence, he was susceptible enough to marked civility. This, indeed, he never expected, and he was ever ready to return, with interest, some fancied slight; but Christina had never known him rude to anyone going out of his way to be polite to him, as Lord Manister was doing this morning. She divined that politeness from a nobleman was not less gratifying to Herbert because he happened to have maligned the nobleman with much industry. Herbert's modest desire was to be treated as an equal by all men, and he was now being treated as an equal by a lord. This was all he required to make him reasonably civil, even to Lord Manister. When Manister asked him, almost deferentially, whether the mare could be taken in the photograph, he offered his lordship a place in it too, the offer being declined, but not without many thanks.

"I'm going to help take it," Manister laughed. "Mind you don't move, Luttrell. I'm going to help your sister. Hadn't you better come too, and leave my man alone in his glory?"

Herbert replied that he would take off the cap or do anything they liked. So the three went down into the meadow, and some infamous negatives resulted later. At the time care seemed to be taken by the photographers, while Lord Manister stood at a little distance, laughing a good deal. He was pressed to stand in the foreground, but not by Christina, and he steadily refused. The conciliation of his enemy seemed assured without that, though he did think of something else to make it doubly sure.

"By the way, Luttrell," he said as the camera was being packed away, "you're a cricketer to a certainty-you're an Australian."

"I'm very fond of it," the Australian replied, "but I haven't played over here; I've never had the slant."

"Well, we play a bit; come over and practice with us."

Herbert thanked him, declaring that he should like nothing better.

"Lord Manister is a great cricketer," Christina observed.

"Come over and practice," repeated his lordship cordially. "The ground isn't at all bad, considering it was only made last winter, and there's a professor to bowl to you. We have some matches coming on presently. Perhaps we might find a place for you."

This was the one thing Lord Manister said which came within measurable distance of offending the touchy Herbert. A minute later they had parted company.

"They *might* find a place for me," Herbert repeated as he and Tiny turned toward the village, while Lord Manister drove off in the opposite direction, with another slightly ornamental sweep of his hat. "Might they, indeed! I wouldn't take it. My troubles about their matches! But I could enjoy a practice."

"He said he would send over for you next time they do practice."

Those had been Lord Manister's last words.

"He did. He is improved. He's a sportsman, after all. It was decent of him to send back the trap for me. But I didn't want to get in —I was jolly scotty with myself for getting in. I say, Tiny!"

"Well?"

He had her by the arm.

"I don't ask any questions. I don't want to know a single thing. I hope he went down on his knees for his sins; I hope you gave him fits! But look here, Tiny: I won't say a word about this inside if you'd rather I didn't."

"I'd rather you did," Tiny said at once. "There's nothing to hide. But-you can be a dear, good boy when you like, Herbs!"

"Can I? Then you can be offended if you like-but he's on the job now if he never was in his life before!"

"I won't say I hope he isn't," Tiny whispered.

So she was not offended.

Chapter VII
The Shadow of the Hall.

Such was Christina's first meeting with Lord Manister in his own county. It occurred while his mother's invitation was exhilarating so many homes, and on the day when the Mundham mail bag would not hold the first draught of prompt replies. Until the garden party itself, however, no one at the rectory saw any more of Lord Manister, who had gone for a few days to the Marquis of Wymondham's place in Scotland, where he shot dreadfully on the Twelfth and was otherwise in queer form, considering that Miss Garth was also one of the guests. But under all the circumstances it is not difficult to imagine Manister worried and unhappy during this interval; which, on the other hand, remained in the minds of the people at the rectory, Christina included, as the pleasantest part of their month there.

Not that they suspected this at the time. Mrs. Erskine especially found these days a little slow. Having knowledge of Lord Manister's whereabouts, she was impatient for his return, and the more so because Christina seemed to have forgotten his existence. Christina was indeed puzzling, and on one embarrassing occasion, which with some girls would have led to a scene, she puzzled Ruth more than ever. Ruth tried to follow her presumptive example, and to put aside the thought of Lord Manister for the time being. Her consolation meanwhile was the lively *camaraderie* between Christina and Erskine, wherein Erskine's wife took a delight for which we may forgive her much.

"How well you two get on!" she would say gladly to each of them.

"He's a man and a brother," Tiny would reply.

To which Ruth was sure to say tenderly: "It's sweet of you, dear, to look upon him as a brother.

"Ah, but don't you forget that he's a man, and not my brother really, but just the very best of pals!" Tiny said once. "That's the beauty of him. He's the only man who ever talked sense to me right through from the beginning, so he's something new. He's the only man I ever liked without having the least desire to flirt with him, if you particularly want to know! And I don't believe his being my brother-in-law has anything to do with that," added the girl reflectively; "it would have been the same in any case. What's better still, he's the only man who ever understood me, my dear."

"He's very clever, you see," observed Ruth slyly, but also in all seriousness.

"That's the worst of him; he makes you feel your ignorance."

"I assure you, Tiny, he thinks *you* very clever."

"So you're crackin'!" laughed Tiny; and as the old bush slang filled her mouth unbidden, the smell of a hot wind at Wallandoon came into her nostrils; and there seemed no more to be said.

But that last assurance of Ruth's was still ringing in her ears when her thoughts got back from the bush. She did not believe a word of it. Yet it was more or less true. Nor was Erskine far wrong in any opinion he had expressed to his wife concerning Christina, of whom, perhaps, he had said even less than he thought.

She was not, indeed, to be called an intellectual girl, in these days least of all. That was her misfortune, or otherwise, as you happen to think. Intellectual possibilities, however, she possessed: raw brain with which much might have been done. Not much can be done by a governess on a station in the back-blocks. Merely in curing the girls of the twang of Australia, more successfully than of its slang, and in teaching Tiny to sing rather nicely, the governess at Wallandoon had done wonders. But gifts that were of more use to Christina were natural, such as the quick perception, the long memory, and the ready tongue with which she defended the doors of her mind, so that few might guess the poverty of the store within. Nor had the governess been able to add much to that store. The liking for books had not come to Christina at Wallandoon; but in Melbourne she had taken to reading, and had reveled in a deal of trash; and now in England she read whatever Erskine put in her hands, and honestly enjoyed most of it, with the additional relish of being proud of her enjoyment. Erskine thought her discriminating, too; but converts to good books are apt to flatter the saviors of their taste, and perhaps her brother-in-law was a poor judge of the girl's judgment. He liked her for finding *Colonel Newcome's* life more touching than his death, and for placing the *Colonel* second to *Dr. Primrose* in the order of her gods after reading "The Vicar of Wakefield." He was delighted with her confession that she should "love to be loved by Clive Newcome," while her defense of *Miss Ethel*, which was vigorous enough to betray a fellow-feeling, was interesting at the time, and more so later, when there was occasion to remember it. Similar interest attached to another confession, that she had long envied *Œnone* and *Elaine* "because they were really in love." She seemed to have mixed some good poetry with the bad novels that had contented her in Melbourne. Two more books which she learned to love now were "Sesame and Lilies" and "Virginibus Puerisque." It was Erskine Holland's privilege to put each into her hands for the first time, and perhaps she never pleased him quite so much as when she said: "It makes me think less of myself; it has made me horribly unhappy; but if they were going to hang me in the morning I would sit up all night to read it again!" That was her grace after "Sesame and Lilies."

"Why don't you make Ruth read too?" she asked him once, quite idly, when they had been talking about books.

"She has a good deal to think about," Erskine replied after a little hesitation. "She's too busy to read."

"Or too happy," suggested Tiny.

Mr. Holland made a longer pause, looking gratefully at the girl, as though she had given him a new idea, which he would gladly entertain if he could. "I wonder whether that's possible?" he said at last.

"I'm sure it is. Ruth is so happy that books can do nothing for her; the happy ones show her no happiness so great as her own, and she thinks the sad ones stupid. The other day, when I insisted on reading her my favorite thing in 'Virginibus——'"

"What is your favorite thing?" interrupted Erskine.

"'El Dorado'—it's the most beautiful thing you have put me on to yet, of its size. I could hardly see my way through the last page—I can't tell you why-only because it was so beautiful, I think, and so awfully true! But Ruth saw nothing to cry over; I'm not sure that she saw much to admire; and that's all because you have gone and made her so happy."

For some minutes Erskine looked grim. Then he smiled.

"But aren't you happy too, Tiny?"

"I'm as happy as I deserve to be. That's good enough, isn't it?"

"Quite. You must be as happy as you're pleased to think Ruth."

"Well, then, I'm not. I should like to be some good in the world, and I'm no good at all!"

"I am sorry to see it take you like that," said Erskine gravely. "I wouldn't have thought this of you, Tiny!"

"Ah, there are many things you wouldn't think of me," remarked Tiny. She spoke a little sadly, and she said no more. And this time her sudden silence came from no vision of the bush, but from what she loved much less—a glimpse of herself in the mirror of her own heart.

There was one thing, certainly, that none of them would have thought of her; for she never told them of her little quiet meddlings in the village. But I could tell you. Pleasant it would be to write of what she did for Mrs. Clapperton (who certainly seemed to have been unfairly treated) and of the memories that lived after her in more cottages than one. But you are to see her as they did who saw most of her, and to remember that nothing is more delightful than being kind to the grateful poor, especially when one is privately depressed. Little was ever known of the liberties taken by Christina's generosity, and nothing shall be recorded here. She must stand or fall without that, as in the eyes of her friends. Suffice it that she did amuse herself in this way on the sly, and found it good for restoring her vanity, which was suffering secretly all this time. She would have been the last to take credit for any good she may have done in Essingham. She knew that it wiped out nothing, and also that it made her happier than she would have been otherwise. For though a worse time came later, even now she was not comfortable in her heart. And she had by no means forgotten the existence of Lord Manister, as someone feared.

Ruth, however, put her own conversation under studious restraint during these days, many of which passed without any mention of Lord Minister's name at the rectory. The distracting proximity of his stately home was apparently forgotten in this peaceful spot. But the wife of one clerical neighbor, a Mrs. Willoughby, who accompanied her husband when he came to play lawn tennis with Mr. Holland, and indeed wherever the poor man went, cherished a grudge against the young nobleman's family, of which she made no secret. It was only natural that this lady should air her grievance on the lawn at Essingham, whence there was a distant prospect of lodge and gates to goad her tongue. Yet, when she did so, it was as though the sun had come out suddenly and thrown the shadow of the hall across the rectory garden.

"As for this garden party," cried Mrs. Willoughby, as it seemed for the benefit of the gentle-men, who had put on their coats, and were handing teacups under the trees, "I consider it an insult to the county. It comes too late in the day to be regarded as anything else. Why didn't they do something when first they came here? They have had the place a year. Why didn't they give a ball in the winter, or a set of dinner parties if they preferred that? Shall I tell you why, Mr. Holland? It was because the general election was further off then, and it hadn't occurred to them to put up Lord Manister for the division."

"They haven't been here a year, my dear, by any means," observed Mrs. Willoughby's husband; "and as for dinner parties, we, at any rate, have dined with them."

"Well, I wouldn't boast about it," answered Mrs. Willoughby, who had a sharp manner in conversation, and a specially staccato note for her husband. "We dined with them, it is true; I suppose they thought they must do the civil to a neighboring rector or two. But as their footman had the insolence to tell our coachman, Mrs. Holland, they considered things had reached a pretty pass when it came to dining the country clergy!'"

"Their footman considered," murmured Mr. Willoughby.

"He was repeating what he had heard at table," the lady affirmed, as though she had heard it herself. "They had made a joke of it-before their servants. So they don't catch me at their garden party, which is to satisfy our social cravings and secure our votes. I don't visit with snobs, Mrs. Holland, for all their coronets and Norman blood-of which, let me tell you, they haven't one drop between them. Who was the present earl's great-grandfather, I should like to know? He never had one; they are not only snobs but upstarts, the Dromards."

"At any rate," Mr. Holland said mildly, "they can't gain anything by being civil to *us*. We don't represent a single vote. We are here for one calendar month."

"Ah, it is wise to be disinterested here and there," rejoined Mrs. Willoughby, whose sharpness was not merely vocal; "it supplies an instance, and that's worth a hundred arguments. Now I shouldn't wonder, Mr. Holland, if they didn't go out of their way to be quite nice to you. I shouldn't wonder a bit. It would advertise their disinterestedness. But wait till you meet them in Piccadilly."

"Mrs. Willoughby is a cynic," laughed Erskine, turning to the clergyman, whose wife swallowed her tea complacently with this compliment to sweeten it. To so many minds a charge of cynicism would seem to imply that intellectual superiority which is cheap at the price of a moral defect.

Now Erskine had a lawn tennis player staying with him for the inside of this week; and the lawn tennis player was a fallen cricketer, who had played against the Eton eleven when young Manister was in it; and he ventured to suggest that the division might find a worse candidate. "He was a nice enough boy then," said he, "and I recollect he made runs; he's a good fellow still, from all accounts."

"From all *my* accounts," retorted Mrs. Willoughby, refreshed by her tea, "he's a very fast one!"

Erskine's friend had never heard that, though he understood that Manister had fallen off in his cricket; he had not seen the young fellow for years, nor did he think any more about him at the moment, being drawn by Herbert into cricket talk, which stopped his ears to the general conversation just as this became really interesting.

"That reminds me," Mrs. Willoughby exclaimed, turning to Ruth. "Was Lord Manister out in Australia in your time?"

Ruth said "No," rather nervously, for Mrs. Willoughby's manner alarmed her. "I was married just before he came out," she added; "as a matter of fact, our steamers crossed in the canal."

"Well, you know what a short time he stayed there, for a governor's aid-de-camp?"

"Only a few months, I have heard. Do let me give you another cup of tea, Mrs. Willoughby!"

"Now I wonder if you know," pursued this lady, having cursorily declined more tea, "how he came to leave so suddenly?"

Poor Mrs. Holland shook her head, which was inwardly besieged with impossible tenders for a change of subject. No one helped her: Tiny had perhaps already lost her presence of mind; Erskine did not understand; the other two were not listening. Ruth could think of no better expedient than a third cup for Christina; as she passed it her own hand trembled, but venturing to glance at her sister's face, she was amazed to find it not only free from all sign of self-consciousness or of anxiety, but filled with unaffected interest. For this was the occasion on which Christina's coolness quite baffled Ruth, who for her part was preparing for a scene.

"Shall I tell you?" asked Mrs. Willoughby.

"Do," said Christina, to whom the well-informed lady at once turned.

"He formed an attachment out there, Miss Luttrell! He could only get out of it by fleeing the country; so he fled. You look as though you knew all about it," she added (making Ruth shudder), for the girl had smiled knowingly.

"About which?" asked Tiny.

"What! Were there more affairs than one?"

"Some people said so."

Mrs. Willoughby glanced around her with a glittering eye, and was sorry to notice that two of her hearers were not listening. "That is just what I expected," she informed the other four. "If you tell me that Melbourne became too hot to hold him I shall not be surprised."

"Melbourne made rather a fuss about him," replied Christina in an excusing tone that pierced Ruth's embarrassment and pricked to life her darling hopes. "He was not greatly to blame."

"But he broke the poor girl's heart. I should blame him for that, to say the least of it."

"You surprise me," said Christina gravely; "I thought that people at home never blamed each other for anything they did in the colonies? Over here you are particular, I know; but I thought it was correct not to be too particular when out there. Your writers come out: we treat them like lords, and then they do nothing but abuse us; your lords come out: we treat them like princes, and, you see, they break our hearts. Of course they do! We expect it of them. It's all we look for in the colonies."

"You are not serious, Miss Luttrell," said Mrs. Willoughby in some displeasure. "To my mind it is a serious thing. It seems a sad thing, too, to me. But I may be old-fashioned; the present generation would crack jokes across an open grave, as I am well aware. Yet there isn't much joke in a young girl having her heart broken by such as Lord Manister, is there? And that's what literally happened, for my friend Mrs. Foster-Simpson knows all about it. She knows all about the Dromards-to her cost!"

"Ah, we know the Foster-Simpsons; they called on us last year," remarked Erskine, who devoutly trusted that they would not call again. His amusement at Christina hardly balanced his weariness of Mrs. Willoughby, and he took off his coat as he spoke.

"Does your friend know the poor girl's name, Mrs. Willoughby?" Tiny asked when the men had gone back to the court; and her tone was now as sympathetic as could possibly be desired.

"I'm sorry to say she does not; it's the one thing she has been unable to find out," said Mrs. Willoughby naïvely. "Perhaps you could tell me, Miss Luttrell?"

"Perhaps I could," said Christina, smiling, as she rose to seek a ball which had been hit into the churchyard. "Only, you see, I don't know which of them it was. It wouldn't be fair to give you a list of names to guess from, would it?"

Fortunately Mrs. Willoughby put no further questions to Ruth, who was intensely thankful. "For," as she told Christina afterward, "*I* was on pins and needles the whole time. I never did know anyone like you for keeping cool under fire!"

"It depends on the fire," Tiny said. "Mrs. Willoughby went off by accident, and luckily she was not pointing at anybody."

"And I'm glad she did, now it's over!" exclaimed Ruth. "Don't you see that I was quite right about your name? So now you need have no more qualms about the garden party."

"Perhaps I've had no qualms for some time; perhaps I've known you were right."

"Since when? Since-since you saw Lord Manister?"

Tiny nodded.

"Do you mean to say you talked about it?" Ruth whispered in delicious awe.

"I mustn't tell you what *he* talked about. He was as nice as he could be-though I should have preferred to find him less beautifully dressed in the country; but I always felt that about him. I am sure, however, of one thing: he was no more to blame than —I was. I have always felt this about him, too."

"Tiny, dear, if only I could understand you!"

"If only you could! Then you might help me to understand myself."

Chapter VIII
"Countess Dromard at Home."

The hall gates were plain enough from the rectory lawn, but plainer still from the steps whence, on the afternoon of the garden party, Mr. Holland watched them from under the brim of the first hard hat he had worn for a fortnight. He was ready, while the ladies were traditionally late, but he did not lose patience; he was too much entertained in watching the hall gates and the hedgerow that hid the road leading up to them. Vehicles were filing along this road in a procession which for the moment was continuous. Erskine could see them over the hedge, and it was difficult to do so without sharing some opinions which Mrs. Willoughby had expressed regarding the comprehensive character of the social measure taken not before it was time by the noble family within those gates. There were county clergymen driving themselves in ill-balanced dogcarts, and county townspeople in carriages manifestly hired, and county bigwigs-as big as the Dromards themselves-in splendid equipages, with splendid coachmen and horseflesh the most magnificent. Greater processional versatility might scarcely be seen in southwestern suburbs on Derby Day; and the low phaeton which he himself was about to contribute to the medley made Erskine laugh.

"We should follow the next really swagger turnout-we should run behind it," he suggested to the girls when at length they appeared; and Ruth took him seriously.

"No, get in front of them," said Herbert, who was lounging on the steps, in dirty flannels which Erskine envied him. "Get in front of them and slow down. That'd be the sporting thing to do! They couldn't pass you in the drive. It would do 'em good."

However, the procession was not without gaps, and to Ruth's satisfaction they found themselves in rather a wide one. As they drove through those august gates a parson's dogcart was rounding a curve some distance ahead, but nothing was in sight behind. Ruth sat beside her husband, who drove. She looked rather demure, but very charming in her little matronly bonnet; her costume was otherwise somewhat noticeably sober, and certainly she had never felt more sensibly the married sister than now, as she glanced at Christina with furtive anxiety, but open admiration. Tiny was neatly dressed in white, and her hat was white also. "Do you know why I wear a white hat?" she asked Erskine on the way; but her question proved merely to be an impudent adaptation of a very disreputable old riddle, and beyond this she was unusually silent during the short drive. Yet she seemed not only self-possessed, but inwardly at her ease. She sat on the little seat in front, often turning round to gaze ahead, and her curiosity and interest were very frank and natural. So were her admiration of the park, her anxiety to see the house itself, and even her wonder at the great length of the drive, which ran alongside the cricket field, and then bent steadily to the left. When at last the low red-brick pile became visible, Gallow Hill was seen immediately behind it, which surprised Christina; the lawn in front was alive with people, which put her on her mettle; and the inspiriting outburst of a military band at that moment forced from her an admission of the pleasure and excitement which had been growing upon her for some minutes.

"I like this!" she exclaimed. "This is first-rate England!"

Countess Dromard stood on the edge of the lawn at the front of the house, and apparently the carriages were unloading at this side of the drive. Ruth whispered hurriedly that she was sure they were, but she was not so sure in reality, and she now saw the disadvantage of arriving in a wide gap, which deprives the inexperienced of their lawful cue. She was quite right, however, and when some minutes elapsed before the arrival of another carriage to interrupt the charming little conversation Ruth had with Lady Dromard, the good of the gap became triumphantly apparent. The countess was very kind indeed. She was a tall, fine woman, with whom the shadows of life had scarce begun to lengthen to the eye; her face was not only handsome, but wonderfully fresh, and she had a trick of lowering it as she chatted with Ruth, bending over her in a way which was comfortable and almost motherly from the first. She had heard of Mrs. Holland, whom she was glad to meet at last, and of whom she now hoped to see something more. Ruth observed that they had the rectory only till September; she was sorry her time was so short. Lady Dromard very flatteringly echoed her sorrow, and also professed an envious admiration for the rectory, which she described as idyllic. That was practically all. What was said of the weather hardly counted; and a repetition of her ladyship's hopes of seeing something more of Mrs. Holland and her party was not worth remembering, according to Erskine, who declared that this meant nothing at all.

Ruth, however, was not likely to forget it; though she treasured just as much the memory of a certain glance which she had caught the countess leveling at her sister. She thought that other eyes also were attracted by the white-robed Tiny, and the smooth-shaven turf was air to Ruth's tread as she marched off with her husband and that cynosure. Nor was her satisfaction decreased when the first person they came across chanced to be no other than Mrs. Willoughby. This meeting was literally the unexpected treat that Ruth pronounced it to be, for the clergyman's wife was smiling in a manner which showed that she had witnessed the countess' singular civility to her friend.

"Yes, I'm here after all," said Mrs. Willoughby grimly. "Henry made me very angry by insisting on coming, but of course I wasn't going to let him come alone. I hope you think he looks happy now he's here!" (Mr. Willoughby and a brother rector might have been hatching dark designs against their bishop, who was himself present, judging by their looks.) "I call him the picture of misery. Well, Mrs. Holland, I hope you are gratified at your reception! Oh, it was quite gushing, I assure you; we have all been watching. But wait till you meet them in Piccadilly, my dear Mrs. Holland."

Mrs. Holland left the reply to her husband, who, however, contented himself with promising Mrs. Willoughby a telegraphic report of the proceedings at that meeting, if it ever took place.

"Ah, there won't be much to report," said that redoubtable woman; "they won't look at you. But I shouldn't be surprised to see them make a deal of you in the country, if you let them."

It did not seem conducive to the enjoyment of the afternoon to prolong the conversation with Mrs. Willoughby. The party of three wandered toward the band, admiring the scarlet coats of the bandsmen against the dark green of the shrubbery, and their bright brass instruments flaming in the sun. The music also was of much spirit and gayety, and it was agreed that a band was an immense improvement to a rite of this sort. Then these three, who, after all, knew very few people present, followed the example of others, and made a circuit of the house, in high good humor. But Tiny found herself between two conversational fires, for Ruth would compel her to express admiration for the premises, which might have been taken for granted, while Erskine called her attention to the people, who were much more entertaining to watch. As they passed a table devoted to refreshments, at which a large lady was being waited upon very politely by a small boy in a broad collar, they overheard one of those scraps of conversation which amuse at the moment.

"So you're a Dromard boy, are you?" the lady was saying. "I've never seen you before. What Dromard boy are *you*, pray?"

"My name's Douglas."

"Oh! So you're the Honorable Douglas Dromard, are you?"

The boy handed her an ice without answering as the three passed on.

"I said you'd see and hear some queer things," whispered Mr. Holland; "but you won't hear anything much finer than that. The woman is Mrs. Foster-Simpson; her husband's a solicitor, and may be the Conservative agent, if his wife doesn't disqualify him. She professes to know all about the Dromards, as you heard the other day. You can guess the kind of knowledge. Even the boy snubs her. Yet mark him. The mixture of politeness and contempt was worth noticing in a small boy like that. There's a little nobleman for you!"

"No, a little Englishman," said Tiny. "Now that's a thing I do envy you-your schoolboys, your little gentlemen! We don't grow them so little in the colonies; we don't know how."

They were walking on a majestic terrace in the shadow of the red-brick house, their figures mirrored in each mullioned window as they passed it.

"I call Lord Manister the luckiest young man in England," Ruth exclaimed during a pause between the other two. "To think that all this will be his!"

"It rather reminds me of Hampton Court on this side," remarked Tiny indifferently.

"And it's by no means their only place, you know; there are others they never use, are there not, Erskine? —to say nothing of all those squares and streets in town!"

But Erskine sounded the thick sibilant of silence as they passed a shabby looking person with a slouching walk and a fair beard.

"I wonder how *he* got here?" Tiny murmured next moment.

"He has a better right than most of us."

"What do you mean, Erskine?"

"Well, it's the earl."

"Earl Dromard? I should have guessed his gardener!"

"No, that's the earl. Old clothes are his special fancy in the country. It's his particular form of side, so they say."

"Well," said Tiny, "I prefer it to his son's, which has always appeared to me to be the other extreme."

"I am sure Lord Manister is not over-dressed," remonstrated Ruth, with her usual alacrity in defense of his lordship.

"No, that's the worst of him," answered her sister. "There is nothing to find fault with, ever; that's what makes one think he employs his intellect on the study of his appearance."

They had seen Lord Manister in the distance. Presumably he had not seen them, but he might have done so; and Ruth supposed it was the doubt that made her sister speak of him more captiously than usual. But the criticism was not utterly unfair, as Ruth might presently have seen for herself; for as they came back to the front of the house, Lord Manister detached himself from a group, and approached them with the suave smile and the slight flourish of the hat which were two of his tricks. Christina asked afterward if the flourish was not dreadfully continental, but she was told that it was merely up to date, like the hat itself. At the time, however, she introduced Lord Manister to her sister Mrs. Erskine Holland, and to Mr. Holland, taking this liberty with charming grace and tact, yet with a becoming amount of natural shyness. Manister, for one, was pleased with the introduction on all grounds. From the first, however, he addressed himself to the married lady, speaking partly of the surrounding country, for which Ruth could not say too much, and partly of Melbourne, which enabled him to return her compliments. His manner was eminently friendly and polite. Discovering that they had not yet been in the house for tea, he led the way thither, and through a throng of people in the hall, and so into the dining room. Here he saved the situation from embarrassment by making himself equally attentive to another party. To Ruth, however, Lord Manister's civility was still sufficiently marked, while he asked her husband whether he was a cricketer; and this reminded him of Herbert, for whom he gave Miss Luttrell a message. He said they had just arranged some cricket for the last week of the month; he thought they would be glad of Miss Luttrell's brother in one or two of the matches. But he seemed to fear that most of the teams were made up; his young brother was arranging everything. Christina gathered that in any case they would be glad to see Herbert at the nets any afternoon of the following week, more especially on the Monday. Lord Manister made a point of the message, and also of the cricket week, "when," he said, "you must all turn up if it's fine." And those were his last words to them.

"I see you know my son," said the countess in her kindliest manner as Ruth thanked her for a charming afternoon.

"My sister met him the other day at Lady Almeric's," replied Ruth, "and before that in Australia."

"I knew Lord Manister in Melbourne," added Tiny with freedom.

"Do you mean to tell me you are Australians?" said Lady Dromard in a tone that complimented the girls at the expense of their country. "Then you must certainly come and see me," she added cordially, though her surprise was still upon her. "I am greatly interested in Australia since my son was there. I feel I have a welcome for all Australians-you welcomed him, you know!"

Christina afterward expressed the firm opinion that Lady Dromard had said this rather strangely, which Ruth as firmly denied. Tiny was accused of an imaginative self-consciousness, and the accusation provoked a blush, which Ruth took care to remember. Certainly, if the countess had spoken queerly, the queerness had escaped the one person who was not on the lookout for something of the kind; Erskine Holland had perceived nothing but her ladyship's condescension, which had been indeed remarkable, though Erskine still told his wife to expect no further notice from that quarter.

"And I'm selfish enough to hope you'll get none, my dears," he said to the girls that evening as they sauntered through the kitchen garden after dinner; "because for my part I'd much rather not be noticed by them. We were not intended to take seriously anything that was said this afternoon; honey was the order of the day for all comers-and can't you imagine them wiping their foreheads when we were all gone? I only hope they wiped us out of their heads! We're much happier as we are. I'm not rabid, like Mrs. Willoughby; but she prophesied a very possible experience, when all's said and done, confound her! I have visions of Piccadilly myself. And seriously, Ruth, you wouldn't like it if you became friendly with these people here and they cut you in town; no more should I. I think you can't be too careful with people of that sort; and if they ask us again I vote we don't go; but they won't ask us any more, you may depend upon it."

"I don't depend upon it, all the same," replied Ruth, with some spirit. "Lady Dromard was most kind; and as for Lord Manister, *I* was enchanted with him."

"Were you?" Tiny said, feeling vaguely that she was challenged.

"I was; I thought him unaffected and friendly, and even simple. I am sure he is simple-minded! I am also sure that you won't find another young man in his position who is better natured or better hearted — —"

"Or better mannered-or better dressed! You are quite right; he is nearly perfect. He is rather too perfect for me in his manners and appearance; I should like to untidy him; I should like to put him in a temper. Lord Manister was never in a temper in his life; he's nicer than most people-but he's too nice altogether for me!"

"You knew him rather well in Melbourne?" said Erskine, eyeing his sister-in-law curiously; her face was toward the moon, and her expression was set and scornful.

"Very well indeed," she answered with her erratic candor.

"I might have guessed as much that time in town. I say, if we meet *him* in Piccadilly we may score off Mrs. Willoughby yet! Wait till we get back — —"

"All right; only don't let us wait out here," Ruth interrupted —"or Tiny and I may have to go back in our coffins!"

Chapter IX
Mother and Son.

A clever man is not necessarily an infallible prophet; and the clever man who is married may well preserve an intellectual luster in the eyes of his admirer by never prophesying at all. But should he take pleasure in predicting the thing that is openly deprecated at the other side of the hearth, let him see to it that his prediction comes true, for otherwise he has whetted a blade for his own breast, from whose justifiable use only an angel could abstain. There was no angel in the family which had been brought up on Wallandoon Station, New South Wales. When, within the next three days, Ruth received a note from Lady Dromard inviting them all to dinner at a very early date, she did not fail to prod Erskine as he deserved. But her thrust was not malignant; nor did she give vexatious vent to her own triumph, which was considerable.

"You are a very clever man," she merely told him, and with the relish of a wife who can say this from her heart; "but you see, you're wrong for once. Lady Dromard *did* mean what she said. She wants us all to dine there on Friday evening, when, as it happens, we have no other engagement; and really I don't see how we can refuse."

"You mean that you would like to get out of it if you could?" her husband said.

"You don't need to be sarcastic," remarked Ruth with a slight flush. "Who wants to get out of it?"

"I thought perhaps you did, my dear; to tell you the truth, I rather hoped so."

"You don't want to go!"

"I can't say I jump."

Ruth colored afresh.

"I have no patience with you, Erskine! Nobody is dying to go; but I own I can't see any reason against going, nor any excuse for stopping away; and considering what you yourself said about going to the garden party, dear, I must say I think you're rather inconsistent."

Holland gazed down into the flushed, frowning face, that frowned so seldom, and flushed so prettily. Always an undemonstrative husband, very properly he had been more so than ever since others had been staying in the house. But neither of those others was present now, and rather suddenly he stooped and kissed his wife.

"There is no reason, and there would be no excuse; so you are quite right," he said kindly. "It's only that one has a constitutional dislike to being taken up-and dropped. I have visions of all that. I'm afraid Mrs. Willoughby has poisoned my mind; we will go, and let us hope it'll prove an antidote."

They went, and that dinner party was not the formidable affair it might have been; as Lady Dromard herself said, most graciously, it was not a dinner party at all. Ten, however, sat down, of whom four came from the rectory; for Herbert had been over to practice at the nets, and was fairly satisfied with his treatment on that occasion, which accounted for his presence on this. The only other guests were an inevitable divine and his wife. The earl was absent. As if to conserve Christina's impression of the old clothes in which, as the natives said, his lordship "liked himself," Earl Dromard had left for London rather suddenly that morning. Lord Manister filled his place impeccably, with Ruth at her best on his right. Herbert was less happy with Lady Mary Dromard, a very proud person, who could also be very rude in the most elegant manner. But Christina fell to the jolliest scion of the house, Mr. Stanley Dromard; and this pair mutually enjoyed themselves.

Young in every way was the Honorable Stanley Dromard. He had just left Eton, where he had been in the eleven, like his brother before him; he was to go into residence at Trinity in October. With a quantum of gentlemanly interest he heard that Miss Luttrell's brother was also going up to Cambridge next term; but not to Trinity. Said Mr. Dromard, "Your brother's a bit of a cricketer, too; he came over for a knock the other day; he means to play for us next week, if we're short, doesn't he?" Christina fancied so. Mr. Dromard said "Good!" with some emphasis, and Herbert's name dropped out of the conversation. This became Anglo-Australian, as it was sure to, and led to some of those bold comparisons for which Christina was generally to be trusted; but the bolder they were, the more Mr. Dromard enjoyed them, for the girl glittered in his eyes. He was a delightfully appreciative youth, if easily amused, and his laughter sharpened Tiny's wits. She shone consciously, but yet calmly, and made a really remarkable impression upon her companion, without once meeting Lord Manister's glance, which rested on her sometimes for a second.

So the flattering attentions of young Dromard were not terminated, but merely interrupted, by the flight of the ladies. When the men followed them to the drawing room the younger son shot to Miss Luttrell's side with the fine regardlessness of nineteen, and furthered their friendship by divulging the Mundham plans for the following week. The cricket was to begin on the Tuesday. The men were coming the day before: half the Eton eleven, Tiny understood, and some older young fellows of Manister's standing. The first two were to be two-day matches against the county and a Marylebone team. The Saturday's match would be between Mundham Hall and another scratch eleven, "and that's when we may want your brother, Miss Luttrell," added Mr. Dromard, "though we *might* want him before. Our team has been made up some time, but somebody is sure to have some other fixture for Saturday."

"I think he may like to play," said Christina.

Mr. Dromard seemed a little surprised.

"It's a jolly ground," he remarked, "and there will be some first-rate players."

"I am sure he would like a game on your ground," Christina went so far as to say.

"Do you dance, Miss Luttrell?" asked the young man, after a pause.

"When I get the chance," said Christina.

He gazed at her a moment, and could imagine her dancing-with him.

"Suppose we were to do something of the kind here one evening between the matches; would you come?"

"If I got the chance," said Christina.

Dromard considered what he was saying. "We ought to have a dance," he added in a doubtful tone, as though the need were greater than the chance; "we really ought. But I don't suppose we shall; nothing is arranged, you see."

"You needn't hedge, Mr. Dromard," said the girl, smiling.

"Eh?"

"I shan't expect an invitation!"

She nodded knowingly as he blushed; but he had the great merit of being easily amused, and with another word she made him merry and at ease again. Not unreasonably, perhaps, a casual spectator might have suspected these two of a mild but immediate flirtation. Stanley, however, was at a safe and privileged age, and no eye was on him but his brother's. Lord Manister gave the impression of being a rather dignified person in his own home, but he was doing his gracious duty by the guests, none of whom seemed especially to occupy his attention, while he was reasonably polite to all. It was he, too, who at length suggested to Lady Dromard that Miss Luttrell would probably sing something if she were asked.

So Christina sang something-it hardly matters what. Her song was not a classic, neither was it grossly popular. It was a pleasant song, pleasantly sung, and the entire absence of pretentiousness and of affectation in the song and the singing was more noticeable than the positive excellence of either. The girl had no greater voice than one would have expected of so small a person, but what she had was in keeping. Lady Dromard, however, had a more sensitive appreciation of good taste than of good music, and she asked for more. Christina sang successively something of Lassen's, and then "Last Night," taking the English words in each case. She played her own accompaniments, and felt little nervousness until her last song was finished, when it certainly startled her to find Lady Dromard standing at her side.

"Thank you!" said the countess with considerable enthusiasm. "You sing delightfully, and you sing delightful songs. You must have been very well taught."

"Mostly in the bush," said Christina truthfully.

"You come from the bush?"

"But you had some lessons in Melbourne," put in Ruth, who was visibly delighted.

"Oh, yes, a few," Tiny said, smiling; "as many as I was worth."

"Ah, you shall tell me about Melbourne one day soon," said Lady Dromard to the young girl. "Your sister has promised to come over and watch the cricket. I do hope you will come with her."

Christina expressed her pleasure at the prospect, and, taking the nearest seat, found Lord Manister leaning over the end of the piano and looking down upon her with a rather sardonic smile.

"You haven't looked at me this evening," he said to her under cover of the general conversation, which was now renewed. "May I ask what I have done?"

"Certainly you may ask, Lord Manister," answered the girl with immense simplicity; "but I can't tell you, because I am not aware that you have done anything beyond making us all very happy and at home."

"Well, I'm glad to hear that," said Manister, whose quasi-humorous tone lacked the lightness to deceive; "I was afraid I had offended you."

"Offended me!" cried Christina, with widening eyes and a puzzled look. "When have you seen me to offend me! I haven't seen you since your garden party, and you certainly didn't offend me then-you were awfully nice to us all!"

"Ah, that wasn't seeing you," Lord Manister murmured. "I don't reckon that I've seen you since-the photographs. I had to go to Scotland; I meant to tell you."

"It wouldn't have interested me," said Christina, with a shrug. "It might have interested me if you had said-you were *not* going," she added next moment. Her tone had dropped. She looked at him and smiled.

Her smile stayed with him after she was gone; but from his face you would not have guessed that he was nursing a kind look. She had given him one smile, which made up for many things. But you would have thought, with his people, that he had been suffering the whole evening from acute boredom: you might well have fancied, with Lady Mary, that a remark disparaging Australian women would have met with a grateful response from him. The response it did meet with was anything but grateful to Lady Mary Dromard. It drove her from the room, in which Manister and his mother were presently left alone.

"I think you were just," the countess said critically. "They are pleasant people, and quite all right. The young man is their weak point."

"They always are," her son remarked, rather savagely still. "They're larrikins!"

"The young girl was especially nice, and sang like a lady."

"Ah, you approve of her," said Lord Manister dryly.

"Entirely, I think. Evidently you don't. I only saw you speak to her once, toward the end. Yet she has met you in Australia; I should have recognized that, I think. Now her people," Lady Dromard added tentatively, "will be rather superior, I suppose, as colonials go?"

"Well, they're rich; I suppose that's how colonials go."

For one moment Lady Dromard fancied that the sneer was for the colonials, and it surprised her; the next, she took it to herself, and very meekly for so proud a heart.

"My dear boy!" she murmured indulgently. "Apart from their people, these girls-for the married one is as young as she has any right to be-strike one as fresh, and free, and pleasing. And they are ladies. Am I to believe that the majority out there are like them?"

Manister shrugged his shoulders.

"That's as you please, my dear mother. These people didn't strike me as the only decent ones in Melbourne. I did meet others."

The countess tapped her foot upon the fender, and took counsel with her own reflection in the mirror, for she was standing before the fireplace while her son wandered about the room-her son with the reputation for a childlike devotion to his mother. There had been little of that sort of devotion since his return from Australia. Nothing between them was as it had been before. This bitter coldness had been his domestic manner-his manner with her, of all people-longer than the mother could bear. She knew the reason; she had tried to tell him so; she had tried to speak freely to him of the whole matter-even penitently, if he would. But he had never spoken freely to her; and once he had refused to speak at all, thence or thenceforth. Lady Dromard had made a resolve then which she remembered now.

"Really, Harry, I can't make you out," she said lightly at length. "You knock down the colonials with one hand, and you set them up with the other, as though they were so many ninepins. I am puzzled to know what you really mean, and what you mean satirically. You never used to be satirical, Harry! I should like to know whether you really approve of these people, or whether you don't."

"I do approve of them," said Lord Manister, halting on the rug before his mother. "I won't put it more strongly. But I am glad that you should have seen there are such things as ladies in Australia!"

Their eyes met, and the mother forgot her resolve; for he had raised the subject himself, and for the first time.

"You think of her still!" whispered Lady Dromard.

"Of course I do," returned Manister, roughly; and again he was striding about the room.

Never in her life, perhaps, had the countess received a sharper hurt; for he had refused to see the hand she had reached out to him involuntarily. Yet assuredly Lady Dromard had never spoken in a more ordinary tone than that of her next words, a minute later.

"It occurred to me, Harry, that if we really think of dancing one evening during the cricket week, we might do worse than ask these people from the rectory. You must have girls to dance with. Still, if you think better not, you have only to say so."

"I think it's for you to decide; but, if you ask me, I don't see the least objection to it," said Lord Manister, with a smooth ceremony that had a sharper edge than his rough words. "I'm not sure, however, that they will come every time you ask them."

"Pourquoi?"

"Because they're the most independent people in the world, the Australians."

"It would scarcely touch their independence," said Lady Dromard with careless contempt; "but we can really do without them, and I am glad of your hint, because now I shall not think of asking them."

"Now, my dear mother," cried Lord Manister, no longer either hot or cold, but his old self for once in his anxiety —"you misunderstand me entirely! I'm not great on a dance at all, but if we're to have one we must, as you say, have somebody to dance with; and I *want* you to ask these people."

Chapter X
A Threatening Dawn.

"I like a dance where you can dance," said Herbert, who was looking at himself in a glass and wondering how long his white tie had been on one side. "It was worth fifty of the swell show you took us to in town, Ruth."

"I am glad you two have enjoyed it so," returned Ruth, with her eye, however, upon her husband. "Of course there's a great difference between a big dance in town and a little one in the country."

Tiny seemed busy. She was tearing her programme into small pieces, and dropping them at her feet, so that when she had gone up to bed it was as though a paper chase had passed through the rectory study, where they had all gathered for a few moments on their return from the dance. Christina, however, was not too preoccupied to chime in on her own note:

"It's like the difference between Riverina and Victoria-there were acres to the sheep instead of sheep to the acre."

Now there was no merit in this speech, but to those who understood it the comparison was apt, and Erskine knew enough of Australia to understand. Moreover, he had taught Tiny to listen for his laugh. So when he made neither sound nor sign the girl felt injured, but remembered that he had been extremely silent on the way home. And he was the first to go upstairs.

"It has bored him," observed Christina.

"He don't like dancing," said Herbert. "He's no sportsman."

"I am afraid he cares for nothing but lawn tennis when he's here," sighed Ruth, who looked a little troubled. "I am afraid he dislikes going out in the country."

They were silent for some minutes before Tiny exclaimed with conviction:

"No; it's the Dromards he dislikes."

And presently they made a move from the room. But on the stairs they met Erskine coming down, having changed his dress suit for flannels; and Ruth followed him back to the study, eying the change with dismay.

"Surely you're not going to sit up at this hour?"

Ruth had raised her glance from his flannels to his face, which troubled her more.

"I'm afraid the fine weather's at an end," Erskine answered crookedly; "it's most awfully close, at any rate. And I want a pipe."

He proceeded to fill one with his back to her.

"Erskine!"

"Well, dear?"

"I won't be 'dear' to you when you're cross with me. I want to know what I have done to vex you."

He had struck a match, and he lit his pipe before answering. Then he said gently enough:

"If you think I'm cross with you I should run away to bed; I certainly don't mean to be."

But he had not turned round.

"You succeed, at any rate! As you seem to wish it, I shall take your advice."

Erskine heard her on the stairs with a twinge in his heart. He went to the door to call her down and be frank with her, but the shutting of her own door checked him. Setting this one ajar, he threw up the window, and stood frowning at the opaque pall that seemed to have been let down behind it like an outer blind. So he remained for some minutes before remembering the easy-chair. No one knew better than Erskine that he had just been unkind to his wife. He was not pleased with her, but he had refused to explain his displeasure when she invited him to do so. There was this difficulty in explaining it-that he knew it to be unreasonable, since the person who had vexed him most was not Ruth, but Christina. And not more reasonable was his disappointment in Christina, as he also knew. Yet the one thing in life not disappointing to him at the moment was his pipe; even the fine weather was most surely at an end.

He was tired of the rectory, which, wet or fair, had no longer either light or shadow of its own, for both were now absorbed in the deepening shadow of the hall. A week ago they had all dined there, now they had been dancing there, and meanwhile the girls had watched one of the matches, and were going to another. Erskine had been opposed to the dance, but the wife had prevailed; he was against their going to another match, but doubtless Ruth would have her way again, for she had shown a tenacity of purpose that surprised him in her, while he was crippled by a conscious lack of logic in his objections. He was not an arbitrary person, and it seemed that Ruth would stop for nothing less than a command where her heart was set; and her sister was with her. The whole trouble was, where their hearts were set.

He tried hard not to think the worst of Tiny, or rather the worst as it seemed to him. To make it easier, he called to mind various things she had said to him at various times concerning Lord Manister, of whom she had seldom failed to make fun. It amused and consoled Erskine to remember the fun; there must be hope for her still. Then he recalled common gossip about Lord Manister and his affairs; and there was hope on that side too. In less than a week the danger would be past, and those two would never see each other again. Consideration of the danger he had in mind, *quá* danger, provoked a smile. Tiny herself would have enjoyed the humor of that, she was so quick to see and to enjoy. But she could appreciate more than a joke, or did she only pretend to like those books? And the soul that shone sometimes in her eyes, did it lie much deeper? She interested Erskine the more because he could not be sure. She was a fascinating study to him, whatever she did or was trying to do. In any case, there was much good in her that he had fathomed, and more was suggested; and the finer the nature, the stronger the contrasts. Now as to contrasts-yet he had never seen that in Australia.

"A penny for your thoughts!"

Ten thousand pounds would not have bought them. It was his wife on the threshold, in a pale pink wrapper.

"My dear! I pictured you asleep hours ago."

"Were you picturing me when I spoke?" Ruth said, with a smile. "I'm not sleepy-and I want to talk to you. May I sit down? An hour more or less makes no difference at this time of the morning."

Erskine rose from the easy-chair in which he had been smoking, and settled his wife in it against her will, and drew the curtains across the open window.

"I'm glad you've come down, Ruth, for I want to speak to you, too. I was a brute to you when I sent you away just now."

"Well, I really think you were; but I know you must have had some reason; so I've come down to have it out and be done with it."

"My dear Ruth!" said Mr. Holland uncomfortably; for was there any call to be frank with her at all? It would hurt; and could it do any good?

"I suppose," pursued Ruth in a tone not perfectly free from defiance, "it's all because we went to this horrid dance! And I'll say I'm sorry we did go, if you like; though why you should have such a down on the Dromards I can't for the life of me imagine."

"My dear girl," said Erskine, smiling now that he had determined not to say everything, "I really have no down on them at all. They're the most amiable family I know, considering who they are. They have a charming place, and they treat you delightfully while you're there. Considering who *we* are, and that we have no root in this soil, I grant you they're particularly kind to us; but don't you think their kindness is just a little trying? I do, though I have nothing against them, personally or otherwise. I am not even a political opponent; if I had a vote for the division young Manister should have it. But I'm not keen on so much notice from them; I've said so before; there's no sense in it!"

"Ah, well, if only you would show me the harm in it!"

"Harm? Heaven forbid there should be any. One finds it a bore, that's all. It's a selfish reason, but it's the truth —I should have had a better time this last week if the Dromards had been far enough!"

"And we should have had a worse-Tiny and I. No, Erskine, I know you better than you think. You're not so selfish as all that; there's some other reason."

Erskine turned away with a shrug, to avoid her glance.

"Something has annoyed you to-night. One of us has behaved badly. Was it Tiny or was it ——"

"You?" said Erskine, with a smile. "From what I saw of your behavior, my dear, it was entirely creditable to you as a chaperon. Your face was seventeen, but your air was a frank fifty!"

"Then it was Tiny. I suppose she danced too much with those boys they have staying in the house. I should have thought there was respectability in numbers; I really don't see how *they* could matter."

"They seemed to matter to Manister," remarked Erskine dryly.

Ruth winced, but he had wondered whether she would, or he would never have noticed it.

"Surely you don't think Lord Manister cares who dances with our Tiny?"

The amusement in her tone and manner was cleverly feigned, but instead of deceiving Erskine it spurred him to speak out, after all.

"I hardly like to tell you what I think about Tiny and Lord Manister," he said gravely.

"What on earth do you mean, Erskine?" cried Ruth, reddening. "Now you *must* tell me!"

Erskine temporized, already regretting that he had said so much. "It would hurt your feelings," he warned her grimly.

"Not so much as your silence."

"I wouldn't say it if I didn't look on her as my own sister by this time, and if I didn't think her the best little girl in the world-but one."

Now he spoke tenderly.

"Say it, in any case," said Ruth, who had been uncommonly calm.

"Then I am afraid she is making up to him, if you must know."

"Which is absurd," said Ruth lightly; but in her anxiety to remain cool she forgot to seem surprised; and that was a mistake.

"I wonder if you really think so?" said her husband very quietly. "If you do I can't agree with you; I wish I could."

"You must!" cried Ruth desperately. "Do you know how many dances she gave him to-night?"

Erskine knew only of one; his eyes rested on the remains of her programme lying on the floor in many fragments.

"Well, that one was the lot!" he was informed severely. "And pray did you count how many times she spoke to him the other evening when we dined at the hall?"

"Not often, I grant you; I noticed that."

"Yet you think she is making up to him!"

"It's a strong way of putting it, I know," said Erskine reluctantly; "but really I can't think of any other. I wonder you don't realize that there are more ways of making up to a man than the dead-set method. Can't you see that a far more effective method is a little judicious snubbing and avoiding, which is coquetry? You take my word for it, that's the touch for a man like Manister, who is probably accustomed to everything but being snubbed and avoided. Then you speak of the one dance she gave him. Now I happen to know that they didn't dance it at all; they spent the time under the stars, for it was my misfortune to see them and their misfortune not to see me."

"Well?" whispered Ruth; and though she had never been so dark until now, that whisper would have drawn his lantern to her real hopes and fears.

"I only saw them for an instant: I bolted; so I may easily be wrong; but it struck me that our Tiny was making up for her snubbing and avoiding. It has since occurred to me that they must have known each other rather well in Melbourne-rather better, at any rate, than you have ever led me to suppose."

As a woman's last resource, Ruth aimed a stone at his temper.

"So that's it!" she exclaimed viciously.

"That's what?"

"The secret of your bad temper."

"Well, to be kept in the dark doesn't sweeten a man, certainly," Erskine answered, in a tone, however, that was far from bitter. "Then one can't help feeling disappointed with Tiny; and in this matter-to be frank with you at last —I am just a little disappointed in you too, my dear."

"I always knew you would be," said Ruth dolefully. For her stone had missed, and there was no more fight in her.

"Now don't be a goose. It's only in this one matter, in which —I can't help telling you —I don't think you've been perfectly straight with me."

"Oh, indeed!" cried Ruth, as her spirit made one spurt more. It was the last. The next moment she was weeping.

It annoys most men to make a woman cry. Those who do not become annoyed make impetuous atonement, partly, no doubt, to drown the hooting in their own heart. But Erskine could not feel himself to blame, and though he spoke very kindly, his kindness was too nearly paternal, and he spoke with his elbow on the chimney-piece. He told Ruth not to do that. He pointed out to her that there was no crime in her want of candor concerning her sister's affairs, which were certainly no business of his. Only, if there really had been something between Christina and Lord Manister in Melbourne-if, for instance, Mrs. Willoughby had gossiped unwittingly to Christina about none other than Christina herself-Erskine put it to his wife that she might have done more wisely to place him in a position silently to appreciate such capital jokes. He would have said nothing; but as it was he might easily have said much to imperil the situation; in fact, he had been in a false position all along, more especially at the hall. But that was all. There was really nothing to cry about. Perhaps to give her the fairest opportunity to compose herself, Erskine crossed the room and drew back the curtains to let in the gray morning; for the birds had long been twittering.

But Ruth had been waiting for the touch of his hand, and he had only given her kind words. She looked up, and saw through her tears his form against the gray window, as he shut down the sash. The lamp burnt faintly, and in the two wan lights it was a chamber of misery, in which one could not sit alone. Ruth rose and ran to Erskine, and laid her hands upon his arm.

"It is raining," he said, without looking at her tears. "I knew we were in for a break up of the fine weather."

"Never mind the rain!" Ruth cried piteously, with her face upon his coat. "Will you forgive me now if I tell you everything that I know-everything? It isn't much, because Tiny has been almost as close with me as I have been with you."

"My dear," he said, patting her head at last, and with his arms around her lightly, "you both had a perfect right to be close."

"But suppose I've been at the bottom of the whole thing? Suppose I turn out a horrid little intriguer-what then?"

She waited eagerly, and the pause seemed long.

"Well, you won't have been intriguing for yourself," sighed Erskine-so that her face rose on his breast, as on a wave.

And then, playing nervously with a button of his coat, Ruth confessed all. As she spoke she gathered confidence, but not enough to watch his face. That was turned to the gray morning, and looked as gray as it. The fine weather had indeed broken up, and Essingham had lost its savor for Erskine Holland.

Chapter XI
In the Ladies' Tent.

And yet, even at the time she made it, Ruth little dreamt how deeply her confession both galled and revolted her husband. He forgave her very kindly in the end, and that satisfied her lean imagination. Perhaps there was not much to forgive. There was enough, at all events, to trouble Erskine (to whom the best excuse there was for her was the least likely to suggest itself); but the matter soon ceased to trouble Erskine's wife, because his smile was as good-tempered as before. He seemed, indeed, to think no more about it. When Ruth would speak confidentially of her hopes and wishes for Tiny (as though Erskine had been in her confidence all the time), he would chat the matter over with interest, which was the next best thing to sympathy. He had to do this oftener than he liked during the next twenty-four hours; for Ruth really thought that excessive candor now was a more or less adequate atonement for an excessive reserve in the past. Moreover, she genuinely enjoyed talking openly at last of the matter which had concerned her so long and so severely in secret.

"Don't you think he means it?" she asked her husband several times.

"I am afraid he thinks he does," was one of Holland's answers.

"That's your way of admitting it," rejoined Ruth, who could bear his repudiation of her desires for the sake of his assent to her opinion, which Erskine was too honest to withhold. "Of course he means it. Have you noticed how he watches her?"

"I have noticed it once or twice."

"And did you see him watching his mother, the night we dined there, to see what impression Tiny made upon her?"

"So you spotted that!" Erskine said curiously, not having given his wife the credit for such acute perception. "Well, I own that I did, too; and that was worse than his watching Tiny. This is a youth with a well-known weakness for his mamma. She has probably more influence over him than any other body in the world. I am prepared to bet that it was she, and she alone, who whistled him back from Australia. Now though she did it partly by her singing-which, by the way, was rather cheap for our Tiny-there's no doubt at all about the impression Tiny has made upon Lady Dromard; and that's the worst of it."

"The worst of it! as if he was beneath her!" said Ruth mockingly. "Or is it that you think her too terribly beneath him?"

"Tiny," said Erskine, shaking his head, "is beneath no man that I have yet come across."

"Then what can you have against it? Is it that you think she will grow so grand that we shall see no more of her! If so, it shows how much you know of our Tiny. Or do you think him too high and mighty to be honest and true? I don't profess to know much about it," continued Ruth scornfully, being stung to eloquence by his perversity, "but I should have said an honest man and his love might be found in a castle, sometimes, as well as in a cottage!"

"'Hearts just as pure and fair may beat in Belgrave Square as in the lowly air of Seven Dials,'" quoted Erskine, with a laugh. "I grant all that; but if you want to know, my point is that Tiny would be thrown away on Belgrave Square! She is far too funny and fresh, and unlike most of us, to thrive in that fine soil; she would need to be clipped and pruned and trimmed in the image of other people. And that would spoil her. Whatever else she may be, she's more or less original as she stands. She's not a copy now; but she will have to become one in Belgrave Square."

"She *will* have to become one!" cried Ruth, jumping at the change of mood. "Then you think that Tiny means it, too?"

"I am afraid she means to marry him," said Erskine, with a sigh. "I have visions of our Tiny ours no more, but my Lady Manister, and Countess Dromard in due course."

So delighted was Ruth with his opinion on this point that his other opinions had no power to annoy her; and in her joy she told him once more, and with much impulsive feeling, how sorry she was for having kept him in the dark so willfully and so long. She called him an angel of good temper and forbearance, and undertook to reward his generosity by never hiding another thing from him in her life. And she would never, never vex him again, she said-so earnestly that he thought she meant it, as indeed she thought herself, for half a minute.

"But you mean to go to the match to-morrow?" he asked her wistfully.

"Oh, we must-if it's fine. It's the last match of the week; besides, Herbert's going to play."

This was an argument, and Erskine said no more. The chances are that he would have said no more in any case. The following afternoon Ruth drove with Tiny to the match, and with a particularly light heart, because she had not heard another word against the plan. Her one remaining anxiety was lest it might rain before they got to the cricket field.

For the day was one of those dull ones of early autumn when there is little wind, a gray sky, and more than a chance of rain; but none had fallen during the morning, which reduced the chance; while the clouds were high, and occasionally parted by faint rays of sunshine. The ground was so beautiful in itself that it was the greater pity there was no more sun, since, without it, well-kept turf and tall trees are like a sweet face saddened. The trees were the fine elms of that country, and they flanked two sides of the ground; but one missed their shadows, and the foliage had a dingy, lack-luster look in the tame light. On the third side a ha-ha formed a natural "boundary," and the red, spreading house stood aloof on the fourth, giving a touch of welcome warmth to a picture whose highest lights were the white flannels of the players and the canvas tents. The tents were many, and admirably arranged; but one beneath the elms had a side on the ground to itself; and thither drove Mrs. Holland, alighting rather nervously as a groom came promptly to the pony's head, because this was the ladies' tent.

To-day, however, the tent was not formidably full, as it had been when the girls had watched the cricket from it earlier in the week; this was only the Saturday's match. Ruth looked in vain for Lady Dromard, but received a cold greeting from her daughter, Lady Mary, upon whom the guinea stamp was disagreeably fresh and sharp. The sight of Mrs. Willoughby and her friend Mrs. Foster-Simpson on a front seat was a relief at the moment (the sight of anything to nod to is a relief sometimes); but Ruth was discreet enough to sit down behind these ladies, not beside them. She congratulated herself on her presence of mind when she heard the tone and character of some of their comments on the game. It would have done Ruth no good to be seen at the side of loud Mrs. Foster-Simpson or of loquacious Mrs. Willoughby, and it might have done Tiny grave harm. Mrs. Willoughby's husband, who had good-naturedly become eleventh man at the eleventh hour, was conspicuous in the field from his black trousers, clerical wide-awake, and shirt-sleeves of gray flannel. "I hope you admire him," said his wife over her shoulder to Ruth; "I tell him he might as well take a funeral in flannels!"

"Or dine in his surplice," added her friend Mrs. Foster-Simpson in a voice that carried to the back of the tent.

"I just do admire Mr. Willoughby," Ruth said softly; "he has a soul above appearances."

"You're not his wife," replied the lady who was.

"You may thank your stars!" shouted her too familiar friend.

Little Mrs. Holland turned to her sister and speculated aloud as to the state of the game, but her tone was an example to the ladies in front, who nevertheless did not lower theirs to supply the gratuitous information that the Mundham players had been fielding all day.

"They're getting the worst of it," declared Mrs. Willoughby, perhaps prematurely.

"Do them good," her friend said viciously, but with the soft pedal down for once. "There would have been no holding them. That young Dromard, now-it will take it out of *him*. He wants it taking out of him!"

Mr. Stanley Dromard, who had been scoring heavily all the week, happened to be in the deep field close to the tent. Ruth nudged her sister, and they moved further along their row in order to avoid the bonnets in front.

"Horrid people!" whispered Ruth.

"That's the earl by the canvas screen," answered Tiny. "I should like to send him a new straw hat!"

"Hush!" whispered Ruth in terror. "You're as bad as they are. Tell me, do you see Herbert?"

"Yes, there he is, all by himself. There's a man out."

"Is there? How tired they seem! That's Lord Manister sprawling on the grass. What a boy he looks! You wouldn't think he was anybody in particular, would you?"

"I should hope not, indeed, on the cricket field!"

"I only meant he looked rather nice."

"Certainly he looks nicer in flannels than in anything else; his tailor has less to do with it."

The patience of Ruth was inexhaustible. She watched the game until another wicket fell. Then it was her admiration for the scene that escaped in more whispers.

"*Isn't* it a lovely place, Tiny?"

"Oh, it's all that."

"I've never seen one to touch it, and I have seen two or three, you know, since we were married. But the house is the best part of it all. I would give anything to live in a house like that-wouldn't you?"

"I? My immortal soul!"

And Tiny sighed, but Ruth, looking round quickly, saw laughter in her eyes, and said no more. Tiny was very trying. Was she half in earnest, or wholly in jest? Ruth could never tell; and now, while she wondered, a lady who knew her sat down on her right. Ruth was glad enough to shake hands and talk, and not sorry in this case to be seen doing so, while at the moment it was a very human pleasure to her to leave Tiny to take care of herself. And that was a thing at which Tiny may be said to have excelled, so far as one saw, and no further. The attacks of most tongues she was capable of repelling with distinction; against those of her own thoughts she made ever the feeblest resistance; and at this stage of Christina's career her own thoughts were a swarm of flies upon a wound in her heart. That was the truth-and no one suspected it.

During the next quarter of an hour the innings came to an end, and the fielders trooped over to the group of tents at another side of the ground. Tiny hoped that one of them would have the good taste to come to the ladies' tent and talk to her; an Eton boy would do very well; Herbert would be better than nobody: but she hoped in vain. On her right Ruth had turned her back, and was quite taken up with the lady with whom she was not sorry to be seen in conversation. The chairs on her left were all empty; and those flies were fighting for her heart. It was the rustle of silk disturbed them in the end; and Lady Dromard who sat down in the empty chair on Tiny's left.

"I am so glad to see you both," said the countess as though she meant it; and she leant over to shake hands with Ruth, whose back was now turned upon her new found friend. Not so much was said to the pair in front, though those ladies had something to say for themselves. Lady Dromard gave them very small change in smiles, but made the conversation general for a minute or two, with that graceful tact at which, perhaps, she was, in a manner, a professional. With equal facility she dropped them from her talk one after another, much as the last wickets had fallen in the match, and until only Tiny was left in. For the countess had come there expressly to talk to Miss Luttrell, as she herself stated with charming directness.

"I was afraid you were feeling dull; though really you deserve to, Miss Luttrell."

"I was," said Tiny honestly; "but I don't know what I have done to deserve to, Lady Dromard."

"It's the last match, and a poor one, which nobody cares anything about. You should have come earlier in the week."

"We were here on Wednesday afternoon."

"But why not oftener? My second son made ninety-three on Thursday. I do wish you had seen that!"

"It wasn't my fault that I didn't," remarked Miss Luttrell. "I suppose things came in the way."

"Then you are a cricketer!" exclaimed the countess. "I am glad to hear it, for I am a great cricketer myself. No, I don't play, Miss Luttrell; only I know all about it."

Christina candidly confessed that she was not a cricketer in any sense-that, in fact, she knew very little about cricket; and the countess, who considered how many girls would have pretended to know much, was more pleased with this answer than she would have been with an exhibition of real knowledge of the game.

"My only interest in this match, however," explained Lady Dromard, "is in my eldest son. I do so want him to make runs! He has been dreadfully unsuccessful all the week."

Christina was discreetly sympathetic.

"He is going in first," murmured the countess presently in suppressed excitement. "We must watch the match."

So they sat without speaking during the first few overs, and the silence did much for Christina, by putting her at her ease in the hour when she needed all the ease at her command. Cool as she was outwardly, in her heart she was not a little afraid of Lady Dromard, whose manner toward herself had already struck her as rather too kind and much too scrutinizing. She now entertained a perfectly private conviction that Lady Dromard either knew something about her or had her suspicions. Not that this made Christina particularly uncomfortable at the moment. The countess had eyes and wits for the game only, following it intently through a heavy field glass grown light now that Manister was batting.

It was difficult to realize that this eager, animated woman was the mother of the young fellow at the wicket, she looked so very little older than her son; or so it seemed to Tiny, who now had ample opportunity to study not only her face and figure, but her quiet, handsome bonnet and faultless dress. Even Tiny could not help admiring Lady Dromard. Suddenly, however, the hand that held the field-glass was allowed to drop, and the fine face flushed with disappointment as a round of applause burst from the field and found no echo in the tents.

"Manister is out!" exclaimed the countess. "He has only made two or three!"

"How fond she is of him," thought the girl, still watching her companion's face, which somehow softened Christina toward both mother and son; so that now it was with real sympathy that she remarked, "Poor Lord Manister! I am very sorry."

Some expressions of condolence from the seats in front threw the young girl's words into advantageous relief.

The countess said presently to Christina, "I am sorry it has turned out so dull a day; the ground looks really nice when it is fine and sunny."

"It is a beautiful ground," answered Tiny simply; "the trees are so splendid."

"Ah, but you're used to splendid trees."

"In Australia? Well, we are and we are not, Lady Dromard. I mean to say, there are tremendous trees in some parts; in others there are none at all, you know. Up the bush, where we used to live, the trees were of very little account."

"I thought the bush was nothing *but* trees," remarked Lady Dromard; and Christina could not help smiling as she explained the comprehensive character of "the bush."

"So you were actually brought up on a sheep farm!" said Lady Dromard, looking flatteringly at the graceful young girl.

"Yes-on a station. It was in the bush, and very much the bush," laughed Tiny, "for we were hundreds of miles up country. But most of the trees were no higher than this tent, Lady Dromard. The homestead was in a clump of pines, and they were pretty tall, but the rest were mere scrub."

"Then how in the world," cried her ladyship, "did you manage to become educated? What school could you go to in a place like that?"

"We never went to school at all," Tiny informed her confidentially. "We had a governess."

"Ah, and she taught you to sing! I should like to meet that governess. She must be a very clever person."

Her ladyship's manner was delightfully blunt.

"Now, Lady Dromard, you're laughing at me! I know nothing —I have read nothing."

"I rejoice to hear it!" cried the countess cordially. "I assure you, Miss Luttrell, that's a most refreshing confession in these days. Only it's too good to be true. I don't believe you, you know."

Christina made no great effort to establish the truth of her statement; for some minutes longer they watched the game.

But the countess was not interested, though her younger son had gone in, and had already begun to score. "What were they?" she said at length with extreme obscurity; but Christina was polite enough not to ask her what she meant until she had put this question to herself, and while she still hesitated Lady Dromard recollected herself, appreciated the hesitation, and explained. "I mean the trees in the bush, at your farm. Were they gum trees?"

"Very few of them-there are hardly any gum trees up there."

"Do you know that *I* have a young gum tree?" said Lady Dromard amusingly, as though it were a young opossum.

"No!" said Tiny incredulously.

"But I have, in the conservatory; you might have seen it the other evening."

"How I wish I had!"

The young girl's face wore a flush of genuine animation. Lady Dromard regarded it for a moment, and admired it very much; then she bent forward and touched Ruth on the arm.

"Mrs. Holland, will you trust your sister to me for half an hour? I want to show her something that will interest her more than the cricket."

"Oh, Lady Dromard, I can't think of taking you away from the match," cried Christina, while Ruth's eyes danced, and the bonnets in front turned round.

"My dear Miss Luttrell, it will interest *me* more, now that Lord Manister is out."

"But there's Mr. Dromard."

"Oh, that boy! He has made more runs this week than are good for him. Miss Luttrell, am I to go alone?"

The bonnets in front knocked together.

Chapter XII
Ordeal by Battle.

If Tiny Luttrell suffered at all from self-consciousness as she followed Lady Dromard from the tent, she hid it uncommonly well. Her color did not change, while her expression was neither bashful nor bold, and unnatural only in its entire naturalness. Considering that the conversation in the ladies' tent underwent a momentary lull, by no means so slight as to escape a sensitive ear, the girl's serene bearing at the countess' skirts was in its way an achievement of which no one thought more highly than Lady Dromard herself. Christina had not merely imagined that she was being systematically watched. No sooner were they in the open air than the countess wheeled abruptly, expecting to surprise some slight embarrassment, not unpardonable in so young a face; and this was not the only occasion on which she was agreeably disappointed in little Miss Luttrell. The short cut to the house was a narrow path that crossed an intervening paddock. They followed this path. But now Lady Dromard walked behind, with eyes slightly narrowed; and still she approved.

Presently they reached the conservatory. It was large and lofty, and the smooth white flags and spreading fronds gave it an appearance of coolness and quiet very different from Christina's recollection of the place on the night of the dance, when Chinese lanterns had shone and smoked and smelt among the foliage, and a frivolous hum had filled the air. The gum tree proved to be a sapling of no great promise or pretensions. Nor was it seen to advantage, being planted in the central bed, in the midst of some admirable palms and tree-ferns. But Tiny made a long arm to seize the leaves and pull them to her nostrils, setting foot on the soft soil in her excitement; and when she started back, with an apology for the mark, her face was beaming.

"But that was a real whiff of Australia," she added gratefully —"the first I've had since I sailed. It was very, very good of you to bring me, Lady Dromard. If you knew how it reminds me!"

"I thought it would interest you," remarked Lady Dromard, who was herself more interested in the footprint on the soil, which was absurdly small. "If you like I will show you something that should remind you still more."

"Oh, of course I like to see anything Australian; but I am sure I am troubling you a great deal, Lady Dromard!"

"Not in the least, my dear Miss Luttrell. I have something extremely Australian to show you now."

Countess Dromard led the way through the room in which Tiny had danced. It was still carpetless and empty, and the clatter of her walking shoes on the floor which her ball slippers had skimmed so noiselessly struck a note that jarred. The desire came over Tiny to turn back. As they passed through the hall, a side door stood open; the girl saw it with a gasp for the open air. It was an odd sensation, as of the march into prison. It made her lag while it lasted; when it passed it was as though weights had been removed from her feet. She ran lightly up the shallow stairs; Lady Dromard was waiting on the landing, and led her along a corridor.

Here Tiny forgot that her feet had drummed vague misgivings into her mind; she could no longer hear her own steps the corridor was so thickly carpeted. It was a special corridor, leading to a very special room of delicate tints and dainty furniture, and Christina was so far herself again as to enter without a qualm. But her qualms had been a rather singular thing.

"This is my own little chapel of ease, Miss Luttrell," the countess explained; "and now do you not see a fellow-countryman?"

She pointed to the window; and in front of the window was a pedestal supporting a gilded cage, and in the cage a pink-and-gray parrot, of a kind with which the girl had been familiar from her infancy. "Oh, you beauty!" cried Christina, going to the cage and scratching the bird's head through the wires. "It's a galar," she added.

"Indeed," said Lady Dromard, watching her; "a galar! I must remember that. By the way, can you tell me why he doesn't talk?"

Christina answered, in a slightly preoccupied manner, that galars very seldom did. She had become quite absorbed in the bird; she seemed easily pleased. She went the length of asking whether she might take him out, and received a hesitating permission to do so at her own risk, Lady Dromard confessing that for her own part she was quite afraid to touch him through the wires. In a twinkling the girl had the bird in her hand, and was smoothing its feathers with her chin. The sun was beginning to struggle through the clouds; the window faced the west; and the faint rays, falling on the young girl's face and the bird's bright plumage, threw a good light on a charming picture. Lady Dromard was reminded of the artificial art of her young days, when this was a favorite posture, and searched narrowly for artifice in her guest. Finding none she admired more keenly than before, but became also more timid on the other's account, so that she could fancy the blood sliding down the fair skin which the beak actually touched.

"Dear Miss Luttrell, do put him back! I tremble for you."

Tiny put the quiet thing back on the perch. Then she turned to Lady Dromard with rather a comic expression.

"Do you know what we used to do with this gentleman up on the station?" said Tiny shame-facedly. "We poisoned him wholesale to save our crop. But this one seems like an old friend to me. Lady Dromard, you have taken me back to the bush this afternoon!"

"So it appears," observed the countess dryly, "or I think you would admire my little view. That's Gallow Hill, and I'm rather proud of my view of it, because it is the only hill of any sort in these parts. Then the sun sets behind it, and those three trees stand out so."

"Ah! I have often wanted to climb up to those three trees," said Tiny, who took a tantalized interest in Gallow Hill; "but I mayn't, because I'm in England, where trespassers will be prosecuted."

For a moment Lady Dromard stared. Then she saw that Christina had merely forgotten. "Dear me, that stupid notice board!" exclaimed the countess. "Lord Dromard never meant it to apply to everybody. Next time you come here come over Gallow Hill, and through the little green gate you can just see. You will find it a quarter of the distance."

Christina had indeed spoken without thinking of Gallow Hill as a part of the estate, or of the warning to trespassers as Lord Dromard's doing. Now she apologized, and was naturally a little confused; but this time the countess would not have had her otherwise. "You shall go back that way this very evening," she said kindly, "and I promise you shan't be prosecuted." But Christina had to pet her fellow-countryman for a minute or two before she quite regained her ease, while her ladyship touched the bell and ordered tea.

"How fond you must be of the bush!" Lady Dromard exclaimed as the girl still lingered by the cage.

"I like it very much," said Christina soberly.

"Better than Melbourne?"

"Oh, infinitely."

"And England?"

"Yes, better than England —I can't help it," Tiny added apologetically.

"There's no reason why you should," said Lady Dromard, with a smile. "I could imagine your quite disliking England after Australia. I'm sure my son disliked it when he first came back."

"Did he?" the girl said indifferently. "Ah, well! I don't dislike England. I admire it very much, and, of course, it is ever so much better than Australia in every way. We have no villages like Essingham out there, no red tiles and old churches, and certainly no villagers who treat you like a queen on wheels when you walk down the street. We've nothing of that sort-nor of this sort either-no splendid old houses and beautiful old grounds! But I can't help it, I'd rather live out there. Give me the bush!"

"You *are* enthusiastic about the bush," said Lady Dromard, laughing; "yet you don't know how fresh enthusiasm is to one nowadays."

"I'm afraid I'm not enthusiastic about anything else, then," answered Christina with engaging candor. "They tell me I don't half appreciate England; I disappoint all my friends here."

"Ah, that is perhaps your little joke at our expense!"

Christina was on the brink of an audacious reply when a footman entered with the tea tray. That took some of the audacity out of her. She had not heard the order given. Once more she reflected where she was, and with whom, and once more she wished herself elsewhere. It was a mild return of her panic downstairs. Now she felt vaguely apprehensive and as vaguely exultant. In the uncertain fusion of her feelings she was apt to become a little unguarded in what she said; there was safety in her sense of this tendency, however.

Lady Dromard was reflecting also. As the footman withdrew she had told him not to shut the door. The truth was she had got Christina to herself by pure design, though she had not originally intended to get her to herself up here. That had been an inspiration of the moment, and even now Lady Dromard was by no means sure of its wisdom. She had gone so far as to closet herself with this girl, but she did not wish the proceeding to appear so pronounced either to the footman or to the girl herself. It would make the footman talk, while it might frighten the girl. That, at any rate, was the idea of Countess Dromard, who, however, had not yet learnt her way about the young mind with which she was dealing.

The tea tray had been placed on a small table near the window. Lady Dromard promptly settled herself with her back to the light, and motioned Christina to a chair facing her.

"Now you'll be able to watch your beloved bird," said her ladyship craftily. "I thought we might as well have tea now we are here. I thought it would be so much more comfortable than having it in the tent."

Tiny settled a business matter by stating that she took two pieces of sugar, but only one spot of cream. Unconsciously, however, she had followed Lady Dromard's advice, for her eyes were fixed on the parrot in the cage.

"I have only had him a few months," observed the countess suggestively. "Something less than a year, I should say."

"Yes?" And Tiny lowered her eyes politely to her hostess' face.

"Yes," repeated Lady Dromard affirmatively. "My son brought him home for me. It was the only present he had time to get, so I rather value it."

The girl's gaze returned involuntarily to the bird she had caressed; apparently her interest was neither diminished nor increased by this information as to its origin.

"He was in a great hurry to run away from us, was he not?" she remarked inoffensively; but there was no attempt in her manner to conceal the fact that Christina knew what she was talking about.

"He was obliged to return rather suddenly," said the countess after a moment's hesitation. She made a longer pause before slyly adding, "I consider myself very lucky to have got him back at all."

"How is that, Lady Dromard?"

And Christina outstared the countess, so that she was asked whether she would not take another cup of tea. She would, and her hand neither rattled it empty nor spilt it full. Then Lady Dromard smiled at the coronet on her teaspoon, and said to it:

"The fact is I was terrified lest he should go and marry one of you."

"One of *us*?"

"Some fascinating Australian beauty," said Lady Dromard hastily. "So many aids-de-camp have done that."

"Poor-young-men!" said Tiny, as slowly and solemnly as though her words were going to the young men's funeral. "It would have been a calamity indeed."

So far from showing indignation Lady Dromard leant forward in her chair to say in her most winning manner:

"I should have been all the more terrified had I known *you*, Miss Luttrell!"

Clearly this was meant for one of those blunt effective compliments to which Lady Dromard had the peculiar knack of imparting delicacy and grace. But the words were no sooner uttered than she saw their double meaning, and grimly awaited the obvious misconstruction. Tiny, however, had a quick perception, and plenty of common sense in little things. Instead of a snub the countess received a good-tempered smile, for which she could not help feeling grateful at the time; but now her instinct told her that she was dealing with a person with whom it might be well to be a little more downright, and she obeyed her instinct without further delay.

"Miss Luttrell, I am sure there is no occasion for me to beat about the bush-with you," she began in an altered, but a no less flattering tone; "I see that one is quite safe in being frank with you. The fact is-and you know it-my son very nearly did marry someone out there. Now you met him out there in society, and you probably knew everyone there who was worth knowing, so pray don't pretend that you know nothing about this."

Their eyes were joined, but at the moment Christina's was the cooler glance.

"I couldn't pretend that, Lady Dromard, for it happens that I know *all* about it."

The countess was perceptibly startled. "The girl was a friend of yours?" she inquired quickly.

"A great friend," answered Tiny, nodding.

"How I wish you would tell me her name!"

"I mustn't do that." This was said decidedly. "But it seems a strange thing that you don't know it."

"It is a strange thing," Lady Dromard allowed; "nevertheless it's the truth. I never heard her name. You may imagine my curiosity. Miss Luttrell, I seem to have felt ever since I met you that you knew something about this-that you could tell one something. And I don't mind confessing to you now-since I see you are not the one to misunderstand me willfully-that I have purposely sought an opportunity of sounding you on the subject."

Christina smiled, for this was not news to her.

"My son will tell me nothing," continued Lady Dromard, "and I have, of course, the greatest curiosity to know everything. It is no idle curiosity, Miss Luttrell. I am his mother, and he has never got over that attachment."

"Has he not?" said Tiny with dry satire.

"He has never got over it," repeated Lady Dromard in a tone which was a match for the other. "Has the girl?"

Tiny was startled in her turn. She hesitated before replying, and seemed to waver over the nature of her reply. It was the first sign she had shown of wavering at all, and Lady Dromard drew her breath. The girl was hanging her head, and murmuring that she really could not answer for the other girl. Suddenly she flung up her face, and it was hot, but not hotter than her words:

"Yes, Lady Dromard, you are his mother. But the girl was my friend. He treated her abominably!"

"It wasn't his fault-it was mine," said Lady Dromard steadily.

"I'm afraid that does not make one think any better of him," murmured the young girl. Her chin was resting in her hand. The flush had passed from her face as suddenly as it had come. Her eyes were raised to the sky out of the window, and there was in them the sad, hardened, reckless look that those who knew her best had seen too often, latterly, in her silent moments. The sun was dropping clear of the clouds, and the brighter rays fell kindly over Tiny's dark hair and pale, piquant face. The keen eye that was on her had never watched more closely nor admired so much.

"Consider!" said Lady Dromard presently, and rather gently. "Try to put yourself in our place-and consider. We have a position, here in England, of which very few people can be got to take a sensible view; half the country professes an absurd contempt for it, while the other half speaks of it and of us with bated breath. We ourselves naturally think something of our position, and we try, as we say, to keep it up. Of course we are worldly, in the popular sense. We bring up our children with worldly ideas. They must make worldly marriages in their own station. Is it so very contemptible that we should see to this, and dread beyond most things an unwise or an unequal marriage? Now do consider: we let our son go out to Australia, because it is good for a young man to see the world before he marries and settles down-and mind! that was what he was about to do. If he had not gone to Australia then, he would have been married at once. He was all but engaged. It was a case of putting off the engagement instead of the marriage. We do not believe in long, formal engagements; we do not permit them. We find them undesirable for many reasons. So, you see, he goes out to Australia as good as engaged, but unable to say so, and very young, and no doubt very susceptible. Can you wonder that I tremble for him when he has gone? Well, he is the best son in the world, and has told me everything always. That is my comfort. But presently he tells one things in his letters which make one tremble more than ever, though he tells them jokingly. Then a cousin of Lord Dromard's stays a day or two in Melbourne and comes home with a report — —"

Christina's face twitched in the sunlight. "I suppose that was Captain Dromard?" she said quietly; "I never met him, but I saw him." She seemed to see him then, and that was why her face twitched. She was still staring out of the window at the yellowing sky.

"Captain Dromard had forgotten the girl's name," said the countess pointedly; "but he told me enough to make me write to my boy — I nearly cabled! And do you think I was wrong?"

"Not from your point of view, Lady Dromard," answered Christina judicially, with her eyes half closed in the slanting sunbeams which she chose to face. "Certainly you cannot have had very much faith in Lord Manister's judgment; but the case is altered if he was to all intents and purposes engaged to a girl in England; and, at all events, that's the worst that could be said of you-looking at it from your own point of view. But is not the girl out there entitled to a point of view as well?" And the hardened reckless eyes were turned so suddenly upon Lady Dromard that the youth and grace and bitterness of the girl smote her straight to the heart.

There was a slight tremor and great tenderness in the voice that whispered, "Did she feel it very much? Come, come-don't tell me it broke her heart!"

"No, I won't tell you that," said the girl briskly, but with a laugh which hurt. "That doesn't break so easily in these days. No, it didn't break her heart, Lady Dromard-it did much worse. It got her talked about. It poisoned her mind, it killed her faith, it spoilt her temper. It did all that-and one thing worse still. Though it didn't *break* her heart, Lady Dromard, it cracked it, so that it will never ring true any more; it made her hate those she had loved-those who loved her; it made it impossible for her ever to care for anybody in the whole wide world again!"

Lady Dromard had drawn her chair nearer to the girl, and nearer still. Lady Dromard was no longer mistress of herself.

"Did it make her hate *you*, my dear?"

"It made her loathe-me."

Lady Dromard was seen to battle with a strong womanly impulse, and to lose. Her fine eyes filled with tears. Her soft, white hands flew out to Christina's, and drew them to her bosom. At this moment a young man in flannels appeared at the door, and the young man was Lord Manister; but the rich carpet had muffled his tread, and the two women had eyes for one another only-the girl he had loved-the mother who had drawn him from her. The same sunbeam washed them both.

"Now I know her name-now I know it!"

"I think you cannot have found it out this minute, Lady Dromard."

"But I have. I have never known whether to believe it or not, since it first crossed my mind, the night you dined here. You see, I know him so well! But he didn't tell me, and after all I had no reason to suppose it. Oh, he has told me nothing-and you are the gulf between us, for which I have only myself to thank. Ah, if I had only dreamt-of you!"

Tiny suffered herself to be kissed upon the cheek.

"Pray say no more, dear Lady Dromard," she said quietly. "Shall I tell you why?" she added, drawing back. "Why, because it's quite a thing of the past."

"It is not a thing of the past," cried Lady Dromard passionately. "He has never loved anyone else. He bitterly regrets having listened to me, and I, now that I know you — I bitterly regret everything! And he loves you … and I would rather … and I have told him what is the simple truth-how I have admired you from the first!"

The last sentence was doubtless a mistake. It was the only one that would let itself be uttered, however, and before another could be added by either woman Lord Manister had tramped into the room. They fell the further apart as he came between them and stooped down, laying his hands heavily on the little table. His eyes sped from the girl to his mother, and back to the girl, on whom they stayed. One hand held his crumpled cap. His hair was disordered. In many ways he looked at his best, as Tiny had always said he did in flannels. But never before had Tiny seen him half so earnest and sad and handsome.

"My mother is right," he said firmly. "I love you, and I ask you to forgive us both, and to give me what I don't deserve-one word of hope!"

The young girl glanced from his grave, humble face to that of his mother, through whose tears a smile was breaking. Lady Dromard's lips were parted, half in surprise at the humility of her son's words, half in eagerness for the answer to them. Tiny Luttrell read her like a printed book, and rose to her feet with a smile that was equally unmistakable, for it was a smile of triumph.

Chapter XIII
Her Hour of Triumph.

Now Herbert was taking part in the match, and Ruth was in the ladies' tent, trying not to think of Christina, who was playing a single-wicket game in another place. But Erskine Holland was rolling the rectory court gloomily and quite alone, and he was tired of Essingham. Not only had the day kept fine in spite of its threats, but toward the end of the afternoon it turned out very fine indeed, and the light became excellent for lawn tennis, because there was nobody to play with poor Erskine. Even the good Willoughby was on the accursed field over yonder; and he mattered least. Ruth was there. Tiny was there. Herbert was not only there, but playing for Lord Manister, who was notoriously short of men. One can hardly wonder at Erskine's condemnation of his brother-in-law, out of his own mouth, as a stultified young fraud in the matter of Lord Manister. As to the girls, some old tenets of his concerning women in general returned to taunt him for the ship-wreck of his holiday at least. Yet Ruth had but plotted for her sister's advancement, not her own. Whether Christina cared in the least for the man whom she evidently meant to marry, if she could, was, after all, Christina's own affair. Erskine had only heard her disparage him behind his back-at which Herbert himself could not beat her-whereas Ruth had at least been openly in favor of the fellow from the very first. But if Herbert was a fraud, what was the name for Tiny? Clearly the only trustworthy person of the three was Ruth, who at least-yet alone-was consistent.

To this conclusion, which was not without its pleasing side, Erskine came with his eyes on the ground he was rolling. But as he pushed the roller toward the low stone wall dividing the lawn from the churchyard, into which the balls were too often hit, one came whizzing out of it for a change, and struck the roller under Erskine's nose. And leaning with her elbows on the low wall, and her right hand under her chin, as though it were the last right hand that could have flung that ball, stood the girl for whom a bad enough name had yet to be found.

"Where on earth did you spring from?" Holland asked, a little brusquely, as he stopped for a moment and then rolled on toward the wall.

"If you mean the ball," replied Tiny, "it must be the one we lost the last time we played. I have just found it among the graves, and it slipped out of my hand."

"I meant you," said Erskine, with an unsuccessful smile; and he pushed the roller close up to the wall, and folded his arms upon the handle.

"Oh, I have come from the hall by the forbidden path over Gallow Hill; but it seems that wasn't meant for us, and at any rate I have leave to use it whenever I like." She was puzzling him, and she knew it, but she met his eyes with a mysterious smile for some moments before adding: "You can't think what a view there is from the top of the hill —I mean a view of the hall. Just now the sun was blazing in all the windows, like the flash of a broadside from an old two-decker; you see it made such an impression on me that I thought of that for your benefit."

Erskine acknowledged the benefit rather heavily with a nod.

"What have you done with Ruth?"

"To the best of my belief she is watching the match; at least she was an hour ago."

"Something *has* happened!" exclaimed Erskine Holland, starting upright and leaving the roller handle swinging in the air like an inverted pendulum. His eyes were unconsciously stern; those of the girl seemed to quail before them.

"Something has happened," she admitted to the top of the wall. "I suppose you would get to know sooner or later, so I may as well tell you myself now. The fact is Lord Manister has just proposed to me."

Erskine dropped his eyes and shrugged slightly; then he raised them to the setting sun, and tried to look resigned; then, with a noticeable effort, he brought them back to her face, and forced a smile.

"I'm not surprised. I saw it coming, though I hardly expected it so soon. Well, Tiny, I congratulate you! He is about the most brilliant match in England."

"Quite the most, I thought?"

"And I am sure he is a first-rate fellow," added Erskine with vigor, regretting that he had not said this first, and disliking what he had said.

"Oh, he is a very good sort," acknowledged Tiny to the wall.

"So you ought to be the happiest young woman in the world, as you are perhaps the luckiest — I mean in one sense. And I congratulate you, Tiny, I do indeed!"

To clinch his congratulations he held out his hand, from which she raised her eyes to him at last-with the look of a cabman refusing his proper fare.

"And I took you for the most discerning person I knew!" said Tiny very slowly.

"You don't mean to say ——"

His eagerness and incredulity arrested his speech.

"I *do* mean to say."

"That you have-refused him?"

Tiny nodded. "With thanks-not too many."

They stared at one another for some moments longer. Then Erskine sat down on the roller and folded his arms and looked extremely serious, though already the corners of his mouth were beginning to twitch.

"Now, you know, Tiny, I'm *in loco parentis* as long as you're in England. In this one matter you've no business to chaff me. Honestly, now, is it the truth that Lord Manister has asked you to marry him, and that you have said him nay?"

"It is the truest truth I ever uttered in my life. I refused him point-blank," added Tiny, with eyes once more lowered, as though the memory were not unmixed with shame, "and before his own mother!"

"In the presence of Lady Dromard?"

She nodded solemnly, but with a blush.

"Good Lord!" murmured Erskine. "And I was ass enough to think you were leading him on!"

She whispered, "And so I was."

For one moment Erskine stared at her more seriously than ever; then the reaction came, and she saw him shaking. He shook until the tears were in his eyes; and when he was rid of them he perceived the same thing in Tiny's eyes, but obviously not from the same cause.

"*I* don't think it's such a joke," said the girl, in the voice of one pained when in pain already. "I am pretty well ashamed of myself, I can tell you. If you really consider yourself responsible for me I think you might let me tell you something about it; for you must tell Ruth —I daren't. But if you're going to laugh ... let me tell you it's no laughing matter to me, now I've done it."

"Forgive me," said Holland instantly; "I am a brute. Do tell me anything you care to; I promise not to laugh unless you do. And I might be able to help you."

"Ah, you would if anybody could; but nobody can; I have behaved just scandalously, and I know it as well as you do, now that it's too late. Yet I wish that you knew all about it, Erskine!" She looked at him wistfully. "You understand things so. Would it bore you if I were to tell you how the whole thing happened?"

The gilt hands of the church clock made it ten minutes to six when Erskine shook his head and bent it attentively. When the hour struck he had opened his mouth only once, to answer her question as to how much he knew of her affair with Lord Manister in Melbourne. He had known for a day and a half as much as Ruth knew; and he did not learn much more now, for the girl could speak more freely of recent incidents, and dwelt principally on those of that afternoon, beginning with Lady Dromard's extraordinary attentiveness on the cricket field.

"I felt there was something behind that, though I didn't know what; I could only be sure that she had her eye on me. However, I took a tremendous vow to face whatever came without moving a muscle. I think I succeeded, on the whole, but I was on the edge of a panic when she took me upstairs. I wanted to clear! I had qualms!"

She was startlingly candid on another point.

"I also made up my mind to behave as prettily as possible, just to show her. I was really pleased with the interest she seemed to take in what I told her about the bush, and I was quite delighted to see a galar again. But I needn't have made the fuss I did in taking it out of its cage; that was purely put on, and all the time I was mortally afraid that it would peck me. Yet I suppose," added Tiny, after some moments, "you won't believe me when I tell you that I am ashamed of all that already?"

Erskine declared that there was nothing in the world to be ashamed of; on the contrary, in his opinion she was perfectly justified in all she had done. With kind eyes upon her, he added what he very nearly meant, that he was proud of her; and his remark wrought a change in her expression which convinced him finally that at least she was not proud of herself.

"Ah, you weren't there, Erskine," said Christina sadly, her blue eyes clouded with penitence; "you don't know how kind poor Lady Dromard was with all her dodges! She said it would be more comfortable to have tea up there. Comfortable was the last thing I felt in my heart, but I never let her see that; and besides, I didn't as yet guess what was coming. Even when she wanted me to tell her my own name, I couldn't be sure that she suspected me. I wasn't sure until she asked me whether the girl had got over it, when I knew from her voice. And I saw then that she really rather liked me, and half wished it to be; and I was sorry because I liked her; and though I spoke my mind to her about her son, I should have made a clean breast of everything to her if he hadn't come in just then. I should have told her straight that I didn't care *that* for him-not now-and that I had been flirting with him disgracefully just to try to make him smart as I had smarted. That's the whole truth of it, Erskine; and I meant to tell her so in another second, because I couldn't stand her kissing me and crying, and all that. I should have been crying myself next moment. But just then *he* came in, and I remembered everything. I remembered, too, what she had had to do with it, on her own showing; and when I saw what she wanted me to say I think I became possessed."

Her brother-in-law was very curious to know all that Christina had said, but she would not tell him. She merely remarked that he would think all the worse of her if he knew, even though at the moment she could hardly remember any one thing that she had said. Then she paused, and recalled a little, and the little made her blush.

"I didn't come well out of it," she declared.

Erskine threw discredit on her word in this particular matter; he sniffed an extravagant remorse.

"Talk of hitting a man when he's down!" exclaimed Tiny miserably. "I hit Lady Dromard when the tears were in her eyes, and Lord Manister when he was hitting himself. He took it splendidly. He is a gentleman. I don't care what else he is-lord or no lord, he would always be a perfect gentleman. What's more, I am very sorry for him."

"Why on earth be sorry for him?" asked Erskine with a touch of irritation; for when Tiny spoke of Lady Dromard's tears, her own eyes swam with them; and to do a thing like this and start crying over it the moment it was done seemed to Erskine a bad sign. The event was so very fresh, and so entirely contrary to his own most recent apprehensions, that at present his only feeling in the matter was one of profound satisfaction. But the symptoms she showed of relenting already interfered not a little with that satisfaction, while, even more than by the remark that had prompted his question, he was alarmed by her answer to it:

"Because I believe he does care for me, a little bit, in his own way-or he thinks he does, which comes to the same thing; and because, when all's said and done, I have treated him like a little fiend!"

"My good girl!" said Holland uneasily, "I should remember how he treated you."

"Ah, no," answered Christina, shaking her head; "I have remembered that far too long as it is. That's ancient history."

"Well, be sorry for him if you like; be sorry for yourself as well."

That was the best advice that occurred to him at the moment, but it set her off at a tangent.

"I should think I am sorry for myself—I should be sorry for any girl who could so far forget herself!" cried Christina, speaking bitterly and at a great pace. "Shall I tell you the sort of thing I said? When I told him I could not possibly believe in his really caring for me, after the way in which he left Melbourne without so much as saying good-by to me or sending me word that he was going, he said it wasn't then he really loved me, but now. So I told him I was sorry to hear it, as in my case it might perhaps have been then, but it certainly wasn't now. I actually said that! Then Lady Dromard spoke up. She had been staring at me without a word, but she spoke up now, and it served me right. I can't blame her for being indignant, but she didn't say half she could have said, and it was more what she implied that sticks and stings. It didn't sting then, though; I was thinking of all the talk out there. It was when Lord Manister stopped her, and held out his hand to me and said, 'Anyway you forgive me now? I thought you *had* forgiven me'—it was then I began to tingle. I said I forgave him, of course; and then I bolted. But I was sorry for him, and I *am* sorry for him, whatever you say, for I had cut him to the heart....And he looked most awfully nice the whole time!"

With these frivolous last words there came a smile: the normal girl shone out for an instant, as the sun breaks through clouds; and Erskine took advantage of the gleam.

"To the heart of his vanity-that's where you cut. You've humiliated him certainly; but surely he deserved it? In any case, you've given young Manister the right-about; and upon my soul that's rather a performance for our Tiny! I should only like to have seen it."

"It's good of you to call me your Tiny," returned the young girl rather coldly. "But don't talk to me about performances, please, unless you mean disgraceful performances. I wish I had never come to England—I wish I was back in Australia—I wish I was up at the station!" she cried with sudden passion. "I am miserable, and you won't understand me; and Ruth couldn't if she tried."

"My dear girl," Erskine said in rather an injured tone, "surely you're a little unfair on us both? Ruth will understand when I tell her; and as for me—I think I understand you already."

"Not you!" answered Tiny disdainfully. "You call it a performance! You treat it as a joke!" And she left him, with the tears in her eyes.

He watched her enter the garden by the little gate lower down, and saunter toward the house with lagging steps. The low sun streamed upon her drooping figure. Even at that distance, and with her face hidden from him, she seemed to Erskine the incarnation of all that was wayward and willful and sweet in girlhood. And her tears and temper made her doubly sweet, as the rain draws new fragrance from a flower; but they had also made her doubly difficult to understand. One moment he had seen her plainly, as in the lime light; in another, she had retired to a deeper shade than before. The explanation of her conduct toward Lord Manister had been a sufficiently startling revelation, yet a perfectly lucid one; but what of this prompt transition to tears and penitence? The only interpretation which suggested itself to Erskine was one that he refused to entertain. He preferred to attribute Christina's present state of mind to mere reaction; if the reaction had taken a rather hysterical form, that, perhaps, was not to be wondered at. Moreover, this seemed to be indeed the case; for the girl was seen no more that day, save by Ruth, who by night was perhaps the most disappointed person in the parish; only she managed to conceal her disappointment in a way that it was impossible not to admire.

Nevertheless dinner at the rectory was a dismal meal, and the more so for the high spirits of Herbert, which, meeting with no response, turned to silence. Poor Herbert happened to have distinguished himself in the match, which, indeed, he had been largely instrumental in winning for his side; but neither Ruth nor her husband showed any interest in his exploit, and Tiny was not there. Erskine was no cricketer; Herbert hated him for it, and made a sullen attack on the claret. But at length it dawned upon him that there was some special reason for the silence and glum looks at either end of the table, for which Christina's alleged headache would not in itself account; and when Ruth left the table early to look after Tiny, he said bluntly to Erskine:

"You're enough to give a fellow the blues, the pair of you! What's wrong? Have I done anything, or has Tiny?"

Erskine temporized, pushing forward the claret. "I understand *you* have done something," he said with a first approach to geniality; "but, upon my word, old fellow, I don't know what it is. I couldn't listen, for the life of me; and you must forgive me. Tiny's upset, and that's upset Ruth, which I suppose has upset me in my turn. Please call me names —I deserve them-and then tell me again what you have done."

Herbert did not require two invitations to do this. He had not only acquitted himself brilliantly, but there was a peculiar piquancy in his success; he had saved the side which had treated him with unobtrusive but galling contempt until the last moment, when he opened their eyes, and their throats too. They had put him to field at short leg; during the intervals, after the fall of a wicket, not one of them had spoken a word to him, save good-natured Mr. Willoughby; and they had sent him in last, with hopeless faces, when there were many runs to get. The good batsmen, beginning with Lord Manister, had mostly failed miserably. The Honorable Stanley Dromard, who had been in fine form all the week, had alone done well; and he was still at the wicket when Herbert whipped in, with his ears full of gratuitous instructions to keep his wicket up, and not to try to hit the professional, and his heart full of other designs. Those instructions were given without much knowledge of this young Australian, who took a sincere delight in disregarding them. He had hit out from the very first, particularly at the professional, who disliked being hit, and who was also somewhat demoralized by the extreme respect with which he had been treated by preceding batsmen. There were thirty runs to make when Herbert went in, and in a quarter of an hour he made them nearly all from his own bat, exhibiting an almost insolent amount of coolness and nerve at the crisis. The best of it was that no one had considered it a crisis when he went in; but his truculent batting had immediately made it one, and ultimately, in a scene of the greatest excitement, of which Herbert was the hero, an almost certain defeat had been converted into a glorious victory. All this was confirmed by the local newspaper next day; considering his achievement and his character, the hero himself told his tale with modesty.

"He bowled like beggary," he concluded, in allusion to the discomfited professional; "but I tell you, old toucher, we were too many measles for him!"

"They were more civil to you after that?"

"My oath!" said Herbert complacently. "Those Eton jokers kicked up hell's delight! Stanley Dromard shook hands with me between the wickets, and said I ought to be going up to Trinity; but he's a real good sportsman, with less side than you'd think. His governor, the earl, congratulated me in person-you bet I felt it down my marrow! He wants to know how it is I'm not playing for the Australians. The only man who didn't say a word to me was that dam' fool Manister."

"Ah, he was on the ground, then?"

"He turned up as I went in; and when I came out he didn't look at me. Who the blazes does he think he is? I'm as good a man as him, though I'm a larrikin and he's a twopenny lord. I don't care what he is, I had the bulge over him to-day —he made four!"

"Perhaps someone else has had the bulge over him, too," suggested Erskine gently.

"Has someone?"

Erskine nodded.

"Our Tiny?"

"Yes; he has asked her to marry him, and she has refused him on the spot."

Herbert shot out of his chair.

"So're you crackin'! I thought something was *wrong*, man? O Lord, this is a treat!"

"It's a treat she didn't prepare one for. I had visions of a very different upshot."

"Aha! you never know where you have our Tiny. No more does old Manister. Oh, but this is a treat for the gods!"

"I told Tiny it was a performance," Erskine said reflectively; "it struck me as one, and I was trying to cheer her up-but that wasn't the way."

"No? She's a terror, our Tiny!" murmured Herbert, with a running chuckle. "Now I know why the brute was so civil to me the first time I met him in these parts. Even then my hand itched to fill his eye for him, but I didn't say anything, because Tiny seemed on the job herself. To think this was her game! I must go and shake hands with her. I must go and tell her she's done better than filling up his eye."

"Don't you," said Erskine quietly. "I wouldn't say much to her afterward, either, if I may give you a hint. She doesn't take quite our view of this matter. Not that we can pretend that ours is at all a nice view of it, mind you; only I really do regard it as a bit of a performance on our Tiny's part, and I should like to have seen it."

"By ghost, so should I! And seriously," added Herbert, "he deserved all he's got. I happen to know."

Chapter XIV
A Cycle of Moods.

But the girl herself chose to think otherwise. That was her perversity. She could now see excuses for her own ill-treatment in the past, but none for the revenge she had just taken on the man who had treated her badly. A revenge it had certainly been, plotted systematically, and carried out from first to last in sufficiently cold blood. But already she was ashamed of it. So sincerely ashamed was Christina, now that she had completed her retaliation and secured her triumph, that she very much exaggerated the evil she had done, and could imagine no baser behavior than her own. She had, indeed, felt the baseness of it while yet there was time to draw back, but the memory of her own humiliation had been her goad whenever she hesitated; and then the way had been made irresistibly easy for her. But this was no comfort to her now. Neither was that goad any excuse to her self-accusing mind; for she could feel it no longer, which made her wonder how she had ever felt it at all. Her judgment was obscured by the magnitude of her meanness in her own eyes. The revulsion of feeling was as complete as it was startling and distressing to herself.

In her trouble and excitement that night it became necessary for her to speak to someone, and she spoke with unusual freedom to Ruth, who displayed on this occasion, among others, a really lamentable want of tact. Tiny sought to explain her trouble: it was not that she could possibly care for Lord Manister again, or dream of marrying him under any circumstances (Ruth said nothing to all this), but that she half believed he really cared for her (Ruth was sure of it), in his own way (Ruth seemed to believe in his way); and in any case she was very sorry for him. So was Ruth. In all the circumstances the sorrow of Ruth might well have received a less frank expression than she thought fit to give it.

But it is only fair to say that this did not occur to Ruth. She was in and out of the room until at last Christina was asleep, and dreaming of the hall windows ablaze against the sunset, while again and again in her sleep the warm, broken voice of Lady Dromard turned hard and cold. Ruth watched her affectionately enough as she slept, and consoled herself for her own disappointment by the reflection that at least they understood one another now. Therefore it was a rude shock to her when Christina came down next day and would hardly look at any of them.

Her mood had changed; it was now her worst. She was pale still, but her expression was set, and there was a quarrelsome glitter in her eyes; the fact being that she was a little tired of chastising herself, and exceedingly ready to begin on some second person. So Erskine himself was badly snubbed at his own breakfast table, and when Tiny afterward took herself into the kitchen garden Ruth followed her for an explanation, in the fullness of her confidence that they understood one another at last. No explanation was given, Tiny merely remarking that she was sorry if she had been rude, but that she was in an evil state all through, and unfit for human society. To Ruth, however, this only meant that Tiny was unfit to be alone. So Ruth remained in the kitchen garden too, and was good enough to resume gratuitously her consolations of the night before. But in a very few minutes she returned, complaining, to her husband.

"My dear," said he at once, "you oughtn't to have gone near her. Above all, you shouldn't have broached the subject of her affairs; you should have left that to her. She seems considerably ashamed of herself, and though I must say I think that's absurd, you can't help liking her the better for it. She surprised us all, but she surprised herself too, because she has found that she can't strike a blow without hurting herself at least as badly as anybody else; and that shows the good in her. Personally, I think the blow was justified; but that has nothing to do with it. The point is that if she's mortified about the whole concern, as is obviously the case, it must increase her mortification to know that we know all about it, and that she herself has told us. Which applies more to me than to you. It was natural she should tell you; she only told me because I happened to be the first person she saw, and I can quite understand her hating me by this time for listening. We must ignore the whole matter except when it pleases her to bring it up, and then we must let her make the running."

"I hate people to require so much humoring!" exclaimed Ruth, with some reason.

"Well, I must say I'm glad that *you* don't," her husband said prettily. "As to Tiny, her faults are very sweet, and her moods are really interesting-but I'm thankful they don't run in the family!"

He seemed thankful.

"Yet you're a wonderful man for understanding other people," returned Ruth as prettily; and her eyes were full of admiration.

"Ah, well! Tiny's not like other people. I think she must enjoy startling one. Our best plan is to expect the unexpected of her from this time forth, and to let her be until she comes to herself."

And that came to pass quite in good time. Having effaced herself all the morning and again during the afternoon, and having been grotesquely polite to the others (when it was necessary to speak to them) at midday dinner, Tiny appeared at tea in another frock and flying signals of peace. She seemed anxious to acquiesce with things that were said. So Erskine forced jokes which were sufficiently terrible in themselves, but they served a good purpose very well. Christina recovered her old form, and after tea made a winsome assault upon no less redoubtable a defender of his own inclinations than her brother Herbert. Him she successfully importuned to take her to church in the evening, although not to the church close at hand, where there was never, necessarily, any service in the rector's absence. Tiny, however, had heard from her friends in the village of a gifted young Irishman who wore a stole and held forth extempore in a neighboring parish; they found their way to it across the twilight fields. They did not return till after nine, when Christina seemed much brighter than before. Her brightness, however, was seemingly more grateful to Mr. than to Mrs. Holland, who enticed her brother into the garden after supper, to ask him whether Tiny had not mentioned Lord Manister.

"Why, yes, she did just mention him," said Herbert; "but that's all. I wasn't going to say a word about the joker, and just as we came back to the drive here she got a hold of my arm and thanked me for not having asked her any questions; so I was glad I hadn't. She said she wasn't by any means proud of herself, and that she wanted to forget the whole thing, if we'd only let her. She doesn't want to be bothered about it by anybody. Those were her very words, as we came up the drive. She was jolly enough all the way there, talking mostly about Wallandoon. You'll have noticed how keen she is on the station ever since she went up there with the governor last April; I think the old place was a treat to her after Melbourne, to tell you the truth."

Ruth nodded, as much as to say that she knew. She asked, however, whether Tiny had talked also of Wallandoon on the way home.

"No; she was a bit quiet on the way home. I think the sermon must have made an impression on her, but I didn't hear it myself; I put in a sleep instead. In the hymns, though, she sang out immense-by ghost, as if she meant it! I rather wished I'd heard the sermon," remarked Herbert thoughtfully, "because it seemed to set her thinking. I believe she's given to thinking of those things now and then; I shouldn't be surprised to see her go religious some day, if she don't marry; I'd rather she did, too, than marry a thing like Manister!"

The next day was their last at Essingham, for which not even Ruth could grieve, in view of recent events. The day, however, was its own consolation; it was cold and dull and damp, though not actually wet, so that Erskine, who spent the greater part of the morning in front of a barometer, had hopes of some final sets in the afternoon, when the Willoughbys were coming to say good-by. Nor was he disappointed when the time arrived, though the court was dead and the light bad; his own service was the more telling under these conditions. But to the two girls, who had been brought up to better things, it was a repulsive day from all points of view, and they were very glad to spend the morning in packing up before a hearty fire.

"This is the kind of thing that makes one sigh for Wallandoon," Tiny happened to say once as she stood looking out of the window at gray sky and sullied trees. The thought was spoken just as it came into her head with an imaginary beam of bush sunshine. There was no other thought behind it-no human mote in that sunbeam certainly. But Ruth had raised her head swiftly from the trunk over which she was bending, and she knelt gazing at her sister's back as a dog pricks its ears.

"Why Wallandoon? Why not Melbourne?"

"Because I have had enough of Melbourne," replied Christina quietly, and without turning round.

"I thought you took so kindly to it?"

"Perhaps I did; I have taken kindly to many things that were bad for me in my time. And that's all the more reason why I should hanker after Wallandoon. I only wish we could all go back there to live!"

"Well, I must say I shouldn't care to live there now," remarked Ruth, with a little laugh; "and I don't see how you could like it either, after civilization."

"Ah, that's because you never cared for the station as I did," replied Christina, with her back still turned; "you liked the veranda better than the run, and you hated the dust from the sheep when you were riding. I can smell it now! Just think: they'll be in the middle of shearing by this time. They were going to have thirty-six shearers on the board, and they expected the best clip they've had for years. Can't you hear the blades clicking and the tar boys tearing down the board, and the bales being heaved about at the back of the shed-or see the fleeces thrown out on the table and rolled up and bounced into the bins-and father drafting in a cloud of dust at the yards? Can't I! Many's the time I've brought him a mob of woollies myself. And how good the pannikin of tea was, and the shearer's bun! I can taste 'em now. You never cared for tea in a pannikin. Yet perhaps if you'd ever gone back to see the place since we left it, as I did, you might be as keen on it as I am. I own I wasn't so keen when we lived there. When I went back and saw it the other day, though, I thought it the best place in the world; and you would, too."

"Is Jack Swift managing it now?" Ruth asked indifferently.

"You knew he was."

"Really I'm afraid I don't know much about it; but if you're so fond of the place as all that, Tiny, I should just marry Jack Swift, and live there ever after."

"I suppose you're joking," said the young girl rather scornfully; "but in case you aren't perhaps it will relieve you to hear that, if ever I do marry, I shall marry a man-not a place."

And she turned round and stared hard through another window, which commanded a view of the Mundham gates and grounds; and Ruth made no more jokes; but neither, on the other hand, did Tiny expatiate any further on the attractions of station life at Wallandoon.

The Willoughbys came in the afternoon, when Mrs. Willoughby was severely disappointed, owing to the rudeness of Christina, who had disappeared mysteriously, although she knew that these people were coming. Mrs. Willoughby had seen her last leaving the cricket ground at Mundham under the wing of Lady Dromard-Mrs. Willoughby had looked forward immensely to seeing her again. But Christina had gone out, and none knew whither; the visitor's idea was some private engagement at the hall; and this was not the only idea she expressed, a little too freely for the entire ease of Christina's sister. Happily they were only ideas. Mrs. Willoughby knew nothing.

Tiny, as it turned out later, had spent the whole afternoon in the village, saying good-by to her friends there. Ruth found this rather difficult to believe, as she had heard so little of the friends in question. Nevertheless it was strictly true, and Tiny had taken tea with Mrs. Clapperton, whose tears she had kissed away when they said good-by; but that was only the end of a scene which would have been a revelation to some who prided themselves on knowing their Tiny as well as anyone could know so unaccountable a person. At dinner that evening she seemed chastened and subdued, yet her temper, certainly, had never been sweeter. It was noticeable that, while she had a responsive smile for most things that were said, she made fun of nothing herself; and she was far too fond of making fun of everything. But for two whole days her moods had come and gone like the shadows of the clouds when sun and wind are strong together; and the last of her whims was not the least puzzling at the time. Later Ruth read it to her own extreme satisfaction; but at the time it did seem odd to her that anyone should desire a walk on so chilly and unattractive a night. Yet when they had left the men to themselves this was what Tiny said she would like above all things. And Ruth, who humored her, had her reward.

For she found herself being led through the churchyard; and when she hesitated as they came to the notice to trespassers, Tiny muttered in a dare-devil way:

"Lady Dromard gave me leave to come this way whenever I liked, and I mean to make use of my privilege while I can. I want to see the hall once again-it has a sort of fascination for me!"

More amazed than before, Ruth followed her leader up the western slope of Gallow Hill. The night was so dark that they heard the rustle of the beeches on top before they could discern their branches against the sky; and standing under them presently, panting from their climb, they gazed down upon a double row of warm lights embedded in blackness. These were the hall windows, in even tier, with here and there one missing, like the broken teeth of a comb. Outline the building had none; only the windows were bitten upon a sable canvas in ruddy orange and glimmering yellow, from which there was just enough reflection on the lawn and shrubs to chain them to earth in the mind of one who watched.

"Only the windows," murmured Tiny musingly. "Those windows mean to haunt me for the rest of my time."

"I wish it were moonlight," Ruth said. "I wish we could see everything."

"No, I like it best as it is," remarked Tiny, after further meditation. "It leaves something to your imagination. Those windows are going to leave my imagination uncommonly well off!"

They stood together in silence, and the beeches talked in whispers above them. When Ruth spoke next she whispered too, as though they were just outside those lighted windows:

"Yet you would rather live at Wallandoon than anywhere else on earth!"

Tiny said nothing to that; but after it, at a distance, there came a sigh.

"What's the matter, Ruth?"

"I'd rather not tell you, dear; it might make you angry."

"I think I like being made angry just at present," said Christina, with a little laugh; "but you've spiked my guns by saying that first; you are quite safe, my dear."

"Then I was thinking —I couldn't help thinking-that one day you might have been mistress — —"

"Of the windows? Then it's high time we turned our backs on them! That's just what I was thinking myself!"

Chapter XV
The Invisible Ideal.

On the flags of a London square, some days later, Ruth repeated the sigh that had succeeded on Gallow Hill, and once more Christina asked her what was the matter.

"I was thinking," said Ruth with a confidence born of the former occasion, "that one day all this, too, would have been more or less yours."

"All what, pray?"

"Every brick and slate that you can see! All this is part of the Dromard estate; they own every inch hereabouts."

Christina's next remark was a perfectly pleasant one in itself, only it referred to a totally different matter. And thus she treated poor Ruth. At other times she would herself rush into the subject without warning, and out of it the moment it wearied or annoyed her; to follow her closely in and out required a nimble tact indeed. Nor was it easy to know always the right thing to say, or at all delightful to feel that the right thing to-day might be the wrong thing to-morrow. But into this one subject Ruth was as ready to enter at a hint from Tiny as she was now contented to quit it at her caprice. The elder sister's patience and good temper were alike wonderful, but still more wonderful was her faith. Instinctively she felt that all was not over between Tiny and Lord Manister, and like many people who do not pretend to be clever, and are fond of saying so, she believed immensely in her instincts. It must not, however, be forgotten that her wishes for Tiny were the very best she could conceive; and it should be remembered that she had nobody but Tiny to watch over and care for, to think about and make plans for, during the long days when Erskine was in the City. This was the great excuse for Ruth, which never occurred to her husband, and was unknown even to herself. Christina was her baby, and a very troublesome, bad baby it was.

But what could you expect? The girl was sufficiently worried and unsettled; she was suffering from those upsetting fluctuations of mind which few of her kind entirely escape, but which are violent in characters that have grown with the emotional side to the sun and the intellectual side to the wall. In such a case the mind remains hard and green, while the emotions ripen earlier than need be; and the fault is the gardener's, and the gardener is the girl's mother. Now Mrs. Luttrell was a soulless but ladylike nonentity, with an eye naturally blind to the soul in her girls. All she herself had taught them was an unaffected manner and the necessity of becoming married. So Ruth had married both early and well by the favor of the gods, and Christina had restored the average by committing more follies of all sizes than would appear possible in the time. That in which Lord Manister was concerned had doubtless been the most important of the series, but its sting lay greatly in its notoriety. It had caused a light-hearted girl to see herself suddenly in the pupils of many eyes, and to recoil in shame from her own littleness. It had made her hate both herself and the owners of all those eyes, but men especially, of whom she had seen far too much in a short space of time. What she had done in England only heightened her poor opinion of herself now that it was done. She had seen her way to an incredibly sweet revenge, only to find it incredibly bitter. In striking hard she had hurt herself most, as Erskine had divined; instead of satisfying her naturally vindictive feeling toward Lord Manister that blow had killed it. Now she forgave him freely, but found it impossible to forgive herself; and so the generosity that was in a disordered heart asserted itself, because she had omitted to allow for it, not knowing it was there. Worse things asserted themselves too, such as the very solid attractions of the position which might have been hers; to these she could not help being fully alive, though this was one more reason why she hated herself. Her first judgment on herself, if a mere reaction at the beginning, became ratified and hardened as time went on. She became what she had never been before, even when notoriety had made her reckless-an introspective girl. And that made her twisty and queer and unaccountable; for, to be introspective with equanimity, you must have a bluff belief in yourself, which is not necessarily conceit, but Tiny was not blessed with it.

"She has lost her sense of fun-that's the worst part of the whole business!" exclaimed Erskine, one night when Christina had gone early to bed, as she always would now. "She has ceased to be amusing or easily amused. The empty town is boring her to the bone, and if I don't fix up our Lisbon trip we shall have her wanting to go back to Australia. However, I am bound to be in Lisbon by the end of next month, and I'm keener than ever on having you two with me. I know the ropes out there, and I could promise you both a good time-but that depends on Tiny. Let us hope the bay will blow the cobwebs out of her head; she wasn't made to be sentimental. I only wish I could get her to jeer at things as she used before we went to Essingham and while we were there!"

"Don't you think it's rather a good thing she has dropped that?" Ruth asked. "She had no respect for anything in those days."

"And her humor saved her! Pray what does she respect now?"

"Two or three people that I know of-my lord and master for one, and another person who is only a lord."

"Look here, Ruth, I don't believe it," cried Erskine, who by this time was pacing his study floor. "Why, she hasn't set eyes on him since the day she refused him-with variations."

"I know-but she's had time to reflect."

"Then I hope and pray she may never have the opportunity to recant!"

"Well, I won't deny that I hope differently," replied Ruth quietly; "but I've no reason to suppose there's any chance of it; and whatever happens, Erskine, you needn't be afraid of my-of my meddling any more."

"My dear girl, I know that," said he cordially enough; "but of course you tell her you're sorry for this, and you wish that. It's only natural that you should."

"Ah, I daren't say as much to her as you think," said Ruth, with a nod and a smile, for she was glad to know more than he did, here and there. "You needn't be afraid of me; I have little enough influence over her. She has only once opened her heart to me-once, and that's all."

Which was perfectly true, at the time.

But a few days later the restless girl was seized with a sudden desire to spend her money (which is really a good thing to do when you are troubled, if, like Christina, you have the money to spend), and as her most irregular desires were sure to be gratified by Ruth when they were not quite impossible, this whim was immediately indulged. It was rather late in the afternoon, but, on the other hand, the afternoon was extremely fine; and it was a Thursday, when men stay late in Lombard Street on account of next day's outward mails. Consequently there was no occasion for hurry; and so fascinated was Christina with the attractions and temptations of several well-known establishments, and last, as well as most of all, with those of the stores, that it was golden evening before they breathed again the comparatively fresh air of Victoria Street. It was like Christina to wish, at that hour, to walk home, and "through as many parks as possible"; it was even more like her to be extravagantly delighted with the first of these, and to insist on "shouting" Ruth a penny chair overlooking the ornamental water in St. James' Park.

Glad as she was to meet her sister's wishes, when she would only express them, which she was doing with inconvenient freedom this afternoon, Ruth did take exception to the penny chairs. Her feeling was that for the two of them to sit down solemnly on two of those chairs was not an entirely nice thing to do, and certainly not a thing that she would care to be seen doing. Knowing, however, that this would be no argument with Tiny, she merely said that it would make them too late in getting home; and that happened to be worse than none.

"Erskine said he wouldn't be home till eight o'clock; and he told us not to dress, as plain as he could speak," Tiny reminded her. "The other parks won't beat this; and you shall not be late, because I'll shout a hansom, too."

So Ruth made no more objections, though she felt a sufficient number; and they sat down with their eyes toward the pale traces of a gentle, undemonstrative September sunset, and were silent. Already the lamps were lighted in the Mall, where the trees were tanned and tattered by the change and fall of the leaf; at each end of the bridge, too, the lamps were lighted, and reflected below in palpitating pillars of fire; and every moment all the lights burnt brighter. Eastward a bluish haze mellowed trees and chimneys, making them seem more distant than they were; the noise of the traffic seemed more distant still, but it floated inward from the four corners, like the breaking of waves upon an islet; and here in the midst of it the stillness was strange, and certainly charming; only Tiny was immoderately charmed. She sat so long without speaking that Ruth leant back and watched her curiously. Her face was raised to the pale pink sky, with wide-opened eyes and tight-shut lips, as though the desires of her soul were written out in the tinted haze, as you may scratch with your finger in the bloom of a plum. She never spoke until the next quarter rang out from Westminster and was lingering in the quiet air, when she said, "Why have we never done this before, Ruth?"

"Well," answered Ruth, "I never did it myself before to-day; and I must own I think it's rather an odd thing to do."

"Ah, well, heaven may be odd —I hope it is!"

Ruth began to laugh. "My dear Tiny, you don't mean to say you call this heavenly?"

"It's near enough," said the young girl.

"But, my dear child, what stuff! The couples keep it sufficiently earthly, I should say-and the smell of bad tobacco, and that child's trumpet, and the midges and gnats-but principally 'Arry and 'Arriet."

"Now I just like to see them," said Christina, for once the serious person of the two, "they're so awfully happy."

"Awfully, indeed!" cried Ruth, with a superior little laugh. "Very vulgarly happy, I should say!" And Tiny did not immediately reply, but her eyes had fallen as far as the fretwork of the shabby foliage in the Mall, over which the sky still glowed; and when she spoke her words were the words of youthful speculation. She seemed, indeed, to be thinking aloud, and not at all sure of the sense of her thoughts.

"Very vulgarly happy!" she repeated, so long after the words had been spoken that it took Ruth some moments to recall them. "I am trying to decide whether there isn't something rather vulgar about all happiness of that kind-from the highest to the lowest. Forgive me, dear —I don't mean anything the least bit personal —I find I don't mean a word I've said! I wasn't thinking of the happiness itself so much, but of the desire for it. Oh, there must be something better for a girl to long for! There *is* something, if one only knew what it was; but nobody has ever shown me, for instance. Still there must be something between misery and marriage-something higher."

Her eyes had not fallen, but they shone with tears.

"I don't know anything higher than marrying the man you love," said Ruth honestly.

"Ah, if you love him! There is no need for *you* to know a higher happiness, even if one were possible in your case. But look at me!"

"You must marry, too," said Ruth with facility.

"As I probably shall; but to be happy, as you are happy, one ought to be fond of the person first, as you were; and-well, I don't think I have ever in my life felt as you felt."

"Stuff!" said Ruth, but with as much tenderness as the word would carry.

"I wish it were," returned Christina sadly; "it's the shameful truth. I have been going over things lately, and that's never a very cheerful employment in my case, but I think it has taught me my own heart this time. And I know now that I have never cared for anyone so much as for myself-much less for Lord Manister! If I had ever really cared for him I couldn't have treated him as I have done-no, not if he had behaved fifty times worse in the beginning. I was flattered by him, but I think I liked him, though I know I was dazzled by-the different things. I would have married him; I never loved him-nor any of the others!"

"Ah, well, Tiny, I am quite sure he loves you."

"Not very deeply, I hope; I can't altogether believe in him, and I don't much want to. It is bad enough to have one of them in deadly earnest," added Christina after a pause, but with a laugh.

"Is one of them —I mean another one?" asked Ruth, correcting herself quickly.

Tiny nodded. She would not say who it was. "I don't care for him either-not enough," she, however, vouchsafed.

"Then you don't think of marrying him, I hope?"

"No, not the man I mean" —she shook her head sadly at trees and sky —"I like him too much to marry him unless I loved him. Only if anyone else asked me-someone I didn't perhaps care a scrap for —I don't know what mightn't happen. I feel so reckless sometimes, and so sick of everything! This comes of having played at it so often that one is incapable of the real thing; more than all, it comes of growing up with no higher ideal than a happy marriage. And there must be something so much nobler-if one only knew what!"

Very wistfully her eyes wandered over the fading sky. The thin, floating clouds, fast disappearing in the darkness, were not less vague than her desires, and not more lofty. Her soul was tugging at a chain that had been too seldom taut.

"I know of nothing-unless you're a bluestocking," suggested poor Ruth, "or go in for Woman's Rights!"

Then the sights and sounds of the place came suddenly home to Christina, and her eyes fell. A child rattled by with an iron hoop. A pleasure boat, villainously rowed, passed with hoarse shouts through the pillar of fire below the bridge and left it writhing. Her eyes as she lowered them were greeted with the smarting smoke of a cigar, and her nostrils with the smell that priced it. The smoker took a neighboring chair, or rather two, for he was not without his companion.

Christina was the first to rise.

"I have been talking utter nonsense to you, Ruth," she whispered as they walked away; "but it was kind of you to let me go on and on. One has sometimes to say a lot more than one means to get out a little that one does mean; you must try to separate the little from the lot. I've been talking on tiptoe-it was good of you not to push me over!"

They crossed the bridge, throbbing beneath the tread of many feet; in the Mall, under the half-clothed trees, they hailed a hansom, and Ruth greeted her reflection in the side mirror with a sigh of relief.

"We should never have done this if we hadn't been Australians," she remarked, as though exceedingly ashamed of what they had done, as indeed she was.

"Then that's one more good reason for thanking Heaven we *are* Australians!" answered Tiny, with some of her old spirit. "You may think differently, Ruth, but for my part that's the one point on which I have still some lingering shreds of pride."

And that was how Tiny Luttrell opened her heart a second time to Ruth, her sister, who was of less comfort to her even than before, because now her open heart was also the cradle of a waking soul. More things than one need name, for they must be obvious, had of late worked together toward this awakening, until now the soul tossed and struggled within a frivolous heart, and its cries were imperious, though ever inarticulate. To Ruth they were but faint echoes of the unintelligible; scarce hearing, she was contented not to try to understand. When Tiny said she had been "talking on tiptoe," to Ruth's mind that merely expressed a queer mood queerly. She did not see how accurately it figured the young soul straining upward; indeed the accuracy was unconscious, and Christina herself did not see this.

Queer as it may have been, her mood had made for nobility, and was, therefore, memorable among the follies and worse of which, unhappily, she was still in the thick. It passed from her not to return, yet to lodge, perhaps, where all that is good in our lives and hearts must surely gather and remain until the spirit itself goes to complete and to inhabit a new temple, and we stand built afresh in the better image of God.

Chapter XVI
Foreign Soil.

There is in Cintra a good specimen of the purely Portuguese hotel, which is worth a trial if you can speak the language of the country and eat its meats; if you want to feel as much abroad as you are, this is the spot to promote that sensation. The whole concern is engagingly indigenous. They will give you a dinner of which every course (there must be nearly twenty) has the twofold charm of novelty and mystery combined; and you shall dine in a room where it is safe, if unsportsmanlike, to criticise aloud your fellow-diners, when their ways are most notably not your ways. Then, after dinner, you may make music in a pleasant drawing room or saunter in the quaint garden behind the hotel; only remember that the garden has a view which is necessarily lost at night.

The view is good, and it improves as the day wears on by reason of the beetling crag that stands between Cintra and the morning sun. So close is this crag to the town, and so sheer, that at dawn it looms the highest mountain on earth; but with the afternoon sunlight streaming on its face you see it for what it is, and there is much in the sight to satisfy the eye. Halfway up the vast wall is forested with fir trees picked out with bright villas and streaked with the white lines of ascending roads. The upper portion is of granite, rugged and bare and iron gray. The topmost angle is surmounted by square towers and battlements that seem a part of the peak, as indeed they are, since the Moors who made them hewed the stones from the spot; and the serrated crest notches the sky like a crown on a hoary head. Finer effects may recur very readily to the traveled eye, but to one too used to flat regions this is fine enough: thus Tiny Luttrell was in love with Cintra from the moment when she and Ruth and Erskine first set foot in the garden of the Portuguese hotel, and let their eyes climb up the sunlit face of the rock.

They were a merrier party now than when leaving Plymouth. They had left fog and damp behind them (it was near the end of October), and steamed back to summer in a couple of days; and that alone was inspiriting. Then they had already stayed a day or two in Lisbon, where Erskine had spent as many years when Ruth was an infant at the other end of the world, so that he was naturally a good guide. There, too, Ruth and Tiny made some friends, being charmingly treated by people with whom they were unable to converse, while Erskine attended to the business matter which had brought him over. The girls were not sorry to hear that this matter was hanging fire, as such matters have a way of doing in Lisbon, for they were enjoying themselves thoroughly. Ruth felt prouder than ever of her big husband when she saw him among his Portuguese friends, and she thought him very clever to speak their language so fluently. As for Tiny, she seemed herself again; she was willing to be amused, and luckily there was much to amuse her. Much, on the other hand, she could seriously admire, and her high opinion of Portugal was itself amusing after the fault she had found with another country; she even made comparisons between the two, which gave considerable pleasure when translated by Erskine. Cintra pleased her most, however. She delighted in the hotel, where there were no English tongues but their own; she even pretended to enjoy the dinner. So Erskine felt proud of his choice of quarters; only he missed his English paper, and had to go to the English hotel and purchase unnecessary refreshment on the chance of a glimpse of one. Your man-Briton abroad is miserable without that. It is a male weakness entirely. Holland took with him on that pilgrimage no sympathy from the ladies, who only derided him when he came back confessing that he had thrown his money away, as some other fellow was staying at the English inn and reading the paper in his room.

"But I'm very sorry there's another Englishman in the place," announced Christina; "though I suppose one ought to be thankful he didn't choose our hotel. It is something like being abroad, staying here; one more Englishman would have spoilt the fun."

"When you see the steeds I've ordered for the morning," said Erskine, with a laugh, "you'll feel more abroad than ever."

And they did, indeed, when the morning came; for their steeds were three small asses in charge of a dark-eyed child who was whacking them for his amusement while he smoked a cigarette. A small but picturesque crowd had collected in the street to see the start, and were greatly entertained by the spectacle of the Senhor Inglez (a giant among them) astride a donkey little taller than a big dog. Interest was also shown in the camera legs, which Erskine carried like a lance in rest, while the camera itself was nursed by Christina, who had spoilt a power of plates in Lisbon without becoming discouraged. The small boy threw away his cigarette, and having asked Erskine for another, which was sternly denied him, smote each donkey in turn and set the cavalcade in motion.

They passed the palace in the little market place, and were unable to admire it; they passed the loathly prison, which is the worst feature of Cintra, and were duly abused by the prisoners at the barred windows; they were glad to reach the outskirts of the town, and to begin their ascent of the rock up which their eyes had already climbed. They were to devote the day to the ruined Moorish fort they had seen against the sky, and to the Palace of Pena, which stands on a peak hidden from the town; and Erskine, who was confident that they were all going to enjoy themselves very particularly, declared that the day was only worthy of the cause. There was not a cloud in the sky, and the weather was just warm enough for the work in hand. As the donkeys wended their way up the steep roads, Mr. Holland was advised to get off and carry his carrier; but he knew the Cintra donkey of old, and sat ignobly still. He also knew the Cintra donkey boy, and aired his Portuguese upon the attendant imp, who passed on the way, and greeted with jeers, a professional friend waiting with only one donkey in front of a pretty house overlooking the road.

"Ah," said Erskine, "that's the English hotel; and no doubt that moke is for the opposition Senhor Inglez-whose name is Jackson."

"Then pray let us push on," cried Christina anxiously. "Do you suppose he is coming our way, Erskine?"

"Most probably, to begin with; but he may turn off for Monserrat or the cork convent."

"Let us hope so. If he should pass us, Erskine, just talk Portuguese to us as loud as ever you can!"

"Far better to hurry up and not be overtaken," added Ruth, who was thinking of her appearance, with which she was far from satisfied.

Accordingly the imp (with whose good looks Christina had already expressed herself as enamored) was employed for some moments at his favorite occupation. But for the pursuing Englishman, however, Tiny, instead of leading the way upward, would have dismounted more than once to set up her camera; for low parapets were continually on their left, high walls on their right; and wherever there was a gap in the fir trees growing below the parapets, a fresh view was presented of the town below. First it was a bird's-eye view of the palace, seen to better advantage through the trees of the Rua de Duque Saldanha than before, from the street; then a fair impression of the town as a whole, with its gay gardens and cheap looking stuccoed houses; and then successive editions of Cintra, each one smaller than the last, and each with a wider tract of undulating brown land beyond, and a broader band of ocean at the horizon. Then they plunged into mountain gorges; there were no more distant views, but mighty walls on either side, and reddening foliage interlacing overhead, as though woven upon the strip of pure blue sky. And the atmosphere was clear as distilled water in a crystal vessel; but in the shade the air had a sweet keenness, an inspiriting pungency, under whose influence the enthusiast of the party grew inevitably eloquent in the praises of Portugal.

"I can't tell you how I like it!" she said to Erskine, with a color on her cheeks and a light in her eyes which alone seemed worth the voyage. "I call it a real good country, which has never had justice done to it. If I could write I would boom it. Of course I haven't seen Italy or Switzerland, nor yet France, but I have seen England. If I were condemned to live in Europe at all, I'd rather live at this end of it than at yours, Erskine. Look at the climate-it's as good as our Australian climate, and very like it-and this is all but November. You have no such air in England, even in summer, but when you think of what we left behind us the other day, it's ditch water unto wine compared with this. Ah, what a day it is, and what a place, and how fresh and queer and un-English the whole thing is!"

"I am perhaps spoiling it for you," suggested Erskine apologetically, "by being not un-English myself?"

"No, Erskine, it's only me you're spoiling," returned the girl unexpectedly, and with a grateful smile for Ruth as well. "But I don't know another Briton-home or colonial-who wouldn't rather spoil the day and the place for me."

"That's a pity, because I happen to smell the blood of an Englishman at this moment-at least I hear his donkey."

They stopped to listen, and following hoofs were plainly audible.

"Then he hasn't turned off for the other places!" exclaimed Ruth, smoothing her skirt.

Erskine shrugged his shoulders like a native of the country. "No, he is evidently bound for our port; and as the chances are that he is under sixteen stone, he's sure to overtake us. It is I that am keeping you all back."

"We won't look round," exclaimed Tiny decisively; "and you shall shout at us in Portuguese as he comes up, and we'll say 'Sim, Senhor!'"

So they kept their eyes most rigorously in front of them; and such was the authority of Tiny that Erskine was in the midst of an absurd speech in Portuguese when they were overtaken. That harangue was interrupted by the voice of the interloping Englishman; and was never resumed, as the voice was Lord Manister's.

The meeting was plainly an embarrassing one for all concerned, but it had at least the appearance of a very singular coincidence; and nothing will go further in conversation than the slightest or most commonplace coincidence. You must be very nervous indeed if you are incapable of expressing your surprise, of which much may be made, while the little bit of personal history to follow need not entail a severe intellectual effort. Lord Manister accounted very simply, if a little eagerly, for his presence in Portugal; he went on to explain that he had heard much of Cintra, but not, as he was glad to find, one word too much. Personally, he was delighted and charmed. Was not Mrs. Holland charmed and delighted? It was at Ruth's side that Lord Manister rode forward, falling into the position very naturally indeed.

Quite as naturally the other two dropped behind. "So now I suppose your day will be spoilt, Tiny," murmured Erskine, with a wry smile.

"The day is doomed-unless he has the good taste to see he isn't wanted."

"Well, I wouldn't let him see that, even if he does bore you," said Erskine, who had his doubts on this point. "I don't think he's looking very well," he added meditatively.

As for Christina, she was staring fixedly at Lord Manister's back; for once, however, his excellent attire earned no gibe from her; and while she was still seeking for some more convincing mode of parading her immutable indifference toward that young man, a turn in the road brought them suddenly before the gates of Pena. The four closed up and rode through the gates abreast; and, presently dismounting, they left their small steeds to the sticks of the Cintra donkey boys, and walked together up the broad, sloping path.

"By the way," remarked Holland, "I was told there was only one other Englishman in Cintra at the moment —a man of the name of Jackson; have you arrived this morning?"

"I am afraid —I'm Jackson!" confessed Manister, with a blush and a noisy laugh.

"Oh, I see," said Mr. Holland, laughing also; and he saw a good deal.

"Of course you have to do that sometimes; I can quite understand it," Ruth said in a sympathetic voice. "Still I think we must call you Mr. Jackson!" she added slyly.

Christina said nothing at all. Her extreme silence and self-possession hardly tended to promote the common comfort; her only comment on Lord Manister's alias was a somewhat scornful smile. As they all pressed upward by well-kept paths, in the shadow of tall fir trees, she kept assiduously by Erskine's side. The ascent, however, was steep enough to touch the breath, and conversation was for some minutes neither a pleasure nor a necessity. Then, above the firs, the palace of Pena reared hoary head and granite shoulders; for, like the ruined fort visible from the town below, the palace is built upon the summit of a rock. Still a steeper climb, and the party stood looking down upon the fir trees which had just shadowed them, with their backs to the palace walls, that seem, and often are, a part of the rugged peak itself. For this is a palace not only founded on a rock, and on the rock's topmost crag, but the foundation has itself supplied so many features ready-made that nature and the Moors may be said to have collaborated in its making. Three of the party, having taken breath, played catch with this idea; but Christina barely listened. Her attitude was regrettable, but not unnatural. In the last place on earth where she would have expected to meet anyone she knew, she had met the last person whom she expected to meet anywhere. She remembered telling him of her mooted trip to Portugal with the Hollands, she remembered also his telling her to be sure to go to Cintra; her recollection of the conversation in question, and of Lady Almeric's conservatory, where it had taken place, was sufficiently clear, now that she thought of it; but certainly she had never thought of it since. Had he? She might have mentioned the time when the trip was likely to take place; she was not so sure of this, but it seemed likely; and in that case, was a certain explanation of his sojourn in Portugal, other than the explanation he had been so careful to give, either preposterous in itself or the mere suggestion of her own vanity?

These questions were now worrying Christina as she had seldom been worried before, even about Lord Manister, who had been much in her thoughts for many weeks past. Yet Manister was not the only person on her mind at the moment. Just before leaving London she had experienced the fulfillment of a prophecy, by receiving from Countess Dromard a stare as stony as the pavement they met on, which was near enough to Piccadilly to inspire a superstitious respect for sibylline Mrs. Willoughby. In the disagreeable moment following Tiny's thoughts had flown straight to that lady-indeed her only remark at the time had been "Good old Mrs. Willoughby!" to which Ruth (who suffered at Tiny's side, and for her part turned positively faint with mortification) had been in no condition to reply. Little as she showed it, however, Christina had felt the affront far more keenly than Ruth-chiefly because she took it all to herself, and was unable to think it utterly undeserved. In any event she felt it now. It was but the other day that the countess had cut her. The wound was still tender; the sight of Lord Manister scrubbed it cruelly. And long afterward the scar had its own little place among the forces driving Christina in a certain direction, whether she went on feeling it or not.

Hardly less preoccupied than herself was the man whose side Christina would not leave. Wherefore, though the place was old ground to him, as a guide he was instructive rather than amusing. He spoke the requisite Portuguese to the janitors, whose stock facts he also translated into intelligible English; he led the way up the winding staircase of the round tower, and from the giddy gallery at the top he did not omit to point out Torres Vedras and such like landmarks; descending, he had stock facts of his own connected with chapel and sacristy, but he failed to make them interesting. A paid guide could not have been more perfunctory in method, though it is certain that the most entertaining showmanship would have failed to entertain Erskine's hearers, each one of whom was more or less nervous and ill at ease. He himself was thinking only of Christina, who would not leave his side. He saw her watching Lord Manister; though she would hardly speak to him, he saw pity in her glance. He heard Lord Manister talking volubly to Ruth; he did not know about what, and he wondered if Manister knew, himself. Erskine did not understand. The girl seemed to care, and if she did-if this thing was to be-he would never say another word against it. If she cared there would not be another word to say, save in joyous and loving congratulation. That was the whole question: whether she cared. For the first time Erskine was not sure; it was a toss-up in his mind whether Tiny was sure herself. Certainly there seemed to be hope for the man who was being watched yet avoided; however, Erskine was resolved to give him the very first opportunity of learning his fate.

Accordingly he reminded Tiny that he had been carrying the camera ever since they had dismounted: and was his arm to ache for nothing? The suggestion of the square tower, with the steps below, as an admirable target, also came from Erskine. Lord Manister helped to take the photograph. That, again, was Erskine's doing; and he even did more. When they all turned their backs on Pena, and their faces to the ruin on the opposite peak, it was her husband who rode ahead with Ruth. His reward was the smile of an angel over a lost soul saved. He returned the smile cynically. But round the first corner he belabored his ass with the camera legs, and shot ahead, Ruth gladly following.

In the hollow between the peaks the bridle path passes an ancient and picturesque mosque, with a lime tree growing in the center; from this the ruin derives a roof in summer, a carpet in winter, and had now a little of each.

"What a romantic place!" said Ruth, peeping in. Her husband had waited for her to do so.

"Then let us leave it to more romantic people," he answered, dropping the tripod in the doorway. "They may like to have a photograph of it-for every reason! You and I had better climb up to the fort and chuck stones into Cintra till they come."

This looked quite possible when at last they sat perched upon the antique battlements; they seemed so to overhang the little town. Erskine lit a Portuguese cigarette, which the wind finished for him in a minute. Ruth kept a hand upon her hat. Then she spoke out, with the wind whistling between their faces.

"Erskine, I know what you think-that this isn't an accident!"

"Of course it isn't."

"And I dare say you think *I* have had something to do with it?"

"Have you, I wonder? You may easily have said that we thought of coming here-quite innocently, you know."

"Then I never said so at all. I thought-you know what I thought would have happened last August. Erskine, I have had absolutely nothing to do with it this time!"

"My dear, you needn't say that. I know neither you nor Tiny have had anything to do with it-so far as you are aware; but Tiny must have told him we were coming here, and this is his roundabout dodge of seeing her again. Certainly that looks as if he were in earnest."

"I always said he was."

"And as for Tiny, I don't pretend to make her out. You see, they do not come. I shouldn't be surprised at anything."

"No more should I; but I should be thankful. Even when I hid things from you, Erskine, I never pretended I shouldn't be thankful if this happened, did I? Oh, and you'll be thankful, too, when you see them happy-as we are happy!"

Holland sat for some minutes with bent head, picking lichen from granite.

"My dear girl," he said at length, and tenderly, "don't let us talk any more about it. I dare say I have taken a rotten view of it all along. I only thought-that he didn't deserve her, and that neither of them could care enough. It seems I was more or less wrong; but there is nothing further to be said until we know."

He leant over the battlements, gazing down into the toy town below. Ruth brooked his silence for a time. Then he heard her saying:

"They are a very long while. He's certainly helping her to take a photograph."

"I hope he'll get a negative," said Erskine, with a laugh.

They came at last.

"How long have you been there, Erskine?" shouted Tiny from below. She held one end of the tripod, by which Manister was tugging her uphill.

"About ten minutes."

"Not as much, Erskine," said Ruth.

"We have been photographing that charming mosque," Manister said, as he set down the camera and wiped his forehead; "you meant us to, didn't you, Holland?"

"Of course I did."

"And have you got a negative?" asked poor Ruth.

"A month to make up her mind!" cried Erskine Holland, on hearing at second hand what had actually happened in the mosque. "No wonder he wouldn't stay and dine, and no wonder he is going back to Lisbon to-morrow. By Jove! he *must* be fond of her to stand it at all. To go and wait a month!"

"He offered to wait six," said Ruth.

"Then he's a fool," said Erskine quietly. "Tell me, Ruth, is it a thing one may speak about? One would like, of course, to say something pleasant. After all, it's very like an engagement, and I could at least tell her that I like him. I did like him to-day. Under the circumstances he behaved capitally; only I do think him a fool not to have insisted on her deciding one way or the other."

"I don't think I'd mention the matter unless she does," Ruth said doubtfully. "She told me to tell you she would rather not speak of it at present. You see she has thought of you already! She says you will find her the same as ever if only you will try to look as though you didn't know anything about it. She declares that she means to make the most of her time for the next month wherever she may be, and she hopes you have ordered the donkeys for to-morrow. Still she is troubled, and if she thought you didn't disapprove-if she thought you approved —I can see that it would make a difference to her. She thinks so much of your opinion-only she doesn't want to speak to you herself about this until it is a settled thing. But if you would send her your blessing, dear, I know she would appreciate that."

"Then take it to her by all means," said Erskine, heartily enough. "Tell her I think she is very wise to have left it open-you needn't say what I think of Manister for letting her do so. But you may say, if she likes to hear it, that I think him a jolly good fellow, who will make her very happy if she can really feel she cares for him. Tell her it all hangs on that. That's what we have to impress upon her, and you're the proper person to do so. I only felt one ought to say something pleasant. Wait a moment-tell her I'll do my best to give her a good time until December if none of us are ever to have one again!"

Tiny was sitting at the dressing table in her room, slowly and deliberately burning a photograph in the flame of a candle. The photograph was on a yellow mount which Ruth remembered, and as she drew near Tiny turned it face downward to the flame, which smacked still more of a former occasion.

"Tiny!" cried Ruth in alarm, laying her hand on the young girl's shoulder. "What on earth are you burning, dear?"

"My boats," replied Christina grimly; and turning the photograph over, the face of Jack Swift was still uncharred.

"So you've carried *his* photograph with you all this time?"

"He is as good a friend as I shall ever have."

"Then why burn him if he is only a friend?"

"Perhaps he would like to be more; and perhaps there was once a moment when he might have been. But now I shall duly marry Lord Manister-if he has patience."

"Then why keep poor Lord Manister in suspense, Tiny, dearest?"

"Because I'm not in love with him; and I question whether he's as much in love with me as he imagines —I told him so."

"As it is, you may find it difficult to draw back."

"Exactly; so I am burning my boats. Jack, my dear, that's the last of you!"

Her voice satisfied Ruth, who, however, could see no more of her face than the curve of her cheek, and beyond it the blackened film curling from the burning cardboard.

Chapter XVII
The High Seas.

"He's done it at last!"

Erskine brandished a letter as he spoke, and then leant back in his chair with a guffaw that alarmed the Portuguese waiters. The letter was from Herbert Luttrell, a Cambridge man of one month's standing, of whose academic outset too little had been heard. His sisters were anxious to know what it was that he had done at last; they put this question in the same breath.

"Oh, it might be worse," said Erskine cheerfully. "He has stopped short of murder!"

"We should like to know how far he got," Tiny said, while Ruth held out an eager hand for the letter.

"I don't think you must read it, my dear; but the fact is he has at last filled up somebody's eye!"

Tiny breathed a sigh of relief.

"Is he in prison?" asked Ruth.

"No, not yet; but I am afraid he must be in bad odor, though perhaps not with everybody."

"Whose was the eye?" Christina wanted to know.

"The proctor's!" suggested Ruth.

"Not yet, again-you must give the poor boy time, my dear. It may be the proctor's turn next, but at present your little brother has contented himself with filling the eye of the man who was coaching his college trials. It's a time-honored privilege of the coach to use free language to his crew, and it doesn't give offense as a rule; but it seems to have offended Herbert. Young Australia don't like being sworn at, and Herbert admits that he swore back from his thwart, and said that he fancied he was as good a man as the coach, but he hoped to find out when they got to the boathouse. They did find out; and Herbert has at last filled up an old country eye; and for my part I don't think the less of him for doing so."

"The less!" cried Tiny, whose blue eyes were alight. "*I* think all the more of him. I'm proud of Herbs! You have too many of those savage old customs, Erskine; you need Young Australia to come and knock them on the head!"

"Well, as long as he doesn't knock a proctor on the head, as Ruth seems to fear! If he does that there's an end of him, so far as Cambridge is concerned. He tells me the eye was unpopular, otherwise I'm afraid he would have had a warm time of it; though a quick fist and an arm that's stronger than it looks are wonderful things for winning the respect of men, even in these days."

"And mayn't we really see the letter?" Tiny said wistfully.

Erskine shook his head.

"I am very sorry, but I'm afraid I must treat it as private. It's a verbatim report. I can only tell you that Herbert seems to have been justified, more or less, though he is perhaps too modest to report himself as fully as he reports the eye. He says nothing else of any consequence. He doesn't mention work of any kind; but he's not there only, or even primarily, to pass exams. On the whole, we mustn't fret about the eye, so long as the dear boy keeps his hands off the authorities."

Their hotel was no longer at Cintra, but in Lisbon, where Mr. Holland was being sadly delayed by the business men of the most unbusinesslike capital in Europe. Already it was the middle of November. They had left Cintra as long ago as the 5th of the month, expecting to sail from Lisbon on the 7th; but out of his experience Erskine ought to have known better. It is true that on landing in the country he had attended first to business. The business was connected with the forming of a company for certain operations on Portuguese territory in the East, the capital coming from London; a board was necessary in both cities, and very necessary indeed were certain negotiations between the London directors, as represented by Erskine Holland, and their colleagues in Lisbon. The latter had promised to do much while Erskine was at Cintra, and duly did nothing until he returned; knowing their kind of old, he ought never to have gone. He quite deserved to have to wait and worry and smoke more Portuguese cigarettes than were either agreeable or good, with the women on his hands; with all his knowledge of the country and the people he might have known very well how it would be-as indeed Erskine was told in a letter from Lombard Street, where an amusing dispatch of his from Cintra had rather irritated the senior partners.

Thus Mr. Holland had his own worries throughout this trip, but it is a pleasure to affirm that his sister-in-law did not add to them after that first day at Cintra. Thenceforward she had behaved herself as a perfectly rational and even a contented being. She had appreciated the other sights of Cintra even more than Pena (which had hardly been given a fair chance), and most of all that gorgeous garden of Monserrat, where the trees of the world are grouped together, and among them the gum trees which were so dear to Christina. She had even been overcome by a bloodthirsty desire to witness the bullfight on the Sunday; and Erskine had taken her, because her present frame was not one to discourage; but it must be confessed that Tiny was disappointed by the tameness of this sport rather than revolted by its cruelty. Negatively, she had been behaving better still; the Cintra donkey, the locality of the English hotel, and other associations of the first day never once perceptibly affected either her spirits or her temper. She had shown, indeed, so dead a level of cheerfulness and good sense as to seem almost uninteresting after the accustomed undulations; but in point of fact she had never been more interesting to those in her secret. She had promised to give Lord Manister his answer in a month, and meanwhile she was displaying all the even temper and equable spirits of settled happiness. She ate healthily, she declared that she slept well, and otherwise she was amazingly and consistently serene. That was her perversity, once more, but on this occasion her perversity admitted of an obvious explanation. The explanation was that she had never been in doubt about her decision, that in her heart she was more than satisfied, and that she had asked for a month's respite chiefly for freedom's sake. The matter was discussed no more between the sisters, because Tiny refused to discuss it, declaring that she had dismissed it from her mind till December. And to Erskine she never once mentioned it while they were in Portugal, nor had she the least intention of doing so on the homeward voyage, which they were able ultimately to make within a week of the arrival of Herbert's letter.

But the voyage was rough, and Tiny happened to be a remarkably good sailor, which made her very tiresome once more. Holland had his hands full in attending to his wife in the cabin, while keeping an eye on her sister, who would remain on deck. Through the worst of the weather the unreasonable girl clung like a limpet to the rail, staring seaward at the misty horizon, or downward at the milky wake, until her pale face was red and rough and sparkling with dried spray.

"I do wish you would come below," Erskine said to her, in a tone of entreaty, toward dusk on the second day, but by no means for the first time. "There's not another woman on deck; and you've chosen the one spot of the whole vessel where there's most motion."

Until he joined her Tiny had indeed been the only soul on the hurricane deck, where she stood, leaning on the after-rail, with eyes for nothing but the steamer's track. They were on the hem of the bay and the wind was ahead, so the boat was pitching; and you must be a good sailor to enjoy leaning over the after-rail with this motion-but that is what Christina was. The wind welded her garments to the wire network underneath, and loosened her hair, and lit lamps in her ears; but it seemed that she liked it, and that the long, frothy trail had a strong fascination for her; for when she answered, it was without lifting her eyes from the sea.

"You see, I like being different from other people; that's what I go in for! Honestly, though, I love being up here, and I think you might let me stay. However, that's no reason why you should stay too-if it makes you feel uncomfortable."

"Thanks, I think I am proof," returned Erskine rather brusquely, for this is a point on which most men are either vain or sensitive; "but of course I'll leave you, if you prefer it."

"On the contrary, I should like you to stay," Christina murmured-in such a lonely little voice that Erskine stayed.

It was difficult to believe in this young lady's sincerity, however. She not only made no further remark herself, but refused to acknowledge one of Erskine's. Men do not like that, either. Tiny's eyes had never been lifted from the endless race of white water, now rising as though to their feet, now sinking from under them as the steamer labored end on to the wind. Apparently she had forgotten that Erskine was there, as also that she had asked him to remain. He was on the point of leaving her to her reverie when she swung round suddenly, with only one elbow on the rail, and looked up at him with a pout that turned slowly to a smile.

"Erskine, you've come and spoilt everything!"

"My dear child, I told you I would go if you liked, you know."

"Ah, that was too late; you'd spoilt it then. It won't come back."

"Do you mean that I have broken some spell? If that's the case I am very sorry."

"That won't mend it-you can't mend spells," said Tiny, laughing ruefully. "Perhaps it's as well you can't; and perhaps it's a good thing you came," she added more briskly. "I had humbugged myself into thinking I was on my way back to Australia. That was all."

"But if I were to go mightn't you humbug yourself again?"

"I don't think I want to," the girl answered thoughtfully; "at any rate I don't want you to go. Don't you think it's jolly up here? To me it's as good as a gallop up the bush-and I think we're taking our fences splendidly! But it was jollier still thinking that England was over there," nodding her head at the wake, "and that every five minutes or so it was a mile further away-instead of the other thing."

"Poor old England!"

"No, Erskine, I meant a mile nearer Australia-that was the jolly feeling," Tiny made haste to explain. "You know I didn't mean anything else-you know how I have enjoyed being with you and Ruth. Only I can't help wishing I was on my way back to Melbourne instead of to Plymouth. I'd give so much to see Australia again."

"Well, so you will see it again."

Her eyes sped seaward as she shook her head.

"Why on earth shouldn't you?" said Erskine, laughing.

"You know why."

Now he saw her meaning, and held his tongue. This was the subject on which he understood it to be her desire that they should not speak. To himself, moreover, it was a highly unattractive topic, and he was thoroughly glad to have it ignored as it had been; but if she alluded to the matter herself that was another thing, and he must say something. So he said:

"Is it really so certain, Tiny?"

"On my part absolutely. I'm only climbing down!"

Erskine was reminded of the pleasant things he had thought of saying to her at Cintra; they had been by him so long that he found himself saying them now as though he meant every word.

"My congratulations must keep till the proper time; but when that comes they may surprise you. My dear girl, I should like you to understand that you're not the only person whose opinion has changed since we were at Essingham. If I may say so at this stage of the proceedings, and if it is any satisfaction to you to hear it, I for one am going to be very glad about this thing, I think him such a first-rate fellow, Tiny!"

For a moment Christina gazed acutely at her brother-in-law. "I wonder if that's sincere?" she said reflectively. Then her eyes hurried back to the sea.

"I think he's a very good fellow indeed," said Erskine with emphasis.

The girl gave a little laugh. "Oh, he's all that; the question is whether that's enough."

"It is, if he really loves you-as I think he must."

"Oh, if it's enough for him to be in love!"

There followed a great pause, during which the thought of pleasant things to say was thrown overboard and left far astern.

"I only hope," Erskine said at last, with an earnest ring in his voice which was new to Christina, "that you are not going to make the greatest mistake of your life!"

"I hope not also."

"Ah, don't make light of it!" he cried impetuously. "If you marry without love you'll ruin your life, I don't care who it is you marry! To marry for affection, or for esteem, or for money-they're all equally bad; there is no distinction. Take affection-for a time you might be as happy as if it were something more; but remember that any day you might see somebody that you could really love. Then you would know the difference, and it would embitter your whole existence with a quiet, private, unsuspected bitterness, of which you can have no conception. And so much the worse if you have married somebody who is honestly and sufficiently fond of you. His love would cut you to the heart-because you could only pretend to return it-because your whole existence would be a living lie!"

He was extremely unlike himself. His voice trembled, and in the dying light his face was gray. These things made his words impressive, but the girl did not seem particularly impressed. Had she remembered the one previous occasion when a similar conversation had taken place between them, the strangeness of his manner must have been driven home to her by contrast; but the contrast was a double one, and her own share in it kept her from thinking of the time when she had been serious and he had not, and now, when he was more serious than she had ever known him, she met him with a frivolous laugh.

"Well, really, Erskine, I've never heard you so terribly in earnest before! I think I had better not tell Ruth what you have said; my dear man, you speak as though you'd been there!"

It was some time before he laughed.

"If only you yourself would be more in earnest, Tiny! You may say this comes badly from me. I know there has been more jest than earnest between me and you. But if I was never serious in my life before I am now, and I want you, too, to take yourself seriously for once. You see, Tiny, I am not only an old married man by this time, but I am your European parent as well. I am entitled to play the heavy father, and to give you a lecture when I think you need one. My dear child, I have been in the world about twice as long as you have, and I know men and have heard of women who have poisoned their whole lives by marrying with love on the other side only; and the greater their worldly goods, the greater has been their misery! And rather than see you do as they have done — —" The sentence snapped. "You shan't do it!" he exclaimed sharply. "You're far too good to spoil yourself as others have done and are doing every day."

"Who told you I was good?" inquired Christina, with a touch of the coquetry which even with him she could not entirely repress. "You never had it from me, most certainly. Let me tell you, Erskine, that I'm bad-bad-bad! And if I haven't shocked you sufficiently already it is evidently time that I did; so you'll please to understand that if I marry Lord Manister it is partly because I think I owe it to him; otherwise it's for the main chance purely. And I think it's very unkind of you to make me confess all this," she added fretfully. "I never meant to speak to you about it at all. Only I can't bear you to think me better than I am."

Erskine shook his head sadly.

"At least you have a better side than this, Tiny-this is not you at all! You love and admire all that is honest and noble, and fresh and free; you should give that love and admiration a chance. But I'm not going to say any more to worry you. If you really, with your eyes open, are going to marry a man whom you do not love, I can only tell you that you will be doing at best a very cynical thing. And yet —I can understand it." This he added more to himself than to the girl.

He was turning away, but she laid a restraining hand upon his arm.

"Don't go," she exclaimed impulsively. "I can't let you go when-when you understand me better than anyone else ever did-and when I am never, never going to speak to you like this again."

"If only I could help you!"

"You cannot!" Tiny cried out. "I'm too far gone to be helped. I feel hopelessly bad and hard, and nobody can mend that. But if there's one grain of goodness in my composition that wasn't there when I came over to England, you may know, Erskine, if you care to know it, that it's you, and you alone, who have put it there!"

"Nonsense," he said; "what good have I done you?"

"You have talked sense to me, as only one other man ever did-and he wasn't as clever as you are. You've given me books to read, and they're the first good books I ever read in my life; you have dug a sort of oyster knife into my miserable ignorance! You have been a real good pal to me, Erskine, and you must never turn your back on me, whatever I do. I know you never will. I believe in you as I believe in very few people on this footstool; but there's one thing you can do for me now that will be even kinder than anything that you have ever done yet."

"There's nothing that I wouldn't do for you, Tiny," said Erskine tenderly. "What is it?"

The corners of her mouth twitched-her eyes twinkled.

"It's not to say another serious word to me this month! I know I began it this time; I won't do so again. I'm trying to be happy in my own way, if you'll only let me. I'm trying to make the most of my time. When I'm really engaged I shall need all the help and advice you can give me; for I mean to be very good to him, Erskine; I do indeed! Then of course I shall need to cultivate the finest manners; but until it actually comes off I'm trying to forget about it-don't you see? I'm doing my level best to forget!"

What Erskine saw was the tears in her eyes, but he saw them only for an instant; instead of his leaving Christina on the deck it was she who left him; and there he stood, between the high seas and the gathering shades of night, until both were black.

It was their last conversation of the kind.

One more night was spent at sea; the next they were all back in Kensington. Here they were greeted with a pleasant surprise: Herbert was in the house to meet them. Cambridge seemed already to have done him good; he was singularly polite and subdued, though a little uncommunicative. They, however, had much to tell him, so this was not noticed immediately. His sisters supposed that he was in London for the night only, as he said he had come down from Cambridge that day. It was not until later that they knew that he had been sent down. Erskine broke the news to them.

"I'm afraid," he added, "that they've sent him down for good and all. The fact is, Ruth, your fears have been realized. He has done his best to fill another eye; and this time the proctor's! He says he shall go back to Melbourne immediately."

"Never!" cried Ruth; and she went straight to her brother, who was smoking viciously in another room.

"Yes, by ghost!" drawled Herbert through his hooked nose. "I'm going to clear out. I'm full up of England, Ruth, and I guess England's full up of me. The best thing I can do is to go back, and turn boundary rider or whim driver. That's about all I'm fit for, and it's what I'm going to do. The *Ballaarat* sails on the 2d —I've been to the office and taken my berth already. My oath, I drove there straight from Liverpool Street this afternoon!"

Nor was there any moving him from his purpose, though Ruth tried for half an hour there and then. Twice that time Herbert spent afterward in Tiny's room; but it was not known whether Tiny also had attempted to dissuade him. When he left her the girl stood for five minutes with a foot on the fender and an elbow on the mantelpiece. Then she sought Ruth in haste.

Ruth had just gone upstairs. Erskine was surprised to see her back in his study almost immediately, and startled by her mode of entrance, which suggested sudden illness in the house.

"What in the world has happened?" he said, sitting upright in his chair.

"Happened?" cried Ruth bitterly. "It is the last straw! I give her up. I wash my hands of her. I wish she had never come over!"

"Tiny? Why, what has she been doing now?"

"It isn't what she has been doing-it is what she says she's going to do. You may be able to bring her to reason, but I never shall. I won't try —I wash my hands of her. I will say no more to her. But it is simply disgraceful! She is far worse than Herbert!"

"Has she unmade her mind," Holland asked eagerly.

"No, no, no! But worse, I call it. O Erskine, if you knew what she says — —"

"I am waiting to hear."

"You'll never guess!"

“No, I give it up.”
“So must Tiny —I never heard a madder idea in my life!”
”Than *what*, my dear?”
”Her going out with Herbert in the *Ballaarat*!”

Chapter XVIII
The Third Time of Asking.

December was at hand soon enough, and with the month came Lord Manister for his answer. Though more than slightly nervous he entered the modest house in Kensington with his head very high; and certain inappropriate sensations visited him during the few minutes he was kept waiting in the drawing room. He did not sit down. Then it was Tiny Luttrell who opened the door, and those sensations made good their escape from a bosom in which they had no business. In the living presence of the person one proposes to marry there are some misgivings that had need be impossible-Christina little suspected her privilege of shutting the door on Manister's with her own hand. He sat down at her example.

But if he was nervous so was she, and as he came bravely to the point she found it more and more difficult to meet his hungry eyes. It was rather rare for Christina to experience any difficulty of the kind. She rose, and stood in front of the fire, with her back to the room and Lord Manister. There, with her forehead resting on the rim of the mantelpiece (for Tiny that was not far to bend), and while the hot fire scorched her plain gray skirt and gave a needed color to the downcast face, she heard what Manister had to say. Soon she knew that he was saying it with his elbow on one end of the mantelpiece; and liked him for facing her so, and compelling her to face him. But when she found him waiting for his answer, she gave him it without lifting her eyes from the fire.

"No!"

He had asked her whether she had been able to make up her mind. The answer she had given was, indeed, the truth; but it had been prepared for a more conclusive question. She was vexed with him for the question he had chosen to put first; and the more so because it had snatched from her an admission which she had not intended to make. But she had not made up her mind-that was the simple truth; and now she trusted that he would make up his.

Instead of which he said sadly, after a pause:

"I wanted to give you six months!"

"It was very wrong of you to give me one," she answered with startling ingratitude.

"Why wrong?"

"You might have seen that I was unworthy of you."

"I might have given up loving you, I suppose, in a second!"

"I wish you would ——"

"I never shall!"

"If you ever began," Christina added to her own sentence. At last her face was raised, and now it was his eyes that fell before the cool acumen of her smile.

"You don't believe in me yet!" he groaned. "Not yet, though I wait, wait, wait."

"No one asked you to wait," Lord Manister was reminded.

"But you see that I can't help it! You see that I am miserable about you!"

This indeed was sufficiently plain; and the sight of his misery was softening Christina by degrees. She said more kindly:

"Listen to me, Lord Manister. It is a month since you saw me. At this moment you may feel what you are saying. Very well, then, you *do* feel it; but have you felt it throughout the last month? Have you felt so patient-you are far too patient-all the time? Has it never seemed to you that my keeping you in doubt, even for one month, was a piece of impertinence you ought never to have stood? Wouldn't your friends simply think you mad if they knew how you were allowing me to use you? Haven't you yourself occasionally remembered who you are, and who I am, and burst out laughing? I must say I have; it sometimes seems to me so utterly absurd —— And you see you can't answer my questions!"

He could not; one after another they had penetrated to the quick.

"They are not fair questions," Manister said doggedly. "What may have crossed my mind when I have felt worried and wretched has nothing to do with it. Isn't it enough that I tell you I can wait your own good time-that I feel a pride in waiting, now we are together and I am looking in your eyes?"

"No, I don't think that's quite enough," replied Christina softly. "It would hardly be enough, you know, if you only felt me worth waiting for while you were with me. That would mean that for some reason I fascinated you. And fascination isn't love, Lord Manister. I don't want to be rude-much less unkind-but I can't believe that you have ever been really in love with me; I simply can't!"

Yet she had never felt so near to that belief before. Her words, however, helped Lord Manister back to his dignity.

"Of course you must believe only what you choose," said he loftily. "One cannot force you to believe in one's sincerity. I suppose I spoilt you for believing in mine some time since. At all events you were fond of me once! Only a month ago you liked me all but well enough to marry me. Yet now you do not know!"

"Therefore the decision is left to you, Lord Manister; you must give me up."

"Never! while you are free."

His teeth were clenched.

"But do consider. Most probably I shall never care enough for you to marry you. And oh! I wonder how you can look at me when no other girl in the world would refuse you!"

"Can't you see that this is part of your charm?" cried the young man impulsively. "You are the one girl I know who is not worldly. You are the one girl I want!"

Christina shook her head.

"If I have any charm at all, you oughtn't to know what it is-you ought to love me you can't say why-there's no sizing up real love!" she informed him rapidly, but with a smile. "There's another thing, too. You cannot be used to being treated as I have treated you in many ways. I have often been intensely rude to you. I can't help thinking there must be a good deal of pique in your feeling toward me."

"There is more real love," returned Manister, "if I know it!"

"I wonder if you do know it?" said the girl, with a laugh; but she was wondering very seriously in her heart. He protested no more; she liked him for that, too, as also for the briskness in his tone and manner when he spoke next.

"You say you don't care for me enough, and you say I don't care for you properly, and we won't argue any more about either matter for the moment." He had flung back his head from the hand that had shaded his eyes; his elbow remained on the chimney-piece, but now he was standing erect. "There is something else," said Lord Manister, "that has prevented you from coming to a decision."

"There is certainly one thing that has had something to do with it."

"May I ask what it is?"

"Certainly, Lord Manister. I am going back to Australia."

"Soon?" This was after a pause, during which their eyes had not met.

"Sooner than was intended."

"Is it-is it for any special reason that-that you have kept from me?"

He was agitated by a sudden thought, which she read. She shook her head reassuringly.

"No, it is not to get married, nor yet engaged."

"Then there is no one out there?"

"There is no one anywhere that I could marry for love. That's the simple truth. I am going back to Australia because Herbert is going. Cambridge doesn't suit him, and I'm sorry to say he doesn't suit Cambridge. We came over together, so we are going back together. That, I promise you, is the whole and only explanation. I myself did not want to go so soon."

"But surely you are not going this year?"

"We are-before Christmas."

As Tiny spoke her glance went to the window: she was very anxious to see the snow before she sailed, but none had fallen yet, though December had come in dull and raw.

"But your people here must be very much against that?"

"They were, but now it is settled."

"You must have promised to come back!"

Christina seemed surprised.

"Yes, I said I would come back some day."

"And you shall!" cried Manister passionately. "You shall come back as my wife! Do you suppose I am going to stop short at this, when but for your brother you would have been mine to-day? I don't mean to say he has influenced you, except by going back so soon; you love Australia, and you must needs go back with him. Then go! I told you to take six months; you have taken one of them. When the other five are up I am coming to you again wherever you may be. Till then I will take no answer; and whatever it may be in the end I bow to it —I bow to it!"

His passion surprised and even moved Christina; but his humility stirred up in her soul a contempt which mingled strangely with her pity. Women of spirit cannot admire the man who will submit to anything at their hands. Christina would willingly have given admiration in exchange for the love in which she was beginning to believe; it would have pleased her sense of justice, it would have promoted her self-respect to make some such small payment on account. With Manister's patience she had none at all. She was disappointed in him. Her foot tapped angrily on the fender.

"But I don't want you to wait!" exclaimed Christina ungraciously. "I have told you so already."

"Still I mean to do so, and it serves me right."

This touched her generosity.

"Ah, don't say that!" she cried earnestly. "Oh, Lord Manister, I have forgotten all old scores —I never think of them now! The balance has been the other way so long; and I do not deserve another chance."

"Ah, but Tiny-darling-it is I who am asking for that!"

His tone compelled her to meet his gaze-its intensity made her wince.

"You believe in me!" he cried joyously. "Say only that you believe in me, and I will go away now. I will go away happy and proud-to wait-for you."

Then Tiny laid her little hand on his arm, and her eyes that had filled with tears answered him to his present satisfaction. He held her hand for just a few seconds before he went, and in kindness she returned his pressure. Then the shutting of the front door down below made her realize that he was gone. And she had time to dry her eyes and to gather herself together before Ruth, whose hopes had been dead some days, came into the room with a dejected mien and pointedly abstained from asking questions.

"If it interests you to hear it," Tiny said lightly, "I am converted to your creed at last; I believe in Lord Manister!"

"But you are not engaged to him," Ruth said wearily; "I see you are not."

"I am not; but he insists on waiting. If only he wasn't so tame! But I can't help believing in him now; and that settles it."

"Nothing is settled until you are engaged," said the matter-of-fact sister, with a sigh.

"Nevertheless I'm going to try with all my might to care for him, now that I see that he must really care for me. And let me tell you that I shall consider myself all the more bound to him because I haven't *said* yes, and because we're *not* actually engaged!"

"Yes?" said the other incredulously. "That is so like you, Tiny!"

And Ruth almost sneered.

Chapter XIX
Counsel's Opinion.

The worst of it all was this: that the young man himself had not invariably that confidence in his own affections which displayed itself so bravely and so convincingly at a psychological moment. Not that Manister was insincere, exactly. If you come to think of it, you may deceive others with perfect innocence, having once deceived yourself. And this was exactly what had happened.

There was one distinctive feature of the case: away from Christina Luttrell the poor fellow had already had his doubts of himself; in her presence those doubts were as certain to evaporate as snowflakes in the warmth of the sun.

Even as he went down Mrs. Holland's stairs Manister was joined by certain invisible companions-the misgivings that had made their escape as Christina entered the room. They had waited for him on the landing outside the door. They led and followed him downstairs. They linked arms with him in the street. They stifled him in his hansom, which they boarded ruthlessly. In one of the silent rooms of the club to which he drove they talked to him silently, sitting on the arms of his saddle-back chair and arguing all at once. Powerless to shake them off he was forced to bear with them, to hear what they had to say, to answer them where he could.

Mingling with the importunate voices of his inner consciousness were the remembered words of the girl. She had asked him whether he had never burst out laughing as the affair presented itself in certain lights; he did so now, silently, it is true, but with exceeding bitterness. She had told him that it was not enough that he should feel willing to wait for her when they were together; and now that he had left her, though so lately, he was certainly less inclined to be patient. She had suggested that he was more fascinated than in love; and already he knew that her suggestion had given shape and utterance to a vague suspicion of his own soul. She had gone so far as to hint at the possible secret of his infatuation, and there again she had hit the mark; though apart from her talent of torture her sweet looks and charming ways had been strong wine to Manister from the first. Still her snubs had piqued his passion in the beginning of things out in Melbourne; and here in Europe she had virtually refused him three times. Modest he might be, and yet know that this were a rare experience for such as himself at the hands of such as Tiny Luttrell. On the whole, the experience was sufficiently complete as it stood; yet he could not help wishing to win; indeed, he had gone too far to draw back, and for that reason alone the idea of defeat in the end was intolerable to him. And this was the one spring of his actions which seemed to have escaped Christina's notice; the others she had detected with an acuteness which made him wonder, for the first time, whether on her very merits she would be a comfortable person to live with, after all.

Gradually, however, these echoes of the late interview grew fainter in his ears, and its upshot came home to Manister with sensations of chagrin sharper than any he had endured in all his life before. His feelings when refused by this girl in the previous August, and under peculiarly humiliating circumstances, were enviable compared with his feelings now. Then he had deserved his humiliation-at least he was generous enough to say so-and he had taken what he called his punishment in a very manly spirit. But the desire to win had sent him on a secret mission to Cintra, on the chance of seeing her there, and his present feelings reminded him of those with which he had beaten his retreat from Portugal. For he had gone there for a final answer, and had come back without one; and to-day he had suffered afresh that selfsame humiliation, only in an aggravated form, and more voluntarily than ever. She had never asked him to wait; he had offered on both occasions to wait six months-nay, he had insisted on waiting. Even now, within a couple of hours after the event, he could scarcely credit his own weakness and stultification. He was by no means so weak in affairs wherein the affections played no part. He firmly believed that no other woman could have twisted him round her finger as this one had done. But here, perhaps, we have merely the everyday spectacle of a young man discerning exceptional excuses for a realized infirmity; and the point is that Manister realized his weakness this evening as he had never done before. The girl herself had made him look inward. She had suggested fascination, not love. That suggestion stuck painfully. Yet he was not sure.

Never had he felt so horribly unsure of himself; in the midst of his self-distrust there came to him, suddenly, the recollection that she distrusted him no longer, and there was actually some comfort in this thought, which is strange when you note its fellows, but due less to the contradictoriness of human nature than to the supremacy of a young man's vanity. He stood well with her now. She believed in him at last. Propped up by these reflections, he began almost to believe in himself. At least a momentary complacency was the result.

The improvement in his spirits allowed Lord Manister to give heed to another portion of his organism which had for some time been inviting him to go into another room and dine. Now he did so, with a sharp eye for acquaintances, whom he had no desire to meet. For this reason he had driven to the club which he had joined most recently; it was not a young man's club, so he felt fairly safe from his friends. Yet he had hardly ordered his soup, and was searching the wine list for the choice brand which the circumstances seemed to demand, when a heavy hand dropped upon his shoulder, and his glance leapt from the wine list to the last face he expected or wished to see-that of his kinsman Captain Dromard.

Captain Dromard was a cousin of the present earl, and notoriously the rolling stone of his house. Manister had seen him last in Melbourne, and ever since had borne him a grudge which he was not likely to forget. Had he dreamt that the captain (who had been last heard of in Borneo) was in London, Manister would have shunned this club in order to avoid the risk of meeting him; but it seemed that Captain Dromard had landed in England only that morning: and they dined together, of course; and Manister made the best of it. His kinsman was a big, grizzled, florid man, with an imperial, and with a comic wicked cut about him which made one laugh. But he retained an unpleasant trick of treating Manister as a mere boy: for instance, he was in time to choose the brand, and, as he said before the waiter, to prevent Manister from poisoning himself. He was, however, an entertaining person, and at his best to-night, being wont to delight in London for a day or two before realizing the infernal qualities of the climate and arranging fresh travels. But Manister was not entertained; he tried to appear so, but the captain saw through the pretense, and immediately scented a woman. There were reasons why the rolling stone was particularly good at detecting this element-which always interested him. His interest was unusual in the present instance, owing to certain reminiscences of Manister in Melbourne during his own flying visit to that port. It was during a subsequent week-end in England that Captain Dromard had alarmed the countess, with a result of which he was as yet unaware; but he did not hesitate to make inquiries now, and he began by asking Manister how he had managed to get out of the scrape in which he had left him.

"I remember no scrape," said Manister stiffly.

"You don't? Well, perhaps I put it too strongly," conceded the captain. "We'll say no more about it, my boy. Devilish pretty little thing, though; remember her well, but could never recall her name. By the bye, I'm afraid I terrified your mother over that; feared she was going to cable you home next day; was sorry I spoke."

"So was I," Manister said dryly, but, by an effort, not forbiddingly, so that the captain saw no harm in raising his glass.

"Well, here's to the lady's health, my boy, whoever she was, and wherever she may be!"

Manister smiled across his glass and drained it in silence. There was a glitter in his young eyes which made it difficult for the captain to drop the subject finally. Manister had been drinking freely, without becoming flushed, which is another sign of trouble. The captain could not help saying confidentially:

"You know, Harry, your mother was so keen for you to marry one of old Acklam's daughters. That's what frightened her. But it is to come off some day, isn't it?"

"Can't say," said Lord Manister.

"It ought to, Harry. I like to see a young fellow with your position marry properly, and settle down. I don't know which of the Garths it is, but I've always heard one of 'em was the girl you liked."

"Suppose the girl you like won't marry you?" Manister exclaimed, with a sudden change of manner, and in the tone of one consulting an authority.

"Well, there's an end on't."

"Ah, but suppose she can't make up her mind?"

"You might give her a month-though I wouldn't."

"Suppose a month is not enough for her?"

The captain stared; his bronzed forehead became barred with furrows; his eyes turned stony with indignation.

"A month not enough for her to make up her mind-about you?" he said at length incredulously. "Good God, sir, see her to the devil!"

Then Lord Manister showed his teeth. Though he had consulted the captain, he took his advice badly. He said you could not be much in love to be choked off so easily; he hinted that his kinsman had never been much in love. Captain Dromard intimated in reply that whether that was the case or not he was not without experience of a sort, and he could tell Harry that no woman under heaven was worth kneeling in the mud to, which Harry said hotly was unnecessary information. So they went elsewhere to smoke, and later on to a music hall, the subject having been left for good in the club coffee room. The following afternoon, however, Lord Manister drove through the snow with a very resolute front to show to Tiny Luttrell, who was just then passing Deal in the *Ballaarat*, without having given him the faintest notion yesterday that she was to sail to-day.

Chapter XX
In Honor Bound.

Aboard the *Ballaarat* Christina committed a new eccentricity, but it may be well to state at once, a perfectly harmless one. She confided in another girl —a practice which Tiny had avoided all her life. And this very girl had offended her at first sight by looking aggressively happy when the boat sailed and all nice women were in tears.

There had been a time when Christina seldom cried, but in England she had grown very soft in some ways, and she looked her last at it, and at the snow that had fallen in the night as if to please her, through blinding tears. She had never in her life felt more acutely wretched than when saying good-by to Ruth and Erskine, and her sorrow was heightened by the feeling that she had been both unkind and ungrateful to Ruth, to whom she clung for forgiveness at the last moment. The reason why her parting words were jocular, though broken, was because the sight of an honest, smiling face, which might have blushed for smiling then, sent a fleam of irritation through her heart that awoke the latent mischief in her wet eyes.

"I do wish you would ask Erskine to throw a snowball at that depressing person," she whispered to Ruth, "who does nothing but laugh and look really happy! If it was only put on for the sake of her friends I could forgive her; but it isn't. Tell him I mean it-there's no fun in me to-day; and you may also tell him that it would have been only brotherly of him to kiss me on this occasion, when we may all be going to the bottom!"

Erskine, who had crossed the gangway before his wife, so that she need not feel that he overheard her final words to her own kin, shook his head at Tiny when Ruth joined him on the quay. But his smile was lifeless; there was no fun in him either to-day. He drew his wife's arm through his own, and Tiny saw the last of them standing together thus. They stood in snow and mud, but the railway shed behind them was a great sheet of unsullied whiteness, softly edging the bright December sky, and Christina never forgot her first glimpse of the snow and her last of Ruth and Erskine. When their figures were gone and only the snow was left for Christina's eyes, they filled afresh, and she broke hastily from Herbert, who was himself uncommonly dejected. She hurried unsteadily to her cabin, to find her cabin companion singing softly to herself as she unstrapped her rugs; for her cabin companion was, of course, the odiously cheerful person who already on deck had done violence to Christina's feelings.

Thus the acquaintance began in a particularly unpromising manner; but the cheerful person turned out to be as bad a sailor as Christina was a good one, and she met with much practical kindness at Christina's hands, which had a clever, tender way with them, though in other respects the good sailor was not from the first so sympathetic. It is harder than it ought to be to sympathize with the seasick when one is quite well one's self; still Christina found it impossible not to admire her extraordinary companion, who kept up her spirits during a whole week spent in her berth, and was more cheerful than ever at the end of it, when she could scarcely stand. Then Christina expressed her admiration, likewise her curiosity, and received a simple explanation. The cheerful person was on her way to Colombo and the altar-rails. Her *trousseau* was in the hold.

The two became exceeding fast friends, and their friendship was founded on mutual envy. Tiny was envied for the various qualities which made her greatly admired on board, for that admiration itself, and for the marked manner in which she paid no heed to it; and she envied her friend a very ordinary love story, now approaching a very ordinary end. The cheerful girl was plain, unaccomplished, and not at all young. But there was one whom she loved better than herself; she was properly engaged; she was happy in her engagement; her soul was settled and at peace. Also she was good, and Christina envied her far more than she envied Christina, who would listen wistfully to the commonplace expression of a commonplace happiness, but was herself much more reserved. It was only when the other girl guessed it that she admitted that she also was "as good as engaged." The other girl clamored to know all about it; and ultimately, in the Indian Ocean, she discovered that Christina was not the least in love with the man to whom she was as good as engaged. Then this honest person spoke her mind with extreme freedom, and Christina, instead of being offended, opened her own heart as freely, merely keeping to herself the man's name and never hinting at his high degree. She declared that she was morally bound to him, adding that she had treated him badly enough already; her friend ridiculed the bond, and told her how she would be treating him worse than ever. Christina argued-it was curious how fond she was of arguing the matter, and how she allowed herself to be lectured by a stranger. But these two were not strangers now; the cheerful girl was the best friend Tiny had ever made among women. They parted with a wrench at Colombo, where Tiny saw the other safely into the arms of a gentleman of a suitably happy and ordinary appearance; and so one more friend passed in and out of the young girl's life, leaving a deeper mark in the three weeks than either of them suspected.

The rest of the voyage dragged terribly with Christina, which is an unusual experience for the prettiest girl aboard an Australian liner; only on this voyage the prettiest girl was also the most unsociable. Beyond her late companion (whose berth remained empty to depress Christina whenever she entered the cabin) Miss Luttrell had formed few acquaintances and no friendships between London and Colombo; between Colombo and Melbourne she simply preyed upon herself. Herbert remonstrated with her, and the third officer-who had been fourth on the boat in which they had come over-was excessively interested, remembering the difference six months earlier. Then, indeed, Christina had found a good deal to say to all the officers, including the captain, whom she had chaffed notoriously; but now she would stay out late and alone on the starlit deck without ever breaking the rules by conversing with the officer of the watch (her pet trick formerly), and only the third, who knew her of old, had the right to bid her good-day. Tiny's cheerful friend had left her wretched and apprehensive. She saw the Southern Cross rise out of the Southern Sea without a thrill of welcome, but rather with a vague dismay; from the after-rail she said good-by to the Great Bear with a shudder at the thought of seeing it again. Neither end of the earth presented a very peaceful prospect to Christina as she hovered between the two on the steamer's deck. She had quite made up her mind to return to England, however, and to reward Lord Manister's long-suffering docility by marrying him at the end of the six months. Meanwhile she would enjoy Australia and tell only one of her friends there. One she must tell, and with her own lips, in case she should be misjudged. And thinking not a little of her own justification, she invented a small sophistry with which to defend herself as occasion might arise. She argued that two men were in love with her, that she herself was in love with neither, but that she liked one of them too well to marry him without love. Therefore, she said, the easiest way out of it was to marry the other, who not only had less in him to satisfy, but who had more to give in place of real happiness. She was proud of this argument. She was sorry it had not occurred to her before stopping at Colombo-forgetting that she had told her friend of only one man who was in love with her. But the heart starves on sophistry with nothing to it; and with Christina the voyage dragged cruelly to its end.

But the moment she landed in Melbourne a good thing happened to her-she was snatched out of herself. A common shock and anxiety awaited both Christina and Herbert Luttrell: they found their mother in tears over a piece of very bad news from Wallandoon. It seemed that Mr. Luttrell had gone up to the station the week before to choose the site for a well which he was about to sink at considerable expense, and that he was now lying at the old homestead with a broken leg, the result of a buggy accident with a pair of young horses. He was able to write with his own hand in pencil, and he mentioned that Swift had fetched a surgeon from the river in the quickest time ever known; that the surgeon had set the leg quite successfully, so that there was no occasion for anxiety, though naturally he should be unable to leave Wallandoon for some weeks. He expressed forcibly the hope that his wife would not think of joining him there; she was not strong enough, and he needed no attention. Nevertheless, had the *Ballaarat* arrived one day later, Mrs. Luttrell would have gone. Her two children were in time to restrain her, but only by undertaking to go instead. Before they could realize that they had spent an afternoon and a night in Melbourne they had left the city and had embarked on an inland voyage of five hundred miles up country.

So their first full day ashore was spent in a railway carriage; but all that night the stars were in their eyes, and the gum trees racing by on either hand, and the warm wind fanning their faces, because Tiny would never travel inside the coach. They were back in Riverina. The Murray coiled behind them; the Murrumbidgee lay before. And the night after that they were creeping across the desert of the One Tree Plain, with the Lachlan lying ahead and the Murrumbidgee left behind. Here the leather-hung coach labored in the mud, for the Lachlan district was suffering before it could profit from a rather heavy rainfall three days old; and the driver flogged seven horses all night long instead of mildly chastening five, and the girl at his side could not have slept if she had tried, but she did not try. To her the night seemed too good to miss. The stars shone brilliantly from rim to rim of the unbroken plain, and upward from the overflowing crab-holes, and even in the flooded ruts, where the coach wheels split and scattered them like quicksilver beneath the thumb. There was no conversation on the coach. On the eve of facing his father Herbert was rehearsing his defense, while Tiny was just reveling in the night, and feeling very happy, so she said.

For a couple of hours before dawn they rested at Booligal. But Booligal is notorious for its mosquitoes, and there had been three inches of rain there, so the rest was a mockery. Tiny had a bed to lie down on, but she did not lie long. She was found by Herbert (who smoked six pipes in those two hours), leaning against one of the veranda posts as if asleep on her feet, but with eyes fixed intently upon a dull, reddening arc on the very edge of the darkling plain.

"By the time we get there," said Herbert severely, "you'll be just about dished! What on earth are you doing out here instead of taking a spell when you can get it?"

"I'm watching for the sun," murmured Christina, without moving. "It's a regular Australian dawn; you never saw one like it in England. Here the sun gets up in the middle of the night, and there he very often doesn't get up at all. Oh, but it's glorious to be back-don't *you* think so, old Herbs?"

"I might-if it wasn't for the governor."

Tiny flushed with shame. She had forgotten the accident. Being reminded of it she turned her back on the sunrise in deep contrition, but she had not taken Herbert's meaning.

"I funk facing him," said he gloomily. "I have nothing to say for myself, and if I had a fellow couldn't say it with the poor governor lying on his back."

"Poor old Herbs!" said Tiny kindly. "I don't think you have much to fear, however. It was our mistake in wanting you to go to Cambridge when you'd been your own boss always. You were born for the bush —I'm not sure that we both weren't!"

He did not hear her sigh.

"It's all very well for you to talk, Tiny! You haven't to make your peace with anybody-you haven't to confess that you've made a ghastly fool of yourself!"

"Have I not?" exclaimed the girl bitterly.

"I thought you weren't going to mention his name?" Herbert said in surprise.

"No more I am," replied Tiny, recovering herself. "So, as you say, it is all very well for me to talk." And as she turned a ball of fire was balanced on the distant rim of the plain, and the arc above was now a semicircle of crimson, which blended even yet with the lingering shades of night.

Even Herbert was not in all Tiny's secrets. He never dreamt that she had before her an ordeal far worse than his own. When they sighted the little township where the station buggy always met the coach, he thought her excitement due to obvious and natural causes. The township roofs gleamed in the afternoon sun for half an hour before one could distinguish even a looked-for object, such as a buggy drawn up in the shade at the hotel veranda. Herbert had time to become excited himself, in spite of the ignoble circumstances of his return.

"I see it!" he exclaimed with confidence, at five hundred yards. "And good old Bushman and Brownlock are the pair. I'd spot 'em a mile off."

"Can you see who it is in the buggy?" asked Tiny, at two hundred. She was sitting like a mouse between Herbert and the driver.

"I shall in a shake; I think it's Jack Swift."

He did not know how her heart was beating. At fifty yards he said, "It isn't Swift; it's one of the hands. I've never seen this joker before."

"Ah!" said Tiny, and that was all. Herbert had no ear for a tone.

The manager of Wallandoon was harder at work that afternoon than any man on the run. This was generally the case when there was hard work to be done; when there was not, however, Swift had a way of making work for himself. He had made his work to-day. Nothing need have prevented his meeting the coach himself; but it had occurred to Swift that he would be somewhat in the way at the meeting between Mr. Luttrell and his children, while with regard to his own meeting with Christina he felt much nervousness, which night, perhaps, would partly cloak. This, however, was an instinct rather than a motive. Instinctively also he sought by violent labor to expel the fever from his mind. He was absurdly excited, and his energy during the heat of the day was little less than insane. So at any rate it seemed to the youth who was helping him by looking on, while Swift covered in half a tank with brushwood. The tank had been almost dry, but was newly filled by the rains, and the partial covering was designed to delay evaporation. But Swift himself would execute his own design, and thought nothing of standing up to his chest in the water, clothed only in his wide-awake, though he was the manager of the station. The young storekeeper did not admire him for it, though he could not help envying the manager his thick arms, which were also bronzed, like the manager's face and neck, and in striking contrast to the whiteness of his deep chest and broad shoulders. There had been a change in storekeepers during recent months, a change not by any means for the better.

Near the tank were some brushwood yards, which were certainly in need of repairs, but the need was far from immediate. Swift, however, chose to mend up the fences that night, while he happened to be on the spot, and his young assistant had no choice but to watch him. It was dark when at last they rode back together to the station, silent, hungry, and not pleased with one another; for Swift was one of those energetic people whom it is difficult to help unless you are energetic yourself; and the new storekeeper was not. This youth did little for his rations that day until the homestead was reached. Then the manager left him to unsaddle and feed both horses, and himself walked over to the veranda, whence came the sound of voices.

Mr. Luttrell was lying in the long deck chair which had been procured from a neighboring station, and Herbert was smoking demurely at his side. Christina was not there at all.

"You will find her in the dining room," Mr. Luttrell said, as his son and the manager shook hands. "She has gone to make tea for you; she means to look after us all for the next few weeks."

The dining room was at the back of the house, and as Swift walked round to it he stepped from the veranda into the heavy sand in which the homestead was planted. He could not help it. His love had grown upon him since that short week with her, nine months before. He felt that if his eyes rested upon her first he could take her hand more steadily. So he stood and watched her a moment as she bent over the tea table with lowered head and busy fingers, and there was something so like his dreams in the sight of her there that he almost cried out aloud. Next instant his spurs jingled in the veranda. She raised her head with a jerk; he saw the fear of himself in her eyes-and knew.

It did not blind him to her haggard looks.

When they had shaken hands he could not help saying, "It is evident that the old country doesn't agree with you, as you feared." And when it was too late he would have altered the remark.

"Seeing that it's six weeks since I left it, and that I have been traveling night and day since I landed, you are rather hard on the old country."

So she answered him, her fingers in the tea caddy, and her eyes with them. The lamplight shone upon her freckles as Swift studied her anxiously. Perhaps, as she hinted, she was only tired.

"I say, I can't have you making tea for me!" Swift exclaimed nervously. "You are worn out, and I am accustomed to doing all this sort of thing for myself."

"Then you will have the kindness to unaccustom yourself! I am mistress here until papa is fit to be moved."

And not a day longer. He knew it by the way she avoided his eyes. Yet he was forced to make conversation.

"Why do you warm the teapot?"

"It is the proper thing to do."

"I never knew that!"

"I dare say it isn't the only thing you never knew. I shouldn't wonder if you swallowed your coffee with cold milk?"

"Of course we do-when we have coffee."

"Ah, it is good for you to have a housekeeper for a time," said Christina cruelly, she did not know why.

"It's my firm belief," remarked Swift, "that you have learnt these dodges in England, and that you did *not* detest the whole thing!"

The words had a far-away familiar sound to Christina, and they were spoken in the pointed accents with which one quotes.

"Did I say I should detest the whole thing?" asked Christina, marking the tablecloth with a fork.

"You did; they were your very words."

"Come, I don't believe that."

"I can't help it; those were your words. They were your very last words to me."

"And you actually remember them?"

She looked at him, smiling; but his face put out her smile, and the wave of compassion which now swept over hers confirmed the knowledge that had come to him with her first frightened glance.

The storekeeper, who came in before more was said, was the unconscious witness of a well-acted interlude of which he was also the cause. He approved of Miss Luttrell at the tea tray, and was to some extent recompensed for the hard day's work he had not done. He left her with Swift on the back veranda, and they might have been grateful to him, for not only had his advent been a boon to them both at a very awkward moment, but, in going, he supplied them with a topic.

"What has happened to my little Englishman?" Christina asked at once. "I hoped to find him here still."

"I wish you had. He was a fine fellow, and this one is not."

"Then you didn't mean to get rid of my little friend?"

"No. It's a very pretty story," Swift said slowly, as he watched her in the starlight. "His father died, and he went home and came in for something; and now that little chap is actually married to the girl he used to talk about!"

Tiny was silent for some moments. Then she laughed.

"So much for my advice! His case is the exception that proves my rule."

"I happen to remember your advice. So you still think the same?"

"Most certainly I do."

He laughed sardonically. "You might just as well tell me outright that you are engaged to be married."

The girl recoiled.

"How do you know?" she cried. "Who has told you?"

"You have-now. Your eyes told me twenty minutes ago."

"But it isn't true! Nobody knows anything about it! It isn't a real engagement yet!"

"I have no doubt it will be real enough for me," answered Swift very bitterly; and he moved away from her, though her little hands were stretched out to keep him.

"Don't leave me!" she cried piteously. "I want to tell you. I will tell you now, if you will only let me."

He faced about, with one foot on the veranda and the other in the sand.

"Tell me," he said, "if it is that old affair come right; that is all I care to know."

"It is; but it hasn't come right yet-perhaps it never will. If only you would let me tell you everything!"

"Thank you; I dare say I can imagine how matters stand. I think I told you it would all come right. I am very glad it has."

"Jack!"

But Jack was gone. In the starlight she watched him disappear among the pines. He walked so slowly that she fancied him whistling, and would have given very much for some such sign of outward indifference to show that he cared; but no sound came to her save the chirrup of the crickets, which never ceased in the night time at Wallandoon. And that made her listen for the champing of the solitary animal in the horse yard, until she heard it, too, and stood still to listen to both noises of the night. She remembered how once or twice in England she had seemed to hear these two sounds, and how she had longed to be back again in the old veranda. Now she was back. This was the old, old veranda. And those two old sounds were beating into her brain in very reality-without pause or pity.

"Why, Tiny," said Herbert later, "this is the second time to-day! I believe you *can* sleep on end like a blooming native-companion. You're to come and talk to the governor; he would like you to sit with him before we carry him into his room."

"Would he?" Tiny cried out, and a moment later she was kneeling by the deck chair and sobbing wildly on her father's breast.

"Just because I told her she'd dish herself," remarked Herbert, looking on with irritation, "she's been and gone and done it. That's still her line!"

Chapter XXII
Summum Bonum.

For a month Christina declined to leave her father's side, much against his will, but the girl's will was stronger. She was as though tethered to the long deck chair until the lame man became able to leave it on two sticks. Then she flew to the other extreme.

North of the Lachlan the recent rains had been less heavy than in Lower Riverina. On Wallandoon less than two inches had fallen, and by February it was found necessary to resume work at the eight-mile whim. But the whim driver had gone off with his check when the rain gave him a holiday, and he had never returned. There was a momentary difficulty in finding a man to replace him, and it was then that Miss Tiny startled the station by herself volunteering for the post. At first Mr. Luttrell would not hear of the plan, but the manager's opinion was not asked, and he carefully refrained from giving it, while Herbert (who was about to be intrusted with a mob of wethers for the Melbourne market) took his sister's side. He pointed out with truth that any fool could drive a whim under ordinary circumstances, and that, as Tiny would hardly petition to sleep at the whim, the long ride morning and evening would do her no harm. Mr. Luttrell gave in then. He had tried in vain to drive the young girl from his side. She had watched over him with increasing solicitude, with an almost unnatural tenderness. She had shown him a warmer heart than heretofore he had known her to possess, and an amount of love and affection which he felt to be more than a father's share. He did not know what was the matter, but he made guesses. It had been his lifelong practice not to "interfere" with his children; hence the earliest misdeeds of his daughter Tiny; hence, also, the academic career of his son Herbert. Mr. Luttrell put no questions to the girl, and none concerning her to her brother, which was nice of him, seeing that her ways had made him privately inquisitive; but he took Herbert's advice and let Christina drive the eight-mile whim.

The experiment proved a complete success, but then plain whim driving is not difficult. Christina spent an hour or so two or three times a day in driving the whim horse round and round until the tank was full, after which it was no trouble to keep the troughs properly supplied. The rest of her time she occupied in reading or musing in the shadow of the tank; but each day she boiled her "billy" in the hut, eating very heartily in her seclusion, and delighting more and more in the temporary freedom of her existence, as a boy in holidays that are drawing to an end. The whim stood high on a plain, the wind whistled through its timbers, and each evening the girl brought back to the homestead a higher color and a lighter step. In these days, however, very little was seen of her. She would come in tired, and soon secrete herself within four newspapered walls; and she went out of her way to discourage visitors at the whim. Of this she made such a point that the manager, on coming in earlier than usual one afternoon, was surprised when Herbert, whom he met riding out from the station, informed him that he was on his way to the eight-mile to look up the whim driver. Herbert seemed to have something on his mind, and presently he told Swift what it was. He had awkward news for Tiny, which he had decided to tell her at once and be done with it. But he did not like the job. He liked it so little that he went the length of confiding in Swift as to the nature of the news. The manager annoyed him-he had not a remark to make.

Herbert rode moodily on his way. He was sorry that he had spoken to Swift (whose stolid demeanor was a surprise to him, as well as an irritation); he had undoubtedly spoken too freely. With Swift still in his thoughts, Luttrell was within a mile of the whim, and cantering gently, before he became aware that another rider was overtaking him at a gallop; and as he turned in his saddle, the manager himself bore down upon him with a strange look in his good eyes.

"I want you to let me-tell Tiny!" Jack Swift said hoarsely, as Herbert stared. Jack's was a look of pure appeal.

"You?"

"Yes — —You understand?"

"That's all right! I thought I couldn't have been mistaken," said Herbert, still looking him in the eyes. "By ghost, Jack, you're a sportsman!"

He held out his hand, and Swift gripped it. In another minute they were a quarter of a mile apart; but it was Swift who was riding on to the whim, very slowly now, and with his eyes on the black timbers rising clear of the sand against the sky. He could never look at them without hearing words and tones that it was still bitter to remember; and now he was going-to break bad news to Tiny? That was his undertaking.

He found the whim driver with her book in the shadow of the tank.

"Good-afternoon," Christina said very civilly, though her eyebrows had arched at the sight of him. "Have you come to see whether the troughs are full, or am I wanted at the homestead?"

"Neither," said Swift, smiling; "only the mail is in, and there are letters from England."

"How good of you!" exclaimed the girl, holding out her hand.

Swift was embarrassed.

"Now you will pitch into me! I haven't seen the letters, and I don't know whether there is one for you: but I met Herbert, and he told me he had heard from your sister; and-and I thought you might like to hear that, as I was coming this way."

"It is still good of you," said Christina kindly; and that made him honest.

"It isn't a bit good, because I came this way to speak to you about something else."

"Really?"

"Yes, because one sees so little of you now, and soon you will be going. The truth is something has been rankling with me ever since the night you arrived-nothing you said to me; it was my own behavior to you — —"

"Which wasn't pretty," interrupted Tiny.

"I know it wasn't; I have been very sorry for it. When you offered to tell me about your engagement I wouldn't listen. I would listen now!"

"And now I shouldn't dream of telling you a word," Tiny said, staring coolly in his face; "not even if I *were* engaged."

"Well, it amounts to that," Swift told her steadfastly, for he knew what he meant to say, and was not to be deterred by the snubs and worse to which he was knowingly laying himself open.

"Pray how do you know what it amounts to?"

"On your side, at any rate, it amounts to an engagement; for you consider yourself bound."

"Upon my word!" cried Tiny hastily. "Do you mind telling me how you come to know so much about my affairs?"

"I am naturally interested in them after all these years."

"How very kind of you! How interested you were when I foolishly offered to tell you myself! So you have been talking me over with Herbert, have you?"

"We have spoken about you to-day for the first time; that is why I'm here."

Christina was white with anger.

"And I suppose," she sneered, "that you have told him things which I have forgotten, and which you might have forgotten as well!"

"I don't think you do suppose that," Swift said gently. "No, he merely told me about your engagement."

"Then why do you want me to tell you?"

"Because you alone can tell me what I most want to know."

"Oh, indeed!"

"Yes-whether you are happy!"

She had found her temper, which enabled her to put a keener edge on the words, "That, I should say, is not your business"; and she stared at Swift coldly where he stood, with his hands behind him, looking down upon her without wincing.

"I am not so sure," said he sturdily. "I loved you dearly; *I* could have made you happy."

"It is well you think so," was the best answer she could think of for that; and she did not think of it at once. "Do you know who he is?" she added later.

"Herbert told me. It seems you have tampered with a splendid chance."

"I have tampered with three. I shall jump at the next-if I get another."

"And if you don't?"

Involuntarily she drew a deep breath at the thought. Her head was lifted, and her blue eyes wandered over the yellow distance of the plains with the look of a prisoner coming back into the world.

"Nobody could blame him," she said at last, "and I should be rightly served."

Swift crouched in front of her, almost sitting on his heels to peer into her face.

"Tiny," he suddenly cried, "you don't love him one bit!"

"But I think he loves me," she answered, hanging her head, for he held her hand.

"Not as I do, Tiny! Never as I have done! I have loved you all the time, and never anyone but you. And you-you care for me best; I see it in your eyes; I feel it in your hand. Don't you think that you, too, may have loved me all the time?"

"If I have," she murmured, "it has been without knowing it."

It was without knowing it that she trod upon the truth. Their voices were trembling.

"Darling," he whispered, "this would be home to you. It's the same old Wallandoon. You love it, I know; and I think-you love — —"

She snatched her hand from his, and sprang to her feet. He, too, rose astounded, gazing on every side to see who was coming. But the plain was flecked only with straggling sheep, bleating to the troughs. His gaze came back to the girl. Her straw hat sharply shadowed her face like a highwayman's mask, her blue eyes flashing in the midst of it, and her lips below parted in passion.

"You? I hate you! I *do* consider myself bound, and you would make me false-you would tempt me through my love for the bush, for this place-you coward!"

Swift reddened, and there was roughness in his answer:

"I can't stand this, even from you. I have heard that all women are unfair; you are, certainly. What you say about my tempting you is nonsense. You have shown me that you love me, and that you don't love the other man; you know you have. You have now to show whether you have the courage of your love-to give him up-to marry me."

This method must have had its attractions after another's; but it hurt, because Tiny was sensitive, with all her sins.

"You have spoken very cruelly," she faltered, delightfully forgetting how she had spoken herself. "I could not marry anyone who spoke to me like that!"

"Oh, forgive me!" he cried, covered with contrition in an instant. "I am a rough brute, but I promise — —" He stopped, for her head had drooped, and she seemed to be crying. He stood away from her in his shame. "Yes, I am a rough brute," he repeated bitterly; "but, darling, you don't know how it roughens one, bossing the men!"

Still she hung her head, but within the widened shadow of her hat he saw her red mouth twitching at his clumsiness. Yet, when she raised her face, her smile astonished him, it was so timorous; and the wondrous shyness in her lovely eyes abashed him far more than her tears.

"I dare say —I need that!" he heard her whisper in spurts. "I think I should like-you-to boss-me-too."

These things and others were tersely told in a letter written in the hot blast of a north wind at Wallandoon, and delivered in London six weeks later, damp with the rain of early April. The letter arrived by the last post, and Ruth read it on the sofa in her husband's den, while Erskine paced up and down the room, listening to the sentences she read aloud, but saying little.

"So you see," said Ruth as she put the thin sheets together and replaced them in their envelope, "she accepted him before she knew of Lord Manister's engagement. *He* knew of it, and had undertaken to tell her, but that was only to give himself a last chance. Had she heard of it first he would never have spoken again."

"I question that," Erskine said thoughtfully. "He might not have spoken so soon; but his love would have proved stronger than his pride in the end. Yet I like him for his pride. That was what she needed, and what Manister lacked. It is very curious."

"I wonder if you really would like him," said Ruth, who no longer cared for the sound of Lord Manister's name. "I don't remember much about him, except that we all thought a good deal of him; but somehow I don't fancy he's your sort."

"I wasn't aware that I had a sort," Erskine said, smiling.

"Oh, but you have. *I* am not your sort. But Tiny was!"

He laughed heartily.

"Then we four have chosen sides most excellently! It is quite fatal to marry your own sort. Didn't you know that, my dear?"

"No, I didn't," said Ruth, watching him from the sofa; "but I am very glad to hear it, and I quite agree. You and Tiny, for instance, would have jeered at everything in life until you were left jeering at one another. Don't you think so?" she added wistfully, after a pause.

"I think you're an uncommonly shrewd little person," Erskine remarked, smiling down upon her kindly, so that her face shone with pleasure.

"Do you?" she said, as he helped her to rise. "You used to think me so dense when Tiny was here; and I dare say I was-beside Tiny."

"My dearest girl," said Erskine, taking his wife in his arms, and speaking in a troubled tone, "you have never said that sort of thing before, and I hope you never will again. Tiny was Tiny-our Tiny-but surely wisdom was not her strongest point? She amused us all because she wasn't quite like other people; but how often am I to tell you that I am thankful you are not like Tiny?"

"Ah, if you really were!" Ruth whispered on his shoulder.

"But I always was," he answered, kissing her; and they smiled at one another until the door was shut and Ruth had gone, for there was now between them an exceeding tenderness.

Ruth had left him her letter, so that he might read it for himself; but though he lit a pipe and sat down, it was some time before Erskine read anything. Had Ruth returned and asked him for his thoughts, he would have confessed that he was wondering whether Tiny's husband would understand the girl he had managed to tame; and whether he had a fine ear for a joke. As wondering would not tell him, he at length turned to the letter; and that did not tell him either; but before he turned the first of the many leaves, it was as though the child herself was beside him in the room.

The qualities she mentioned in her beloved were all of a serious character, and the praises she bestowed upon him, at her own expense, were a little tiresome to one who did not know the man. Erskine turned over with excusable impatience, and was rewarded on the next page by a sufficiently just summary of Lord Manister; even here, however, Tiny took occasion to be very hard on herself. She declared-possibly she would have said it in any case, but it happened to be true-that she had never loved Lord Manister. On the way she had ill-used him she harped no more; his own solution of his difficulties had, indeed, broken that string. But she spoke of her "temptation" (incidentally remarking that the hall windows haunted her still), and said she would perhaps have yielded to it outright but for her visit to Wallandoon before sailing for England; and that she would certainly have done so at the third asking had it not been for that stronger temptation to go back with Herbert to Australia. As it was, she had gone back fully determined to marry Lord Manister in the end. And if that decision had been furthered to the smallest extent by any sort of consideration for another, she did not say so; neither did she seek to defend her own behavior at any point, for this was not Tiny's way. However, with Jack she had burned to justify herself, because love puts an end to one's ways. She had longed to tell him everything with her own lips, and to have him forgive and excuse her on the spot. This she admitted. But she denied having known what her unreasonable longing really was. Did Ruth remember the "burning of the boats" at Cintra? Well, she had spoken the truth about Jack then; she had never "known" until the night of her last arrival at the station; she had never been quite miserable until the succeeding days. Reverting to Manister, she supposed the discovery of her departure the day after their interview-in which she had studiously refrained from revealing its imminence-had proved the last straw with him; she added that such a result had been vaguely in her mind at the time, but that she had never really admitted it among her hopes. Yet it seemed she had cured him just when she gave him up for incurable-and how thankful she was! A well-felt word about Lord Manister's future happiness and so on led her to her own; and Erskine slid his eye over that, but had it arrested by a loving little description of the old home to which she was coming back for good. It was a hot wind as she wrote, and the beginning of a word dried before she got to the end of it-so she affirmed. The roof was crackling, and the shadows in the yard were like tanks of ink. Out on the run the salt-bush still looked healthy after the rains. She had given up whim driving; the manager had put in his word. But she was taking long rides, all by herself; and the lonely grandeur of the bush appealed to her just as it had when she first came back to it nearly a year ago; and the deep sky and yellow distances and dull leaves were all her eyes required; and she thought this was the one place in the world where it would be easy to be good.

The letter came rather suddenly to its end. There were some very kind words about himself, which Erskine read more than once. Then he sat staring into the fire, until, by some fancy's trick, the red coals turned pale and took the shape of a girl's sweet face with blemishes that only made it sweeter, with dark hair, and generous lips, and eyes like her own Australian sky. And the eyes lightened with fun and with mischief, with recklessness, and bitterness, and temper; and in each light they were more lovable than before; but last of all they beamed clear and tranquil as the blue sea becalmed; and in their depths there shone a soul.

The Boss of Taroomba

Chapter I
The Little Musician

They were terribly sentimental words, but the fellow sang them as though he meant every syllable. Altogether, the song was not the kind of thing to go down with a back-block audience, any more than the singer was the class of man.

He was a little bit of a fellow, with long dark hair and dark glowing eyes, and he swayed on the music-stool, as he played and sang, in a manner most new to the young men of Taroomba. He had not much voice, but the sensitive lips took such pains with each word, and the long, nervous fingers fell so lightly upon the old piano, that every one of the egregious lines travelled whole and unmistakable to the farthest corner of the room. And that was an additional pity, because the piano was so placed that the performer was forced to turn his back upon his audience; and behind it the young men of Taroomba were making great game of him all the time.

In the moderate light of two kerosene lamps, the room seemed full of cord breeches and leather belts and flannel collars and sunburnt throats. It was not a large room, however, and there were only four men present, not counting the singer. They were young fellows, in the main, though the one leaning his elbow on the piano had a bushy red beard, and his yellow hair was beginning to thin. Another was reading *The Australasian* on the sofa; and a sort of twist to his mustache, a certain rigor about his unshaven chin, if they betrayed no sympathy with the singer, suggested a measure of contempt for the dumb clownery going on behind the singer's back. Over his very head, indeed, the red-bearded man was signalling maliciously to a youth who with coarse fat face and hands was mimicking the performer in the middle of the room; while the youngest man of the lot, who wore spectacles and a Home-bred look, giggled in a half-ashamed, half-anxious way, as though not a little concerned lest they should all be caught. And when the song ended, and the singer spun round on the stool, they had certainly a narrow escape.

"Great song!" cried the mimic, pulling himself together in an instant, and clapping out a brutal burlesque of applause.

"Shut up, Sandy," said the man with the beard, dropping a yellow-fringed eyelid over a very blue eye. "Don't you mind Mr. Sanderson, sir," he added to the musician; "he's not a bad chap, only he thinks he's funny. We'll show him what funniment really is in a minute or two. I've just found the very song! But what's the price of the last pretty thing?"

"Of 'Love Flees before the Dawn?'" said the musician, simply.

"Yes."

"It's the same as all the rest; you see — —"

Here the mimic broke in with a bright, congenial joke.

"Love how much?" cried he, winking with his whole heavy face. "I don't, chaps, do you?"

The sally was greeted with a roar, in which the musician joined timidly, while the man on the sofa smiled faintly without looking up from his paper.

"Never mind him," said the red-bearded man, who was for keeping up the fun as long as possible; "he's too witty to live. What did you say the price was?"

"Most of the songs are half a crown."

"Come, I say, that's a stiffish price, isn't it?"

"Plucky stiff for fleas!" exclaimed the wit.

The musician flushed, but tossed back his head of hair, and held out his hand for the song.

"I can't help it, gentlemen. I can't afford to charge less. Every one of these songs has been sent out from Home, and I get them from a man in Melbourne, who makes *me* pay for them. You're five hundred miles up country, where you can't expect town prices."

"Keep your hair on, old man!" said the wit, soothingly.

"My what? My hair is my own business!"

The little musician had turned upon his tormentor like a knife. His dark eyes were glaring indignantly, and his nervous fingers had twitched themselves into a pair of absurdly unserviceable white fists. But now a freckled hand was laid upon his shoulder, and the man with the beard was saying, "Come, come, my good fellow, you've made a mistake; my friend Sanderson meant nothing personal. It's our way up here, you know, to chi-ak each other and our visitors too."

"Then I don't like your way," said the little man, stoutly.

"Well, Sandy meant no offence, I'll swear to that."

"Of course I didn't," said Sanderson.

The musician looked from one to the other, and the anger went out of him, making way for shame.

"Then the offence is on my side," said he, awkwardly, "and I beg your pardon."

He took a pile of new music from the piano, and was about to go.

"No, no, we're not going to let you off so easily," said the bearded man, laughing.

"You'll have to sing us one more song to show there's no ill feeling," put in Sanderson.

"And here's the song," added the other. "The very thing. I found it just now. There you are —'The World's Creation!'"

"Not that thing!" said the musician.

"Why not?"

"It's a comic song."

"The very thing we want."

"We'll buy up your whole stock of comic songs," said Sanderson.

"Hear, hear," cried the silent youth who wore spectacles.

"I wish you would," the musician said, smiling.

"But we must hear them first."

"I hate singing them."

"Well, give us this one as a favor! Only this one. Do."

The musician wavered. He was a very sensitive young man, with a constitutional desire to please, and an acute horror of making a fool of himself. Now the whole soul of him was aching with the conviction that he had done this already, in showing his teeth at what had evidently been meant as harmless and inoffensive badinage. And it was this feeling that engendered the desperate desire at once to expiate his late display of temper, and to win the good opinion of these men by fairly amusing them after all. Certainly the song in demand did not amuse himself, but then it was equally certain that his taste in humor differed from theirs. He could not decide in his mind. He longed to make these men laugh. To get on with older and rougher men was his great difficulty, and one of his ambitions.

"We must have this," said the man with the beard, who had been looking over the song. "The words are first chop!"

"I can't stand them," the musician confessed.

"Why, are they too profane?"

"They are too silly."

"Well, they ain't for us. Climb down to our level, and fire away."

With a sigh and a smile, and a full complement of those misgivings which were a part of his temperament, the little visitor sat down and played with much vivacity a banjo accompaniment which sounded far better than anything else had done on the antiquated, weather-beaten bush piano. The jingle struck fire with the audience, and the performer knew it, as he went on to describe himself as "straight from Old Virginia," with his head "stuffed full of knowledge," in spite of the fact that he had "never been to 'Frisco or any other college;" the entertaining information that "this world it was created in the twinkling of two cracks" bringing the first verse to a conclusion. Then came the chorus-of which there can scarcely be two opinions. The young men caught it up with a howl, with the exception of the reader on the sofa, who put his fingers in his ears. This is how it went:

> Oh, walk up, Mr. Pompey, oh, walk up while I say,
> Will you walk into the banjo and hear the parlor play?

Will you walk into the parlor and hear the banjo ring?
Oh, listen to de darkies how merrily dey sing!

The chorus ended with a whoop which assured the soloist that he was amusing his men; and having himself one of those susceptible, excitable natures which can enter into almost anything, given the fair wind of appreciation to fill their sails, the little musician began actually to enjoy the nonsense himself. His long fingers rang out the tinkling accompaniment with a crisp, confident touch. He sang the second verse, which built up the universe in numbers calculated to shock a religious or even a reasonably cultivated order of mind, as though he were by no means ashamed of it. And so far as culture and religion were concerned he was tolerably safe-each fresh peal of laughter reassured him of this. That the laugh was with him he never doubted until the end of the third verse. Then it was that the roars of merriment rose louder than ever, and that their note suddenly struck the musician's trained ear as false. He sang through the next verse with an overwhelming sense of its inanity, and with the life gone out of his voice and fingers alike. Still they roared with laughter, but he who made them knew now that the laugh was at his expense. He turned hot all over, then cold, then hotter than ever. A shadow was dancing on the music in front of him; he could hear a suppressed titter at the back of the boisterous laughter; something brushed against his hair, and he could bear it all no longer. Snatching his fingers from the keys, he wheeled round on the music-stool in time to catch the heavy youth Sanderson in the mimic act of braining him with a chair; his tongue was out like a brat's, his eyes shone with a baleful mirth, while the red-bearded man was rolling about the room in an ecstasy of malicious merriment.

The singer sprang to his feet in a palsy of indignation. His dark eyes glared with the dumb rage of a wounded animal; then they ranged round the room for something with which to strike, and before Sanderson had time to drop the chair he had been brandishing over the other's head, the musician had snatched up the kerosene lamp from the top of the piano, and was poising it in the air with murderous intent. Yet his anger had not blinded him utterly. His flashing eyes were fixed upon the fat mocking face which he longed to mark for life, but he could also see beyond it, and what he saw made him put down the lamp without a word.

At the other side of the room was a door leading out upon the veranda; it had been open all the evening, and now it was the frame of an unlooked-for picture, for a tall, strong girl was standing upon the threshold.

"Well, I never!" said she, calmly, as she came into their midst with a slow, commanding stride. "So this is the way you play when I'm away, is it? What poor little mice they are, to be sure!"

Sanderson had put down the chair, and was looking indescribably foolish. The boy in the spectacles, though he had been a merely passive party to the late proceedings, seemed only a little less uncomfortable. The man on the sofa and the little trembling musician were devouring the girl with their eyes. It was the personage with the beard who swaggered forward into the breach.

"Good-evening, Naomi," said he, holding out a hand which she refused to see. "This is Mr. Engelhardt, who has come to tune your piano for you. Mr. Engelhardt-Miss Pryse."

The hand which had been refused to the man who was in a position to address Miss Pryse as Naomi, was held out frankly to the stranger. It was a firm, cool hand, which left him a stronger and a saner man for its touch.

"I am delighted to see you, Mr. Engelhardt. I congratulate you on your songs, and on your spirit, too. It was about time that Mr. Sanderson met somebody who objected to his peculiar form of fun. He has been spoiling for this ever since I have known him!"

"Come, I say, Naomi," said the man who was on familiar terms with her, "it was all meant in good part, you know. You're rather rough upon poor Sandy."

"Not so rough as both you and he have been upon a visitor. I am ashamed of you all!"

Her scornful eyes looked black in the lamplight; her eyebrows *were* black. This with her splendid coloring was all the musician could be sure of; though his gaze never shifted from her face. Now she turned to him and said, kindly:

"I have been enjoying your songs immensely-especially the comic one. I came in some time ago, and have been listening to everything. You sing splendidly."

"These gentlemen will hardly agree with you."

"These gentlemen," said Miss Pryse, laying an unpleasant stress on the word, "disagree with me horribly at times. They make me ill. What a lot of songs you have brought!"

"I brought them to sell," said the young fellow, blushing. "I have just started business-set up shop at Deniliquin —a music-shop, you know. I am making a round to tune the pianos at the stations."

"What a capital idea! You will find ours in a terrible state, I'm afraid."

"Yes, it is rather bad; I was talking about it to the boss before I started to make a fool of myself."

"To the boss, do you say?"

"Yes."

"And pray which is he?"

The piano-tuner pointed to the bushy red beard.

"Why, bless your life," cried Naomi Pryse, as the red beard split across and showed its teeth, "*he's* not the boss! Don't you believe it. If you've anything to say to the boss, you'd better come outside and say it."

"But which is he, Miss Pryse?"

"He's a she, and you're talking to her now, Mr. Engelhardt!"

Chapter II
A Friend Indeed

"Do you mean to say that you have never heard of the female boss of Taroomba?" said Naomi Pryse, as she led the piano-tuner across the veranda and out into the station-yard. The moon was gleaming upon the galvanized-iron roofs of the various buildings, and it picked out the girl's smile as she turned to question her companion.

"No, I never heard of you before," replied the piano-tuner, stolidly. For the moment the girl and the moonlight stupefied him. The scene in the room was still before his eyes and in his ears.

"Well, that's one for me! What station have you come from to-day?"

"Kerulijah."

"And you never heard of me there! Ah, well, I'm very seldom up here. I've only come for the shearing. Still, the whole place is mine, and I'm not exactly a cipher in the business either; I rather thought I was the talk of the back-blocks. At one time I know I was. I'm very vain, you see."

"You have something to be vain about," said the piano-tuner, looking at her frankly.

She made him a courtesy in the moonlit yard.

"Thank you kindly. But I'm not satisfied yet; I understand that you arrived in time for supper; didn't you hear of me at table?"

"I just heard your name."

"Who mentioned it?"

"The fellow with the beard."

"Prettily?"

"I think so. He was wondering where you were. He seems to know you very well?"

"He has known me all my life. He is a sort of connection. He was overseer here when my father died a year or two ago. He is the manager now."

"But you are the boss?"

"I am so! His name, by the way, is Gilroy-my mother was a Gilroy, too. See? That's why he calls me Naomi; I call him Monty when I am not wroth with him. I am disgusted with them all to-night! But you mustn't mind them; it's only their way. Did you speak to the overseer, Tom Chester?"

"Which was he?"

"The one on the sofa."

"No, he hardly spoke to me."

"Well, he's a very good sort; you would like him if you got to know him. The new chum with the eye-glasses is all right, too. I don't believe those two were to blame. As for Mr. Sanderson, I wouldn't think any more about him if I were you; he really isn't worth it."

"I forgive him," said the musician, simply; "but I shall never forgive myself for playing the fool and losing my temper!"

"Nonsense! It did them good, and they'll think all the more of you. Still, I must say I'm glad you didn't dash the kerosene lamp in Mr. Sanderson's face!"

"The what?" cried Engelhardt, in horror.

"The lamp; you were brandishing it over your head when I came in."

"The lamp! To think that I caught up the lamp! I can't have known what I was doing!"

He stood still and aghast in the sandy yard; they had wandered to the far side of it, where the kitchen and the laundry stood cheek-by-jowl with the wood-heap between them, and their back-walls to the six-wire fence dividing the yard from the plantation of young pines which bordered it upon three sides.

"You were in a passion," said Miss Pryse, smiling gravely. "There's nothing in this world that I admire more than a passion-it's so uncommon. So are you! There, I owed you a pretty speech, you know! Do you mind giving me your arm, Mr. Engelhardt?"

But Engelhardt was gazing absently at the girl, and the road between ear and mind was choked with a multitude of new sensations. Her sudden request made no impression upon him, until he saw her stamping her foot in the sand. Then, and awkwardly enough, he held out his arm to her, and her firm hand caught in it impatiently.

"How slow you are to assist a lady! Yet I feel sure that you come from the old country?"

"I do; but I have never had much to do with ladies."

The piano-tuner sighed.

"Well, it's all right; only I wanted you to take my arm for Monty Gilroy's benefit. He's just come out on to the veranda. Don't look round. This will rile him more than anything."

"But why?"

"Why? Oh, because he showed you the hoof; and when a person does that, he never likes to see another person being civil to the same person. See? Then if you don't, you'd better stand here and work it out while I run into the kitchen to speak to Mrs. Potter about your room."

"But I'm not going to stay!" the piano-tuner cried, excitedly.

"Now what are you giving us, Mr. Engelhardt? Of course you are going to stay. You're going to stay and tune my poor old piano. Why, your horse was run out hours ago!"

"But I can't face those men again — —"

"What rubbish!"

"After the way I made a fool of myself this evening!"

"It was they who made fools of themselves. They'll annoy you no more, I promise you. In any case, they all go back to the shed to-morrow evening; it's seven miles away, and they only come in for Sunday. You needn't start on the piano before Monday, if you don't like."

"Oh, no, I'll do it to-morrow," Engelhardt said, moodily. He now felt bitterly certain that he should never make friends with the young men of Taroomba, and shamefully thankful to think that there would be a set occupation to keep him out of their way for the whole of the morrow.

"Very well, then; wait where you are for two twos."

Engelhardt waited. The kitchen-door had closed upon Miss Naomi Pryse; there was no sense in watching that any longer. So the piano-tuner's eyes climbed over the waterspout, scaled the steep corrugated roof, and from the wide wooden chimney leapt up to the moon. It was at the full. The white clear light hit the young man between his expressive eyes, and still he chose to face it. It gave to the delicate eager face an almost ethereal pallor; and as he gazed on without flinching, the raised head was proudly carried, and the little man looked tall. To one whom he did not hear when she lifted the kitchen-latch and opened the door, he seemed a different being; she watched him for some moments before she spoke.

"Well, Mr. Engelhardt?"

"Well," said he, coming down from the moon with an absent smile, and slowly.

"I have been watching you for quite a minute. I believe it would have been an hour if I hadn't spoken. I wish I hadn't! We're going to put you in that little building over there-we call it the 'barracks.' You'll be next door to Tom Chester, and he'll take care of you. There's no occasion to thank me; you can tell me what you've been thinking about instead."

"I wasn't thinking at all."

"Now, Mr. Engelhardt!" said Naomi, holding up her finger reprovingly. "If you weren't thinking, I should like to know what you were doing?"

"I was waiting for you."

"I know you were. It was very good of you. But you were smiling, too, and I want to know the joke."

"Was I really smiling?"

"Haven't I told you so? Have you signed the pledge against smiles? You look glum enough for anything now."

"Yes?"

"Very much yes! I wish to goodness you'd smile again."

"Oh, I'll do anything you like." He forced up the corners of his mouth, but it was not a smile; his eyes ran into hers like bayonets.

"Then give me your arm again," she said, "and let me tell you that I'm very much surprised at you for requiring to be told that twice."

"I'm not accustomed to ladies," Engelhardt explained once more.

"That's all right. I'm not one, you know. I'm going to negotiate this fence. Will you have the goodness to turn your back?"

Engelhardt did so, and saw afar off in the moonlit veranda the lowering solitary figure of the manager, Gilroy.

"Yes, he sees us all right," Miss Pryse remarked from the other side of the fence. "It'll do him good. Come you over, and we'll make his beard curl!"

The piano-tuner looked at her doubtfully, but only for one moment. The next he also was over the fence and by her side, and she was leading him into the heart of the pines, her strong kind hand within his arm.

"We'll just have a little mouch round," she said, confidentially. "You needn't be frightened."

"Frightened!" he echoed, defiantly. The hosts of darkness could not have frightened such a voice.

"You see, I'm the boss, and I'm obliged to show it sometimes."

"I see."

"And you have given me an opportunity of showing it pretty plainly."

"Oh!"

"Consequently, I'm very much obliged to you; and I do hope you don't mind helping me to shock Monty Gilroy?"

"I am proud."

But the kick had gone out of his voice, and to her hand his arm was suddenly as a log of wood. She mused a space. Then —

"It isn't everyone I would ask to help me in such-in such a delicate matter," she said, in a troubled tone. "You see I am a woman at the mercy of men. They're all very kind and loyal in their own way, but their way *is* their own, as *you* know. I thought as I had given you a hand with them-well, I thought you would be in sympathy."

"I am, I am-Heaven knows!"

The log had become exceedingly alive.

"Then let us skirt in and out, on the edge of the plantation, so that Mr. Gilroy may have the pleasure of seeing my frock from time to time."

"I'm your man."

"No, not that way-this. There, I'm sure he must have seen me then."

"He must."

"It's time we went back; but this will have done him all the good in the world," said Naomi.

"It's a pity you haven't a manager whom you can respect and like," the piano-tuner remarked.

Naomi started. She also stopped to lace up her shoe, which necessitated the withdrawal of her hand from the piano-tuner's arm; and she did not replace it.

"Oh, but I do like him, Mr. Engelhardt," she explained as she stooped. "I like Mr. Gilroy very much; I have known him all my life, you know. However, that's just where the disadvantage comes in-he's too much inclined to domineer. But don't you run away with the idea that I dislike him; that would never do at all."

The piano-tuner felt too small to apologize. He had made a deadly mistake-so bad a one that she would take his arm no more. He looked up at the moon with miserable eyes, and his brain teemed with bitter self-upbraiding thoughts. His bitterness was egregiously beyond the mark; but that was this young man's weakness. He would condemn himself to execution for the pettiest sin. So ashamed was he now that he dared not even offer her his hand when they got back to the veranda, and she consigned him to the boy in spectacles, who then showed him his room in the barracks. And his mistake kept him awake more than half that night; it was only in the gray morning he found consolation in recollecting that although she had declared so many times that she liked Monty Gilroy, she had never once said she respected him.

Had he heard a conversation which took place in the station-yard later that night, but only a little later, and while the full moon was in much the same place, the piano-tuner might have gone to sleep instead of lying awake to flagellate his own meek spirit; though it is more likely that he would have lain quietly awake for very joy. The conversation in question was between Naomi Pryse and Montague Gilroy, her manager, and it would scarcely repay a detailed report; but this is how it culminated:

"I tell you that I found you bullying him abominably, and whenever I find you bullying anybody I'll make it up to that body in my own way. And I won't have my way criticised by you."

"Very good, Naomi. Very good indeed! But if you want to guard against all chance of the same thing happening next week, I should recommend you to be in for supper next Saturday, instead of gallivanting about the run by yourself and coming in at ten o'clock at night."

"The run is mine, and I'll do what I like while I'm here."

"Well, if you won't listen to reason, you might at least remember our engagement."

"You mean *your* engagement? I remember the terms perfectly. I have only to write you a check for the next six months' salary any time I like, to put an end to it. And upon my word, Monty, you seem to want me to do so to-night!"

Chapter III
"Hard Times"

It was the middle of the Sunday afternoon, when the young men of Taroomba were for the most part sound asleep upon their beds. They were wise young men enough, in ways, and to punctuate the weeks of hard labor at the wool-shed with thoroughly slack Sundays at the home station was a practice of the plainest common-sense. To do otherwise would have been to fly in the face of nature. Yet just because Naomi Pryse chose to settle herself in the veranda outside the sitting-room door with a book, the young man who had worked harder than any of the others during the week must needs be the one to spend the afternoon of rest at her feet, and with nothing but a lean veranda-post to shelter his broad back from the sun.

This was Tom Chester, of whom Naomi had spoken highly to her *protégé*, the piano-tuner. Tom was newly and beautifully shaved, and he had further observed the Sabbath by putting on a white shirt and collar, and a suit of clothes in which a man might have walked down Collins Street; but he seemed quite content to sit in them on the dirty veranda boards, for the sake of watching Naomi as she read. She had not a great deal to say to him, but she had commanded him to light his pipe, and as often as she dropped the book into her lap to make a remark, she could reckon upon a sympathetic answer, preceded by a puff of the tobacco-smoke she loved.

"It is a dreadful noise, though, isn't it?" Naomi had observed more than once.

"It is so," Tom Chester would answer, with a smile and another puff.

"He made such a point of setting to work this morning, you know, and it's so good of him to work on Sunday. I don't see how we can stop him."

Then Naomi would sit silent, but not reading, and would presently announce that she had counted the striking of that note twenty-nine times in succession. Once she made it sixty-six; but the piano-tuner behind the closed door had broken his own record, and seemed in a fair way of hammering out the same note a hundred times running, when Monty Gilroy came tramping along the veranda with blinking yellow eyelashes, and his red face pale with temper. Miss Pryse was keeping tally aloud when the manager blundered upon the scene.

"I say, Naomi, how long is this to go on?" exclaimed Gilroy, in a tone that was half-complaining, half-injured, but wholly different from that which he had employed toward her the night before.

"Eighty-three, eighty-four, eighty-five," counted Naomi, giving him a nod and a smile.

"I hadn't been asleep ten minutes when he awoke me with his infernal din."

"Ninety, ninety-one, ninety-two, ninety-three ——"

"It's no joke when a man has been over the board the whole week," said Gilroy, trying to smile nevertheless.

"Ninety-seven, ninety-eight —well, I'll be jiggered!"

"Ninety-eight it is," said Tom Chester.

"Yes, he's changed the note. He might have given it a couple more! Still, it's the record. Now, Monty, please forgive us; we're trying to make the best of a bad job, as you see."

"It is a bad job," assented Gilroy, whose rueful countenance concealed (but not from the girl) a vile temper smouldering. "It's pretty rough, I think, on us chaps who've been working like Kanakas all the week."

"Well, but you were pretty rough upon poor Mr. Engelhardt last night; so don't you think that it serves you quite right?"

"Poor Mr. Engelhardt!" echoed Gilroy, savagely. "So it serves us right, does it?" He forced a laugh. "What do you say, Tom?"

"*I* think it serves you right, too," answered Tom Chester, coolly.

Gilroy laughed again.

"So you're crackin', old chap," said he, genially. He generally was genial with Tom Chester, for whom he entertained a hatred enhanced by fear. "But I say, Naomi, need this sort of thing go on all the afternoon?"

"If it doesn't he will have to stay till to-morrow."

"Ah! I see."

"I thought you would. The piano was in a bad way, and he said there was a long day's work in it; but he seems anxious to get away this evening, that's why he began before breakfast."

"Then let him stick to it, by all means, and we'll all clear out together. I'll see that his horse is run up —I'll go now."

He went.

"That's the most jealous gentleman in this colony," said Naomi to her companion. "He'd rather suffer anything than leave this little piano-tuner and me alone together!"

"Poor little chap," said Chester of the musician; he had nothing to say about Gilroy, who was still in view from the veranda, a swaggering figure in the strong sunlight, with his hands in his cross-cut breeches' pockets, his elbows sticking out, and the strut of a cock on its own midden. Tom Chester watched him with a hard light in his clear eye, and a moistening of the palms of his hands. Tom was pretty good with his fists, and for many a weary month he had been spoiling for a fight with Monty Gilroy, who very likely was not the only jealous gentleman on Taroomba.

All this time the piano-tuner was at his fiendish work behind the closed door, over which Naomi Pryse had purposely mounted guard. Distracting repetitions of one note were varied only by depressing octaves and irritating thirds. Occasionally a chord or two promised a trial trip over the keys, but such promises were never fulfilled. At last Naomi shut her book, with a hopeless smile at Tom Chester, who was ready for her with an answering grin.

"Really, I can't stand it any longer, Mr. Chester."

"You have borne it like a man, Miss Pryse."

"I wanted to make sure that nobody bothered him. Do you think we may safely leave him now?"

"Quite safely. Gilroy is up at the yards, and Sanderson only plays the fool to an audience. Let me pull you out of your chair."

"Thanks. That's it. Let us stroll up to the horse-paddock gate and back; then it will be time for tea; and let's hope our little tuner will have finished his work at last."

"I believe he has finished now," Tom Chester said, as they turned their backs on the homestead. "He's never run up and down the board like *that* before."

"The board!" said Miss Pryse, laughing. "No, don't you believe it; he won't finish for another hour."

Tom Chester was right, however. As Naomi and he passed out of earshot, the piano-tuner faced about on the music-stool, and peered wistfully through the empty room at the closed door, straining his ear for their voices. Of course he heard nothing; but the talking on the veranda had never been continuous, so that did not surprise him. It gladdened him, rather. She was reading. She might be alone; his heart beat quicker for the thought. She had sat there all day, of her own kind will, enduring his melancholy performance; now she should have her reward. His eyes glistened as he searched in his memory for some restful, dreamy melody, which should at once soothe and charm her ears aching from his crude unmusical monotonies. Suddenly he rubbed his hands, and then stretching them out and leaning backward on the stool he let his fingers fall with their lightest and daintiest touch upon Naomi's old piano.

He had chosen a very simple, well-known piece; but it need not be so well known in the bush. Miss Pryse might never have heard it before, in which case she could not fail to be enchanted. It was the "Schlummerlied" of Schumann, and the piano-tuner played it with all the very considerable feeling and refinement of which he was capable, and with a smile all the time for its exceeding appropriateness. What could chime more truly with the lazy stillness of the Sunday afternoon than this sweet, bewitching lullaby? Engelhardt had always loved it; but never in his life had he played it half so well. As he finished-softly, but not so softly as to risk a single note dropping short of the veranda-he wheeled round again with a sudden self-conscious movement. It was as though he expected to find the door open and Naomi entranced upon the threshold. It is a fact that he sat watching the door-handle to see it turn, first with eagerness, and at last with acute disappointment. His disappointment was no greater when he opened the door himself and saw the book lying in the empty chair. That, indeed, was a relief. To find her sitting there unmoved was what his soul had dreaded.

But now that his work was done, the piano-tuner felt very lonely and unhappy. To escape from these men with whom he could not get on was his strongest desire but one; the other was to stay and see more of the glorious girl who had befriended him; and he was torn between the two, because his longing for love was scarcely more innate than his shrinking from ridicule and scorn. He knew this, too, and had as profound a scorn for himself as any he was likely to meet with from another. His saving grace was the moral courage which enabled him to run counter to his own craven inclinations.

Thus in the early morning he had apologized to Sanderson, the store-keeper, for the loss of his temper overnight; after lying awake for hours chewing the bitterness of this humiliating move, he had determined upon it in the end. But determination was what he had-it takes not a little to bring you to apologize in cold blood to a rougher man than yourself. Engelhardt had done this, and more. At breakfast and at dinner he had made heroic efforts to be affable and at ease with the men who despised him; though each attempt touched a fresh nerve in his sensitive, self-conscious soul. And now, because from the veranda he could descry Gilroy and Sanderson up at the stock-yards, and because these men were the very two whose society he most dreaded, his will was that he must join them then and there.

He was a man himself; and if he could not get on with other men, that was his own lookout. No doubt, too, it was his own fault. It was a fault of which he swore an oath that he would either cure himself or suffer the consequences like a man. He may even have taken a private pride in being game against the grain. There is no fathoming the thoughts that generate action in egotistical, but noble, natures, whose worst enemy is their own inner consciousness.

Gilroy and Sanderson were in the horse-yard, leaning backward against the heavy white rails. Their pipes were in their mouths, and they were watching Sam Rowntree stalk a wiry bay horse that took some catching. Sam was the groom, and he had just run up all the horses out of the horse-paddock. The yard was full of them. Gilroy hauled a freckled hand out of a cross pocket to point at the piano-tuner's nag.

"Poor-looking devil," said he.

"Yes, the kind you see when you're out without a gun," remarked the wit. "Quite good enough for a thing like him, though." Some association of ideas caused him to glance round toward the homestead through the rails. "By the hokey, here's the thing itself!" he cried.

The pair watched Engelhardt approach.

"I'd like to break his beastly head for him," muttered the manager. "The cheek of him, spoiling our spell with that cursed row!"

The piano-tuner came up with a pleasant smile that was an effort to him, and pretended not to notice Sanderson's stock remark, that "queer things come out after the rain."

"You'll be glad to hear, gentlemen, that I've finished my job," said he, airily.

"Thank God," growled Gilroy.

"I know it's been a great infliction — —"

"Oh, no, not at all," said Sanderson, winking desperately. "We liked it. It's just what we *do* like. You bet!"

The wiry bay horse had been caught by this time, and Sam Rowntree was saddling it, by degrees, for the animal was obviously fresh and touchy. Engelhardt watched the performance with a bitter feeling of envy for all Australian men, and of contempt for himself because they contemned him. The fault was his, not theirs. He was of a different order from these rough, light-hearted men-of an altogether inferior order, as it seemed to his self-criticising mind. But that was no excuse for his not getting on with them, and as a rider puts his horse at a fence again and again, so Engelhardt spurred himself on to one more effort to do so.

"That's your horse, Mr. Gilroy?"

"Yes."

"I saw the 'G' on the left shoulder."

"You mean the near shoulder; a horse hasn't a left."

"No? I'm not well up in horses. What's his name?"

"Hard Times."

"That's good! I like his looks, too-not that I know anything about horses."

Here Sanderson whispered something to Gilroy, who said carelessly to Engelhardt:

"Can you ride?"

"I can ride my own moke."

"Like a turn on Hard Times?"

"Yes! I should."

This was said in a manner that was all the more decided for the moments of deliberation which preceded it. The piano-tuner was paler even than usual, but all at once his jaw had grown hard and strong, and there was a keen light in his eyes. The others looked at him, unable to determine whether it was a good rider they were dealing with or a born fool.

"Fetch him out of the yard, Sam," said Gilroy to the groom. "This gentleman here is going to draw first blood."

Sam Rowntree stared.

"You'd better not, mister," said he, looking doubtfully at the musician. "He's fresh off the grass-hasn't had the saddle on him for two months."

"Get away, Sam. The gentleman means to take some of the cussedness out of him. Isn't that it, Engelhardt?"

"I mean to try," said Engelhardt, quietly.

A lanky middle-aged bushman, who had loafed across from the men's hut, here spat into the sand without removing the pipe from his teeth, and put in his word.

"Becod, then ye're a brave man! He bucks like beggary. He's bucked me as high as a blessed house!"

"We'll see how high he can buck me," said Engelhardt.

Gilroy was losing interest in the proceedings. The little fool could ride after all; instead of being scored off, he was going to score. The manager thrust his hands deep in his cross pockets, and watched sullenly, with his yellow eyelashes drooping over his blue eyes. Suddenly he strode forward, crying:

"What the blazes are you up to, you idiot?"

Engelhardt had shown signs of mounting on the off-side, but was smiling as though he had done it on purpose.

"He's all right," said the long stockman with the pipe. "He knows a thing or two, *my* word."

But his style of mounting in the end hardly tallied with this theory. The piano-tuner scrambled into the saddle, and kicked about awkwardly before finding his stirrups; and the next thing he did was to job the horse's mouth with the wanton recklessness of pure innocence. The watchers held their breath. As for Hard Times, he seemed to know that he was bestridden by an unworthy foeman, to appreciate the humor of the situation, and to make up his evil mind to treat it humorously as it deserved. Away he went, along the broad road between homestead and yards, at the sweetest and most guileless canter. The rider was sitting awkwardly enough, but evidently as tight as he knew how. And he needed all the grip within the power of his loins and knees. Half-way to the house, without a single premonitory symptom, the wiry bay leapt clean into the air, with all its legs gathered up under its body, its head tucked between its knees, and its back arched like a bent bow. Down it came, with a thud, then up again like a ball, again and again, and yet again.

At the first buck Engelhardt stuck nobly; he evidently had been prepared for the worst. The second displayed a triangle of blue sky between his legs and the saddle; he had lost his stirrups and the reins, but was clinging to the mane with all ten fingers, and to the saddle with knees and shins.

"Sit tight!" roared Gilroy. "Stick to him!" yelled Sanderson. "Slide off as he comes down!" shouted the groom.

But if Engelhardt heard them he did not understand. He only knew that for the first time in his life he was on a buck-jumper, and that he meant to stay there as long as the Lord would let him. A wild exhilaration swamped every other sensation. The blue sky fell before him like a curtain at each buck; at the fifth his body was seen against it like a burst balloon; and after that, Hard Times was left to the more difficult but less exciting task of bucking himself out of an empty saddle.

They carried Engelhardt toward the house. But Naomi came running out and met them half-way, and Tom Chester was at her back. From the veranda the two had seen it happen. And in all that was done during the next minutes Naomi was prime mover.

"You call yourselves men. Men indeed! There's more manhood lying here than ever there was or will be in the two of you put together!"

"Hear, hear!"

The voices were those of Miss Pryse and Tom Chester. They were the first that Engelhardt heard when his senses came back to him. But the first thing that was said to him when he opened his eyes was said by Gilroy:

"Why the devil didn't you tell us you couldn't ride?"

He did not answer, but Tom Chester said coolly before them all:

"He can ride a jolly sight better than you can, Gilroy. You sit five bucks and I'll give you five notes."

There was bad blood in the air. The piano-tuner could not help it. His head was all wrong, and his right arm felt red-hot from wrist to elbow; he discovered that it was bare, and in the hands of Miss Pryse. He felt ashamed, it was such a thin arm. But Miss Pryse smiled at him kindly, and he smiled faintly back at her; he just saw Tom Chester tearing the yellow backs off a novel, and handing them to the kneeling girl; then once more he closed his eyes.

"He's off again," said Naomi. "Thank God I can set a joint. There's nothing to watch, all of you! Sam, you may as well turn out this gentleman's horse again. If anybody thought of getting rid of him to-night, they've gone the wrong way about it, for now he shall stay here till he's able to go on tuning pianos."

And as she spoke Naomi looked up, and sent her manager to the rightabout with a single stare of contempt and defiance.

Chapter IV
The Treasure in the Store

When Engelhardt regained consciousness he found himself spread out on his bed in the barracks, with Tom Chester rather gingerly pulling off his clothes for him as he lay. The first thing he saw was his own heavily splintered arm stretched stiffly across his chest. For the moment this puzzled him. His mind was slow to own so much lumber as a part of his person. Then he remembered, and let his lids fall back without speaking. His head ached abominably, but it was rapidly clearing, both as to what had happened and what was happening now. With slight, instinctive movements, first of one limb, then another, he immediately lightened Tom Chester's task. Presently he realized that he was between the sheets and on the point of being left to himself. This put some life in him for perhaps the space of a minute.

"Thank you," he said, opening his eyes again. "That was awfully good of you."

"What was?" asked the other, in some astonishment. "I thought you were stunned."

"No, not this last minute or two; but my head's splitting; I want to sleep it off."

"Poor chap! I'll leave you now. But what induced you to tackle Hard Times, when you weren't a rider, sweet Heaven only knows!"

"I was a fool," said Engelhardt, wearily.

"You leave that for us to say," returned the other. "You've got some pluck, whatever you are, and that's about all you want in the bush. So long."

He went straight to Naomi, who was awaiting him outside with considerable anxiety. They hovered near the barracks, talking all things over for some time longer. Then Naomi herself stole with soft, bold steps to the piano-tuner's door. There she hesitated, one hand on the latch, the other at her ear. It ended in her entering his room on tiptoe. A moment later she was back in the yard, her fine face shining with relief.

"He's sleeping like a baby," she said to Chester. "I think we may perhaps make our minds easy about him now-don't you? I was terribly frightened of concussion; but that's all right, or he wouldn't be breathing as he is now. We'll let him be for an hour or two, and then send Mrs. Potter to him with some toast and tea. Perhaps you'll look him up last thing, Mr. Chester, and give him a hand in the morning if he feels well enough to get up?"

"Certainly I would, Miss Pryse, if I were here; but we were all going out to the shed to-night, as usual, so as to make an early start — —"

"I know; I know. And very glad I shall be to get quit of the others; but I have this poor young man on my mind, and you at least must stop till morning to see me through. I shall mention it myself to Mr. Gilroy."

"Very well," said Chester, who was only too charmed with the plan. "I'll stop, with all my heart, and be very glad to do anything that I can."

With Chester it was certainly two for himself and one for the unlucky Engelhardt. He made the most of his evening with Naomi all to himself. It was not a very long evening, for Gilroy delayed his departure to the last limit, and then drove off in a sullen fury, spitting oaths right and left and lashing his horses like a madman. This mood of the manager's left Chester in higher spirits than ever; he had the satisfaction of feeling himself partly responsible for it. Moreover, he had given Gilroy, whom he frankly detested, the most excellent provocation to abuse him to his face before starting; but, as usual, the opening had been declined. Such were the manager of Taroomba and his subordinate the overseer; the case was sufficiently characteristic of them both. As for Chester, he made entertaining talk with Naomi as long as she would sit up, and left her with an assurance that he would attend to the piano-tuner like a mother. Nor was he much worse than his word; though the patient knew nothing until awakened next morning by the clatter and jingle of boots and spurs at his bedside.

"What is it?" he cried, struggling to sit up.

"Me," said Chester. "Lie perfectly tight. I only came to tell you that your breakfast's coming in directly, and to see how you are. How are you? Had some sleep?"

"Any quantity," said Engelhardt, with a laugh that slipped into a yawn. "I feel another man."

"How's the arm?"

"I don't feel to have one. I suppose it's broken, is it?"

"No, my boy, only dislocated. So Miss Pryse said when she fixed it up, and she knows all about that sort of thing. How's the head?"

"Right as the bank!"

"I don't believe you. You're the color of candles. If you feel fit to get up, after you've had something to eat, I'm to give you a hand; but if I were you I'd lie in."

"Die first," cried the piano-tuner, laughing heartily with his white face.

"Well, we'll see. Here comes Mother Potter with your breakfast. I'll be back in half an hour, and we'll see about it then."

Chester came back to find the piano-tuner half dressed with his one hand. He was stripped and dripping to the waist, and he raised his head so vigorously from the cold water, at the overseer's entrance, that the latter was well splashed.

"Dry me," he cried.

The overseer did his best.

"I feel as fit as a Strad," panted Engelhardt.

"What may that be?"

"A fiddle and a half."

"Then you don't look it."

"But I soon shall. What's a dislocated arm? Steady on, I say, though. Easy over the stones!"

Chester was nonplussed.

"My dear fellow, you're bruised all over. It'd be cruel to touch you with a towel of cotton-wool."

"Go on," said Engelhardt. "I must be dried and dressed. Dry away! I can stand it."

The other exercised the very greatest care; but ribs and shoulders on the same side as the injured arm were fairly dappled with bruises, and it was perfectly impossible not to hurt. Once he caught Engelhardt wincing. He was busy at his back, and only saw it in the mirror.

"I am hurting you!" he cried.

"Not a bit, sir. Fire away!"

The white face in the mirror was still racked with pain.

"Where did you get your pluck?" asked Chester, casually, when all was over.

"From my mother," was the prompt reply; "such as I possess."

"My boy," said Chester, "you've as much as most!" And, without thinking, he slapped the other only too heartily on the bruised shoulder. Next moment he was sufficiently horrified at what he had done, for this time the pain was more than the sufferer could conceal. In an instant, however, he was laughing off his friend's apologies with no less tact than self-control.

"You're about the pluckiest little devil I've ever seen," said the overseer at last. "I thought so yesterday — I know so to-day."

The piano-tuner beamed with joy. "What rot," however, was all he said.

"Not it, my boy! You're a good sort. You've got as much pluck in one hair of your head—though they *are* long 'uns, mind—as that fellow Gilroy has in his whole composition. Now I must be off to the shed. I should stroll about in the air, if I were you, but keep out of the sun. If you care to smoke, you'll find a tin of cut-up on the corner bracket in my room, and Miss Pryse'll give you a new pipe out of the store if you want one. You'll see her about pretty soon, I should say. Oh, yes, she had breakfast with me. She means to keep you by main force till you're up to piano-tuning again. Serve Gilroy jolly well right, the brute! So we'll meet again this week-end; meanwhile, good-by, old chap, and more power to the arm."

Engelhardt watched the overseer out of sight, with a mingled warmth and lightness of heart which for the moment were making an unusually happy young man of him. This Chester was the very incarnation of a type that commonly treated him, as he was too ready to fancy, with contempt; and yet that was the type of all others whose friendship and admiration he coveted most. All his life he had been so shy and so sensitive that the good in him, the very best of him, was an unknown quantity to all save those who by accident or intimacy struck home to his inner nature. The latter was true as steel, and brave, patient, and enduring to an unsuspected degree; but a cluster of small faults hid this from the ordinary eye. The man was a little too anxious to please-to do the right thing-to be liked or loved by those with whom he mixed. As a natural consequence, his anxiety defeated his design. Again, he was a little too apt to be either proud or ashamed of himself-one or the other-he never could let himself alone. Wherefore appreciation was inordinately sweet to his soul, and the reverse proportionately bitter. Mere indifference hurt him no less than active disdain; indeed, where there was the former, he was in the bad habit of supposing the latter; and thus the normal current of his life was never clear of little unnecessary griefs of which he was ashamed to speak, but which he only magnified by keeping them to himself. Perhaps he had his compensating joys. Certainly he was as often in exceedingly high spirits as in the dumps, and it is just possible that the former are worth the latter. In any case he was in the best of spirits this morning; nor by any means ashamed of his slung arm, but rather the reverse, if the whole truth be told. And yet, with a fine girl like Naomi, and a smart bushman like Tom Chester, both thinking well of him together, there surely was for once some slight excuse for an attack of self-satisfaction. It was transitory enough, and rare enough, too, Heaven knows.

In this humor, at all events, he wandered about the yard for some time, watching the veranda incessantly with jealous eyes. His saunterings led him past the rather elaborate well, in the centre of the open space, to the store on the farther side. This was a solid isolated building, very strongly built, with an outer coating of cement, and a corrugated roof broken on the foremost slope by a large-sized skylight. A shallow veranda ran in front, but was neither continued at the ends nor renewed at the back of the building. Nor were there any windows; the piano-tuner walked right round to see, and on coming back to the door (a remarkably strong one) there was Naomi fitting in her key. She was wearing an old black dress, an obvious item of her cast-off mourning, and over it, from her bosom to her toes, a brilliantly white apron, which struck Engelhardt as the most charming garment he had ever seen.

"Good business!" she cried at sight of him. "I know how you are from Mr. Chester. Just hold these things while I take both hands to this key; it always is so stiff."

The things in question, which she reached out to him with her left hand, consisted of a box of plate-powder, a piece of chamois leather, a tooth-brush, and a small bottle of methylated spirits; the lot lying huddled together in a saucer.

"That does it," continued Naomi as the lock shot back with a bang and the door flew open. "Now come on in. You can lend me your only hand. I never thought of that."

Engelhardt followed her into the store. Inside it was one big room, filled with a good but subdued light (for as yet the sun was beating upon the hinder slope of corrugated iron), and with those motley necessaries of station life which are to be seen in every station store. Sides of bacon, empty ration-bags, horse-collars and hames, bridles and reins, hung promiscuously from the beams. Australian saddles kept their balance on stout pegs jutting out from the walls. The latter were barely lined with shelves, like book-cases, but laden with tinned provisions of every possible description, sauces and patent medicines in bottles, whiskey and ink in stone jars, cases of tea, tobacco, raisins, and figs. Engelhardt noticed a great green safe, with a couple of shot-guns and a repeating-rifle in a rack beside it, and two or three pairs of rusty hand-cuffs on a nail hard by. The floor was fairly open, but for a few sacks of flour in a far corner. It was cut up, however, by a raised desk with a high office-stool to it, and by the permanent, solid-looking counter which faced the door. A pair of scales, of considerable size and capacity, was the one encumbrance on the counter. Naomi at once proceeded to remove it, first tossing the weights onto the flour bags, one after the other, and then lifting down the scales before Engelhardt had time to help her. Thereafter she slapped the counter with her flat hand, and stood looking quizzically at her guest.

"You don't know what's under this counter," she said at last, announcing an obvious fact with extraordinary unction.

"I don't, indeed," said the piano-tuner, shaking his head.

"Nor does your friend Mr. Sanderson, though he's the store-keeper. He's out at the shed during shearing-time, branding bales and seeing to the loading of the drays. But all the rest of the year he keeps the books at that desk or serves out rations across this counter; and yet he little dreams what's underneath it."

"You interest me immensely, Miss Pryse."

"I wonder if I dare interest you any more?"

"You had better not trust me with a secret."

"Why not? Do you mean that you couldn't keep one?"

"I don't say that; but I have no right — —"

"Right be bothered," cried Naomi, crisply; "there's no question of right."

Engelhardt colored up.

"I was only going to say that I had no right to get in your way and perhaps make you feel it was better to tell me things than to turn me out," he explained, humbly. "I shall turn myself out, since you are too kind to do it for me. I meant in any case to take a walk in the pines."

"Did I invite you to come in here, or did I not?" inquired Miss Pryse.

"Well, only to carry these things. Here they are."

He held them out to her, but she refused to look at them.

"When I tell you I don't want you, then it will be time for you to go," she said. "Since you don't live here, there's not the least reason why you shouldn't know what no man on the place knows, except Mr. Gilroy. Besides, you can really help me. So now will you be good?"

"I'll try," said Engelhardt, catching her smile.

"Then I forgive everything. Now listen to me. My dear father was the best and kindest man in all the world; but he had his fair share of eccentricity. I have mine, too; and you most certainly have yours; but that's neither here nor there. My father came of a pretty good old Welsh family. In case you think I'm swaggering about it, let me tell you I'd like to take that family and drop the whole crew in the well outside-yes, and heat up the water to boil 'em before they'd time to drown! I owe them nothing nice, don't you believe it. They treated my father shamefully; but he was the eldest son, and when the old savage, *his* father, had the good taste to die, mine went home and collared his dues. He didn't get much beyond the family plate; but sure enough he came back with that. And didn't the family sit up, that's all! However, his eccentricity came in then. He must needs bring that plate up here. It's here still. I'm sitting on it now!"

Indeed, she had perched herself on the counter while speaking; and now, spinning round where she sat, she was down on the other side and fumbling at a padlock before her companion could open his mouth.

"Isn't it very dangerous?" he said at length, as Naomi stood up and set the padlock on the desk.

"Hardly that. Mr. Gilroy is absolutely the only person who knows that it is here. Still, the bank would be best, of course, and I mean to have it all taken there one of these days. Meanwhile, I clean my silver whenever I come up here. It's a splendid opportunity when my young men are all out at the shed. I did a lot last week, and I expect to finish off this morning."

As she spoke the top of the counter answered to the effort of her two strong arms, and came up with a jerk. She raised it until it caught, when Engelhardt could just get his chin over the rim, and see a huge, heavily clamped plate-chest lying like a kernel in its shell. There were more locks to undo. Then the baize-lined lid of the chest was raised in its turn. And in a very few minutes the Taroomba store presented a scene which it would have been more than difficult to match throughout the length and breadth of the Australian bush.

Chapter V
Masterless Men

Naomi had seated herself on the tall stool at the bookkeeper's desk, on which she had placed in array the silver that was still unclean. This included a fine old epergne, of quaint design and exceedingly solid proportions; a pair of candlesticks, in the familiar form of the Corinthian column-more modern, but equally handsome in their way; a silver coffee-pot with an ivory handle; and a number of ancient skewers. She tackled the candlesticks first. They were less tarnished than might have been expected, and in Naomi's energetic hands they soon regained their pristine purity and lustre. As she worked she talked freely of her father, and his family in Wales, to Engelhardt, for whose benefit she had unpacked many of the things which she had already cleaned, and set them out upon the counter after shutting it down as before. He, too, was seated, on the counter's farther edge, with his back half-turned to the door. And the revelation of so much treasure in that wild place made him more and more uneasy.

"I should have thought you'd be frightened to have this sort of thing on the premises," he could not help saying.

"Frightened of what?"

"Well-bushrangers."

"They don't exist. They're as extinct as the dodo. But that reminds me!"

She broke off abruptly, and sat staring thoughtfully at the door, which was standing ajar. She even gave the steps of her Corinthian column a rest from tooth-brush and plate-powder.

"That reminds you?"

"Yes-of bushrangers. We once had some here, before they became extinct."

"Since you've had the plate?"

"Yes; it was the plate they were after. How they got wind of it no one ever knew."

"Is it many years ago?"

"Well, I was quite a little girl at the time. But I never shall forget it! I woke in the night, hearing shots, and I ran into the veranda in my night-dress. There was my father behind one of the veranda posts, with a revolver in each hand, roaring and laughing as though it were the greatest joke in the world; and there were two men in the store veranda, just outside this door. They were shooting at father, all they knew, but they couldn't hit him, though they hit the post nearly every time. I'll show you the marks when we go over to lunch. My father kept laughing and shooting at them the whole time. It was just the sort of game he liked. But at last one of the men fell in a heap outside the door, and then the other bolted for his horse. He got away, too; but he left something behind him that he'll never replace in this world or the next."

"What was that?" asked Engelhardt with a long breath.

"His little finger. My father amputated it with one of his shots. It was picked up between this and the place where he mounted his horse. Father got him on the wing!" said Naomi, proudly.

"Was he caught?"

"No, he was never heard of again."

"And the man who was shot?"

"He was as dead as sardines. And who do you suppose he turned out to be?"

Engelhardt shook his head.

"Tigerskin the bushranger! No less! It was a dirty burgling business for a decent bushranger to lose his life in, now wasn't it? For they never stuck up the station, mind you; they were caught trying to burst into the store. Luckily, they didn't succeed. The best of it was that at the inquest, and all that, it never came out what it was they really wanted in our store. Soon afterward my father had the windows blocked up and the whole place cemented over, as you see it now."

Naomi was done. Back went the tooth-brush to work on the Corinthian column, and Engelhardt saw more of the pretty hair, but less of the sweet face, as she bent to her task with redoubled vigor. Sweet she most certainly was in his sight, and yet she could sit there, and tell him of blood spilt and life lost before her own soft eyes, as calmly as though such sights were a natural part of a young girl's education. For a space he so marvelled at her that there was room in his soul for no other sensation. Then the towering sun struck down through the skylight, setting light to the silver, and brushing the girl's hair as she leant forward, so that it shone like spun copper. From that moment the piano-tuner could only and slavishly admire; but he was not allowed much time for this slightly perilous recreation. Abruptly, impulsively, as she did most things, Naomi raised her face and gave him a nod.

"Now, Mr. Engelhardt, it's your turn to talk. I've done my share. Who are you, where do you come from, and what's your ambition in life? It really is time I knew something more about you."

The poor fellow was so taken aback, and showed it so plainly, that Naomi simplified her question without loss of time.

"It doesn't matter who you are, since you're a very nice young man-which is the main thing. And I know that you hail from old England, which is all I have any business to know. But come! you must have some ambitions. I like all young men to have their ambitions. I distrust them when they have none. So what's yours? Out with it quick!"

She discerned delight behind his blushes.

"Come on, I can't wait! What is it?"

"I suppose it's music."

"I knew it. Oh, but that's such a splendid ambition!"

"Do you really think so?"

"It's grand! But what do you aspire to do? Mephistopheles or Faust in the opera? Or sentimental songs in your dress-suit, with a tea-rose in your button-hole and a signet-ring plain as a pike-staff to the back row? Somehow or other I don't think you're sleek enough for a tenor or coarse enough for a bass. Certainly I know nothing at all about it."

"Oh, Miss Pryse, I can't sing a bit!"

"My dear young man, I've heard you."

"I only tried because they made me-and to sell my wretched songs."

"Then is it to be solos on the piano?"

"I'm not good enough to earn my rations at that."

"The organ-and a monkey? Burnt cork and the bones?"

"Oh, Miss Pryse!"

"Well, then, what?"

"How can I say it? I should like, above everything else-if only I ever could! —to write music-to compose." He said it shyly enough, with downcast eyes, and more of his blushes.

"And why not?"

"Well, I don't know why not-one of these days."

His tone had changed. He had tossed up his head erect. She had not laughed at him after all!

"I should say that you would compose very well indeed," remarked Naomi, naïvely.

"I don't know that; but some day or other I mean to try."

"Then why waste your time tuning pianos?"

"To keep myself alive meanwhile. I don't say that I shall ever do any good as a composer. Only that's what you'd call my ambition. In any case, I don't know enough to try yet, except to amuse myself when I'm alone. I have no technique. I know only the rudiments of harmony. I do get ideas; but they're no use to me. I haven't enough knowledge-of treatment-of composition-to turn them to any account. But I shall have some day! Miss Pryse, do you know why I'm out here? To make enough money to go back again and study-and learn my trade-with plenty of time and pains-which all trades require and demand. I mean all artistic trades. And I'm not doing so very badly, seeing I've only been out three years. I really am beginning to make a little. It was my mother's idea, my coming out at all. I wasn't twenty-three at the time. It was a splendid idea, like everything she does or says or thinks! How I wish you knew my mother! She is the best and cleverest woman in all the world, though she is so poor, and has lived in a cottage all her life. My father was a German. He was clever, too, but he wasn't practical. So he never succeeded. But my mother is everything! One day I shall go back to her with my little pile. Then we shall go abroad together-perhaps to Milan-and I shall study hard-all, and we'll soon find out whether there's anything in me or not. If there isn't, back I come to the colonies to tune pianos and sell music; but my mother shall come with me next time."

"You will find that there is something in you," said Naomi. "I can see it."

Indeed, it was not unreasonable to suppose that there was something behind that broad, high forehead and those enthusiastic and yet intelligent eyes. The mouth, too, was the delicate, mobile mouth of the born artist; the nostrils were as sensitive as those of a thoroughbred race-horse; and as he spoke the young man's face went white-hot with sheer enthusiasm. Clearly there was reason in what Naomi thought and said, though she knew little about music and cared less. He beamed at her without answering, and she spoke again.

"Certainly you have ambition," she said; "and honestly, there's nothing I admire so much in a young man. Please understand that I for one am with you heart and soul in all you undertake or attempt. I feel quite sure that I shall live to see you famous. Oh, isn't it splendid to be a man and aim so high?"

"It is," he answered, simply, out of the frankness of his heart.

"Even if you never succeed, it is fine to try!"

"Thank Heaven for that. Even if you never succeed!"

"But you are going to — —"

"Or going to know the reason why!"

To a sympathetic young woman who believes in him, and thus stimulates his belief in himself; who is ready with a nod and a smile when his mind outstrips his tongue; who understands his incoherences, and is with him in his wildest nights; to such a listener the ordinary young man with enthusiasm can talk by the hour together, and does. Naomi was one such; she was eminently understanding. Engelhardt had enthusiasm. He had more than it is good for a man to carry about in his own breast. And there is no doubt that he would have spent the entire morning in putting his burden, bit by bit, upon Naomi as she sat and worked and listened, had no interruption occurred. As it was, however, she interrupted him herself, and that in the middle of a fresh tirade, by suddenly holding up her finger and sharply enjoining silence.

"Don't you hear voices?" she said.

He listened.

"Yes, I do."

"Do you mind seeing who it is?"

He went to the door. "There are two men hanging about the station veranda," he said. "Stay! Now they have seen me, and are coming this way."

Naomi said not one word, but she managed to fetch over the office-stool in the haste with which she sprang to the ground. At a run she rounded the counter, and reached the door just as the men came up. She pushed Engelhardt out first, and then followed him herself, locking the door and putting the key in her pocket before turning to the men. Last of all, but in her most amiable manner, she asked them what they wanted.

"Travellers' rations," said one.

"Especially meat," added the other.

"Very good," said Naomi, "go to the kitchen and get the meat first. Mr. Engelhardt, you may not know the station custom of giving rations to travellers. We don't give meat here as a rule; so will you take these men over to the kitchen, and tell Mrs. Potter I wish them each to have a good helping of cold mutton? Then bring them back to the store."

"We don't seek no favors," growled the man who had spoken first.

"No?" said Naomi, with a charming smile. "But I'm sure you need some meat. What's more, I mean you to have some!"

"Suppose we take the tea and flour first, now we are at the store!"

"Ah, I can't attend to you for a few minutes," said the girl, casually. As she spoke she turned and left them, and Engelhardt gathered her unconcern from the snatch of a song as she entered the main building. The men accompanied him to the kitchen in a moody silence. As for himself, he already felt an extraordinary aversion for them both.

And indeed their looks were against them. The one who had spoken offensively about the meat was a stout, thick-set, middle-aged man, who gave an impression of considerable activity in spite of his great girth. Half his face was covered with short gray bristles, like steel spikes. Though his hands were never out of his pockets, he carried his head like a man of character; but the full force of a bold, insolent, vindictive expression was split and spoilt by the most villanous of squints. Nevertheless the force was there. It was not so conspicuous in his companion, who was, however, almost equally untoward-looking in his own way. He was of the medium size, all bone and gristle like a hawk, and with no sign upon his skin of a drop of red blood underneath. The hands were brown and furry as an ape's, with the nails all crooked and broken by hard work. The face was as brown, and very weather-beaten, with a pair of small black eyes twinkling out of the ruts and puckers like pools in the sun upon a muddy road. This one rolled as he walked, and wore brass rings in his ears; and Engelhardt, who had come out from England in a sailing ship, saw in a moment that he was as salt as junk all through. Decidedly he was the best of the two, though his eyes were never still, nor the hang of his head free and honest. And on the whole the piano-tuner was thankful when his share of the trouble with these men was at an end, and they all came back to the store.

Rather to his surprise, Naomi was there before them, and busy weighing out the traveller's quantum of sugar, tea, and flour, for each man. What was really amazing, however, was the apparent miracle that had put every trace of the silver out of sight.

"No work for us on the station?" said the stout man, before they finally sheered off, and in a tone far from civil, to Engelhardt's thinking.

"None, I'm afraid," said Naomi, again with a smile.

"Nor yet at the shed?" inquired the other, civilly enough.

"Nor yet at the shed, I am sorry to say."

"So long, then," said the fat man, in his impudent manner. "Mayhap we shall be coming to see you again, miss, one o' these fine days or nights. My dear, you look out for us! You keep your spare-room in readiness! A feather-bed for me — —"

"Stow it, mate," said the other tramp, as he hitched his swag across his shoulders. "Can't you hump your bluey and come away decent?"

"If you don't," cried Engelhardt, putting in his little word in a gigantic voice, "it will be the worse for you!"

The big fellow laughed and swore.

"Will it, my little man?" said he. "Are *you* going to make it the worse? I've a blessed good mind to take and crumple you up for manure, I have. And a blessed bad barrerful you'd make! See here, my son, I reckon you've got one broke bone about you already; mind out that I don't leave a few pals to keep it company. A bit more of your cheek, and I'll make you so as your own sweetheart —a fine girl she is, as ought to be above the likes of you; but I suppose you're better than nothing —I tell you I'll make you so as your sweetheart — —"

It was the man's own mate who put a stop to this.

"Can't you shut it and come on?" he cried, with a kind of half-amused anger. "Wot good is this going to do either me or you, or any blessed body else?"

"It'll do somebody some harm," returned the other, "if he opens his mouth again. Yes, I'll clear out before I smash 'im! Good-by, my dear, and a bigger size to you in sweethearts. So long, little man. You may thank your broke arm that your 'ead's not broke as well!"

They were gone at last. Naomi and Engelhardt watched them out of sight from the veranda, the latter heaving with rage and indignation. He was not one to forget this degradation in a hurry. Naomi, on the other hand, who had more to complain of, being a woman, was in her usual spirits in five minutes. She took him by the arm, and told him to cheer up. He made bitter answer that he could never forgive himself for having stood by and heard her spoken to as she had been spoken to that morning. She pointed to his useless arm, and laughed heartily.

"As long as they didn't see the silver," said she, "I care very little what they said."

"But I care!"

"Then you are not to. Do you think they saw the silver?"

"No; I'm pretty sure they didn't. How quickly you must have bundled it in again!"

"There was occasion for quickness. We must put it to rights after lunch. Meanwhile come along and look here."

She had led the way along the veranda, and now stood fingering one of the whitewashed posts. It was pocked about the middle with ancient bullet-marks.

"This was the post my father stood behind. Not much of a shelter, was it?"

Engelhardt seemed interested and yet distrait. He made no answer.

"Why don't you speak?" cried Naomi. "What has struck you?"

"Nothing much," he replied. "Only when you heard the voices, and I went to the door, the big brute was showing the little brute this very veranda-post!"

Naomi considered.

"There's not much in that," she said at last. "It's the custom for travellers to wait about a veranda; and what more natural than their spotting these holes and having a look at them? As long as they didn't spot my silver! Do you know why I came over to the house before putting it away?"

"No."

"To get this," said Naomi, pulling something from her pocket. She was laughing rather shyly. It was a small revolver.

"And what is your other name, Mr. Engelhardt?"

"Hermann."

"Hermann Engelhardt! That's a lovely name. How well it will look in the newspapers!"

The piano-tuner shook his head.

"It will never get into them now," said he, sadly.

"What nonsense!" exclaimed the girl. "When you have told me of all the big things you dream of doing one day! You'll do them every one when you go home to England again; I'll put my bottom dollar on you."

"Ah, but the point is whether I shall ever go back at all."

"Of course you will."

"I have a presentiment that I never shall."

"Since when?" inquired Naomi, with a kindly sarcasm.

"Oh, I always have it, more or less."

"You had it very much less this morning, when you were telling me how you'd go home and study at Milan and I don't know where-all, once you'd made the money."

"But I don't suppose I ever shall make it."

"Bless the man!" cried Naomi, giving him up, for the moment in despair. She continued to gaze at him, however, as he leant back in his wicker chair, with hopeless dark eyes fixed absently upon the distant clumps of pale green trees that came between glaring plain and cloudless sky. They were sitting on the veranda which did not face the station-yard, because it was the shady one in the afternoon. The silver had all been properly put away, and locked up as carefully as before. As for the morning's visitors, Naomi was herself disposed to think no more of them or their impudence; it is therefore sad to relate that her present companion would allow her to forget neither. With him the incident rankled characteristically; it had left him solely occupied by an extravagantly poor opinion of himself. For the time being, this discolored his entire existence and prospects, draining his self-confidence to the last drop. Accordingly, he harped upon the late annoyance, and his own inglorious share in it, to an extent which in another would have tried Naomi very sorely indeed; but in him she rather liked it. She had a book in her lap, but it did not interest her nearly so much as the human volume in the wicker chair at her side. She was exceedingly frank about the matter.

"You're the most interesting man I ever met in my life," was her very next remark.

"I can't think that!"

He had hauled in his eyes some miles to see whether she meant it.

"Nevertheless, it's the case. Do you know why you're so interesting?"

"No, that I don't!"

"Because you're never the same for two seconds together."

His face fell.

"Among other reasons," added Naomi, nodding kindly.

But Engelhardt had promptly put himself upon the spit. He was always doing this.

"Yes, I know I'm a terribly up-and-down kind of chap," said he, miserably; "there's no happy medium about *me*."

"When you are good you are very good indeed, and when you are bad you are horrid! That's just what I like. I can't stand your always-the-same people. They bore me beyond words; they drill me through and through! Still, you were very good indeed this morning, you know. It is too absurd of you to give a second thought to a couple of tramps and their insolence!"

"I can't help it. I'm built that way. To think that I should have stood still to hear you insulted like that!"

"But you didn't stand still."

"Oh, yes, I did."

"Well, I wish you wouldn't bother about it. I wish you wouldn't bother about yourself."

"When I am bad I am horrid," he said, with a wry smile, "and that's now."

"No, I tell you I like it. I never know where I've got you. That's one reason why you're so interesting."

His face glowed, and he clasped her with his glance.

"How kind you are!" he said, softly. "How you make the best of one, even at one's worst! But oh, how bitterly you make me wish that I were different!"

"I'm very glad that you're not," said Naomi; "everybody else is different."

"But I would give my head to be like everybody else-to be hail-fellow with those men out at the shed, for instance. *They* wouldn't have stood still this morning."

"Wouldn't you as soon be hail-fellow with me?" asked the girl, ignoring his last sentence.

"A million times sooner, of course! But surely you understand?"

"I think I do."

"I know you do; you understand everything. I never knew anyone like you, never!"

"Then we're quits," said Naomi, as though the game were over. And she closed her eyes. But it was she who began it again; it always was.

"You have one great fault," she said, maternally.

"I have a thousand and one."

"There you are. You think too much about them. You take too much notice of yourself; that's your great fault."

"Yet I didn't think I was conceited."

"Not half enough. That's just it. Yet you *are* egotistical."

He looked terribly crestfallen. "I suppose I am," he said, dolefully. "In fact, I am."

"Then you're not, so there!"

"Which do you mean?"

"I only said it to tease you. Do you suppose I'd have said such a thing if I'd really thought it?"

"I shouldn't mind what you said. If you really do think me egotistical, pray say so frankly."

"Of course I don't think anything of the kind!"

"Is that the truth?"

"The real truth."

(It was not.)

"If it's egotistical to think absolutely nothing of yourself," continued Naomi, "and to blame yourself and not other people for every little thing that goes wrong, then I should call you a twenty-two-carat egotist. But even then your aims and ambitions would be rather lofty for the billet."

"They never seemed so to me," he whispered, "until you sympathized with them."

"Of course I sympathize," said Naomi, laughing at him. It was necessary to laugh at him now and then. It kept him on his feet; this time it led him from the abstract to the concrete.

"If only I could make enough money to go home and study, to study even in London for one year," murmured Engelhardt, as his eyes drifted out across the plains. "Then I should know whether my dreams ever were worth dreaming. But I have taken root out here, I am beginning to do well, better than ever I could have hoped. At our village in the old country I was glad enough to play the organ in church for twelve pounds a year. Down in Victoria they gave me fifty without a murmur, and I made a little more out of teaching. Oh! didn't I tell you I started life out here as an organist? That's how it was I was able to buy this business, and I am doing very well indeed. Two pounds for tuning a piano! They wouldn't credit it in the old country."

"The man before you used to charge three. A piano-tuner in the bush is an immensely welcome visitor, mind. I don't think I should have lowered my terms at all, especially when you have no intention of doing this sort of thing all your days."

"Ah, well, I shall never dare to throw it up."

"Never's not a word I like to hear you use, Mr. Engelhardt. Remember that you've only been out here three years, and that you are not yet twenty-six. You told me so yourself this morning."

"It's perfectly true," said Engelhardt. "But there's one's mother to consider. I told you about her. I am beginning to send her so much money now. It would be frightful to give that up, just because there are tunes in my head now and then, and I can't put them together in proper harmony."

"I should say that your mother would rather have you than your money, Mr. Engelhardt."

"Perhaps so, but not if I were on her hands composing things that nobody would publish."

"That couldn't be. You would succeed. Something tells me that you would. I see it in your face; I did this morning. I know nothing about music, yet I feel so certain about you. The very fact that you should have these ambitions when you are beginning to do well out here, that in itself is enough for me."

He shook his head, without turning it to thank her by so much as a look. The girl was glad of that. Though he had so little confidence in himself, she knew that the dreams of which he had spoken more freely and more hopefully in the morning were thick upon him then, as he sat in the wicker chair and looked out over the plains, with parted lips and such wistful eyes that Naomi's mind went to work at the promptings of the heart in her which he touched. It was a nimble, practical mind, and the warm heart beneath it was the home of noble impulses, which broke forth continually in kind words and generous acts. Naomi wore that heart upon her sweet frank face, it shone with a clear light out of the fearless eyes that were fixed now so long and so steadily upon the piano-tuner's eager profile. She watched him while the shadow of the building grew broader and broader under his eyes, until all at once it lost its edges, and there were no more sunlit patches on the plain. Still he neither moved nor looked at her. At last she touched him on the arm. She was sitting on his right, and she laid her fingers lightly upon the splints and bandages which were her own handiwork.

"Well, Mr. Engelhardt?"

He started round, and she was smiling at him in the gloaming, with her sweet warm face closer to his than it had ever been before.

"I have been very rude," he stammered.

"I am going to be much ruder."

"Now you are laughing at me."

"No, I am not. I was never farther from laughing in my life, for I fear that I shall offend you, though I do hope not."

He saw that something was upon her mind.

"You couldn't do it if you tried," he said, simply.

"Then I want to know how much money you think you ought to have to go home to England with a clear conscience, and to give yourself heart and soul to music for a year certain? I *am* so inquisitive about it all."

She was employing, indeed, and successfully, a tone of pure and indefensible curiosity. He thought for some moments before answering. Then he said, quite innocently:

"Five hundred pounds. That would leave me enough to come back and start all over again out here if I failed. I wouldn't tackle it on less."

"But you wouldn't fail. I know nothing about it, but I have my instincts, and I see success in your face. I see it there! And I want to bet on you. I have more money than is good for any girl, and I want to back you for five hundred pounds."

"It is very kind of you," he said, "but you would lose your money." He did not see her meaning. The southern night had set in all at once; he could not even see her strenuous eyes.

"How dense you are," she said, softly, and with a little nervous laugh. "Can't you see that I want to *lend* you the money?"

"To lend it to me!"

"Why not?"

"Five hundred pounds!"

"My dear young man, I'm ashamed to say that I should never feel it. It's a sporting offer merely. Of course I'd charge interest-you'd dedicate all your nice songs to me. Why don't you answer? I don't like to see you in the bush, it isn't at all the place for you; and I do want to send you home to your mother. You might let me, for her sake. Have you lost your tongue?"

Her hand had remained upon the splints and bandages; indeed, she had forgotten that there was a living arm inside them, but now something trivial occurred that made her withdraw it, and also get up from her chair.

"Are you on, or are you not?"

"Oh, how can I thank you? What can I say?"

"Yes or no," replied Naomi, promptly.

"No, then. I can't —I can't — —"

"Then don't. Now not another word! No, there's no offence on either side, unless it's I that have offended you. It was great cheek of me, after all. Yes, it was! Well, then, if it wasn't, will you have the goodness to lend me your ears on an entirely different matter?"

"Very well; with all my heart; yet if only I could ever thank you — —"

"If only you would be quiet and listen to me! How are the bruises behaving? That's all I want to hear now."

"The bruises? Oh, they're all right; I'd quite forgotten I had any."

"You can lean back without hurting?"

"Rather! If I put my weight on the left side it doesn't hurt a bit."

"Think you could stand seven miles in a buggy to-morrow morning?"

"Couldn't I!"

"Then I thought of driving over to the shed in the morning; and you shall come with me if you're good."

For an instant he looked radiant. Then his face clouded over as he thought again of her goodness and his own ingratitude.

"Miss Pryse," he began-and stuck-but his tone spoke volumes of remorse and self-abasement.

Evidently she was getting to know that tone, for she caught him up with a look of distinct displeasure.

"Only if you're good, mind!" she told him, sharply. "Not on any account unless!"

And Engelhardt said no more.

Chapter VII
The Ringer of the Shed

A sweet breeze and a flawless sky rendered it an exquisite morning when Naomi and her piano-tuner took their seats behind the kind of pair which the girl loved best to handle. They were youngsters both, the one a filly as fresh as paint, the other a chestnut colt, better broken, perhaps, but sufficiently ready to be led astray. The very start was lively. Engelhardt found himself holding on with his only hand as if his life depended on it, instead of on the firm gloved fingers and the taut white-sleeved arm at his side. He looked from the pair of young ones to that arm and those fingers, and back again at the pair. They were pulling alarmingly, especially the filly. Engelhardt took an anxious look at the driver's face. He was prepared to find it resolute but pale. He found it transfigured with the purest exultation. After all, this was the daughter of the man who had returned the bushranger's fire with laughter as loud as his shots; she was her father's child; and from this moment onward the piano-tuner felt it a new honor to be sitting at her side.

"How do you like it?" she found time to ask him when the worst seemed over.

"First-rate," he replied.

"Not in a funk?"

"Not with you."

"That's a blessing. The filly needs watching-little demon! But she sha'n't smash your other arm for you, Mr. Engelhardt, if I can prevent it. No screws loose, Sam, I hope?"

"Not if I knows it, miss!"

Sam Rowntree had jumped on behind to come as far as the first gate, to open it. Already they were there, and as Sam ran in front of the impatient pair the filly shied violently at a blue silk fly-veil which fluttered from his wide-awake.

"That nice youth is the dandy of the men's hut," explained Naomi, as they tore through the gates, leaving Sam and his fly-veil astern in a twinkling. "I daren't say much to him, because he's the only man the hut contains just at present. The rest spend most nights out at the shed, so I should be pretty badly off if I offended Sam. I wasn't too pleased with the state of the buggy, as a matter of fact. It's the old Shanghai my father used to fancy, and somehow it's fallen on idle days; but it runs lighter than anything else we've got, and it's sweetly swung. That's why I chose it for this little trip of ours. You'll find it like a feather-bed for your bruises and bones and things-if only Sam Rowntree used his screw-hammer properly. Feeling happy so far?"

Engelhardt declared that he had never been happier in his life. There was more truth in the assertion than Naomi suspected. She also was happy, but in a different way. A tight rein, an aching arm, a clear course across a five-mile paddock, and her beloved Riverina breeze between her teeth, would have made her happy at any time and in any circumstances. The piano-tuner's company added no sensible zest to a performance which she thoroughly enjoyed for its own sake; but with him the exact opposite was the case. She was not thinking of him. He was thinking only of her. She had her young bloods to watch. His eyes spent half their time upon her grand strong hand and arm. Suddenly these gave a tug and a jerk, both together. But he was in too deep a dream either to see what was wrong or to understand his companion's exclamation.

"He didn't!" she had cried.

"Didn't what?" said Engelhardt. "And who, Miss Pryse?"

"Sam Rowntree didn't use his screw-hammer properly. Wretch! The near swingle-tree's down and trailing."

It took Engelhardt some moments to grasp exactly what she meant. Then he saw. The near swingle-tree was bumping along the ground at the filly's heels, dragged by the traces. Already the filly had shown herself the one to shy as well as to pull, and it now appeared highly probable that she would give a further exhibition of her powers by kicking the Shanghai to matchwood. Luckily, the present pace was too fast for that. The filly had set the pace herself. The filly was keeping it up. As for the chestnut, it was contentedly playing second fiddle with traces drooping like festoons. Thus the buggy was practically being drawn by a single rein with the filly's mouth at one end of it and Naomi's hand at the other.

"Once let the bar tickle her hoofs, and she'll hack us to smithereens," said the latter, cheerfully. "We'll euchre her yet by keeping this up!" And she took her whip and flogged the chestnut.

But this did not ease the strain on her left hand and arm, for the chestnut's pace was nothing to the filly's, so that even with the will he had not the power to tighten his traces and perform his part. Engelhardt saw the veins swelling in the section of wrist between the white sleeve and the dogskin glove. He reached across and tried to help her with his left hand; but she bade him sit quiet, or he would certainly tumble out and be run over; and with her command she sent a roar of laughter into his ear, though the veins were swelling on her forehead, too. Truly she was a chip of the old block, and the grain was as good as ever.

It came to an end at last.

"Hurray!" said Naomi. "I see the fence."

Engelhardt saw it soon after, and in another minute the horses stood smoking, and the buggy panting on its delicate springs, before a six-bar gate which even the filly was disinclined to tackle just then.

"Do you think you can drive through with your one hand, and hold them tight on t'other side?" said Naomi. "Clap your foot on the break and try."

He nodded and managed creditably; but before opening the gate Naomi made a temporary fixture of the swingle-tree by means of a strap; and this proved the last of their troubles. The shed was now plainly in sight, with its long regular roof, and at one end three huts parallel with it and with each other. To the left of the shed, as they drove up, Naomi pointed out the drafting yards. A dense yellow cloud overhung them like a lump of London fog.

"They're drafting now," said Naomi. "I expect Mr. Gilroy is drafting himself. If so, let's hope he's too busy to see us. It would be a pity, you know, to take him away from his work," she added next instant; but Engelhardt was not deceived.

They drove down the length of the shed, which had small pens attached on either side, with a kind of port-hole opening into each. Out of these port-holes there kept issuing shorn sheep, which ran down little sloping boards, and thus filled the pens. At one of the latter Naomi pulled up. It contained twice as many sheep as any other pen, and a good half of them were cut and bleeding. The pens were all numbered, and this one was number nineteen.

"Bear that in mind," said Naomi. "Nineteen!"

Engelhardt looked at her. Her face was flushed and her voice unusually quiet and hard. But she drove on without another word, save of general explanation.

"Each man has his pen," she said, "and shears his sheep just inside those holes. Then the boss of the shed comes round with his note-book, counts out the pens, and enters the number of sheep to the number of each pen. If a shearer cuts his sheep about much, or leaves a lot of wool on, he just runs that man's pen-doesn't count 'em at all. At least, he ought to. It seems he doesn't always do it."

Again her tone was a singular mixture of hard and soft.

"Mr. Gilroy is over the shed, isn't he?" said Engelhardt, a little injudiciously.

"He is," returned Naomi, and that was all.

They alighted from the buggy at the farther end of the shed, where huge doors stood open, showing a confused stack of wool-bales within, and Sanderson, the store-keeper, engaged in branding them with stencil and tar-brush. He took off his wide-awake to Naomi, and winked at the piano-tuner. The near-sighted youth was also there, and he came out to take charge of the pair, while Engelhardt entered the shed at Naomi's skirts.

Beyond the bales was the machine which turned them out. Here the two wool-pressers were hard at work and streaming with perspiration. Naomi paused to see a bale pressed down and sewn up. Then she led her companion on to where the wool-pickers were busy at side tables, and the wool-sorter at another table which stood across the shed in a commanding position, with a long line of shearers at work to right and left, and an equally long pen full of unshorn sheep between them. The wool-sorter's seemed the softest job in the shed. Boys brought him fleeces-perhaps a dozen a minute-flung them out upon the table, and rolled them up again into neat bundles swiftly tied with string. These bundles the wool-sorter merely tossed over his shoulder into one or other of the five or six bins at his back.

"He gets a pound a thousand fleeces," Naomi whispered, "and we shear something over eighty thousand sheep. He will take away a check of eighty odd pounds for his six weeks' work."

"And what about the shearers?"

"A pound a hundred. Some of them will go away with forty or fifty pounds."

"It beats piano-tuning," said Engelhardt, with a laugh. They crossed an open space, mounted a few steps, and began threading their way down the left-hand aisle, between the shearers and the pen from which they had to help themselves to woolly sheep. The air was heavy with the smell of fleeces, and not unmusical with the constant swish and chink of forty pairs of shears.

"Well, Harry?" said Naomi, to the second man they came to. "Harry is an old friend of mine, Mr. Engelhardt-he was here in the old days. Mr. Engelhardt is a new friend, Harry, but a very good one, for all that. How are you getting on? What's your top-score?"

"Ninety-one, miss —I shore ninety-one yesterday."

"And a very good top-score, too, Harry. I'd rather spend three months over the shearing than have sheep cut about and wool left on. What was that number I asked you to keep in mind, Mr. Engelhardt?"

"Nineteen, Miss Pryse."

"Ah, yes! Who's number nineteen, Harry?"

Harry grinned.

"They call him the ringer of the shed, miss."

"Oh, indeed. That means the fastest shearer, Mr. Engelhardt-the man who runs rings round the rest, eh, Harry? What's *his* top-score, do you suppose?"

"Something over two hundred."

"I thought as much. And his name?"

"Simons, miss."

"Point him out, Harry."

"Why, there he is; that big chap now helping himself to a woolly."

They turned and saw a huge fellow drag out an unshorn sheep by the leg, and fling it against his moleskins with a clearly unnecessary violence and cruelty.

"Come on, Mr. Engelhardt," said Naomi, in her driest tones; "I have a word to say to the ringer of the shed. I rather think he won't ring much longer."

They walked on and watched the long man at his work. It was the work of a ruffian. The shearer next him had started on a new sheep simultaneously, and was on farther than the brisket when the ringer had reached the buttocks. On the brisket of the ringer's sheep a slit of livid blue had already filled with blood, and blood started from other places as he went slashing on. He was either too intent or too insolent to take the least heed of the lady and the young man watching him. The young man's heart was going like a clock in the night, and he was sufficiently ashamed of it. As for Naomi, she was visibly boiling over, but she held her tongue until the sheep rose bleeding from its fleece. Then, as the man was about to let the poor thing go, she darted between it and the hole.

"Tar here on the brisket!" she called down the board.

A boy came at a run and dabbed the wounds.

"Why didn't you call him yourself?" she then asked sternly of the man, still detaining his sheep.

"What business is that of yours?" he returned, impudently.

"That you will see presently. How many sheep did you shear yesterday?"

"Two hundred and two."

"And the day before?"

"Two hundred and five."

"That will do. It's too much, my man, you can't do it properly. I've had a look at your sheep, and I mean to run your pen. What's more, if you don't intend to go slower and do better, you may throw down your shears this minute!"

The man had slowly lifted himself to something like his full height, which was enormous. So were his rounded shoulders and his long hairy arms and hands. So was his face, with its huge hook-nose and its mouthful of yellow teeth. These were showing in an insolent yet savage grin, when a good thing happened at a very good time.

A bell sounded, and someone sang out, "Smoke-oh!"

Instantly many pairs of shears were dropped; in the ensuing two minutes the rest followed, as each man finished the sheep he was engaged on when the bell rang. Thus the swish and tinkle of the shears changed swiftly to a hum of conversation mingled with deep-drawn sighs. And this stopped suddenly, miraculously, as the shed opened its eyes and ears to the scene going forward between its notorious ringer and Naomi Pryse, the owner of the run.

In another moment men with pipes in their hands and sweat on their brows were edging toward the pair from right and left.

"Your name, I think, is Simons?" Naomi was saying, coolly, but so that all who had a mind might hear her. "I have no more to say to you, Simons, except that you will shear properly or go where they like their sheep to have lumps of flesh taken out and lumps of wool left on."

"Since when have you been over the board, miss?" asked Simons, a little more civilly under the eyes of his mates.

"I am not over the board," said Naomi, hotly, "but I am over the man who is."

She received instant cause to regret this speech.

"We wish you was!" cried two or three. "*You* wouldn't make a blooming mull of things, you wouldn't!"

"I'll take my orders from Mr. Gilroy, and from nobody else," said Simons, defiantly.

"Well, you may take fair warning from me."

"That's as I like."

"It's as *I* like," said Naomi. "And look here, I won't waste more words upon you and I won't stand your impertinence. Better throw down your shears now-for I've done with you-before I call upon your mates to take them from you."

"We don't need calling, miss, not we!"

Half a dozen fine fellows had stepped forward, with Harry at their head, and the affair was over. Simons had flung his shears on the floor with a clatter and a curse, and was striding out of the shed amid the hisses and imprecations of his comrades.

Naomi would have got away, too, for she had had more than enough of the whole business, but this was not so easy. Someone raised three cheers for her. They were given with a roar that shook the iron roof like thunder. And to cap all this a gray old shearer planted himself in her path.

"It's just this way, miss," said he. "We liked Simons little enough, but, begging your pardon, we like Mr. Gilroy less. He doesn't know how to treat us at all. He has no idea of bossing a shed like this. And mark my words, miss, unless you remove that man, and give us some smarter gentleman like, say, young Mr. Chester — —"

"Ay, Chester'll do!"

"He knows his business!"

"He's a man, he is — —"

"And the man for us!"

"Unless you give us someone more to our fancy, like young Mr. Chester," concluded the old man, doing his best to pacify his mates with look and gesture, "there'll be further trouble. This is only the beginning. There'll be trouble, and maybe worse, until you make a change."

Naomi felt inexpressibly uncomfortable.

"Mr. Gilroy is the manager of this station," said she, for once with a slight tremor in her voice. "Any difference that you have with him, you must fight it out between you. I am quite sure that he means to be just. I, at any rate, must interfere no more. I am sorry I interfered at all."

So they let her go at last, the piano-tuner following close upon her heels. He had stuck to her all the time with shut mouth and twitching fingers, ready for anything, as he was ready still. And the first person these two encountered in the open air was Gilroy himself, with so white a face and such busy lips that they hardly required him to tell them he had heard all.

"I am very sorry, Monty," said the girl, in a distressed tone which highly surprised her companion; "but I simply couldn't help it. You can't stand by and see a sheep cut to pieces without opening your mouth. Yet I know I was at fault."

"It's not much good knowing it now," returned Gilroy, ungraciously, as he rolled along at her side; "you should have thought of that first. As it is, you've given me away to the shed, and made a tough job twice as tough as it was before."

"I really am very sorry, Monty. I know I oughtn't to have interfered at all. At the same time, the man deserved sending away, and I am sure you would have been the first to send him had you seen what I saw. I know I should have waited and spoken to you; but I shall keep away from the shed in future."

"That won't undo this morning's mischief. I heard what the brutes said to you!"

"Then you must have heard what I said to them. Don't try to make me out worse than I am, Monty."

She laid her hand upon his arm, and Engelhardt, to his horror, saw tears on her lashes. Gilroy, however, would not look at her. Instead, he hailed the store-keeper, who had passed them on his way to the huts.

"Make out Simons's account, Sandy," he shouted at the top of his voice, "and give him his check. Miss Pryse has thought fit to sack him over my head!"

Instantly her penitence froze to scorn.

"That was unnecessary," she said, in the same quiet tone she had employed toward the shearer, but dropping her arm and halting dead as she spoke. "If this is the way you treat the men, no wonder you can't manage them. Come, Mr. Engelhardt!"

And with this they turned their back on the manager, but not on the shed; that was not Naomi's way at all. She was pre-eminently one to be led, not driven, and she remained upon the scene, showing Engelhardt everything, and explaining the minutest details for his benefit, much longer than she would have dreamt of staying in the ordinary course of affairs. This involved luncheon in the manager's hut, at which meal Naomi appeared in the highest spirits, cracking jokes with Sanderson, chaffing the boy in spectacles, and clinking pannikins with everyone but the manager himself. The latter left early, after steadily sulking behind his plate, with his beard in his waistcoat and his yellow head presented like a bull's. Tom Chester was not there at all. Engelhardt was sorry, though the others treated him well enough to-day—Sanderson even cutting up his meat for him. It was three o'clock before Naomi and he started homeward in the old Shanghai.

With the wool-shed left a mile behind, they overtook a huge horseman leading a spare horse.

"That's our friend Simons," said Naomi. "I wonder what sort of a greeting he'll give me. None at all, I should imagine."

She was wrong. The shearer reined up on one side of the track, and gave her a low bow, wide-awake in hand, and with it a kind of a glaring grin that made his teeth stand out like brass-headed nails in the afternoon sunshine. Naomi laughed as they drove on.

"Pretty, wasn't it? That man loves me to distraction, I should say. On the whole we may claim to have had a rather lively day. First came that young lady on the near side, who's behaving herself so angelically now; and then the swingle-tree, which they've fixed up well enough to see us through this afternoon at any rate. Next there was our friend Simons; and after him, poor dear Monty Gilroy-who had cause to complain, mind you, Mr. Engelhardt. We mustn't forget that I had no sort of right to interfere. And now, unless I'm very much mistaken, we're on the point of meeting two more of our particular friends."

In fact, a couple of tramps were approaching, swag on back, with the slow swinging stride of their kind. Engelhardt colored hotly as he recognized the ruffians of the day before. They were walking on opposite sides of the track, and as the buggy cut between them the fat man unpocketed one hand and saluted them as they passed.

"Not got a larger size yet?" he shouted out. "Why, that ain't a man at all!"

The poor piano-tuner felt red to his toes, and held his tongue with exceeding difficulty. But, as usual, Naomi and her laugh came to his rescue.

"How polite our friends are, to be sure! A bow here and a salute there! Birds of a feather, too, if ever I saw any; you might look round, Mr. Engelhardt, and see if they're flocking together."

"They are," said he, next minute.

Then Naomi looked for herself. They were descending a slight incline, and, sure enough, on top of the ridge stood the two tramps and the mounted shearer. Stamped clean against the sky, it looked much as though horses and men had been carved out of a single slab of ebony.

Chapter VIII
"Three Shadows"

That night the piano-tuner came out in quite a new character, and with immediate success. He began repeating poetry in the moonlit veranda, and Naomi let him go on for an hour and a half; indeed, she made him; for she was in secret tribulation over one or two things that had happened during the day, and only too thankful, therefore, to be taken out of herself and made to think on other matters. Engelhardt did all this for her, and in so doing furthered his own advantage, too, almost as much as his own pleasure. At all events, Naomi took to her room a livelier interest in the piano-tuner than she had felt hitherto, while her own troubles were left, with her boots, outside the door.

It was true she had been interested in him from the beginning. He had so very soon revealed to her what she had never come in contact with before —a highly sensitized specimen of the artistic temperament. She did not know it by this name, or by any name at all; but she was not the less alive to his little group of interesting peculiarities, because of her inability to label the lot with one phrase. They interested her the more for that very reason; just as her instinct as to the possibilities that were in him was all the stronger for her incapacity to reason out her conviction in a satisfactory manner. Her intellectual experience was limited to a degree; but she had seen success in his face; and she now heard it in his voice when he quoted verses to her, so beautifully that she was delighted to listen whether she followed him or not. Her faith in him was sweetly unreasonable, but it was immensely strong. She was ready and even eager to back him heavily; and there are those who would rather have one brave girl do that on instinct, than win the votes of a hundred clear heads, basing their support upon a logical calculation.

For reasons of her own, however, Naomi decided overnight to take her visitor a little less seriously to his face. She had been too confidential with him concerning station affairs past and present; that she must drop, and at the same time discourage him from opening his heart to her, as he was beginning to do, on the slightest provocation. These resolutions would impose a taboo on nearly all the subjects they had found in common. She quite saw that, and she thought it just as well. Too much sympathy with this young man might be bad for him. Naomi realized this somewhat suddenly in the night, and it kept her awake rather longer than she liked. But she rose next morning fully resolved to eschew conversation of too sympathetic a character, and to encourage her young friend in quotations from the poets instead. Obviously this was quite as great a pleasure to him, while it was a much safer one-or so Naomi thought in her innocence. But then it was a very genuine pleasure to her, too, because the poetry was entirely new to her, and her many-sided young man knew so much and repeated it so charmingly.

It was incredible, indeed, what a number of the poets of all ages he had at his finger-ends, and how justly he rendered their choicest numbers. Their very names were mostly new to Naomi. There was consequently an aboriginal barbarity about many of her comments and criticisms, and more than once the piano-tuner found it impossible to sit still and hear her out. This was notably the case at their second poetical séance, when Naomi had got over her private depression on the one hand, and was full of her new intentions toward the piano-tuner on the other. He would jump out of his chair, and fume up and down the veranda, running his five available fingers through his hair until the black shock stood on end. It was at these moments that Naomi liked him best.

He had been giving her "Tears, idle tears" (because she had "heard of Tennyson," she said) on the Wednesday morning in the veranda facing the station-yard. He had recited the great verses with a force and feeling all his own. Over one of them in particular his voice had quivered with emotion. It was the dear emotion of an æsthetic soul touched to the quick by the sheer beauty of the idea and its words. And Naomi said:

"That's jolly; but you don't call it poetry, do you?"

His eyes dried in an instant. Then they opened as wide as they would go. He was speechless.

"It doesn't rhyme, you know," Naomi explained, cheerfully.

"No," said Engelhardt, gazing at her severely. "It isn't meant to; it's blank verse."

"It's blank *bad* verse, if you ask me," said Naomi Pryse, with a nod that was meant to finish him; but it only lifted him out of his chair.

"Well, upon my word," said the piano-tuner, striding noisily up and down, as Naomi laughed. "Upon my word!"

"Please make me understand," pleaded the girl, with a humility that meant mischief, if he had only been listening; but he was still wrestling with his exasperation. "I can't help being ignorant, you know," she added, as though hurt.

"You can help it-that's just it!" he answered, bitterly. "I've been telling you one of the most beautiful things that Tennyson himself ever wrote, and you say it isn't verse. Verse, forsooth! It's poetry-it's gorgeous poetry!"

"It may be gorgeous, but I don't call it poetry unless it rhymes," said Naomi, stoutly. "Gordon always does."

Gordon, the Australian poet, she was forever throwing at his head, as the equal of any of his English bards. They had already had a heated argument about Gordon. Therefore Engelhardt said merely:

"You're joking, of course?"

"I am doing nothing of the sort."

"Then pray what do you call Shakespeare" —pausing in front of her with his hand in his pocket —"poetry or prose?"

"Prose, of course."

"Because it doesn't rhyme?"

"Exactly."

"And why do you suppose it's chopped up into lines?"

"Oh, *I* don't know-to moisten it perhaps."

"I beg your pardon?"

"To make it less dry."

"Ah! Then it doesn't occur to you that there might be some law which decreed the end of a line after a certain number of beats, or notes-exactly like the end of a bar of music, in fact?"

"Certainly not," said Naomi. There was a touch of indignation in this denial. He shrugged his shoulders and then turned them upon the girl, and stood glowering out upon the yard. Behind his back Naomi went into fits of silent laughter, which luckily she had overcome before he wheeled round suddenly with a face full of eager determination. His heart now appeared set upon convincing her that verse might be blank. And for half an hour he stood beating his left hand in the air, and declaiming, in feet, certain orations of Hamlet, until Mrs. Potter, the cook-laundress, came out of the kitchen to protect her young mistress if necessary. It was not necessary. The broken-armed gentleman was standing over her, shaking his fist and talking at the top of his voice; but Miss Pryse was all smiles and apparent contentment; and, indeed, she behaved much better for awhile, and did her best to understand. But presently she began to complain of the "quotations" (for he was operating on the famous soliloquy), and to profane the whole subject. And the question of blank verse was discussed between them no more.

She could be so good, too, when she liked, so appreciative, so sympathetic, so understanding. But she never liked very long. He had a tendency to run to love-poems, and after listening to five or six with every sign of approval and delight, Naomi would suddenly become flippant at the sixth or seventh. On one occasion, when she had turned him on by her own act aforethought, and been given a taste of several past-masters of the lyric, from Waller to Locker, and including a poem of Browning's which she allowed herself to be made to understand, she inquired of Engelhardt whether he had ever read anything by "a man called Swinton."

"Swinburne," suggested Engelhardt.

"Are you sure?" said Naomi, jealously. "I believe it's Swinton. I'm prepared to bet you that it is!"

"Where have you come across his name?" the piano-tuner said, smiling as he shook his head.

"In the preface to Gordon's poems."

Engelhardt groaned.

"It mentions Swinton-what are you laughing at? All right! I'll get the book and settle it!"

She came back laughing herself.

"Well?" said Engelhardt.

"You know too much! Not that I should accept anything that preface says as conclusive. It has the cheek to say that Gordon was under his influence. You give me something of his, and we'll soon see."

"Something of Swinburne's?"

"Oh, you needn't put on side because you happen to be right according to a preface. I'll write and ask *The Australasian*! Yes, of course I mean something of his."

Engelhardt reflected. "There's a poem called 'A Leave-taking,'" said he, tentatively, at length.

"Then trot it out," said Naomi; and she set herself to listen with so unsympathetic an expression on her pretty face, that he was obliged to look the other way before he could begin. The contrary was usually the case. However, he managed to get under way:

> "Let us go hence, my songs; she will not hear.
> Let us go hence together without fear;
> Keep silence now, for singing-time is over,
> And over all old things and all things dear.
> She loves not you nor me as all we love her.
> Yea, though we sang as angels in her ear,
> She would not hear.

> "Let us rise up and part; she will not know.
> Let us go seaward as the great winds go,
> Full of blown sand and foam; what help is there?
> There is no help, for all these things are so,
> And all the world is bitter as a tear.
> And how these things are, though ye strove to show
> She would not know.

"Let us go home and hence; she will not weep — —"

"Stop a moment," said Naomi, "I'm in a difficulty. I can't go on listening until I know something."

"Until you know what?" said Engelhardt, who did not like being interrupted.

"Who it's all about-who *she* is!" cried Naomi, inquisitively.

"Who-she-is," repeated the piano-tuner, talking aloud to himself.

"Yes, exactly; who *is* she?"

"As if it mattered!" Engelhardt went on in the same aside. "However, who do *you* say she is?"

"I? She may be his grandmother for all I know. I'm asking you."

"I know you are. I was prepared for you to ask me anything else."

"Were you? Then why is she such an obstinate old party, anyway? She won't hear and she won't know. What will she do? Now it seems that you can't even make her cry! 'She will not weep' was where you'd got to. As you seem unable to answer my questions, you'd better go on till she does."

"I'm so likely to go on," said Engelhardt, getting up.

Naomi relented a little.

"Forgive me, Mr. Engelhardt; I've been behaving horribly. I'm sorry I spoke at all, only I did so want to know who she was."

"I don't know myself."

"I was sure you didn't!"

"What's more, I don't care. What *has* it got to do with the merits of the poem?"

"I won't presume to say. I only know that it makes all the difference to my interest in the poem."

"But why?"

"Because I want to know what she was like."

"But surely to goodness," cried Engelhardt, "you can imagine her, can't you? You're meant to fill her in to your own fancy. You pays your money and you takes your choice."

"I get precious little for my money," remarked Naomi, pertinently, "if I have to do the filling in for myself!"

Engelhardt had been striding to and fro. Now he stopped pityingly in front of the chair in which this sweet Philistine was sitting unashamed.

"Do you mean to say that you like to have every little thing told you in black and white?"

"Of course I do. The more the better."

"And absolutely nothing left to your own imagination?"

"Certainly not. The idea!"

He turned away from her with a shrug of his shoulders, and quickened his stride up and down the veranda. He was visibly annoyed. She watched him with eyes full of glee.

"I do love to make you lose your wool!" she informed him in a minute or two, with a sudden attack of candor. "I like you best when you give me up and wash your hands of me!"

This cleared his brow instantaneously, and brought him back to her chair with a smile.

"Why so, Miss Pryse?"

"Must I tell you?"

"Please."

"Then it's because you forget yourself, and me, too, when I rile you; and you're delightful whenever you do that, Mr. Engelhardt."

Naomi regretted her words next moment; but it was too late to unsay them. He went on smiling, it is true, but his smile was no longer naïve and unconsidered; no more were his recitations during the next few hours. His audience did her worst to provoke him out of himself, but she could not manage it. Then she tried the other extreme, and became more enthusiastic than himself over this and that, but he would not be with her; he had retired into the lair of his own self-consciousness, and there was no tempting him out any more. When he did come out of himself, it was neither by his own will nor her management, and the moment was a startling one for them both.

It was late in the afternoon of that same Wednesday. They were sitting, as usual, in the veranda which overlooked not the station-yard but the boundless plains, and they were sitting in silence and wide apart. They had not quarrelled; but Engelhardt had made up his mind to decamp. He had reasoned the whole thing out in a spirit of mere common-sense; yet he was reasoning with himself still, as he sat in the quiet veranda; he thought it probable that he should go on with his reasoning-with the same piece of reasoning-until his dying hour. He looked worried. He was certainly worrying Naomi, and annoying her considerably. She had given up trying to take him out of himself, but she knew that he liked to hear himself saying poetry, and she felt perfectly ready to listen if it would do him any good. Of course she was not herself anxious to hear him. It was entirely for his sake that she put down the book she was reading, and broached the subject at last.

"Have you quite exhausted the poetry that you know by heart, Mr. Engelhardt?"

"Quite, I'm afraid, Miss Pryse; and I'm sure you must be thankful to hear it."

"Now you're fishing," said Naomi, with a smile (not one of her sweetest); "we've quarrelled about all your precious poets, it's true, but that's why I want you to trot out another. I'm dying for another quarrel, don't you see? Out with somebody fresh, and let me have shies at him!"

"But I don't know them all off by heart —I'm not a walking Golden Treasury, you know."

"Think!" commanded Naomi. When she did this there was no disobeying her. He had found out that already.

"Have you ever heard of Rossetti-Dante Gabriel?"

"Kill whose cat?" cried Naomi.

He repeated the poet's name in full. She shook her head. She was smiling now, and kindly, for she had got her way.

"There is one little thing of his-but a beauty-that I once learnt," Engelhardt said, doubtfully. "Mind, I'm not sure that I can remember it, and I won't spoil it if I can't; no more must you spoil it, if I can."

"Is there some sacred association, then?"

He laughed. "No, indeed! There's more of a sacrilegious association, for I once swore that the first song I composed should be a setting for these words."

"Remember, you've got to dedicate it to me! What's the name of the thing?"

"'Three Shadows.'"

"Let's have them, then."

"Very well. But I love it! You must promise not to laugh."

"Begin," she said, sternly, and he began:

> "I looked and saw your eyes
> In the shadow of your hair,
> As the traveller sees the stream
> In the shadow of the wood;
> And I said, 'My faint heart sighs
> Ah me! to linger there,
> To drink deep and to dream
> In that sweet solitude.'"

"Go on," said Naomi, with approval. "I hope you *don't* see all that; but please go on."

He had got thus far with his face raised steadfastly to hers, for he had left his chair and seated himself on the edge of the veranda, at her feet, before beginning. He went on without wincing or lowering his eyes:

> "I looked and saw your heart
> In the shadow of your eyes,
> As a seeker sees the gold
> In the shadow of the stream;
> And I said, 'Ah me! what art
> Should win the immortal prize,
> Whose want must make life cold
> And heaven a hollow dream?'"

"Surely not as bad as all that?" said Naomi, laughing. He had never recited anything so feelingly, so slowly, with such a look in his eyes. There was occasion to laugh, obviously.

"Am I to go on," said Engelhardt, in desperate earnest, "or am I not?"

"Go on, of course! I am most anxious to know what else you saw."

But the temptation to lower the eyes was now hers; his look was so hard to face, his voice was grown so soft.

> "I looked and saw your love
> In the shadow of your heart,
> As a diver sees the pearl
> In the shadow of the sea;
> And I murmured, not above
> My breath, but all apart — —"

Here he stopped. Her eyes were shining. He could not see this, because his own were dim.

"Go on," she said, nodding violently, "do go on!"

"That's all I remember."

"Nonsense! What did you murmur?"

"I forget."

"You do no such thing."

"I've said all I mean to say."

"But not all I mean you to. I *will* have the lot."

And, after all, his were the eyes to fall; but in a moment they had leapt up again to her face with a sudden reckless flash.

"There are only two more lines," he said; "you had much better not know them."

"I must," said she. "What are they?"

> "Ah! you can love, true girl,
> And is your love for me?"

"No, I'm afraid not," said Naomi, at last.

"I thought not."

"Nor for anybody else-nor for anybody else!"

She was leaning over him, and one of her hands had fallen upon his neck-so kindly-so naturally-like a mother's upon her child.

"Then you are not in love with anybody else!" he cried, joyously. "You are not engaged!"

"Yes," she answered, sadly. "I am engaged."

Then Naomi learnt how it feels to quench the fire in joyous eyes, and to wrinkle a hopeful young face with the lines of anguish and despair. She could not bear it. She took the head of untidy hair between her two soft hands, and pressed it down upon the open book on her knees until the haunting eyes looked into hers no more. And as a mother soothes her child, so she stroked him, and patted him, and murmured over him, until he could speak to her calmly.

"Who is he?" whispered Engelhardt, drawing away from her at last, and gazing up into her face with a firm lip. "What is he? Where is he? I want to know everything!"

"Then look over your shoulder, and you will see him for yourself."

A horseman had indeed ridden round the corner of the house, noiselessly in the heavy sand. Monty Gilroy sat frowning at them both from his saddle.

"I'm afraid I have interrupted a very interesting conversation?" said Gilroy, showing his teeth through his beard.

Naomi smiled coolly.

"What if I say that you have, Monty?"

"Then I'm sorry, but it can't be helped," replied the manager, jumping off his horse, and hanging the bridle over a hook on one of the veranda-posts.

"Ah, I thought as much," said Naomi, dryly. She held out her hand, however, as she spoke.

But Gilroy had stopped before setting foot in the veranda. He stood glaring at Engelhardt, who was not looking at him, but at the fading sky-line away beyond the sand and scrub, and with a dazed expression upon his pale, eager face. The piano-tuner had not risen; he had merely turned round where he sat, at the sound of Gilroy's voice.

Now, however, he seemed neither to see nor to heed the manager, though the latter was towering over him, white with mortification.

"Now then, Mr. Piano-tuner, jump up and clear; I've ridden over to see Miss Pryse on urgent business ———"

"Leaving your manners behind you, evidently," observed that young lady, "or I think you would hardly be ordering my visitors out of my veranda *and* my presence!"

"Then will you speak to the fellow?" said Gilroy, sulkily. "He seems deaf, and I haven't ridden in for my own amusement. I tell you it's an important matter, Naomi."

"Mr. Engelhardt!" said Naomi, gently. He turned at once. "Mr. Gilroy," she went on to explain, "has come from the shed to see me about something or other. Will you leave us for a little while?"

"Certainly, Miss Pryse." He rose in sudden confusion. "I —I beg your pardon. I was thinking of something else."

It was only Naomi's pardon that he begged. He had not looked twice at Gilroy; but as he rounded the corner of the building, he glanced sharply over his shoulder. He could not help it. He felt instinctively that a glimpse of their lovers' greeting would do something toward his cure. All that he saw, however, was Naomi with her back to the wall, and her hands laid firmly upon the wicker chair-back where her head had rested a moment before. Across this barrier Gilroy had opened so vehement a fire upon her that Engelhardt thought twice about leaving them alone together. As he hesitated, however, the girl shot him a glance which commanded him to be gone, while it as plainly intimated her perfect ability to take care of herself.

Once out of her sight, the piano-tuner turned a resolute back upon the homestead, determining to get right away from it for the time being-to get away and to think. He did not, however, plunge into the plantation of pines, in which Naomi and he had often wandered during these last few days, that seemed a happy lifetime to him now that he felt they were over. He took the broad, sandy way which led past the stables to the men's hut on the left, and to the stock-yards on the right. Behind the yards the sun was setting, the platform for the pithing of bullocks, and the windlass for raising their carcasses, standing out sharp and black against the flaming sky; and still farther to the right, where there were sheep-yards also, a small yellow cloud rose against the pink like a pillar of sand. Engelhardt knew little enough of station life, but he saw that somebody was yarding-up a mob of sheep for the night. He went on to have a look at the job, which was over, however, before he reached the spot. Three horses were trotting off in the direction of the horse-paddock, while, coming away from the yard, carrying their saddles and bridles, were two of the station hands and the overseer, Tom Chester.

"Hulloa, Engelhardt, still here?" said the latter, cheerily, as they met. "How goes the arm?"

"First-rate, thanks. I'm off to-morrow."

"Yes? Come on back to the homestead, and help me shave and brush up. I've been mustering seventeen miles from the shed. We've run the mob into these yards for the night, and I'm roosting in the barracks."

"So is Mr. Gilroy, I fancy."

"The devil he is! Has he come in from the shed, then?"

"Yes; within the last ten minutes."

Chester looked black.

"You didn't hear what for, I suppose?"

"To speak to Miss Pryse about some important matter; that's all I know."

"I should have thought they'd had enough to say to each other yesterday, to last Gilroy for a bit. I'm mustering, you know; but I heard all about it when I got back to the shed last night. Some of the men came to me in a sort of deputation. They hate Gilroy about as much as I do, and they want him out of that. If he's a sensible man he's come in to chuck up the sponge himself."

Tom Chester flung his saddle and bridle over the rail as they passed the stable, and walked on to the station-yard, and across it to the little white barracks, without another word. Engelhardt followed him into his room and sat down on the bed. He felt that they understood one another. That was what made him say, while Chester was stropping his razor:

"You don't love Gilroy, I imagine."

"No, I don't," replied Tom Chester, after a pause.

"But Miss Pryse does!" Engelhardt exclaimed, bitterly.

The other made a longer pause. He was lathering his chin. "Not she," said Tom, coolly, at length.

"Not! But she's engaged to him, I hear!"

"There's a sort of understanding."

"Only an understanding?"

"Well, she doesn't wear a ring, for one thing."

"I wish you would tell me just how it stands," said Engelhardt, inquisitively. His heart was beating, nevertheless.

"Tell you?" said Tom Chester, looking only into the glass as he flourished his razor. "Why, certainly. I don't wonder at your wanting to know how a fine girl like that could go and engage herself to a God-forsaken image like Gilroy. *I* don't know, mind you. I wasn't here in Mr. Pryse's time; but everyone says he was a good sort, and that the worse thing he ever did was to take on Gilroy, just because he was some sort of relation of his dead wife's. He's second cousin to Miss Pryse, that's what Gilroy is; but he was overseer here when the boss was his own manager, and when he died Gilroy got the management, naturally. Well, and then he got the girl, too-the Lord knows how. She knew that her father thought well of the skunk, and no doubt she herself felt it was the easiest way out of her responsibilities and difficulties. Ay, she was a year or two younger then than she is now, and he got the promise of her; but I'll bet you an even dollar he never gets her to keep."

The piano-tuner had with difficulty sat still upon the bed, as he listened to this seemingly impartial version of the engagement which had numbed his spirit from the moment he heard of it. Tom Chester had spoken with many pauses, filled by the tinkle of his razor against a healthy beard three days old. When he offered to bet the dollar, he was already putting the razor away in its case.

"I won't take you," said Engelhardt. "You don't think she'll marry him, then?" he added, anxiously.

"Tar here on the brisket," remarked Chester, in the shearer's formula, as he dabbed at a cut that he had discovered under his right jaw. "What's that! Marry him? No; of course she won't."

Engelhardt waited while the overseer performed elaborate ablutions and changed his clothes. Then they crossed over together to the front veranda, which was empty; but as they went round to the back the sound of voices came fast enough to their ears. The owner and her manager were still talking in the back veranda, which was now in darkness, and their voices were still raised. It was Tom Chester's smile, however, that helped Engelhardt to grasp the full significance of the words that met their ears. Gilroy was speaking.

"All right, Naomi! You know best, no doubt. You mean to paddle your own canoe, you say, and that's all very well; but if Tom Chester remains on at the shed there'll be a row, I tell you straight."

"Between whom?" Naomi inquired.

"Between Tom Chester and me. I tell you he's stirring up the men against me! You yourself did mischief enough yesterday; but when he came in he made bad worse. It may be an undignified thing to do, for the boss of the shed; but I can't help that, I shall have to fight him."

"Fight whom?" said Chester, in a tone of interest, as he and Engelhardt came upon the scene together.

"You," replied Naomi, promptly. "You have arrived in the nick of time, Mr. Chester. I am sorry to hear that you two don't hit it off together at the shed."

"So that's it, is it?" said Tom Chester, quietly, glancing from the girl to Gilroy, who had not opened his mouth. "And you're prepared to hit it off somewhere else, are you? I'm quite ready. I have been wanting to hit it off with you, Gilroy, ever since I've known you."

His meaning was as plain as an italicised joke. They all waited for the manager's reply.

"Indeed!" said he, at length, out of the kindly dark that hid the color of his face. "So you expect me to answer you before Miss Pryse, do you?"

"On the contrary, I'd far rather you came down to the stables and answered me there. But you might repeat before Miss Pryse whatever it is you were telling her about me behind my back."

"I shall do nothing of the sort."

"Then I must do it for you," said Naomi, firmly.

"Do," said Gilroy. And diving his hands deep into his cross-pockets, he swaggered off the scene with his horse at his heels and his arm through the reins.

"I think I can guess the kind of thing, Miss Pryse," Tom Chester waited to say; "you needn't trouble to tell me, thank you." A moment later he had followed the manager, and the piano-tuner was following Tom; but Naomi Pryse remained where she was. She had not lifted a finger to prevent the fight which, as she saw for herself, was a good deal more imminent than he had imagined who warned her of it five minutes before.

"Will you take off your coat?" said Chester, as he caught up to Gilroy between homestead and stables.

"Is it likely?" queried Gilroy, without looking round.

"That depends whether you're a man. The light's the same for both. There are lanterns in the stables, whether or no. Will you take off your coat when we get there?"

"To you? Manager and overseer? Don't be a fool, Tom."

"I'll show you who's the fool in a brace of shakes," said Tom Chester, following Gilroy with a swelling chest. "I never thought you had much pluck, but, by God, I don't believe you've got the pluck of a louse!"

Gilroy led on his horse without answering.

"Have you got the pluck of a louse?" the overseer sang into his ear. Gilroy was trembling, but he turned as they reached the stable.

"Take off your coat, then," said he, doggedly; "I'll leave mine inside."

Gilroy led his horse into the stable. Instead of taking off his coat, however, Tom Chester stood waiting with his arms akimbo and his eyes upon the open stable-door.

"Aren't you going to take it off?" said an eager yet nervous voice at his side. "Don't you mean to fight him after all?"

It was the piano-tuner, whose desire to see the manager soundly thrashed was at war with his innate dread of anything approaching a violent scene. He could be violent himself when his blood was up, but in his normal state the mere sound of high words made him miserable.

"Hulloa! I didn't see that you were there," remarked Chester, with a glance at the queer little figure beside him. "Lord, yes; I'll fight him if he's game, but I won't believe that till I see it, so we'll let him strip first. The fellow hasn't got the pluck of —— I knew he hadn't! That's just what I should have expected of him!"

Before Engelhardt could realize what was happening, a horse had emerged from the shadow of the stable-door, a man's head and wide-awake had risen behind its ears as they cleared the lintel, and Gilroy, with a smack of his whip on the horse's flank and a cut and a curse at Tom Chester, was disappearing in the dusk at a gallop. Chester had sprung forward, but he was not quick enough. When the cut had fallen short of him, he gathered himself together for one moment, as though to give chase on foot; then stood at ease and watched the rider out of sight.

"Next time, my friend," said he, "you won't get the option of standing up to me. No; by the Lord, I'll take him by the scruff of his dirty neck, and I'll take the very whip he's got in his hand now, and I'll hide him within an inch of his miserable life. That's the way we treat curs in these parts, d'ye see? Come on, Engelhardt. No, we'll stop and see which road he takes when he gets to the gate. I can just see him opening it now. I might have caught him up there if I'd thought. Ah! he's shaking his fist at us; he shall smell mine before he's a day older! And he's taken the township track; he'll come back to the shed as drunk as a fool, and if the men don't dip him in the dam I shall be very much surprised."

"And Miss Pryse is going to marry a creature like that," cried Engelhardt, as they walked back to the house.

"Not she," said Chester, confidently.

"Yet there's a sort of engagement."

"There is; but it would be broken off to-morrow if I were to tell Miss Pryse to-night of the mess he's making of everything out at the shed. The men do what they like with him, and he goes dropping upon the harmless inoffensive ones, and fining them and running their sheep; whereas he daren't have said a word to that fellow Simons, not to save his life. I tell you there'd have been a strike last night if it hadn't been for me. The men appealed to me, and I said what I thought. So his nibs sends me mustering again, about as far off as he can, while he comes in to get Miss Pryse to give me the sack. Of course that's what he's been after. That's the kind of man he is. But here's Miss Pryse herself in the veranda, and we'll drop the subject, d'ye see?"

Naomi herself never mentioned it. Possibly from the veranda she had seen and heard enough to enable her to guess the rest pretty accurately. However that may be, the name of Monty Gilroy never passed her lips, either now in the interval before dinner, or at that meal, during which she conversed very merrily with the two young men who faced one another on either side of her. She insisted on carving for them both, despite the protests of the more talkative of the two. She rattled on to them incessantly-if anything, to Engelhardt more than to the overseer. But there could be no question as to which of these two talked most to her. Engelhardt was even more shy and awkward than at his first meal at Taroomba, when Naomi had not been present. He disappeared immediately after dinner, and Naomi had to content herself with Tom Chester's company for the rest of the evening.

That, however, was very good company at all times, while on the present occasion Miss Pryse had matters for discussion with her overseer which rendered a private interview quite necessary. So Engelhardt was not wanted for at least an hour; but he did not come back at all. When Chester went whistling to the barracks at eleven o'clock he found the piano-tuner lying upon his bed in all his clothes.

"Hulloa, my son, are you sick?" said Tom, entering the room. The risen moon was shining in on all sides of the looking-glass.

"No, I'm well enough, thanks. I felt rather sleepy."

"You don't sound sleepy! Miss Pryse was wondering what could be the matter. She told me to tell you that you might at least have said good-night to her."

"I'll go and say it now," cried Engelhardt, bounding from the bed.

"Ah, now you're too late, you see," said Chester, laughing a little unkindly as he barred the doorway. "You didn't suppose I'd come away before I was obliged, did you? Come into my room, and I'll tell you a bit of news."

The two rooms were close together; they were divided by the narrow passage that led without step or outer door into the station-yard. It was a lined, set face that the candle lighted up when Tom Chester put a match to it; but that was only the piano-tuner's face, and Tom stood looking at his own, and the smile in the glass was peculiar and characteristic. It was not conceited; it was merely confident. The overseer of Taroomba was one of the smartest, most resolute, and confident young men in the back-blocks of New South Wales.

"The news," he said, turning away from the glass and undoing his necktie, "may surprise you, but I've expected it all along. Didn't I tell you before dinner that Miss Pryse would be breaking off her rotten engagement one of these days! Well, then, she's been and done it this very afternoon."

"Thank God!" cried Engelhardt.

"Amen," echoed Chester, with a laugh. He had paid no attention to the piano-tuner's tone and look. He was winding a keyless watch.

"And is he going on here as manager?" Engelhardt asked, presently.

"No, that's the point. Naomi seems to have told him pretty straight that she could get along without him, and on second thoughts he's taken her at her word. She got a note an hour ago to say she would never see him again. He'd sent a chap with it all the way from the township."

"Do you mean to say he isn't coming back?"

"That's the idea. You bet he had it when he shook his fist at us as he opened that gate. He was shaking his fist at the station and all hands on the place, particularly including the boss. She's to send his things and his check after him to the township, where they'll find him drunk, you mark my words. Good riddance to the cur! Of course he was going to marry her for her money; but she's tumbled to him in time, and a miss is as good as a mile any day in the week."

He finished speaking and winding his watch at the same moment. It was a gold watch, and he set it down carelessly on the dressing-table, where the candle shone upon the monogram on its back.

"He has nothing of his own?" queried Engelhardt, with jealous eyes upon the watch.

"Not a red cent," said Tom Chester, contemptuously. "He lived upon the old boss, and of course he meant to live upon his daughter after him. He was as poor as a church-mouse."

So indeed was the piano-tuner. He did not say as much, however, though the words had risen to his lips. He said no more until the overseer was actually in bed. Then a flash of inspiration caused him to ask, abruptly,

"Are you anything to do with Chester, Wilkinson, & Killick, the big wool-people down in Melbourne?"

"To do with 'em?" repeated Tom, with a smile. "Well, yes; at least, I'm Chester's son."

"I've heard that you own more Riverina stations than any other firm or company?"

"Yes; this is about the only one around here that we haven't got a finger in. That's why I came here, by the way, for a bit of experience."

"Then *you* don't want to marry her for her money. You'll have more than she ever will! Isn't that so?"

"What the blue blazes do you mean, Engelhardt?"

Chester had sat bolt upright in his bed. The piano-tuner was still on the foot of it, and all the fire in his being had gone into his eyes.

"Mean?" he cried. "Who cares what *I* mean! I tell you that she thinks more of you than ever she thought of Gilroy. She has said so to me in as many words. I tell you to go in and win!"

He was holding out his left hand.

"I intend to," said Tom Chester, taking it good-naturedly enough. "That's exactly my game, and everybody must know it, for I've been playing it fair and square in the light of day. I may lose; but I hope to win. Good-night, Engelhardt. Shall I look you up in the morning? We make a very early start, mind.”

“Then you needn’t trouble. But I do wish you luck!”

“Thanks, my boy. I wish myself luck, too.”

Chapter X
Missing

Naomi's room opened upon the back veranda, and in quitting it next morning it was not unnatural that she should pause to contemplate the place where so many things had lately happened, which, she felt, must leave their mark upon her life for good or evil. It was here that she might have seen the danger of unreserved sympathy with so sensitive and enthusiastic a nature as that of the piano-tuner. Indeed, she had seen it, and made suitable resolutions on the spot; but these she had broken, and wilfully shut her eyes to that danger until the young man had told her, quite plainly enough, that he loved her. Nay, she had made him tell her that, and until he did so she had purposely withheld from him the knowledge that she was already engaged. That was the cruel part of it, the part of which she was now most sincerely ashamed. Yet some power stronger than her own will had compelled her to act as she had done, and certainly she had determined beforehand to take the first opportunity of severing all ties still existing between herself and Monty Gilroy. And it was here that she had actually broken off her engagement with him within a few minutes of her announcement of it to Hermann Engelhardt. Still she was by no means pleased with herself as she stepped out into the flood of sunshine that filled the back veranda of a morning, and saw everything as it had been overnight, even to the book she had laid aside open when Gilroy rode up. It was lying shut in the self-same spot. This little difference was the only one.

She went round to the front of the house, looking out rather nervously for Engelhardt on the way. Generally he met her in the front veranda, but this morning he was not there. Mrs. Potter was laying the breakfast-table, but she had not seen him either. She looked searchingly at her young mistress as she answered her question.

"Are you quite well, miss?" she asked at length, without preamble. "You look as though you hadn't slep' a wink all night."

"No more I have," said Naomi, calmly.

"Good gracious, miss!" cried Mrs. Potter, clapping down the plate-basket with a jingle. "Whatever has been the matter? That nasty toothache, I'll be bound!"

"No, it wasn't a tooth this time. I may as well tell you what it was," added Naomi, "since you're bound to know sooner or later. Well, then, Mr. Gilroy has left the station for good, and I am not ever going to marry him. That's all."

"And I'm thankful — —"

Mrs. Potter checked herself with a gulp.

"So am I," said her mistress, dryly; "but it's a little exciting, and I let it keep me awake. You are to pack up his boxes, please, so that I may send them to the township in the spring-cart. But now make haste with the tea, for I need a cup badly, and I'll go and sing out to Mr. Engelhardt. Did you call him, by the way?"

"Yes, miss, I called him as usual."

Naomi left the breakfast-room, and was absent some three or four minutes. She came back looking somewhat scared.

"I've called him, too," she said, "at the top of my voice. But there's no making him hear anything. I've hammered at his door and at his window, too; both are shut, as if he wasn't up. I do wish that you would come and see whether he is."

A moment later Mrs. Potter was crossing the sandy yard, with Naomi almost treading on her ample skirts until they reached the barracks, which the elderly woman entered alone. No sooner, however, had she opened Engelhardt's door than she called her mistress to the spot. The room was empty. It was clear at a glance that the bed had not been slept in.

"If he hasn't gone away and left us without a word!" cried Mrs. Potter, indignantly.

"I am looking for his valise," said Naomi. "Where has he generally kept it?"

"Just there, underneath the dressing-table. He has taken it with him. There's nothing belonging to him in the room!"

"Except that half-crown under the tumbler, which is evidently meant for you. No, Mrs. Potter, I'm afraid you're right. The half-crown settles it. I should take it if I were you. And now I'll have my breakfast, if you please."

"But, miss, I can't understand — —"

"No more can I. Make the tea at once, please. A little toast is all that I require with it."

And Naomi went slowly back toward the house, but stopped half way, with bent head and attentive eyes, and then went slower still. She had discovered in the sand the print of feet in stockings only. These tracks led up to the veranda, where they ended opposite the sitting-room door, which Naomi pushed open next moment. The room wore its ordinary appearance, but the pile of music which Engelhardt had brought with him for sale had been removed from the top of the piano to the music-stool; and lying conspicuously across the music, Naomi was mortified to find a silk handkerchief of her own, which the piano-tuner had worn all the week as a sling for his arm. She caught it up with an angry exclamation, and in doing so caught sight of some obviously left-handed writing on the topmost song of the pile. She stooped and read:

"These songs for Miss Pryse, with deep gratitude for all her kindness to Hermann Engelhardt."

It was a pale, set face that Mrs. Potter found awaiting her in the breakfast-room when the toast was ready and the tea made. Very little of the toast was eaten, and Mrs. Potter saw no more of her young mistress until the mid-day meal, to which Naomi sat down in her riding-habit.

"Just wait, Mrs. Potter," said she, hastily helping herself to a chop. "Take a chair yourself. I want to speak to you."

"Very good, miss," said the old lady, sitting down.

"I want to know when you last set eyes on Sam Rowntree."

"Let me see, miss. Oh, yes, I remember; it was about this time yesterday. He came to the kitchen, and told me he was going to run up a fresh mob of killing-sheep out of Top Scrubby, and how much meat could I do with? I said half a sheep, at the outside, and that was the last I saw of him."

"He never came near you last night?"

"That he didn't, miss. I was looking out for him. I wanted — —"

"You didn't see him in the distance, or hear him whistling?"

"No, indeed I didn't."

"Well, he seems to have vanished into space," said Naomi, pushing away her plate and pouring out a cup of tea.

"It's too bad," said Mrs. Potter, with sympathy and indignation in equal parts. "I can't think what he means-to go and leave us alone like this."

"I can't think what Mr. Chester meant by not telling me that he was gone," remarked Naomi, hotly.

"I 'xpect he knew nothing about it, miss. He went off before daylight, him and the two men that come in with the sheep they was to take on to the shed."

"How can you know that?" inquired Naomi, with a touch of irritation. Her tea was very hot, and she was evidently in a desperate hurry.

"Because Mr. Chester asked me to put his breakfast ready for him overnight; and I did, too, and when I got up at six he'd had it and gone long ago. The teapot was cold. The men had gone, too, for I gave 'em their suppers last night, and they asked for a snack to take before their early start this morning. They must all have got away by five. They wouldn't hardly try to disturb Sam so early as all that; so they weren't to know he wasn't there."

"Well, he wasn't," said Naomi, "and it's disgraceful, that's what it is! Here we are without a man on the place, and there are nearly a hundred at the shed! I have had to catch a horse, and saddle it for myself." As she spoke Naomi made a last gulp at her hot tea, and then jumped up from the table.

"You are going to the shed, miss?"

"No; to the township."

"Ah, that's where you'll find him!"

"I hope I may," said Naomi, softly, and her eyes were far away. She was in the veranda, buttoning her gloves.

"I meant Sam Rowntree, miss."

Naomi blushed.

"I meant Mr. Engelhardt," said she, stoutly. "They are probably both there; but I have no doubt at all about Mr. Engelhardt. I am going to fetch the mail, but I hope I shall see that young gentleman, too, so that I may have an opportunity of telling him what I think of him."

"I should, miss, I should that!" cried Mrs. Potter, with virtuous wrath. "I should give him a piece of my mind about his way of treating them that's good and kind to him. I'm sure, miss, the notice you took of that young man ———"

"Come, I don't think he's treated *you* so badly," interrupted Naomi, tartly. "Moreover, I am quite sure that he must have had some reason for going off so suddenly. I am curious to know what it was, and also what he expects me to do with his horse. If he had waited till this morning I would have sent him in with the buggy, and saved him a good old tramp. However, you don't mind being left in charge for an hour or so-eh, Mrs. Potter? No one ever troubles the homestead during shearing, you know."

"Oh, I shall be all right, miss, thank you," Mrs. Potter said, cheerfully; and she followed Naomi out into the yard, and watched her, in the distance, drag a box out of the saddle-room, mount from it, and set off at a canter toward the horse-paddock gate.

But Naomi did not canter all the way. She performed the greater part of her ride at a quiet amble, leaning forward in her saddle most of the time, and deciding what she should say to the piano-tuner, while she searched the ground narrowly for his tracks. She had the eagle eye for the trail of man or beast, which is the natural inheritance of all children of the bush. Before saddling the night-horse, she had made it her business to discover every print of a stocking sole that had been left about the premises during the night; and there were so many that she had now a pretty definite idea of the movements of her visitor prior to his final departure from the station. He had spent some time in aimless wandering about the moonlit yard. Then he had stood outside the kitchen, just where she had left him standing on the night of his arrival; and afterward had crossed the fence, just where they had crossed it together, and steered the very same course through the pines which she had led him that first evening. Still in his stockings, carrying his boots in his one hand and his valise under that arm (for she came to a place where he had dropped one boot, and, in picking it up, the valise also), he had worked round to the back veranda, and sat long on the edge, with his two feet in the soft sand, staring out over the scrub-covered, moonlit plain, just as he had sat staring many a time in broad daylight. Of all this Naomi was as certain as though she had seen it, because it was child's play to her to follow up the trail of his stockinged feet and to sort them out from all other tracks. But it ought to have been almost as easy to trace him in his boots on the well-beaten road to the township, and it was not.

The girl grew uncomfortable as she rode on and on without ever striking the trail; and the cutting sentences which she had prepared for the piano-tuner escaped her mind long before she reached the township, and found, as she now expected, that nobody answering to his description had been seen in the vicinity.

Naomi was not the one to waste time in a superfluity of inquiries. She saw in a moment that Engelhardt had not been near the place, and a similar fact was even more easily ascertained in the matter of Sam Rowntree. The township people knew him well. His blue fly-veil had not enlivened their hotel verandas for a whole week. So Naomi received her mail-bag and rode off without dismounting. A glimpse which she had caught of a red beard, at the other side of the broad sandy road, and the sound of a well-known voice shouting thickly, added to her haste. And on this journey she never once drew rein until her horse cantered into the long and sharp-cut shadows of the Taroomba stables.

As Naomi dismounted, Mrs. Potter emerged from the homestead veranda. The good woman had grown not a little nervous in her loneliness. Her looks as she came up were in striking contrast to those of her mistress. The one was visibly relieved; the other had come back ten times more anxious than she had gone away.

"No one been near you, Mrs. Potter?"

"Not a soul, miss. Oh, but it's good to see you back! I thought the afternoon was never coming to an end."

"They are neither of them at the township," said Naomi, with a miserable sigh.

"Nor have they been there at all-neither Mr. Engelhardt nor Sam Rowntree!"

Mrs. Potter cudgelled her poor brains for some-for any-kind of explanation.

"Sam did tell me" —she had begun, when she was promptly shut up.

"Who cares about Sam?" cried Naomi. "He's a good bushman; he can take care of himself. Besides, wherever he is, Sam isn't bushed. But anything may have happened to Mr. Engelhardt!"

"What do you think has happened?" the old lady asked, inanely.

"How am I to know?" was the wild answer. "I have nothing to go on. I know no more than you do."

Yet she stood thinking hard, with her horse still bridled and the reins between her fingers. She had taken off the saddle. Suddenly she slipped the reins over a hook and disappeared into the saddle-room. And in a few moments she was back, with a blanched face, and in her arms a packed valise.

"Is this Mr. Engelhardt's?"

Mrs. Potter took one look at it.

"It is," she said. "Yes, it is his!"

"Take it, then," said Naomi, mastering her voice with difficulty, "while I hunt up his saddle and bridle. If they are gone, all the better. Then I shall know he has his horse; and with a horse nothing much can happen to one."

She disappeared again, and was gone a little longer; but this time she came back desperately self-possessed.

"I have found his saddle. His bridle is not there at all. I know it's his saddle, because it's a pretty good one, and all our decent saddles are in use; besides, they all have the station brand upon them. This one has no brand at all. It must be Mr. Engelhardt's; and now I know exactly what he has done. Shall I tell you?"

Mrs. Potter clasped her hands.

"He has taken his bridle," said Naomi, still in a deadly calm, "and he has set out to catch his horse. How he could do such a thing I can't conceive! He knows the run of our horse-paddock no more than you do. He has failed to find his horse, tried to come back, and got over the fence into Top Scrubby. You don't know what that means! Top Scrubby's the worst paddock we have. It's half-full of mallee, it's six miles whichever way you take it, and the only drop of water in it is the tank at the township corner. Or he may be in the horse-paddock all the time. People who don't know the bush may walk round and round in a single square mile all day long, and until they drop. But it's no good our talking here; wherever he is, I mean to find him."

As she spoke she caught her saddle from the rail across which she had placed it, and was for flinging it on to her horse again, when Mrs. Potter interposed. The girl was trembling with excitement. The sun was fast sinking into the sand and scrub away west. In half an hour it would be dark.

"And no moon till ten or eleven," said Mrs. Potter, with sudden foresight and firmness. "You mustn't think of it, miss; you mustn't, indeed!"

"How can you say that? Why should you stop me? Do you mean me to leave the poor fellow to perish for want of water?"

"My dear, you could do no good in the dark," said Mrs. Potter, speaking as she had not spoken to Naomi since the latter was a little girl. "Besides, neither you nor the horse is fit for anything more until you've both had something to eat and drink."

"It's true!"

Naomi said this in helpless tones and with hopeless looks. As she spoke, however, her eyes fastened themselves upon the crimson ball just clear of the horizon, and all at once they filled with tears. Hardly conscious of what she did or said, she lifted up her arms and her voice to the sunset.

"Oh, my poor fellow! My poor boy! If only I knew where you were-if only I could see you now!"

Chapter XI
Lost in the Bush

Had Naomi seen him then she would have found some difficulty in recognizing Hermann Engelhardt, the little piano-tuner whom already she seemed to have known all her life. Yet she had made a singularly shrewd guess at his whereabouts. Top Scrubby held him fast enough. And when Naomi stretched her arms toward the sunset, it is a strange fact that she also stretched them toward the lost young man, who was lying between it and her, not three miles from the spot on which she stood.

Within a mile of him ran the horse-paddock fence, which he had crossed by mistake at three o'clock that morning. He had never seen it again. All day he had wandered without striking track, or fence, or water. Once indeed his heart had danced at the sudden revelation of footprints under his very nose. They were crisp and clean and obviously recent. All at once they took a fatally familiar appearance. Slowly he lifted his right foot and compared the mark of it with the marks he had discovered. They were identical. To put the matter beyond a doubt he got both his feet into a couple of the old footprints. They fitted like pipes in a case. And then he knew that he was walking in circles, after the manner of lost men, and that he stood precisely where he had been three hours before.

That was a bitter moment. There were others and worse before sundown. The worst of all was about the time when Naomi flung out her arms and cried aloud in her trouble.

His staggering steps had brought him at last, near sundown, within sight of a ridge of pines which he seemed to know. The nearer he came to them the surer did he become that they were the station pines themselves. Footsore and faint and parched as he was, he plucked up all his remaining strength to reach those pines alive. If he were to drop down now it would be shameful, and he deserved to die. So he did not drop until he gained the ridge, and found the pines merely the outer ranks of a regular phalanx of mallee scrub. There was no mallee among the station pines. Nor would it have been possible to get so near to the homestead without squeezing through the wires of two fences at least. He had made a hideous and yet a fatuous mistake, and, when he realized it, he flung himself on his face in the shade of a hop-bush and burst into tears. To think that he must perish miserably after all, when, not five minutes since, he had felt the bottle-neck of the water-bag against his teeth-the smell of the wet canvas in his nostrils-the shrinking and lightening of the bag between his palms as the deep draught of cold water brought his dead throat to life.

It was all over now. He turned his face to the sand, and waited sullenly for the end. And presently a crow flew down from a pine, and hopped nearer and nearer to the prostrate body, with many a cautious pause, its wise black head now on one side, now on the other. Was it a dead body or a man asleep? There would have been no immediate knowing had not the crow been advancing between the setting sun and the man. Its shadow was a yard long when it came between Engelhardt's eyes, which were wide open, and the patch of sand that was warm with his breath. An instant later the crow was away with a hoarse scream, and Engelhardt was sitting up with a still hoarser oath upon his lips; indeed, he was inarticulate even to his own ears; but he found himself shaking his only fist at the crow, now a mere smut upon the evening sky, and next moment he was tottering to his feet.

He could hardly stand. His eyes were burning, his tongue swollen, his lips cracking like earth in a drought. He was aching, too, from head to foot, but he was not yet food for the crows. He set his teeth, and shook his head once or twice. Not yet-not yet.

The setting sun made a lane of light through the pines and mallee. The piano-tuner looked right and left along this lane, wondering which way to turn. He had no prejudice in the matter. All day he had been making calculations, and all day his calculations had been working out wrong. Like the struggles of a fly in a spider's web, each new effort left him more hopelessly entangled than the last. So now, without thinking, for thought was of no avail, he turned his face to the sunset, and, after half an hour's painful stumbling, was a mile farther from the station, and a mile deeper in the maze of Top Scrubby.

Night had fallen now, and the air was cool and sweet. This slightly refreshed him, and the continual chewing of leaves also did him some little good, as indeed it had done all day. But he was becoming troubled with a growing giddiness in addition to his other sufferings, and he well knew that the sands of his endurance were almost run. When the stars came out he once more altered his course, taking a new line by the Southern Cross; but it could not be for long, he was losing strength with every step. About this time it occurred to him to cut a branch for a staff, but when he took out his knife he was too weak to open the blade. A fatal lassitude was creeping over him. He could no longer think or even worry. Nothing mattered any more! Naomi-his mother-the plans and aspirations of his own life-they were all one to him now, and of little account even in the bulk. It had not been so a few hours earlier, but body and mind were failing together, and with no more hope there was but little more regret. His head and his heart grew light together, and when at last he determined to sit down and be done with it all, his greatest care was the choice of a soft and sandy place. It was as though he had been going to lie down for the night instead of for all time. And yet it was this, the mere fad of a wandering mind, that saved him; for before he had found what he wanted, suddenly-as by a miracle-he saw a light.

In a flash the man was alive and electrified. All the nerves in his body tightened like harp-strings, and the breath of life swept over them, leaving his heart singing of Naomi and his mother and the deeds to be done in this world. And the thrill remained; for the light was no phantom of a rocking brain, but a glorious reality that showed brighter and lighter every moment.

Yet it was a very long way off. He might never reach it at all. But he rushed on with never a look right or left, or up or down, as if his one chance of life lay in keeping his grip of that light steadfast and unrelaxed. His headlong course brought him twice to his knees with a thud that shook him to the very marrow. Once he ran his face into a tangle of small branches, and felt a hot stream flowing over his lips and chin; he sucked at it as it leapt his lips, and reeled on, thanking heaven that he could still see out of his eyes. The light had grown into a camp-fire, and he could hear men's voices around it. Their faces he could not see-only the leaping, crackling fire. He tried to coo-ee, but no sound would come. The thought crossed him that even now, within sight and ear-shot of his fellow-men, he might drop for good. His heart kept throbbing against his ribs like an egg boiling in a pan, and his every breath was as a man's last gasp. He passed some horses tethered among the trees. Then before the fire there stood a stout figure with shaded eyes and pistols in his belt; another joined him; then a third, with a rifle; and the three loomed larger with every stride, until Engelhardt fell sprawling and panting in their midst, his hat gone, his long hair matted upon his forehead, and the white face beneath all streaming with sweat and blood.

"By God, he's dying!" said one of the men, flinging away his fire-arm. "Yank us the water-bag, mate, and give the cuss a chance."

Engelhardt looked up, and saw one of his two enemies, the swagmen, reaching out his hand for the bag. It was the smaller and quieter of the pair-the man with the weather-beaten face and the twinkling eye-and as Engelhardt looked further he saw none other than Simons, the discharged shearer, handing the dripping bag across. But a third hand stretched over and snatched it away with a bellowing curse.

"What a blessed soft pair you are! Can't you see who 'e is? It's 'is bloomin' little nibs with the broke arm, and not a damned drop does he get from me!"

"Come on, Bill," said the other tramp. "Why not?"

"He knows why not," said Bill, who, of course, was the stout scoundrel with the squint. "Don't you, sonny?" And he kicked Engelhardt in the side with his flat foot.

"Easy, mate, easy. The beggar's dying!"

"All the better! If he don't look slippy about it I'll take an' slit his throat for him!"

"Well, give him a drop o' water first."

"Ay, give 'im a drink, whether or no," put in Simons. "No tortures, mate! The plain thing's good enough for me."

"And me, too!"

"Why, Bo's'n," cried Bill, "you've got no more spunk than a blessed old ewe! You sailors and shearers are plucky fine chaps to go mates with in a job like ours! You wouldn't have done for poor old Tigerskin!"

"To hell with Tigerskin," said Simons, savagely. "We've heard more than enough of him. Give the beggar a drink, or, by cripes, I'm off it!"

"All right, boys, all right. You needn't get so scotty about it, matey. But he sha'n't drink more than's good for 'im, and he sha'n't drink much at a time, or 'e'll burst 'is skin!"

As he spoke Bill uncorked the water-bag, hollowed a filthy palm, flooded it, and held it out to the piano-tuner, who all this time had been sitting still and listening without a word.

"Drink out o' my hand," said he, "or not at all."

But Engelhardt could only stare at the great hairy paw thrust under his nose. It had no little finger. He was trying to remember what this meant.

"Drink out o' that, you swine," thundered Bill, "and be damned to you!"

Human nature could endure no more. Instead of drinking, Engelhardt knocked the man's hand up, and made a sudden grab at the water-bag. He got it, too, and had swallowed a mouthful before it was plucked away from him. The oaths came pouring out of Bill's mouth like sheep racing through a gate. But the piano-tuner had tasted what was more to him than blood, and he made a second dash at the bag, which resulted in a quantity of water being spilled; so without struggling any more, he fell upon his face with his lips to the wet sand.

"Let the joker suck," said Bill; "I'll back the sand!"

But Engelhardt rolled over on his left side and moved no more.

Simons knelt over him.

"He's a stiff 'un, mates. My blessed oath he is! That's number two, an' both on 'em yours, Bill."

Bill laughed.

"That'll be all right," said he. "Where's my pipe got to? I'm weakenin' for a smoke."

Chapter XII
Fallen Among Thieves

There was life in Engelhardt yet, though for some time he lay as good as dead. The thing that revived him was the name of Naomi Pryse on the lips of the late ringer of the Taroomba shed. The piano-tuner listened for more without daring to open his eyes or to move a muscle. And more came with a horrifying flow of foul words.

"She had the lip to sack me! But I'll be even with her before the night's out. Yes, by cripes, by sunrise she'll wish she'd never been born!"

"It's not the girl we're after," said Bill's voice, with a pause and a spit. "It's the silver." And Engelhardt could hear him puffing at his pipe.

"It's gold and silver. She's the gold."

"I didn't dislike her," said the sailor-man. "I'd leave her be."

"She didn't sack you from the shed. Twelve pound a week it meant, with that image over the board!"

"Bo's'n'd let the whole thing be, I do believe," said Bill, "if we give 'im 'alf a chance."

"Not me," said Bo's'n. "I'll stick to my messmates. But we've stiffened two people already. It's two too many."

"What about your skipper down at Sandridge?"

"Well, I reckon he's a stiff 'un, too."

"Then none o' your skite, mate," said Bill, knocking out a clay pipe against his heel. "Look ye here, lads; it's a blessed Providence that's raked us together, us three. Here's me, straight out o' quod, coming back like a bird to the place where there's a good thing on. Here's Bo's'n, he's bashed in his skipper's skull and cut and run for it. We meet and we pal on. The likeliest pair in the Colony! And here's old Simons, knocked cock-eye by this 'ere gal, and swearing revenge by all that's bloody. He has a couple of horses, too-just the very thing we wanted-so he's our man. Is he on? He is. Do we join hands an' cuss an' swear to see each other through? We do-all three. Don't we go to the township for a few little necessaries an' have a drink on the whole thing? We do. Stop a bit! Doesn't a chap and a horse come our way, first shot off? Don't we want another horse, an' take it, too, ay and cook that chap's hash in fit an' proper style? Of course we do. Then what's the good o' talking? Tigerskin used to say, 'We'll swing together, matey, or by God we'll drive together in a coach-and-four with yeller panels and half-a-dozen beggars in gold lace and powdered wigs.' So that's what I say to you. There's that silver. We'll have it and clear out with it at any blessed price. We've let out some blood already. A four-hundred-gallon tankful more or less can make no difference now. We can only swing once. So drink up, boys, and make your rotten lives happy while you have 'em. There's only one thing to settle: whether do we start at eleven, or twelve, or one in the morning?"

Engelhardt heard a pannikin passed round and sucked at by all three. Then a match was struck and a pipe lit. His veins were frozen; he was past a tremor.

"Eleven's too early," said Simons; "it's getting on for ten already. I'm for a spell before we start; there's nothing like a spell to steady your nerve."

"I'd make it eight bells-if not seven," argued the Bo's'n. "The moon'll be up directly. The lower she is when we start, the better for us. You said the station lay due east, didn't you, Bill? Then it'll be easy steering with a low moon."

The other two laughed.

"These 'ere sailors," said Bill, "they're a blessed treat. Always in such an almighty funk of getting bushed. I've known dozens, and they're all alike."

"There's no fun in it," said the Bo's'n. "Look at this poor devil."

Engelhardt held his breath.

"I suppose he *is* corpsed?" said Bill.

"Dead as junk."

"Well, he's saved us the trouble. I'd have stuck the beggar as soon as I'd stick a sheep. There's only one more point, lads. Do we knock up her ladyship, and make her let us into the store — —"

"Lug her out by her hair," suggested Simons. "I'll do that part."

"Or do we smash into it for ourselves? That's the game Tigerskin an' me tried, ten years ago. It wasn't good enough. You know how it panned out. Still, we ain't got old Pryse to reckon with now. He was a terror, he was! So what do you say, boys? Show hands for sticking-up —and now for breaking in. Then that settles it."

Engelhardt never knew which way it was settled.

"The she-devil!" said Simons. "The little snake! I can see her now, when she come along the board and sang out for the tar-boy all on her own account. That little deader, there, he was with her. By cripes, if she isn't dead herself by morning she'll wish she was! I wonder how she'll look to-night? Not that way, by cripes, that's one thing sure! You leave her to me, mates! I shall enjoy that part. She sha'n't die, because that's what she'd like best; but she shall apologize to me under my own conditions-you wait and see what they are. They'll make you smile. The little devil! Twelve pound a week! By cripes, but I'll make her wish she was as dead as her friend here. I'll teach her — —"

"Stiffen me purple," roared Bill, "if the joker's not alive after all!"

The rogues were sitting round their fire in a triangle, Simons with his back to the supposed corpse; when he looked over his shoulder, there was his dead man glaring at him with eyes like blots of ink on blood-stained paper.

Engelhardt, in fact, had been physically unable to lie still any longer and hear Naomi so foully threatened and abused. But the moment he sat up he saw his folly, and tried, quick as thought, to balance it by gaping repeatedly in Simons's face.

"I beg your pardon, I'm sure," said he, in the civilest manner. "I'd been asleep, and couldn't think where I was. I assure you I hadn't the least intention of interrupting you."

His voice was still terribly husky. Bill seized the water-bag and stuck it ostentatiously between his knees. Simons only scowled.

"Please go on with what you were saying," said Engelhardt, crawling to the fire and sitting down between these two worthies. "All I ask is a drink and a crust. I've been out all day without bite or sup. Yes, and all last night as well! That's all I ask. I am dead tired. I'd sleep like a stone."

No one spoke, but presently, without a word, Bill took a pannikin, filled it from the water-bag, and sullenly handed it to the piano-tuner. Then he knifed a great wedge from a damper and tossed it across. Engelhardt could scarcely believe his eyes, so silently, so unexpectedly was it done. He thanked the fellow with unnecessary warmth, but no sort of notice was taken of his remarks. He was half afraid to touch without express permission the water which he needed so sorely. He even hesitated, pannikin in hand, as he looked from one man to the other; but the villanous trio merely stared at him with fixed eyeballs, and at last he raised it to his lips and swallowed a pint at one draught.

Even the mouthful he had fought for earlier in the evening-even that drop had sent a fresh stream of vitality swimming through his veins. But this generous draught made a new man of him in ten seconds. He wanted more, it is true; but the need was now a mere desire; and then there was the damper under his eyes. He never knew how hungry he was until he had quenched his thirst and started to eat. Until he had finished the slice of damper, he took no more heed of his companions than a dog with a bone. Bill threw him a second wedge, and this also he devoured without looking up. But his great thirst had never been properly slaked, and the treatment he was now receiving emboldened him to hold out the pannikin for more water. Even this was granted him, but still without a word. Since he had arisen and joined them by the fire, not one of the men had addressed a single remark to him, and his own timid expressions of thanks and attempts at affability had been received all alike in impenetrable silence. Nor were the ruffians talking among themselves. They just sat round the fire, their rough faces reddened by the glow, their weapons scintillating in the light, and stared fixedly at the little man who had stumbled among them. Their steady taciturnity soon became as bad to bear as the conversation he had overheard while feigning insensibility. There was a kind of sinister contemplation in their looks which was vague, intangible, terrifying. Then their vile plot ringing in his ears, with dark allusions to a crime already committed, made the piano-tuner's position sickening, intolerable. He spoke again, and again received no answer. He announced that he was extremely grateful to them for saving his life, but that he must now push on to the township. They said nothing to this. He wished them good-night; they said nothing to that. Then he got to his feet, and found himself on the ground again quicker than he had risen. Bill had grabbed him by the ankle, still without a syllable. When Engelhardt looked at him, however, the heavy face and squinting eyes met him with a series of grimaces, so grotesque, so obscene, that he was driven to bury his face in his one free hand, and patiently to await his captors' will. He heard the Bo's'n chuckling; but for hours, as it seemed to him, that was all.

"Who *is* the joker?" said Bill, at last. "What does he do for his rations?"

"They say as 'e tunes pianners," said Simons.

"Then he don't hang out on Taroomba?"

"No; 'e only come the other day, an' goes an' breaks his arm off a buck-jumper. So they were saying at the shed."

"Well, he enjoyed his supper, didn't he? It's good to see 'em enjoying theirselves when their time is near. Boys, you was right; it would have been a sin to send 'im to 'ell with an empty belly an' a sandy throat. If ever I come to swing, I'll swing with a warm meal in my innards, my oath!"

Engelhardt held up his head.

"So you mean to kill me, do you?" said he, very calmly, but with a kind of scornful indignation. Bill gave him a horrible leer, but no answer.

"I suppose there's nothink else for it," said Simons, half-regretfully; "though mark you, mates, I'm none so keen on the kind o' game."

"No more ain't I," cried the Bo's'n, with vigor. "I'd give the cove a chance, Bill."

"How?" said Bill.

"I'd lash the beggar to a tree and leave him to snuff out for hisself."

Engelhardt laughed aloud in mock gratitude.

"Oh, I ain't partickler as to ways," said Bill. "One way's as good as another for me. There's no bloomin' 'urry, any'ow. The moon ain't up yet, and before we go this beggar's got to tell us things. He heard what we was saying, mates. I seen it in his eye. Didn't you, you swine?"

Engelhardt took no kind of notice.

"Didn't you-you son of a mangy bandicoot?"

Still Engelhardt would have held his tongue; but Bill started kicking him on one side, and Simons on the other; and the pain evoked an answer in a note of shrill defiance.

"I did!" he cried. "I heard every word."

"We're after that silver."

"I know you are."

"You've seen it?"

"I have."

"Tell us all about it."

"Not I!"

For this he got a kick on each side.

"Is it in the store yet?"

No answer.

"Is the chest easy to find?"

No answer.

"Is it covered up?"

"Or underground?"

"Or made to look like something else?"

Each man contributed a question; none elicited a word; no more did their boots; it was no use kicking him.

There was a long pause. Then Bill said:

"You've lost your hat. You need another. Here you are."

He had blundered to his feet, stepped aside out of the ring of light, and spun a wide-awake into Engelhardt's lap. He started. It was adorned with a blue silk fly-veil.

"Recognize it?"

He had recognized it at once; it was Sam Rowntree's; and Sam Rowntree had been missing, yesterday, before Engelhardt himself said his secret farewell to the homestead.

He looked for more. No more was said. The villains had relapsed into that silence which was more eloquent of horror than all their threats. But Bill now flung fresh branches on the fire; the wood crackled; the flames spurted starward; and in the trebled light, Engelhardt, peering among the trees for some further sign of Sam, saw that which set the pores pringling all over his skin.

It was the glint of firelight upon a pair of spurs that hung motionless in the scrub-not a yard from the ground-not ten paces from the fire.

He looked again; the spurs were fixed to a pair of sidespring boots; the boots hung out of a pair of moleskins, with a few inches of worsted sock in between. All were steady, immovable as the stars above. He could see no higher than the knees; but that was enough; a hoarse cry escaped him, as he pointed with a quivering finger, and turned his white face from man to man.

Neither Simons nor the Bo's'n would meet his look; but Bill gripped his arm, with a loud laugh, and dragged him to his feet.

"Come and have a look at him," he said. "He isn't pretty, but he'll do you good."

Next instant Engelhardt stood close to the suspended body of the unfortunate Rowntree. Both hands were tied behind his back, his hair was in his eyes, and the chin drooped forward upon his chest like that of a man lost in thought.

"See what you'll come to," said Bill, giving the body a push that set it swinging like a pendulum, while the branch creaked horribly overhead. "See what you'll come to if you don't speak out! It was a good ten minutes before he stopped kicking and jingling his spurs; you're lighter, and it'd take you longer. Quarter of an hour, I guess, or twenty minutes."

Engelhardt had reeled, and would have fallen, but the Bo's'n jumped up and caught him in his arms.

He did more.

"Listen to reason, messmate," said the sailor, with a touch of rude friendliness in his lowered tone. "There ain't no sense in keeping mum with us. If you won't speak, you'll swing at the yard-arm along with t'other cove in a brace of shakes; if you will, you'll get a chance whether or no. Besides, what good do you think you can do? We know all that's worth knowing. Anything you tell us'll make less trouble in at the homestead-not more."

"All right," said Engelhardt, faintly. "Let me sit down; I'll tell you anything you like."

"That's more like. Take my place, then you'll be stern-on to that poor devil. Now then, Bill, fire away. The little man's hisself again."

"Good for him," growled Bill. "Look at me, you stuck pig, and answer questions. Where's that chest?"

"In the store."

"Didn't I say so! Never been shifted! Whereabouts in the store?"

"Inside the counter."

"Much of a chest to bust into?"

"Two locks, and clamps all over."

"Where's the keys?"

"I don't know. Miss Pryse keeps them."

"She won't keep 'em long. See here, you devil, if you look at me again like that I'll plug your eyes into your mouth! You seem to know a fat lot about this silver. Have you seen it, or haven't you?"

"I have."

"What is there?"

"Not much. A couple of candlesticks; a few spoons; some old skewers; a biscuit-box; a coffee-pot —but it's half ivory; an epergne — —"

"What the 'ells that? None o' your Greek, you swine!"

"It's a thing for flowers."

"Why didn't you say so, then? What else?"

"Let me see — —"

"You'd best look slippy!"

"Well, there's not much more. A cake-basket, some napkin-rings, and a pair of nut-crackers. And that's about all. It's all *I* saw, anyhow."

"All silver?"

"I shouldn't think it."

"You liar! You plucky well know it is. And not a bad lot neither, even if it *was* the lot. By the Lord, I've a good mind to strip and sit you on that fire for not telling me the truth!"

"Easy, mate, easy!" remonstrated the Bo's'n. "That sounds near enough."

"By cripes," cried Simons, "it's near enough for me. 'Tain't the silver I want. It's the gold, and that's the girl!"

"You won't get her," said Engelhardt.

"Why not?"

"She'll put a bullet through you."

"Can she shoot straight?"

"As straight as her father, I should say. I never saw him. But I've seen her."

"What do?"

"Stand in the veranda and knock a crow off the well fence-with her own revolver."

"By cripes, *that's* a lie."

(It was.)

"I'm not so blooming sure," said Bill. "I recollect how the old man dropped Tigerskin at nigh twenty yards. She was with him, too, at the time —a kid out of bed. I took a shot at her and missed. She'd be as likely as not to knock a hole through one or other of us, lads, if you hadn't got me to see you through. You trust to Bill for ideas! He's got one now, but it'll keep. See here, you swine, you! When was it you saw all what you pretend to have seen, eh?"

Engelhardt laughed. His answer could do no harm, and it gave him a thrill of satisfaction to score even so paltry a point against his bestial antagonist.

"It was the day you two came around the station."

"That morning?"

"Yes."

"Where did you see it?"

"In the store."

"Before we came?"

"While you were there. When Miss Pryse locked the door, it was all over the place. While we were in the kitchen she got it swept out of sight."

"Good God!" screamed Bill; "if only I'd known. You little devil, if only I'd guessed it!"

His vile face was convulsed and distorted with greed and rage; his hairy, four-fingered fist shaking savagely in Engelhardt's face. Bo's'n remonstrated again.

"What's the sense o' that, messmate? For God's sake shut it! A fat lot we could ha' done without a horse between us."

"We could have rushed the store, stretched 'em stiff— —"

"And carried a hundredweight o' silver away in our bluies! No, no, my hearty; it's a darn sight better as it is. What do you say, Simons?"

"I'm glad you waited, but I'm bleedin' dry."

"An' me, too," said Bill, sulkily, as he uncorked a black bottle. "Give us that pannikin, you spawn!"

Engelhardt handed it over unmoved. He was past caring what was said or done to him personally. Bill drank first.

"Here's fun!" said he, saluting the other two simultaneously with a single cross-eyed leer.

"'An' they say so-an' we hope so!'" chanted the Bo's'n, who came next. "Anyway, here's to the moon, for there she spouts!"

As he raised his pannikin, he pointed it over Engelhardt's shoulder, and the latter involuntarily turned his head. He brought it back next moment, with a jerk and a shudder. Far away, behind the scrub, on the edge of the earth, lay the moon, with a silvery pathway leading up to her, and a million twigs and branches furrowing her face. But against the top of the great white disc there fell those horrible boots and spurs, in grisly silhouette, and still swaying a little to the mournful accompaniment of the groaning bough above. Surely the works of God and man were never in ghastlier contrast than when Engelhardt turned his head without thinking and twitched it back with a shudder. And yet to him this was not the worst; he was now in time to catch that which made the blood run colder still in all his veins.

Simons was toasting Naomi Pryse. It took Engelhardt some moments to realize this. The language he could stand; but no sooner did he grasp its incredible application than his self-control boiled over on the spot.

"Stop it!" he shrieked at the shearer. "How dare you speak of her like that? How dare you?"

The foul mouth fell open, and the camp-fire flames licked the yellow teeth within. Engelhardt was within a few inches of them, with a doubled fist and reckless eyes. To his amazement, the man burst out laughing in his face.

"The little cuss has spunk," said he. "I like to see a cove stick up for 'is gal, by cripes I do!"

"So do I," said Bo's'n. "Brayvo, little man, brayvo!"

"My oath," said Bill, "I'd have cut 'is stinkin' throat for 'alf as much if I'd been you, matey!"

"Not me," said Simons. "I'll give 'im a drink for 'is spunk. 'Ere, kiddy, you wish us luck!"

He held out the pannikin. Engelhardt shook his head. He was, in fact, a teetotaler, who had made a covenant with himself, when sailing from old England, to let no stimulant pass his lips until his feet should touch her shores again. The covenant was absolutely private and informal, as between a man and his own body, but no power on earth would have made him break it.

"Come on," said Simons. "By cripes, we take no refusals here!"

"I must ask you to take mine, nevertheless."

"Why?"

"Because I don't drink."

"Well, you've got to!"

"I shall not!"

Simons seemed bent upon it. Perhaps he had taken a drop too much himself; indeed, none of the three were entirely above such a suspicion; but it immediately appeared that this small point was to create more trouble than everything that had gone before. Small as it was, neither man would budge an inch. Engelhardt said again that he would not drink. Simons swore that he should either drink or die. The piano-tuner cheerfully replied that he expected to die in any case, but he wasn't going to touch whiskey for anybody; so he gave Simons leave to do what he liked and get it over-the sooner the better. The shearer promptly seized him by his uninjured wrist, twisted it violently behind his back, and held out his hand to Bo's'n for the pannikin. Engelhardt was now helpless, his left arm a prisoner and in torture, his right lying useless in a sling. Bo's'n, however, came to his rescue once more, by refusing to see good grog wasted when there was little enough left.

"What's the use?" said he. "If the silly devil won't drink, we'll make him sing us a song. He says he tunes pianners. Let him tune up now!"

"That's better," assented Bill. "The joker shall give us a song before we let his gas out; and I'll drink his grog. Give it here, Bo's'n."

The worst of a gang of three is the strong working majority always obtainable against one or other of them. Simons gave in with a curse, and sent Engelhardt sprawling with a heavy kick. As he picked himself up, they called upon him to sing. He savagely refused.

"All right," said Bill, "we'll string him up an' be done with him. I'm fairly sick o' the swine — I am so!"

"By cripes, so am I."

"Then up he goes."

"The other beggar's got the rope," said Bo's'n.

"Then cut him down. He won't improve by hanging any longer. We ain't a-going to eat him, are we? Cut him down, and sling this one up. It's your job, Bo's'n."

Bo's'n was disposed to grumble. Bill cut him short.

"All right," said he, getting clumsily to his feet, "I'll do it myself. You call yourself a bloomin' man! I'd make a better bloomin' man than you with bloomin' baccy-ash. Out of the light, you cripple, an' the thing'll be done in half the time you take talking about it!"

Engelhardt was left sitting between Simons and the ill-used Bo's'n. The latter had his grumble out, but Bill took no more account of him. As for the shearer, the ferocity of his attitude toward the doomed youth was now second to none. He sat very close to him, with a hellish scowl and a great hand held ready to blast any attempt at escape. But none was made. The piano-tuner stuck his thumbs into his ears, covered his closed eyes with his palms, and tried both to think and to pray. He could not think; vague visions of Naomi crowded his mind, but they formed no thought. Nor could he pray for anything but courage to meet his fate. Within a few yards of him was the body of a dead man murdered by these thieves among whom he himself had fallen. He could not but doubt that they were about to murder him too. His last hour had come. He wanted courage. That was all he asked for as he sat with plugged ears and tight-shut eyes.

He was aroused by a smart kick in the ribs. As he got up to go to his doom, Bill seized him by the shoulders and pushed him roughly toward the hanging rope; it hung so low, it bisected the rising moon.

"Let me alone," he cried, wriggling fiercely. "I can get there without your help."

"Well, we'll see."

He got there fast enough. A little deeper in the scrub he could see a shapeless mass of moleskin and Crimean shirting, with a spurred boot half covered by a stiff hand. He was thankful to turn his face to the blazing camp-fire, even though the noose went round his neck as he did so.

"Now then," said Bill, hauling the rope taut, "will you give us a song or won't you?"

He could not speak.

"If you sing us a song we may give you another hour," said the Bo's'n from the ground. Simons and he had been whispering together. Bill shook his head at them.

"That rests with me," said he to Engelhardt. "Don't you make any mistake."

"Another hour!" cried the young man, bitterly, as he found his voice. "What's another hour? If you're men at all, put an end to me now and be done with it."

"How's that?" said Bill, hauling him upon tip-toe. "No, no, sonny, we want our song first," he added, as he let the rope fall slack again.

"Sing up, and there's no saying what'll happen," cried the Bo's'n, cheerily.

"What shall I sing?"

"Anything you like."

"Something funny to cheer us up."

"Ay, ay, a comic song!"

Engelhardt wavered-as once before under the eyes and ears of a male audience. "I'll do my best," he said at last. And Bo's'n clapped.

A minute later the bushrangers' camp was the scene of as queer a performance as ever was given. A very young man, with a pallid, blood-stained face, and a rope round his neck, was singing a "comic" song to a parcel of cut-throats who were presently to hang him, as they had hanged already the corpse at his heels. Meanwhile they surrendered themselves like simple innocents to a thorough enjoyment of the fine fun provided. The replenished camp-fire lit their villanous faces with a rich red glow. They grinned, they laughed, they displayed their pleasure and satisfaction each after his own fashion. The fat man shook in his fat; the long man showed his grinning teeth; the sailor-man slapped his thighs and rolled on the ground in paroxysms of spirituous mirth. It must have been the humor of the situation, rather than that of the song, which so powerfully appealed to them. The former had the piquant charm of being entirely their own creation. The latter was that poetic paraphrase of the early chapters of the Book of Genesis which the singer had tried upon another back-block audience but a few nights before. Of the two, this audience, as such, was decidedly the better. At any rate they let him get to the end. And when that came, and Bo's'n clapped again, even the other two joined in the applause.

"By cripes," said Simons, "that's not so bad!"

"Bad?" cried the enthusiastic Bo's'n. "It's as good as fifty plays. We'll have some more, and I'll give you a song myself."

"Right!" said Bill. "The night's still young. Stiffin me purple if we haven't forgot them weeds we laid in at the township! Out with 'em, mateys, an' pass round the grog; we'll make a smokin' concert of it. A bloomin' smoker, so help me never!"

The cigars were unearthed from the pockets of Bill himself. He and Simons at once put two of them in full blast. Meantime, Bo's'n was trying his voice.

"Any of you know any sailors' chanties?" said he.

A pause, and then —

"Yes, I do."

The voice was none other than Engelhardt's.

"*You?* The devil you do! How's that, then?"

"I came out in a sailing ship."

"What do you know?"

"Some of the choruses."

"'Blow the land down?'"

"Yes-best of all."

"Then we'll have that! Messmates you join his nibs in the chorus. I sing yarn and chorus too. Ready? Steady! Here goes!"

And in a rich, rolling voice, that had been heard above many a gale on the high seas, he began with the familiar words:

> Oh, where are you going to, my pretty maid? —
> Yo-ho, blow the land down!
> Oh, where are you going to, my pretty maid? —
> And give us some time to blow the land down!

The words were not long familiar. They quickly became detestable. The farther they went, of course, the more they appealed to Simons, Bill, and the singer himself. As for Engelhardt, obviously he was in no position to protest; nor could mere vileness add at all to his discomfort, with that noose still round his neck, and the rope-end still tight in Bill's clutch. Then the refrain for every other line was no bad thing in itself; at all events, he joined in throughout, and at the close stood at least as well with his persecutors as before.

It now appeared, however, that sailors' chanties were the Bo's'n's weakness. He insisted on singing two more, with topical and impromptu verses of his own. As, for instance:

> The proud Miss Pryse may toss 'er 'ead —
> *An' they say so-an' we hope so* —
> The proud Miss Pryse will soon be dead —
> The poor-old-gal!

Or again, and as bad:

> Oh, they call me Hanging Johnny —
> Hurray! Pull away!
> An' I'll soon hang you, my sonny —
> Hang-boys-hang!

These are but opening verses. There were many more in each case, and they were bad enough in all respects. And yet Engelhardt chimed in at his own expense-even at Naomi's —because it might be that his life and hers depended upon it. He was beginning to have his hopes, partly from the delay, partly from looks and winks which he had seen exchanged; and his hopes led to ideas, because his brain had never been clearer and busier than it was now become. He was devoutly thankful not to have been twice forced to sing. The second time, however, was still to come. It was announced by a jerk of the rope that went near to dislocating his neck.

"This image is doing nothink for 'is living, an' yet we're letting 'im live!" cried Bill, in a tone of injured and abused magnanimity. "Sing, you swine, or swing! One o' the two."

"What sort will you have this time?" asked Engelhardt, meekly. His meekness was largely put on, however. The black bottle had been going round pretty freely; in fact, it was quite empty. Another had been broached, and the men were both visibly and audibly in their cups.

"Another comic!" cried Simons and the Bo's'n in one breath.

"No, something serious this trip," Bill said, contradictiously. "You know warri mean, you lubber-somethin' soothin' for a night-cap —somethin' Christy-mental. Go ahead an' be damned to ye!"

Engelhardt had no time to consider, to reflect, to choose. The signal to start instantly was given by a series of sharp, throttling jerks at the rope. Almost before he was himself aware of it, he was giving them the well-known "Swannee River." It was the first "Christy-mental" song that had risen to his mind and lips. Moreover, he gave it with all the pathos and expression of which he was capable, and that, as we know, was not inconsiderable. They did not join in the chorus. This made it the easier. He tried to forget that these men were there, and, throwing his gaze aloft, sung softly-even sweetly-to the stars. Doubtless it was all acting, and by a cunning instinct that he went so slow in the final chorus:

> Oh, my heart is sad and weary,
> Everywhere I roam;
> Oh, darkies, but my heart is weary,
> Far from the old folks at home.

And yet one knows that it is possible to act and to feel at one and the same time; and, incredible as it may seem in the circumstances, Engelhardt found it so just then. He *did* think of the dear old woman at home; and being an artist to his boots, he gave his emotions their head, and sang to these blackguards as he would have sung to Naomi herself. And the effect was extraordinary-if in part due to the whiskey. When the young man lowered his eyes there was the maudlin Bo's'n snivelling like a babe, and the other two sucking their cigars to life with faces as long as lanterns.

"Lads," said Bill, "the night's still young. What matter does it make when we tackle the station? It'll keep. We on'y got to get there before mornin'. 'Tain't midnight yet." His voice was thickish.

"If the moon gets much higher," hiccoughed the Bo's'n, "we'll never get there at all. We'll never find it!" And he dried his eyes on his sleeve.

Bill took no notice of this. But he shook up his companions, linked arms between the two, and halted them in front of Engelhardt. They all three swayed a little as they stood, yet all three were still dangerously sober; and the second bottle was empty now; and there was no third. Engelhardt confronted them with hope, but not confidence, and listened, more eagerly than he dared to show, to Bill's harangue.

"Young man," said he, "you're not such a cussed swine's I thought. Sing or swing, says I. You sings like a man. So you sha'n't swing at all-not yet. No saying what we'll do in an hour or two. P'r'aps we're going to take you along with us to the station, to show us things, an' p'r'aps we ain't. You make your miseral life happy, to go on with. You bloomin' beggar, you, we respite you! Bo's'n, take the same rope an' lash the joker to that tree."

Bill stopped to see it done. He was quite sober enough to be sufficiently particular in this matter; as was Bo's'n, to perform his part in sailor-like fashion. In five minutes the thing was done.

"What do you think of that?" cried the seaman, with a certain honest sort of deep-sea pride.

"It'll do, matey."

"By cripes, he'll never get out of that!"

In fact, from his chin to his knees, the poor piano-tuner was encased in a straight-waistcoat of rope-the rope that had been round his neck for the last half-hour. Even the injured arm was inside. Nor could he move his feet, for they were tied separately at the ankles. Otherwise there was only one knot in what was indeed a masterpiece of its kind.

"I hope you'll be comfortable," said the Bo's'n, with a quaint touch of remorse, "for split me if you didn't sing like a blessed cock-angel! And never you fear," he added, under his breath, "for we ain't agoin' to hang you. Not us! And if there's anything we can do for you afore we take our spell, say the word, messmate, say the word."

The piano-tuner shook his head.

"Then so long and ——"

"Stop! you might give us a cigar."

It was given readily.

"Thanks; and now you might light it."

This also was done, with a brand from the dying fire.

"Good-night," said Bo's'n.

"And thank you," added Engelhardt.

The sailor stopped to give a last admiring glance at his handiwork; then he joined his companions, who were already spread out upon the broad of their backs; and Engelhardt was left to himself at last-unable to move hand or foot-with a corpse at hand and the murderers under his eyes-with the risen moon shining full upon his face, and the vilest of vile cigars held tight between his teeth.

And he was no smoker; tobacco made him sick.

Nevertheless, he kept that bad weed alight, and very carefully alight, for ten minutes by guess-work. Then he depressed his chin, knocked off an inch of ash against the top-most coil, applied the red end to the rope, and sucked and puffed for his life and Naomi's.

Chapter XIV
The Raid on the Station

Those same dark hours of this eventful night were also the slowest and the dreariest on record in the mind of Naomi Pryse. She too had waited for the moon. At sundown she had stabled her horse, and left it with a fine feed of chaff and oats as priming for the further work she had in view. This done, she had consented, under protest, to eat something herself; but had jumped up early to fill with her own hands a water-bag and a flask of which she could have no need for hours. It made no matter. She must be up and doing this or that; it was intolerable sitting still even to eat and drink. Besides, how could she eat, how could she drink, when he who should have shared her meal was perhaps perishing of hunger and thirst in Top Scrubby? It was much more comforting to cut substantial slices of mutton and bread, to put them up in a neat packet, and to set this in readiness alongside the flask and the water-bag. Then came the trouble. There was nothing more to be done.

It was barely eight o'clock, and no moon for two hours and a half.

Naomi went round to the back veranda, picked up the book she had been reading the day before, and marched about with it under her arm. She had not the heart to sit down and read. Her restless feet took her many times to the kitchen and Mrs. Potter, who shook her good gray head and remonstrated with increasing candor and asperity.

"Go to look for him?" she cried at last. "When the time comes for that, you'll be too dead tired to sit in your saddle, miss. If you start before the moon's well up, there'll be no telling a hoof-mark from a foot-print without getting off every time. You've said so yourself, Miss Naomi. Then why not go straight to your bed and lie down for two or three hours? I'll bring you a cup of tea at half-past eleven, and you can be away by twelve."

Naomi sighed.

"It is so long to wait-doing nothing! He may be dying, poor fellow; and yet what can one do in the dark?"

"Lie down and rest," said Mrs. Potter, dryly.

"Well, I will try, but not on my bed-on the sitting-room sofa, I think. Will you light the lamp there, please? And bring the tea at eleven; I'll start at half-past."

Naomi took a short stroll among the darkling pines-the way that she had taken the piano-tuner in the first moments of their swift friendship-the way that he had taken alone last night. She reached the sitting-room with moist, wistful eyes, which startled themselves as she confronted the mirror over the chimney-piece whereon stood the lamp. She stood for a little, however, looking at herself-steadfastly-inquisitively-as though to search out the secrets of her own heart. She gave it up in the end, and turned wearily away. What was the use of peering into her own heart now, when so often aforetime she had seemed to know it, and had not? There was no use; and as it happened, no need. For the first thing her eyes fell upon, as she turned, was the pile of music lying yet where Engelhardt had placed it, on the stool. The next was his little inscription on the uppermost song. She knelt to read it again; when she had done so the two uncertain, left-handed, pencilled lines were wet and blotched with her tears, and she rose up knowing what she had never known before.

At eleven-thirty —she had set her heart upon that extra half hour if let alone-Mrs. Potter rattled the tea-tray against the sitting-room door and entered next moment. She found her mistress on the sofa certainly, but lying on her back and staring straight at the ceiling. Her face was very white and still, but she moved it a little as the door opened. She had not slept? Not a wink. Her book was lying in her lap; it had never been opened. Mrs. Potter was not slow to exhibit her disappointment, not to say her disgust. But Naomi sprang up with every sign of energy, and finished her tea in five minutes. In ten she had her horse saddled. In twelve she had cantered back to the veranda, and was receiving from Mrs. Potter the water-bag, the flask, and the packet of bread and meat.

"Have his room nice and ready for him," said the girl, excitedly, "and the kettle boiling, so that we may both have breakfast the instant we get in. It will be a pretty early breakfast, you'll see! Do you think you can do without sleep as long as I can?"

"Well, I know I sha'n't lie down while you're gone, miss."

"Then I'll be tremendously quick, I will indeed. I only wish I'd started long ago. The moon is splendid now. You can see miles — —"

"Then look there, Miss Naomi!"

"Where?"

"Past the stables-across the paddock-toward the fence."

Naomi looked. A black figure was running toward them in the moonlight.

"Who can it be, Mrs. Potter? Not Mr. Engelhardt — —"

"Who else?"

"But he is reeling and staggering! Could it be some drunken roustabout? And yet that's just his height-it must be-it *is* —thank God!"

Her curiosity first, and then her amazement, kept Naomi seated immovable in her saddle. She wondered later why she had not cantered to meet him. She did not stir even when his stertorous breathing came painfully to her ears. It was only when the quivering, spent, and speechless young man threw his arms across the withers of her horse, and his white face fell forward upon the mane, that Naomi silently detached the water-bag which she had strapped to her saddle, and held it to his lips with a trembling hand. At first he shook his head. Then he raised his wild eyes to hers with a piteously anxious expression.

"You have heard-that they are coming?"

"No-who?"

"You have heard, or why are you on horseback?"

"To look for you. I was on the point of starting. I made sure you must be bushed."

"I was. But I got to a camp. They looked after me; I am all right. And now they are coming in here-they're probably on their way!" Each little sentence came in a fresh gasp from his parched throat.

"But who?"

"Those two tramps who came the other day, and Simons, the ringer of the shed. Villains-villains every one!"

"Ah! And what do they want?"

"Can't you guess? The silver! The silver! That fat brute who insulted you so, who do you suppose he is? Tigerskin's mate-just out of prison-the man whose finger your father shot off ten years ago! You remember how he kept his hands in his pockets the other day? Well, that was the reason. Now there isn't a moment to lose. I listened to their plans. Half an hour ago-or it may be an hour-they lay down for a spell. They were drunk, but not very. They only meant to rest for a bit; then they're coming straight here. They left me tied up-they were going to bring me with them —I'll tell you afterward how I got loose. I daren't stop a moment, even to cut adrift their horses. I just bolted for the moon —I'd heard them say the station lay due east-and here I am. Thank God I've found you up and mounted! It couldn't have been better; it's providential. Now you mustn't get off at all; you must just ride right on to the shed."

"Must I?" said Naomi, with a tight lip and a keen eye, but a touch of the old banter in her tone.

"We could follow on foot. Meanwhile you would rouse them out at the shed — —"

"And my silver?"

Engelhardt was silent. The girl leant forward in her saddle, and laid a hand upon his shoulder.

"No, no, Mr. Engelhardt! Captains don't quit their ships in such a hurry as all that. I'm captain here, and I'll stick to mine. It isn't only the silver. Still my father smelt powder for that silver, and the least I can do is to follow his lead."

She slid to the ground as she spoke.

"You will barricade yourself in the store?" said Engelhardt.

"Exactly. It was fixed up for this very kind of thing, after the first fuss with Tigerskin. They'll never get in."

"And you mean to stick to your guns inside?"

"To such as I have-most certainly."

"Then I mean to stick to you."

"Very well."

"But think-think before it's too late! They are devils, Miss Pryse-beasts! I have seen them and heard them. Better a hundred times be dead than at their mercy. For God's sake, take the horse before they are upon us!"

"I stop here," said Naomi, decidedly.

"Yet Mrs. Potter and I could hold the store as easily as you could. They shall not get your silver while I'm alive."

"My mind is made up," said the girl, in a voice which silenced his remonstrances; "but I agree with you that somebody ought to start off for the shed. I think that you should, Mr. Engelhardt, if you feel equal to it."

"Equal to it! It's so likely I would ride off and leave two women to the mercy of those brutes! If it really must be so, then I think the sooner we all three get into the store — —"

It was Mrs. Potter who here put in her amazing word. While the young people stood and argued, her eyes had travelled over every point of the saddled horse. And now she proposed that she should be the one to ride to the shed for help.

"You!" the two cried in one breath, as they gazed at her ample figure.

"And why not?" said the hardy woman. "Wasn't I born and bred in the bush? Couldn't I ride-bareback, too-before either of you was born? I'm not so light as I used to be, and I haven't the nerve either; but what I have is all there in the hour of need, Miss Naomi. Let me go now. I'm ready this minute."

Naomi had seemed lost in thought.

"Very well!" cried she, whipping her eyes from the ground. "But you don't know the way to the shed, and I must make your directions pretty plain. Run to the back of the kitchen, Mr. Engelhardt, you'll see a lot of clothes-props. Bring as many as you can to the store veranda."

Engelhardt darted off upon his errand. Already they had wasted too many minutes in words. His brain was ablaze with lurid visions of the loathsome crew in Top Scrubby; of the murderous irruption imminent at any moment; of the unspeakable treatment to be suffered at those blood-stained hands-not only by himself-that mattered little-but by a woman-by Naomi of all women in the world. God help them both if the gang arrived before they were safe inside the store! But until the worst happened she need not know, nor should she guess, how bad that worst might be. Poor Rowntree's fate, and even his own ill-usage by those masterless men, were things which Engelhardt was not the man to tell to women in the hour of alarm. He was clear enough as to that; and having done up to this point all that a man could do, he jumped at the simple task imposed by Naomi, and threw himself into it with immense vigor and a lightened heart. As he dropped his first clothes-prop in the store veranda, Naomi and the housekeeper were still talking, though the latter was already huddled up in the saddle. When he got back with a second, both women were gone; with a third, Naomi was unlocking the store door; with the fourth and last, she had lit a candle inside, and was sawing one of the other props in two.

"That'll do," she said, as her saw ran through the wood. "Now hold this one up for me."

She pointed to another of the stout poles. She made him hold it with one end inside, and the other protruding through the opening. Then she made a mark on the prop at the level of the door, sawed it through at her mark, and cut down the other two in the same fashion. In less than five minutes the four poles had become eight, which cumbered the floor within. Then Naomi rose from her knees, flung the saw back into the tool-box, and made a final survey with the candle. A few flakes of sawdust lay about the shallow veranda. She fetched a broom from a corner of the store and whisked them away. Then she removed the key to the inside, and was about to lock the door upon herself and Engelhardt when he suddenly stopped her.

"Hold on!" he cried. "I want your boots."

"My boots?"

"Yes, those you've got on-with the dust on 'em, just as they are. They must be left outside your door, and your door must be locked; you must keep the key."

Naomi gave him a grateful, an admiring smile.

"That *is* a happy thought. I'll get it myself. While I'm gone you might fetch in the axe from the wood-heap; I'd almost forgotten it."

They ran off in different directions. Next minute they were both back in the store, Engelhardt with the axe. Naomi took it from him, and set it aside without a word. Her face was blanched.

"I heard something," she whispered. "I heard a cry. Oh, if they've seen me!"

"We'll lock the door as quietly as possible."

This was done.

"Now the props," said Naomi.

Engelhardt had guessed what they were for. He helped her to fix them, with one wedged between floor and counter, and the other pressing the heavy woodwork of the door. It now appeared how craftily Naomi had cut her timbers. They met the door, two at the top, two at the bottom, and four about the centre. Still the brave engineer was distressed.

"I meant to hammer them down," she murmured. "Now I daren't."

"We'll put all our weight on them instead," said Engelhardt. They did so with a will, until each prop had creaked in turn. Then they listened.

"Out with the light," said Naomi. "There are no windows to give us away-but still!"

He blew it out. As yet his own ears had heard nothing, and he was beginning to wonder whether Naomi had been deceived. They listened a little longer. Then she said:

"We're provisioned for a siege. Did you see the flask and things on the counter?"

"I did. How in the world did you find time to get them ready?"

"I had them ready before you came. They were for you."

The two were crouching close together between the props. It was a natural though not a necessary attitude. The moon was shining through the skylight upon one of the walls; the multifarious tins and bottles on the shelves made the most of the white light; and faint reflections reached the faces of Naomi and the piano-tuner —so close to each other, so pale, so determined, and withal so wistful as their eyes met. Engelhardt first looked his thanks, and then stammered them out in a broken whisper. Even as he did so the girl raised a finger to her lips.

"Hark! There they are."

"Yes, I hear them. They won't hear us yet a bit."

"They mustn't hear us at all; but off with your boots-we may have to move about."

She had already kicked off her shoes, and now, because he had only one of his own, she pulled off his boots with her two hands.

"You should not have done that!"

"Why not?"

"It's dreadful! Just as though you were my servant."

"Mr. Engelhardt, we must be everything to each other — —"

She shot up her hand and ceased. The voices without were now distinguishable.

"To-night!" he muttered, bitterly, before heeding them.

Naomi, on the other hand, was at the last pitch of attention; but not to him. She inclined her head as she knelt to hear the better. The voices were approaching from one side.

"Ay, that's where he dropped-just there!" said one. It was Tigerskin's mate, Bill.

"Take the key from the door!" Engelhardt whispered to Naomi, who was the nearer it. They had forgotten to do this. For one wild moment the girl hesitated, then she cautiously reached out her hand and withdrew the key without a scratch.

"So this is the crib!" they heard Bo's'n say.

"The same old crib," said Bill. "Same as it was ten years ago, only plastered up a bit. I suppose it *is* locked, mate?"

The handle was tried. The door shook ever so little. The two inside gazed at the props and held their breath. If one of them should be shaken down!

"Ay, it's locked all right; and I reckon it's true enough about the girl sleeping with the key under her pillow, and all."

"Blast your reckonings!" said Bill. "Make sure the key ain't in the door on t'other side."

The thimbleful of starlit sky which Naomi had been watching for the last minute and a half was suddenly wiped away. She heard Bo's'n breathing hard as he stooped and peered. The key grew colder in her hand.

"No, there ain't no key, Bill."

"That's all right. They're both in their beds then, and that little suck-o'-my-thumb hasn't got here yet. When he does, God 'elp him!"

The voices were those of Bill and Bo's'n. For the moment these two seemed to be alone together.

"Ay, ay, we'd string the beggar up fast enough another time!"

"String him up? Yes, by his heels, and shoot holes through him while he dangled."

"Beginning where you don't kill. Holy smoke! but I wish he'd turn up now."

"So do I—the swine! But here comes the ringer. What cheer, matey?"

"It's right," said Simons. "The little devil's locked her door; but there are her boots outside, same as if she was stoppin' at a blessed 'otel. A fat lot she cared whether her precious pal was bushed or whether he wasn't! We thought you was telling us lies, mother, but, by cripes, you wasn't!"

"I should think not!" said a fourth voice. "She wouldn't believe he was lost, but I knew he was; so I just saddled the night-horse after she was in bed and asleep, and was going straight to the shed to raise a search-party!"

The pair within were staring at each other in dumb horror. That fourth voice was but too well known to them both. It was Mrs. Potter's.

Chapter XV
The Night Attack

"See here, mother!" said Bill. "There's one or two things we want to know. Spit out the truth, and that'll be all right. Tell us one lie, and there'll be an end of *you*. Understand?"

"I ought to."

"Right you are, then; now you know. What about this key?"

"She keeps it in her room."

"Under her pillow, eh?"

"That I can't say; but she will tell you."

"So we reckon. Now look here. Will you take your oath there's not another soul on the premises but you and her?"

The pair within again held their breath. They must be discovered; but the longer they could postpone it the shorter would be their danger. Mrs. Potter's heart was stout, however, and her tongue ready.

"I swear it," she cried, heartily.

"What makes you so cussed sure?"

"Why, it stands to reason. By rights there ought to be four of us. That's with Sam Rowntree and Mr. Engelhardt. Sam's gone off on his own hook somewhere"—Bill chuckled—"but nobody knows where. Mr. Engelhardt's lost, as I told you. So there's nobody left but mistress and me. How could there be?"

"I don't know or care a curse how there could be. I only know that if there *is*, you'll have a pill to take without opening your mouth for it. About this chap that's lost; you'll take your oath he didn't turn up before you left the station just now?"

"I told you he hadn't, as soon as ever you overtook me."

"You've got to swear it!" said Bill, savagely.

"I swore it then."

"So she did," said Simons, who had been grumbling openly during this cross-examination. "What's the good of going over the same track twice, mate? Let her give us the feed she promised, and then let's get to work."

"And so say I!" cried the Bo's'n.

"You shall have your supper in five minutes," said Mrs. Potter, "if you'll let me get it."

"All right, missus," said Bill, after a pause. "Only mind, if we catch you in any hanky-panky, by God I'll screw your neck till I put your face where your back-hair ought to be. Don't you dare get on the cross with us, or there'll be trouble! Come on, chaps. You show the way to the dining-room, mother, and light up; then we'll...."

The rest sounded indistinct in the store. The low crunching of the foot-falls in the sandy yard changed to a crisp clatter upon the homestead veranda. Naomi waited for that sign; then with a white face and eager hands she began to tear down, prop by prop, the barricade on which their very lives depended.

"She shall not suffer for this, whoever else does," she muttered. "At least she sha'n't suffer alone."

"You mean to open the door?"

"Yes, and catch her as she passes. To get to the kitchen she must pass close to the store. We'll open the door, and if she's wise she'll pass three or four times without turning her head; she'll wait till they're well at work; then she'll come back for something else-and slip in."

As she spoke Naomi went round to the gun-rack, took down the Winchester repeating-rifle, loaded it and came back to the front of the store. Then she directed Engelhardt to unlock the door, she helping him to be gentle with the key. The lock was let back by degrees. A moment later the door was wide open, with Naomi standing as in a frame, the Winchester in her hands.

The station-yard lay bathed and purified in the sweet moonlight. The well-palings opposite, and the barracks beyond, were as though newly painted white. The main building Naomi could not see without putting out her head, for it ran at right angles with the store, and she was standing well inside. But the night wind that blew freshly in her face bore upon it the noise of oaths and laughter from the dining-room, and presently that of footsteps, too. At this Naomi laid a finger on the trigger and stood like a rock, with the piano-tuner, like its shadow, at her side. But it was only Mrs. Potter who stepped into the moonlight. So far all was as Naomi had hoped and calculated.

But no further. When the poor soul saw the open door she stopped dead, hesitated half a second, and then ran like a heavy doe for it and Naomi. The latter had made adverse signals in vain. She drew aside to let the woman in, and was also in time to prevent Engelhardt from slamming the door. She shut it gently, turned the key with as much care as before, and with a sternly whispered "hush!" kept still to listen. The other two stood as silent, though Mrs. Potter, in the moment of safety and of reaction, was heaving and quivering all over, shedding tears like rain, and swaying perilously where she stood. But she kept her feet bravely during that critical minute; it was but one; the next, a shout of laughter from the distance made it clear that by a miracle the incident had passed unobserved and unsuspected.

"We may think ourselves lucky," said Naomi, severely. Next moment she had thrown her arms round the old woman's neck, and was covering her honest wrinkled face with her tears and kisses.

The practical Engelhardt was busily engaged in replacing the props against the door. His one hand made him slow at the work. Naomi was herself again in time to help him, and now there was sturdy Mrs. Potter to lend her weight. The supports were soon firmer than ever, with gimlets and bradawls driven into the door above those at the greatest slant, which were thus in most danger of being forced out of place. Then came a minute's breathing-space.

"I had just got through the first gate," Mrs. Potter was saying, "when I heard a galloping, and they were on me. Nay, Miss Naomi, it isn't anything to be proud of. I just said the first things that came into my head about you both; there was no time to think. It's only a mercy it's turned out so well."

"It was presence of mind," said Naomi. "We have scored an hour through it, and may another if they are long in missing you. If we can hold out till morning, someone may ride in from the shed. Don't you hear them talking still?"

"Yes; they're more patient than I thought they'd be."

"They think you're busy in the kitchen. When they find you're not, they'll waste their time looking all over the place for you-everywhere but here."

"Ay, but they'll come here in the end, and then may the Lord have mercy on our souls!"

"Come, come. They're not going to get in as easily as all that. And if they do, what with the Winchester ——"

"Hush!" said Engelhardt. He was kneeling among the props, with his ear close to the bottom of the door.

All three listened. The voices were louder and more distinct. The men had come outside.

"I don't believe she's there at all," said one. "I see no light."

"Go you and have a look, Bo's'n. Prick the old squaw up with the p'int o' your knife. But if you find her trying to hide, or up to any o' them games, I'd slit her throat and save the barney."

"By cripes, so would I!"

"Ay, ay, messmates, but we'll see-we'll see."

All the voices were nearer now. Naomi had taken Mrs. Potter's hand, and was squeezing it white. For some moments they could make out nothing more. Bo's'n had evidently gone over to the kitchen. The other two were talking in low tones somewhere near the well-palings. Suddenly a muffled shout from the kitchen reached every ear.

"She's not here at all."

"Not there!"

"Come and look for yourselves."

"By gock," cried Bill, "let me just get my grip on her fat neck!"

A moment later the three could be heard ransacking the kitchen, and calling upon the fugitive to come out, with threats and imprecations most horrible to hear even in the distance; but as they drew nearer, working swiftly from out-building to out-building, like ferrets in a rabbit-warren, the ferocity of their language rose to such a pitch that the hunted woman within fell back faint and trembling upon the counter. Naomi was quick as thought with the flask; but her own cool hand and steady eyes were as useful as the brandy, and the fit passed as swiftly as it had come. While it lasted, however, the only one to follow every move outside was the assiduous Engelhardt. He had not yet risen from his knees; but he raised himself a little as Mrs. Potter stood upright again, supported by Naomi.

"It's all right," he whispered. "They've no idea where you are. Simons has had a look in the barracks, and Bo's'n in the pines. But they've given you up now. They're holding a council of war within five yards of us!"

"Let's listen," said Naomi. "Their language won't kill us."

They had quite given up Mrs. Potter. This was evident from the tail-end of a speech in which Bill bitterly repented not having "stiffened" both her and Engelhardt at sight.

"As for getting to the shed," said Simons, who was the obvious authority on this point, "that'll take her a good hour and a half on foot. It'd be a waste of time and trouble to ride after her, though I'd like to see Bill at work on her—I should so! If she had her horse, it'd be another thing."

"Ay, ay," cried the Bo's'n. "Let the old gal rip."

Bill had been of the same opinion a moment before; but this indecent readiness to be beaten by an old woman was more than he could share or bear. He told his mate so in highly abusive terms. They retorted that he was beaten by that same old woman himself. Bill was not so sure of that; what about the bedroom with the boots outside? Nobody had looked in there.

A brisk debate ensued, in which the voice of Simons rose loudest. Bill, on the other hand, spoke in a much lower tone than usual; his words did not penetrate into the store; it was as though they were meant not to. And yet it was Bill who presently cried aloud:

"Then that's agreed. We all three go together to rouse her up anyhow, whether the old gal's there or whether she isn't. Come on!"

Apparently they went then and there.

"Nice for me!" whispered Naomi. "Nice for us both, Mrs. Potter, if we weren't safe ——"

A bovine roar seemed to burst from their very midst. It was Bill outside the door.

"Tricked 'em, by God!" he yelled. "Here they are. Never mind that room. I tell you they're here-both of 'em; I heard 'em whispering."

"Bill, you're a treat," said the Bo's'n, running up. "I never saw such a man ——"

"Where's Simons?"

"He was bound to have a look for hisself. Here he comes. Well, messmate, where is she?"

"Not there," cried Simons, with an oath. "The room's as empty as we are. There's been no one in it all night."

Bill laughed.

"I knew that, matey. You might have saved yourself the trouble when I sang out. She's—in-here." And he kicked the store door three times with all his might.

"Who is?" said Simons.

"Both on 'em. What did I tell you? They started whisperin' the moment they thought we'd sheered off."

"They're not whisperin' now," said Simons, at the keyhole. "By cripes, let's burst the door in!"

"Hold on," said Bill. "If they're not born fools they'll listen to reason. Out o' the light, matey. See here, ladies, if you walk out now you may live to spin the yarn, but if you don't —" He broke away into nameless blasphemies.

The cruel voice came hoarse and hot through the keyhole. Engelhardt opened his mouth to reply, but Naomi clapped a warm palm upon it, and with the other hand signalled silence to Mrs. Potter.

"We've given 'em their chance," said Bill, after a pause. "Come on, chaps. One, two, all together-now!"

There was a stampede of feet in the shallow veranda, and then a thud and a crash, as the three men hurled themselves against the door. But for their oaths outside, in the store it was as though nothing had happened. Not a timber had given, not a prop was out of place. Naomi's white face wore a smile, which, however, was instantly struck out by a loud report and a flash through the keyhole.

Engelhardt crouched lower, picked something from the floor, and passed it up to Naomi in his open hand.

She carried it into the moonlight. It was a wisp of the musician's long hair, snipped out by the bullet.

They stood aside from the keyhole. More bullets came through, but all at the same angle. The women caught up a sack of flour, rolled it over the counter, and with Engelhardt's help jammed it between the props, so that the top just covered the keyhole. Next moment there was a rush against the door, and for the second time all the harm was done to the besiegers, not the besieged.

"We'll be black and blue before we've anything to show for it!" they heard the Bo's'n groaning.

"There's more than women in this," said Bill. "There's that spawn that I should have strung up if it hadn't been for you two white-feathers. It's yourselves you've got to thank for this. I might have known it the moment I caught sight o' that lump o' lard on horseback. The swine's been in here all the time!"

"He has!" shouted Engelhardt at the top of his excited voice; "and it's where you'll never get, not a man of you! You take that from me!"

For a short space there was a hush outside. Then arose such a storm of curses and foul threats that the women within put their fingers in their ears. When they withdrew them, all was silence once more, and this time it lasted.

"They must have gone for something!" exclaimed Naomi.

"They have," said the piano-tuner, coolly. "A battering-ram!"

"Then now's our time," cried the girl. "It's absurd to think of our being cooped up here with any quantity of fire-arms, and no chance of using one of them! First we must light up. Chop that candle in two, Mrs. Potter. It'll see us through to daybreak, and there's nothing to keep dark any longer, so the more light now the better. Ah, here's the tool-box, and yes! here's the brace and bits. Now this is my little plan."

She took the brace, fitted it with the largest bit, and was making for the door.

"What are you going to do?" said Engelhardt.

"Make a loop-hole to fire through."

"And for them to fire through, too!"

"Well, that can't be helped."

"Excuse me, I think it can. I've been puzzling the thing out for the last hour. I've a better plan than that!"

"Let me hear it."

"A tomahawk!"

She gave him one from the tool-box.

"May I hack the roofing a bit?"

"As much as ever you like."

"Now a pile of boxes-here-just at the left of the door-and four feet high."

The women had it ready in a twinkling. They then helped him to clamber to the top-no easy matter with an arm that was not only useless, but an impediment at every turn. When he stood at his full height his head touched the corrugated iron some twenty inches from the obtuse angle between roof and wall.

He reached out his hand for the tomahawk, and at the height of his eyes he hacked a slit in the iron, prising the lower lip downward until he could see well out into the yard. Then, a handbreadth above the angle, he made a round hole with the sipke of the tomahawk, and called for a revolver. Naomi produced a pair. He took one, and worked the barrel in the round hole until it fitted loosely enough to permit of training. Then he looked down. There was no sign of the thieves.

"Have you plenty of cartridges, Miss Pryse?"

"Any amount."

"Well, I don't expect to spill much blood with them; but, on the other hand, I'm not likely to lose any myself." The work and the danger had combined to draw his somewhat melancholy spirit out of itself. Or perhaps it was not the danger itself, but the fact that he shared it with Naomi Pryse. Whatever the cause, the young man was more light-hearted than was his wont. "They'll fire at the spot I fire from," he explained, with a touch of pride; "they'll never think of my eyes being two feet higher up, and their bullets must strike the roof at such an angle that no charge on earth would send them through. Mind, it'll be the greatest fluke if I hit them; but they aren't to know that; and at any rate I may keep them out of worse mischief for a time."

"You may and you will," said Naomi, enthusiastically. "But still we shall want my loop-hole!"

"Why so?"

"The veranda!"

For some moments Engelhardt said nothing. When at last he found his voice it was to abuse himself and his works with such unnecessary violence that again that soft warm palm lay for an instant across his lips. His pride in his own ingenuity had been cruelly humbled, for he had to confess that he had entirely forgotten to reckon with the store-veranda, a perfect shelter against even the deadliest fusillade from his position.

"Very well," he cried at last. "We'll drill a hole through the door, but we must drill it near the top, and at an angle, so that they can't put a bullet through it at a distance."

"Then let me do it," said Naomi. She sprang upon the flour-bag, and the hole was quickly made. Still the men did not return. "Lucky thing I remembered the axe in time!" she continued, remaining where she was. "They would have hacked in the door in no time with that. I say, Mr. Engelhardt, this is my post. I mean to stick here."

"Never!" he cried.

"But you can't work both revolvers."

"Well, then, let us change places. You'll probably shoot straighter than I should. I'll stand on the flour-bag with the barrel of the other revolver through the hole you've made. If any one of them gets in a line with it — —well, there'll be a villain less!"

"And Mrs. Potter shall load for us," cried Naomi. "Do you know how?"

"Can't say I do, miss."

"Then I'll show you."

This was the work of a moment. The old bush-woman was handy enough, and cool enough too, now that she was getting used to the situation. It was her own idea to bring round the storekeeper's tall stool, to plant it among the props, within reach of Naomi on the boxes and of Engelhardt on the flour-bag, and to perch herself on its leather top with the box of cartridges in her lap. Thus prepared and equipped, this strange garrison waited for the next assault.

"Here they come," cried Naomi at last, with a sudden catch in her voice. "They're carrying a great log they must have fished out from the very bottom of the wood-heap. All the top part of the heap was small wood, and I guess they've wasted some more time in hunting for the axe. But here they are!" She pushed her revolver through the slit in the roof, and the sharp report rang through the store.

"Hit anybody?" said Engelhardt next moment.

"No. They're stopping to fire back. Ah, you were right."

As she spoke there was a single report, followed by three smart raps on the sloping roof. The bullet had ricochetted like a flat stone flung upon a pond. Another and another did the same, and Naomi answered every shot.

"For God's sake take care!" cried the piano-tuner.

"I am doing so."

"Hit any one yet?"

"Not yet; it's impossible to aim; and they've never come nearer than the well-palings. Ah!"

"What now?"

"They're charging with the log."

Engelhardt slipped his revolver into his pocket, and grasped the shelf that jutted out over the lintel. He felt that the shock would be severe, and so it was. It came with a rush of feet and a volley of loud oaths —a crash that smashed the lock and brought three of the clothes-props clattering to the ground. But those secured by gimlet and bradawl still held; and though the lower part of the door had given an inch the upper fitted as close as before, and the hinges were as yet uninjured.

"One more does it!" cried Bill. "One more little rush like the last, and then, by God, if we don't make the three of you wish you was well dead, send me to quod again for ten year! Aha, you devil with the pistol! Very nice you'd got it arranged, but it don't cover us here. No, no, we've got the bulge on you now, you swine you! And you can't hit us, neither! We're going to give you one chance more when we've got our breath-just one, and then — —"

By holding on to the shelf when the crash came Engelhardt had managed to stand firm on the flour-bag. Seeing that the door still held, though badly battered, he had put his eye to the loop-hole bored by Naomi, and it had fallen full on Bill. A more bestial sight he had never seen, not even in the earlier hours of that night. The bloated face was swimming with sweat, and yet afire with rage and the lust for blood. The cross-eyes were turned toward the holes in the roof, hidden from them by the veranda, and the hairy fist with the four fingers was being savagely shaken in the same direction. The man was standing but a foot from the door, and when Engelhardt removed his eye and slipped his pistol-barrel in the place, he knew that it covered his midriff, though all that he could see through the half-filled hole was a fragment of the obscene, perspiring face. It was enough to show him the ludicrous change of expression which followed upon a sudden lowering of the eyes and a first glimpse of the protruding barrel. Without a moment's hesitation Engelhardt pressed the trigger while Bill was stupidly repeating:

"And then-and then — —"

A flash cut him short, and as the smoke and the noise died away, Engelhardt, removing the pistol once more and applying his eye, saw the wounded brute go reeling and squealing into the moonshine with his hand to his middle and the blood running over it. To the well-palings he reeled, dropping on his knees when he got there, but struggling to his feet and running up and down and round and round like a mad bull, still screaming and blaspheming at the top of his voice, and with the blood bubbling over both his hands, which never ceased to hug his wound. His mates rushed up to him, but he beat them off, cursing them, spitting at them, and covering them with blood as he struck at them with his soaking fists. It was their fault. They should have let him have his way. He would have done for that hell-begotten swine who had now done for him. It was they who had killed him-his own mates-and he told them so with shrieks and curses, varied with sobs and tears, and yet again with wild shots from a revolver which he plucked from his belt. But he dropped the pistol after madly discharging it twice, and clapping his hand to his middle, as though he could only live by pressing the wound with all his force, he rushed after them, foaming at the mouth and squirting blood at every stride. At last he seemed to trip, and he fell forward in a heap, but turned on one side, his knees coming up with a jerk, his feet treading the air as though running still. And for some seconds they so continued, like the screws of a foundering steamer; then he rolled over heavily; his two companions came up at a walk; one of them touched him with his foot; and Engelhardt stepped down from the flour-bag with a mouth that had never relaxed, and a frown that had never gone.

Naomi was no longer standing on the boxes; but she was sitting on them, with her face in her hands; and in the light of the two candle-ends, Mrs. Potter was watching her with a white dazed face.

"Cheer up!" said Engelhardt. "The worst is over now."

"Is he dead?" said Naomi, uncovering her face.

"As dead as a man can be."

"And you shot him?"

She knew that he had; but the thing seemed incredible as she sat and looked at him; and by the time it came fully home to her, the little musician was inches taller in her eyes.

"Yes, I shot the brute; and I'll shoot that shearer, too, if I get half a chance."

Naomi felt nervous about it, and sufficiently shocked. She was dubiously remarking that they had not committed murder, when she was roughly interrupted.

"Haven't they!"

"Whom have they murdered?"

"You'll see."

"I know!" cried Mrs. Potter, with sudden inspiration; but even as they looked at her, a voice was heard shouting from a respectful distance outside.

"We're going," it cried. "We've had enough of this, me and Simons have. Only when they find that chap in the paddock, recollect it was Bill that hung him. But for us he'd have hung you, too!"

They listened very closely, but they heard no more. Then Naomi stood up to look through the slit in the roof.

"The yard is empty," she cried. "Their horses are gone! Oh, Mr. Engelhardt-Mr. Engelhardt-we are saved!"

Chapter XVI
In the Midst of Death

The candle-ends had burnt out in the store; the moon no longer shone in through the skylight; but the latter was taking new shape, and a harder outline filled with an iron-gray that whitened imperceptibly, like a man's hair. The strange trio within sat still and silent, watching each other grow out of the gloom like figures on a sensitive film. The packet of meat and bread was reduced to a piece of paper and a few crumbs; the little flask was empty, and the water-bag half its former size; but now that all was over, the horror of the night lay heavier upon them than during the night itself. It was Naomi who broke the long silence at last.

"They have evidently gone," she said. "Don't you think we might venture now?"

"It is for you to decide," said Engelhardt.

"What do you think, Mrs. Potter?"

"If you ask me, Miss Naomi, I think it's beneath us to sit here another minute for a couple of rascals who will be ten miles away by this time."

"Then let us go. I will take the Winchester, and if they are still about we must just slip in again quicker than we came out. But I think it's good enough to chance."

"So do I," said the piano-tuner, "most decidedly."

"Then down with the props. They have served us very well, and no mistake! You must keep them in your kitchen, Mrs. Potter, as a trophy for all time."

The old woman made no reply. Of what she was thinking none ever knew. Her life had run in a narrow, uneventful groove. Its sole adventure was probably the one now so nearly at an end. Ten years ago she had been ear-witness of a somewhat similar incident. And now she had played a part, and no small part, in another and a worse. At her age she might have come out shaken and shattered to the verge of imbecility, after such a night. Or she might have felt inordinately proud of her share in the bushrangers' repulse. But when at last the battered door stood wide open, and the keen morning air chilled their faces, and the red morning sky met their eyes, the old woman looked merely sad and thoughtful, and years older since the day before. Her expression touched Naomi. Once more she threw her young arms about the wrinkled neck, and left kisses upon the rough cheek, and words of grateful praise in the old ears. Meanwhile Engelhardt had pushed past them both and marched into the middle of the yard.

"It's all right, I think," said he, standing purposely between the women and the hideous corpse by the well-palings. "Yes, the coast is clear. But there's the horse you rode, Mrs. Potter, and Bill's horse, too, apparently, tied side by side to the fence."

"May God forgive them all," said Mrs. Potter, gravely, as she walked across the yard at Naomi's side.

They were the last words she ever uttered. As she spoke, the crack of a rifle, with the snap of a pistol before and after, cut the early stillness as lightning cuts the sky. Naomi wheeled round and levelled her Winchester at the two men who were running with bent backs from a puff of smoke to a couple of horses tethered among the pines beyond kitchen and wood-heap. She sighted the foremost runner, but never fired. A heavy fall at her side made her drop the Winchester and turn sharply round. It was Mrs. Potter. She was lying like a log, with her brave old eyes wide open to the sky, and a bullet in her heart.

"Take me away," said the girl, faintly, as she got up from her knees. "I can bear no more."

"There are the horses," answered the piano-tuner, pointing to the two that were tied up to the fence. "I should dearly like to give chase!"

"No, no, no!" cried Naomi, in an agony. "Hasn't there been enough bloodshed for one night? We will ride straight to the shed. They have taken the very opposite direction. Let us start at once!"

"In an instant," he said, and ran indoors for something to throw over the dead woman. The girl was again kneeling beside her, when he came back with a table-cloth. And she was crying bitterly when, a minute later, he slipped his left hand under her foot and helped her into the saddle.

They never drew rein until the long, low wool-shed was well in sight. The sun was up. It was six o'clock. They could see the shearers swarming to the shed like bees to a hive. The morning air was pungent as spiced wine. Some color had come back to Naomi's cheeks, and it was she who first pulled up, forcing Engelhardt to do the same.

"Friday morning!" she said, walking her horse. "Can you realize that you only came last Saturday night?"

"I cannot."

"No more can I! We have been through so much ——"

"Together."

"Together and otherwise. I think you must have gone through more than I can guess, when you were lost in Top Scrubby, and when you fell in with those fiends. Will you tell me all about it some time or other?"

"I'm afraid there will be no opportunity," said Engelhardt, speaking with unnatural distinctness. "I must be off to-day."

"To-day!"

Her blank tone thrilled him to the soul.

"Of course," he said, less steadily. "Why not? I did my best to get away the night before last. Thank God I didn't succeed in that!"

"Why did you go like that?"

"You know why."

"I know why! What do you mean? How can I know anything?"

"Very easily," he bitterly replied, staring rigidly ahead with his burning face. "Very easily indeed, when I left you that letter!"

"What letter, Mr. Engelhardt?"

"The awful nonsense I was idiot enough to slip into your book!"

"The book I was reading?"

"Yes."

"Then I have never had your letter. I haven't opened that book since the day before yesterday, though more than once I have taken it up with the intention of doing so."

"Well, thank Heaven for that!"

"But why?"

"Because I said ——"

"Well, what *did* you say?"

She caught his bridle, and, by stopping both horses, forced him to face her at last.

"Surely you can guess? I had just got to know about Tom Chester, and I felt there was no hope for me, so I thought ——"

"Stop! what had you got to know about Tom Chester, please?"

"That he cared for you."

"Indeed! To me that's a piece of news. Mind, I care for him very much as a friend-as a hand."

"Then you don't ——"

"No, indeed I don't."

"Oh, Naomi, what am I to say? In that letter I said it all-when I had no hope in my heart. And now ——"

"And now you have called that letter awful nonsense, and yourself an idiot for writing it!"

She was smiling at him-her old, teasing smile-across the gap between their horses. But his eyes were full of tears.

"Oh, Naomi, you know what I meant!"

"And I suppose it has never occurred to you what I mean?"

He stared at her open-eyed.

"Will you marry me?" he blurted out.

"We'll see about that," said Naomi, as he took her hand and they rode onward with clasped fingers. "But I'll tell you what I *am* on to do. I'm on to put Taroomba in the market this very day, and to back you for all that it fetches. After that there's Europe-your mother-Milan-and anything you like, my dear fellow, for the rest of our two lives."

The Unbidden Guest

Chapter I
The Girl from Home.

Arabella was the first at the farm to become aware of Mr. Teesdale's return from Melbourne. She was reading in the parlour, with her plump elbows planted upon the faded green table-cloth, and an untidy head of light-coloured hair between her hands; looking up from her book by chance, she saw through the closed window her father and the buggy climbing the hill at the old mare's own pace. Arabella went on reading until the buggy had drawn up within a few feet of the verandah posts and a few more of the parlour window. Then she sat in doubt, with her finger on the place; but before it appeared absolutely necessary to jump up and run out, one of the men had come up to take charge of the mare, and Arabella was enabled to remove her finger and read on.

The parlour was neither very large nor at all lofty, and the shut window and fire-place closely covered by a green gauze screen, to keep the flies out, made it disagreeably stuffy. There were two doors, but both of these were shut also, though the one at the far end of the room, facing the hearth, nearly always stood wide open. It led down a step into a very little room where the guns were kept and old newspapers thrown, and where somebody was whistling rather sweetly as the other door opened and Mr. Teesdale entered, buggy-whip in hand.

He was a frail, tallish old gentleman, with a venerable forehead, a thin white beard, very little hair to his pate, and clear brown eyes that shone kindly upon all the world. He had on the old tall hat he always wore when driving into Melbourne, and the yellow silk dust-coat which had served him for many a red-hot summer, and was still not unpresentable. Arabella was racing to the end of a paragraph when he entered, and her father had stolen forward and kissed her untidy head before she looked up.

"Bad girl," said he, playfully, "to let your old father get home without ever coming out to meet him!"

"I was trying to finish this chapter," said Arabella. She went on trying.

" I know, I know! I know you of old, my dear. Yet I can't talk, because I am as bad as you are; only I should like to see you reading something better than the Family Cherub There were better things in the little room adjoining, where behind the shooting lumber was some motley reading, on two long sagging shelves; but that room was known as the gun-room, and half those books were hidden away behind powder-canisters, cartridge-cases, and the like, while all were deep in dust.

"You read it yourself, father," said Arabella as she turned over a leaf of her Family Cherub,

" I read it myself. More shame for me! But then I've read all them books in the little gun-room, and that's what I should like to see you reading now and then. Now why have you got yon door shut, Arabella, and who's that whistling in there ? "

" It's our John William," Miss Teesdale said; and even as she spoke the door in question was thrown open by a stalwart fellow in a Crimean shirt, with the sleeves rolled up from arms as brown and hard-looking as mellow oak. He had a breech-loader in one hand and a greasy rag in the other.

" Holloa, father! " cried he, boisterously.

"Well, John William, what are you doing?"

" Cleaning my gun. What have you been doing, that's more like it ? What took you trapesing into Melbourne the moment I got my back turned this morning ? "

"Why, hasn't your mother told you?"

" Haven't seen her since I came in."

"Well, but Arabella "

"Arabella! I'm full up of Arabella," said John William contemptuously; but the girl was still too deep in the Family Cherub to heed him. " There's no getting a word out of Arabella when she's on the read; so what's it all about, father?"

" I'll tell you ; but you'd better shut yon window, John William, or I don't know what your mother'll say when she comes in and finds the place full o' flies."

It was the gun-room window that broke the law of no fresh air, causing Mr. Teesdale uneasiness until John William shut it with a grumble; for in this homestead the mistress was law-maker, and indeed master, with man-servant and maid-servant, husband and daughter, and a particularly headstrong son, after her own heart, all under her thumb together.

"Now then, father, what was it took you into Melbourne all of a sudden like that?"

" A letter by the English mail, from my old friend Mr. Oliver."

"Never heard tell of him," said John William, making spectacles of his burnished bores, and looking through them into the sunlight. Already he had lost interest.

Mr. Teesdale was also occupied, having taken from his pocket a very large red cotton handkerchief, with which he was wiping alternately the dust from his tall hat and the perspiration from the forehead whereon the hat had left a fiery rim. Now, however, he nodded his bald head and clicked his lips, as one who gives another up.

" Well, well! Never heard tell of him — you who've heard me tell of him time out of mind! Nay, come; why, you've called after him yourself! Ay, we called you after John William Oliver because he was the best friend that ever we had in old Yorkshire or anywhere else; the very best; and you pretend you've never heard tell of him."

"What had he got to say for himself ?" said Mr. Oliver's namesake, with a final examination of the outside of his barrels.

"Plenty; he's sent one of his daughters out in the Parramatta that got in with the mail yesterday afternoon; and of course he had given her an introduction to me."

"What's that?" exclaimed John William, looking up sharply, as he ran over the words in his ear. "I say, father, we don't want her here," he added earnestly.

"Oh, did you find out where she was." Have you seen her? What is she like." cried Arabella, jumping up from the table and joining the others with a face full of questions. She had that instant finished her chapter.

"I don't know what she's like; I didn't see her; I couldn't even find out where she was, though I tried at half a dozen hotels and both coffee-palaces," said the farmer with a crestfallen air.

" All the better ! " cried John William, grounding his gun with a bang. "We don't want none of your stuck-up new chums or chumesses here, father."

" I don't know that; for my part, I should love to have a chance of talking to an English young lady," Arabella said, with a backward glance at her Family Cherub. "They're very rich, the Olivers" she added for her brother's benefit; "that's their house in the gilt frame in the best parlour, the house with the tower; and the group in the frame to match, that is the Olivers, isn't it, father?"

"It is, my dear; that's to say, it was, some sixteen years ago. We must get yon group and see which one it is that has come out, and then I'll read you Mr. Oliver's letter, John William. If only he'd written a mail or two before the child started! However, if we've everything made snug for her to-night, I'll lay hands on her to-morrow if she's in Melbourne; and then she shall come out here for a month or two to start with, just to see how she likes it."

" How d'ye know she'll want to come out here at all ? " asked John William. " Don't you believe it, father; she wouldn't care for it a little bit."

"Not care for it? Not want to come out and make her home with her parents' old friends? Then she's not her father's daughter," cried Mr. Teesdale indignantly; " she's no child of our good old friends. Why, it was Mr. Oliver who gave me the watch I hush! Was that your mother calling ?"

It was. " David ! David! Have you got back, David ?" the harsh voice came crying through the lath-and-plaster walls.

Mr. Teesdale scuttled to the door. "Yes, my dear, I've just got in. No, I'm not smoking. Where are you, then ? In the spare room ? All right, I'm coming, I'm coming." And he was gone.

" Mother's putting the spare room to rights already," Arabella explained.

"I'm sorry to hear it; let's hope it won't be wanted."

" Why, John William ? It would be such fun to have a young lady from Home to stay with us!"

"I'm full up o' young ladies, and I'm just sick of the sound of Home. She'll be a deal too grand for us, and there won't be much fun in that. What's the use o' talking ? If it was a son of this here old Oliver's it 'd be a different thing; we'd precious soon knock the nonsense out of him; I'd undertake to do it myself; but a girl's different, and I jolly well hope she'll stop away. We don't want her here, I tell you. We haven't even invited her. It's a piece of cheek, is the whole thing! "

John William was in the parlour now, sitting on the horse-hair sofa, and laying down the law with freckled fist and blusterous voice, as his habit was. It was a good-humoured sort of bluster, however, and indeed John William seldom opened his mouth without displaying his excellent downright nature in one good light or another. He had inherited his mother's qualities along with her sharp, decided features, which in the son were set off by a strong black beard and bristling moustache. He managed the farm, the men, Arabella, and his father; but all under Mrs. Teesdale, who managed him. Not that this masterful young man was so young in years as you might well suppose; neither John William nor Arabella was under thirty; but their lives had been so simple and so hard-working that, going by their conversation merely, you would have placed the two of them in their teens. For her part, too, Arabella looked much younger than she was, with her wholesome, attractive face and dreamy, inquisitive eyes; and as for the brother, he was but a boy with a beard, still primed with rude health and strength, and still loaded with all the assorted possibilities of budding manhood.

" I've taken down the group," said Mr. Teesdale, returning with a large photograph in a gilt frame ; " and here is the letter on the chimney-piece. We'll have a look at them both again."

On the chimney-piece also were the old man's spectacles, which he proceeded to put on, and a tobacco jar and long clay pipe, at which he merely looked lovingly; for Mrs. Teesdale would have no smoking in the house. His own chair stood in the cosy corner between the window and the hearth; and he now proceeded to pull it up to his own place at the head of the table as though it were a meal-time, and that gilt-framed photograph the only dish. Certainly he sat down to it with an appetite never felt during the years it had hung in the unused, ornamental next room, without the least prospect of the Teesdales ever more seeing any member of that group in the flesh. But now that such a prospect was directly at hand, there was some sense in studying the old photograph. It was of eight persons: the parents, a grandparent, and five children. Three of the latter were little girls, in white stockings and hideous boots with low heels and elastic sides; and to the youngest of these three, a fair-haired child whose features, like those of the whole family, were screwed up by a strong light and an exposure of the ancient length, Mr. Teesdale pointed with his finger-nail.

"That's the one," said he. "She now is a young lady of five or six and twenty."

" Don't think much of her looks," observed John William.

"Oh, you can't tell what she may be like from this," Arabella said, justly. " She may be beautiful now; besides, look how the sun must have been in her eyes, poor little thing! What's her name again, father ? "

" Miriam, my dear."

" Miriam! I call it a jolly name, don't you. Jack ? "

" It's a beast of a name," said John William.

" Stop while I read you a bit of the letter," cried the old man, smiling indulgently. " I won't give you all of it, but just this little bit at the end. He's been telling me that Miriam has her own ideas about things, has already seen something of the world, and isn't perhaps quite like the girls I may remember when we were both young men ".

" Didn't I tell you?" interrupted John William, banging the table with his big fist. " She's stuck-up! We don't want her here."

"But just hark how he ends up. I want you both to listen to these few lines: — 'It may even be that she has formed habits and ways which were not the habits and ways of young girls in our day, and that you may like some of these no better than I do. Yet her heart, my dear Teesdale, is as pure and as innocent as her mother's was before her, and I know that my old friend will let no mere modem mannerisms prejudice him against my darling child, who is going so far from us all. It has been a rather sudden arrangement, and though the doctors ordered it, and Miriam can take care of herself as only the girls nowadays can, still I would never have parted with her had I not known of one tried friend to meet and welcome her at the other end. Keep her at your station, my dear Teesdale, as long as you can, for an open-air life is, I am convinced, what she wants above all things. If she should need money, an accident which may always happen, let her have whatever she wants, advising me of the amount immediately. I have told her to apply to you in such an extremity, which, however, I regard as very unlikely to occur. I have also provided her with a little note of introduction, with which she will find her way to you as soon as possible after landing. And into your kind old hands, and those of your warm-hearted wife, I cheerfully commend my girl, with the most affectionate remembrances to you both, and only regretting that business will not allow me to come out with her and see you both once more.' Then he finishes — calls himself my affectionate friend, same as when we were boys together. And it's two-and-thirty years since we said good-bye ! " added Mr. Teesdale as he folded up the letter and put it away.

He pushed his spectacles on to his forehead, for they were dim, and sat gazing straight ahead, through the inner door that stood now wide open, and out of the gun-room window. This overlooked a sunburnt decline, finishing, perhaps a furlong from the house, at the crests of the river timber, that stood out of it like a hedge, by reason of the very deep cut made by the Yarra, where it formed the farm boundary on that side. And across the top of the window (to one sitting in Mr. Teesdale's place) was stretched, like a faded mauve ribbon, a strip of the distant Dandenong Ranges; and this and the timber were the favourite haunts of the old man's eyes, for thither they strayed of their own accord whenever his mind got absent elsewhere, as was continually happening, and had happened now.

" It's a beautiful letter! " exclaimed Arabella warmly.

"I like it, too," John William admitted; "but I shan't like the girl. That kind don't suit me at all; but I'll try to be civil to her on account of the old man, for his letter is right enough."

Mr. Teesdale looked pleased, though he left his eyes where they were.

"Ay, ay, my dears, I thought you would like it. Ah, but all his letters are the same! Two-and-thirty years, and never a year without at least three letters from Mr. Oliver. He's a business man, and he always answers promptly. He's a rich man now, my dears, but he doesn't forget the early friends, not he, though they're at the other end of the earth, and as poor as he's rich."

"Yet he doesn't seem to know how we're situated, for all that," remarked John William thoughtfully. " Look how he talks about our station,' and of your advancing money to the girl, as though we were rolling in it like him! Have you never told him our circumstances, father ? "

At the question, Mr. Teesdale's eyes fell twenty miles, and rested guiltily upon the old green tablecloth.

"I doubt a station and a farm convey much the same thing in the old country" he answered crookedly.

" That you may bet they do!" cried the son, with a laugh; but he went on delivering himself of the most discouraging prophecies touching the case in point. The girl would come out with false ideas; would prove too fine by half for plain people like themselves; and at the best was certain to expect much more than they could possibly give her.

" Well, as to that," said the farmer, who thought himself lucky to have escaped a scolding for never having told an old friend how poor he was —" as to that, we can but give her the best we've got, with may be a little extra here and there, such as we wouldn't have if we were by ourselves. The eggs'll be fresh, at any rate, and I think that she'll like her sheets, for your mother is getting out them 'at we brought with us from Home in '51. There was just two pairs, and she's had 'em laid by in lavender ever since. We can give her a good cup o' tea, an' all; and you can take her out 'possum-shooting, John William, and teach her how to ride. Yes, we'll make a regular bush-girl of her in a month, and send her back to Yorkshire the picture of health; though as yet I'm not very clear what's been the matter with her. But if she takes after her parents ever so little she'll see that we're doing our best, and that'll be good enough for any child of theirs."

From such a shabby waistcoat pocket Mr. Tees-dale took so handsome a gold watch, it was like a ring on a beggar's finger; and he fondled it between his worn hands, but without a word.

"Mr. Oliver gave you that watch, didn't he, father?" Arabella said, watching him.

"He did, my dear," said the old man proudly. " He came and saw us off at the Docks, and he gave me the watch on board, just as we were saying good-bye; and he gave your mother a gold brooch which neither of you have ever seen, for I've never known her wear it myself."

Arabella said she had seen it. "Now his watch," continued Mr. Teesdale, "has hardly ever left my pocket — save to go under my pillow — since he put it in my hands on July 3, 1851. Here's the date and our initials inside the case; but you've seen them before. Ay, but there are few who came out in '51 — and stopped out — who have done as poorly as me. The day after we dropped anchor in Hobson's Bay there wasn't a living soul aboard our ship; captain, mates, passengers and crew, all gone to the diggings. Every man Jack but me! It was just before you were born, John William, and I wasn't going. It may have been a mistake, but the Lord knows best. To be sure, we had our hard times when the diggers were coming into Melbourne and shoeing their horses with gold, and filling buckets with champagne, and standing by with a pannikin to make everybody drink that passed; if you wouldn't, you'd got to take off your coat and show why. I remember one of them offering me a hundred pounds for this very watch, and precious hard up I was, but I wouldn't take it, not I, though I didn't refuse a sovereign for telling him the time. Ay, sovereigns were the pennies of them days; not that fingered many; but I never got so poor as to part with Mr. Oliver's watch, and you never must either, John William, when it's yours. Ay, ay," chuckled Mr. Teesdale, as he snapped-to the case and replaced the watch in his pocket, "and it's gone like a book for over thirty years, with nothing worse than a cleaning the whole time"

" You must mind and tell that to Miriam, father," said Arabella, smiling.

"I must so. Ah, my dear, I shall have two daughters, not one, and you'll have a sister while Miriam is here."

"That depends what Miriam is like," said John William, getting up from the sofa with a laugh and going back idly to the little room and his cleaned gun.

"I know what she will be like," said Arabella, placing the group in front of her on the table. "She will be delicate and fair, and rather small; and I shall have to show her everything, and take tremendous care of her."

" I wonder if she'll have her mother's hazel eyes and gentle voice ? " mused the farmer aloud, with his eyes on their way back to the Dandenong Ranges. "I should like her to take after her mother; she was one of the gentlest little women that ever I knew, was Mrs. Oliver, and I never clapped eyes "

The speaker suddenly turned his head; there had been a step in the verandah, and some person had passed the window too quick for recognition.

"Who was that?" said Mr. Teesdale.

" I hardly saw," said Arabella, pushing back her chair. "It was a woman."

" And now she's knocking! Run and see who it is, my dear."

Arabella rose and ran. Then followed such an outcry in the passage that Mr. Teesdale rose also. He was on his legs in time to see the door flung wide open, and the excited eyes of Arabella reaching over the shoulder of the tall young woman whom she was pushing into the room.

"Here is Miriam," she cried. "Here's Miriam found her way out all by herself!"

Chapter II
A Bad Beginning.

At the sound of the voices outside, John William, for his part, had slipped behind the gun-room door; but he had the presence of mind not to shut it quite, and this enabled him to peer through the crack and take deliberate stock of the fair visitant.

She was a well-built young woman, with a bold, free carriage and a very daring smile. That was John William's first impression when he came to think of it in words a little later. His eyes then fastened upon her hair. The poor colour of her face and lips did not strike him at the time any more than the smudges under the merry eyes. The common stamp of the regular features never struck him at all, for of such matters old Mr. Teesdale himself was hardly a judge; but the girl's hair took John William's fancy on the spot. It was the most wonderful hair: red, and yet beautiful. There was plenty of it to be seen, too, for the straw hat that hid the rest had a backward tilt to it, while an exuberant fringe came down within an inch of the light eyebrows. John William could have borne it lower still. He watched and listened with a smile upon his own hairy visage, of which he was totally unaware.

" So this is my old friend's daughter! " the farmer had cried out.

" And you're Mr. Scarsdale, are you ? " answered the girl, between fits of intermittent, almost hysterical laughter.

" Eh ? Yes, yes; I'm Mr. Teesdale, and this is my daughter Arabella. You are to be sisters, you two."

The visitor turned to Arabella and gave her a sounding kiss upon the lips.

" And mayn't I have one too ? " old Teesdale asked. " I'm that glad to see you, my dear, and you know you're to look upon me like a father as long as you stay in Australia. Thank you, Miriam. Now I feel as if you'd been here a week already ! "

Mr. Teesdale had received as prompt and as hearty a kiss as his daughter before him.

" Mrs. Teesdale is busy, but she'll come directly," he went on to explain. " Do you know what she's doing ? She's getting your room ready, Miriam. We knew that you had landed, and I've spent the whole day hunting for you in town. Just to think that you should have come out by yourself after all! But our John William was here a minute ago. John William, what are you doing?"

"Cleaning my gun," said the young man, coming from behind his door, greasy rag in hand.

" Nay, come! You finished that job long ago. Come and shake hands with Miriam. Look, here she is, safe and sound, and come out all by herself !"

" I'm very glad to see you," said the son of the house, advancing, dirty palms foremost, "but I'm sorry I can't shake hands!"

" Then I'd better kiss you too!"

She had taken a swinging step forward, and the red fringe was within a foot of his startled face, when she tossed back her head with a hearty laugh.

" No, I think I won't. You're too old and you're not old enough — see ? "

" John William'll be three-and-thirty come January," said Mr. Teesdale gratuitously.

" Yes ? That's ten years older than me," answered the visitor with equal candour. "Exactly ten!"

"Nay, come — not exactly ten," the old gentleman said, with some gravity, for he was a great stickler for the literal truth; "only seven or eight, I understood from your father?"

The visitor coloured, then pouted, and then burst out laughing as she exclaimed, "You oughtn't to be so particular about ladies' ages! Surely two or three years is near enough, isn't it ? Fm ashamed of you, Mr. Teesdale; I really am!" And David received such a glance that he became exceedingly ashamed of himself; but the smile that followed it warmed his old heart through and through, and reminded him, he thought, of Miriam's mother.

Meantime, the younger Teesdale remained rooted to the spot where he had been very nearly kissed. He was still sufficiently abashed, but perhaps on that very account a plain speech came from him too.

" You're not like what I expected. No, I'm bothered if you are! "

" Much worse ?" asked the girl, with a scared look.

" No, much better. Ten thousand times better! " cried the young man. Then his shyness overtook him, and, though Tie joined in the general laughter, he ventured no further remarks. As to the laughter, the visitor's was the most infectious ever heard in the weather-board farm-house. Arabella shook within the comfortable covering with which nature had upholstered her, and old David had to apply the large red handkerchief to his furrowed cheeks before he could give her the message to Mrs. Teesdale, for which there had not been a moment to spare out of the crowded minute or two which had elapsed since the visitor's unforeseen arrival.

"Go, my dear," he said now, "and tell your mother that Miriam is here. That's it. Mrs. T. will be with us directly, Miriam. Ah, I thought this photograph 'd catch your eye sooner or later. You'll have seen it once or twice before, eh ? Just once or twice, I'm thinking." The group still lay on the table at Mr. Teesdale's end.

" Who are they ? " asked the visitor, very carelessly; indeed, she had but given the photograph a glance, and that from a distance.

"Who. Why, yourselves; your own family.

All the lot of you when you were little," cried David, snatching up the picture and handing it across. "We were just looking at it when you came, Miriam; and I made you out to be this one, look — this poor little thing with the sun in her eyes."

The old man was pointing with his finger, the girl examining closely. Their heads were together. Suddenly she raised hers, looked him in the eyes, and burst out laughing.

" How clever you are! " she said. " I'm not a bit like that now, now am I?"

She made him look well at her before answering. And in all his after knowledge of it, he never again saw quite so bold and debonnaire an expression upon that cool face framed in so much hot hair. But from a mistaken sense of politeness, Mr. Teesdale made a disingenuous answer after all, and the subject of conversation veered from the girl who had come out to Australia to those she had left behind her in the old country.

That conversation would recur to Mr. Teesdale in after days. It contained surprises for him at the time. Later, he ceased to wonder at what he had heard. Indeed, there was nothing wonderful in his having nourished quite a number of misconceptions concerning a family of whom he had set eyes on no member for upwards of thirty years. It was those misconceptions which the red-haired member of that family now removed. They were all very natural in the circumstances. And yet, to give an instance, Mr. Teesdale was momentarily startled to ascertain that Mrs. Oliver had never been so well in her life as when her daughter sailed. He had understood from Mr. Oliver that his wife was in a very serious state with diabetes. When he now said so, the innocent remark made Miss Oliver to blush and bite her lips. Then she explained. Her mother had been threatened with the disease in question, but that was all. The real fact was, her father was morbidly anxious about her mother, and to such an extent that it appeared the anxiety amounted to mania.

She put it in her own way.

"Pa's mad on ma," she said. "You can't believe a word he says about her."

Mr. Teesdale found this difficult to believe of his old friend, who seemed to him to write so sensibly about the matter. It made him look out of the gun-room window. Then he recollected that the girl herself lacked health, for which cause she had come abroad.

"And what was the matter with you, Miriam," said he, " for your father only says that the doctors recommended the voyage ? "

"Oh, that's all he said, was it?"

" Yes, that's all."

"And you want to know what was the matter with me, do you ? "

" No, I was only wondering. It's no business of mine."

"Oh, but I'll tell you. Bless your life, I'm not ashamed of it. It was late nights — it was late nights that was the matter with me."

"Nay, come," cried the farmer; yet, as he peered through his spectacles into the bright eyes sheltered by the fiery fringe, he surmised a deep-lying heaviness in the brain behind them; and he noticed now for the first time how pale a face they were set in, and how gray the marks were underneath them.

" The voyage hasn't done you much good, either," he said. " Why, you aren't even sunburnt."

"No? Well, you see, I'm such a bad sailor. I spent all my time in the cabin, that's how it was."

"Yet the Argus says you had such a good voyage?"

" Yes ? I expect they always say that. It was a beast of a voyage, if you ask me, and quite as bad as late nights for you, though not nearly so nice."

" Ah, well, we'll soon set you up, my dear. This is the place to make a good job of you, if ever there was one. But where have you been staying since you landed, Miriam? It's upwards of twenty-four hours now."

The guest smiled.

"Ah, that's tellings. With some people who came out with me — some swells that I knew in the West End, if you particularly want to know; not that I'm much nuts on 'em, either."

" Don't you be inquisitive, father," broke in John William from the sofa. It was his first remark since he had sat down.

"Well, perhaps I mustn't bother you with any more questions now," said Mr. Teesdale to the girl; "but I shall have a hundred to ask you later on. To think that you're Mr. Oliver's daughter after all! Ay, and I see a look of your mother and all now and then. They did well to send you out to us, and get you right away from them late hours and that nasty society — though here comes one that'll want you to tell her all about that by-and-by."

The person in question was Arabella, who had just re-entered.

" Society ? " said she. " My word, yes, I shall want you to tell me all about society, Miriam."

"Do you hear that, Miriam?" said Mr. Teesdale after some moments. She had taken no notice.

"What's that? Oh yes, I heard; but I shan't tell anybody anything more unless you all stop calling me Miriam."

This surprised them; it had the air of a sudden thought as suddenly spoken.

" But Miriam's your name," said Arabella, laughing.

"Your father has never spoken of you as anything else," remarked Mr. Teesdale.

" All the same, I'm not used to being called by it," replied their visitor, who for the first time was exhibiting signs of confusion. "I like people to call me what I'm accustomed to being called. You may say it's a pet name, but it's what I'm used to, and I like it best."

" What is, missy ? " said old Teesdale kindly ; for the girl was staring absently at the opposite wall.

"Tell us, and we'll call you nothing else," Arabella promised.

The girl suddenly swept her eyes from the wall to Mr. Teesdale's inquiring face. "You said it just now," she told him, with a nod and her brightest smile. "You said it without knowing when you called me 'Missy.' That's what they always call me at home — Missy or the Miss. You pays your money and you takes your choice."

" Then I choose Missy," said Arabella. " And now, father, I came with a message from my mother; she wants you to take Missy out into the verandah while we get the tea ready. She wasn't tidy enough to come and see you at once, Missy, but she sends you her love to go on with, and she hopes that you'll excuse her."

"Of course she will," answered Mr. Teesdale for the girl; "but will you excuse me. Missy, if I bring my pipe out with me? I'm just wearying for a smoke."

" Excuse you ? " cried Missy, taking the old man's arm as she accompanied him to the door. "Why, bless your life, I love a smoke myself."

John William had jumped up to follow them; had hesitated; and was left behind.

" There!" said Arabella, turning a shocked face upon him the instant they were quite alone.

"She was joking," said John William.

"I don't think it."

" Then you must be a fool, Arabella. Of course she was only in fun."

" But she said so many queer things; and oh, John William, she seems to me so queer altogether !"

"Well, what the deuce did you expect?" cried the other in a temper. " Didn't her own father say that she was something out of the common? What do you know about it, anyway ? What do you know about 'modem mannerisms'? Didn't her own father let on that she had some? Even if she did smoke, I shouldn't be surprised or think anything of it; depend upon it they smoke in society, whether they do or they don't in your rotten Family Cherub. But she was only joking when she said that; and I never saw the like of you, Arabella, not to know a joke when you hear one." And John William stamped away to his room; to reappear in a white shirt and his drab tweed suit, exactly as though he had been going into Melbourne for the day.

It was Mrs. Teesdale, perhaps, who put this measure into her son's head; for, as he quitted the parlour, she pushed past him to enter it, in the act of fastening the final buttons of her gray-stuff chapel-going bodice. "Now, then, Arabella," she cried sharply, "let blind down and get them things off table." And on to it, as she spoke, Mrs. Teesdale flung a clean white folded table-cloth which she had carried between elbow and ribs while busy buttoning her dress. As for Arabella, she obeyed each order instantly, displaying an amount of bustling activity which only showed itself on occasions when her mother was particularly hot and irritable; the present was one.

Mrs. Teesdale was a tall, strong woman who at sixty struck one first of all with her strength, activity, and hard, solid pluck. Her courage and her hardness too were written in every wrinkle of a bloodless, weather-beaten face that must have been sharp and pointed even in girlhood; and those same dominant qualities shone continually in a pair of eyes like cold steel — the eyes of a woman who had never given in. The woman had not her husband's heart full of sympathy and affection for all but the very worst who came his way. She had neither his moderately good education, nor his immoderately ready and helping hand even for the worst. Least of all had she his simple but adequate sense of humour; of this quality and all its illuminating satellites Mrs. Teesdale was totally devoid. Yet, but for his wife, old David would probably have found himself facing his latter end in one or other of the Benevolent Asylums of that Colony; whereas with the wife's character inside the husband's skin, it is not improbable that the name of David Teesdale would have been known and honoured in the land where his days had been long indeed, but sadly unprofitable.

Arabella, then, who had inherited some of David's weak points, just as John William possessed his mother's strong ones, could work with the best of them when she liked and Mrs. Teesdale drove. In ten minutes the tea was ready; and it was a more elaborate tea than usual, for there was quince jam as well as honey, and, by great good luck, cold boiled ham in addition to hot boiled eggs. Last of all, John William, when he was ready, picked a posy of geraniums from the bed outside the gun-room outer door (which was invisible from the verandah, where David and the visitor could be heard chatting), and placed them in the centre of the clean table-cloth. Then Mrs. Teesdale drew up the blind; and a nice sight met their eyes. Mr. Teesdale was discovered in earnest expostulation with the girl from England, who was smoking his pipe. She had jumped on to the wooden armchair upon which, a moment ago, she had no doubt been seated; now she was dancing upon it, slowly and rhythmically, from one foot to the other, and while holding the long clay well above the old man's reach, she kept puffing at it with such immense energy that the smoke hung in a cloud about her rakish fringe and wicked smile, under the verandah slates. A smile flickered also across the entreating face of David Teesdale; and it was this his unpardonable show of taking the outrage in good part, that made away with the wife's modicum of self-control. Doubling a hard-working fist, she was on the point of knocking at the window with all the might that it would bear, when her wrist was held and the blind let down. And it was John William who faced her indignation with the firm front which she herself had given him.

" I am very sorry, mother," said he quietly, " but you are not going to make a scene."

Such was the power of Mrs. Teesdale in her own home, she could scarcely credit her hearing. " Not going to ." she cried, for the words had been tuned neither to question nor entreaty, but a command. " Let go my hands this moment, sir!"

"Then don't knock," said John William, complying ; and there was never a knock; but the woman was blazing.

" How dare you ? " she said; and indeed, man and boy, he had never dared so much before.

" You were going to make a scene," said he, as kindly as ever; " and though we didn't invite her, she is our guest "

"You may be ashamed of yourself! I don't care who she is; she shan't smoke here."

" She is also the daughter of your oldest friends; and hasn't her own father written to say she has ways and habits which the girls hadn't when you were one ? Not that smoking's a habit of hers: not likely. I'll bet she's only done this for a lark. And you're to say nothing more about it, mother, do you see ? "

" Draw up the blind," said Mrs. Teesdale, speaking to her son as she had spoken to him all his life, but, for the first time, without confidence. " Draw up the blind, and disobey me at your peril."

" Then promise to say nothing about it to the girl."

They eyed each other for a minute. In the end the mother said: " To the girl ! No, of course I won't say anything to her — unless it happens again." It was not even happening when the blind was drawn up, and it never did happen again. But Mrs. Teesdale had given in, for once in her life, and to one of her own children. Moreover, there was an alien in the case, who was also a girl; and this was the beginning between these three.

Chapter III
Au Revoir.

It was not a very good beginning, and the first to feel that was John William himself. He felt it at tea. During the meal his mouth never opened, except on business; but his eyes made up for it.

He saw everything. He saw that his mother and Missy would never get on; he knew it the moment they kissed. There was no sounding smack that time. The visitor, for her part, seemed anxious to show that even she could be shy if she tried ; and as for Mrs. Teesdale and her warm greeting, it was very badly done. The tone was peevish, and her son, for one, could hear between the words. "You're our old friends' child," he heard her saying in her heart, " but I don't think I shall like you ; for you've come without letting me know, you've smoked, and you've set my own son against me — already." He was half sorry that he had checked, what is as necessary to some as the breath they draw, a little plain speaking at the outset. But sooner or later, about one thing or another, this was bound to come; and come it did.

"I can't think, Miriam," said Mrs. Teesdale, " how you came by that red hair o' yours! Your father's was very near black, and your mother's a light brown wi' a streak o' gold in it; but there wasn't a red hair in either o' their heads that I can remember."

At this speech John William bit off an oath under his beard, while David looked miserably at his wife, and Arabella at their visitor, who first turned as red as her hair, and then burst into a fit of her merriest laughter.

" Well, I can't help it, can I ? " cried she, with a good-nature that won two hearts, at any rate. "I didn't choose my hair; it grew its own colour — all I've got to do is to keep it on !"

" Yes, but it's that red! " exclaimed Mrs. Tees-dale stolidly, while John William chuckled and looked less savage.

"Ah, you could light your old pipe at it," said Missy to the farmer, making the chuckler laugh outright.

Not SO Mr. Teesdale. " My dear," he said to his wife ; " my dear! "

"Well, but I could understand it, David, if her parents' hairs had any red in them. In the only photograph we have of you, Miriam, which is that group there taken when you were all little, you look to have your mother's fair hair. I can't make it out."

" No ? " said Missy, sweetly. " Then you didn't know that red always comes out light in a photograph ? "

"Oh, I know nothing at all about that," said Mrs. Teesdale, with the proper disregard for a lost point. " Then have the others all got red hair too?"

" N—no, I'm the only one."

"Well, that's a good thing, Miriam, I'm sure it is! "

" Nay, come, my dear, that'll do," whispered David; while John William said loudly, to change the subject, " You're not to call her Miriam, mother."

" And why not, I wonder ? "

" Because she's not used to it. She says they call her Missy at home; and we want to make her at home here, surely to goodness!"

Missy had smiled gratefully on John William and nodded confirmation of his statement to Mrs. Teesdale, who, however, shook her head.

" Ay, but I don't care for nicknames at all," said she, without the shadow of a smile; "I never did and I never shall, John William. So, Miriam, you'll have to put up with your proper name from me, for I'm too old to change. And I'm sure it's not an ugly one," added the dour woman, less harshly. " Is your cup off, Miriam t " she added to that; she did not mean to be quite as she was.

It was at this point, however, that the visitor asked Mr. Teesdale the time, and that Mr. Tees-dale, with a sudden eloquence in his kind old eyes, showed her the watch which Mr. Oliver had given him ; speaking most touchingly of her father's goodness, and kindness, and generosity, and of their lifelong friendship. Thus the long hand marked some minutes while the watch was still out before it appeared why Missy wanted to know the time. She then declared she must get back to Melbourne before dark, a statement which provoked some brisk opposition, notably on the part of Mr. Teesdale. But the girl showed commendable firmness. She would go back as she had come, by the six o'clock 'bus from the township. None of them, however, would hear of the 'bus, and John William waited until a compromise had been effected by her giving way on this point; then he went out to put-to.

This proved a business. The old mare had already made one journey into Melbourne and back; and that was some nine miles each way. There was another buggy-horse, but it had to be run up from the paddock. Thus twenty minutes elapsed before John William led horse and trap round to the front of the house. He found the party he had left mildly arguing round the tea-table, now assembled on the grass below the red-brick verandah. They were arguing still, it seemed, and not quite so mildly. Missy was buttoning a yellow glove, the worse for wear, and she was standing like a rock, with her mouth shut tight. Mr. Tees-dale had on his tall hat and his dust-coat, and the whip was once more in his hand; at the sight of him his son's heel went an inch into the ground.

" Only fancy ! " cried the old man in explanation. "She says she's not coming back to us any more. She doesn't want to come out and stay with us! "

Arabella echoed the " Only fancy! " while Mrs. Teesdale thought of the old folks who had been young when she was, and said decisively, " But she'll have to."

John William said nothing at all; but it was to him the visitor now looked appealingly.

"It isn't that I shouldn't like it —that isn't it at all — it's that you wouldn't like me! Oh, you don't know what I am. You don't, I tell you straight. I'm not fit to come and stay here — I should put you all about so — there's no saying what I shouldn't do. You can't think how glad I am to have seen you all. It's a jolly old place, and I shall be able to tell 'em all at home just what it's like. But you'd far better let me rest where I am — you — you — you really had."

She had given way, not to tears, indeed, but to the slightly hysterical laughter which had characterised her entry into the parlour when John William was looking through the crack. Now she once more made her laughter loud, and it seemed particularly inconsequent. Yet here was a sign of irresolution which old David, as the wisest of the Teesdales, was the first to recognise. Moreover, her eyes were flying from the weather-board farmhouse to the river timber down the hill, from the soft cool grass to the peaceful sky, and from hay-stack to hen-yard, as though the whole simple scene were a temptation to her; and David saw this also.

"Nonsense," said he firmly; and to the others, " She'll come back and stay with us till she's tired of us — we'll never be tired of you. Missy. Ay, of course she will. You leave her to me, Mrs. T."

"Then," said Missy, snatching her eyes from their last fascination, a wattle-bush in bloom, " will you take all the blame if I turn out a bad egg ? "

"A what?" said Mrs. Teesdale.

" Of course we will," cried her husband, turning a deaf ear to John William, who was trying to speak to him.

" You promise, all of you!"

"Of course we do," answered the farmer again; but he had not answered John William.

" Then I'll come, and your blood be on your own heads."

For a moment she stood smiling at them all in turn; and not a soul of them saw her next going without thinking of this one. The low sun struck full upon the heavy red fringe, and on the pale face and the devil-may-care smile which it overhung just then. At the back of that smile there was a something which seemed to be coming up swiftly like a squall at sea; but only for one moment; the next, she had kissed the women, shaken hands with the young man, mounted into the buggy beside Mr. Teesdale, and the two of them were driving slowly down the slope.

" I think, John William," said his mother, " that you might have driven in this time, instead o' letting your father go twice."

" Didn't I want to ? " replied John William, in a bellow which made Missy turn her head at thirty yards. " He was bent on going. He's the most pig-headed old man in the Colony. He wouldn't even answer me when I spoke to him about it just now."

He turned on his heel, and mother and daughter were at last alone, and free to criticise.

" For a young lady fresh from England," began the former, " I must say I thought it was a shabby dress — didn't you ? "

" Shabby isn't the word," said Arabella; " if you ask me, I call her whole style flashy — as flashy as it can stick."

Chapter IV
A Matter of Twenty Pounds.

"This is jolly! " exclaimed Missy, settling herself comfortably at the old man's side as she handed him back the reins. They had just jogged out of the lowest paddock, and Mr. Teesdale had been down to remove the slip-rails and to replace them after Missy had driven through.

"Very nicely done," the farmer said, in his playful, kindly fashion. "I see you've handled the ribbons before."

" Never in my life ! "

" Indeed ? I should have thought that with all them horses and carriages every one of you would have learnt to ride and drive."

" Yes, you would think so," Missy said, after a pause; "but in my case you'd think wrong. I can't bear horses, so I tell you straight. One flew at me when I was a little girl, and I've never gone near 'em since."

" Flew at you! " exclaimed Mr. Teesdale. " Nay, come!"

"Well, you know what I mean. I'd show you the bite "

" Oh, it bit you ? Now I see, now I see."

" You saw all along! "

" No, it was such a funny way of putting it."

"You knew what I meant," persisted Missy. "If you're going to make game of me, I'll get down and walk. Shall we be back in Melbourne by seven ? "

Mr. Teesdale drew out his watch with a proud smile and a tender hand. He loved consulting it before anybody, but Missy's presence gave the act a special charm. He shook his head, however, in answer to her question.

"We'll not do it," said he; "it's ten past six already."

"Then how long is it going to take us?"

" Well, not much under the hour; you see "

A groan at his side made Mr. Teesdale look quickly round; and there was trouble under the heavy fringe.

"I must be there soon after seven!" cried the girl petulantly.

" Ay, but where, Missy ? I'll do my best," said David, snatching up the whip, "if you'll tell me where it is you want to be."

"It's the Bijou Theatre — I'm supposed to be there by seven — to meet the people I'm staying with, you know."

David had begun to use the whip vigorously, but now he hesitated and looked pained. " I am sorry to hear it's a theatre you want to get to," said he gravely.

"Why, do you think them such sinks of iniquity — is that it ?" asked the girl, laughing.

" I never was in a theatre in my life, Missy; I don't approve of them, my dear."

" No more do I —no more do I! But when you're staying with people you can't always be your own boss, now can you ? "

"You could with us. Missy."

" Well, that's bully; but I can't with these folks. They're regular terrors for the theatre, the folks I'm staying with now, and I don't know what they'll say if I keep 'em waiting long. Think you can do it?"

" Not by seven; but I think we might get there between five and ten minutes past."

"Thank God!"

Mr. Teesdale wrinkled his forehead, but said nothing. Evidently it was of the first importance that Missy should not keep her friends waiting. Of these people, however, she had already spoken so lightly that David was pleased to fancy her as not caring very much about them.

He was pleased, not only because they took her to the theatre, but because he wanted no rival Australian friends for his old friend's child; the farm, if possible, must be her only home so long as she remained in the Colony. When, therefore, the girl herself confirmed his hopes the very next time she opened her mouth, the old man beamed with satisfaction.

"These folks I'm staying with," said Missy — " I'm not what you call dead nuts on 'em, as I said before."

"I'm glad to hear it," chuckled David, "because we want you all to ourselves, my dear."

"So you think! Some day you'll be sorry you spoke."

"Nonsense, child. What makes you talk such rubbish ? You've got to come and make your home with us until you're tired of us, as I've told you already. Where is it they live, these friends of yours ?"

" Where do they live ?" repeated Missy. " Oh, in Kew."

"Ah —Kew."

The name was spoken in a queer, noticeable tone, as of philosophic reflection. Then the farmer smiled and went on driving in silence; they were progressing at a good speed now. But Missy had looked up anxiously.

"What do you know about Kew ?" said she.

" Not much," replied David, with a laugh; " only once upon a time I had a chance of buying it — and had the money too!"

"You had the money to buy Kew ?"

"Yes, I had it. There was a man who took me on to a hill and showed me a hollow full of scrub and offered to get me the refusal of it for an old song. I had the money and all, as it happened, but I wasn't going to throw it away. The place looked a howling wilderness; but it is now the suburb of Kew."

"Think of that. Aren't you sorry you didn't buy it ? "

" Oh, it makes no difference."

" But you'd be so rich if you had! "

" I should be a millionaire twice over," said the farmer, complacently, as he removed his ruin of a top-hat to let in the breeze upon his venerable pate. Missy sat aghast at him.

" It makes me sick to think of it," she exclaimed. " I don't know what I couldn't do to you! If I'd been you I'd have cut my throat years ago. To think of the high old time you could have had! "

"I never had that much desire for a high old time," said Mr. Teesdale with gentle exaltation.

" Haven't I, then, that's all! cried his companion in considerable excitement. "It makes a poor girl feel bad to hear you go on like that."

"But you're not a poor girl."

Missy was silenced.

" Yes, I am," she said at last, with an air of resolution. It was not, however, until they were the better part of a mile nearer Melbourne.

"You are what ?"

"A poor girl."

" Nonsense, my dear. I wonder what your father would say if he heard you talk like that."

"He's got nothing to do with it."

" Not when he's worth thousands, Missy ?"

" Not when he's thousands of miles away, Mr. Teesdale."

Mr. Teesdale raised his wrinkled forehead and drove on. A look of mingled anxiety and pain aged him years in a minute. Soon the country roads were left behind, and the houses began closing up on either side of a very long and broad high road. It was ten minutes to seven by Mr. Teesdale's watch when he looked at it again. It was time for him to say the difficult thing which had occurred to him two or three miles back, and he said it in the gentlest tones imaginable from an old man of nearly seventy.

” Missy, my dear, is it possible ” (so he put it) ” that you have run short of the needful ? ”

” It’s a fact,” said Missy light-heartedly.

“But how, my dear, have you managed to do that?”

” How ? Let’s see. I gave a lot away — to a woman in the steerage — whose husband went and died at sea. He died of dropsy. I nursed him, I did. Rather! I helped lay him out when he was dead. But don’t go telling anybody — please.”

Mr. Teesdale had shuddered uncontrollably; now, however, he shifted the reins to his right hand in order to pat Missy with his left.

” You’re a noble girl. You are that! Yet it’s only what I should have expected of their child. I might have known you’d be a noble girl.”

” But you won’t tell anybody ? ”

” Not if you’d rather I didn’t. That proves your nobility ! About how much would you like, my dear, to go on with ? ”

“Oh, twenty pounds.”

Mr. Teesdale drew the breeze in through the broken ranks of his teeth.

” Wouldn’t — wouldn’t ten do, my dear ? ”

” Ten ? Let’s think. No, I don’t think I could do with a penny less than twenty. You see, a wave came into the cabin and spoilt all my things. I want everything new.”

“But I understood you had such a good voyage. Missy ? ”

” Not from me you didn’t! Besides, it was my own fault: I gone and left the window open, and in came a sea. Didn’t the captain kick up a shine! But I told him it was worse for me than for him; and look at the old duds I’ve got to go about in all because! Why, I look quite common — I know I do. No; I must have new before I come out to stay at the farm.”

“I’m sure our Arabella dresses simple,” the farmer was beginning; but Missy cut him short, and there was a spot of anger on each of her pale cheeks as she broke out:

” But this ain’t simple — it’s common! I had to borrow the most of it. All my things were spoilt. I can’t get a new rig-out for less than twenty pounds, and without everything new ”

” Nay, come ! ” cried old David, in some trouble. ” Of course I’ll let you have anything you want — I have your father’s instructions to do so. But — but there are difficulties. It’s difficult at this moment. You see the banks are closed, and — and ”

“Oh, don’t you be in any hurry. Send it when you can; then I’ll get the things and come out afterwards. Why, here we are at Lonsdale Street! ”

” But I want you to come out soon. How long would it take you to get everything ? ”

” To-day’s Thursday. If I had it to-morrow I could come out on Monday.”

“Then you shall have it to-morrow,” said David, closing his lips firmly. ” Though the banks are closed, there’s the man we send our milk to, and he owes me a lump more than twenty pound. I’ll go to him now and get the twenty from him.

or I’ll know the reason why! Yes, and I’ll post it to you before I go back home at all! What address must I send it to, Missy ?”

” What address ? Oh, to the General Post Office. I don’t want the folks I am staying with to know. They offered to lend me, and I wouldn’t. Will you stop, please ? ”

” Quite right, my dear, quite right. I was the one to come to. You’ll find it at the ”

” Do you mind stopping ?”

” Why, we’re not there yet. We’re not even in Bourke Street.”

” No, but please stop here.”

“Very well. Here we are, then, and it’s only six past. But why not drive right on to the theatre — that’s what I want to know ? ”

Missy hesitated, and hesitated, until she saw the old man peering into her face through the darkness that seemed to have fallen during the last five minutes. Then she dropped her eyes. They had pulled up alongside the deep-cut channel between road-metal and curb-stone, whereby you shall remember the streets of Melbourne. Nobody appeared to be taking any notice of them.

" I see," said David very gently. " And I don't wonder at it. No, Missy, it's not at all the sort of turn-out for your friends to see you in. Jump down, my dear, and I'll just drive alongside to see that nothing happens you. But I won't seem to know you. Missy — I won't seem to know you! "

Lower and lower, as the old man spoke, the girl had been hanging her head; until now he could see nothing of her face on account of her fringe; when suddenly she raised it and kissed his cheek. She was out of the buggy next moment.

She walked at a great rate, but David kept up with her by trotting his horse, and they exchanged signals the whole way. Close to the theatre she beckoned to him to pull up again. He did so, and she came to the wheel with one of her queer, inscrutable smiles.

" How do you know," said she, " that Fm Miriam Oliver at all?"

The rays from a gas-lamp cut between their faces as she looked him full in the eyes.

" Why, of course you are ! "

" But how do you know ? "

" Nay, come, what a question! What makes you ask it, Missy ?"

"Because I've given you no proof. I brought an introduction with me and I went and forgot to give it to you. However, here it is, so you may as well put it in your pipe and smoke it."

She took some letters out of her pocket as she spoke, and shifted the top one to the bottom until she came to an envelope that had never been through the post. This she handed up to David, who recognised his old friend's writing, which indeed had caught his eye on most of the other envelopes also. And when she had put these back in her pocket she held out her dirty-gloved hand.

"So long," she said. "You won't know me when I turn up on Monday."

" Stop!" cried David. " You must let me know when to send the buggy for you, and where to. It'll never do to have you coming out in the 'bus again."

"Right you are. I'll let you know. So long again — and see here. I think you're the sweetest and trustingest old man in the world!"

She was far ahead, this time, before the buggy was under way again.

"Naturally," chuckled David, following her hair through the crowd. "I should hope so, indeed, when it's a child of John William Oliver, and one that you can love for her own sake an' all! But what made her look so sorry when she gave me the kiss ? And what's this ? Nay, come, I must have made a mistake!"

He had flattered himself that his eyes never left the portals where they had lost sight of the red hair, and when he got up to it what should it be but the STAGE DOOR? The words were painted over it as plain as that. The mistake might be Missy's; but a little waiting by the curb convinced Mr. Teesdale that it was his own; for Missy never came back, as he argued she must have done if she really had gone in at the stage door.

Chapter V
A Watch and a Pipe.

Mr. Teesdale drove on to the inn at which he was in the habit of putting up when in town with the buggy. His connection with the house was very characteristic. Many years before the landlord had served him in a menial capacity, but for nearly as many that worthy had been infinitely more prosperous than poor David, who, indeed, had never prospered at all. They were good friends, however, for the farmer had a soul too serene for envy, and a heart too simple to be over-sensitive concerning his own treatment at the hands of others. Thus he never resented his old hand's way with him, which would have cut envy, vanity, or touchiness, to the quick. He came to this inn for the sake of old acquaintance; it never occurred to him to go elsewhere; nor had he ever been short or sharp with his landlord before this evening, when, instead of answering questions and explaining what had brought him into Melbourne twice in one day, Mr. Teesdale flung the reins to the ostler, and himself out of the yard, with the rather forbidding reply that he was there on business. He was, indeed; though the business was the birth of the last half-hour.

It led him first to a little bare office overlooking a yard where many milk-carts stood at ease with their shafts resting upon the ground; and the other party to it was a man for whom Mr. Teesdale was no match.

" I must have twenty pounds," said David, beginning firmly.

"When?" replied the other coolly.

"Now. I shan't go home without it."

"I am very sorry, Mr. Teesdale, but I'm afraid that you'll have to."

"Why should I," cried David, smacking his hand down on the table, "when you owe me a hundred and thirty ? Twenty is all I ask, for I

know how you are situated; but twenty I must and shall have."

"We simply haven't it in the bank."

"Nay, come, I can't believe that."

"I'll show you the pass-book."

"I won't look at it. No, I shall put the matter into the hands of a solicitor. Good evening to you. I dare say it isn't your fault; but I must have some satisfaction, one way or the other. I am not going on like this a single day longer."

"Good evening, then, Mr. Teesdale. If you do what you say, we shall have to liquidate; and then you will get nothing at all, or very little."

David had heard this story before. "It was an evil day for me when I sent you my first load of milk," he cried out bitterly; but in the other's words there had been such a ring of truth as took all the sting out of his own.

"It will be a worse one for us when you send me your last," replied the man of business. " That would be enough to finish us in itself, without your solicitor, in our present state; whereas, if you give us time "

" I have given you too much time already," said the farmer, heaving the sigh which was ever the end of all his threats; and with a sudden good-humoured resignation (which put his nature in a nutshell), he got up and went away, after an amicable discussion on the exceeding earliness of summer with the man for whom he was no match at all. Throughout his life there had been far too many men who were more than a match for poor David in all such matters.

But the getting of the twenty pounds was a matter apart. He did not want it for himself; the person in need of the money was the child of his dear old friend, who had charged her to apply to him, David, in precisely that kind of difficulty which had already arisen. The fact made the old man's heart hot on one side and cold on the other; for while it glowed with pride at the trust reposed in him, it froze within his breast at the thought of his own helplessness to fulfil that trust. This, however, was a thought which he obstinately refused to entertain. He had not twenty pounds in the bank; on the contrary, his account was overdrawn to the utmost limit. For himself, he would have starved rather than borrow from his friend the innkeeper; but he could have brought himself to do so for Miriam, had he not been perfectly certain that his old servant would refuse to lend. In all Melbourne there was no other to whom he could go for the twenty pounds; yet have it he must, by hook or crook, that night; and ten minutes after his fruitless interview with the middleman who sold his milk, a way was shown him.

He was hanging about the corner of Bourke and Elizabeth Streets, watching the multitude with an absent, lack-lustre eye; the post-office clock had chimed the hour overhead, and David, still absently, had taken his own cherished watch from his waistcoat pocket to check its time. It was not on his last day in Melbourne, nor on his last but one, that the watch had been set by the post-office clock, yet it was still right to the minute; and before the eighth clang from above had been swallowed in the city's hum, David had got his idea. He closed the gold case with a decisive snap, and next moment went in feverish quest of the nearest pawnbroker.

It was with a face strangely drawn between joy and regret, between guilt and triumph, that Mr. Teesdale at length returned to his inn. Here, in the writing-room, now with the scared frown of a forger, and now with a senile giggle, he cowered over a blotting-pad for some minutes; and thereafter returned to the post-office with a sealed envelope, which he shot into safety with his own hands. It was well after nine before the horse was put to, and David seated once more in the buggy, with the collar of his dust-coat turned up about his ears and the apron over his long lean legs.

"Never knew you so late before, old man," said his former servant, who was smoking a cigar in the yard, and perhaps still thinking of his first snub from David Teesdale.

" No, I don't think you ever did," replied David, blandly.

"Second time in to-day, too."

"Second time in," repeated Mr. Teesdale, drawing the reins through his fingers.

"And it'll take you a good hour to get home. I say, you'll be getting into trouble. You won't be there before What time is it now, old man?"

"Look at the post-office," said David, as he took up his whip.

" I can't see it without going out into the street; besides, I always thought they took their time from that wonderful watch of yours ? "

" You're a clever fellow!" cried David, as the other had never heard him speak in the whole course of their previous acquaintance; and he was gone without another word.

He drove away with a troubled face; but the Melbourne street-lamps showed deeper furrows under the old tall hat than David carried with him into the darkness beyond the city, for the more he thought of it, the surer did he become that his late action was not only defensible, but rather praiseworthy into the bargain. There was about it, moreover, a dramatic fitness which charmed him no less because he did not know the name for it. Throughout his unsuccessful manhood he had treasured a watch, which was as absurd in his pocket as a gold-headed cane in a beggarman's hand, because Oliver had given it to him. For years it must have mocked him whenever he took it from his shabby pocket, but in the narrowest straits he had never parted with it, nor had his gold watch ever ceased to be David Teesdale's most precious possession. And now, after two-and-thirty years, he had calmly pawned it, on the spur of the moment, and, as it seemed to himself, for the most extraordinary and beautiful reason in the world; for what he could never bring himself to do in his own need be had done in a moment for the extravagant behoof of his friend's daughter; and his heart beat higher than for many a year in the joy of his deed. So puffed up was he, indeed, that he forgot the fear of Mrs. Teesdale, and some other things besides; for at the foot of the last hill, within a mile of the farm, the horse shied so suddenly that David, taken off his guard, found his near wheels in the ditch before he could haul in the slack of the reins; and when another plunge might have overturned the buggy, a man ran out of the darkness to the horse's head, and before David could realise what had happened his ship had righted itself and was at anchor in the middle of the road.

" My fault, as I'm a sinner!" cried a rich voice from near the horse's ears.

"Nay, I'm very much obliged to you," said Mr. Teesdale, with a laugh, for he made no work of a bit of danger, much less when past.

" But it was me your horse shied at," returned the other, and fell to petting the frightened animal with soft words and a soothing hand. " I was going to take the liberty of stopping you for a moment."

" I never saw you," said David; " it was that dark, and I was that busy thinking. What is it I can do for you ? The horse'll stand steady now, thank you, if you'll come this way."

The wayfarer came round to the buggy wheels and stood still, feeling in all his pockets before answering questions. The near lamp shot its rays upon a broad, deep chest, and showed a pair of hairy hands searching one pocket after another. The rays reached as high as a scarlet neckcloth, but no higher, so that the man's face was not very easily visible; and David was only beginning to pick out of the night a heavy moustache, and a still heavier jaw, when from between the two there came the gleam of teeth, and the fellow was laughing a little and swearing more. He had given up his search, and stood empty-handed under the lamp.

" I'm not a bushranger," said he, " but you might easily think me one."

"Why so?" asked David.

" Because I stopped you to ask for a match to light my pipe, and now I'm hanged if I can find my pipe in any of my pockets; and it was the best one ever I smoked," said the man, with more of his oaths.

"That's a bad job," said David, sympathetically, in spite of a personal horror of bad language, which was one of his better peculiarities.

" A bad job ?" cried the man. " It would be that if I'd lost my pipe, but it's a damned sight worse when it's a girl that goes and shakes it from you, and she the biggest little innocent you ever clapped eyes on. Yet she must have shook it. Confound her face!"

He was feeling in his pockets again, but as unsuccessfully as before. The farmer inquired whether he was on his way back to Melbourne, and suggested it was a long walk.

"It is so," said the man; "but it's a gay little town when you get there, is Melbourne — what ?"

"Very," said Mr. Teesdale, to be civil; but he was beginning to find this difficult.

" You prefer the country — what ? " continued the other, who was now leaning on the wheel, and showing a face which the old man liked even less than the rest of him, it was so handsome and yet so coarse. "Well, so do I, for a change. And talk of the girls!" The fellow winked. "Old Country or Colonies, it's all the same — you give me a country lass for a lark that's worth having.

But damn their souls when they lose your favourite pipe!"

"What sort of a pipe was it?" asked David, to change a conversation which he disliked. " If I come across it I'll send it to you, if you tell me where to."

" Good, old man ! " cried the stranger. " It was a meerschaum, with a lady's hand holding of the bowl, and coloured better than any pipe ever you saw in your life. If you do find it, you leave it with the boss of the 'Bushman's Rest'; then I'll get it again when next I come this way-to see my girl. For I can't quite think she's the one to have touched it, when all's said and done."

"Very good," said David, coldly, because both look and word of this roadside acquaintance were equally undesirable in his eyes. "Very good, if I find it. And now, if you'll allow me, I'll push on home."

The other showed himself as ready with a sneer as with an oath. " You are in a desperate hurry ! " said he.

" I am," said David; " nevertheless, I'm much obliged to you for being so clever with the horse just now, and I wish you a very good night." And with that, showing for once some little decision, because this kind of man repelled him, old Tees-dale cracked his whip and drove on without more ado.

Nor is it likely he would have thought any more about so trifling an incident, but for another which occurred before he finally reached home. It was at his own slip-rails, not many minutes later; he had got down and taken them out, and was in the act of leading through, when his foot kicked something hard and small, so that it rattled against one of the rails, and shone in the light of the buggy lamp at the same instant. The farmer stopped to pick it up, found it a meerschaum pipe, and pulled a grave face over it for several moments. Then he slipped it into his pocket, and after putting up the rails behind him, was in his own yard in three minutes. Here one of the men took charge of horse and buggy, and the master went round to the front of the house, but must needs stand in the verandah to spy on Arabella, who was sitting with her Family Cherub under the lamp and the blind never drawn. She was not reading; her head was lifted, and she was gazing at the window — at himself, David imagined; but he was wrong for she never saw him. Her face was flushed, and there was in it a wonder and a stealthy joy, born of the romantic reading under her nose, as the father thought; but he was wrong again; for Arabella had finished one chapter before the coming of Missy, and had sat an hour over the next without taking in a word.

"So you've got back, father ?" she was saying presently, in an absent, mechanical sort of voice.

"Here I am," said Mr. Teesdale; "and I left Missy at the theatre, where it appears she had to meet "

" Missy! " exclaimed Arabella, remembering very suddenly. "Oh yes! Of course. Where do you say you left her, father."

" At the Bijou Theatre, my dear, I am sorry to say; but it wasn't her fault; it was the friends she is staying with whom she had to meet there. Well, let's hope it won't do her any harm just once in a way. And what have you been doing, my dear, all the evening?"

" I? Oh, after milking I had a bit of a stroll outside."

" A stroll, eh ? Then you didn't happen to see a man hanging about our slip-rails, did you?"

Mr. Teesdale was emptying his pockets, with his back to Arabella, so he never knew how his question affected her.

" I wasn't near the slip-rails, I was in the opposite direction," she said presently. " Why do you ask ? "

" Because I found this right under them," said Mr. Teesdale, showing her the meerschaum pipe before laying it down on the chimney-piece; "and as I was getting near the township, I met a man who told me he'd lost just such a pipe. And I didn't like him, my dear, so I only hope he's not coming after our Mary Jane, that's all."

Mary Jane was the farm-servant. She had not been out of the kitchen since milking-time, said Arabella; and her father was remarking that he was glad to hear this, when the door flew open, and Mrs. Teesdale whistled into the room like a squall of wind.

" At last!" she cried. " Do you know how long you've been, David ? Do you know what time it is? "

" I don't, my dear," said he.

"Then look at your watch."

"My dear," he said, "I've left my watch in Melbourne."

" In Melbourne!" cried Mrs. Teesdale among her top notes. "And what's the meaning of that?"

"It means," said Mr. Teesdale, struggling to avoid the lie direct, " that it hasn't been cleaned for years, and that it needed cleaning very badly indeed."

"But you told Miriam how well it was going; time we were having our teas!"

"Yes, I know, and — that's the curious thing, my dear. It went and stopped on our way in."

For there was no avoiding it, after all; yet in all the long years of their married life, it was his first.

Chapter VI
The Ways of Society.

The Monday following was the first and the best of some bad days at the farm; for Missy had never written to tell Mr. Teesdale when and where he might call for her, so he could not call at all, and she did not come out by herself. This they now firmly expected her to do, and David wasted much time in meeting every omnibus; but when the last one had come in without Missy, even he was forced to give her up for that day. There would be a letter of explanation in the morning, said David, and shut his ears to his wife's answer. She had been on tenter-hooks all day, for ever diving into the spare room with a duster, dodging out again to inquire what time it was now, and then scolding David because he had not his watch — a circumstance for which that simpleton was reproaching himself before long.

For there was no letter in the morning, and no Missy next day, or the next, or the next after that. It was then that Mr. Teesdale took to lying awake and thinking much of the friendly ticking that had cheered his wakefulness for thirty years, and even more of a few words in the Thursday's Argosy which he had not shown to a soul. And strange ideas concerning the English girl were bandied across the family board; but the strangest of all were John William's, who would not hear a word against her; on the contrary, it was his father, in his opinion, who was to blame for the whole matter, which the son of the house declared to be a mere confusion of one Monday with another.

"You own yourself," said he, "that the girl wanted a new rig-out before she'd come here to stay. Did she say so, father, or did she not ? Very well, then. Do you mean to tell me she could get measured, and tried on, and fixed up all round in four days, and two of 'em Saturday and Sunday? Then I tell you that's your mistake, and it wasn't Monday she said, but Monday week, which is next Monday. You mark my words, we'll have her out here next Monday as ever is! "

How John William very nearly hit the mark, and how shamefully Arabella missed it with the big stones she had been throwing all the week — how rest returned to the tortured mind of Mr. Teesdale, and how Mrs. T. was not sorry that she had left the clean good sheets on the spare bed in spite of many a good mind to put them away again — all this is a very short story indeed. For Missy reappeared on the Saturday afternoon while they were all at tea.

Arabella was the one who caught first sight of the red sunshade bobbing up the steep green ascent of the farmhouse, for Arabella sat facing the window; but it was left to John William to turn in his chair and recognise the tall, well-dressed figure at a glance as it breasted the hill.

"Here she is — here's Miriam!" he cried out instantly. "Now what did I tell you all?" He was rolling down his shirt-sleeves as he' spoke, flushed with triumph.

Mr. Teesdale had risen and pressed forward to peer through the window, and as he did so the red sunshade waved frantically. Beneath it was a neat straw hat, and an unmistakable red-fringed face nodding violently on top of a frock of vestal whiteness. Arabella flew out to meet the truant, and John William to put on a coat.

"Well, well!" said Mr. Teesdale, holding both her hands when the girl was once more among them. "Well, to be sure; but you've just in time for tea, that's one good thing."

" Nay, I must make some fresh," cried his wife, without a smile. " Mind, I do think you might have written, Miriam. You have led us a pretty dance, I can tell you that." She caught up the teapot and whisked out of the room.

"Have I?" the girl asked meekly of the old man.

" No, no, my dear," and " Not you," the two Teesdales answered in one breath; though the father added, "but you did promise to write."

" I know I did. But you see "

Missy laughed.

"You should have written, my dear," David said gently, as she got no further, and he had no wish to cross-question her. " I didn't know what had got you."

"None of us could think," added Arabella.

" Except me, Miriam," said John William, proudly. "You were getting your new rig-out; wasn't that it?"

The girl nodded and beamed at him as she said that it was. The sunshade was lying on the sofa now, and Missy sitting at the table in Arabella's place.

" I thought," said Mr. Teesdale, " that you had gone off to Sydney, and weren't coming near us any more. Do you know why? There was a Miss Oliver in the list of the overland passengers in Thurday's Argus,"

"Indeed," said the girl.

"Yes, and it was a Miss M, Oliver, and all."

" Well, I never! That's what you'd call a coincident, if you like."

" I'm very glad it was nothing worse," said Mr. Teesdale heartily. " I made that sure it was you."

"You never mentioned it, father." said John William.

" No, because I was also quite sure that she would write if we only gave her time. You ought to have written, Missy, and then I'd have gone in and fetched you "

"But that's just what I didn't want. All this way! No, the 'bus was quite good enough for me."

"But what about your trunk?" Arabella inquired.

Missy made answer in the fewest words that her trunk was following by carrier; and because Mrs. Teesdale entered to them now, with a pot of fresh tea, Missy said little more just then, except in specific apology for her remissness in not writing. This apology was made directly to Mrs. Teesdale, whose manner of receiving it may or may not have discouraged the visitor from further conversation at the moment. But so it seemed to one or two, who heard and saw and felt that such discouragement would exist eternally between that old woman and that young girl.

Milking-time was at hand, however, and Missy was left to finish her tea with only Mr. Teesdale to look after her. John William and his mother were the two best milkers on the farm, and Arabella was a fair second to them when she liked, but that was not this evening. Her heart was with Missy in the parlour. But Missy herself was far better suited in having the old farmer all to herself. With him she was entirely at her ease. The moment they were alone she was thanking David for the twenty pounds duly received at the post-office, and his immediate stipulation that the matter of the loan must be a secret made it also an additional bond of sympathy between these two. They sat chatting about England and Miriam's parents, but not more than Missy could help. She referred but lightly to a home-letter newly received, as though there was no news in it; she was much more ready to hear how Mr. Teesdale had had the coat torn off his back in rescuing his first home-letters from the tiny post-office of the early days, which had been swept away by the first wave of the gold-rush. Again he spoke of that golden age, and of his own lost chances, without a perceptible shade of regret, and again Missy marvelled; as did Mr. Teesdale yet again, and in his turn, at her tone about money who had been brought up in the midst of it. It only showed the good sense of his old friend in keeping his children simple and careful amid all their rich surroundings; but Mr. Oliver had been ever the most sensible, as well as the kindest of men. The farmer said this as he was walking slowly in the paddock, with a pipe in his mouth and Missy on his arm, and his downcast eyes upon the long, broken shadow of his own bent figure. Missy's trunk came about this time, but she let it alone. And these two were feeding the chickens together — old David's own department — when Arabella came seeking Missy, having escaped from the milking-stool a good hour before her time.

" Oh, here you are! Come, and I'll help you unpack. Mother said I was to," said she hurriedly. She was only in a hurry for Missy's society. So Missy went with her, getting a good-humoured nod from the old man, whose side she was sorry to leave.

And David watched her out of sight, smiling his calm, kind smile. "She's her father's daughter," said he to the chickens. " Her ways are a bit new to me-but that's where I like 'em. Mannerisms she may have — I wouldn't have her otherwise. She's one of the rising generation — but she has her father's heart, and that's the best kind that ever beat time."

In Missy's bedroom much talking was being done by Arabella. Her curiosity was insatiable, but she herself never gave it a chance. She wanted to know this, but before there was time for an answer she must know that. One thing, when the trunk was unpacked and its contents put away in drawers, she was left entirely unable to understand; and that was, how Missy came to have everything brand-new.

"Why, because everything was spoilt," said Missy, in apparent wonder at the other's wonderment.

" By that one wave ? "

"Why, of course."

" But how did it happen ? "

" Didn't I tell you ? We'd left the window open, and in comes a green sea and half fills the cabin. The captain, he was ever so wild, and, oh my! didn't he give it us ! Of course, all our things were spoilt — me and the other girls. We finished the voyage in borrowed everything, and in borrowed everything I came here the other day. Did you think them things were mine ? Not much, my dear. Not much! But I was forced to have things of my own before I could come out here and stay."

Arabella, sitting on the bed, studied the tall figure with arms akimbo that struck sharp through the dusk against the square-paned window. She was wondering whether the Olivers were such well-to-do people after all. Her own English was not perfect, but her ear was better than her tongue, and the young ladies in the Family Cherub spoke not at all as Missy spoke. Arabella's next question seemed irrelevant.

"Did you see much society at home, Missy?"

" You bet I did! " was the answer, and the fuzzy head was nodding against the window.

" Real high society, like you read about in tales, Missy ?"

"Rather!"

"Lords ?"

" Any jolly quantity of lords ! "

"You really mean it, Missy ?"

" Mean it? What do you mean? Look here, I won't tell you no more if you think Fm telling lies."

"Missy, I never thought of such a thing — never!" Arabella hastened to aver. " I was only surprised, that's all I was. 'Tisn't likely I meant to doubt your word."

" Didn't you ? That's all right, then. Why, bless your heart, do you think it so wonderful to know a few lords ?"

" I didn't think they were as common as all that," said Arabella, meekly.

" Common as mud," cried Missy grandly. " Why, you can't swing a cat without knocking a lord's topper off — not in England!"

Arabella laughed. Then her questions ceased for the time being, and Missy was curious to know how she had impressed a rather tiresome interlocutor, for now in the bedroom it was impossible for them to see each other's faces. A few minutes later Missy was satisfied on this point. At the supper-table she had no more attentive listener than Arabella, who watched her in the lamplight as one who has merely read watches another who has seen and done, while Missy rattled on more freely than she had done yet before Mrs. Teesdale. Even Mrs. Teesdale was made to smile this time, though she did her best to conceal it. The visitor was in such racy form.

"I may have to go back home again any day," she told them all. "It'll depend how my mother is, and how they all get on without me. I'll bet they manage pretty badly. But while I am here I mean to make the most of my time. A short life and a merry one, them's my sentiments, ladies and gentlemen! So I want to learn to shoot and milk and do everything but ride. I could ride if I wanted to; I learnt when I was a kid; but a horse once ”

She broke off, laughing and nodding knowingly at Mr. Teesdale, who explained how Missy had been once bitten and was twice shy. John William said that he could very well understand it; and he offered to take Missy out ’possum-shooting as soon as ever there was a moon.

” Have you ever fired a gun, Missy ? ” said Mr. Teesdale; and Missy shook her head.

” P’r’aps you wouldn’t like to try ? ” said John William.

” Wouldn’t I so!” cried the girl, with flashing eyes. ” You show me how, and I’ll try to-morrow.”

“To-morrow’s Sunday,” Mrs. Teesdale said solemnly. ” Is your cup off, Miriam ? ”

It was not, and because the cocoa was too hot for her Missy poured it into the saucer, and drank until her face was all saucer and red fringe. This impressed Arabella.

“We’ll soon teach Missy to shoot,” remarked Mr. Teesdale, smiling into his plate, ” if she’ll hold the gun tight and not mind the noise.”

“I’ll do my level,” said Missy gamely.

John William proceeded to assure her that she could not be taught by a better man than his father, whom he declared to be the best shot in that colony for his age. The old man looked pleased, praise from his son being a very rare treat to him. But Arabella had been neglecting her supper to watch and listen to the guest, and now she asked, ” Do the fine ladies shoot in England, Missy ?”

” Not they ! ” replied Missy promptly. ” I should like to catch them.”

“What ladies do you mean, my dear?” asked the farmer of his daughter.

” Grand ladies — countesses and viscountesses and the rest. Missy knows heaps of them — don’t you. Missy ? ”

“Well, a good few,” said Missy, with some show of modesty.

“To be sure you would,” murmured Mr. Tees-dale, adding, as his eyes glistened, ” and yet you’ll come and stay with the likes of us! You aren’t too proud to take us as you find us-you aren’t above drinking cocoa with your supper.”

” What do the lords and ladies drink with their suppers ? ” asked Arabella, as Missy smiled and blushed.

But the farmer cried, ” Their dinners, she means; I’ll warrant they dine late every night o’ their lives.”

Missy nodded to this.

” But what do they drink with their dinners ? ” repeated Arabella.

” Oh, champagne.”

“What else?”

” What else ? Oh! claret, and port, and sherry wine. And beer and spirits for them that prefers ’em!”

” All that with their dinners ? ”

” Rather! I should think they did. The whole lot, one after the other!”

“What! Beer and brandy and sherry wine ?” Arabella’s incredulity was disagreeably apparent.

” Yes, everything you can think of ; but look here, if you don’t want to believe me, you needn’t, you know!” said Missy, turning as red as her fringe as she stared the other girl full in the eyes across the supper-table. In the awkward pause following John William turned and glared furiously at his sister; but it was their father who cleared the air by saying mildly:

“Arabella, my dear, I’m afraid you don’t know a joke when you hear one.”

Then Arabella coloured in her turn.

” Do you mean to say you were joking. Missy ? ” she leant forward to ask as though she could no more believe this than recent statements.

But Missy had given one quick glance at Mr. Teesdale, and then, with a little gasp, had burst into an immoderate fit of laughter.

" Of course I was," she cried out as soon as she could speak; " of course I was joking —
you old silly!"

Chapter VII
Moonlight Sport.

So the first few days were largely spent in teaching Missy to shoot. A very plucky pupil she made, too, if not a particularly apt one; but head and chief of her sporting qualities was her enthusiasm. That was intense. The girl was never happy without a gun in her hand. So far as safety went, she took palpable pains to follow every injunction in the matter of full-cock and half-cock, and laid to heart all the rules given her for the carrying and handling of a loaded firearm. Thus, no one feared her prowling about the farm on tiptoe with John William's double-barrels pointing admirably to earth; least of all, the sparrows and parrots which she never hit. Old Teesdale would go with her and stand chuckling at her side when she missed a sparrow sitting; once he snatched the smoking gun from her, and with the other barrel picked off the same small bird on the wing. Then there was much practice at folded newspapers, of which Missy could sometimes make a sieve, at her own range; and altogether these two shots enjoyed themselves. Certainly it was a sight to see them together — the weak-kneed old man, who could shoot so cleverly still, when he had a mind, and the jaunty young woman who was all slang and fun and rollicking good-nature, plus a cockney lust for blood and feathers.

Missy's first feathers, however, were not such as she might stick in her hat, and her first blood was exceedingly ill-shed. To be sure, she knew no better until the deed was done, and the quaint dead bird with the big head and beak carried home in triumph to Mr. Teesdale. That triumph was short-lived.

" Got one at last!" cried Missy, as she dropped her prey at the old man's feet. Mr. Teesdale was smoking in the verandah, and he pulled a long face behind his smile.

" So I see," said he; " but do you know what it is you have got. Missy ? "

" No, I don't, but I mean to have him stuffed, whatever he is."

" I think I wouldn't, Missy, if I were you. It's a laughing jackass."

"Yes? Well, I guess he won't laugh much more! "

"And there's a five-pound penalty for shooting him, Missy. He kills the snakes, therefore you are not allowed by law to kill him. You have broken the law, my dear, and the best thing that we can do is to bury the victim and say nothing about it to anybody." He was laughing, but the girl stood looking at her handiwork with a very red face.

" I thought I was to shoot everything," she said. " I thought that everything eat the fruit and things. I never knew I was so beastly cruel! "

She put away the gun, and spent most of that summer's day in reading to Mr. Teesdale, for whom she had developed a very pretty affection. They read longest in the parlour, with the window shut, and the blind down, and a big fly buzzing between it and the glass. The old man fell sound asleep in the end, whereupon Missy sat very still indeed, just to watch him. And what it was exactly in the worn and white-haired face that fetched the tears to her eyes and the shame to her cheeks. On this particular occasion, there is no saying; but Missy was scarcely Missy during the remainder of the afternoon.

That evening, however, had already been pitched upon for some 'possum-shooting, given a good moon. From the moment she was reminded of this, at tea-time, the visitor was herself again, and something more. It is saying a good deal, but they had not hitherto seen her in such excessively high spirits as overcame her now. She lent Mr. Tees-dale a hand to load some cartridges in the gunroom while the others were milking; but she was rather a hindrance than a help to that patient old man. She would put in the shot before the powder. Then she got into pure infantile mischief, letting off caps under David's coat-tails, and doing her best to make him sharp with her. Herein she failed; nevertheless, the elder was glad enough to hand her over to the younger Teesdale when the time came, and with it a moon without a cloud. Neither Arabella nor her father was going, but three of the men were who worked on the place, and with whom John William was obliged to leave Missy alone in the yard while he went for the dogs. It was only for a minute or two; but the men were in fits of laughter when he returned. It appeared that Missy had been giving them some sort of a dance under that limelit moon.

” Down, Major! Down, Laddie ! ” John William cried at the dogs as they leaped up at Missy.

But Missy answered, ” Down yourself, Jack — I like 'em.” And the three men laughed; in fact, they seemed prepared to laugh at Missy whenever she opened her mouth; but John William laughed too as he led the way into the moonlit paddocks.

Here the hunting-ground began without preliminary, for on this side of the farm there were trees and to spare, the land dipping in a gully full of timber before it rose to the high ploughed levels known as the Cultivation. The gully was well grassed for all its trees, which were divers as well as manifold. There were gum-trees blue and red, and stringy-barks, and she-oaks, each and all of them a haunt of the opossum and the native cat. The party promptly surrounded a blue gum at the base of which the dogs stood barking, and Missy found herself doing what the others did — getting the moon behind the branches and searching for what she was told would look more like the stump of a bough or a tangle of leaves than any known animal.

“I believe it's a lie” said John William; “for Laddie barked first, and Laddie always did tell lies.”

” Tell lies ? ” echoed Missy, with a puzzled grin.

“Yes, barking up trees where there's nothing at all — that's what we call telling lies; and old Laddie's started the evening well by telling one already.”

“Not he,” cried a shrill voice; and the youngest of the three farm-hands — a little bit of a fellow — stood pointing to a branch so low that everyone else had overlooked it.

” I see a little bit of a knot on the bough,” said Missy, “but blow me tight if I see anything else!”

“That's it,” cried John William. “That little knot is a native cat.”

Missy lowered her gun at once. “Oh, I didn't come out,” said she, ” to shoot cats ! ”

” But they aren't cats at all,” Teesdale explained (while his men stood and laughed); ” they're much more like little leopards, I assure you. We only call them cats because — because I'm bothered if I know why! It's not the name for them, as you'll say when you've shot this beggar. And you don't know the way they tear our fowls to pieces, Missy, or you wouldn't make so many bones about it; besides which, you won't get an easier shot all night.”

” Oh, if that's the kind of customer, I'm on to try,” said Missy. She raised her gun there and then, pressed it to her shoulder, and took aim at the black notch against the silver disc of the moon. The moonlight licked the barrels from sight to sight, getting into Missy's eyes, but there were barely a dozen feet between muzzle and mark. The report was quickly followed by a lifeless thud upon the ground; and when the smoke cleared, that notch was gone from the bough. Then one of the men struck a match to show Missy what she had done; and she had done it so effectually as to give herself a sensation which she concealed with difficulty. It was not pity; there was no pitying a spotted little horror with so sharp a snout and such devilish fangs: but whatever it was, that sensation kept Missy modest in her success, so that she refused the next shot point-blank. John William took it, with the only possible result.

” A bushy,” someone said, turning over the dead bush-tailed opossum with his foot. It looked very big and soft and gray, lying dead in the moonlight. Missy found it in her heart to pity an opossum.

” Don't you skin them f ” she asked at a respectful range. “Do you make no use of them after all?”

” Ifs so hard not to spoil them,” John William said as he slipped another cartridge into the breech. He would have shown her how this particular skin had been ruined by the shot, but Missy said she quite understood.

He was beginning to think her squeamish. He asked her whether she had not had enough. She would not admit it, and took another shot to prove her spirit. This time she failed, and bore her failure with an equanimity which (in Missy) amounted almost to apathy. That she was neither squeamish nor apathetic, however, was demonstrated very suddenly while the night was still young.

A ring-tailed opossum had been brought to earth by a charge from the muzzle-loader of that stunted young colonial whose eyes were as sharp as his voice — he who had " mooned" the native cat. The others called him Geordie. The three of them were kneeling over the dead "ringy," and Missy was taking no more notice of them than she could help; only Geordie's was a voice that made itself heard. Missy had taken little stock of what the kneeling men were doing or saying until suddenly she heard:

" Young 'uns it is! I told you there was young 'uns! That little beggar's as dead as his mother, but this one ain't. 'Ere, come off 'er back, can't yer f She ain't no more good to you now, do you 'ear ? "

This was Geordie's manner of speech to the bunch of breathing fur that stuck tight to the dead doe's back, whence his fingers were busy disengaging it; but Geordie suddenly found himself on his back in the grass, and when he picked himself up it was Miss Oliver herself who was kneeling where he had knelt, and even going on with his work. It took her some moments, and when done her hands were bloody in the moonshine. Then, first she took that bit of warm fur and nursed it in her neck, stroking it with her chin. And next she turned a calm face up to her companions, and said distinctly to them all, "I call this a damned shame, so I tell you straight! " Indeed she was anything but squeamish.

She lowered her eyes immediately, undid three buttons, and slipped the small opossum into her bosom. There she fixed it, with great care, but not the smallest fuss; and looking up once more, saw the three hirelings walking off together through the trees.

" I tell you," she called after them — shaking her fist at their backs — "I tell you it's the damnedest shame that ever was! "

The words rang clear through the clear night, then found an answer at Missy's side. "You are quite right. It is. And now won't you get up and come back home. Missy ? "

"Jack!" cried the girl faintly, as she stumbled to her feet. " I'd quite forgotten you were there."

"I have been here all the time," said John William.

"Then do tell me what I've been saying," said Missy, anxiously, as she took his arm and they started homeward. " I couldn't see no more and keep my scalp fixed. I hope to God I haven't been swearing, have I ?"

"Not you. Missy. You've only said what was right and proper. It was cruel, and I blame myself for the whole thing."

" No, no, no! I wanted some sport. I thought I could kill things, and never give a —no, never give a thought to 'em. Now I know I can't. That's all. I say, though, if I did use a swear-word, you won't give me away, will you ? I don't know what I said, and that's all about it; but when I lose my scalp — ah well, I know I can trust, you "

" Of course you can," said John William cheerily. And involuntarily he pressed to his side the hand that was still within his arm.

" I wouldn't say swear-words unless I did lose my scalp — you understand t " said Missy, coming back to it again.

"Of course you wouldn't; but you didn't."

" I'm not so sure. I wouldn't have your parents hear of it if I did; they'd take it so terribly to heart."

" They shall hear nothing — not that there's anything for them to hear."

"Now my parents are different; they swear themselves."

" Come, I can't credit that, you know! "

" But they do — like troopers! " persisted the girl. " It's the fashion just now in England. You may not know — how should you ?"

" Missy," said John William, as he opened her the gate into the homestead yard, "it's impossible to tell when you're joking and when you're not."

"Aha, I mean it to be," cried the girl, bowing low to him, with the moon all over her. Then she stood up to her last inch, smiled full in his face, and turning, left him that smile to keep if he could. He would have followed her, but a burst of laughter in the men's room took him off his course, as good reasons occurred to him for calling in there first.

The room was a part of one of the farm outhouses. In each corner was a bunk, and on each bunk a man (counting Geordie), the fourth being one Old Willie, a retired salt, who drove the milk into Melbourne in the middle of every night. Old Willie was sitting on the side of his bunk and chuckling so windily that the sparks were flying out of his cutty like fireworks. There was nothing, however, to show which of the other three was the entertainer, for each turned silent and looked guilty when John William entered and planted himself in their midst.

" I just thought I'd tell you," said he, with forced blandness, "that there is to be no more 'possum-shooting on this place for good and all. The man who shoots another 'possum, I'll hide him with my own hands, and the man who catches me shooting one, he may take and shoot me. For it's a grand shame, men, it's a grand shame! You heard Miss Oliver say it was, didn't you ? " he added sharply, turning to the three.

For the moment they looked blank; the next, it was such a fierce person who was repeating the question, with eyes so like pointed pistols, that one after the other of those three men meekly perjured their souls.

"Exactly," said John William, nodding his head in a deadly calm. "She said it was the grandest shame ever was; and if any man says she said anything else — well, he'd better let me hear him, that's all!"

Chapter VIII
The Saving of Arabella.

One night early in December, Arabella burst into Missy's room with singular abruptness. Missy had said good-night to the others and was very nearly in bed, but she had not seen Arabella, who had been out all the evening. Evidently she had only now come in. She was breathing quickly from hurrying up-hill; and there was a light in her countenance which Missy noticed in due course.

"Missy," she began, as abruptly as she had entered, "do you remember the day you first came, and we showed you that group of you all taken when you were quite little ? "

Missy nodded in the looking-glass. She was busy with her fringe.

"Well," continued Arabella, "you said red came out light, talking of your hair. Do you remember that?"

" Red came out light ? No, I can't say I do."

"You must Missy! You were speaking of your hair in that group "

Missy flourished a brave bare arm. " Now I see. My poor old carrots! Of course they came out light; they couldn't come out red, could they?"

"No; but Fm told that red comes out black — that's all."

Missy faced about in a twinkling. Her bare arms went akimbo. She was pale.

" So that's what excited you, eh ? " she cried derisively; yet it was only in the moment of speaking that she perceived that Arabella was excited at all.

" I'm not excited. Missy ! "

"No ?"

" Not a bit," said Arabella, as she gave herself the scarlet lie from neck to forehead. This amused Missy.

"Then what is it?" said she at last, with a provoking smile which the other could not meet. "Is it only that you're just dying to bowl me out? All right, my dear, we'll put it down to that. Only take care I don't bowl you out too — take very good care that I don't find out something about you I "

Arabella had the pale face now.

"Take very extra special good care," continued Missy, nodding nastily, " that I haven't found out something already! "

" Have you ? "

The hoarse voice was unknown to Missy, and the frightened face seemed a fresh face altogether. She read it in a moment, and was laughing the next.

" Of course I haven't, my good girl! "

" O Missy! "

"Just as if you'd done anything you'd mind being found out! No, my dear, I was only having a lark with you; but you deserved it for having one with me. Now as to my hair in that photograph "

"Oh, but of course I believe you. Missy, and not-and not the person who told me different."

" Now I wonder who that was ? " said Missy to herself; but aloud —"That's a blessing! And now if you'll let me go to bed, my dear, we'll neither of us think any more of all this tommy-rot that we've been talking."

Nevertheless she herself thought about it half that night. And a variety of vague suspicions crystallised at last into a single definite conclusion.

"She has a man on," muttered Missy to her pillow. "Thafs what's the matter with Arabella."

Her mind was fully made up before she slept.

"I must find out something about it; what I do see I don't like; and I've just got to take care of Arabella."

Forthwith she set herself to watch. It was first of all necessary to become really intimate with Arabella. The latter's addiction to personal catechism, to name one thing, had kept Missy not a little aloof hitherto. Now, however, in the nick of time, this weakness passed away, and with it this barrier. There were no more questions asked obviously for the sake of doubting or discrediting the answer. On the other hand, about some things Arabella was as inquisitive as ever; especially to wit, Missy's love affairs. Curiously enough, this was the one point on which Missy was markedly reticent, for very good reasons of her own; but she had no objection to discussing with Arabella the general subject of love. She noted the fascination this had for her companion. When the latter came to speak of her male ideal, from the point of view of his appearance, Missy noted much more. " He has a black moustache and very dark eyes," said she to herself. "That's the kind I trust least of all! " She knew something about it, evidently.

A tiny incident, however, which happened when Missy had been some five or six weeks at the farm, told her more than Arabella had done, directly or indirectly, in any of their conversations. The girls were in the room with Mr. Teesdale, who was looking on the chimney-piece for a lost letter, when he exclaimed suddenly:

"What's got that meerschaum pipe, Arabella?"

"Which one was that, father."" was the only answer, in a suspiciously innocent voice.

" The one I picked up by our slip-rails the night I took Missy back to Melbourne. It belonged to yon man I told you I met on the. road. I was saving it in case I ever set eyes on him again."

" Oh, that one!" cried Arabella; then, after a pause, she added, with a nonchalance which Missy for one admired: " I gave it back to him the other day."

"To whom?"

"Why, the man that lost it."

"You gave it back — to the man that lost it?" cried David, in the greatest surprise, while Missy became buried in the Argus of that morning. " Dear me, where have you seen him, honey ?"

" In the township."

" In the township, eh ? Now what sort of a man was it that you saw in the township ? Tell me what he was like."

" Like ? Oh, he had — let's see — he had very dark eyes; oh, yes, and a dark moustache and all; and he was very — well, rather handsome, I thought him."

"Ay, that's near enough," said Mr. Teesdale, greatly puzzled; " quite near enough to satisfy me that he's the same man; but how in the world did you know that he was ? That's what I can't make out! "

" Why, he told me himself, to be sure !"

" Ay, but how came he to speak to you at all ? That's what I want to know."

" Then Fm sure I can't tell you," said Arabella, with a toss of her head, not badly done. "I suppose he saw where I came from, and I dare say he'd been leaning again our slip-rails that night he lost his pipe. Anyhow, he asked me whether I'd found one, and I said you had, and he described the one he'd lost, and I knew that must be it. So I came back and got it for him. That was all."

Mr. Teesdale seemed just a little put out. " I wonder you didn't say anything about it at the time, my dear," said he, in mild remonstrance.

" Me ? Why, I never thought any more of it," the young woman said, with a slightly superfluous laugh. "I — you see that was the first and last I'd seen of him," added Arabella, as if to end the discussion; but her father had not finished his say.

"I'm glad it was the last, however —I am glad o' that!" he exclaimed with unusual energy. " Why ? Because, my dear, little as I saw of him, I didn't like the cut of that man's jib. No," said Mr. Teesdale, letting his eyes travel through the window to the river-timber, and shaking his head decidedly, as he sat down in his accustomed seat; " no, I didn't like it at all; and very sorry I should have been to think a man of that stamp was coming here after our Mary Jane!"

And Missy said never a word; but neither word, look nor tone had escaped her.

Her eyes were very wide open now. Arabella went out more evenings than one, but never, it appeared, on two consecutive evenings; so the man was not living in the district. And Missy said so much the worse; he was not merely passing his time. To clinch matters, the unhappy girl began to hang out signs of sleepless nights and perpetual nervous preoccupation by day; signs which Missy alone interpreted aright.

At length, a little before Christmas, there came a night when Arabella kissed them all round and went off to her room much earlier than usual. And the fever in her eyes and lips was noted by Missy, and by Missy alone.

It was a night of stars only. The moon by which Missy had killed her one native cat, and nursed an infant opossum, had waxed and waned. The night, when Mr. Teesdale took a breath of it last thing, looked black as soot. Twenty minutes later, the farmhouse was in utter darkness; not a single ray from a single window; and so it remained for nearly two hours.

Then suddenly a light shone in the parlour for a single instant only. The outer door of the little gun-room was now opened, as noiselessly as might be, and shut again, hairbreadth by hairbreadth. The odd thing was, that this happened not once, but twice within five minutes. And each time it was a woman's figure that stood up under the stars, and then stole forth into the night.

There were two of them ; and while the first went swiftly in a given direction (towards the timbered gully), the second made a quick circuit of the premises, and, as it happened, intercepted the first among the trees as though she had been lying in wait there for hours. Then it was " O Missy!" and Arabella uttered a stifled, terrified scream.

" Yes, it's Missy," said that young woman soberly. " And I wonder what we're doing out here at this time of night, both of us ? "

" I'm having a walk," said Arabella, giggling half hysterically.

" That's exactly what I'm doing; so we can walk together."

"You've followed me out, you mean liar!" cried Arabella, with wholly hysterical wrath. She had, indeed, been for pushing forward after the first shock, but when Missy stepped out alongside there was nothing for it but a pitched battle on the spot.

"I have so," said Missy. "I know all about it, you see."

" All about what ?"

" What you are after."

" And what am I after, since you're so mighty clever ?"

" You're meeting that man."

"What man?" Arabella was quaking pitifully.

"The man you're always meeting; but to-night you meant to run away with him."

" Spy! " said Arabella. " What makes you think that ?"

"You have put on all your best things."

" But what makes you think there is a man at all?"

" Oh, I saw that ages ago; though mind you, I have never seen him. It is the man with the meerschaum pipe, now isn't it?"

Arabella's first answer was a shaking fist. Next moment she was shaking all over, in a storm of tears during which Missy took hold of her with both arms, was thrown off, took a fresh hold, and was then suffered to keep it. At last she asked:

" Where were you to meet him, Arabella ?"

The answer came with more sobs than words. " At the top corner of the Cultivation : the road corner: he is to wait there till I come."

" Good! " said Missy. " That's half a mile away, and where we are is out of hearing of the house. Not so sure, eh t Well, come a little, further down the gully. That's better! Now we're safe as the bank, and you'll stop and tell me something about him, won't you, dear, before you go t "

Before she went! Could she ever go now ? All the strength which this poor creature had imbibed from a man as masterful as the woman was weak — an imitative courage, never for a moment her honest own — had been rooted up easily enough from the soul where there was no soil for it, and was now as though it had never existed. Such nerve as she had summoned up was gone. Yes, she would stop and talk; that would be a relief. And Missy should hear all, all there was to tell; but this was very little, incredibly little indeed.

On that first evening, when Missy had come and gone, Arabella had taken a stroll by herself after supper; had been thinking more about the Family Cherub story, in which she was then engrossed than of anything else that she could now remember; but it appeared her head had been full at the time of romantic stuff of one kind or another, so that when she came very suddenly upon a handsome stranger leaning over the slip-rails and smoking his pipe, it was readily revealed to Arabella that she had been waiting for that moment and that stranger all her life. She said as much now, in other words, but wasted time in unnecessary dilatation upon the man's good looks before proceeding with her confession. He had spoken soft words to her in the soft night air. He had kissed her across the slip-rails. And Arabella had lived thirty years in her tiny corner of the world, but never before had she been kissed by the mouth of man not a Teesdale. Missy might stare as much as she liked; it was the sacred truth, was that.

So much for the first meeting, which was a pure accident. There had been others which were nothing of the kind. Missy nodded, as much as to say she knew all about those other meetings, and hurried Arabella to the point. That the foolish girl knew less than nothing worth knowing about this man was only too evident; but it seemed his name was Stanborough. And to-morrow, said Arabella, with a sudden hauling at the slack of her nerves, this would be her name too.

Then she still meant to go?

Arabella fell to pieces again. She had promised. He was waiting. He would kill her if she broke her promise.

" Kill your grandmother ! " said Missy. " Let him wait. Shall I tell you who'll kill who if you do go?"

"Who?" said Arabella in a whisper.

"Why, you'll kill your father, as sure as ever God made you, my girl."

" But we should soon come back — and with money enough to help them here tremendously! He has promised that; and you don't know how well off he is. Missy. Yes, yes, we should soon come back after we were married!"

"I dare say — after that," said Missy dryly.

"Then you don't think he — means "

"Of course he doesn't."

" How do you know ?"

"Never mind how I know. It's enough that I do know, as sure as I'm standing under this tree. You've told me quite sufficient. I feel as if I knew your man as well as I've known two or three.

The brutes! And I tell you, 'Bella, that if you go to him now, as you thought of doing, your life will be blasted from this night on. He will never marry you. He hasn't gone the right way about that. No, but he'll ruin you and leave you in your ruin; and when he does, may the Lord have mercy on your soul! "

She had said. And the extraordinary emotion which had gathered in her voice as she went on had the effect of taking Arabella out of herself even then.

" Missy," she whispered — " Missy, you are crying ! How can you know so much that is terrible "You seem to know all about it. Missy!"

" Never mind how much I know, or how I came to know it," cried the other. " I know enough to want to save you from what some girls I've known have come to. To say nothing of saving your dear old father's life. For kill him it would."

Arabella had been marvelling; but now her own difficulty clutched her afresh.

"He will kill me if I don't go to him. He has said so," she moaned in her misery, "and he will."

" Not he! He's a coward. I feel as if I knew the beast — and precious soon I shall"

Arabella started. " What do you mean ?" said she.

” I mean that you've got to leave your friend to me. I'll soon settle him.”

Missy spoke cheerily. Her new tone inspired confidence in the breast of Arabella, who whispered eagerly, ” How can you ? Ah, if you only could! ”

“You would like it?”

“I should thank God! O Missy, I have been such a wicked, foolish girl, but you are so strong and brave! I shall love you for this all my life! ”

” Will you ? I wonder,” said Missy. ” But never mind that now. Go you back to the house, and if I don't come to your room in less than half an hour and tell you that I've sent Mr. Stanborough about his business ”

” Hush ! ” exclaimed the other in low alarm. ” I hear him now. He is coming to look for me.”

It was a very faint sound, but terror had sharpened the girl's ears. It was the sound of a walking-stick swishing the dry grass on the further slope of the gully. Missy heard it also when she bent her ear to listen, and the next moment she had her companion by the shoulders.

” Now run” said she, ” and run for your life. No, we've no time for any of that stuff now. Time enough to thank me when I come and tell you I've sent him to the right-about for good and all. Run quickly-keep behind the trees — and all will be well before you're an hour older.”

And so they separated, Arabella hurrying upward to the farm, her heart drumming against her ribs, while Missy trudged down the hill at her full height, with a marble mouth, and both fists clenched.

Chapter IX
Face to Face.

For whatever else this wild girl may have been, she was obviously not a coward. That is the one thing to be said for Missy without any hesitation whatever. Alone, and in the night, she was going to pit herself against an unknown man, who was certainly a villain; yet on she went, with her chin in the air and her arms swinging free. The trees were thickest at the bottom of the low gully. The girl came through them with a brisk glance right and left, but never a lagging step. On the further slope the trees spread out again, and here, on comparatively open ground, she did stop, and suddenly. She could smell the man's pipe in the sweet night air; the man himself was nowhere to be seen.

Missy filled her lungs slowly through her teeth, and emptied them with dilated nostrils. Then she went on, longing in her heart for a moon. In the starlight it was not possible to see clearly very many yards ahead. So far as she could see' —and her eyes were good — there was no one in that paddock but herself. Yet a faint smell of tobacco still slightly fouled the air. And this was the very worst part of the whole business; it had brought Missy at last to a second stand-still, and to the determination of singing out, when, without warning sound, an arm was flung round her neck, soft words were being whispered in her ear, and Missy who was no coward felt the veins freezing in her body.

She flung herself free with a great effort, then reeled against the she-oak from behind which he had crept who now stood taking off his hat to her in the starlight.

" I beg your pardon," said a rich, suave voice in its suavest tones; "upon my word, I beg your pardon from the very bottom of my heart! I thought — I give you my word I thought you were another young lady altogether! "

Missy had recovered a measure of her customary self-control. "So I see — so I see," she managed to say distinctly enough; but her voice was the voice of another person.

"Thank you, indeed! You are very generous" said the man, raising his hat once more; " few women would have understood. The fact is, as I say, I took you for a certain young lady whom I quite expected to meet before this. Perhaps you have seen her, and could tell me where she is? For we have missed each other among these accursed gum-trees."

The fellow's impudence was good for Missy.

" Yes, I have seen her," said she, as calmly as the other.

" And where may she be at this moment ? "

"In her father's house."

The man stood twirling his moustache and showing the white teeth under it. Then he stuck in his mouth a meerschaum he had in his hand, and sucked silently at the pipe for some moments. "I beg your pardon once more; but I fear we are at cross-purposes," said he presently. He had been considering.

"I don't think it," said Missy.

" And why not ? " This with a smile.

" Because I have a message for you, Mr. Stan-borough."

"Ha!"

"A message from Arabella Teesdale" said Missy, who had lowered her tone and drawn the other a pace nearer in his eagerness.

"And?" he asked; but he was made to wait. "Will you have the goodness to give me that message ? Tell me what she says, can't you? "

" Oh, certainly!" replied Missy, with a laugh. " I was to say that she had been very foolish, but has come to her senses in time; and that you will never see her any more, as she has thought better of it, and is done with you for good and all!"

There was a pause first, and then a short sardonic laugh.

” So you were to say all that! It isn't the easiest thing in the world to take it in all at once. Do you mind saying some of it over again t ”

“Once is enough. you've got your warning; it's no good your coming after 'Bella Teesdale no more. If you do, you look out for her brother, that's all!”

” John William, eh ? ” The man laughed again.

” Yes.”

”I know all about the family, you see. I know all about you too — in a way. I never knew you were 'Bella's keeper, I must admit. She merely told me you were a young English lady, of the name of Miss Miriam Oliver, who landed the other week in the Parramatta”

“So I am,” said Missy, trembling violently. Her back was still to the good she-oak, but the man had come so close to her now that she could not have escaped him if she would.

“Now that's very interesting,” he hissed, so that the moisture from his mouth struck her in the face. “If I'd been asked who you were, d'ye see, without first being told, d'ye know what I should have said? I should have said that the other week — just about the time the Parramatta came in — there was a certain member of the Bijou Chorus, who answered to the name of Ada Lefroy. And I should have said that Miss Miriam Oliver, of England, was so exactly the dead-spit of Miss Ada Lefroy, of the Bijou Theatre, Melbourne, Victoria, Australia, in the Southern Hemisphere, that they must be one and the same young lady. As it is, I'll strike a light and see.”

He struck one on the spot. Missy was staring at him with still eyes in a white face. He laughed softly, and used the match to relight his meerschaum pipe, which had gone out.

” Well, if this doesn't lick creation! ” he murmured, nodding his head very slowly, to look the girl up and down. ” To think that I should have missed you from the town and found you in the country! The swell young lady from Home! Good Lord, it's too rich to be true.”

Missy opened her lips that had been fast, and under that she-oak her language would have surprised the Teesdales.

“Come, this is more like,” said the other clapping his hands in mock approval. ” Now you'll feel better, eh ? And now you'll tell me how you worked it, Fm sure.”

Missy said what she would do instead.

“Then I must just tell myself. Let's see now: your father — ha ! ha ! — was old Teesdale's old friend, and luckily for you he'd warned them his daughter was something out of the common. That was luck! And you were out of the common! Hasn't 'Bella told me the things you said and did, till I was sick and tired ”t Faith, I'd have listened better if I'd dreamt it was you! I remember her saying you brought a letter of introduction, however; and that you must have stole, my beauty!”

Missy cleared her throat. ” You're a liar,” she said. “I found it.”

” You found it! That's a lot better, isn't it ? A fat lot! Anyhow, out you came, to pose as my young lady from Home till further orders. And my oath, it was one of the cheekiest games I've heard of yet!”

” I only came out for a lark,” Missy said sullenly. ” It was they that put it into my head to come back and stay. I couldn't help it. It was better here than in Melbourne. Much better! ”

” Morally, eh ? ”

” What do you mean ? ”

“I mean, this is a cleaner life than t'other-what?”

“It is. Thank God!”

Stanborough laughed. (Missy had known him under another name, but she was hardly in a position to gain anything by reminding him of that.) ” A mighty fine life,” said he, ” with a mighty fine lie at the bottom of it! ”

“Yes,” said Missy slowly, “that's true enough. But I'm a better sort than when I came here, I know that! ”

" A better sort, eh ? Ha! ha ! ha! That's good, that is. That's very good indeed."

But the girl was too much in earnest to heed the sneers. "You may laugh as you like — it's God's truth," cried she. "And Melbourne will never see me no more, nor London neither. Why ? 'Cause when I clear out of this, I clear up-country; and up-country I shall live ever after; yes, and very likely marry and die respectable. So you can go on jeering "

" Stop! Not so fast," said Stanborough. " You seem to have got it all cut and dried ; but when did you think of clearing out of this ? Suppose you're safe till there's been time for the mails home and out again. That takes three months; you've been here more than one already, and you meant to stop just one month more. Good! very good indeed. Sorry your one month more has gone so quickly — sorry it's only one more night instead. However, that's the misfortune of war. Quite understand ? Not another month — another night only — that's to-night — and a little bit of tomorrow."

Missy remarked at length :

" So you mean to give me away; I might have known that."

" Of course I do. Six months hard, that's what you will get." Missy shuddered. Her tormentor watched her and continued: " So that makes you sit up, does it, my dear ? She didn't know she was breaking the law, didn't she t She'll find out soon enough — find out what it costs to pass yourself off as another person, in this Colony — find out what the inside of Carlton Jail's like, too ! Not go back to town. That was good, that was."

The girl could only pant and glare and wring her hands. More followed in the same strain.

" Nice night, ain't it ? Nice breeze coming up to kiss the leaves and make 'em cry ! Hark at 'em, tree after tree. There goes this she-oak over our heads! Nice and cool on your face, too, isn't it ? Nice wholesome smell of eucalyptus — and all the rest of it. Oh, a sweet night altogether, and one to remember — for your last night out o' prison ! "

" You brute!" said Missy, and worse.

He listened patiently, nodding his head at each name. And then —

" All that ? Not so fast, my dear, not half so fast, if you please. You're in far too much of a hurry, I do assure you. All that's supposing I do give you away." The man's tone was changed.

"But you're going to."

"No," replied Stanborough, "not if you'll clear right out to-night. Do that and I won't say a word to a soul; not even at the farm will I give you away, once you're gone. It'll just be a case of your going as mysteriously as you came; and they may never find out the truth about you; but even if they do, you'll be far enough before they do. Only clear out to-night! "

"And leave 'Bella to you? I'll see you in blazes "

"And yourself in quod "

" I don't care; you're not going to ruin Arabella."

"What if you're too late to prevent it ?"

"If I was, you wouldn't be here to-night. You see I know you, too."

There was a pause.

" Do you know what I've half a mind to do ? " Stanborough said at length in an exceedingly calm voice.

" Yes; to kill me. But you haven't half the pluck — not you! I know you of old."

" All right, we shall see. I give you the rest of this night to clear out in. If you don't, you may lose me my game; but you may bet your soul, Ada Lefroy, I'll have you locked up before you're a day older."

He shook his fist in her face and went away very abruptly; but in a minute he was back, all eagerness and soft persuasion.

"I have nothing against you, Ada," he began now. "You and I have had fun together. And after all, what have I to gain by getting you locked up ? What is it to me if you hoodwink these old people and run your own risk ? Why should I want you to clear out to-night ? See here, my girl, I don't want you to do anything of the kind. You sit tight as long as you think you can; only go back now, like a sensible sort, and get 'Bella to come along with me, like another."

" I can't."

" You could. It was you who persuaded her not to come. I know it was; so don't tell me you couldn't persuade her that I am all right, and to keep her word with me after all."

"Then I won't say I couldn't. I'll say I never will."

"And you mean that?"

"Of course I mean it."

" Well knowing that I shall come and expose you to-morrow, or the next day, or the day after that ? By God, it'd be sport to keep you waiting!"

" Then have your sport. Have it! I will never leave 'Bella, that's one thing sure."

" You'd go to prison for her ? "

"I'd do anything for any of them."

"Then go to hell for them!"

With that he lifted his clenched fist and struck at the girl's face, but she put up her hands, and only her lip was grazed. When she lowered her hands the man was gone.

And this time he was gone altogether. Missy waited, cowering behind the tree, now on this side, now on that. But there were no more footsteps in the short, dry grass until Missy herself stole out from under that she-oak, and crept down into the gully, with giving knees and her chin on her breast, a very different figure from the bold adventuress who had marched up that same slope a short hour earlier in the night. And the stars were still shining all over the little weather-board homestead, so softly, so peacefully, when Missy got back to it. And in the verandah was the wooden chair in which she would sit to read to Mr. Teesdale, and the wooden chair in which Mr. Teesdale would sit and listen. And Missy glided up and took away their book, which lay forgotten on one of the chairs; and then she glided back, thinking chiefly of the last chapter they had read together. They were hardly likely to read another now. But that was not a nice thought; and the farmhouse lay so still and serene under the stars, it was good to watch it longer; for the little homestead had never before seemed half so sweet or so desirable in the girl's eyes. And these were the only waking eyes just then on the premises, for even Arabella had fallen into a fitful, feverish sleep, from which, however, she was presently awakened in the following manner.

Something hot and dry had touched her hand that was lying out over the coverlet. Something else that was also hot, but not dry, had fallen upon that hand, and more of the same sort were still failing. So Arabella awoke frightened; and there was Missy, kneeling at her bedside, fondling her hand, and sobbing as she prayed aloud. Arabella heard without listening. Days afterwards she took out of her ears two phrases: " whatever I have been" and "bad as I am." These words she put in due season through the mills of her mind; but at the time she simply said:

" Missy ! What are you doing ? Ah, I remember. Have you seen him ? Tell me what he said — what has happened — and what is going to happen now."

"I've seen him and settled him ? Missy whispered firmly as she dried her eyes. "What he said isn't of any account. But nothing's going to happen — nothing — nothing at all."

Chapter X
The Thinning of the Ice.

Old Teesdale sat with his arm-chair drawn close to the table, and his shirt-sleeves rolled up to the elbow. He was. writing a letter in which he had already remarked that it was the hottest Christmas Eve within even his experience of that colony. In the verandah, indeed, the thermometer had made the shade heat upwards of 100" since nine o'clock in the morning, touching no" in the early afternoon. It was now about six (Mr. Teesdale being still without his watch was never positive of the time), and because of Mrs. T.'s theory that to open a window was to let in the heat, to say nothing of the flies, the atmosphere of the parlour with its reminiscences of the day's meals was sufficiently unendurable. A little smoke from Mr. Teesdale's pipe would surely have improved it if anything; but that was against the rules of the house, and the poor gentleman, who was not master of it, wrote on and on with the perspiration standing on his bald head, and the reek of the recent tea in his nose.

He was on the third leaf of a letter for the English mail. "As to Miriam herself" — thus the paragraph began which was still being penned — "I can only say that she is the life and soul of our quiet home, and what we shall do without her when she goes I really do not like to think. Referring again to the letter in which you advised me of her arrival, and to those 'habits and ways' of which you warned me, I cannot deny that I soon saw what you meant; but I must say that I would not have Miriam without her 'mannerisms' even if I could. They may be modern, but they are very entertaining indeed to us, who are so far behind the times. Yes, the young girls of our day may have talked less 'slang' and paid more attention to 'appearances,' but no girl ever had a warmer heart than your Miriam, nor a kinder nature, nor a franker way with her in all her dealings. But her kindness is what has struck me most, from the very first, and especially her kindness to an old man like me. You should see her sit and read to me by the hour, and help me with whatever little thing I may happen to be doing, and listen to my talk as though I were a young man like our John William. Then I think you would understand why I am always saying that she never could have been anybody's daughter but yours, and why I want to keep her as long as ever you will let her stay. She has spoken of going on to other friends after the New Year; but I wish you would insist upon her coming back to us for a real long visit before she leaves the colony for good; and I know that you would do so if you could but see the change which even a few weeks with us has already wrought in her. You must know, my dear Oliver, that we live here very simply indeed; but I am of opinion that simple living and early hours were what Miriam needed more than anything else, for it is no exaggeration to say that she does not look the same girl who first came to see us with your letter of introduction. She has a better colour, her whole face is brighter and healthier, and the tired look I at first noticed in her eyes has gone out of them once and at this point Mr. Teesdale paused, pen in air.

He was a very careful letter-writer, who wrote a beautiful old-fashioned hand, and made provision for perfectly even spaces by means of a black-lined sheet nicely adjusted under the leaf; and he rounded each sentence in his own mind before neatly committing it to paper. Thus a single erasure was a great rarity in his letters, while two would have made him entirely rewrite. On the other hand, many a minute here and there were spent in peering through the gun-room window, and scouring the Dandinong Ranges for the right word; and now several minutes went thus in one lump, because Mr. Teesdale was by nature an even greater stickler for the literal truth than for flawless penmanship, and he had caught himself in the act of writing what was not strictly true. It was a fact that the tired look had gone out of Missy's eyes, but to add "once and for all" was to make the whole statement a lie, according to Mr. Teesdale's standard. For the last thirty-six hours that tired look had been back in those bright eyes, which brightened now but by fits and starts. David did not so define it, but the girl looked hunted. He merely knew that she did not look to-day or yesterday as she had looked for some weeks without a break, therefore he could not and would not say that she did. Accordingly the predicate of the unfinished sentence was radically altered until that sentence stood . . . "and the tired look I at first noticed in her eyes is to be seen in them but very seldom now."

But the erasure had occurred on the fifth page, on a new sheet altogether, which it was certainly worth while to commence afresh; and old Tees-dale had scarcely regained the point at which he had tripped when the door opened, and the subject of his letter was herself in the room beside him, looking swiftly about her, as if to make certain that he was alone, before allowing her eyes to settle upon his welcoming smile.

"Well, Missy, and what have you been doing with yourself since tea?"

" I ?" said the girl absently, as she glanced into the gun-room, and then out of each window, very keenly, before sitting down on the sofa. " I ? Oh, I've been having a sleep, that's what I've been doing."

Mr. Teesdale was watching her narrowly as he leant back in his chair. She did not look to him as though she had been sleeping; but that was of course his own fancy. On the other hand, the strange expression in Missy's eyes, which he could not quite define, struck the old man as stranger and more conspicuous than ever.

"I'm afraid, my dear, that you haven't been getting your proper sleep lately."

"You're right. There's no peace for the wicked these red-hot nights, let alone the extra wicked, like me."

" Get away with you!" said old Teesdale, laughing at the grave girl who was staring him in the face without the glimmer of a smile.

"Get away I will, one of these days; and glad enough you'll be when that day comes and you know all about me. I've always told you a day like that would come sooner or later. It might come to-morrow — it might come to-night! "

"Missy, my dear, I do wish you'd smile and show me you're only joking. Not that it's one of your best jokes, my dear, nor one of your newest either. Ah, that's it —that's better!"

She had jumped up to look once more out of the window: a man was passing towards the hen-yard, it was little Geordie, and Missy sat down smiling.

"Then tell me what it is you're busy with" she began in a different tone; an attempt at the old saucy manner which the farmer loved as a special, sacred perquisite of his own.

" Now you're yourself again ! Fm writing a long, long letter. Missy. Guess who to?"

"To —to Mr. Oliver?"

"Mr. Oliver! Your father, my dear-your own father! Now guess what it's about, if you can!"

"About —me ?"

David nodded his head with great humour.

"Yes, it's about you. A nice character I'm giving you, you may depend!"

"Are you saying that I'm a regular bad lot then ? "

" Ah, that's telling ! "

"If you were, you wouldn't be far from the mark, if you only knew it. But let's hear what you have said."

"Nay, come! You don't expect me to let you hear what I've said about you, do you, Missy ?"

"Of course I do," said Missy firmly.

" But that would be queer! Nay, Missy, I couldn't show you this letter, I really couldn't. For one thing, it would either make you conceited or else very indignant with poor me!"

"So that's the kind of character you've been giving me, is it ? " said Missy, smiling grimly. "Now I must see it."

"Nay, come, I don't think you must, Missy — I don't think you must!"

" But I want to."

So exclaiming, the girl rose resolutely to her feet; and her resolution settled the matter; for it will have been seen that the weak old man himself was all the time wishing her to see what he had written about her. After all, why should she not know how fond he was of her. If it made her ever such a little bit fonder of him, well, there surely could be no harm in that. Still, Mr. Tees-dale chose to walk up and down the room while Missy stood at the window to read his letter, for it was now growing dark.

" I see you mention that twenty pounds." Missy had looked up suddenly from the letter. " How was it you managed to get the money that night, after all." I have often meant to ask you."

Mr. Teesdale stopped in his walk. "What does it matter how I got them, honey . "I neither begged, borrowed nor stole 'em, if that's what you want to know." The old gentleman laughed.

"I want to know lots more than that, because it matters a very great deal, when I went and put you to all that inconvenience."

"Well, I went to the man who buys all our milk. I told you I was going to him, didn't I ? "

" Yes, but I've heard you say here at table that you haven't had a farthing from him these six months."

" Missy, my dear," remonstrated the old man, with difficulty smiling, "you will force me to ask you — to mind "

" My own business ? Right you are. What's the time?"

"The time!" The question did indeed seem irrelevant. " Fm sure I don't know, but I'll go and have a look at the kitchen "

" Then you needn't. I don't really want to know. I was only wondering when John William would be back from Melbourne. But where's your watch t "

"Getting put to rights, my dear," said old Tees-dale faintly, with his eyes upon the carpet.

"What, still?"

"Yes; they're keeping it a long time, aren't they ? "

" They are so," said Missy dryly. She watched the old man as he crossed the room twice, with his weak-kneed steps, his white hands joined behind him and his thin body bent forward. Then she went on reading his letter.

It affected her curiously. At the third page she uttered a quick exclamation; at the fourth she lowered the letter with a quick gesture, and stood staring at David with an expression at which he could only guess, because the back of her head was against the glass.

"This is too much," cried Missy in a broken voice. " I can never let you send this."

"And why not, my dear." laughed Mr. Teesdale, echoing, as he thought, her merriment; for it was to this he actually attributed the break in her voice.

" Because there isn't a word of truth in it; because I haven't a warm heart nor a kind nature, and because I'm not frank in my dealings. Frank, indeed! If you knew what I really was, you wouldn't say that in a hurry!"

Mr. Teesdale could no longer suppose that the girl was in fun. Her bosom was heaving with excitement ; he could see that, if he could not see her face. He said wearily:

"There you go again, Missy! I can't understand why you keep saying such silly things."

" I'm not what you think me. You understand that, don't you?"

" I hear what you say, but I don't believe a word of it."

" Then you must! You shall! I can't bear to deceive you a moment longer — I simply can't bear it when you speak and think of me like this. First of all, then, this letter's no good at all! "

In another instant that letter fluttered upon the floor in many pieces.

"You must forgive me," said Missy, "I couldn't help it; it wasn't worth the paper it was written on; and now I'm going to tell you why."

Old Teesdale, however, had never spoken, and this silenced the girl also, for the moment. But that moment meant a million. One more, and Missy would have confessed everything. She was worked up to it. She was in continual terror of an immediate exposure. Her better nature was touched and cauterised with shame for the sweet affection of which she had cheated this simple old man. She would tell him everything now and here, and the mercy that filled his heart would be extended to her because she had not waited to be unmasked by another. But she paused to measure him with her eye, or, perhaps, to take a last look at him looking kindly upon her. And in that pause the door opened, making Missy jump with fright; and when it was only Arabella who entered with the lighted kerosene lamp. Missy's eyes sped back to the old man's face in time to catch a sorrowful mute reproach that went straight to her palpitating heart. She stooped without a word to help him gather up the fragments of the torn letter.

She had no further opportunity of speaking that night; and supper would have been a silent meal but for what happened as they all sat at table. All, that night, did not include John William, who was evidently spending Christmas Eve in Melbourne. There was some little talk about him. David remarked that a mail would be in with the Christmas letters, and Missy was asked whether she had not told John William to call at the post office. She had not. During her sojourn at the farm she had only once been to the post office herself; had never sent; and had been told repeatedly she was not half anxious enough about her Home letters. They told her so now. Missy generally said it was because she was so happy and at-home with them; but tonight she made no reply; and this was where they were when there came that knock at the window which made Missy spill her cocoa and otherwise display a strange state of mind.

" Who is it ?" she cried. " Who do you think it is ?"

" Maybe some neighbour," said Mrs. T., "to wish us the compliments o' t' season."

" If not old Father Christmas himself!" laughed David to Missy, in the wish that she should forgive herself, as he had forgiven her, for tearing up his letter. But Missy could only stare at the window-blind, behind which the knock had been repeated, and she was trembling very visibly indeed. Then the front-door opened, and it was Missy, not one of the family, that rushed out into the passage to see who it was. The family heard her shouting for joy:

" It's John William. It's only John William after all. Oh, you dear, dear old Jack!"

Very quickly she was back in the room, and down on the horsehair sofa, breathing heavily. John William followed in his town clothes.

"Yes, of course it's me. Good evening, all. Who did you think it was. Missy ? "

"I thought it was visitors. What if it had been? Oh, I hate visitors, that's all". "Then I'm sorry to hear it," remarked Mrs. Teesdale sourly, "for we have visitors coming to-morrow."

"I hate 'em, too," said John William wilfully.

"Then I'll thank you to keep your hates to yourselves," cried Mrs. T. "It's very rude of you both. Your mother wouldn't have spoke so. Missy!"

" Wouldn't she! " laughed the girl. " I wonder if you know much about my mother? But after that I think I'll be off to bed. I am rude, I know I am, but I never pretended to be anything else."

This was fired back at them from the door, and then Missy was gone without saying good-night.

"She's not like her mother," said Mrs. T. angrily ; " no, that she isn't!"

"But why in the name of fortune go and tell her so?" John William blurted out. "I never knew anything like you, mother; on Christmas Eve, too!"

" I think," said David gently, " that Missy is not quite herself. She has been very excitable all day, and I think it would have been better to have taken no notice of what she said. You should remember, my dear, that she is utterly unused to our climate, and that even to us these last few days have been very trying."

Arabella was the only one who had nothing at all to say, either for Missy or against her. But she went to Missy's room a little later, and there she spoke out:

" You thought it was — Stanborough ! I saw you did."

"Then I did — for the moment. But it was very silly of me —I don't know what could have put him into my head, when I've settled him so finely for good and all!"

" God bless you, Missy! But — but do you think there is any fear of him coming back and walking right in like that ? "

"Not the least. Still, if he did-if he did, mark you — I'd tackle him again as soon as look at him. So never you fear, my girl, you leave him to me."

Chapter XI
A Christmas Offering.

In the Melbourne shops that Christmas Eve the younger Teesdale had been perpetrating untold acts of extravagance, for two of which a certain very bad character was entirely and solely responsible. Thus with next day's Christmas dinner there was a bottle of champagne, and the healths of Mr. and Mrs. Oliver, and of Miriam their daughter, were drunk successively, and with separate honours. Missy thereat seemed to suffer somewhat from her private feelings, as indeed she did suffer, but those feelings were not exactly what they were suspected to be at the time. She was wondering how much longer she could keep up this criminal pretence and act this infamous part. And as she wondered, a delirious recklessness overcame her, and emptying her glass she jumped to her feet to confess to them all then and there; but the astonished eye of Mrs. Teesdale went like cold steel to her heart, and she wished them long life and prosperity instead. She found herself seated once more with a hammering heart and sensations that drove her to stare hard at the old woman's unsympathetic face, as her own one chance of remaining cool till the end of the meal. And yet a worse moment was to follow hard upon the last.

Missy had made straight for the nearest and the thickest shelter, which happened to underlie that dark jagged rim of river-timber at which old Teesdale was so fond of gazing. She had thrown herself face downward on a bank beside the sluggish brown stream; her fingers were interwoven under her face, her thumbs stuck deep into her ears. So she did not hear the footsteps until they were close beside her, when she sat up suddenly with a face of blank terror.

It was only John William. "Who did you think it was?" said he, smiling as he sat down beside her.

Missy was trembling dreadfully. " How was I to know?" she answered nervously. "It might have been a bushranger, mightn't it ?"

" Well, hardly?" replied John William, as seriously as though the question had been put in the best of good faith. And it now became obvious that he also had something on his mind and nerves, for he shifted a little further away from Missy, and sat frowning at the dry brown grass, and picking at it with his fingers.

" Anyhow, you startled me," said Missy, as she arranged the carroty fringe that had been shamefully dishevelled a moment before. "I am very easily startled, you see."

" I am very sorry. I do apologise, I'm sure ! And I'll go away again this minute, Missy, if you like."

He got to his knees with the words, which were spoken in a more serious tone than ever.

" Oh, no, don't go away. I was only moping. I am glad you've come."

"Thank you. Missy."

" But now you have come, you've got to talk and cheer me up. See? There's too many things to think about on a Christmas Day — when — when you're so far away from everybody."

John William agreed and sympathised. "The fact is I had something to show you," he added; "that's why I came."

" Then show away " said Missy, forcing a smile. "Something in a cardboard box, eh?"

"Yes. Will you open it and tell me how you like it ? " He handed her the box that he had taken out of his breast-pocket. Missy opened it and produced a very yellow bauble of sufficiently ornate design.

" Well, I'm sure ! A bangle !"

" Yes; but what do you think of it ? " asked John William anxiously. He had also blushed very brown.

" Oh, of course I think it's beautiful — beautiful!" exclaimed Missy, with unmistakable sincerity. "But who's it for? That's what I want to know," she added, as she scanned him narrowly.

" Can't you guess ? "

"Well, let's see. Yes — you're blushing! It's for your young woman, that's evident."

John William edged nearer.

"It's for the young lady — the young lady I should like to be mine-only I'm so far below her," he began in a murmur. Then he looked at her hard. " Missy, for God's sake forgive me," he cried out, "but it's for you!"

" Nonsense!"

" But I mean it. I got it last night. Do, please, have it."

"No," said Missy firmly. "Thank you ever so very awfully much; but you must take it back." And she held it out to him with a still hand.

"I can't take it back — I won't!" cried young Teesdale excitedly. " Consider it only as a Christmas box — surely your father's godson may give you a little bit of a Christmas box? That's me, Missy, and anything else I've gone and said you must forgive and forget too, for it was all a slip. I didn't mean to say it. Missy, I didn't indeed. I hope I know my position better than that. But this here little trumpery what-you-call-it, you must accept it as a Christmas present from us all. Yes, that's what you must do; for I'm bothered if I take it back."

"You must," repeated Missy very calmly. "I think you mean to break my heart between you with your kindness. Here's the box and here's the bangle."

John William looked once and for all into the resolute light eyes. Then first he took the box and put the lid on it, and stowed it away in his breastpocket; and after that he took that gold bangle very gingerly, between finger and thumb, and spun it out into the centre of the brown river, where it made bigger, widening bangles, that took the best part of a minute to fail and die away. Then everything was stiller than before; and stillest of all were the man and the woman who stood facing each other on the bank, speckled with the steep sunlight that came down on them like rain through the leaves of the river-timber overhead.

" That was bad," said Missy at last. Something else was worse. It's not much good your trying to hedge matters with me; and for my part I'm going to speak straight and plain for once. If I thought that you'd gone and fallen in love with me — as sure as we're standing here. Jack, I'd put myself where you've put that bangle."

Her hand pointed to the place. There was neither tremor in the one nor ripple upon the other.

"But why?" Teesdale could only gasp.

"Because I'm so far below you"

"Missy! Missy!" he was beginning passionately, but she checked him at once.

"Let well alone. Jack. I've spoken God's truth. I'm not going to say any more; only when you know all about me — as you may any day now — perhaps even to-day — don't say that I told nothing but lies. That's all. Now must I go back to the house, or will you."

He glanced towards the river with unconscious significance. She shook her head and smiled. He hung his, and went away.

Once more Missy was alone among the river-timber; once more she flung herself down upon the short, dry grass, but this time upon her back, while her eyes and her ears were wide open.

A cherry-picker was frivolling in the branches immediately above her. From the moment it caught her eye. Missy seemed to take great interest in that cherry-picker's proceedings. She had wasted innumerable cartridges on these small birds, but that was in her blood-thirsty days, now of ancient history, and there had never been any ill-feeling between Missy and the cherry-pickers even then. One solitary native cat was all the fair game that she had slaughtered in her time. She now took to wondering why it was that these animals were never to be seen upon a tree in day-time; and as she wondered, her eyes hunted all visible forks and boughs; and as she hunted, a flock of small parrots came whirring like a flight of arrows, and called upon Missy's cherry-picker, and drove him from the branches overhead. But the parrots were a new interest, and well worth watching. They had red beaks and redder heads and tartan wings and emerald breasts. Missy had had shots at these also formerly; even now she shut her left eye and pretended that her right fore-finger was a gun, and felt certain of three fine fellows with one barrel had it really been a gun. Then at last she turned on her elbow towards the river, and opened her mouth to talk to herself. And after a long half-hour with nature this was all she had to say:

"If I did put myself in there, what use would it be ? That beast would get a hold of Arabella then. But it'd be nice never to know what they said when they found out everything. What's more, I'd rather be in there, after this, than in any town. After this !"

She gave that mob of chattering parrots a very affectionate glance; also the dark green leaves with the dark blue sky behind them; also the brown, still river, hidden away from the sun. She had come to love them all, and the river would be a very good place for her indeed.

She muttered on: " Then to think of John William ! Well, I never! It would be best for him too if I snuffed out, one way or another; and as for 'Bella, if that brute doesn't turn up soon, he may not turn up at all. But he said he'd keep me waiting. He's low enough down to do it, too."

She looked behind her shuddering, as she had looked behind her many and many a time during the last few days. Instantly her eyes fell upon that at which one has a right to shudder. Within six feet of Missy a brown snake had stiffened itself from the ground with darting tongue and eyes like holes in a head full of fire. And Missy began to smile and hold out her hands to it.

"Come on," she said. "Come on and do your worst! I wish you would. That'd be a way out without no blame to anybody — and just now they might be sorry. Come on, or I'll come to you. Ah, you wretch, you blooming coward, you!"

She had got to her knees, and was actually making for the snake on all fours; but it darted back into its hole like a streak of live seaweed; and Missy then rose wearily to her feet, and stood looking around her once more, as though for the last time.

"What am I to do?" she asked of river, trees, and sky. "What am I to do? I haven't the pluck to finish myself, nor yet to make a clean breast. I haven't any pluck at all. I might go back and do something that'd make the whole kit of 'em glad to get rid o' me. That's what I call a gaudy idea, but it would mean clearing out in a hurry. And I don't want to clear out — not yet. Not just yet! So I'll slope back and see what's happening and how things are panning out; and I'll go on sitting tight as long as I'm let."

Chapter XII
"The Song of Miriam."

Accordingly Missy reappeared in the verandah about tea-time, and in the verandah she was once more paralysed with the special terror that was hanging over her from hour to hour in these days. An unfamiliar black coat had its back to the parlour window; it was only when Missy discerned an equally unfamiliar red face at the other side of the table that she remembered that Christmas visitors had been expected in the afternoon, and reflected that these must be they. The invited guests were a brace of ministers connected with the chapel attended by the Teesdales, and the red face, which was also very fat, and roofed over with a thatch of very white hair, rose out of as black a coat as that other of which Missy had seen the back. So these were clearly the ministers. And they were already at tea.

As soon as Missy entered the parlour she recognised the person sitting with his back to the window. He had lantern jaws hung with black whiskers, and a very long but not so very clean-shaven upper lip. His name was Appleton, he was the local minister, and Missy had not only been taken to hear him preach, but she had met him personally, and made an impression, judging by the length of time the minister's hand had rested upon her shoulder on that occasion. He greeted her now in a very complimentary manner, and with many seasonable wishes, which received the echo of an echo from the elder reverend visitor, whom Mrs. Teesdale made known to Missy as their old friend Mr. Crowdy.

"Mr. Crowdy," added Mrs. T., reproachfully, " came all the way from Williamtown to preach our Christmas morning sermon. It was a beautiful sermon, if ever I heard one."

"It was that," put in David, wagging his kind old head. "But you should have told Mr. Crowdy, my dear, how Miriam feels our heat. I wouldn't let her go this morning, Mr. Crowdy, on that account. So you see it's me that's to blame."

Mr. Crowdy looked very sorry for Miriam, but very well pleased with himself and the world. Missy was shooting glances of gratitude at her indefatigable old champion. Mr. Crowdy began to eye her kindly out of his fat red face.

"So your name's Miriam? A good old-fashioned Biblical name, is Miriam," he said, in a wheezy, plethoric voice. "Singular thing, too, my name's Aaron; but I'd make an oldish brother for you, young lady, hey?"

Miriam laughed without understanding, and showed this. So Mr. Teesdale explained.

"Miriam, my dear, was the sister of Moses and Aaron, you remember."

Missy did remember.

"Moses and Aaron? Why, of course!" cried she. " Says Moses to Aaron !'"

The quotation was not meant to go any further; but the white-haired minister asked blandly, " Well, what did he say?" So bland, indeed, was the question that Missy hummed forth after a very trifling hesitation —

> "Says Moses to Aaron,
> ' While talking of these times' —
> Says Aaron to Moses,
> I vote we make some rhymes!
> The ways of this wicked world,
> 'Tis not a bed of roses —
> No better than it ought to be —
> ' Right you are!' says Moses."

There was a short but perfect silence, during which Mrs. Teesdale glared at Missy and her husband looked pained. Then the old minister simply remarked that he saw no fun in profanity, and John William (who was visibly out of his element) felt frightfully inclined to punch Mr. Crowdy's white head for him. But the Reverend Mr. Appleton took a lighter view of the matter.

"With all due deference to our dear old friend," said this gentleman, with characteristic unction, "I must say that I am of opinion 'e is labouring under a slight misconception. Miss Miriam, I feel sure, was not alluding to any Biblical characters at all, but to two typical types of the latter-day Levite. Miss Miriam nods! I knew that I was right!"

"Then I was wrong," said Mr. Crowdy, cheerfully, as he nodded to Missy, who had not seriously aggrieved him; "and all's well that ends well."

" Hear, hear!" chimed in David, thankfully. "Mrs. T., Mr. Appleton's cup's off. And Mr. Crowdy hasn't got any jam. Or will you try our Christmas cake now, Mr. Crowdy? My dears, my dears, you're treating our guests very shabbily!"

"Some of them puts people about so — some that ought to know better," muttered Mrs. Tees-dale under her breath; but after that the tea closed over Missy's latest misdemeanour — if indeed it was one for Missy — and a slightly sticky meal went as smoothly as could be expected to its end.

Then Mr. Appleton said grace, and Mr. Crowdy, pushing back his plate and his chair, exclaimed in an oracular wheeze, "The Hundred!"

"The Old 'Undredth," explained the other, getting on his feet and producing a tuning-fork. He was the musical minister, Mr. Appleton. Nevertheless, he led them off too high or too low, and started them afresh three times, before they were all standing round that tea-table and singing in unison at the rate of about two lines per minute —

"All-peo-pie-that-on-earth-do-dwell —
Sing-to-the-Lord-with-cheer-ful-voice —
Him-serve-with-fear-His-praise-forth-tell —
Come-ye-be-fore-Him-and-re-joice."

And so through the five verses, which between them occupied the better part of ten minutes; whereafter Mr. Crowdy knelt them all down with their elbows among the tea-things, and offered up a prayer.

Now it is noteworthy that the black sheep of this mob, that had no business to be in this mob at all, displayed no sort of inclination to smile at these grave proceedings. They took Missy completely by surprise; but they failed to tickle her sense of humour, because there was too much upon the conscience which had recently been born again to Missy's soul. On the contrary, the hymn touched her heart and the prayer made it bleed; for that heart was become like a foul thing cleaned in the pure atmosphere of this peaceful homestead. The prayer was very long and did not justify its length. It comprised no point, no sentence, which in itself could have stung a sinner to the quick. But through her fingers Missy could see the bald pate, the drooping eyelids, and the reverent, submissive expression of old Mr. Teesdale. And they drew the blood. The girl rose from her knees with one thing tight in her mind. This was the fixed determination to undeceive that trustful nature without further delay than was necessary, and in the first fashion which offered.

A sort of chance came almost immediately; it was not the best sort, but Missy had grown so desperate that now she was all for running up her true piratical colours and then sheering off before a gun could be brought to bear upon her. So she seized the opportunity which occurred in the best parlour, to which the party adjourned after tea. The best parlour was very seldom used. It had the fusty smell of all best parlours, which never are for common use, and was otherwise too much of a museum of albums, antimacassars, ornaments and footstools, to be a very human habitation at its best. Though all that met the eye looked clean, there was a strong pervading sense of the dust of decades; but some of this was about to be raised.

In the passage Mr. Appleton had taken Missy most affectionately by the arm, and had whispered of Mr. Crowdy, who was ahead, "A grand old man, and ripe for 'eaven!" But as they entered the best parlour he was complimenting Missy upon her voice, which had quite altered the sound of the late hymn from the moment when John William fetched and handed to her an open hymn-book. And here Mr. Crowdy, seating himself in the least uncomfortable of the antimacassared chairs, had his say also.

"*I* like your voice too," the florid old minister observed, cocking a fat eye at Miriam. "But it is only natural that any young lady of your name should be musical. Surely you remember." And Miriam the prophetess, the sister of Aaron, took a timbrel in her hand; and all the women went out after her with timbrels and with dances — ' and so forth. Exodus fifteenth. I suppose you can't play upon the timbrel, hey, Miss Miriam?"

"No," said Missy; "but I can dance."

"Hum! And sing? What I mean is, young lady, do you only sing hymns?"

Missy kept her countenance.

"I have sung songs as well," she ventured to assert.

"Then give us one now, Missy," cried old Teesdale. "That's what Mr. Crowdy wants, and so do we all."

"Something lively?" suggested Missy, looking doubtfully at the red-faced minister.

"Lively? To be sure," replied Mr. Crowdy. " Christmas Day, young lady, is not like a Sunday unless it happens to fall on one, which I'm glad it hasn't this year. Make it as lively as convenient. I like to be livened up ! " And the old man rubbed his pudgy hands and leant forward in the least uncomfortable chair.

" And shall I give you a dance too ? " "A dance, by all means, if you dance alone. I understand that such dancing has become quite the rage in the drawing-rooms at home. And a very good thing too, if it puts a stop to that dancing two together, which is an abomination in the sight of the Lord. But a dance by yourself — by all manner of means! " cried Mr. Crowdy, snatching off his spectacles and breathing upon the lenses. "But I should require an accompaniment." " Nothing easier. My friend Appleton can accompany anything that is hummed over to him twice. Can't you, Appleton ?"

" Mr. Crowdy," replied the younger man, in an injured voice, as he looked askance at a little old piano with its back to the wall, and still more hopelessly at a music-stool from which it would be perfectly impossible to see the performance; " Mr. Crowdy, I do call this unfair! I — I "

"You — you — I know you, sir!" cried the aged divine, with unmerciful good-humour. " Haven't I heard you do as much at your own teas ? Get up at once, sir, and don't shame our cloth by disobliging a young lady who is offering to sing to us in the latest style from England ! "

" I'm not offering, mind!" said Missy a little sharply. " Still, I'm on to do my best. Come over here, Mr. Appleton, and I'll hum it quite quietly in your ear. It goes something like this."

That conquered Appleton; but the Teesdales, while leaving the whole matter in the hands of Missy and of the venerable Mr. Crowdy, who wanted to hear her sing, had thrown in words here and there in favour of the performance and of Mr. Appleton's part in it; all except Mrs. T., who was determined to have no voice in a matter of which she hoped to disapprove, and who showed her determination by an even more unsympathetic cast of countenance than was usual with her wherever Missy was concerned. Mrs. T. was seated upon a hard sofa by her husband's side, Arabella on a low footstool, John William by the window, and the two ministers we know where. The one at the piano seemed to have got his teeth into a banjo accompaniment which would have sounded very wonderfully like a banjo on that little old tin-pot piano if he had thumped not quite so hard; but now Missy was posing in front of the mantelpiece, and all eyes but the unlucky accompanist's were covering her eagerly.

" Now you're all right, Mr. Appleton. You keep on like that, and I'll nip in when I'm ready. If I stop and do a spout between the verses you can stop too, only don't forget to weigh in with the chorus. But when I dance, you keep on. See ? That'll be all right, then. Ahem!"

Missy had spoken behind her hand in a stage whisper; now she turned to her audience and struck an attitude that made them stare. The smile upon her face opened their eyes still wider — it was so brazen, so insinuating, and yet so terribly artificial. And with that smile she began to dance, very slowly and rhythmically, plucking at her dress and showing her ankles, while Appleton thumped carefully on, little knowing what he was missing. And when it seemed as though no song was coming the song began.

But the dance went on through all, being highly appropriate, at all events to verse one, which ran : —

> ” Yuss ! A fling and a slide with a pal, inside,
> It isn’t ’alf bad — but mind you!
> The spot for a ‘op is in front o’ the shop
> With a fried-fish-breeze be’ind you . . .
> Well! Every lass was bold as brass,
> But divvle a one a Venus;
> An ’Rorty ’Arry as I’m to marry
> The only man between us!”

Here Missy and the music stopped together, Mr. Appleton holding his fingers in readiness over the next notes, while Missy interrupted her dance, too, to step forward and open fire upon her audience in the following prose : —

” Now that’s just ‘ow the ’ole thing ’appened. They wouldn’t give my pore ’Arry no peace — catch them ! Well, ’Arry ’e done ’s level — I will say that for ’im. ’E took on three at once; but ’is legs wouldn’t go round fast enough, an’ ’is arms wouldn’t go round at all — catch them I Now would you believe it ? When ’e’s ’ad enough -o’ the others — a nasty common low lot they was, too — ’e ’as the cheek to come to yours truly. But — catch me! ’ No, ‘Arry,’ I sez, ’ ‘ere’s 2 d, to go and ’ave a pint o’ four-’alf,’ I sez, ‘w’ich you must need it,’ I sez — just like that. So ’e goes an’ ’as ’alf a dozen. That’s my ’Arry all over, that is! An’ w’en ’e come back ’e ’as the impidence to ax me again. But I give ’im a look like this,” cried Missy, leering horribly at the venerable Crowdy. “Such a look! Just like that” —with a repetition of the leer for Mrs. Teesdale’s special benefit — ” ’cause I seen what was wrong with ’im in the twinkling of a dress-improver. An’ after that — chorus-up, Mr. Appleton ! — why, after that —

> ” ’Any ’e ’ad the ’ump,
> An’ I lets ’im know it — plump
> ’E swore ’e’d not,
> So ’e got it ’ot,
> I caught ’im a good ole crump.
> You should ‘a’ seen ’im jump!
> I didn’t give a dump!
> For I yells to ’is pals
> ‘Now look at ’im, gals — Arry,’e ’as the ’ump!’ ”

The dancing had been taken up again with the chorus. There was some dancing plain at the end of it. Then came verse two : —

> ”’E swore and cussed till you thought ’e’d bust,
> W’ich ’is ’abit is when drinky;
> ’E cussed and swore till ’is mouth was sore
> An’ the street was painted pinky.
> So I sez, sez I, to a stander-by
> As was standin’ by to listen,
> ‘We’ve ’ad quite enough o’ the reg’lar rough.
> An’ a bit too much o’ this ‘un!’”

” ‘Yuss,’ ” continued Missy without a break, “ ‘an’ if you’re a man,’ I sez, ‘come an’ ’elp shift this ’ere bloomin’ imitition,’ I sez. ‘Right you are,’ ’e sez, ’since you put it so flatterin’ like. An’ wot do they call you, my dear,' sez 'e. 'That's my bloomin' business,' sez I, 'wot's yours on the charge-sheet.-' 'Ted,'sez'e. 'Right,'sez I. 'You git a holt of 'is 'eels, Ted, an' I'll 'ang on to 'is 'air!'"

Up to this point matters had proceeded without audible let or hindrance. But it appeared that at the psychological moment now reached by the narrator the prostrate hero had regained the command of his tongue, and the use he made of it was represented by Missy in so voluble and violent a harangue, couched in such exceedingly strong language, and all hurled so pointedly at the heads of Mr. and Mrs. Teesdale on the sofa opposite the fire-place, that an inevitable interruption now occurred.

" It's quite disgusting! I won't allow such language in my house. Stop at once!" cried Mrs. T. half rising; but Missy's voice was louder; while old David stretched an arm in front of his wife and fenced her to the sofa.

" Sit still, my dear, and don't be foolish," said he, quite firmly. "Can't you see that it's part of the song, and only in fun?"

" Only in fun! " echoed Missy, whose speaking voice had risen to a hoarse scream. " Ho, yuss, an' I s'pose it was fun between 'Any an' me an' Ted ? You bet your bags it wasn't! Why, time we'd done with 'im, Ted's rigging was gone to glory — all but 'is chest-protector. And as for me, you couldn't ha' made a decent pen-wiper out o' my 'ole attire. An' why? Why 'cause — now then, you at the pianner ! — 'cause —

    " 'Arry 'e 'ad the 'ump —
    The liquorin' lushin' lump —
    So I sez to Ted,
    ' 'Ere, sit on 'is 'ead,
    Or shove 'im under the pump!'
    Ted 'e turns out a trump. We done it with bump an' thump.
    For that 'orrible 'Arry
    Was 'eavy to carry —
    An' 'Arry 'e 'ad the 'ump!"

Now not one of them guessed that this was the end of the song. They had made up their minds to more and worse, and they got it in Missy's final dance. She was wearing a dark blue skirt of some thin material. Already there had been glimpses of a white underskirt and a pair of crimson ankles, but now there were further and fuller views. John William and Arabella had been curiously and painfully fascinated from the beginning. Their father was still barring their mother to the sofa with an outstretched arm. The poor old minister sat forward in his chair with his eyes protruding from his head. His junior, who was still thumping the old piano as though his life depended upon it, was the one person present who saw nothing of what was going on; and he suspected nothing amiss; he had been too busy with his notes to attend even to the words. Every other eye was fixed upon the dancing girl; every other forehead was wet with a cold perspiration. But Mr. Appleton was so far unconsciously infected with the spirit of the proceedings that he was now playing that banjo accompaniment at about double his rate of starting. And the ornaments were rattling on mantelpiece and table and bracket, and a small vase fell with a crash into the fender — Missy had brought it down with the toe of one high-heeled shoe. Then with a whoop she was at the door. The door was flung open. There was a flutter of white and a flare of crimson, neither quite in the room nor precisely in the passage. The door was slammed, and the girl gone.

Mr. Teesdale was the first to rise. His face was very pale and agitated. He crossed the room and laid a hand upon the shoulder of Mr. Appleton, who was still pounding with all his heart at the old piano. Appleton stopped and revolved on the music-stool with a face of very comical ignorance and amazement. Mr. Teesdale went on to the door and turned the handle. It did not open. The key had been turned upon the outer side.

Chapter XIII
On the Verandah.

Night had fallen, and Mr. Teesdale had the homestead all to himself. Arabella and her mother had accompanied the ministers to evening worship in the township chapel. John William was busy with the milking. As for Missy, she had disappeared, as well she might, after her outrageous performance in the best parlour. And Mr. Teesdale was beginning to wonder whether they were ever to see her again; and if never, then what sort of report could he send his old friend now.

He did not know. Her last prank was also incomparably her worst, it had stunned poor David, and it left him unable to think coherently of Missy any longer. Yet her own father had warned him that Miriam was a very modern type of young woman; had hinted at the possibility of her startling simple folks. Then again, David, who took his newspaper very seriously indeed, had his own opinion of modern society in England and elsewhere. And if, as he believed. Missy was a specimen of that society, then it was not right to be hard upon the specimen. Had not he gathered long ago from the newspapers that the music-hall song and dance had found their way into smart London drawing-rooms. Now that he had heard that song, and seen that dance, were they much worse than he had been led to suppose ? If so, then society was even blacker than it was painted, that was all. The individual in any case was not to blame, but least of all in this case, where the individual had shown nothing but kindness to an uninteresting old man, quite aside and apart from her position in the old man's house as the child of his earliest friend.

And yet — and yet — he would do something to blot this last lurid scene out of his mind. There was nothing he would not do, if only he could do that. Yet this only showed him the narrowness of his own mind. That, after all, was half the trouble. Here at the antipodes, in an overlooked corner that had missed development with the colony, just as Mr. Teesdale himself had missed it: here all minds must be narrow. But theirs at the farm were perhaps narrower than most; otherwise they would never have been so shocked at Missy; at all events they would not have shown their feelings, as they evidently must have shown them, to have driven poor Missy off the premises, as they had apparently done.

Mr. Teesdale became greatly depressed as he made these reflections, and gradually got as much of the blame on to his own shoulders as one man could carry. It was very dark. He was sitting out on the verandah and smoking; but it was too dark to enjoy a pipe properly, even if David could have enjoyed anything just then. He was sitting in one of those wooden chairs in which he had so often sat of late while Missy read to him, and one hand rested mournfully upon the seat of the empty chair at his side. Not that he as yet really dreaded never seeing Missy again. He was keeping a look-out for her all the time. Sooner or later she was bound to come back.

She had come back already, but it was so dark that David never saw her until he was putting a light to his second pipe. Then the face of Missy, with her red hair tousled, came out of the night beyond the verandah with startling vividness, and it was the most defiant face that ever David Teesdale had beheld.

" Missy," cried he, " is that you ?"

He dropped the match and Missy's face was gone.

"Yes, it's me," said her voice, in such a tone as might have been expected from her face.

"Then come in, child, come in," said David joyfully, pushing back his chair as he rose. "I'm that glad you've come back, you can't think!"

"But I haven't come back — that's just it," answered the defiant voice out of the night.

" Then I'm going to fetch you back, Missy. I'm going "

"You stop in that verandah. If you come out I'll take to my heels and you'll never see me again — never! Now look here, Mr. Teesdale, haven't I sickened you this time?"

"Done what, Missy?" asked David, uneasily, from the verandah. He could see her outline now.

"Sickened you. I should have thought I'd sickened you just about enough this trip, if you'd asked me. I should have said I'd choked you off for good and all."

"You know you've done no such thing, Missy. What nonsense the child will talk! "

" What! I didn't sicken you this afternoon ?"

"No."

"Didn't disgust you, if you like that better?"

"No."

"Didn't make you perspire, the whole lot of you?"

"Of course you didn't, Missy. How you talk! You amused us a good deal, and you surprised us, too, a bit; but that was all."

" Oh ! So that was all, was it ? So I only surprised you a bit? I suppose you don't happen to know whether it was a big bit, eh ?"

But David now decided that the time was come for firmness.

" Listen to me, Missy ; I'm not going to have any more to say to you unless you come inside at once !"

"But what if I'm not never coming inside — never no more?"

There was that within the words which made David pause to consider. At length he said :

"Very well, then, come into the verandah and we'll have a sensible talk here, and I won't force you into the house; though where else you're to go I don't quite see. However, come here, and I won't insist on your coming a step further."

"Honour bright?"

"Of course."

"Hope to die?"

"I don't understand you. Missy; but I meant what I said."

"Then I'm coming. One moment, though! Is anybody about? Is Mrs. Teesdale in the house?"

" No, she's gone to chapel. So has Arabella, and John William's milking. They'll none of 'em be back just yet. Ah, that's better, my dear girl, that's better!"

Missy was back in her old wooden chair. Mr. Teesdale sat down again in its fellow and put his hand affectionately upon the girl's shoulder.

"So you mean to tell me your hairs didn't stand on end ! " said Missy, in a little whisper that was as unnecessary as it was fascinating just then.

"I haven't got much to boast of," answered the old man cheerily; " but what hair I have didn't do any such thing. Missy."

"Now just you think what you're saying," pursued the girl, with an air as of counsel cautioning a witness. " You tell me I neither sickened you, nor disgusted you, nor choked you off for good and all with that song and dance I gave you this afternoon. Your hairs didn't stand on end, and I didn't even make you perspire — so you say! But do you really mean me to believe you ?"

" Why, bless the child ! To be sure-to be sure!"

"Then, Mr. Teesdale, I must ask you whether you're in the habit of telling lies."

David opened his mouth to answer very promptly indeed, but kept it open without answering at all at the moment. He had remembered something that sent his left thumb and forefinger of their own accord into an empty waistcoat pocket. "No," said he presently with a sigh, "I'm not exactly in the habit of saying what isn't true."

"But you do it sometimes?"

" I have done it, God forgive me ! But who has not ? "

"Not me," cried Missy candidly. "There's not a bigger liar in this world than me! I'm going to tell you about that directly. I'm so glad you've told a lie or two yourself — it gives me such a leg-up — though I never should have thought it of you, Mr. Teesdale. I've told hundreds since I've known you. Have you told any since you've known me?"

The question was asked with all the inquisitive sympathy of one discovering a comrade in sin. " I mean not counting the ones you've just been telling me," added Missy when she got no answer, " about your not being shocked, and all the rest of it."

"That was no falsehood, Missy; that was the truth."

"All right, then, we'll pass that. Have you told any other lies since I've been here ?Just whisper, and I promise I won't let on. I do so want to know."

"But why, my dear — but why?"

"Because it'll be ever so much easier for me to make my confession when you've made yours."

" Your confession ! What can you have to confess, Missy?" The old man chuckled as he patted her hand.

" More than you're prepared for. But you must fire first. Have you or have you not told a wicked story since I've been staying here?"

Mr. Teesdale cleared his throat and sat upright in his chair.

"Missy," said he solemnly, "the only untruth I can remember telling in all my life, I have told since you have been with us; and I've told it over and over again. Heaven knows why I admit this much to you! I suppose there's something in you, my dear, that makes me say more than ever I mean to say. But Tm not going to say another word about this — that's flat."

" Good Lord ! " murmured Missy. " And you've told it over and over and over again ! Oh, do tell me," she whispered coaxingly ; " you might."

" My dear, I've told you too much already." And old Teesdale would have risen and paced the verandah, but a pair of strong arms restrained him. They were Missy's arms thrown round his neck, and the old man was content to sit still.

"Tell me one thing," she wheedled softly: "had it anything to do with me — that wicked story you've told so often ? "

Mr. Teesdale was silent.

"Then it had something to do with me. Let me think. Had it anything — to do with — your watch? . . . Then it had! And anything to do with that twenty pounds you sent me to the post office ? . . . Yes, it had! You pawned that watch to get me that money. You said you had left it mending. I've heard you say so a dozen times. So this is the lie you meant you'd told over and over again. And all for me! O Mr. Teesdale, I am so sorry — I am — so — sorry."

She had broken down and was sobbing bitterly on his shoulder. The old man stroked her head.

" You needn't take it so to heart, Missy dear. Nay, come! Shall I tell you why ? ecause it wasn't all for you. Missy. I hardly knew you then. Nay, honey, it was all for your dear father-no one else."

The effect of this distinction, made with a very touching sort of pride, was to withdraw Missy's arms very suddenly from the old man's neck, and to leave her sitting and trembling as far away from him as possible, though still in her chair. Her moment was come; but her nerve and her courage, her coolness and steadiness of purpose, where were they now?

She braced herself together with a powerful effort. Hours ago she had resolved, under influences that may be remembered, to undeceive the too trustful old man now at her side. To that resolve she still adhered; but as it had since become evident that nothing she could possibly do would lead him to suspect the truth, there was now no way for her but the hardest way of all — that of a full and clean confession. Her teeth were chattering when she began, but Mr. Teesdale understood her to say:

"Before you told your lie I had told you a dozen — I spoke hardly a word of truth all the way into Melbourne that day. But there was one great, big, tremendous lie at the bottom of all the rest. And can't you guess what that was ? You must guess — I can never tell you — I couldn't get it out."

Mr. Teesdale was very silent. "Yes, I think I can guess," he said at last, and sadly enough.

" Then what was it?" exclaimed Missy in an eager whisper. She was shivering with excitement.

"Well, my dear, I suppose it was to do with them friends you had to meet at the theatre. You might have trusted me a bit more, Missy! I shouldn't have thought so much of it, after all."

"Of what?"

"Why, of your going to the theatre alone. Wasn't that it. Missy?"

The girl moaned. " Oh, no — no ! It was something ever so much worse than that."

"Then you weren't stopping with friends at all. Was that it? Yes, you were staying all by yourself at one of the hotels."

" No — no — no. It was ever so much worse than that too. That was one of the lies I told you, but it was nothing like the one I mean."

"Missy " old David said gravely, "I don't want to know what you mean. I don't indeed! I'd far rather know nothing at all about it."

"But you must know!" cried Missy in desperation.

"Why must I?"

"Because this has gone on far too long. And I never meant it to go on at all. No, I give you my oath I only meant to have a lark in the beginning-to have a lark and be done with it! Anyhow I can't keep it up any longer; that's all about it, and — but surely you can guess now, Mr. Teesdale, can't you ? "

Again the old man was long in answering. "Yes," he exclaimed at length, and with such conviction in his voice that Missy grasped her chair-arms tight and sat holding her breath. "Yes, I do see now. You borrowed that money not because you really needed it, but because "

The girl's groans stopped him. "To think that you can't guess," she wailed, "though I've as good as told you in so many words!"

"No, I can't guess," answered David decisively. "What's more, I don't want to. So I give it up. Hush, Missy, not another word! I won't have it! I'll put my fingers in my ears if you will persist. I don't care whether it's true or whether it isn't, I'm not going to sit here and listen to you pitching into yourself when — when "

"When what?"

"Why, when I've grown that fond of you, my dear!"

"And are you fond of me?" said Missy, in a softened voice that quivered badly. She put her arms once more round the old man's neck, and let her tousled head rest again upon his, shoulder. "Are you really so fond of me as all that?"

" My dear, we all are. You know that as well as I do."

Missy made one important exception in her own mind, but not aloud. Kind, worn fingers were now busy with her hair, now patting her shoulder tenderly; and in all her poor life Missy had never known a father or a father's love. Even with the will she could not have spoken for some minutes. When she did speak next it was to echo the old man's last words; "Yes, I know that as well as you do. And I know how it hurts! But tell me, can you possibly be as fond of me after this afternoon ? "

"*I* can," said old Teesdale. "I can only speak for myself. Maybe I think more of you than anyone else does; I've seen more of you, and had more of your kindness. Nothing could make me forget that. Missy — how you've sat with me, and walked with me, and read to me, and taken notice of the old man, no matter who else was by or who wasn't. No, I could never forget all that, my dear; nothing that you could do could make me forget one half of that!"

" And nothing that I have done ?" "Still less anything that you have done." "But if you found out that I'd been deceiving you all along, and obtained every mortal thing on false pretences, and taken the filthiest advantage of your kindness — surely that would wipe out any little good turns which anybody would have done you ? Of course it would! "

" It might. But anybody wouldn't have done 'em — anybody wouldn't," the old man said, leaving a kiss upon the hair between his fingers. "At all events. Missy, there's one thing that nothing could blot out; for whatever you did, you'd still be your dear father's daughter!"

Very slowly and deliberately, Missy unwound her arms and lifted her head, and got out of the chair, and stood to her full height in the dark verandah.

"That's just it," she said calmly, distinctly. "That's just what I was coming to."

But Mr. Teesdale had also risen, and he was not listening to Missy. For footsteps were drawing near through the grass — footsteps and the rustle of stiff Sunday gowns, and the creaking of comfortless Sunday boots — and a harsh voice was crying more harshly than was even its wont:

" Is that you, David ? And is that Miriam beside you ? And how dare she come back and show her face, I wonder? Ay, that's what I want to know!"

David ran to meet and expostulate with his harder half. It was seldom that he even tried to quell that outspoken tongue; but now he both tried and succeeded, though Missy in the verandah could not hear by how much artifice or in what words. In another minute, however, Mr. Teesdale was again at her side, while his wife and daughter went past them and into the house without further parley.

These few words were then exchanged in the verandah :

"Missy, she didn't mean it. You'll hear no more about it — not a word from anybody."

"I deserve to, nevertheless."

"So you'll come in, won't you, and have your supper like a dear good girl ? "

"Ah, yes, I'll come in now."

" I was so afraid — Mrs. T. is that hasty and plain-spoken — that what she said might make you say you'd never come into our house any more."

"Not it," said Missy with a laugh. "That's the sort of thing to have the very opposite effect upon you. Come on in!"

Chapter XIV
A Bolt from the Blue.

Mr. Teesdale sat at his end of the old green tablecloth, reading a singularly unseasonable communication from that middle-man who bought the milk but was never in a position to pay for it. The time was half-past eleven in the forenoon of Boxing Day, and the daily delivery of letters had just taken place. It was naturally a little later than usual, but Mr. Teesdale wished with all his heart that there had been no delivery at all. At length he raised a tired face from his bad news, and let his eyes rest for the comfort of his spirit upon the red head and fringe of his solitary companion in the parlour. Missy was seated on the sofa, and all of her but the top of her head and the bottom of her dress, with a finger or two of each hand, was hidden behind the Argus newspaper. Missy always liked to see the Argus as soon as it came, though by that time it was never less than a day old, because Mr. Teesdale had it from a friend when the friend was done with it. This morning, as usual, he had handed it to the girl before opening his letters. He now sat staring absently at the girl's hair, and was therefore somewhat slow to notice that the narrow strip of forehead under the fringe was gone so white that it was difficult to tell where paper ended and forehead began. No sooner had David seen this, however, than he saw also the paper jumping up and down in the girl's grasp; whereupon the unpleasant letter in his own hands went straightway out of his head.

"Missy," he cried, "what's the matter, my dear? What have you seen?"

Missy dashed down the paper and was on her feet in an instant. There was extraordinary spirit in the action, and her eyes were very bright.

"What have I seen?" she repeated, in a tone that suppressed excitement rather than concern. "Nothing; that is, nothing that could interest any of you; only something about a friend of mine."

Yet she bounced out of the room without another word, and forthwith went in search of Arabella.

She found her in the dairy, which was half under the ground, and wholly out of the way.

"Arabella," she cried wildly, "put down that bowl and shake hands. We're safe!"

Now Arabella was not a person of quick perceptions. She was imaginative, she was inquisitive, she had a romantic side which had very nearly been the ruin of her at the responsible age of thirty-two. Like the parent whom she so strongly resembled in her undiscerning nature and easygoing temperament, she was sufficiently credulous, weak, and unwise in her generation. On the other hand, she was by no means without her father's merits. She had the same talent for affection, the same positive genius for uncommon gratitude. She could never make light of a good turn, not even in her own mind; nor out of her own mouth could she make too much of one. In the family circle she had been very silent and subdued during these last days, but to Missy in private she had opened a contrite and a very grateful heart more times than the other had liked to listen. Vague doubts and suspicions of Missy she had entertained in the beginning; she might have them still; nay, they might well be stronger than ever, after yesterday.

But one thing was now certain concerning these shy misgivings; they might rise to the mind, but they would never again pass the lips. No matter what Missy did or said, henceforth, Arabella would shield her with all the ingenuity at her command: which was not a little: only it was sometimes hindered by a certain slowness to perceive which frequently accompanies a constitutional readiness to imagine. So when Missy wanted her to shake hands because they were safe, Arabella looked perfectly blank.

"How are we safe?" she asked. "What are we safe from ? "

"Why, from your friend."

" My friend ? Ah ! " She understood now.

"Yes, he won't trouble us much more," pursued Missy, sidling rhythmically from one foot to the other, while her eyes lit up the dairy. "O 'Bella, 'Bella, if you knew how I feel "

"Stop a moment," said Arabella, white as the milk that she had spilled in her agitation; "is he — is he — dead?"

"Dead? I wish he was. No, no; he's only in prison."

"In prison?"

"Yes; run in the day before Christmas Eve — the day after I swep' him out o' this — no, the very day itself. See where you'd ha' been! 'Bella, 'Bella, let's drink his health in a pint of cream! It seems too good to be true."

But Arabella was grasping with both hands the shelf which supported the bowls of milk for creaming, and her face was drawn and wretched.

"Don't, Missy!" she exclaimed with tears in her voice. "You wouldn't if you knew how sorry I am. What is he in prison for ? What has he been doing ? "

"Writing a cheque he had no business to write and getting the money. That's what it was this time. But it isn't the first time; no, don't you believe it."

" I am so sorry," repeated Arabella, covering her eyes.

"But why? What for?"

"For him. I —I thought I loved him."

"You thought you loved him," Missy repeated buoyantly. She was all buoyancy now. "Yes, many a girl has thought that before you, my dear. And them that thought it too long, they didn't come to think they hated him. Not they! They jolly soon knew!"

The other's wet eyes were wide open.

"How is this, Missy? You seem to know all about him. You never told me that before."

"No, I didn't. What was the use when I'd got rid of him — for the time being, anyway? I was very much afraid he'd turn up again, and I was keeping what I knew until he did. I thought it'd be time enough to tell you then; but I'll tell you now if you like. It makes no difference one way or the other, now that our friend's in quod. Very well then, as soon as ever I heard his voice that dark night I knew that I'd heard it before. Never mind where — maybe in England, maybe on the ship, maybe after I landed in Melbourne. You mustn't want to know too much. It's good enough, isn't it, that I knew what sort he was, and that when I'd known him before he was sailing under another name altogether? Yes, I thought that'd knock you! You knew Stan-borough, I knew Mowbray, and the police, they've run in a man of the name of Paolo Verini, alias Thomas Stanborough, alias Paul Mowbray. 'A handsome man of foreign appearance,' the Argus says. You may look for yourself. But if that isn't good enough for you I don't know what is."

"It might be someone else for all that," murmured Arabella, shuddering at the thought of the man in prison. "Have you any other reason for making so certain that it is the same?"

"I have. I wouldn't tell you before, but now what does it matter? I've expected him turning up every hour since that night. He swore that he would; and he would have, you may depend, if he hadn't got run in."

Arabella was silent; she felt that also. She had never been able to understand how a man of so firm a purpose as her lover should have made so facile a capitulation to a mere girl like Missy.

Presently she asked a question:

" Did he recognise you Missy ? "

"No," replied Missy, after a little hesitation. "No, he did not," she repeated more firmly. "And look you here, 'Bella, take my advice and never give him another thought. He was a bad egg, that's what he was; you may thank your stars that he is where he is, as I thank mine."

"I can't help being sorry," sighed Arabella, wiping her eyes with her apron; " but that doesn't make me less thankful to you. Missy. You've saved me, body and soul. I was under a spell, but you broke it. I don't understand it. I can't feel it now. But God knows how I felt it then, and what would have got me but for you! So I can never be thankful enough to you, Missy, and I shall never, never be able to tell you how thankful I am."

"Then never try," said Missy lightly; "only think kindly of me when you find it a hard job. That's all you've got to try to do."

And with a light-hearted laugh and a kiss from the fingers Missy was out of the dairy and above ground in the brilliant noonday sun.

There was no one about in the yard. Missy was glad of that, because there was no living soul whom she desired to see or to speak to for hours to come. The naked sword hanging over her head had suddenly been lifted down, snapped, and thrown away; she must be alone to appreciate that. Nevertheless this should be her last day at the farm ; and again, she must be alone to make the most of the last day. Alone to consider all things, especially the life lying ahead; alone to drink for the last time of the sweet sensations of this peaceful spot, and so deeply, that the taste should be with her till her dying day. Then she would depart in peace; and lastly, she must be alone to invent the why and wherefore of this departure.

So she opened the gate leading out of the yard, and going down through the gum-trees into that shallow gully, she mounted the other side, and stopped to stand in triumph under the very tree from behind which Stanborough, or Verini, had sprung and caught her in his arms. She pictured him in his cell at that moment, with only one small iron-barred square of that blue sky which was all for her; and she drew into her throat and nostrils a long draught of eucalyptus perfume. This was one of the sensations which she desired always to remember. At length, still sniffing and glancing ever at the deep blue sky above the tree-tops, yet with both eyes and ears attentive to her friends the parrots, she turned sharp to the left, crossed the road below the Cultivation, and struck into the thick of the timber on the further side.

She had shut out of her light mind every thought of penitence and remorse. There was no further occasion for her to take a serious view of the situation. The very air seemed charged with a new and most delicious sense of freedom ; enough, for the present, to revel in this, without thinking of anything at all. Another comparatively new sense, that of her own iniquity, was a dead nerve for the time being. Missy was too thankful for what she had escaped to consider what she deserved; indeed, she had considered this sufficiently. On the other hand, she was enjoying a natural reaction in the most natural manner imaginable. All by herself, among the gum-trees, she burst into song, or rather the snatch of one. And on the whole one would call it unconscious song, for the snatch ran —

> "You should 'a' seen 'im jump!
> I didn't give a dump!
> For I yells to 'is pals
> 'Now look at him, gals —
> 'Any 'e 'as the '"

Here it broke off. Missy halted too.

"Morning, John William," said she.

He was standing in front of her, with his gun under his arm and a dead hare in the other hand. He returned her salute gravely. Then —

" You seem very happy," he said, with a spice of bitterness.

"Oh, I haven't got it," laughed Missy, "have you?"

"Got what?"

"The 'ump."

He shook his head and grinned; as he looked at her the grin broadened.

"So I didn't shock your head off, either!" exclaimed Missy.

" Not likely. I thought it was splendid myself."

"Then why did you look so glum just now?"

"Missy, I didn't "

" You did! I thought you'd caught the 'ump from 'Arry. I believe you have. You're looking as glum as ever again ! "

It was true. But he said:

"Missy, I don't feel a bit glum."

"No?"

She was examining him coolly, critically, and he knew it.

"Not a bit!" he reiterated, hacking out a tuft of grass with his right heel. Then his miserable eyes rose fiercely upon the girl. She had been waiting for this look, however.

"You are making a great mistake," she said, "if you are imagining yourself the least little atom in love with mey

For the instant her outspokenness enraged him ; then it made him meek.

" I am imagining no such thing, Missy; I know it. But I also know that it is a mistake — when you are so far above me."

" There you go ! That is your mistake. It's the other way about — it's you that's so far above me. John William, if you only knew what a bad lot I am

"I don't care what you are."

"You don't know what I am. That's just it! I'm not what you think I am, I'm not what I make myself out to be ; I'm not — I'm not!"

She was speaking passionately, being, in fact, once more on the verge of a full confession. All in a moment the impulse had come over her, and nothing could have stopped her but the thing that did. John William was not listening to a word she said; he was only gazing in her eyes.

" I don't care what you are. Missy; I shouldn't care if you were as black as sin ! No, I should like it, for the blacker you were, the nearer I should be to you-the more chance I should have. If you were bad-which is all nonsense — you would still be too good for me ; but I should love you. Missy, whether or no. I shall love you all my days!"

He looked at her once with ravening eyes, and then spun round upon his heel. She called him back in a broken voice to tell him everything; but he shook his head without looking round, and the tree-trunks closed behind him like a door. Then Missy drew a very long breath, wiped her eyes, and sat down to think.

Her conscience was wide awake now. For an hour she let it tear and rend her. By the end of the second hour she had hardened her heart once more.

"I'm not meant to confess, that's evident," she exclaimed aloud. " I was a little fool ever to think of it."

A little fool, at that rate, she continued to be; inasmuch as for yet another hour she permitted her mind to dwell upon her attempted confessions, to old Teesdale yesterday, to John William to-day. It hurt her to think of the kindness and credulity of those two. It hurt her so much that she wept bitterly, only thinking of old David and John William his son. Yet she was thankful they had not listened, she was thankful they did not know, she was doubly thankful that she was to go away of her own accord, and without being found out after all. If she could ever make the slightest atonement! But that was for future thought.

The afternoon was well advanced when Missy once more crossed the road below the Culti-vation. She was now in a perfectly philosophic frame of mind. Also she had slightly altered her plans. She would not invent an excuse for her departure; she would go without saying a word to any of them; she would run away in the night. And she would leave all her things behind her. The present value of them would not go far towards redeeming Mr. Teesdale's watch; still they must be worth something.

This she was thinking as she came to the end of the gum-trees, and opened the gate which was grown familiar to her hand and eye. Then suddenly she reflected that dinner must long be over, that she would barely be in time for tea. And the goodness of Mrs. Teesdale's tea was the next thought that filled her mind: she had the smell in her nostrils, she could almost feel the hot fluid coursing over her parched palate as she rounded the hen-yard and caught sight of the verandah. Thereat she came to a sudden standstill, and yet another new set of thoughts. The verandah was half hidden by a two-horse buggy drawn up in front of it.

"More visitors!" said Missy. "Well, I won't shock this lot. I wonder who they are? They must be swells!"

In fact, a man in livery held the reins, the afternoon sun made fireworks with the burnished harness, and the buggy was a .very good one indeed.

Missy kept her eyes upon it as she approached the house. She never saw the faces that appeared for an instant at the parlour window and then disappeared. Her foot was lifted, to be set down in the verandah, when the door was flung open, and Mrs. Teesdale marched forth.

"Stand back!" she screamed. "Not another step! You would dare to set foot inside my doors again!"

Missy fell back in wonderment. As she did so a dainty-looking young lady appeared in the doorway behind Mrs. Teesdale, and screwed up her fair face at the glare of the afternoon sun. And Missy left off wondering, for in an instant she knew who that dainty-looking young lady must be.

Chapter XV
A Day of Reckoning.

Missy retreated a step from the verandah, stood still, and gasped. Then she pressed both hands to her left side. She was as one walking on the down line in order to avoid the up train, only to be cut to pieces by the down express, whose very existence she had forgotten.

Her eyes fastened themselves upon one object. Presently she found that it was Mrs. Teesdale's pebble brooch. Her ears rang with a harsh, shrill voice; it took her mind some moments to capture the words and grasp their meaning.

"You wicked, wicked, ungrateful woman! To dare to come here and pass yourself off as Miriam Oliver, and live with us all these weeks-you lying hussy! If you have anything to say for yourself be sharp and say it, then out you pack!"

The convicted girl now beheld the verandah swimming with people. As her sight cleared, however, she could only count four, including Mrs. Teesdale. There was the veritable Miss Oliver, but Missy took no note of her just then. There was Arabella, white and weeping; and there was Mr. Teesdale, looking years older since the morning, with the saddest expression Missy had ever seen upon human countenance. He was gazing, not at her, but down upon the ground at her feet. John William was not there at all. Missy looked about for him very wistfully, but in vain; and her glance ended, where it had begun, upon the furious face of Mrs. Teesdale. Furious as it was, the wretched girl found it much the easiest face to meet with a firm lip and a brazen front.

" Do you know that you could be sent to prison ?" Mrs. Teesdale proceeded, still at a scream. "Ay, and I'll see that you are sent, and all!"

" Nay, come! " muttered Mr. Teesdale, shaking his head at the grass, but without looking at anybody.

Then suddenly he lifted his eyes, stepped down from the verandah, and went up to Missy.

" Missy," said he, in a low, hoarse voice, " Missy, I'll take your word as soon as the word of a person I've never set eyes on before. Is this true, or is it not ? Are you, or are you not, Miriam Oliver, the daughter of my old friend?"

" It is true," said Missy. " I'm no more Miriam Oliver than you are."

Neither question nor answer had reached the ears of those in the verandah. But they saw David turn towards them with his head hanging lower than before, and he tottered as he rejoined them. Miss Oliver, however, may have guessed what had passed, for she smiled a supercilious smile which no one happened to observe. This young lady was a contrast to her impersonator in every imaginable way. She was not nearly so tall, and she had exceedingly 'fair hair. Her nose was tip-tilted to begin with, but she seemed to have a habit of turning it up even beyond the design of nature. This was perhaps justified on the present occasion. She was very fashionably dressed in a costume of extremely light gray; and in the dilapidated framework of the old verandah she was by far the most incongruous figure upon- the scene.

" Has she anything to say for herself ? " Mrs. Teesdale demanded of her husband. He shook his head despondently.

And then, at last, Missy opened her mouth.

"I have only this to say for myself. It isn't much, but Mr. Teesdale will tell you that it's the truth. It's only that I did do my level best to make a clean breast to him last night."

" She did!" exclaimed the old man, after a moment's rapid consideration. " Now I see what she meant. To think that I never saw then !"

" You were very dense," said Missy; " but not worse than John William. I did my best to tell you last night, and I did my best to tell him only this morning, but neither of you would understand."

As she spoke to the old man her voice was strangely gentle, and a smile was hovering about the corners of her mouth when she ceased. Moreover, her words had brought out a faint ray of light upon Mr. Teesdale's dejected mien.

" It's a fact!" he cried, turning to the others. " She did her best to confess last night. She did confess. I remember all about it now. It was a full confession, if only I'd put two and two together. But — well, I never could have believed it of her. That was it!"

He finished on a sufficiently reproachful note.

Nevertheless, Mrs. Teesdale turned upon him as fiercely as though he had spoken from a brief in Missy's defence.

"What if she had confessed? I'm ashamed of you, David, going on as though that could ha' made any difference! She'd still have deceived us and lied to us all these weeks. Black is black and this — this woman —is that black that God Himself couldn't whiten her! "

And Mrs. Teesdale shook her fist at the guilty girl.

" We have none of us a right to say that," murmured David.

" But I do say it, and I mean it, too. I say that she'd still have stolen Miriam's letter of introduction, and come here deliberately and passed herself off as Miriam, and slept under our roof, and eaten-our bread, under false pretences — false pretences as shall put her in prison if I have anything to do with it! No confession could have undone all that; and no confession shall keep her out of prison neither, not if I know it!"

Some of them were expecting Missy to take to her heels any moment; but she never showed the least sign of doing so.

" No, nothing can undo it," she said herself. "I've known that for some time, and I shan't be sorry to pay the cost."

Then the real Miss Oliver put in her word. It was winged with a sneer.

" It was hardly a compliment," she said, " to take her for me! You might ask her, by the way, when and where she stole my letters. I lost several." She could not permit herself to address the culprit direct.

"I'll tell you that," said Missy, "and everything else too, if you like to listen."

" Do, Missy!" cried Arabella, speaking also for the first time. "And then I'll tell them something."

"Be sharp, then," said Mrs. Teesdale. "We're not going to stand here much longer listening to the likes of you. If you've got much to say, you'd better keep it for the magistrate!"

Missy shook her head at Arabella, stared briefly but boldly at Mrs. Teesdale, and then addressed herself to the fair girl in gray, who raised her eyebrows at the liberty.

" You remember the morning after you landed in the Parramatta It was a very hot day, about a couple of months ago, but in the forenoon you went for a walk with a lady friend. And you took the Fitzroy Gardens on your way.'

Miss Oliver nodded, without thinking whom she was nodding to. This was because she had become very much interested all in a moment; the next, she regretted that nod, and set herself to listen with a fixed expression of disgust.

"You walked through the Fitzroy Gardens, you stopped to look at all the statues, and then you sat down on a seat. I saw you, because I was sitting on the next seat. You sat on that seat, and you took out some letters and read bits of them to your friend. I could hear your voices, but I couldn't hear what you were saying, and I didn't want to, either. I had my own things to think about, and they weren't very nice thinking, I can tell you! That hot morning, I remember, I was just wishing and praying to get out of Melbourne for good and all. And when I passed your seat after you'd left it, there were your letters lying under it on the gravel. I picked them up, and I looked up and down for you and your friend. You were out of sight, but I made for the entrance and waited for you there. Yes, I did — you may sneer as much as you like!

But you never came, and when I went back to my lodgings I took your letters with me."

Still the young lady sneered without speaking, and Missy hardened her heart.

" I read them every one," she said defiantly. " I had nothing to do with myself during the day, and very good reading they were ! And in the afternoon, just for the lark of it, I took your letter of introduction, which was among the rest, and then I took the 'bus and came out here."

She turned now to David, and continued in that softer voice which she could not help when speaking to him.

" It was only for the fun of it! I had no idea of ever coming out again. But you made so much of me; you were all so kind — and the place — it was heaven to a girl like me!"

Here she surprised them all, but one, by breaking down. Mr. Teesdale was not astonished. When she recovered her self-control it was to him she turned her swimming eyes; it was the look in his that enabled her to go on.

" If you knew what my life was! " she wailed ; " if you knew how I hated it! If you knew how I longed to come out into the country, when I saw what the country was like! I had never seen your Australian country before. It was all new to me. I had only been a year out from home, but at home I lived all my life in London. My God, what a life! But I never meant to come back to you — I said I wouldn't — and then I said you must take the consequences if I did. Even when I said good-bye to you, Mr. Teesdale, I never really thought of coming back; so you see I repaid your kindness not only by lies, but by robbing you "

She pulled herself up. David had glanced uneasily towards his wife. The girl understood.

"By robbing you of your peace of mind, for I said that I would come back, never meaning to at all. And now do you know why I was in such a hurry to get to the theatre ? Yes, it was because I had an engagement there. All the rest was lies. And I never should have come out to you again, only at last I saw in the Argus that she — that Miss Oliver — had gone to Sydney. Don't you remember how you'd seen it too ? ell, then I felt safe. I was only a ballet-girl, I'd done better once, for at home I'd had a try in the halls. So I chucked it up and came out to you. I thought I should see in the Argus when Miss Oliver came back from Sydney, but somehow I've missed it. And now "

She flung wide her arms, and raised her eyes, and looked from the sky overhead to the river-timber away down to the right, and from the river-timber to David Teesdale.

"And now you may put me in prison as fast as you like. I've been here two months. They're well worth twelve of hard labour, these last two months on this farm!"

She had finished.

Mrs. Teesdale turned to her husband. "The brazen slut!" she cried. " Not a word of penitence ! She doesn't care — not she ! To prison she shall go, and we'll see whether that makes her care."

But David shook his head. "No, no, my dear! I will not have her sent to prison. What good could it do us or her ? Rather let her go away quietly, and may the Almighty forgive her — and — and make her "

He looked down, and there was Missy on her knees to him. " Can you forgive me ? " she cried passionately. "Say that you forgive me, and then send me to prison or any place you like. Only say that you forgive me if you can."

"I can," said the old man softly, "and I do. But I am not the One. You shall not go to prison, but you must go away from us, and may God have mercy on you and help you to lead a better life hereafter. You — you have been very kind to me in little ways. Missy, and I shall try to think kindly of you too."

He spoke with great emotion, and as he did so his trembling hand rested ever so lightly upon the red head from which the hat was tilted back. And the girl seized that kind, caressing hand, and raised it to her lips, but let it drop without allowing them to touch it. Then she rose and retreated under their eyes. And all the good women had been awed to silence by this leave-taking; but one of them recovered herself in time to put a shot into the retiring enemy.

"Mr. Teesdale is a deal too lenient," cried the farmer's wife. "He's been like that all his life! If I'd had my way, to prison you should have gone — to prison you should have gone, you shameless bad woman, you ! "

Old David heard it without a word. He was seeing the last of Missy as she descended the paddock by the path that led down to the slip-rails; the very last that he saw of her was the sunlight upon her hair and hat.

Arabella had darted into the house, and she now came out with a small bundle of things in her arms. With these she followed Missy, coming up with her at the slip-rails, against which she was leaning with her face buried in her hands.

Now this was the spot where Arabella had first met the man from whom this abandoned girl had rescued her, body and soul. She had desired to tell them all that story, to show them the good in Missy, and so make them less hard upon her. The person who had prevented her, by forbidding look and vigorous gesture, was Missy herself. . . .

It was half an hour later when Arabella returned to the house. This was what she was in time to see and hear.

The real Miss Oliver was sitting in the buggy beside the man in livery, replying, with chilly smiles and decided shakes of her fair head, to the joint remonstrances, exhortations, and persuasions of Mr. and Mrs. Teesdale, who were standing together on the near side of the buggy.

"But I've just made the tea this minute," Arabella heard her mother complain. " Surely you'll stop and have your tea with us after coming all this way?"

"Thank you so much; it is very kind of you; but I promised to be back at the picnic in time for tea, and it is some miles away."

"But Mrs. Teesdale takes a special pride in her tea," said David, "and she has made it, so that we shouldn't keep you waiting at all."

" So kind of you; but I'm afraid I have stayed too long already. I was just waiting to say goodbye to Mrs. Teesdale. Good-bye again "

"Come, Miriam," said Mrs. T., a little testily, "or we shall be offended ! "

" I should be very sorry to offend you, I am sure, but really my friends lent me their buggy on the express condition "

From her manner Mr. Teesdale saw that further pressing would be useless.

"We will let you go now," said he, "if you will come back and stay with us as long as you can."

"For a month at least," added Mrs. T.

Miss Oliver looked askance.

"We are such very old friends of your parents," pleaded David.

"We would like to be your parents as long as you remain in Australia," Mrs. Teesdale went so far as to say. And already her tone was genuinely kind and motherly, as it had never become towards poor Missy in all the past two months.

Miss Oliver raised her eyebrows; luckily they were so light that the grimace was less noticeable than it otherwise might have been.

" Suppose we write about it . " said she at length. "Yes, that would be the best. I have several engagements, and I am only staying out a few weeks longer. But I will certainly come out and see you again if I can."

" And stay with us ? " said Mrs. T.

"And stay a night with you — if I can."

"By this time," exclaimed David, "we might have had our tea and been done with it. Won't you think better of it and jump down now. Come, for your parents' sakes — I wish you would."

" So do I, dear knows!" said Mrs. Teesdale wistfully.

But Miss Oliver, this time without speaking, shook her head more decidedly than ever; gave the old people a bow apiece worthy of Hyde Park; and drove off without troubling to notice the daughter of the house, who, however, was not thinking of her at all, but of Missy.

Chapter XVI
A Man's Resolve.

How to tell John William when he came home, that was the prime difficulty in the mind of Arabella. Tell him she must, as soon as ever he got in. She felt it of importance that he should hear the news first from herself, and not, for example, from their mother. But it was going to be a very disagreeable duty ; more so, indeed, than she ever could have dreamt, until Missy herself warned her, almost with her last words, at the slip-rails. Missy had opened her eyes for her during those few final minutes. Till then she had suspected nothing between her brother and the girl. And now the case seemed so clear and so inevitable that her chief cause for wonderment lay in her own previous want of perception. It made her very nervous, however, with the news still to break to John William. She wished that he would make haste home. He had ridden off early in the afternoon to look up another young farmer several miles distant; not that he wanted to see anyone at all, but because he was ill at ease and anxious to be out of Missy's way, as Arabella now made sure. But poor Missy ! And poor John William ! Would they ever see each other again ? She hoped not. Her heart grieved for them both, but she hoped not. No woman, being also a sister of the man concerned, could know about another woman what Arabella now knew against Missy, and hope otherwise. And the state of her own feelings in the matter was her uppermost trouble, when at last John William trotted his mare into the yard, and Arabella followed him into the stable.

Then and there she hurriedly told all. Her great dread was that their mother might appear on the scene and tell it in her way. But the attitude of the man greatly astonished Arabella. He took the news so coolly — but that was not it. He seemed not at all agitated to hear what Missy was, and who she was not, but very much so on learning how summarily she had been sent about her business. He said very little even then, but Arabella knew that he was trembling all over as he unsaddled the mare.

"My heart bled for the poor thing," she added, speaking the simple truth. "It would have bled even if she hadn't done more for me than ever I can tell anybody. I was thankful I went after her, and saw the last of her at the rails "

" Which way did she go ? "

" To the township to begin with; but she gave me "

"Which way did she mean to go — straight back to Melbourne ? "

"She didn't say. I was going on to tell you that at the slip-rails she gave me some messages for you, John William."

"We will have them afterwards. Let us go in to supper now."

" Very well — but stay! Are you prepared for mother? She is dreadful about it; she makes it even worse than it is."

"I am prepared for anything. I shall not open my mouth."

Nor did he; but the provocation was severe. Mrs. Teesdale was glad of an opportunity of rehearsing the whole story from beginning to end. This enabled her to decide what epithets were too weak for the occasion, and what names were as nearly bad enough for Missy as any that a respectable woman could lay her tongue to; also, by what she now said, this excellent woman strengthened her own rather recent convictions that she had "suspected something of the kind" about Missy from the very first. Certainly she had felt a strong antipathetic instinct from the very first. Quite as certainly she had now just cause for righteous rage and desires the most vindictive. Yet there was not one of those three, her nearest, who did not feel a fresh spasm of pain at each violent word, because every one of them, save the wife and mother, had some secret cause to think softly of the godless girl who was gone, and to look back upon her more in pity than in blame.

For sadness, Mr. Teesdale was the saddest of them all. He crept to his bed a shaken old man, and had to listen to his wife until he thought she must break his heart. Meantime Arabella and

John William foregathered in the latter's room, and talked in whispers in order not to wake two old people who had neither of them closed an eye.

"About those messages," said John William. " What were they ? "

He was sitting on the edge of his bed, and he pared a cake of tobacco as he spoke. His wideawake lay on the quilt beside him, and he had not taken off his boots. Arabella stood uneasily.

"Poor girl! she spoke about you a good deal just at the last"

Arabella hesitated.

" I want to know what she said," observed John William dryly.

"Well, first she was sorry you weren't there."

"If I had been she never should have gone like that!"

"What, not when everything had come out "

"No, not at all; she shouldn't have been kicked out, anyway. I'd have given her time and then driven her back to Melbourne, with all her things. What right have we with them, I should like to know ? "

"She wanted us to keep them, she "

" Wanted us! I'd have let her want, if I'd been here. However, go on. She was sorry I wasn't there, was she?"

"Well, at first she said so, but in a little while she told me that she was glad. And after that she said I didn't know how glad she was for you never to set eyes on her again!"

"Never's a long time," muttered John William.

"Did she explain herself?" he added, as loud as they ventured to speak.

" Y —yes." Arabella was hesitating.

"Then out with it!"

"She told me-it can't be true, but yet she did tell me-that you-fancied yourself in love with her, John William!"

"It isn't true."

"Thank God for that!"

"Stop a moment. Not so fast, my girl! It isn't true-because there's no fancy at all about it, d'ye see?"

Arabella saw. It was written and painted all over his lined yet glowing face ; but where there could be least mistake about it was in his eyes. They were ablaze with love — with love for a woman who had neither name, honour, nor common purity. He could not know this. But Arabella knew all, and it was her business — nay, her solemn undertaking — to repeat all that she knew to John William.

"I was told," she faltered, "what to say to you if you said that."

"Who told you?"

"She did —Missy."

"Then say it right out."

But that was difficult between brother and sister. At first he refused to understand, and then he refused to believe.

"It's a lie!" he cried hoarsely. "I don't believe a word of it!"

" And do you suppose I would make it up ? Upon my sacred honour, John William, it is only what she told me with her own "

" I know that; it's her lie — I never meant it was yours. No, no, it's Missy's lie to choke me off. But it shan't! No, by Heaven, and it shouldn't if it were the living truth ! "

There was no more to be said. The man knew that, and he relit the pipe, which he had scarcely tasted, without looking at the sister whom he had silenced. Presently he said in a perfectly passionless voice, coming back from the unspeakable to a point which it was possible to discuss:

"About those things of hers — all her clothes. Did you say that she wanted us to keep them ? And if so, why?"

"Because," said Arabella with some reluctance, "they were bought with money which — as she said herself — she had obtained from father on false pretences."

It may have been because he was now quite calm outwardly, but at this the man winced more visibly than at what had come out before.

" From father," he repeated at length; " he couldn't let her have much, anyway!"

"He let her have twenty pounds."

"Never; the bank wouldn't let him have it."

"The bank didn't; he got it on his watch."

"On the watch that's — mending?"

The truth flashed across him before the words were out. Arabella nodded her head, and her brother bowed his in trouble.

"Yes, that's bad," said he, as though nothing else had been. "There's no denying it, that is bad." It was a thing he could realise; that was why he took it thus disproportionately to heart.

" Surely it is all bad together!" said Arabella.

John William spent some minutes in a study of the bare boards by his bedside.

"Where do you think she went to?" he said at last, looking up.

"I have no idea."

"Have you told me all that she said? She didn't — she didn't send any other messages?" It was wistfully asked.

" No, none; but she did tell me how she hopes and prays that you will never give her another thought. She declares she has never given a single thought to you. It is true, too, I am sure."

"We shall see-we shall see. So you have no idea where she went ? She gave you no hint of any sort or kind ? "None whatever."

"She has gone back to Melbourne, think you?" "I don't know where else she could go to." "No more do I," said John William, rising from the bed at last. He opened the window softly and looked out into the night. "No more do I see where else she could go to," he whispered over again. Then he turned round to Arabella. She was watching him closely. Neither of them spoke. But John William picked his wideawake from off the bed and jammed it over his brows. Then he took a pair of spurs from the drawers-head and dropped them into his coat pocket. Then he faced Arabella afresh.

"Do you know what I am going to do?" "I can guess. You are going to ride into Melbourne and look for Missy."

"I am — and now, at once. I'm going out by that window. Don't shut it, because I shall be back before milking, and shall come in the same way I get out."

" But you'll never see her, John William; you'll never see her," said Arabella in misery. "It'll be like hunting for a needle in a haystack!"

"You may always find the needle — there is always a chance. For me, if half of what she told you has a word of truth in it I shall have a better chance by night than by day. It can't be much after eleven now, and I guess I shall do it to-night in half an hour."

"But if you don't see her?"

"Then I shall have another try to-morrow night — and another the next — and another the night after that. There are plenty of horses in the paddock; there are some that haven't been ridden this long time, and some that nobody can ride but me. The mare will have to sweat for it to-night, but not after to-night. Only look here. I shall be found out sooner or later, then there will be a row, and you know who'll make it. You'll let it be later, won't you, 'Bella, so far as you're concerned?"

" You must know that I will!"

"Then bless you, my dear, and good night."

They had seldom kissed since they were little children. They were both of them over thirty now, in respect of mere years. But with his beard tickling the woman's cheek, the man whispered, "You said that she had done something for you, too, you know ! "

And the woman answered, "Something more than I can ever tell any of you. You little know what I might have come to, but for Missy. Yet what are you to do with her, poor Jack, if you do find her?"

And the man said, "Make her good again, so help me God!"

Chapter XVII
The Two Miriams.

A Sunday morning early in the following February ; in fact, the first Sunday of the month.

It was, perhaps, the freshest and coolest morning of any kind that the hot young year had as yet brought forth. Nevertheless, neither Mr. nor Mrs. Teesdale had gone to chapel, as was their wont. For this Sabbath day was also one requiring a red letter in the calendar of the Teesdales, insomuch as it was the solitary entire day which a greatly honoured visitor over the week-end had consented, after much ill-bred importuning, to give to her father's old friends at the farm.

The visitor was gone to chapel with Arabella. But the farmer and his wife had stayed at home, the one to shoot a hare, and the other to cook it for the very special Sunday dinner which the occasion demanded.

Naturally David's part was soon performed, because the old man was so good a shot still, and there were plenty of hares about the place. It was less natural in one of his serene disposition to light a pipe afterwards and sit down in the verandah expressly and deliberately to think of things which could only trouble him. This, however, was what he proceeded to do. And the things troubled him more and more the longer he allowed his mind to dwell upon them.

One thing was the whole miserable episode of Missy, of whom the old man could not possibly help thinking, in that verandah.

Another was the manner and bearing of the proper Miriam, which was of the kind to make simple homely folks feel small and awkward.

A third thing was the difference between the two Miriams.

" She is not like her mother, and she certainly is not like her father — not as I knew him," muttered David with reference to the real one. But she's exactly like her portrait in yon group. Put her in the sun, and you see it in a minute. She frowns just like that still. She has much the same expression whenever she isn't speaking to you or you aren't speaking to her. It isn't a kind expression, and I wish I never saw it. I wish it was more like "

He ceased thinking so smoothly, for as a stone stars a pane of glass, that had shot into his mind's eye which made cross-roads of his thoughts. He took one of the roads and sat pulling at his pipe. Here from the verandah there was no view to be had of the river-timber and the distant ranges so beloved of the old man's gaze. But his eyes wandered down the paddock in front of the farmhouse, and thence to the township roofs, shifting from one to another of such as shone salient in the morning sun, and finally running up the parched and yellow hill upon the farther side. That way lay Melbourne, nine or ten miles to the south. And on this hill-top, between withered grass and dark blue sky, the old eyes rested; and the old lips kept clouding with tobacco-smoke the bit of striking sky-line, for the satisfaction of seeing it break through the cloud next instant; while on the worn face the passing flicker of a smile only showed the shadow of pain that was there all the time, until at length no more smoke came to soften the garish brilliance of the southern sky.

Then David lowered his eyes and knocked the ashes out of his pipe. And presently he sighed a few syllables aloud:

" Ay, Missy ! Poor thing ! Poor girl! " For on the top of that hill, between grass and sky, between puff and puff from his own pipe, a mammoth Missy had appeared in a vision to David Teesdale. Nor was it one Missy, but a whole set of her in a perfect sequence of visions. And this sort of thing was happening to the old man every day. There was some reason for it. With all her badness the girl had certainly shown David personally a number of small attentions such as he had never experienced at any hands but hers. She had filled his pipe, and fetched his slippers, and taken his arm whenever they chanced to be side by side for half a dozen steps. His own daughter never dreamt of such things, unless asked to do them, which was rare. But Missy had done them continually and of her own accord. She had taken it into her own head to read to the old man every day; she had listened to anything and all things he had to say to her, as Arabella had never listened in her life. Not that the daughter was at all uncommon in this respect; the wife was just the same. The real Miriam, too, showed plainly enough to a sensitive eye that poor David's conversation interested her not in the least. So it was only Missy who was uncommon — in caring for anything that he had to say. And this led Mr. Teesdale to remember the little good in her, and doubtless to exaggerate it, without thinking of the enormous evil; even so that when he did remember everything the old man, for one, was still unable to think of the impostor without a certain lingering tenderness.

There kept continually recurring to him things that she had said, her way of saying them, the tones of her voice, the complete look and sound of her in sundry little scenes that had actually taken place during her stay at the farm. Two such had been played all over again between the smoke of his pipe, the rim of yellow grass, and the background of blue sky which had formed the theatre of his thoughts. One of the two was the occasion of Missy's first blood-shedding with John William's gun. David recalled her sudden coming round the corner of the house — this corner. A whirlwind in a white dress, the flush of haste upon her face, the light of triumph in her eyes, the trail of the wind about her disorderly red hair. So had she come to him and thrown her victim at his feet as he sat where he was sitting now. And in a trice he had taken the triumph out of her by telling her what it was that she had shot, and why she ought not to have shot it at all. He could still see the look in her face as she gazed at her dead handiwork in the light of those candid remarks: first it was merely crestfallen, then it was ashamed, as her excitement subsided and she realised that she had done a cruel thing at best. She was not naturally cruel — a thousand trifles had proved her to be the very reverse. Her heart might be black by reason of her life, but by nature it was soft and kind. Kindness was something! It made up for some things, too.

Thus David would console himself, fetching his consolation from as far as you please. But even he could extract scant comfort from the other little incident which had come into his head. This was when Missy drank off Old Willie's whisky without the flicker of an eyelid; there has hitherto been no occasion to mention the matter, which was not more startling than many others which happened about the same time. Suffice it now to explain that Mr. Teesdale was in the habit of mixing every evening, and setting in safety on the kitchen mantelpiece, a pannikin of grog for Old Willie, who started townwards with the milk at two o'clock every morning. One fine evening Missy happened to see David prepare this potion, and asked what it was, getting as answer, " Old Willie's medicine"; whereupon the girl took it up, smelt it, and drank it off before the horrified old gentleman had time to interfere. " It's whisky! " he gasped. " Good whisky, too," replied Missy, smacking her lips. " But it was a stiff dose — I make it stiff so as to keep Old Willie from wanting any at the other end. You'd better be off to bed. Missy, before it makes you feel queer." "Queer!" cried Missy. "One tot like that! Do you suppose I've never tasted whisky before." And indeed she behaved a little better than usual during the remainder of the evening.

That alone should have aroused his suspicions — so David felt now. But at the time he had told nobody a word about the trick, and had passed it over in his own mind as one of the many "habits and ways which were not the habits and.ways of young girls in our day." Their name had indeed been legion as applied to the perjured pretender; that sentence in Mr. Oliver's letter, like the remark about "modern mannerisms" was fatally appropriate to her. Remained the question, how could those premonitory touches apply to a young lady so cultivated and so superior as the real Miriam Oliver ?

It was a question which Mr. Teesdale found very difficult to answer; it was a question which was driven to the back of his brain, for the time being, by the return of the superior young lady herself, with Arabella, from the township chapel.

David jumped up and hurried out to meet them. Miss Oliver wore a look which he could not read, because it was the look of boredom, with which David was not familiar. He thought she was tired, and offered her his arm. She refused it with politeness and a perfunctory smile.

"I'm afraid youVe had a very hot walk," said the old man. "Who preached, Arabella."

"Mr. Appleton. Miss Oliver didn't think "

"Ah! I thought he would!" cried David with enthusiasm. "We're very proud of Mr. Appleton's sermons. It will be interesting to hear how he strikes a young lady "

"She didn't think much of him," Arabella went on to state with impersonal candour.

"Nay, come!" And Mr. Teesdale looked for contradiction to the young lady herself; but though the latter raised her eyebrows at Arabella's way of putting it, she did not mince matters in the least. Perhaps this was one of those ways or habits.

"It was better than I expected," she said, with a small and languid smile.

"But didn't you like our minister, Miss Oliver. " We all think so highly of him."

" Oh, I am sure he is an excellent man, and what he said seemed extremely well meant; but one has heard all that before, over and over again, and rather better put."

"Ah, at Home, no doubt. Yes; I suppose you would now, in London. However," added David, throwing up his chin in an attempt to look less snubbed than he felt as they came into the verandah, "as long as you don't regret having gone! That's the main thing-not the sermon. The prayers and the worship are of much more account, and I knew you'd enjoy them. Take this chair, Miss Oliver, and get cooled a bit before you go inside."

Miss Oliver stopped short of saying what she thought of the prayers, which, indeed, had been mostly extemporised by the Rev. Mr. Appleton. But Arabella, had she not gone straight into the house, would have had something to say on this point, for Miss Oliver had been excessively frank with her on the way home, and she was nettled. It was odd how none of them save Mrs. Teesdale (who was not sensitive) thought of calling the real Miriam by her Christian name. That young lady had refused the chair, but she stood for a moment taking off her gloves.

"And why didn't you come to chapel, Mr. Teesdale ?" she asked, for something to say, simply.

"Aha!" said David slyly. "That's tellings. I make a rule of going, and it's a rule I very seldom break; but I'm afraid I broke it this morning — ay, and the Sabbath itself — I've broken that and all!"

Miss Miriam was a little too visibly unamused, because, with all her culture, she had omitted to cultivate the kind art of appreciation. She had never studied the gentle trick of keeping one's companions on good terms with themselves, and it did not come natural to her. So David was made to feel that he had said something foolish, and this led him into an unnecessary explanation.

" You see, in this country, in the hot weather, meat goes bad before you know where you are."

This put up the backs of Miss Oliver's eyebrows to begin with.

"You can't keep a thing a day, so, if I must tell you, I've been shooting a hare for our dinners. Mrs. T. is busy cooking it now. You see, if we'd hung it up even for a couple of hours "

"Please don't go into particulars," cried Miss Oliver, with a terrible face and much asperity of tone. "There was no need for you to tell me at all. You dine late, then, on Sundays ? "

" No, early, just as usual; it will be ready by the time you've got your things off."

"What — the hare that you've only shot since we went out?"

"Why, to be sure."

Miss Oliver went in to take off her things without another word. And David gathered from his guilty conscience that he had said what he had no call to say, what it was bad taste to say, what nobody but a very ill-bred old man would have dreamt of saying; but presently he knew it to his cost.

For nothing would induce the visitor to touch that hare, though Mrs. Teesdale had cooked it with her own hands. She had to say so herself, but Miss Miriam steadily shook her head; nor did there appear to be much use in pressing her. Mrs. Teesdale only made matters worse by so doing. But it is impossible not to sympathise with Mrs. Teesdale. She was by no means so strong a woman as her manifold and varied exertions would have led one to suppose. A hot two hours in the kitchen had left their mark upon her, and being tired at all events, if not in secret bodily pain, she very quickly became angry also. There was, in fact, every prospect of a scene, when David interposed and took the entire blame for having divulged to Miss Oliver the all too modern history of the hare. Then Mrs. Teesdale was angry, but only with her husband. With Miriam she proceeded to sympathise from that instant; indeed, she had set herself to make much of this Miriam from the first; and the matter ended by the young lady at last overcoming her scruples and condescending to one minute slice from the middle of the back. But she had worn throughout these regrettable proceedings a smile, hardly noticeable in itself, but of peculiarly exasperating qualities, if one did happen to remark it. And it had not escaped John William, who sat at the table without speaking a word, feeling, in any case, disinclined to open his mouth before so superior a being as this young lady from England.

In the heat of the afternoon, however, the younger Teesdale found the elder in the parlour, alone too, but walking up and down, as if ill at ease; and John William then had his say.

"Where's everybody?" he asked, putting his head into the room first of all. Then he entered bodily and shut the door behind him. "Where's our precious guest ? " he cried, in no promising tone.

"She's gone to lie down, and so has "

"That's all right ! I shan't be sorry myself if she goes on lying down for the rest of the day. I don't know what you think of her, father, but I do know what I think!"

Mr. Teesdale continued to pace the floor with bent body and badly troubled face, but he said nothing.

"She's what I told you she would be," proceeded the son, " in the very beginning. I told you she'd be stuck up — and good Lord, isn't she ? I said we didn't want that kind here, and no more we do.

No, I'm dashed if we do ! Don't you remember ? It was the time you read us the old man's letter. I liked the letter and I might like the old man, but I'm dashed if I like his daughter! She doesn't take after her father, I'll be bound."

"Not unless he is very much changed," admitted David sadly. "Still, I think you are rather hard upon her, John William."

" Hard upon her! Haven't I been watching her ? Haven't I ears and eyes in my head, like everybody else. It's only one meal I've set down to beside her, so far, but one'll do for me ! With her nasty supercilious smile, and her no-thank-you this and no-thank-you that! I never did know anybody take such a delight in refusing things. Look at her about that hare ! "

" Yes; and your mother had spent all morning at it. I'm very much afraid she's knocked herself up over it, for she's lying down, too. Your mother is not so strong as she was, John William. I'm very much afraid that matter of Missy has been preying on her nerves."

"I'd rather have Missy than this here Miriam," said John William, after a pause, and all at once his voice was full of weariness.

The same thought was in Mr. Teesdale's mind, but he did not give expression to it. Presently he said, still pacing the room with his long-legged, weak-kneed stride:

" I wonder what Mr. Oliver meant when he hinted that I should find Miriam so different from the girls of our day ? Where are the tricks and habits that he alluded to? Poor Missy had plenty, but I can't see any in Miriam."

" Can't you ? Then I can. Ways of another kind altogether. Did the girls in your day turn up their noses at things before people's faces ? "

"No."

" Did they sneer when they talked to their elders and betters ? "

" No; but we are only Miriam's elders, mind — not her betters."

"Could they smile without looking supercilious, and could they open their mouths without showing their superiority?"

"Of course they could."

" There you are then ! One more question —about Mr. Oliver this time. When you left the old country he hadn't the position he has now, had he ? "

"No, no; very far from it. He was just beginning business, and in a small way, too. Now he is a very wealthy man."

"Then he hadn't got as good an education as he's been able to give his children, I reckon t "

" No, you're right. We went to school together, he and I," said Mr. Teesdale simply.

"Then don't you see." cried his son, jumping up from the sofa where he had been sitting, while the old man still walked up and down the room. "Don't you see, father? Mr. Oliver was warning you against what he himself had suffered from. You bet that Miss Miriam picks him up, and snubs him and sneers at him, just as she does with us!"

Which was the cleverest deduction that this unsophisticated young farmer had ever arrived at in his life; but puzzling constantly over another matter had lent a new activity to his brain, and much worry had sharpened his wits.

Old Teesdale accepted his son's theory readily enough, but yet sorrowfully, and the more so because the more he saw of his old friend's child, the less he liked her.

Indeed, she was not at all an agreeable young person. It appeared that she had been merely reading in her own room, so when Arabella owned to having been asleep in hers, she looked duly and consciously superior. There was something comic about that look of conscious superiority which broke out upon this young lady's face upon the least provocation, but it is difficult to give an impression of it in words — it was so slight, and yet so plain. To be sure, she was the social as well as the intellectual superior of the simple folk at the farm, but that in itself was not so very much to be proud of, and at any rate one would not have expected a tolerably well-educated girl to exhale superiority with every breath. But this was the special weakness of Miss Miriam Oliver. Even the fact that some of the Teesdales read the Family Cherub was an opportunity which she could not resist. She took up a number and satirised the Family Cherub most unmercifully. Then she was queer about the poor old piano in the best parlour. She played a few bars upon it — she could play very well —:and then jumped up shuddering. Certainly the piano was terribly out of tune ; but not more so than this young Englishwoman's manners. In conversation with the Teesdales there was only one subject that really interested her.

It was a subject which had been fully dealt with at supper on the Saturday night, when Mrs. Teesdale had waxed very warm thereon. Old Teesdale and Arabella had listened in silence because to them it was not quite such a genial topic. John William had not been there; the misfortune was that he did sit down to the Sunday supper, when Miss Oliver brought up this subject again.

" Did my under-study like cocoa, then ? " she inquired, having herself refused to take any, much to Mrs. T.'s discomfiture.

" You mean that impudent baggage ? " said the latter. "Ay, she was the opposite extreme to you, Miriam. She took all she could get, you may be sure ! She made the best use of her time! "

" Do tell me some more about her," said Miss Oliver. " It is most interesting."

" Nay, I would rather not speak of her," replied Mrs. Teesdale, who was only too delighted to do so when sure of a sympathetic hearing. "It was the most impudent piece of wickedness that ever I heard tell of in my life."

"The queer thing to me," remarked Miss Oliver, "is that you ever should have believed her. Fancy taking such a creature for me! It was scarcely a compliment, Mrs. Teesdale. A more utterly vulgar person one could hardly wish to see."

" My dear," began Mr. Teesdale nervously, " she behaved very badly, we know; yet she had her good points "

" Hold your tongue, David!" cried his wife, whom nothing incensed more than a good word for Missy. "She curry-favoured with you, so you try to whitewash her. I wonder what Miriam will think of you. However, Miriam, I can tell you that I never believed in her-never once! A brazen, shameless, lying, thieving hussy, that's what she ”

A heavy fist had banged the table at the lower end, so that every cup danced in its saucer, and all eyes were turned upon John William, who sat in his place — trembling a little — very pale — but with eyes that glared alarmingly, first at his mother, then at the guest.

” What did she steal ? ” he thundered out. “You may be ashamed of yourself, mother, trying to make the girl out worse than she was. And you, Miss Oliver — I wonder you couldn't find something better to talk about — something in better taste !”

Miss Oliver put up her pale eyebrows.

” This is interesting!” she exclaimed. ” To think that one should come here to learn what is, and what is not good taste ! Perhaps you preferred my-my predecessor to me, Mr. Teesdale.”

“I did so!” said John William stoutly.

“Ah, I thought as much. She was, of course, rather more in your line.”

” By the Lord,” answered the young man, forgetting himself entirely, “if you were more in hers it would be the better for them that have to do with you. She could have taught you common civility, at any rate, and common kindness, and two or three other common things that you seem never to have been taught in your life!”

There was a moment's complete silence. Then Miss Oliver got steadily to her feet.

” After that,” she said to David, ” I think my room is the best place for me — and the safest too.”

She proceeded to the door without let or hindrance. All save herself were too much startled to speak or to act. Mr. Teesdale was gazing through the gun-room window with a weary face; his wife held her side as if it were a physical trouble with her; while Arabella looked in terror at John William, who was staring unflinchingly at the first woman he had lived to insult. The latter had reached the threshold, where, however, she turned to leave them something to keep.

” It serves me right,” she said. ” I might have known what- to expect if I came here.”

Chapter XVIII
The Way of All Flesh.

"Ay, it's been a bad job," said David. "But it's over and done with now — that's one thing."

He meant the whole matter, from Mr. Oliver's letter about Miriam to this young lady's ultimate depressing visit; but in his heart he was thinking more of things and a person that came in between ; and he glanced in wonder at his wife, who for once had missed an opening to loosen her lips and rail at that person and those things.

They were driving into Melbourne, the old couple together, and such a thing was rare. Moreover, the proposal had been Mrs. Teesdale's, which was rarer still. But rarest of all was her reason, namely, that there were several little odds and ends which she wanted to buy for herself. They had been married thirty-five years, but she had never been known deliberately to buy herself any odds or ends before.

" Fal-lals ? " said David chuckling.

" No such thing; you know nothing about it, David?"

" Ribbons ?"

" Rubbish," said Mrs. Teesdale; and David looked at her again, for there was no edge on the word, and, after thirty-five years, there was a something in the woman which was new and puzzling to the man.

What was it? A week and more had passed since Miriam Oliver left them, with undisguised relief in her eyes and the coldest of cold farewells upon her lips, which not even Mrs. Teesdale, who half attempted it, was allowed to kiss in memory of her parents. Since that day Mrs. T. had not been herself; but David was only now beginning to perceive it. When one has lived thirty-five years with another the master-spirit of the pair, it must be hard indeed for the weaker to discern the first false ring, telling of the first flaw in the stronger vessel. And the weaker vessel need not necessarily be the woman, that is the worst of it; in the Teesdales' case it was certainly plain enough which, was which. So the feeble and indolent old man was slow to see infirmity in the active, energetic body, his wife; indeed, the infirmity did not show itself as such quite immediately. It came out first of all in snapping and storming, in continual irritation, culminating in furies as insane as the rage of babes and sucklings. In this stage she would take and tear the unforgotten Missy into little pieces when other irritating matter chanced to flag; and once boxed Arabella's ears for daring to hint that the ways of the genuine Miriam were themselves not absolutely perfect. The name of Missy, whom she could not abuse too roundly, had the excellent effect upon her of taking off the steam; that of Miriam caused certain explosion, because for her Mrs. Teesdale would stick up with her lips while resenting most bitterly in her secret heart every remembered word and look of this young lady. The memory of both girls was gall and wormwood to her. There was only this difference, that she lost her temper in defending Miriam, and found it again in reviling Missy. But now, after not many days, that temper was much less readily lost and found; the sharpness was gone from the tongue to the face; all at once the woman was grown old; and he who had aged before her, though by her side, was the last to realise that she had caught him up.

She could milk no longer. One afternoon she got up from her stool with a very white face and left the shed, walking unsteadily. She never went back to it. She had ceased to be a wonderful woman. It was the very next day that she made David drive her into Melbourne to buy those little odds and ends.

On the way, in the buggy, under a merciless sun, the husband, looking often at his wife, saw at last what manner of changes had taken place. They were outward and visible; they made her look old and ill. It was the worry of recent events, no more, no less. David had been worried himself, he truly said; but there was no sense in anybody's worrying any more about what couldn't be helped, being over and done with, for good and all.

"It's been a bad job," he said again before they got to Melbourne; "a very bad job, as it is. If you let it make you ill, my dear, with thinking about what can't be mended, it'll be a worse job than ever."

He wanted to accompany Mrs. T. upon her unwonted little flutter among the shops. They had put up the mare at their old servant's inn. The landlord had remarked of his former mistress, and to her face, that she was not looking at all well, but, in fact, very poorly. And as David now thought the same, he was very anxious indeed to go with her and hold the odds while she bought the ends. She would not hear of it; but instead of sharply ordering, she entreated him to mind his own business and stay at the inn; so he stayed there, marvelling, for a time. Then a thought struck him.

He went to the pawnbroker's and saw his watch. It was all right. He had it in his hands, and wound it up, and set it right, and listened to its tick as to the beating of some loving heart, while his own went loud and quick with emotion. Then he left, and wandered along the street with eyes that were absent and distraught until they rested for a moment upon a passing face full of misery. He looked again — it was his wife.

They met with a mutual guilty start — hers the guiltier of the two — so that all the questioning came from him.

"Where have you been, my dear?"

"Collins Street."

"And what have you bought, and where is it?"

" Nowhere; I've bought nothing at all. I — I couldn't find what I wanted."

" Not find what you wanted ? Not in Melbourne ? Nonsense, my dear! You've been to the wrong places; you must take me with you after all. What was it that you wanted most particularly ?"

" Nothing, David; I want nothing now. I only want to go home to the farm — only home now, David. There were little things, but — but I couldn't get 'em, and now they don't matter. I am disappointed, but that doesn't matter either. Yes, I am disappointed; but now I only want to get home — to get home!"

She was so disappointed, this tough old woman with the weather-beaten face that was now and suddenly so aged and haggard, that her eyes were full of tears even there in the street; and she let them run over when David forged ahead to push the way; and wiped them up before she took his arm again. This taking of his arm, too, was done more tenderly, more dependently, than ever, perhaps, in their married life before. And David must have felt this himself, for he held up his head and shouldered his way through the crowd like a very brave old gentleman, and drove back to the farm for once the lord and master of his wife — he who had quitted it with less authority than their children.

He was not, of course, exactly aware of it. He was conscious of something, but not so much as all that. He did not know enough to keep him awake that night. But the window-blind took shape out of the darkness, and the wife at David's side saw it with eyes that had never closed. And the gray dawn filled the room: and daylight whitened the face and beard of the sleeping man: and the wife at his side raised herself in the bed and looked long upon David, and wept, and kissed the bedclothes where they covered him, because she was frightened of his waking if she kissed him. But he went on sleeping like a child.

Then Mrs. Teesdale lay back and stared at the ceiling, thinking hard. She thought of their long married life together; and had she been a good wife to David ? She thought of the easy-going, sweet-tempered young man who had made laughing love to her long ago in some Yorkshire lane; of the middle-aged philosopher who had found it rather amusing than otherwise to watch worse men making their fortunes while he stood still and chuckled; of the frail, white-haired sleeper who would presently awake with a smile to one day more of indolence and unsuccess. She still envied that sweet temperament, as she had envied it when a girl, though she knew now what no girl could have dreamt, that two such natures linked together would have found themselves hand in hand at the poor-house door in very much shorter time than thirty-five years. He had had no vices, this poor dear David of hers. Neither drink nor cards, nor the racecourse, nor another woman, had ever tempted him from their own hearthstone, which was the place he had loved best through all the years. Through all the years he had never spoken a harsh word to wife or child. He was full of affection and incapable of unkindness; but he was equally incapable of making a strong man's way in the world. Therefore she had played the man's part, which had been thrust upon her; and if this had hardened her could she help it ? Was it not natural? Hard labour hardens not the hands alone, but the mind, the eye, the face, the tongue, and the heart most of all. It had hardened her; she realised that now, when the strength was gone out of her, and she at last knew what it was to feel soft, and weak, and to need the support which she had hitherto given.

She tried to be just, however. Perhaps the support had not been all on her side through all the years. Perhaps with his even-minded placidity, his unfailing philosophy, David had all along done very nearly as much for her as she for him. Certainly he had never complained, and the life they had led would have been impossible with a complaining man. In their greatest straits he had stood up to her with a smile and a kiss; he had never depressed her with his own depression. That kiss and smile might have seemed impertinent to her at the time, in the actual circumstances, but now she knew how they had helped her by freeing her mind of special care on his account. So after all he had been a good husband to her; nay, the very best; for what other would have borne with her temper as he had done ? What other would have been as calm, and kind, and contented ? But he was not fit to be by himself. That was the dreadful part of it. He was not fit to be left alone.

To be sure, there were the children. They were still children to their mother, and young children, too; their minds seemed to have grown no older for so many years. Their mother saw the possibility of their marrying one day — as though that day might not have come any time those ten years and more. She saw it still; and what would become of David then? Arabella would not so much matter; she was just such another as her poor father; but John William.

Here Mrs. Teesdale's thoughts left the main track for a very ugly turning indeed. She had taken this turning once or twice before, but it was so ugly that she had never followed it very far. Now, however, she followed it until not another moment could she lie in bed, but must jump up and speak to her son with the matter hot in her head.

It was quite late enough. She was going out a-milking no more, either morning or evening, and that was another thing which John William must be told. Mrs. Teesdale, like everybody else, was glad to have more things than one to speak about, when the one was so difficult, and even dangerous. She partially dressed, and left the room as quietly as possible. The first gray light was penetrating into the passage as she stole along it. When she reached John William's door, there was a noise within ; when she opened it, she stood like a rock on the threshold — because she had been a plucky woman all her life — and a man was in the act of getting in by the window.

His middle was across the sill, and the crown of his hat was presented to the door.

"Who are you," said Mrs. Teesdale sternly, "and what do you want?"

The man raised his head instantly; and it was John William himself.

" Holloa, mother !"

" Where have you been ? " said Mrs. Teesdale.

"I didn't want to wake you before your time, so I thought I'd come in like this. That's better!"

He landed lightly on the floor; but his feet jingled; he was spurred as well as booted, and dressed, moreover, in his drab tweed suit.

"Where have you been?" said Mrs. Teesdale.

His bed had not been slept in.

"Been? There was something I had to do. No time during the day. So I've just got it done before "

" Where have you been ? " said Mrs. Teesdale.

The young man stared. His mother had repeated the question thrice, each time in exactly the same tone, without raising her voice or moving a muscle as she stood on the threshold, with the brass door-handle still between her fingers.

"What business is it of yours, mother?" he said sullenly. " Surely to goodness I'm old enough to do what I like ? Tm not what you'd exactly call a boy."

" You are my boy. Where have you been ? "

"In Melbourne — since you so very much want to know."

He had lost patience, and adopted defiance.

" I was sure of it," said Mrs. Teesdale, coming into the room now, and quietly shutting the door behind her. "I was sure of it."

Then, very slowly and deliberately, she raised her left arm, until one lean finger pointed to the wall at his left, and through that wall, as it were, into the room which had been occupied by each of the two visitors. Her eyes flashed into her son's. The lean finger trembled. But she said no word.

"What does that mean?" he asked at last, with an uneasy laugh.

" You have been — with — that woman !"

" I wish I had," said John William.

"You have ."'cried his mother.

"I have not. With her? Why, I haven't set eyes on her since the day you took and — the day she left us," said the angered man, ending quietly.

"Then what have you been doing?"

"I have been looking for her."

"For that woman?"

" Yes."

"Looking in Melbourne?"

"Yes."

"In the streets? —in the streets?"

"Yes."

"And you have never seen her since "

"Never."

" But this isn't the first time! You've been looking night after night! So that's why you ran up them other horses? That's why you're half dead unless you get some sleep of afternoons?"

"Mother," he said, "it is."

" Oh, my God!" cried Mrs. Teesdale, reeling, and breaking down very suddenly. "Oh, my God!"

In an instant strong arms were round her; but she would not have them; she freed herself and sat down on the chair that was by the bedside, warding him off with one hand while with the other she covered her face. It cut him to the heart to hear her sobs; to note the tears trickling through the old fingers, gnarled and knotted by a long life of hard work; to see the light strong frame, that had seemed all bone and muscle, like a hawk, so shaken. But because of her other hand, which forbade him to touch her, he could only stand aloof with his beard upon his chest and his thick arms folded. At length she calmed herself; and sat looking up at him with both hands in her lap. Her poor feet were bare; he had snatched a pillow from the bed and pushed it under them while she was still beside herself; and now, when she saw what he had done, she looked at him more kindly; and when she spoke, her voice was softer than ever he had heard it, boy or man.

"John William, you must give this up."

"Mother, we shall break each other's hearts, you and I. I cannot — I cannot!"

"But I know you will. You will give up looking for that girl; you will promise me this before I leave the room. Why should you look for her? How can you expect to find her? You don't know that she is in Melbourne at all. Why should you think of her "

"Because I've got to think of her, as long as I've a head on my shoulders and a heart in my body."

Mrs. Teesdale had her woman's quick instincts, after all. Hence her very singular omission, on this occasion, to apply a single hard name to the enemy whose deadliest thrust of all was only now coming home to her.

"Very well," she said; "but you must promise to give up looking for her in Melbourne, by night or by day, at any rate while your mother is alive."

"It is all that I can do! It is the only chance!" cried the young man, miserably. "Why should I promise to give up my one chance ?"

"Only while I live," interposed the mother.

"But why should I?"

"Because I shall not live very long. Don't look like that — listen to me. I have been ailing for months; never mind how. Whether it was the worry of lately, or what it was, I don't know; but it's only this last week or two that I've felt too poorly to bide it any longer. I never said a word to anybody — I wouldn't have said a word to you — not this morning, but now I must. And you are not to say a word to anybody — least of all to your father — till I give you leave. But the night before last I felt like dying where I sat milking; so I made your father take me into Melbourne, to buy some odds and ends. So I told him, poor man. But a doctor's opinion was all I wanted; that was my odds and ends. And I got it! No, let me tell you first; I went to Dr. James Murray, in Collins Street East. I had heard of him. So I went to him for the worst; but I never thought it would be the very worst; and it was — it was!"

There was an interruption here.

"My boy! Nay you mustn't fret; I'm sixty-three come August, and it's not a bad age isn't that. I may see August, he says. He says I may live a good few months yet. Nay, never mind what it is that's the matter with me; you'll know soon enough. He says he'll come and see me for nothing. It's an interesting case, he says; wanted me to go into a hospital and be under his eye, he did But that I wouldn't, so he thinks he must come and see me. Nay, never mind — never mind! Only promise not to look for that girl — any more — till I am gone."

The promise was given. John William had long been kneeling at his mother's feet, and kissing her hands, her face, her neck, her eyes. That was the interruption which had taken place. Now he was crying like a child.

Mr. Teesdale awoke as his wife reopened their bedroom door.

" My dear," said he, sweetly, " you've been going about with bare feet! You'll be catching your death of cold !"

He was not to be told just yet; and because Mrs. Teesdale's eyes were full of tears, which he must not see, she made answer in her very sharpest manner.

" Mind your own business, and go to sleep again, do! "

David only smiled.

"All right, my dear, you know best. But if you did catch your death o' cold, it'd be a bad job for the lot of us; it'd be the worst job of all, would that!"

Chapter XIX
To the Tune of Rain.

Towards the close of a depressing afternoon in the following winter Arabella might have been seen (but barely heard) to steal out of the farmhouse by the front door, which she shut very softly behind her. Twilight had set in before its time, thanks to ttie ponderous clouds that were gathered and still gathering overhead; but as she came forth into the open air, Arabella blinked, like one accustomed to no light at all. Rain had fallen freely during the day, but only, it seemed certain, as a foretaste of what was presently to come. At the moment all was very still, which rendered it the more difficult to make no noise; but this time Arabella was not bound upon any secret or private enterprise. She stepped out naturally enough when a few yards from the house, her simple object being a breath of fresh air; and from her white face and tired eyes, of this she was in urgent need. She picked her way as quickly as possible across the muddy yard, but ere she reached the gate was accosted by Old Willie, who was off duty until milk-cart time in the small hours, and who peered at her with a grave, inquiring look before opening his mouth.

" About the same, miss ? "

She shook her head.

"No better, at any rate; if anything, worse."

"And Mr. Teesdale?"

" He is keeping up. The woman who is helping me to nurse has a baby. She had to bring it with her. Father plays with it all day, and it seems to occupy his mind."

"Well, that's something. Now get your snack of air, miss. I mustn't keep you."

" No, you mustn't. I am going to the Cultivation, it is so high and open there. Do you think it will rain before I can get back ? "

Old Willie looked aloft. He was an ancient mariner, who had deserted his ship for the diggings in the early days; hence the aptitude for regular night-work.

" I think we shall catch it before pitch-dark," said he; " so you'd better look sharp, miss; and — good-night!"

"Good-night; and thank you-thank you."

But Arabella walked away wincing, and she opened the gate with her left hand; for the horny-fisted old sea-dog had shown his sympathy by nearly breaking her right.

It was the gate that led one among the gum-trees, down into that shallow gully, and so upward to the Cultivation. The trees were as leafy as ever in summer-time; the grass at their feet was much greener. There was no other striking difference to mark the exchange of seasons, saving always the heavy gray sky and the damp raw air. Arabella drew her shawl skin-tight about her shoulders, and walked rapidly; but far swifter than her feet went her thoughts — to last summer.

Heaven knows there were others to think of first — and last — just then. Yet in a minute or two Arabella was thinking only of the wicked, the dishonest, the immoral Missy. Nothing was known of her at the farm from the day she left it. That was nearly eight months ago, and eight months was time enough, surely, to forget her in ; but here, of all places, Arabella could never forget the woman who had saved her own woman's honour. Here it had happened. It was at the Cultivation corner that she had made the tryst that would infallibly have been her ruin; it was somewhere hereabouts that Missy had kept that tryst for her and saved her from ruin. She could never come this way without thinking only of Missy, and wondering whether she was alive, and where she was, and what doing. Therefore that which happened this evening was in reality less of a coincidence than it looked.

The girl of whom she was thinking stood suddenly in Arabella's path.

The recognition, however, was not so immediate. Missy was clad in garments that were the meanest rags compared even with those in which she had first appeared at the farm; also, she was thin to emaciation, and not a strand of her distinguishing red hair could be seen for the unsightly bonnet which was tightly fastened over her head and ears. Consider, further, the light, and you will have more patience than Missy had with the dumbfounded Arabella.

" Dorit you know me, 'Bella, or won't you know me?"

Arabella did know her then, and her hands flew out to the other's and caught them tight. Then she doubted her knowledge — the hands were harder than her own.

" Missy! No, I don't believe it is you. Where's your fringe ? Why are you — like this t How can it be you ? You never used to have hard hands! "

Yet she held them tight.

" Don't talk so loud," said Missy, nervously; "there might be someone about. You know it's me. I wonder how you can bear to touch me!"

" I can bear a bit more than that," said Arabella warmly, and she flung her arms about the other, and reached up and kissed her lovingly upon the mouth, upon both cheeks. The cheeks were cold, and the back and shoulders were wet to the hands and wrists encircling them.

"You're a good sort, 'Bella," murmured Missy, not particularly touched, but in a grateful tone enough. " You always were. There, that'll do. Fancy you not even being choked off yet — and me like this!"

" Fancy you being back again. Missy ! That's the grand thing. I can hardly credit it even now. But you're terribly wet, poor dear! It's dreadful for you. Missy, it is indeed !"

" Oh, that's nothing; it did rain pretty hard, but there'll be some more in a minute, so it would come to the same thing in any case."

"Then you have walked, and were caught in it on the road ? "

"Do I look as if I'd ridden? Yes, and it was a pretty long road "

"From Melbourne? — I should think it was."

Missy laughed.

"From Melbourne, that's no distance. I've travelled more than twice as far since morning, my dear, and I shall have it to travel all over again before to-morrow morning."

" Then you haven't come from Melbourne ? " cried Arabella, highly amazed.

"Haven't set foot in it since I saw you last."

" Where in the world have you been, then Missy?"

But even as they were speaking, the grass whispered on every hand, the leaves rustled, and down came the rain in torrents. Arabella found herself taken by the arm and led into the shelter of the nearest tree — a spreading she-oak. She was much agitated.

"Oh, what am I to do?" she cried. "I dare not stay many minutes; but I would give anything to stay ever so long, Missy! You don't understand. Tell me quickly where you have been, if you never went back to Melbourne?"

"Nay, if you're in a hurry, it's you that must tell me things. That's what I've come all this way for, 'Bella — just to hear how you're all getting on. How's Mr. Teesdale ?"

" He's as well as he ever is."

"And you, 'Bella?"

"Oh, there's never anything the matter with me."

"And John William?"

" There's not much the matter with him, either."

"Then that's all right," Missy fetched a sigh of relief.

It struck Arabella as very odd indeed that the only one of them after whom Missy did not ask should be Mrs. Teesdale. But was it odd? Quite apart from any rights or wrongs, Mrs. Teesdale had been Missy's natural enemy from the first. Moreover, she had struck Missy as an old woman who would never grow older or die; and Arabella let it pass. She was in a hurry, and it was now her turn to get answers from Missy.

"Where have you been," she repeated, "if you never went back to Melbourne? Be quick and tell me all about it."

Missy shook her head, shaking the rain that had gathered upon her shabby bonnet into Arabella's eyes. It was raining very heavily all this time, and the she-oak's shelter left much to be desired. But Missy was now the one with her arms about the other, who was, as we know, a much shorter woman; so that Arabella, whose back was to the tree-trunk, was being kept wonderfully dry. Missy shook her head.

" I can't tell you much if I'm to tell you quickly. You are in a hurry, I can see, and indeed it's no wonder "

"Oh, you don't understand, Missy!" cried the other in a torment. "If only you would come into the house "

"That I never can."

"I tell you that you don't understand. You could — just now."

"Never," said Missy firmly. "I know my sins pretty well by this time. I've had time to study 'em lately; and the worst of the lot was how I played it upon all of you here. Now don't you begin! You want to know where I've been lying low all this while, and what I've been doing. I'll tell you in two twos; then I'll give you what I've got for Mr. Teesdale, and then you shall run away indoors, and back I go to the place I come from. Where's that ? Over twenty miles away, in the Dandenong Ranges. It's a farm like this — What am I saying? There never was or will be a farm like this! But it isn't so unlike, either, in this and that; and I'm the girl in the kitchen there, same as Mary Jane is here, and help milk the cows, and cook the dinner, and clean up the place, and all that."

"Oh, Missy, I can scarcely believe it! Yet I felt hard work on your hands the moment I touched them — they are as rough and hard as Mary Jane's," said Arabella, taking fresh hold of them, "and your dress is just like hers. Where did you get such a dress t And how did you come to get taken on at the farm? We all thought you'd gone straight back to Melbourne; as for John William "

She hesitated. It was one thing to befriend Missy; but Arabella could not help taking a special and a different view of her in relation to her own brother.

"Yes?" said Missy.

"John William was quite sure of it."

"Then — I suppose — he never thought of looking for me } No, of course he wouldn't. Why should he?"

"You-you could hardly expect it, dear, I think," said John William's sister, very gently.

" Hardly; what a cracked thing it was to say!" cried Missy, laughing down the wistful tone into which she had dropped. "But you none of you could have guessed much about my life there, if you thought I was likely to go straight back to Melbourne from here. No, and you can't have known what it was to me to have lived here for two months, even as a cheat and a liar. There's worse things than cheating and lying, 'Bella; there's things that cheating and lying's a healthy change after! But never mind all that. When I left you, and had got through the township, I didn't take the road to Melbourne at all; I took the other road. Bang ahead of me was them Dandenong Ranges that your dear old father's always looking at as he sits at the table. I wonder does he look at 'em as much as ever? So I said, 'Them ranges is the place for me;' and I stumped for them ranges straight away. I swopped dresses with a woman I met on the road; this is the rags of what I got for mine; and then I stopped at all the farms asking for work. How I got work, after ever so long, and all about it, I'd tell you if you weren't in such a hurry to go. You'll get wet, you know, and here you're as dry as a bone. But I suppose it's only natural! "

"It isn't natural, Missy, and it isn't true," said Arabella, earnestly. "Oh, if only you understood everything! As if I could ever forget what you did for me — in this very paddock!"

"It was under this very tree, for that matter," said Missy, with a laugh. " I found it easily enough, and I was standing under it for old acquaintance when you came along. Do you know what he got?"

Arabella hung her head, because in the Argus she had read his sentence, to whom once she had been prepared to commit body and soul. She did not answer; but in her anxiety to be good to Missy, she forgot that other anxiety concerning her brother.

" If only you would come into the house, and let me give you some dry things and some supper! You must need both ; and you have no idea how clear the coast is. You don't understand!"

"What is it that I don't understand?" asked Missy, pertinently. "You keep on saying that."

"It is my mother — you never asked after her. She is very ill. She is — on her deathbed."

For more than a minute Missy remained speechless, while the fall of the rain on leaf and blade seemed all at once to have grown very loud. Then she shook her head firmly.

" I am so sorry for you all; but it's all the more reason why I mustn't come in. If she were well, I daren't."

They argued the matter. The want of food was admitted; that of dry clothes, obvious.

" If you would only come as far as the cart-shed; there's not the least chance of anyone going there till Old Willie does at two o'clock in the morning; and there I could bring you some supper and a change as well. If you would only do that," Arabella urged, "it would be something."

"You would promise not to tell a soul?"

"I do promise."

"Not even John William?"

Arabella remembered her forgotten anxiety. " Certainly not John William," said she, emphatically. And Missy gave in at last.

Five minutes later they stood, wet and dripping, in the cart-shed. It was one of the many more or less ramshackle shanties which stood around the homestead yard. It had a galvanised iron roof, a back and two sides of wattle and dab, and no front at all. And no sooner had the two women gained this shelter than a man's voice calling through the rain caused them to cling instinctively together. The man was John William, and, low as his voice was purposely pitched, the words carried clear and clean into the cart-shed.

" 'Bella! 'Bella ! Where are you, 'Bella ? "

And the voice was coming nearer.

"I must go," whispered 'Bella.

" Remember your promise !"

Missy could not know how superfluous was her caution; it comforted her to remember that she had given it, now that she was left alone, able to think, and to examine the situation. This was not that situation which she had planned and bargained for in her own mind; this was the better of the two. She had intended to waylay Arabella, but she had never hoped to manage it so far from the house. She had contemplated the impossibility of waylaying her at all — the necessity of knocking at her window as she was going to bed — the circumstances of a more difficult and a more dangerous interview than that which had already taken place. She knew the daily ways of the farm well enough to know also that she was tolerably safe at present where she was. Soon Arabella would return with eatables and dry clothing, and the one would be as welcome as the other. Meantime, Missy had hidden herself under the spring-cart, lest by any chance another should look into the shed before Arabella. When the latter came back, she would confide into her safe keeping that which she had brought for Mr. Teesdale, to be given him not before Missy had been twenty-four hours gone from the premises. And after that —

Nothing mattered after that.

But Arabella did not return so very soon, after all; and it was uncomfortable for body and nerves alike, crouching under the spring-cart; and . the rain made such an uproar on the iron roof that it would be impossible to hear footsteps outside, came they never so near; and this made it worse still for the nerves.

The cow-shed was not far from that which sheltered buggy and carts and Missy in the midst of them. On a perfectly still evening it would have been possible to hear the jet of milk playing on the side of the pail; but to-night Missy could hear nothing but the rain and her own heart beating. It was raining harder than ever. She crouched, watching the sputtering blackness outside until, very suddenly, it ceased to be absolutely black. The light of a lantern came swinging nearer and nearer to the shed.

"What can she want with a lantern?" thought Missy, shrinking for a moment as the rays reached her. Then she extricated herself from the spring-cart wheels, stood upright, and asked the question aloud when the lantern itself was within a yard or two of the shelter. Now you cannot tell who is carrying the ordinary lantern when the night is dark and there is no other light at all; and Missy never dreamt that this was any person but Arabella, until strong arms encircled her and the breath was out of her body.

At last she gasped —

" Arabella told you! She has broken her sacred promise!"

"No one told me; but I saw it in Arabella's face. . . . Missy! Missy! To think that I have got you safe! I shall never let you go any more — never-never!"

Suddenly he swept her off her feet and bore her into the rain.

"Where are you going to take me? Not into the house?"

She could scarcely speak; she was quite past struggling. Without answering, he bore her on.

Chapter XX
The Last Encounter.

It was in the old parlour, an hour later.

Here the change from summer to winter struck the eye more forcibly than it ever can out-of-doors in a country where no leaves fall. The gauze screen which had fitted in front of the fire-place was put away, and a log fire burnt excellently on the whitened hearth; the room was further lighted by the kerosene lamp that stood as of old upon the table; the gun-room door was shut; and a pair of old green curtains, of a different shade from that of the tablecloth, which looked less green and more faded than ever, were drawn across the window.

Mr. Teesdale sat in his accustomed corner, with his chair pushed back and pointing neither towards the table nor the fire, but between the two. On his knee was a bare-legged child, perhaps fourteen months old. Arabella, when she was in the room, took a chair near the table, if she sat down at all, and the lamplight only blackened the inscription of sleepless nights and anxious days that was cut deep upon her pallid face. John Willian sat at that end of the sofa which he had invariably afflected, watching Missy; they all did this, even to Mr. Tees-dale, who was also occupied with the child upon his knee; but all save the child, who sometimes crowed and was checked, sat more like waxworks in a show than living, suffering beings.

When one spoke, it was in a whisper. But there was very little speaking. If Missy had not come back at all they could scarcely have been more silent.

Yet the way they spoke to her when they spoke at all — the way they looked at her, whether they spoke or not — this was much more remarkable than their silence, for which there was good reason. They spoke to Missy as to an old and valued friend, who had come at a cruel time, but who brought her own welcome even so; they looked at her with hospitable, grieved eyes that entreated her to take the kindly will for the kindlier deed. Across their faces, too, there now and then swept looks of apprehension which she did not see; but never a shade that would have led a stranger to suspect that they knew aught but good of this girl, or that she had rendered aught but kindness to them and theirs.

As for Missy, she did not see half their looks, because her own eyes had been either averted or downcast during the whole of the hour that she had already spent in the room. Now they were averted. She was sitting on a stool by the fireside — by that side of the fire which was furthest from Mr. Teesdale and nearest to the door. Her body was bent forward ; her eyes were fixed pensively upon the fire; her left elbow rested upon her knee, and her chin in the hollow of her left hand. Hand and face were brown alike from hard work in all weathers. It was the weather of that day, however, that had quenched the colour from her hair; limp and soaking as it was, it looked much less red than formerly in the glare of midsummer. Also the fringe had disappeared entirely; but this alteration was permanent. Most notable of all changes, however, was the gauntness and angularity of the old good figure, which had struck Arabella even in the darkness; it was painfully conspicuous in the light. Missy had been to her box with Arabella, and was clad in a blouse and skirt that had been made for her ten months earlier. They fitted but loosely now. A hat and jacket, which she had also obtained from her box, had been taken away from her by John William: it lay within reach of his hand upon the sofa, where he appeared content to sit still and stare fixedly at Missy's back. Thus he was not aware that she had taken a small roll of papers out of her blouse, and that her right hand had been for some time fidgeting with it in her lap. And when David, who had a much better view, broke the silence with a low-toned question, the younger Teesdale had to get up in order to understand what his father meant.

" What is it you have got there. Missy ?" " It is something that I — I wanted to talk to you about, Mr. Teesdale." She turned her head and looked a little wistfully at John William and Arabella; but neither of these two perceived that she wished to speak to Mr. Teesdale alone ; and, after all, there was no reason why she should not speak out in front of them.

So Ae proceeded. "It's something rather important — it's the only thing that could ever have brought me back here. Mr. Teesdale, you never took possession of my box after all!"

"'Twasn't likely," said David.

"But I meant you to. I told Arabella. "

" Yes, yes, but you didn't really and truly expect me to take you at your word, Missy?"

"Of course I did. The box was yours. It and all that was in it had been bought with your money."

"I wouldn't have anybody touch the box," said David, with characteristic pride. " I took and locked it up myself, and I've kept the key in my pocket ever since."

" But it was all yours by rights. "

"I care nothing at all about that!"

" The dresses and things, as well as the box itself, were worth something. Not much, perhaps — still, something. And then there were four pounds and some silver which I'd never touched. Here they are — four pounds."

She got up and laid them in a row on the tablecloth under the lamp. The others had risen also ; and John William, for one, had his eyes fixed upon the little roll of paper in her right hand. It was a roll of one-pound notes. She began to lay them one by one upon the table, counting aloud as she did so.

" One, two, three, four, five, six "

"Stop a moment," said David, trembling. "How did you come by them. Missy ? "

" Seven, eight. Didn't I tell you that Fve been working all this time upon a farm? Nine "

" Ah, yes, you did."

There had been a few explanations — a very few — when John William had first brought her in. Then dry clothes, then supper, then silence. It must be remembered that the shadow of death hung over the farm.

" Ten. I was there thirty-three weeks last Saturday. Eleven. They gave me ten shillings a week, and they found me — twelve — in food and clothes. I had things to put up with — thirteen — but nothing I couldn't bear. I was thankful you'd taught me to milk here. Fourteen, fifteen. I was so! Sixteen, and that's the lot. Sixteen and four's twenty. Twenty pound I got out of you, Mr. Tees-dale, because I couldn't resist it when you said what you may recollect saying as you drove me back into Melbourne that first day. I never meant to pay you back; I wasn't half sure that I'd ever let you see me again. I don't say I should have done it if I'd known you'd go and pawn your watch for me; still I did do you out of the twenty pounds, and I meant to do you out of them for good and all. But here they are."

"Thank you, Missy," said David at last. The others said nothing at all.

"Thank me! I don't want you to thank me at all. What have I done but rob you and pay you back again . No —I only want you — to forgive me — if you can !"

"I do forgive you, my dear; but I forgave you long ago," said David, smoothing back her hair and kissing her upon the forehead.

" You two forgive me, I know," she said, turning to the others.

Arabella embraced her tearfully, but John William only laughed sardonically. What had he to forgive ?

" I knew you did. So now there is only one thing more that I want to send me away happy."

"Send you away! Where to? You've only just come," cried Mr. Teesdale, as loud as he dared; but even as he spoke he remembered the special difficulty of the occasion, and his face twitched with the pain. "Why, where did you think of going to?" he added, wiping his lips with his red pocket-handkerchief.

" Back to the Dandenong Ranges. I'm so happy-there, you don't know! Thought I'd left ? Not me, don't you believe it. No, I must get back to my work as quick as I can. And you'll be able to sit in quietness and look out through the gun-room window" — she pointed to the gun-room door — "and across the river-timber to them blue ranges, and you'll be able to say, ' Missy's working there. She's honest now, whatever she was once; and she's trying to make up for her whole life.' Yes, and you may say, 'She's trying to make up for it all, and it was us that taught her; it was us that took her out of hell and gave her a glimpse of the other thing!' That's what you'll be able to say, Mr. Teesdale. And I'll know you're looking at the ranges, and I'll think you're looking at me, every evening in the summer-time, and every dinner-time all the year round. They ain't so blue as they look, when you get there — I guess the sky isn't either when you get there — but they're blue enough for Missy; they're blue enough for me."

The tears were running down her face. John William had interjected, here and there, " You're never going back at all." But she had taken no notice of him; and when he repeated the same speech now, she shook her head and only sobbed the more.

" What is it that would send you away happy ? " asked poor David; for he knew well what the answer was to be; and by now he was himself intensely agitated.

"I want someone else to forgive me, too," said Missy, "if it is not too late." And she looked at the door that led into the passage that led to Mrs. Tees-dale's room. This door, also, was kept carefully closed.

" It is too late for you to see her; it would not be safe," said Mr. Teesdale, sadly shaking his head. " But she lies yonder at peace with all mankind ; she has told me so herself. Rest assured that she forgives you, Missy."

" She would forgive you with all her heart," said Arabella. " She has been so brave and good — and gentle — ever since she first fell ill. She would forgive you, Missy, as freely as my father has done."

" She has forgiven you long ago," declared John William. " She spoke to me about you the morning after she had been to see the doctor without telling us she was going. She spoke of you then without any bitterness; so she had forgiven you as long ago as that.'

Missy received these optimistic assurances with a look of dissatisfied doubt, as though she could accept no forgiveness that was not actual and absolute. Then her eyes found their way back to the passage door; and she could scarce believe them. She sprang backward with a cry of fear. The other three started also with one accord — so that the room shook. For the door was open, and on the threshold, like a spectre, stood none other than the dying woman herself.

" Forgive you! " she said, in a crazy rattle of a voice. " You !"

She entered without stumbling, shut the door behind her, and took two steps forward. They appeared the steps of a decrepit, rather than a dying woman; but they brought her no nearer to Missy, who backed in terror towards the gun-room. Nor was poor Missy worse than any of the rest, who not one of them could put out a hand to uphold this tottering, terrible figure, so scared and shaken were they. And the old woman stood there in her bedclothes, with a ghastly dew upon her emaciated face, and ordered the young girl out of the house.

" Forgive you ! " she said. " Go ; how dare you come back? David-all of you — how dare you take her in — a common slut — with me on my deathbed? How long have you had her here, I wonder? Not long, I know, or I should ha' felt it — I should ha' known ! Do you think I could have died in my bed with that — with that in the house ? God forgive you all; and you, out you go. Do you hear ? Go ! "

She pointed to the gun-room door with a bony, quivering hand; and because the girl she abhorred was paralysed with horror, she brought that hand down passionately upon the table, so that the four sovereigns rang together, and she saw the gold and notes, and fiercdy inquired where they came from.

But now at last David was supporting her in his arms, and he answered soothingly : "They are twenty pounds that Missy borrowed from me when she was with us — I never told you about it. She has come to-night and paid them back to me. That's the only reason she is here. She has been all this time earning them, just to do something to atone."

" Pah! " cried Mrs. Teesdale, stiffening herself in her husband's arms, and reaching her skinny hands to the notes and gold. "How came you to have twenty pounds to give her? How comes she to have them to give you back? How do you think she earned them ? Shall I tell you how ? " the poor woman screamed. " They're the wages of sin — the wages of sin — of sin ! " She snatched up gold and notes alike and flung the lot at the fire with all her feeble might. The gold went ringing round the whitened hearth. The notes fell short.

" Now go," she said to Missy, her scream dropping to a whisper, "and come back at your peril."

Missy got her hat and jacket from the sofa, brushing the wall all the way, and never taking her eyes from that awful, menacing, death-smitten face. Then suddenly she plucked up courage, took one step forward, and stood in profound humility, mutely asking for that forgiveness which she was never to get. A strong hand, young Teesdale's, had laid hold of her arm from behind and given her strength.

David, too, was putting in a quavering word for her.

"She is going," said he. "She was going in any case. You are wrong about the money. She has earned it honestly, as a farm servant, like our Mary Jane. Can't you see how brown her face and hands are? We have all forgiven her, as we hope to be forgiven. Cannot you also forgive her, my dear, and let her go her ways in peace ? "

The sick woman wavered, and for a moment the terrible gaze, transfixing Missy, turned, by comparison, almost soft. Then it shifted and fell upon the bearded face of him who was supporting the unhappy girl, and moment, mood and chance were gone, all three, beyond redemption.

"John William," said his mother, "leave her alone. Do you hear me ? Let her go!"

Nothing happened.

" Let her go!" screamed Mrs. Teesdale. "Choose once and for all between us-your dying mother and — that — woman !"

At first nothing; then the man's hand dropped clear of the girl.

"Now go," said the woman to the girl.

The girl fled into the gun-room, and so out into the night, only pausing to shut the doors behind her, one after the other. With the shutting of the outer door — it was not slammed-they heard the last of Missy.

"Now follow her," said the mother to the man.

But the man remained.

Now there was nothing but wet grass between the gun-room window and the river-timber; and that way lay the Dandenong Ranges; therefore it was clearly Missy's way — until she stopped to think.

This was not until she had very nearly walked into the Yarra itself; it was only then that she came to know what she was doing, to consider what she must do next, and to recall coherently the circumstances of her last and final expulsion from the farmhouse of the Teesdales. Already it seemed to have happened hours ago, instead of minutes. The hat and jacket she had snatched up from the sofa were still upon her arm ; she put them on now, because suddenly she had turned cold. Another moment and she could not have said on which arm she had carried them, she had carried them so short a time. Yet the deathly face and the deathlier voice of Mrs. Teesdale were as a horror of old standing ; there was something so familiar about them; they seemed to have dwelt in her memory so long. But, indeed, her mind was in a mist, through which the remote and the immediate past loomed equally indistinct and far away.

The mist parted suddenly. One face shone through it with a baleful light. It was the dreadful face of Mrs. Teesdale.

" Dying!" exclaimed Missy, eyeing the face judicially in her mind. "Dying.? Not she — not now! She may have been dying; but she won't die now. No, I've saved her by dragging her off her deathbed to curse me and turn me out! I've heard of folks turning the corner like that. She was right enough, though. You can't blame her and call her unkind. The others are more to blame for going on being kind to one of my sort. No, she'd better not die now, she'd much better leave that to me."

Her mind was in a mist. She tried to see ahead. She must live somewhere, and she must do something for her living. But what — but where ?

There was one matter about which she had not spoken the truth even now; neither to Arabella, nor to John William, nor to Mr. Teesdale himself. That was the matter of her new home in the Dandenong Ranges, where she said she had been so happy, they didn't know! It was no home at all. She was particularly wretched there. She had stayed on with one object alone; now that this was accomplished there would be no object at all in going back. She had not intended ever to return, when leaving; but then her intentions had gone no further than the paying back to Mr. Teesdale of the twenty pounds obtained from him once upon a time by fraud. This had been the be-all and end-all of her existence for many months past. It was strange to be without it now; but to go back without it, to that farm in the ranges, would be terrible Yet go somewhere she must; and there was the work which she could do. They would give her that work again, and readily, as before; they would overwork her, bully her, speak hardly to her — but clothe her decently, feed her well, and pay her ten shillings a week, all as before. She nust do some work somewhere. Then what and where else?

Her mind was in a mist.

She saw no future for herself at all, or none that would be tolerable now. If she had dreamt once of unanimous forgiveness at the farm — of getting work there, in the kitchen, in the cow-shed — that dream had come to such utter annihilation that even the memory of it entered her head no more. And she wanted no work elsewhere. So why work at all? She had done enough. Rest was all she wanted now. It was the newborn desire of her heart; rest, and nothing more.

And here was the river at her feet; but that thought did not stay or crystallise just yet.

Before it came the thought of Melbourne and the old life, which parted the mind's mist with a lurid light. That old life need not necessarily be an absolutely wicked one. There were points about that old life, wicked or otherwise. It had warmth, colour, jingle and glare, abundant variety, and superabundant gaiety. But rest 1 And rest was all she wanted now — all. And the mist gathered again in her mind; but the river still ran at her feet.

The river! How little heed she had taken of it until this moment! She had watched without seeing it, but she noted everything now. That the rain must have stopped before her banishment from the house, since her dry clothes were dry still; that overhead there was more clear sky than clouds ; that the clouds were racing past a sickle moon, overwhelming it now and then, like white waves and a glistening rock; that the wind was shivering and groaning through the river-timber, and that it had loosened her own hair; that the river itself was strong, full, noisy and turbulent, and so close, so very close to her own feet.

She stooped, she knelt, she reached and touched it with her fingers. The river was certainly very cold and of so full a current that it swept the finger-tips out of the water as soon as they touched it. But this was only in winter-time. In summer it was a very different thing.

In summer-time the river was low and still and warm to the hand ; the grass upon the banks was dry and yellow; the bottle-green trees were spotted and alive with the vivid reds, emeralds, and yellows of parrot, parrakeet, and cherry-picker; and the blue sky pressed upon the interlacing branches, not only over one's head but under one's feet, if one stood where Missy was standing now and looked where she was looking.

She was imagining all these things, as she had heard and seen and felt them many a time last summer. Last Christmas Day was the one she had especially in mind. It was so very hard to realise that it was the same place. Yet there was no getting over that fact. And Missy was closer than she knew to the spot where she had cast herself upon the ground and shut out sight and hearing until poor John William arrived upon the spot and brought about a little scene which she remembered more vividly than many a more startling one of her own unaided making. Poor Jack, indeed! Since that day he had been daily in her thoughts, and always as poor Jack. Because he had got it into his head that he was in love — and with her — that was why he was to be pitied; or rather, it was why she had pitied him so long, whom she pitied no longer. To-night — now, at any rate, as she stood by the river — of the two she pitied only herself.

To-night she had seen him again ; to-night he had carried her in his arms, but spoken no word of love to her; to-night he had stood aside and allowed her to be turned out of the house by his mother who was not dying — not she.

It was as it should be; it was also as she had prayed that it might be. He did not care. That was all. She only regretted she had so long tormented herself with the thought that he might, nay, that he did care. She felt the need of that torment now as keenly as though it had been a comfort. Without it, she was lonely and alone, and more than ever in need of rest.

Then, suddenly, she remembered how that very day — last Christmas Day-in the gorgeous summer-time, but in this selfsame spot — the idea had come to her which was with her now. And her soul rose up in arms against herself for what she had not done last Christmas Day.

"If only I had," she cried, "the trouble would have been over when it seems it was only just beginning. I shouldn't have disgusted them as I did on purpose that very afternoon. A lot of good it did me! And they would all have forgiven me, when they found out. Even Mrs. Teesdale would have forgiven me then. And Jack — Jack — I shouldn't have lived to know you never cared."

She clasped her hands in front of her and looked up steadily at the moon. It was clear of the clouds now — a keen-edged sickle against a slatey sky; and such light as it shed fell full enough upon the thin brown face and fearless eyes of the nameless girl whom, as Missy, two or three simple honest folk had learnt to like so well that they could think of her kindly even when the black worst was known of her. Her lips moved — perhaps in prayer for those two or three — perhaps to crave forgiveness for herself; but they never trembled. Neither did her knees, though suddenly she knelt. And now her eyes were shut; and it seems, or she must have heard him, her ears also. She opened her eyes again, however, to look her last at sky and moon. But her eyes were full of tears. So she shut them tight, and, putting her hands in front of her, swung slowly forward.

It was then that John William stooped forward and caught her firmly by the waist; but, after a single shrill scream, the spirit left her as surely as it must had he never been there. . . . Only, it came back.

He had taken off his coat. She was lying upon it, while he knelt over her. The narrow moon was like a glory over his head.

" Why did you do it ? " she asked him. " You might have let me get to rest when — when you didn't care!"

" I do care!" he answered; " and I mean you to rest now all the days of your life — your new life, Missy. I have cared all the time. But now I care more than ever."

"Your father and 'Bella "

" Care as much as I do, pretty nearly, in their own way. Missy, dear, don't you care, too, — for me?"

She looked at him gratefully through her starting tears. " How can I help it ? You picked me up out of the gutter between you; but it was you alone that kept me out of it, after I'd gone ; because I sort of felt all the time that you cared. But oh, you must never marry me. I am thinking so of your mother! She will never, never forgive me; I couldn't expect it; and she is going to get quite better, you know — I feel sure that she is better already."

He put his hand upon the hair that was only golden in the moonshine: he peered into the wan face with infinite sadness: for here it was that Missy was both right and wrong.